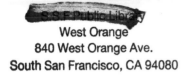

Lincoln Peirce

BiG NATE

WHAT COULD POSSIBLY GO WRONG?

HARPER

An Imprint of HarperCollins*Publishers*

MRS. GODFREY TO THE RESCUE

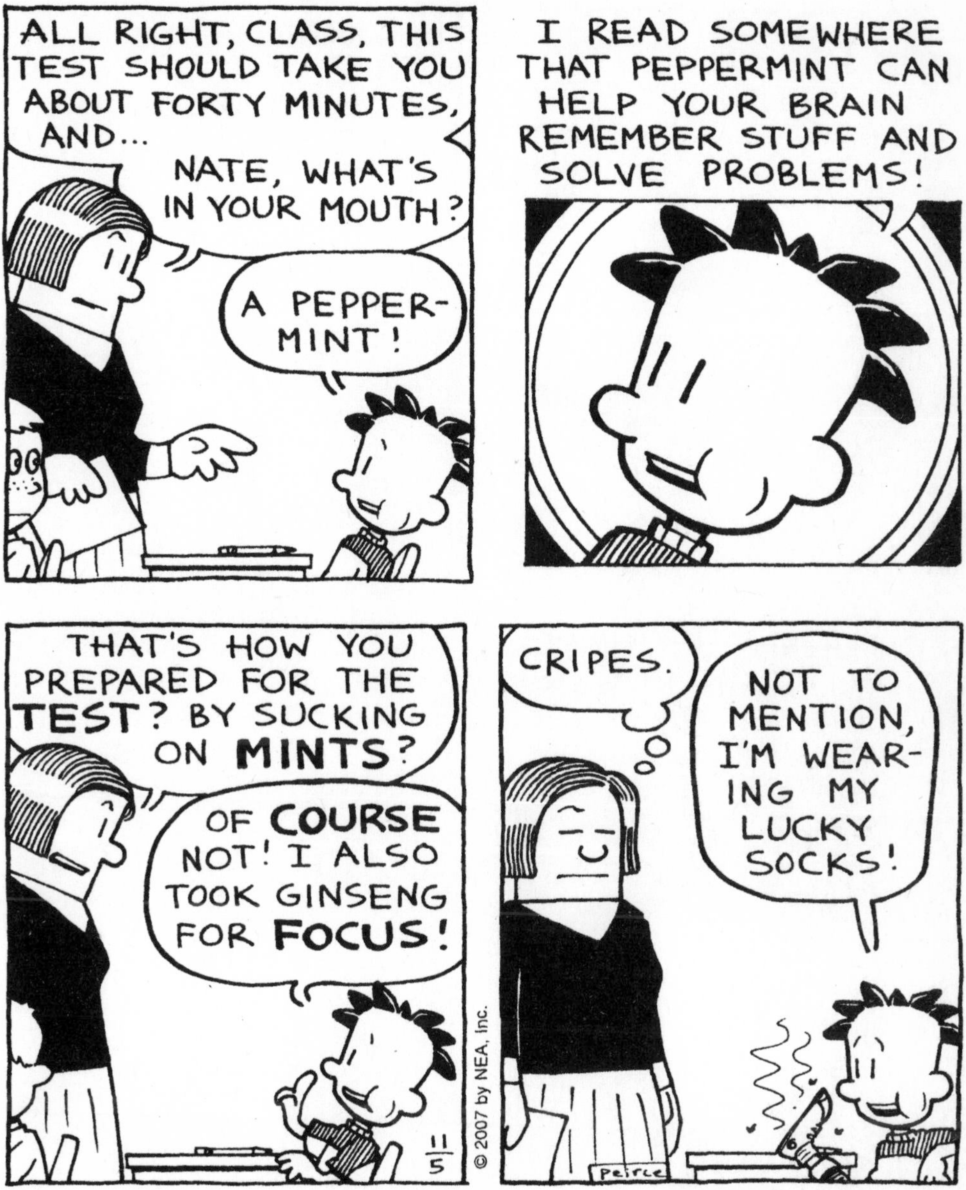
ALL RIGHT, CLASS, THIS TEST SHOULD TAKE YOU ABOUT FORTY MINUTES, AND...
NATE, WHAT'S IN YOUR MOUTH?
A PEPPER-MINT!
I READ SOMEWHERE THAT PEPPERMINT CAN HELP YOUR BRAIN REMEMBER STUFF AND SOLVE PROBLEMS!
THAT'S HOW YOU PREPARED FOR THE **TEST**? BY SUCKING ON **MINTS**?
OF **COURSE** NOT! I ALSO TOOK GINSENG FOR **FOCUS**!
11/5
CRIPES.
NOT TO MENTION, I'M WEAR-ING MY LUCKY SOCKS!
Peirce

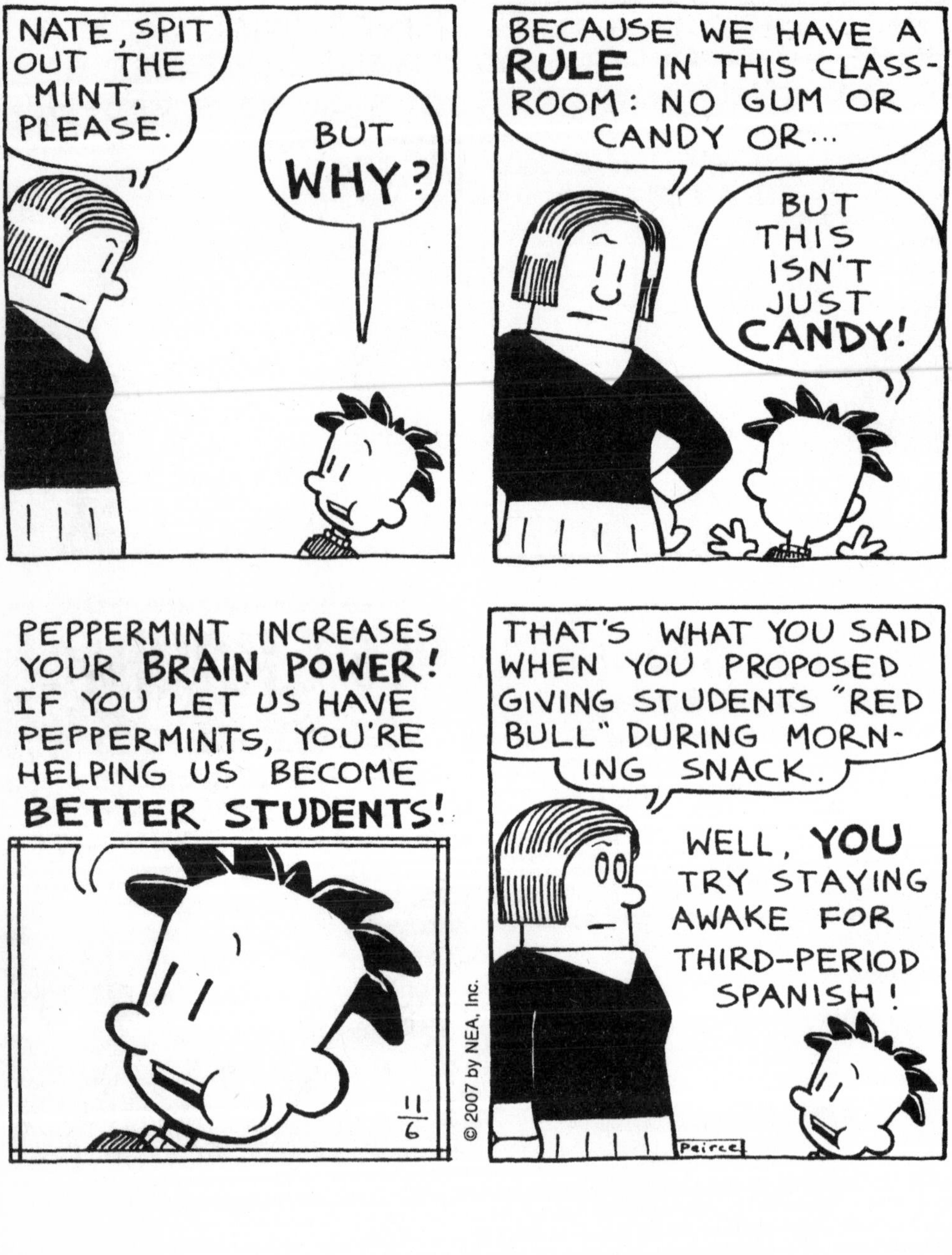
NATE, SPIT OUT THE MINT, PLEASE.
BUT WHY?
BECAUSE WE HAVE A RULE IN THIS CLASS-ROOM: NO GUM OR CANDY OR...
BUT THIS ISN'T JUST CANDY!
PEPPERMINT INCREASES YOUR BRAIN POWER! IF YOU LET US HAVE PEPPERMINTS, YOU'RE HELPING US BECOME BETTER STUDENTS!
11/6
THAT'S WHAT YOU SAID WHEN YOU PROPOSED GIVING STUDENTS "RED BULL" DURING MORN-ING SNACK.
WELL, YOU TRY STAYING AWAKE FOR THIRD-PERIOD SPANISH!
Peirce

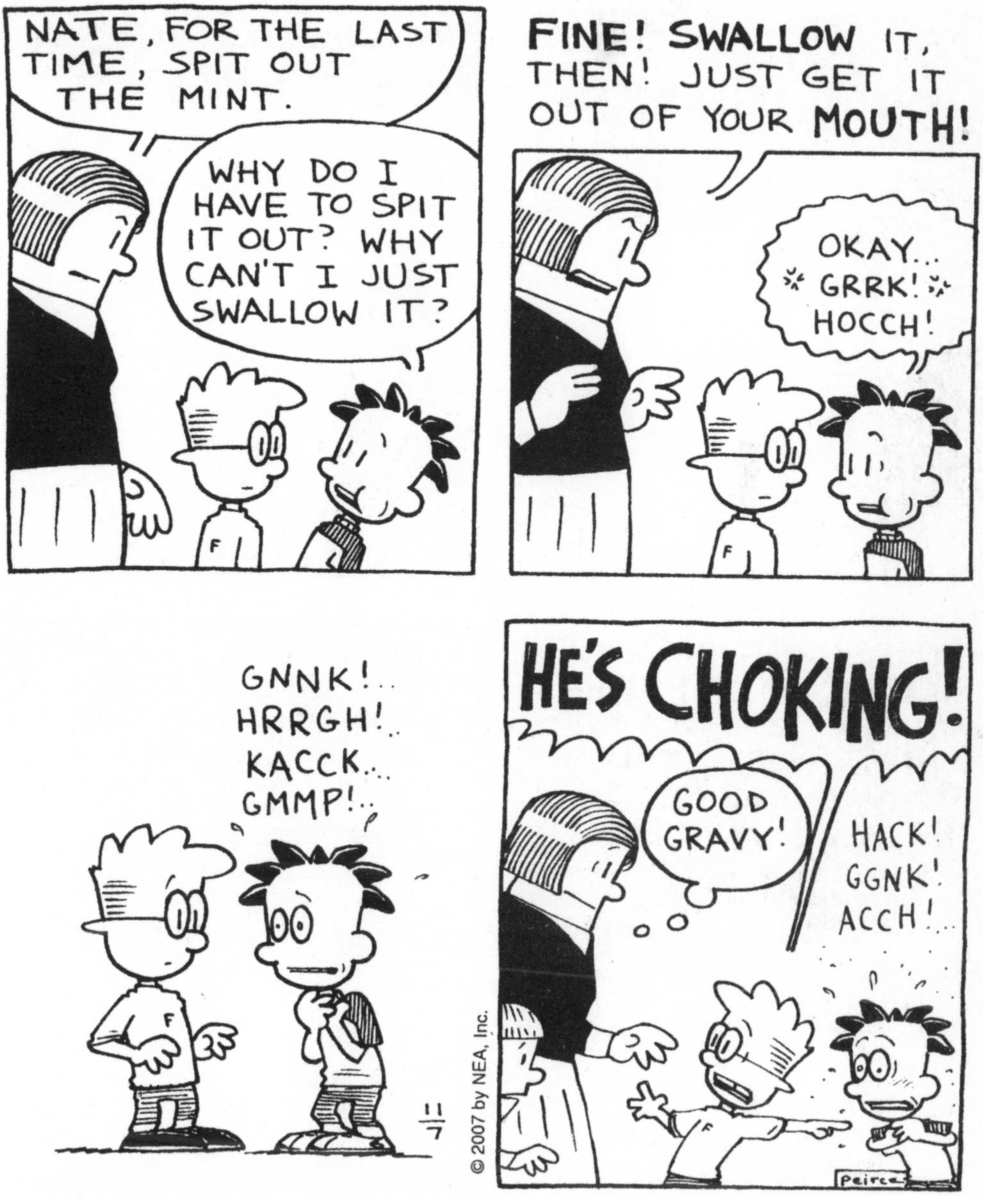
NATE, FOR THE LAST TIME, SPIT OUT THE MINT.
WHY DO I HAVE TO SPIT IT OUT? WHY CAN'T I JUST SWALLOW IT?
FINE! SWALLOW IT, THEN! JUST GET IT OUT OF YOUR MOUTH!
OKAY... GRRK! HOCCH!
GNNK!.. HRRGH!.. KACCK... GMMP!..
11/7
© 2007 by NEA, Inc.
HE'S CHOKING!
GOOD GRAVY!
HACK! GGNK! ACCH!..
Peirce

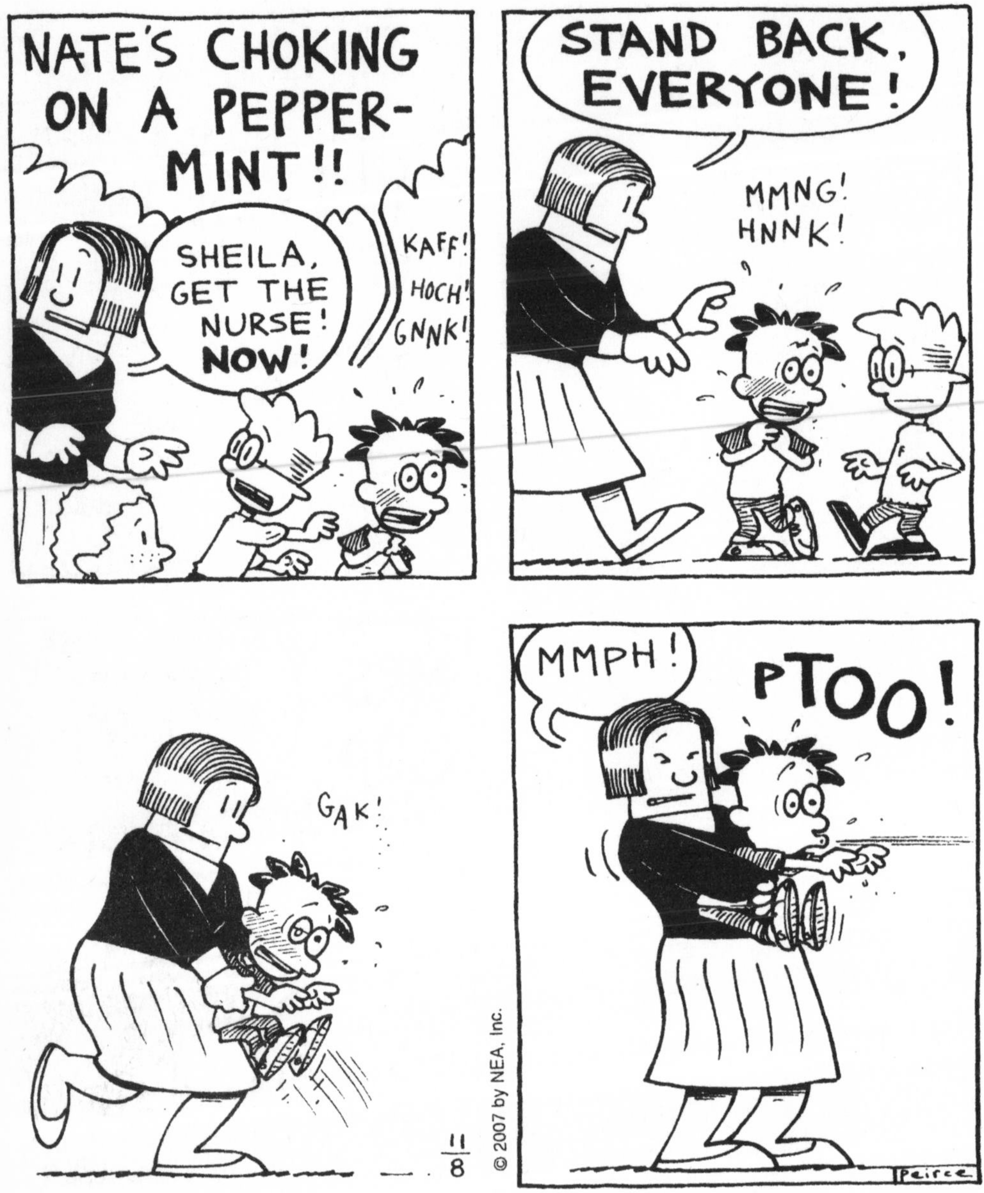
NATE'S CHOKING ON A PEPPER-MINT!!
SHEILA, GET THE NURSE! NOW!
KAFF! HOCH! GNNK!
STAND BACK, EVERYONE!
MMNG! HNNK!
GAK!
MMPH!
PTOO!
11/8
© 2007 by NEA, Inc.
Peirce

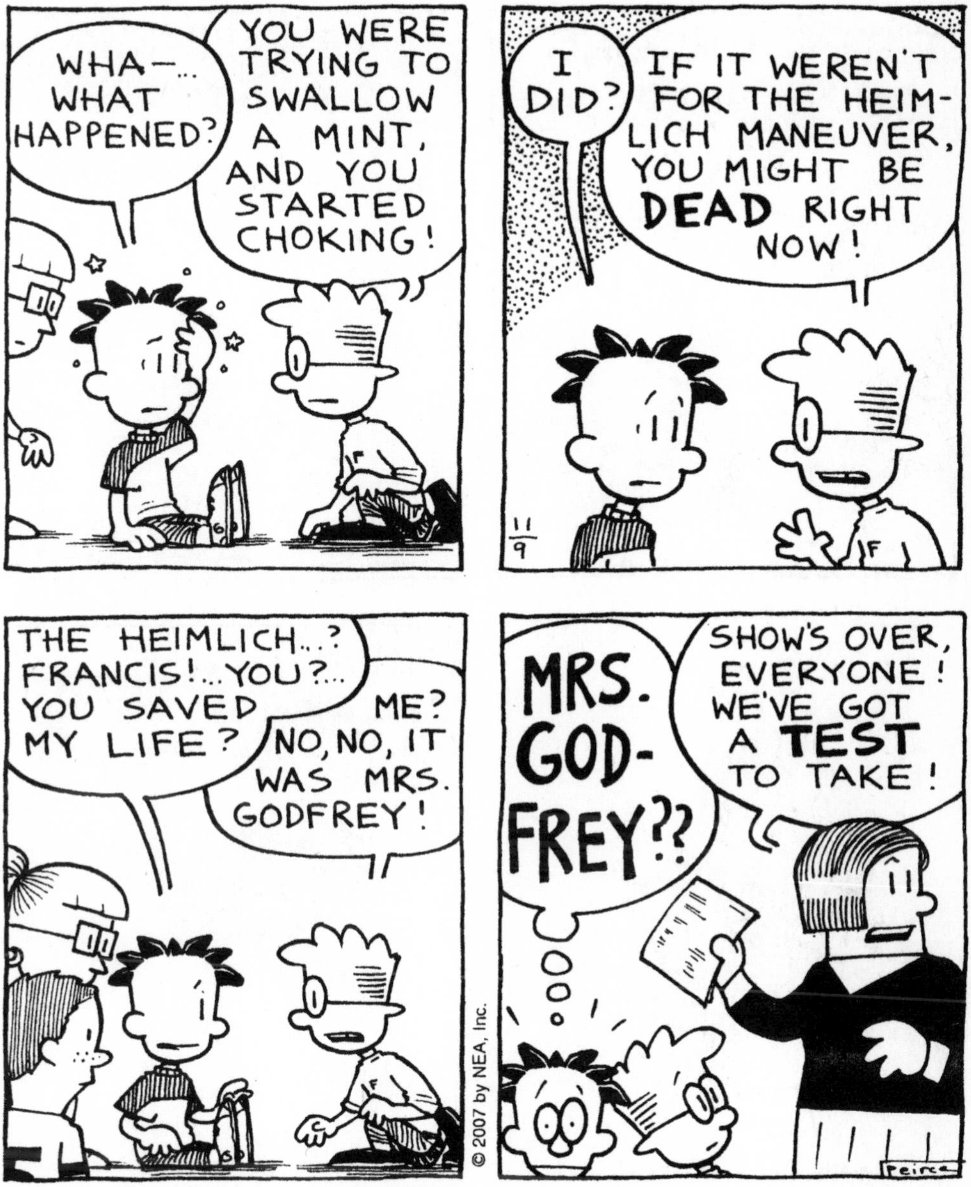
WHA–... WHAT HAPPENED?
YOU WERE TRYING TO SWALLOW A MINT, AND YOU STARTED CHOKING!
I DID?
IF IT WEREN'T FOR THE HEIMLICH MANEUVER, YOU MIGHT BE **DEAD** RIGHT NOW!
THE HEIMLICH...? FRANCIS!...YOU?... YOU SAVED MY LIFE?
ME? NO, NO, IT WAS MRS. GODFREY!
MRS. GODFREY??
SHOW'S OVER, EVERYONE! WE'VE GOT A **TEST** TO TAKE!
Peirce

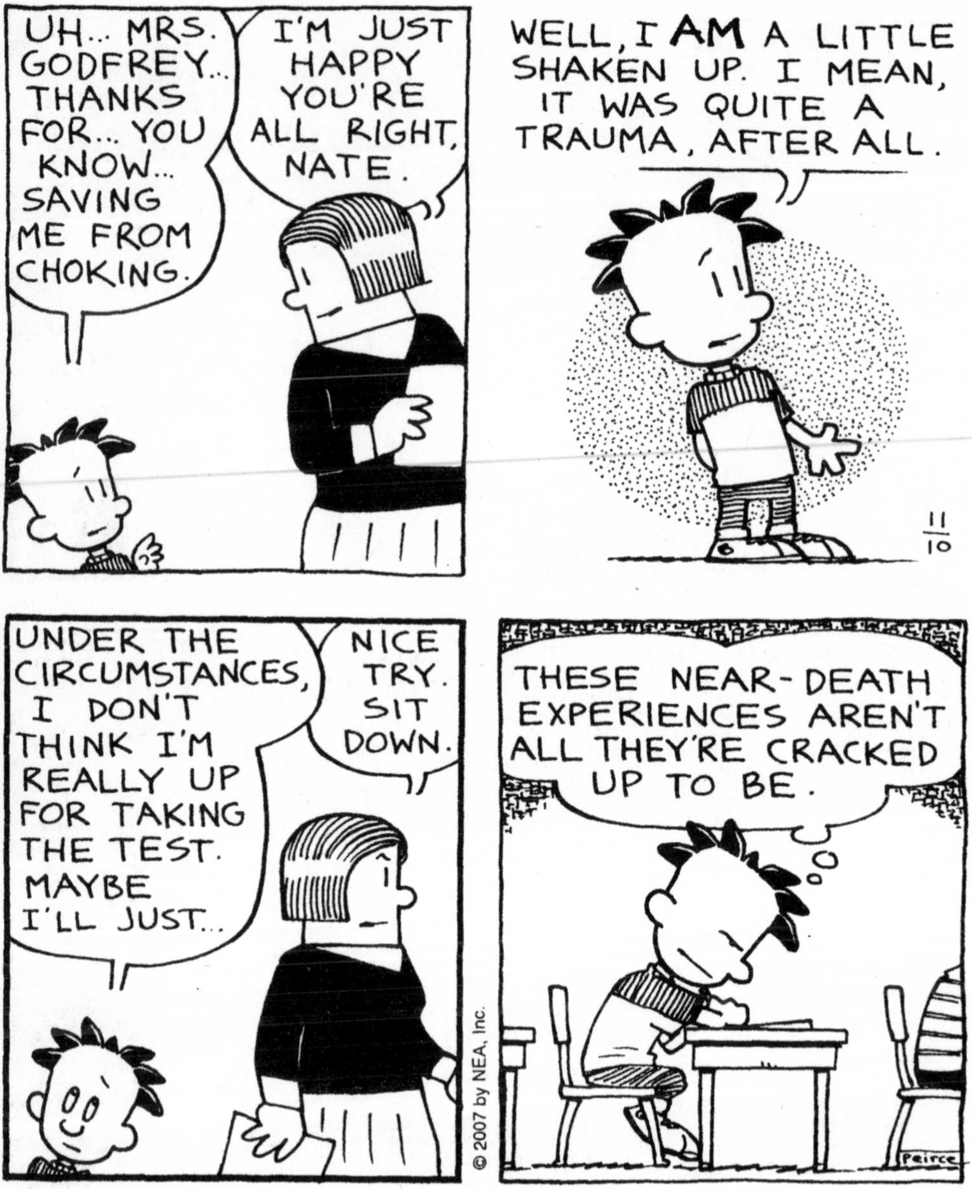
UH... MRS. GODFREY... THANKS FOR... YOU KNOW... SAVING ME FROM CHOKING.
I'M JUST HAPPY YOU'RE ALL RIGHT, NATE.
WELL, I AM A LITTLE SHAKEN UP. I MEAN, IT WAS QUITE A TRAUMA, AFTER ALL.
11/10
UNDER THE CIRCUMSTANCES, I DON'T THINK I'M REALLY UP FOR TAKING THE TEST. MAYBE I'LL JUST...
NICE TRY. SIT DOWN.
THESE NEAR-DEATH EXPERIENCES AREN'T ALL THEY'RE CRACKED UP TO BE.
Peirce

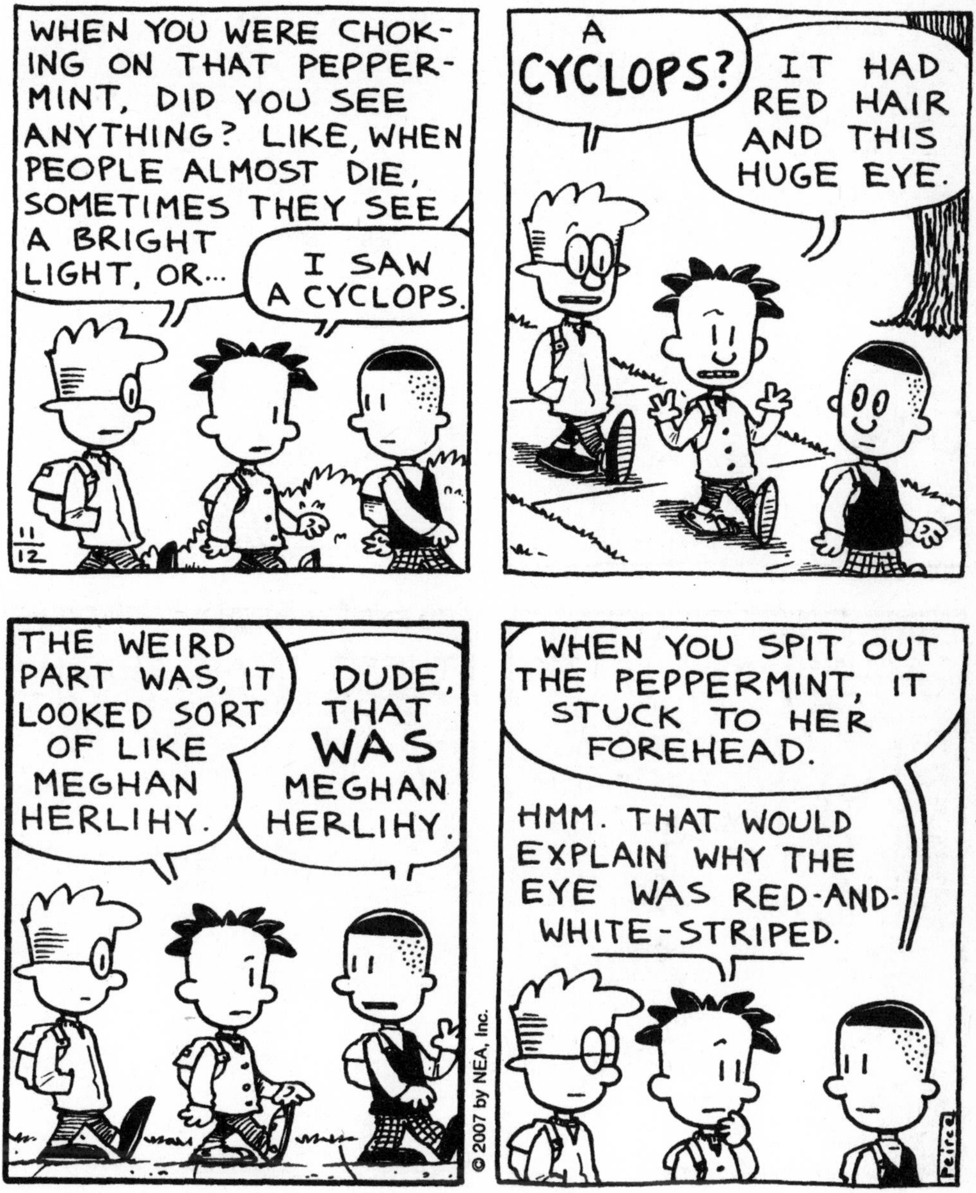
WHEN YOU WERE CHOKING ON THAT PEPPERMINT, DID YOU SEE ANYTHING? LIKE, WHEN PEOPLE ALMOST DIE, SOMETIMES THEY SEE A BRIGHT LIGHT, OR...
I SAW A CYCLOPS.
11/12
A CYCLOPS?
IT HAD RED HAIR AND THIS HUGE EYE.
THE WEIRD PART WAS, IT LOOKED SORT OF LIKE MEGHAN HERLIHY.
DUDE, THAT WAS MEGHAN HERLIHY.
© 2007 by NEA, Inc.
WHEN YOU SPIT OUT THE PEPPERMINT, IT STUCK TO HER FOREHEAD.
HMM. THAT WOULD EXPLAIN WHY THE EYE WAS RED-AND-WHITE-STRIPED.
Peirce

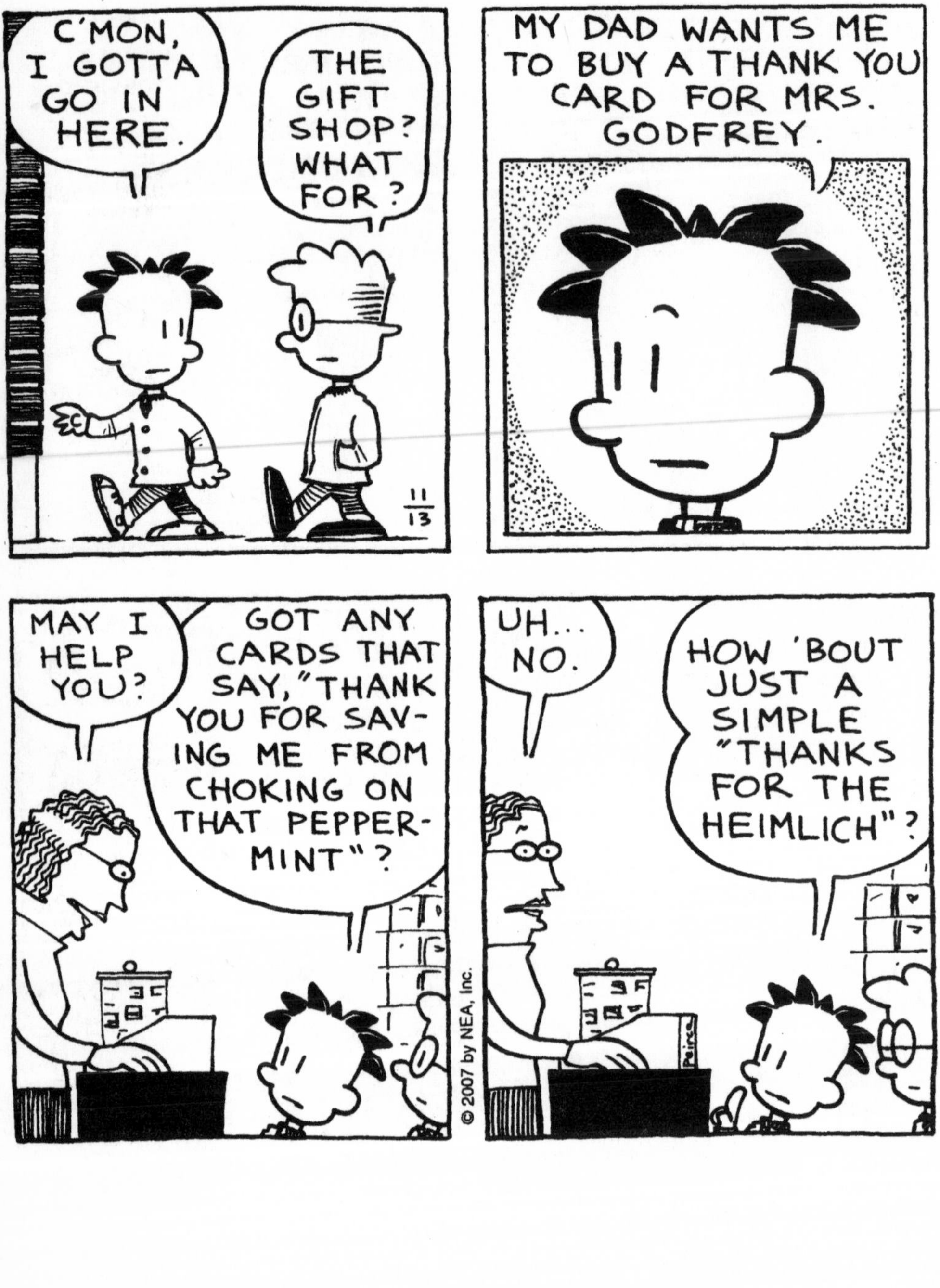

C'MON, I GOTTA GO IN HERE.
THE GIFT SHOP? WHAT FOR?
11
13
MY DAD WANTS ME TO BUY A THANK YOU CARD FOR MRS. GODFREY.
MAY I HELP YOU?
GOT ANY CARDS THAT SAY, "THANK YOU FOR SAVING ME FROM CHOKING ON THAT PEPPERMINT"?
© 2007 by NEA, Inc.
UH... NO.
HOW 'BOUT JUST A SIMPLE "THANKS FOR THE HEIMLICH"?
Peirce

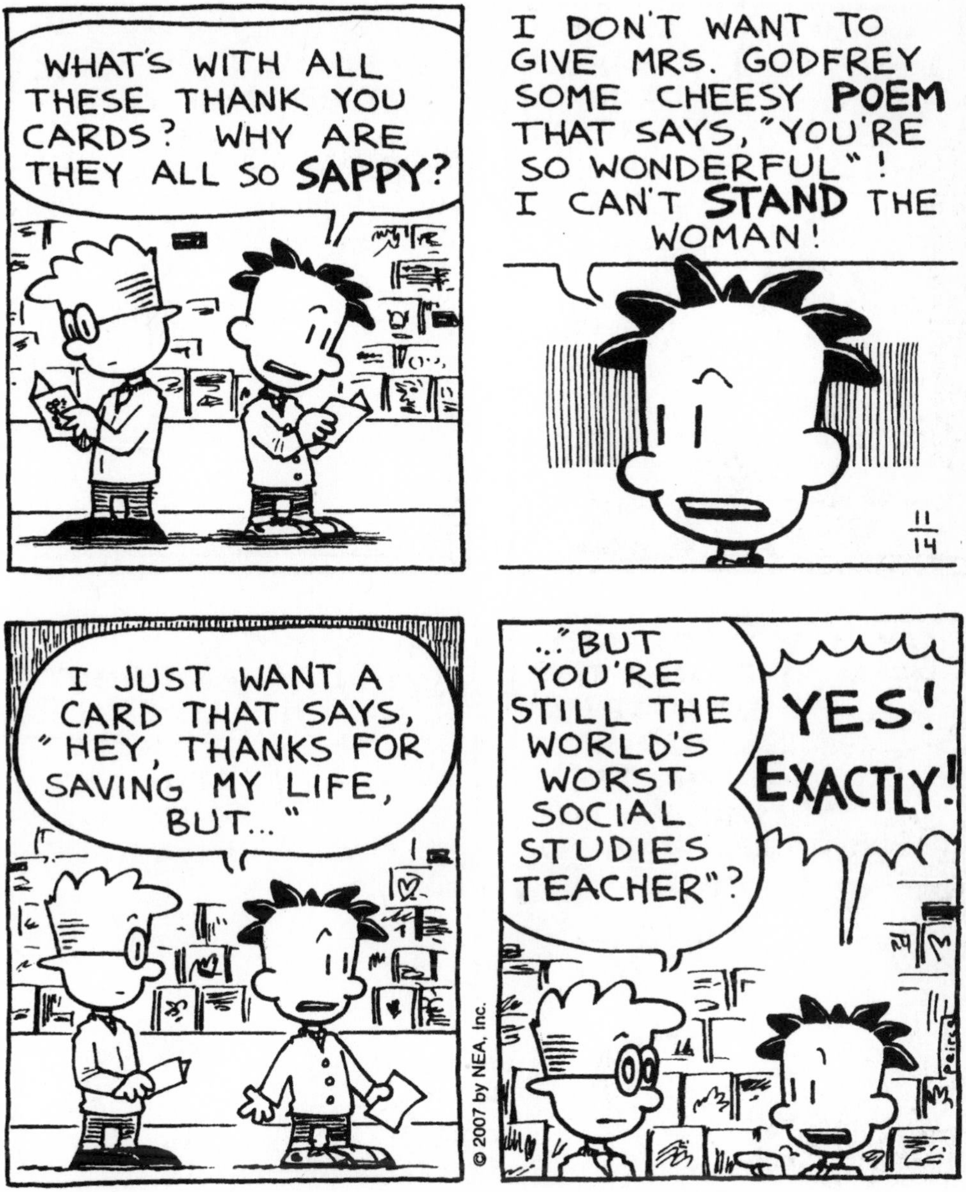
WHAT'S WITH ALL THESE THANK YOU CARDS? WHY ARE THEY ALL SO **SAPPY**?
I DON'T WANT TO GIVE MRS. GODFREY SOME CHEESY **POEM** THAT SAYS, "YOU'RE SO WONDERFUL"! I CAN'T **STAND** THE WOMAN!
I JUST WANT A CARD THAT SAYS, "HEY, THANKS FOR SAVING MY LIFE, BUT..."
..."BUT YOU'RE STILL THE WORLD'S WORST SOCIAL STUDIES TEACHER"?
YES! EXACTLY!

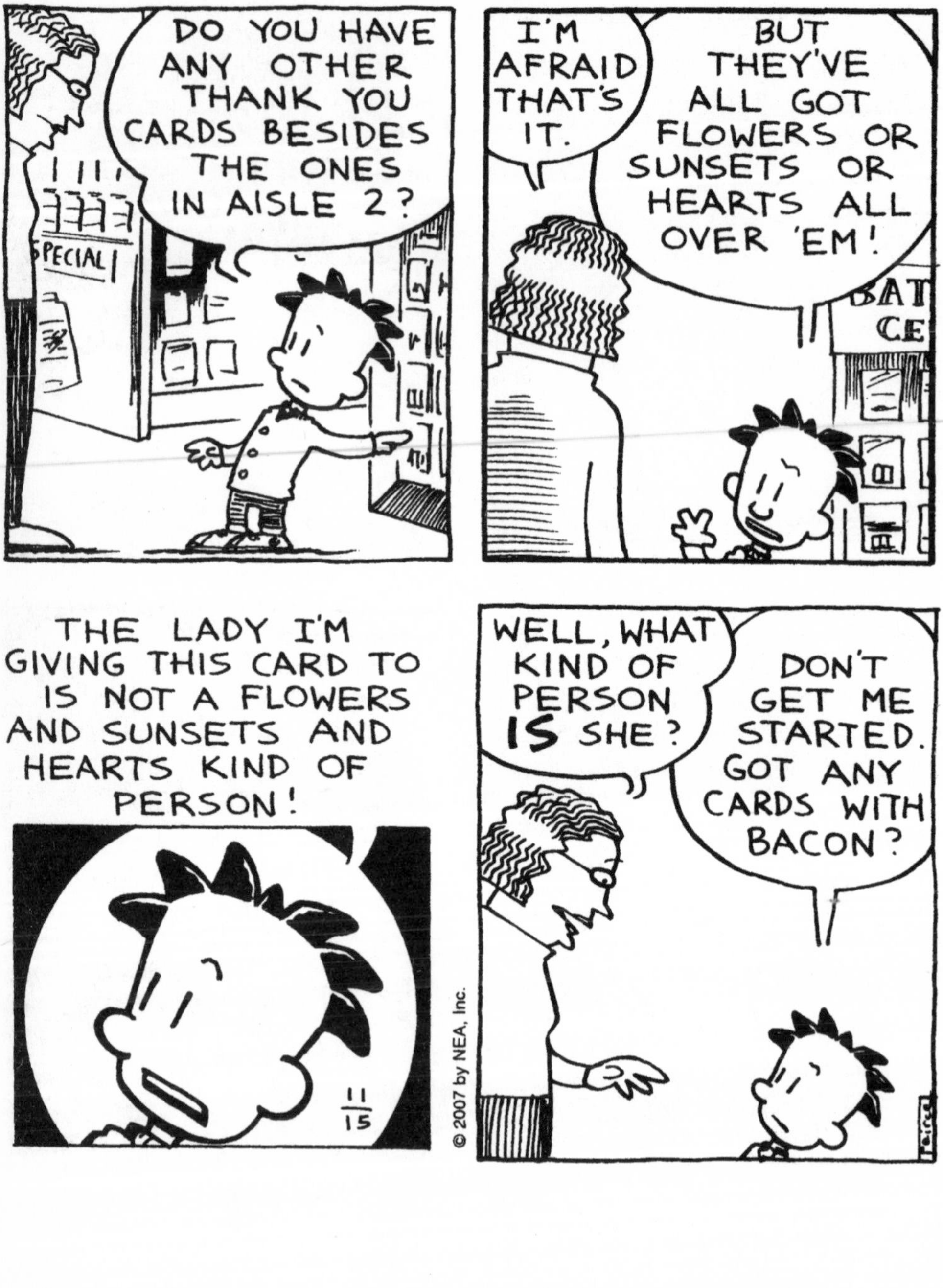
DO YOU HAVE ANY OTHER THANK YOU CARDS BESIDES THE ONES IN AISLE 2?
SPECIAL
I'M AFRAID THAT'S IT.
BUT THEY'VE ALL GOT FLOWERS OR SUNSETS OR HEARTS ALL OVER 'EM!
THE LADY I'M GIVING THIS CARD TO IS NOT A FLOWERS AND SUNSETS AND HEARTS KIND OF PERSON!
11/15
WELL, WHAT KIND OF PERSON **IS** SHE?
DON'T GET ME STARTED. GOT ANY CARDS WITH BACON?

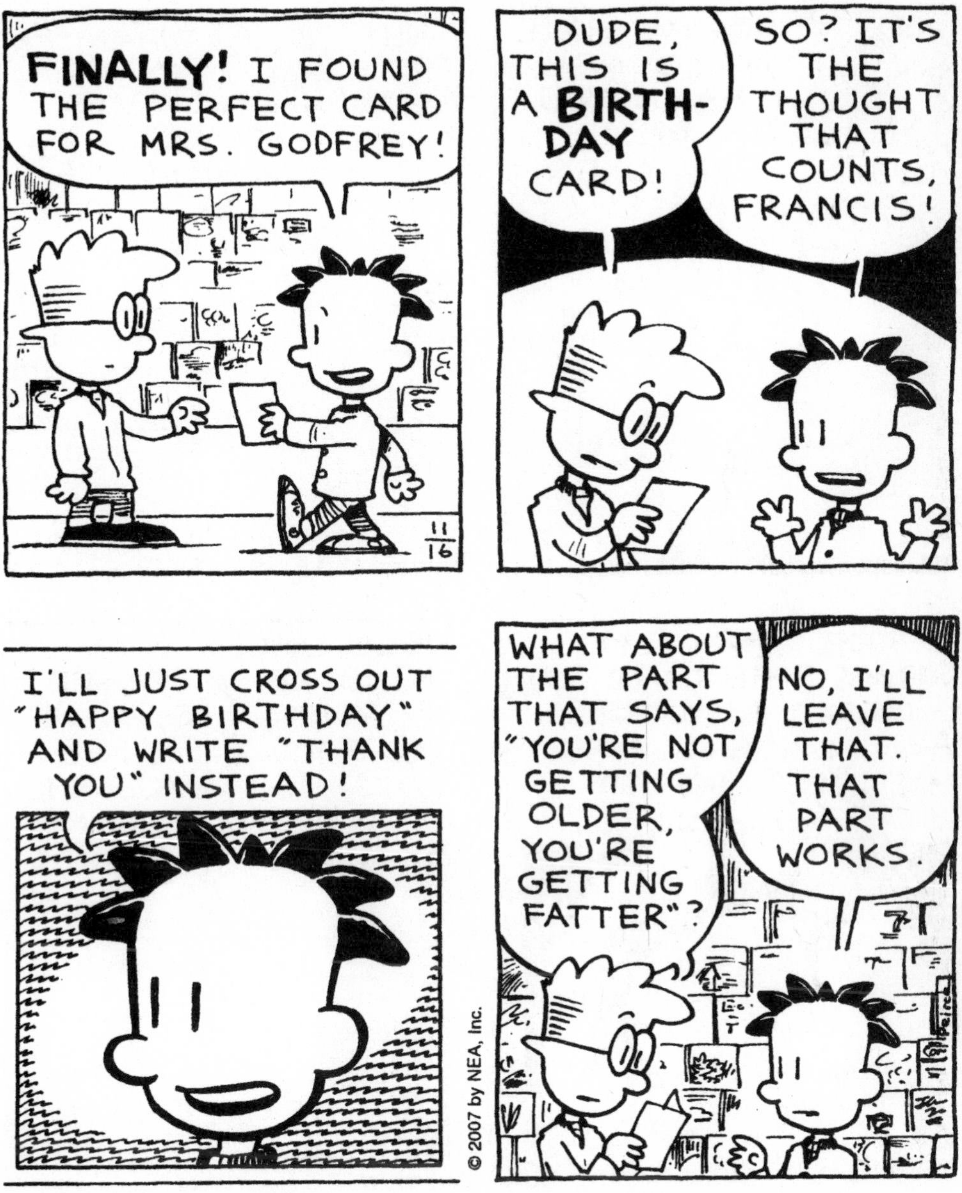
FINALLY! I FOUND THE PERFECT CARD FOR MRS. GODFREY!
11/16
DUDE, THIS IS A BIRTHDAY CARD!
SO? IT'S THE THOUGHT THAT COUNTS, FRANCIS!
I'LL JUST CROSS OUT "HAPPY BIRTHDAY" AND WRITE "THANK YOU" INSTEAD!
WHAT ABOUT THE PART THAT SAYS, "YOU'RE NOT GETTING OLDER, YOU'RE GETTING FATTER"?
NO, I'LL LEAVE THAT. THAT PART WORKS.

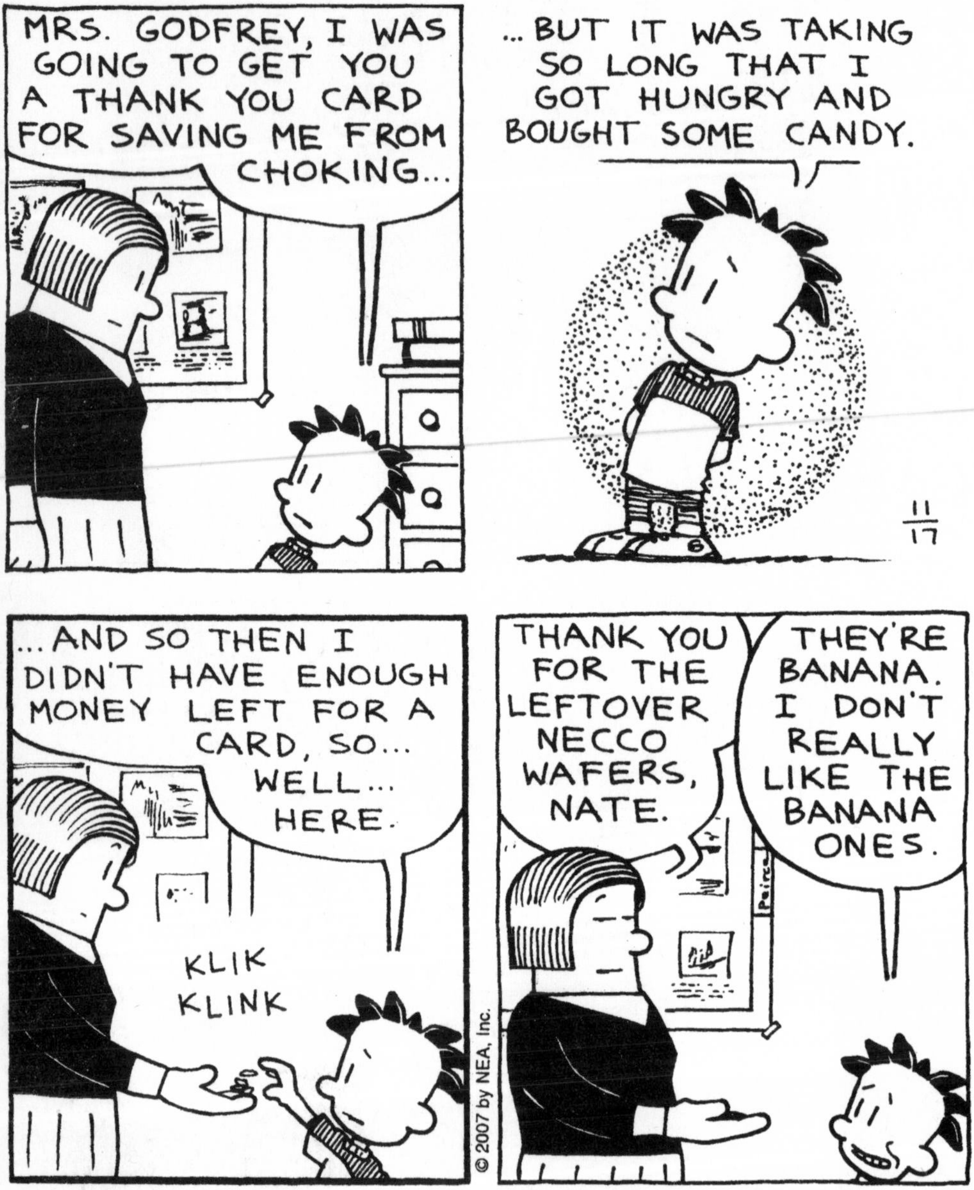
MRS. GODFREY, I WAS GOING TO GET YOU A THANK YOU CARD FOR SAVING ME FROM CHOKING...
...BUT IT WAS TAKING SO LONG THAT I GOT HUNGRY AND BOUGHT SOME CANDY.
11/17
...AND SO THEN I DIDN'T HAVE ENOUGH MONEY LEFT FOR A CARD, SO... WELL... HERE.
KLIK
KLINK
© 2007 by NEA, Inc.
THANK YOU FOR THE LEFTOVER NECCO WAFERS, NATE.
THEY'RE BANANA. I DON'T REALLY LIKE THE BANANA ONES.

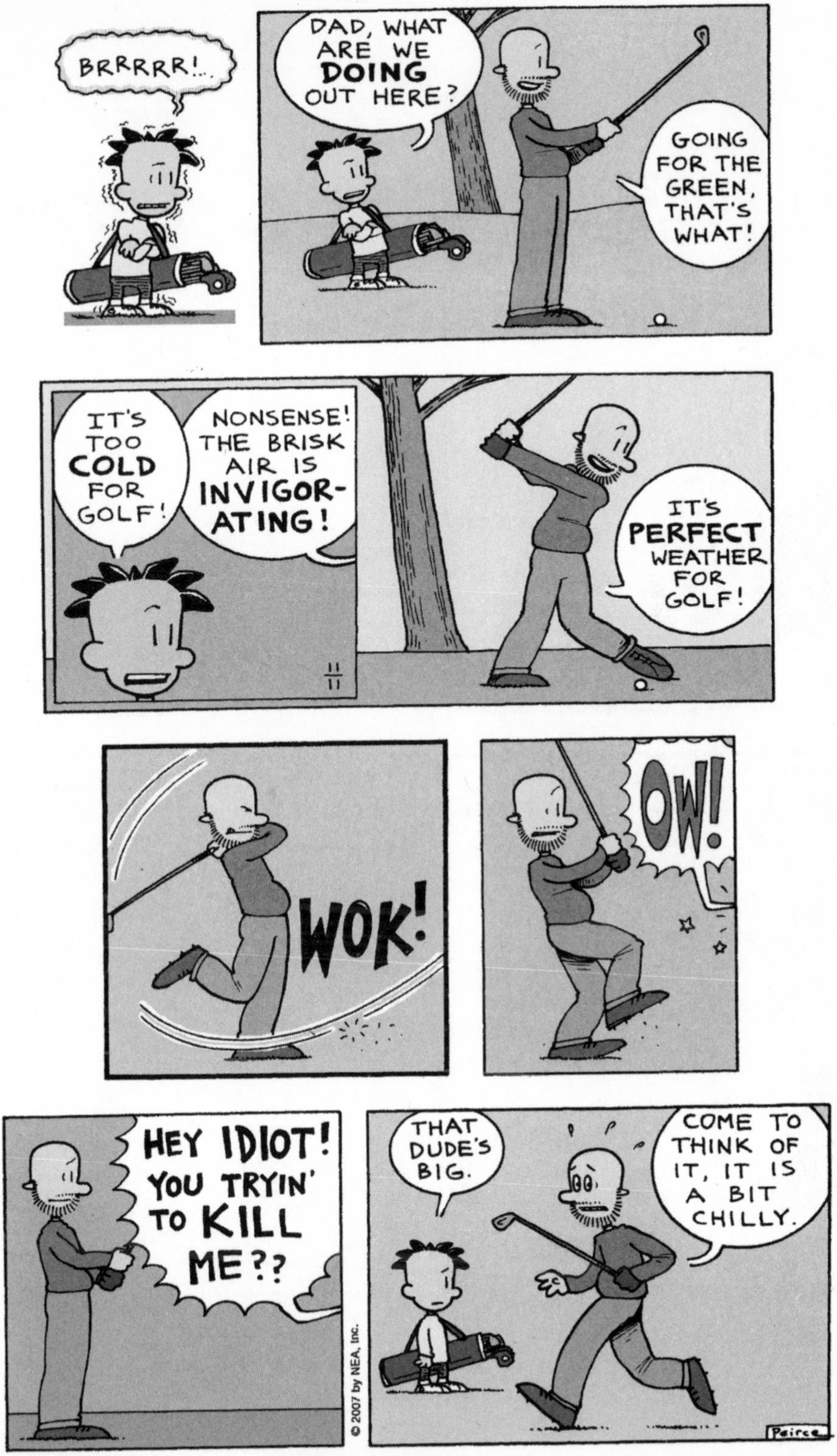
BRRRRR!...
DAD, WHAT ARE WE DOING OUT HERE?
GOING FOR THE GREEN, THAT'S WHAT!
IT'S TOO COLD FOR GOLF!
NONSENSE! THE BRISK AIR IS INVIGOR-ATING!
IT'S PERFECT WEATHER FOR GOLF!
WOK!
OW!
HEY IDIOT! YOU TRYIN' TO KILL ME??
© 2007 by NEA, Inc.
THAT DUDE'S BIG.
COME TO THINK OF IT, IT IS A BIT CHILLY.
Peirce

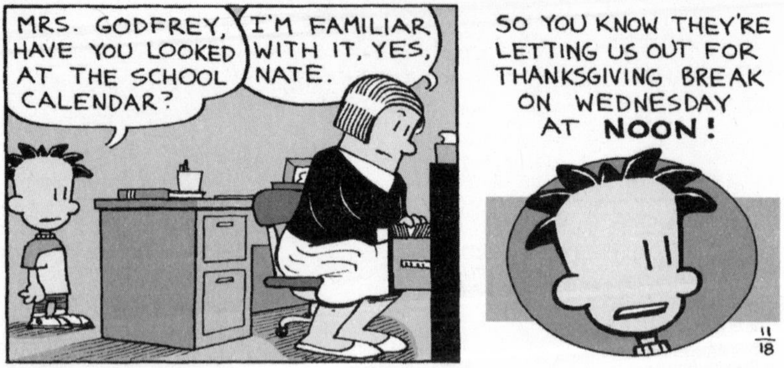
MRS. GODFREY, HAVE YOU LOOKED AT THE SCHOOL CALENDAR?
I'M FAMILIAR WITH IT, YES, NATE.
SO YOU KNOW THEY'RE LETTING US OUT FOR THANKSGIVING BREAK ON WEDNESDAY AT NOON!
11/18

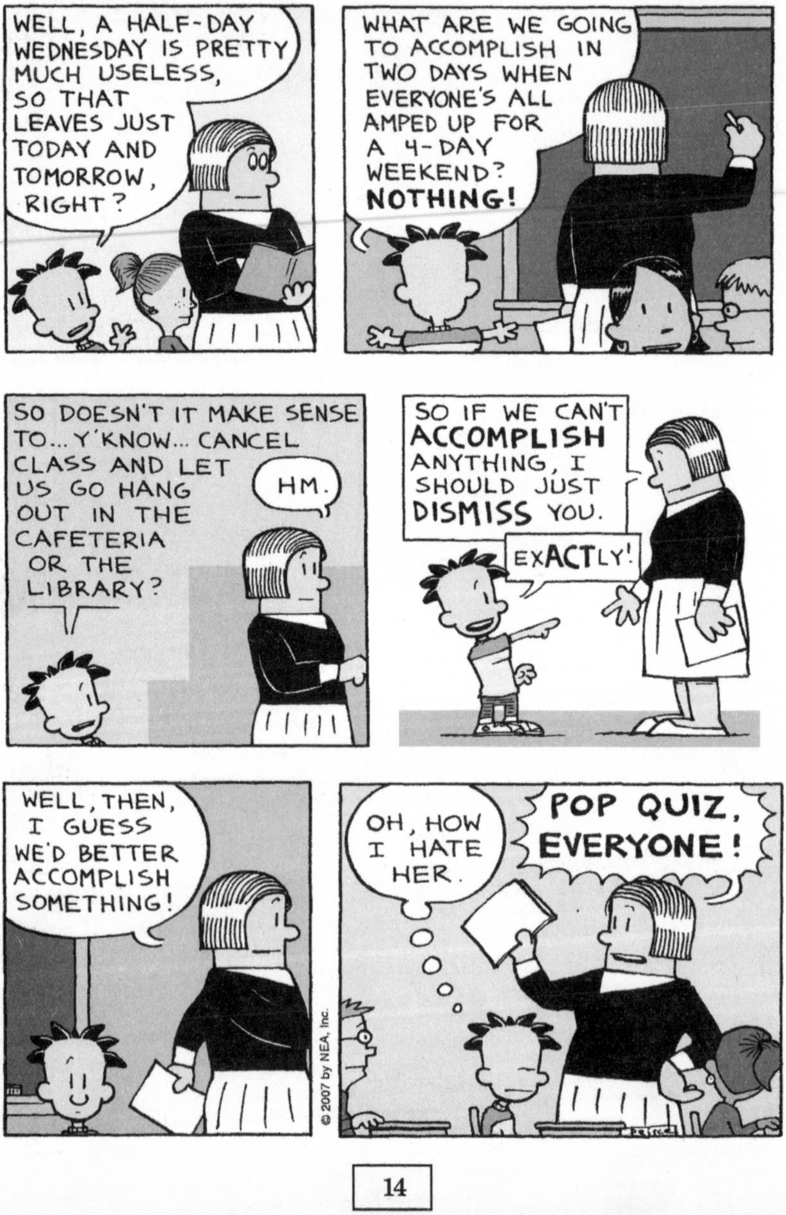
WELL, A HALF-DAY WEDNESDAY IS PRETTY MUCH USELESS, SO THAT LEAVES JUST TODAY AND TOMORROW, RIGHT?
WHAT ARE WE GOING TO ACCOMPLISH IN TWO DAYS WHEN EVERYONE'S ALL AMPED UP FOR A 4-DAY WEEKEND? NOTHING!
SO DOESN'T IT MAKE SENSE TO... Y'KNOW... CANCEL CLASS AND LET US GO HANG OUT IN THE CAFETERIA OR THE LIBRARY?
HM.
SO IF WE CAN'T ACCOMPLISH ANYTHING, I SHOULD JUST DISMISS YOU.
EXACTLY!
WELL, THEN, I GUESS WE'D BETTER ACCOMPLISH SOMETHING!
OH, HOW I HATE HER.
POP QUIZ, EVERYONE!

WHO WANTS TO PLAY SOCIAL STUDIES JEOPARDY?

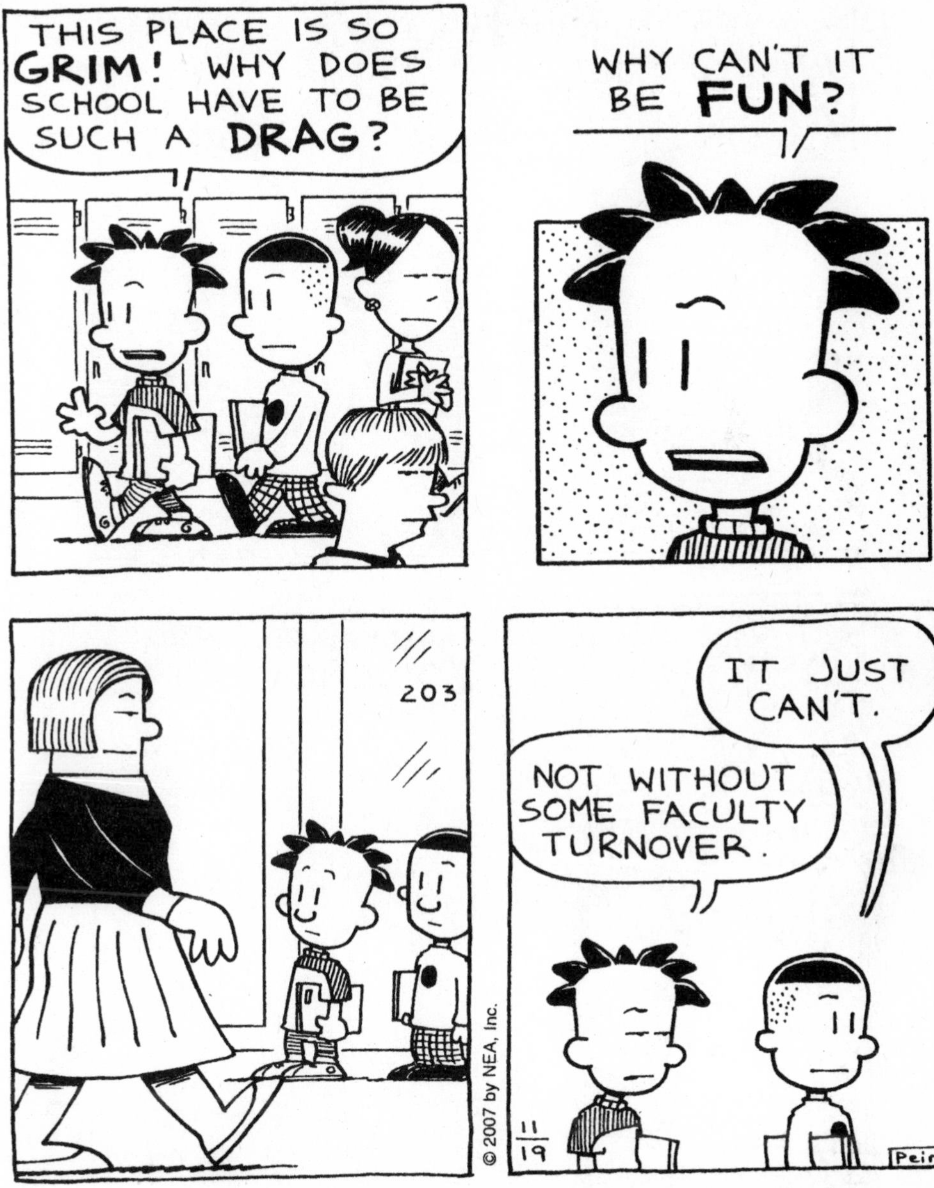
THIS PLACE IS SO GRIM! WHY DOES SCHOOL HAVE TO BE SUCH A DRAG?
WHY CAN'T IT BE FUN?
203
IT JUST CAN'T.
NOT WITHOUT SOME FACULTY TURNOVER.
11/19
Peirce
© 2007 by NEA, Inc.

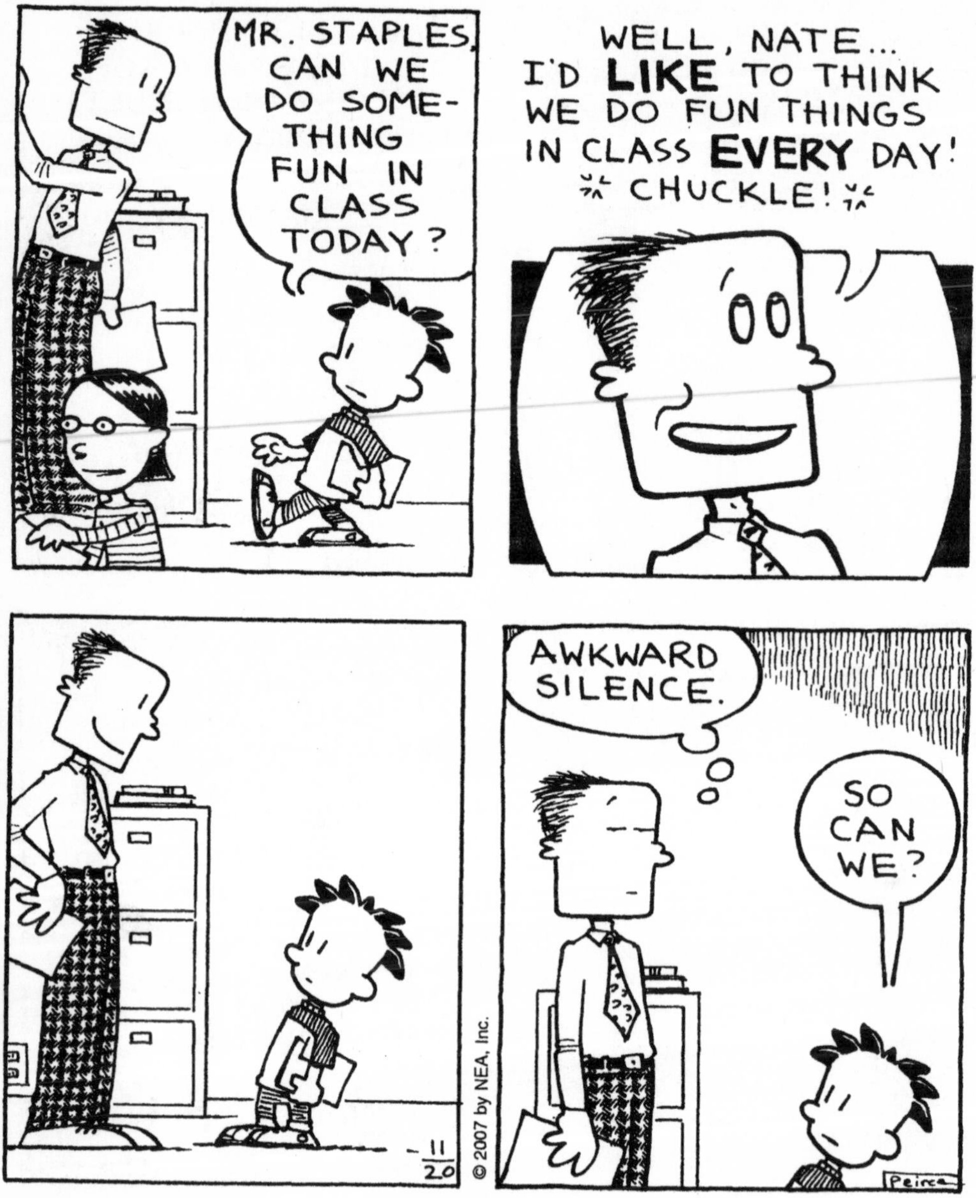
MR. STAPLES, CAN WE DO SOME-THING FUN IN CLASS TODAY?
WELL, NATE... I'D **LIKE** TO THINK WE DO FUN THINGS IN CLASS **EVERY** DAY!
CHUCKLE!
11-20
© 2007 by NEA, Inc.
AWKWARD SILENCE.
SO CAN WE?
Peirce

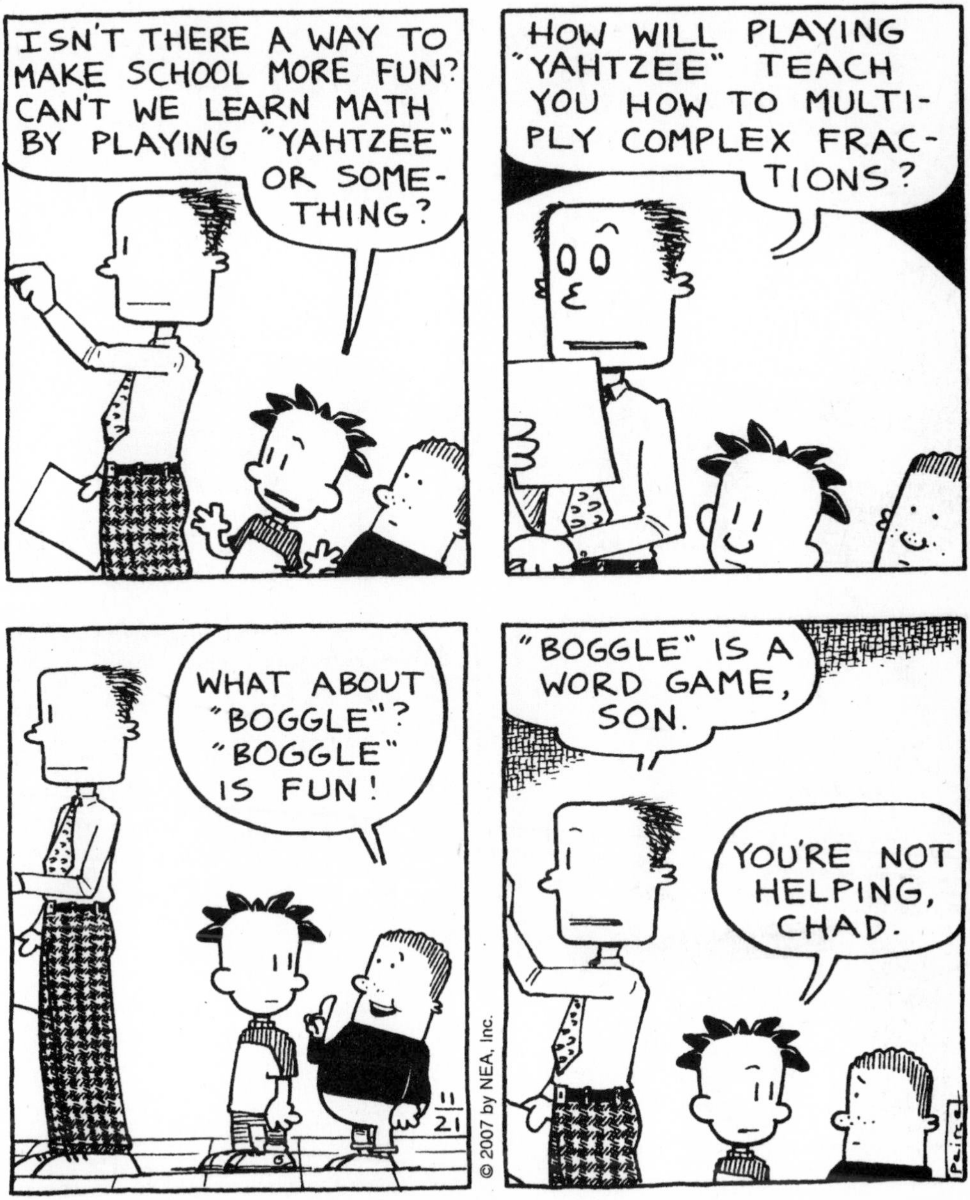
ISN'T THERE A WAY TO MAKE SCHOOL MORE FUN? CAN'T WE LEARN MATH BY PLAYING "YAHTZEE" OR SOMETHING?
HOW WILL PLAYING "YAHTZEE" TEACH YOU HOW TO MULTIPLY COMPLEX FRACTIONS?
WHAT ABOUT "BOGGLE"? "BOGGLE" IS FUN!
11/21
"BOGGLE" IS A WORD GAME, SON.
YOU'RE NOT HELPING, CHAD.
PEIRCE

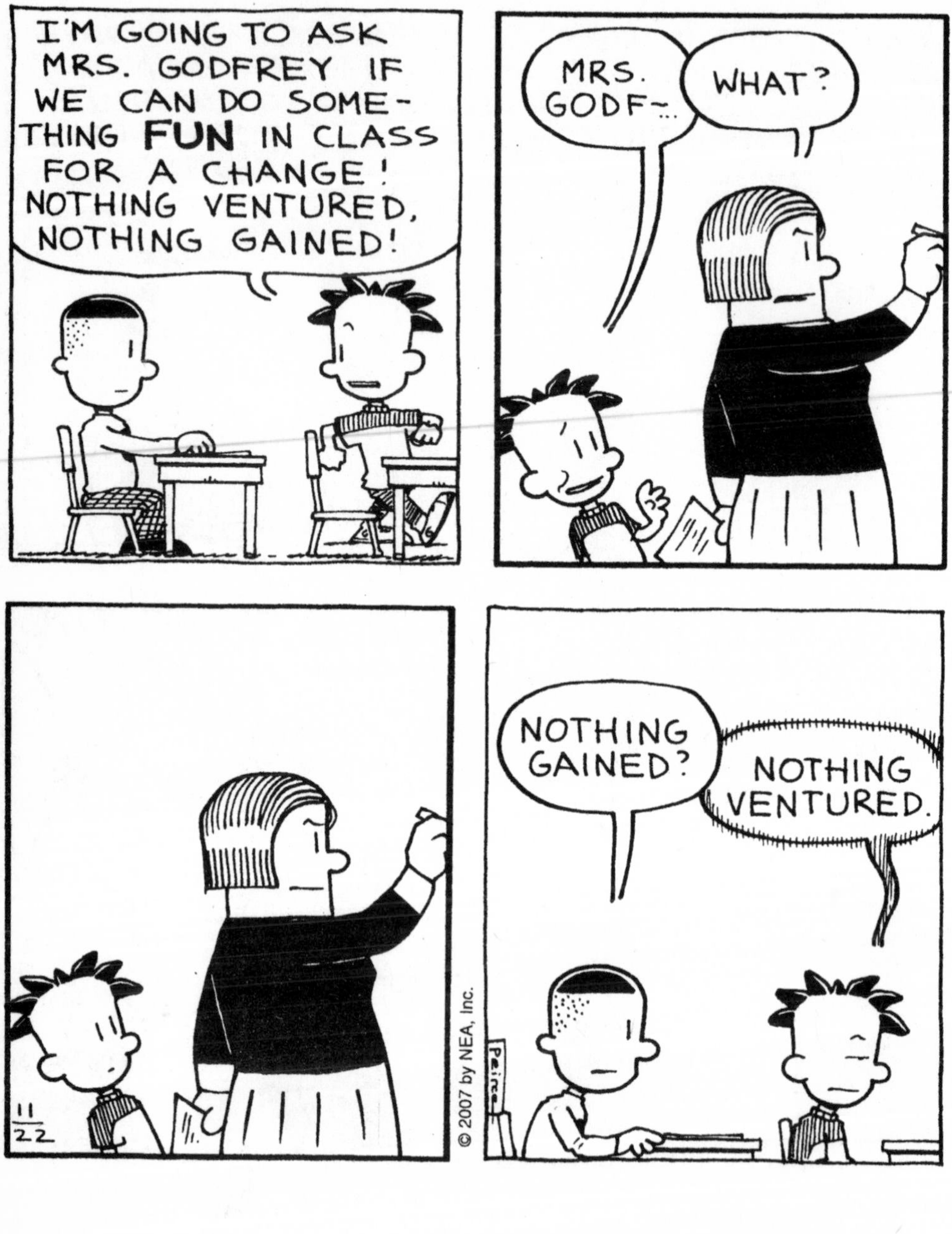
I'M GOING TO ASK MRS. GODFREY IF WE CAN DO SOMETHING **FUN** IN CLASS FOR A CHANGE! NOTHING VENTURED, NOTHING GAINED!
MRS. GODF~...
WHAT?
11/22
© 2007 by NEA, Inc.
Peirce
NOTHING GAINED?
NOTHING VENTURED.

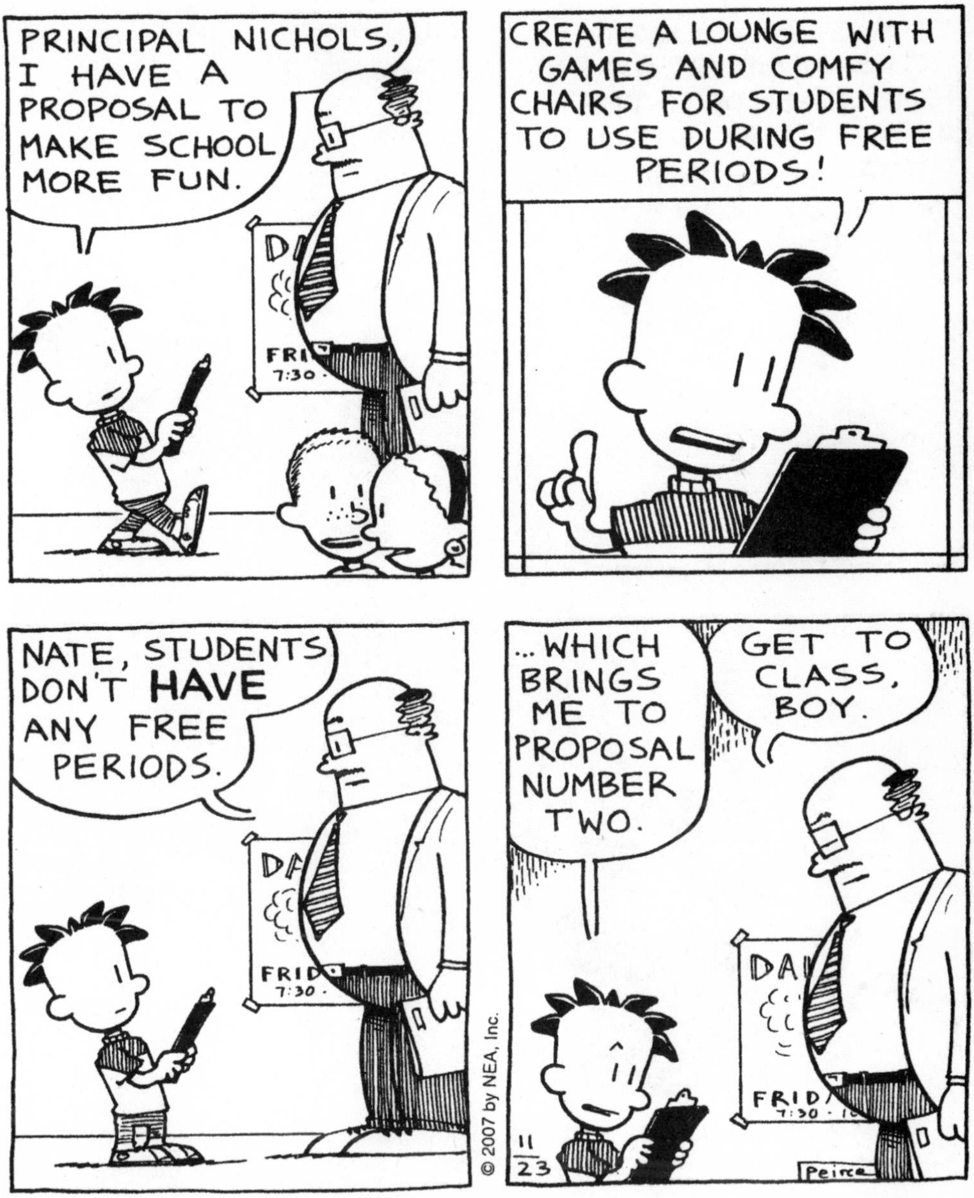
PRINCIPAL NICHOLS, I HAVE A PROPOSAL TO MAKE SCHOOL MORE FUN.
CREATE A LOUNGE WITH GAMES AND COMFY CHAIRS FOR STUDENTS TO USE DURING FREE PERIODS!
NATE, STUDENTS DON'T **HAVE** ANY FREE PERIODS.
...WHICH BRINGS ME TO PROPOSAL NUMBER TWO.
GET TO CLASS, BOY.
11
23
Peirce

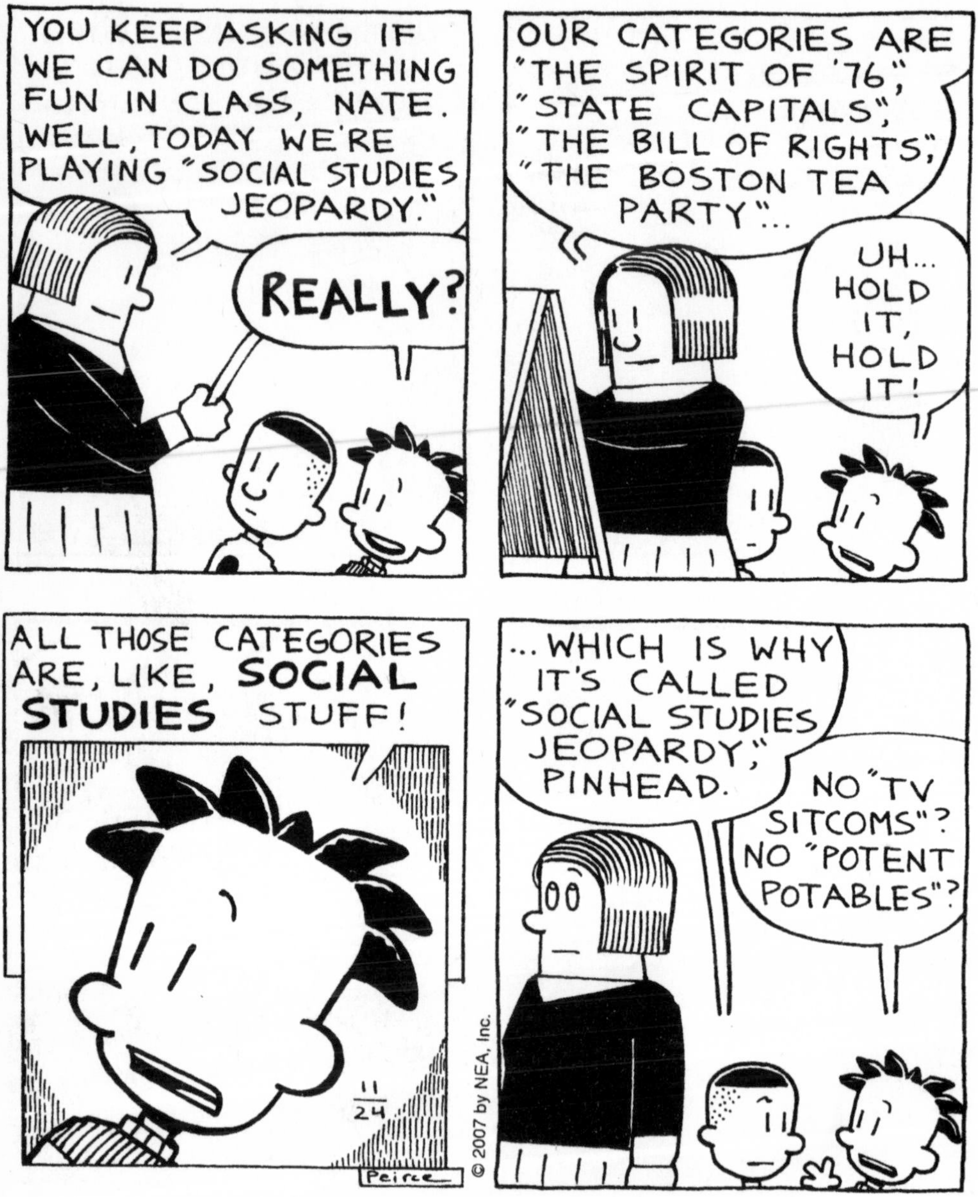
YOU KEEP ASKING IF WE CAN DO SOMETHING FUN IN CLASS, NATE. WELL, TODAY WE'RE PLAYING "SOCIAL STUDIES JEOPARDY."
REALLY?
OUR CATEGORIES ARE "THE SPIRIT OF '76," "STATE CAPITALS," "THE BILL OF RIGHTS," "THE BOSTON TEA PARTY"...
UH... HOLD IT, HOLD IT!
ALL THOSE CATEGORIES ARE, LIKE, SOCIAL STUDIES STUFF!
11/24
Peirce
© 2007 by NEA, Inc.
...WHICH IS WHY IT'S CALLED "SOCIAL STUDIES JEOPARDY," PINHEAD.
NO "TV SITCOMS"? NO "POTENT POTABLES"?

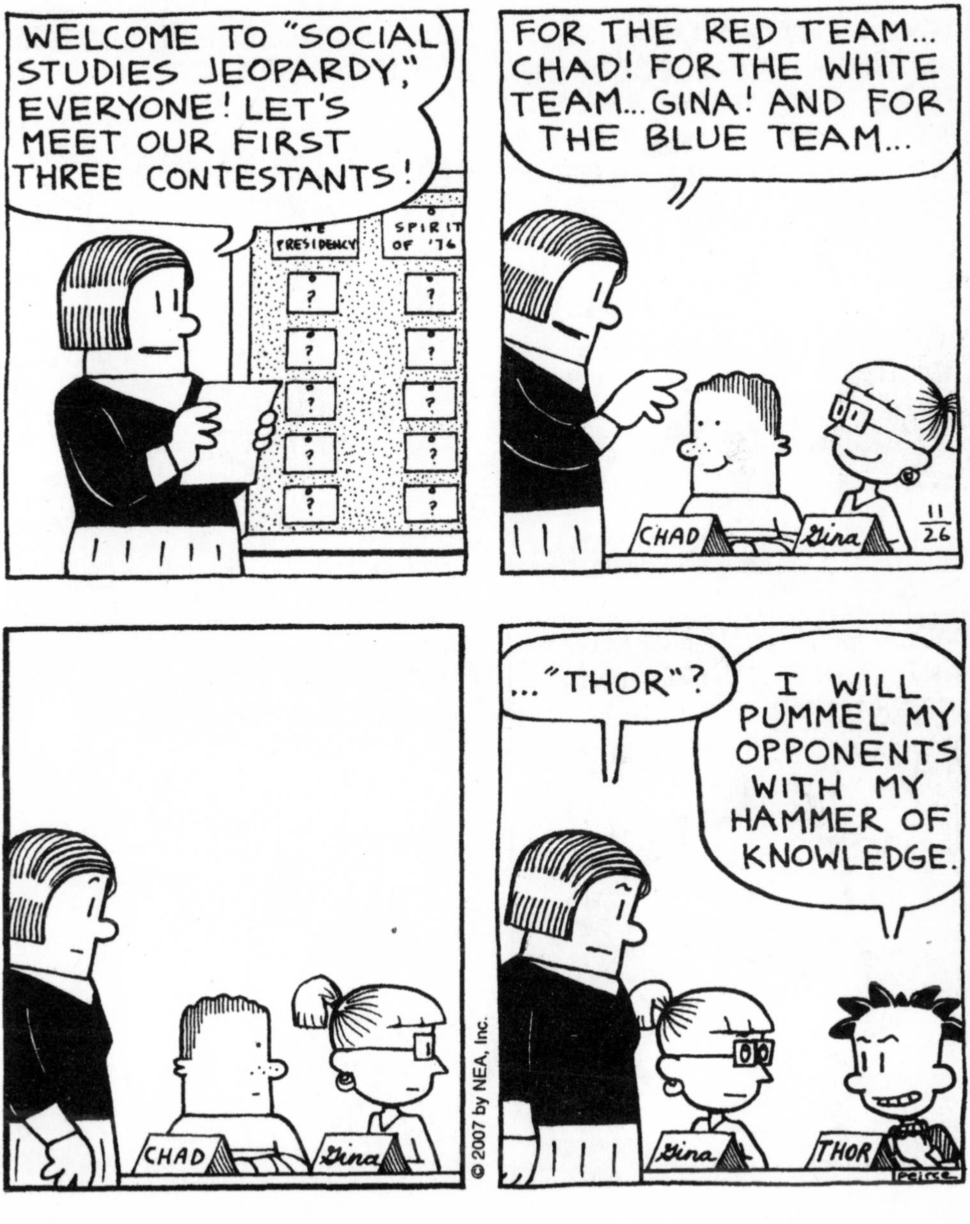
WELCOME TO "SOCIAL STUDIES JEOPARDY," EVERYONE! LET'S MEET OUR FIRST THREE CONTESTANTS!
PRESIDENCY
SPIRIT OF '76
FOR THE RED TEAM... CHAD! FOR THE WHITE TEAM... GINA! AND FOR THE BLUE TEAM...
CHAD
Gina
11/26
CHAD
Gina
..."THOR"?
I WILL PUMMEL MY OPPONENTS WITH MY HAMMER OF KNOWLEDGE.
Gina
THOR
PEIRCE
© 2007 by NEA, Inc.

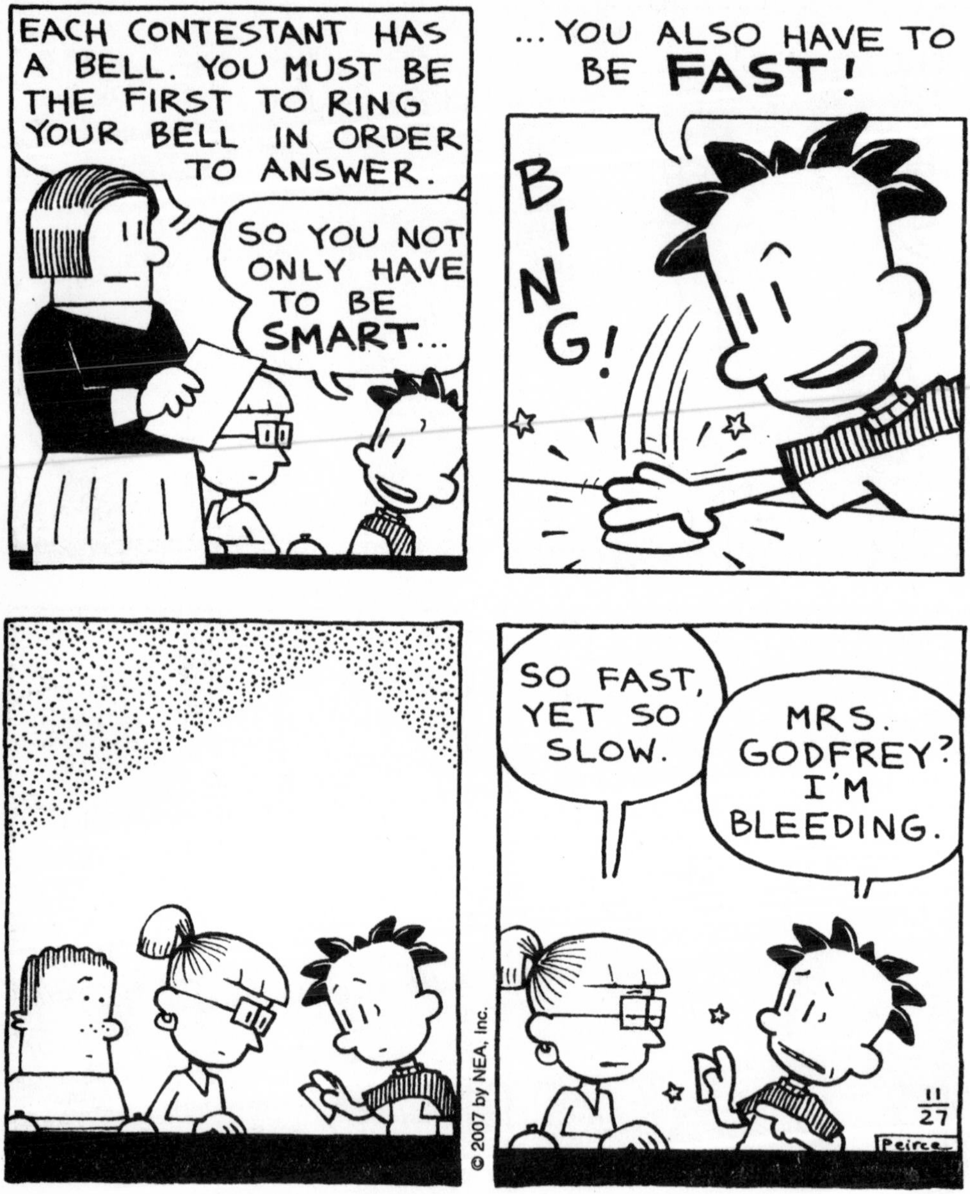
EACH CONTESTANT HAS A BELL. YOU MUST BE THE FIRST TO RING YOUR BELL IN ORDER TO ANSWER.
SO YOU NOT ONLY HAVE TO BE SMART...
...YOU ALSO HAVE TO BE FAST!
BING!
SO FAST, YET SO SLOW.
MRS. GODFREY? I'M BLEEDING.
11/27
Peirce

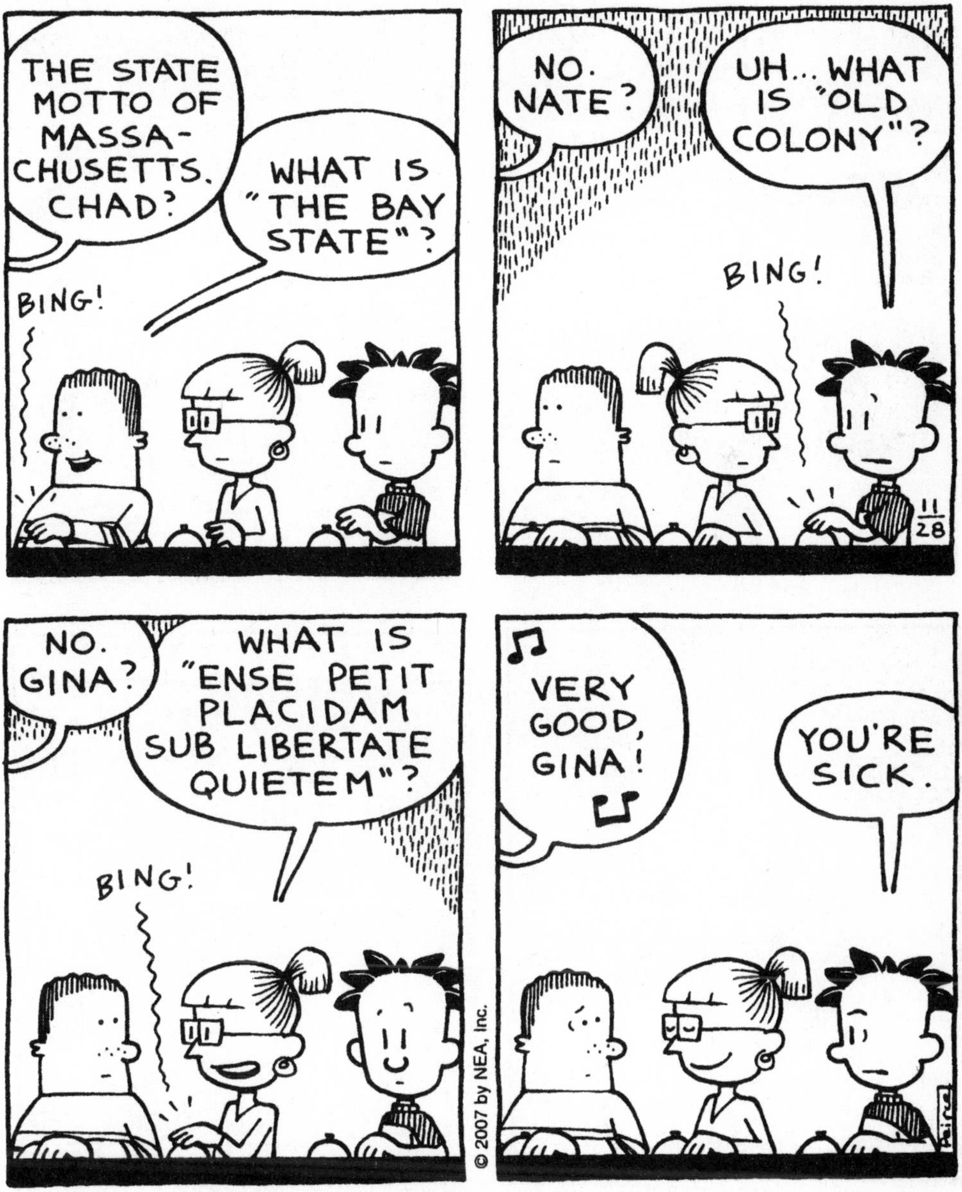
THE STATE MOTTO OF MASSA-CHUSETTS. CHAD?
WHAT IS "THE BAY STATE"?
BING!
NO. NATE?
UH... WHAT IS "OLD COLONY"?
BING!
11/28
NO. GINA?
WHAT IS "ENSE PETIT PLACIDAM SUB LIBERTATE QUIETEM"?
BING!
VERY GOOD, GINA!
YOU'RE SICK.

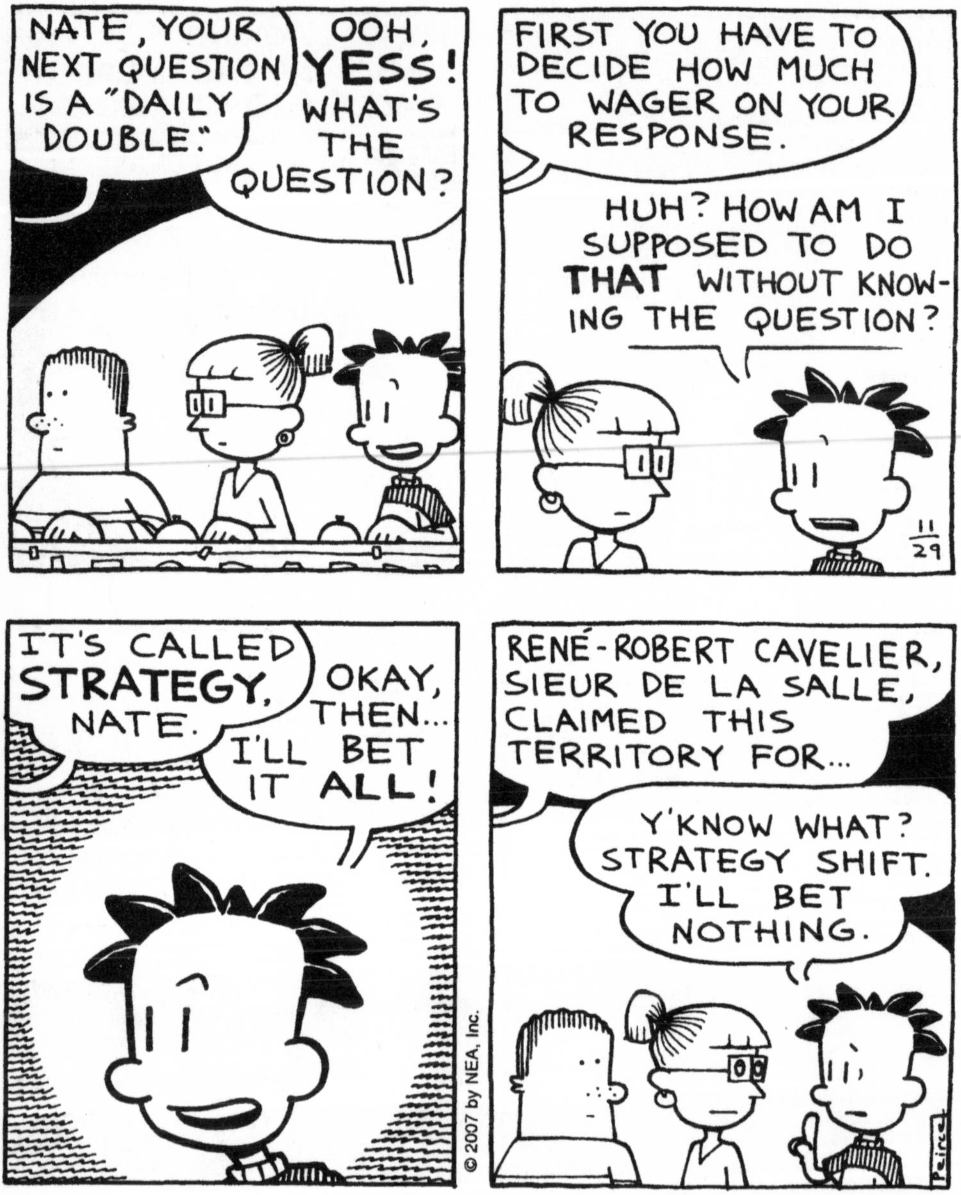
NATE, YOUR NEXT QUESTION IS A "DAILY DOUBLE."
OOH, YESS! WHAT'S THE QUESTION?
FIRST YOU HAVE TO DECIDE HOW MUCH TO WAGER ON YOUR RESPONSE.
HUH? HOW AM I SUPPOSED TO DO THAT WITHOUT KNOWING THE QUESTION?
11/29
IT'S CALLED STRATEGY, NATE.
OKAY, THEN... I'LL BET IT ALL!
© 2007 by NEA, Inc.
RENÉ-ROBERT CAVELIER, SIEUR DE LA SALLE, CLAIMED THIS TERRITORY FOR...
Y'KNOW WHAT? STRATEGY SHIFT. I'LL BET NOTHING.
Peirce

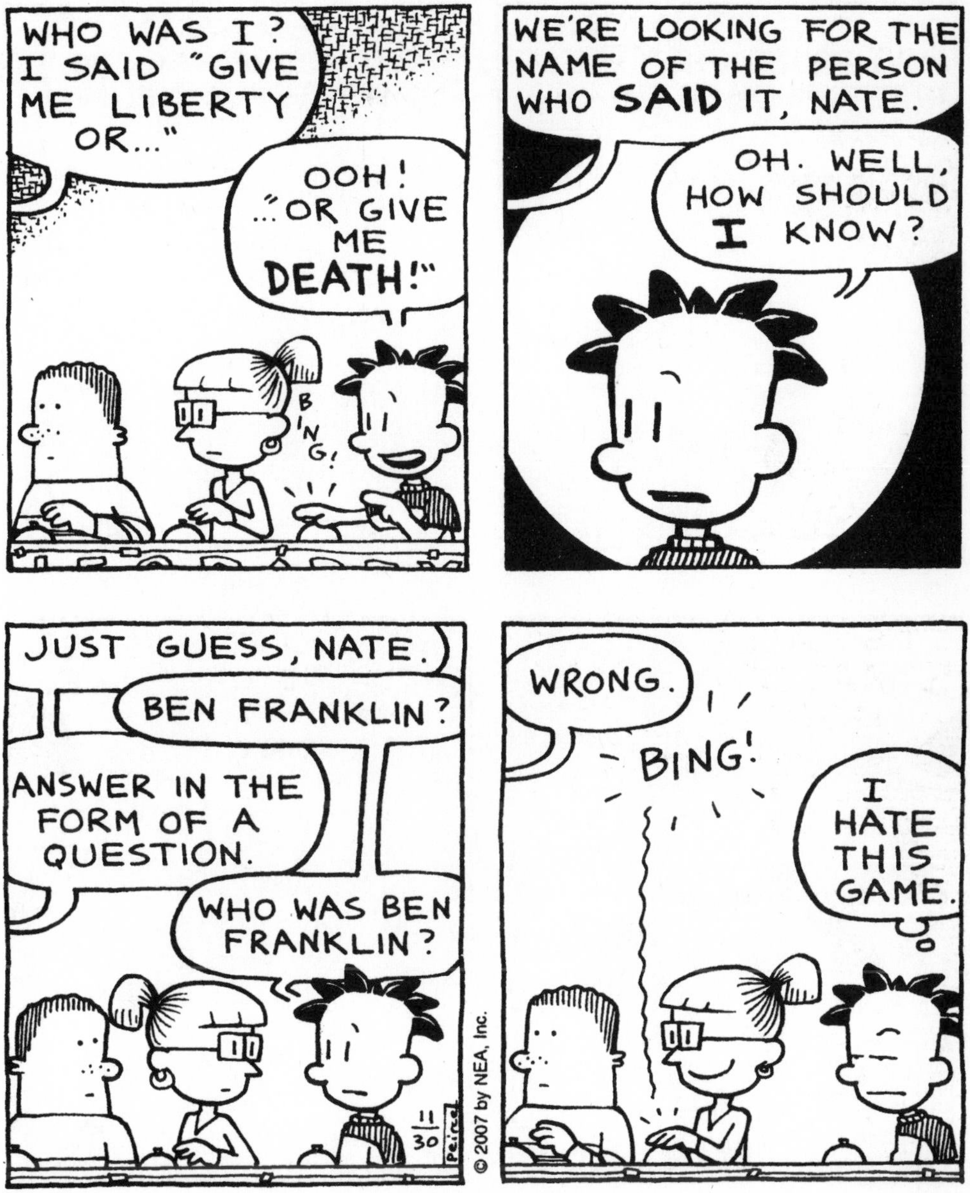
WHO WAS I? I SAID "GIVE ME LIBERTY OR..."
OOH! ..."OR GIVE ME DEATH!"
BING!
WE'RE LOOKING FOR THE NAME OF THE PERSON WHO **SAID** IT, NATE.
OH. WELL, HOW SHOULD **I** KNOW?
JUST GUESS, NATE.
BEN FRANKLIN?
ANSWER IN THE FORM OF A QUESTION.
WHO WAS BEN FRANKLIN?
11/30
Peirce
WRONG.
BING!
I HATE THIS GAME.

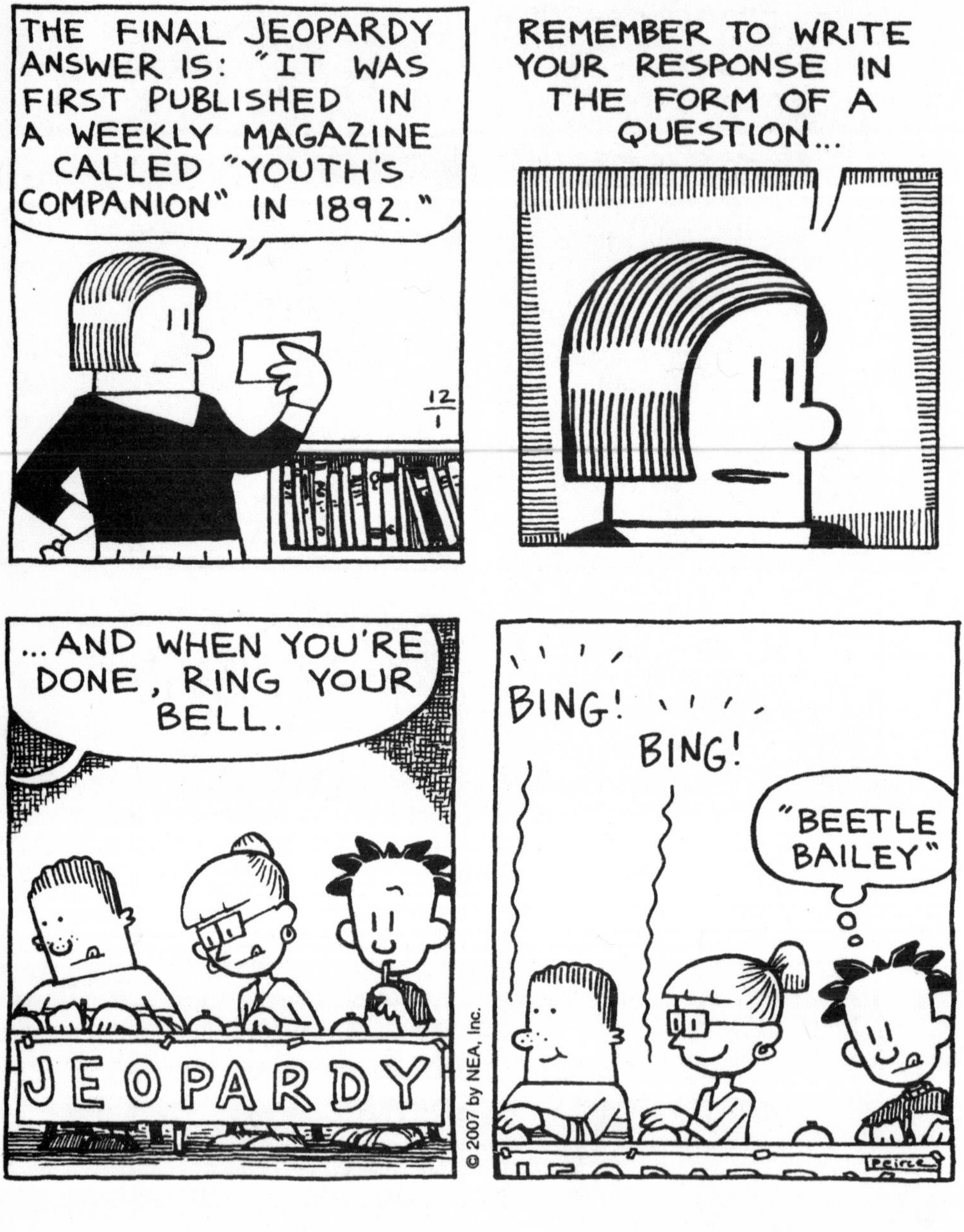
THE FINAL JEOPARDY ANSWER IS: "IT WAS FIRST PUBLISHED IN A WEEKLY MAGAZINE CALLED "YOUTH'S COMPANION" IN 1892."
12/1
REMEMBER TO WRITE YOUR RESPONSE IN THE FORM OF A QUESTION...
...AND WHEN YOU'RE DONE, RING YOUR BELL.
JEOPARDY
BING!
BING!
"BEETLE BAILEY"
Peirce

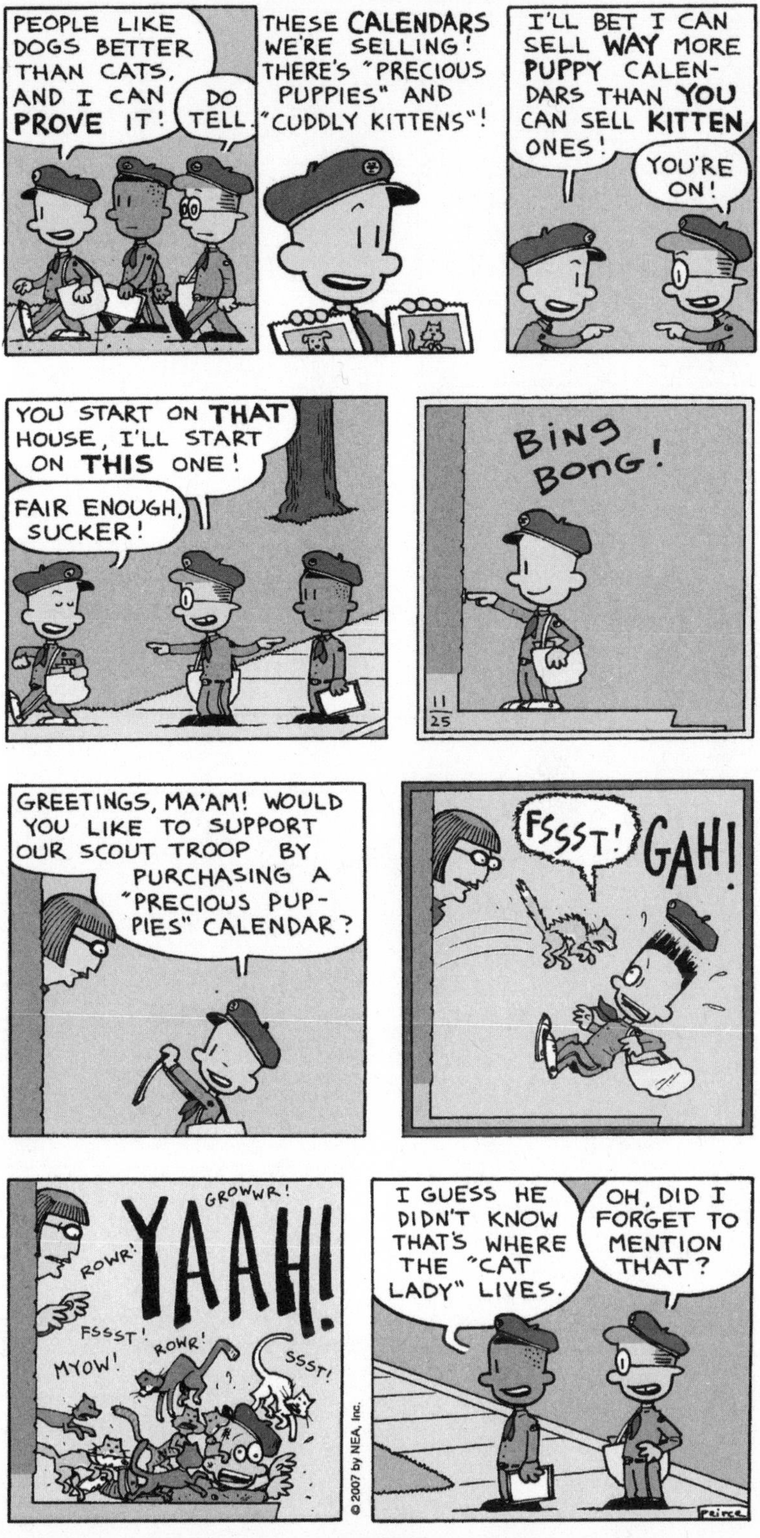
PEOPLE LIKE DOGS BETTER THAN CATS, AND I CAN PROVE IT!
DO TELL.
THESE CALENDARS WE'RE SELLING! THERE'S "PRECIOUS PUPPIES" AND "CUDDLY KITTENS"!
I'LL BET I CAN SELL WAY MORE PUPPY CALENDARS THAN YOU CAN SELL KITTEN ONES!
YOU'RE ON!
YOU START ON THAT HOUSE, I'LL START ON THIS ONE!
FAIR ENOUGH, SUCKER!
BING BONG!
11
25
GREETINGS, MA'AM! WOULD YOU LIKE TO SUPPORT OUR SCOUT TROOP BY PURCHASING A "PRECIOUS PUPPIES" CALENDAR?
FSSST!
GAH!
GROWWR!
YAAH!
ROWR!
FSSST!
ROWR!
MYOW!
SSST!
© 2007 by NEA, Inc.
I GUESS HE DIDN'T KNOW THAT'S WHERE THE "CAT LADY" LIVES.
OH, DID I FORGET TO MENTION THAT?
PEIRCE

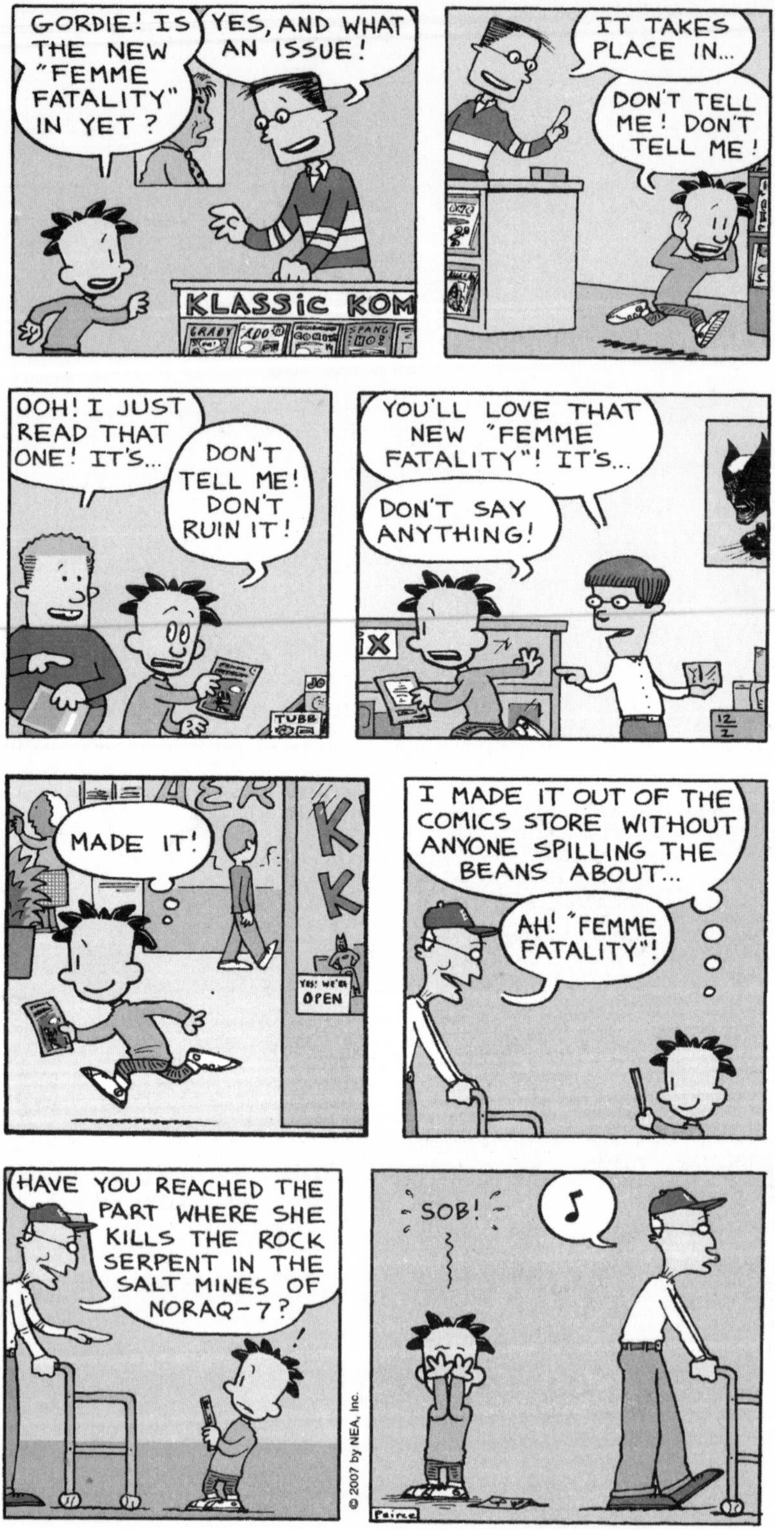
GORDIE! IS THE NEW "FEMME FATALITY" IN YET?
YES, AND WHAT AN ISSUE!
KLASSIC KOM
IT TAKES PLACE IN...
DON'T TELL ME! DON'T TELL ME!
OOH! I JUST READ THAT ONE! IT'S...
DON'T TELL ME! DON'T RUIN IT!
YOU'LL LOVE THAT NEW "FEMME FATALITY"! IT'S...
DON'T SAY ANYTHING!
MADE IT!
YES! WE'RE OPEN
I MADE IT OUT OF THE COMICS STORE WITHOUT ANYONE SPILLING THE BEANS ABOUT...
AH! "FEMME FATALITY"!
HAVE YOU REACHED THE PART WHERE SHE KILLS THE ROCK SERPENT IN THE SALT MINES OF NORAQ-7?
SOB!
© 2007 by NEA, Inc.
Peirce

HERE COMES JENNY!

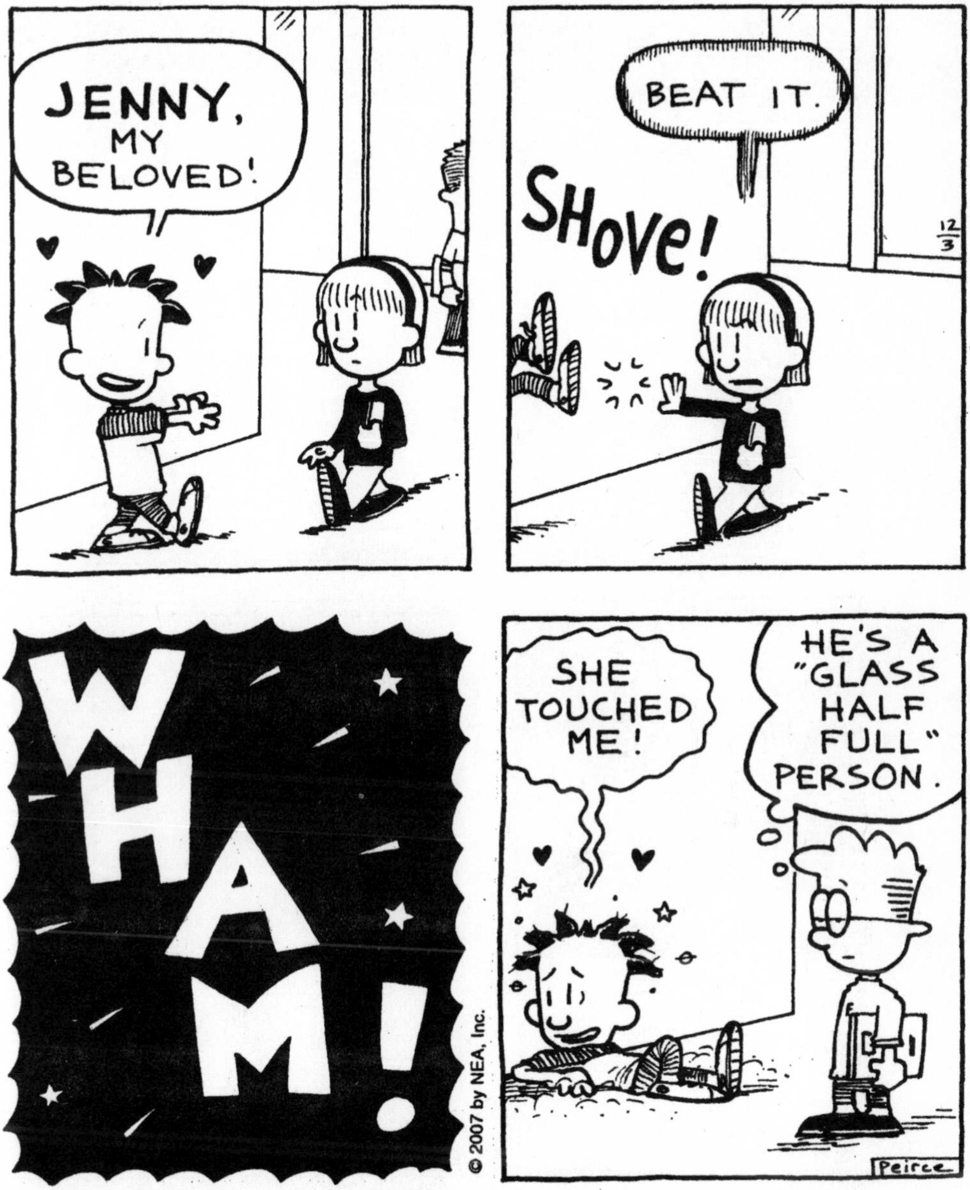
JENNY, MY BELOVED!
BEAT IT.
SHOVE!
12/3
WHAM!
SHE TOUCHED ME!
HE'S A "GLASS HALF FULL" PERSON.
Peirce

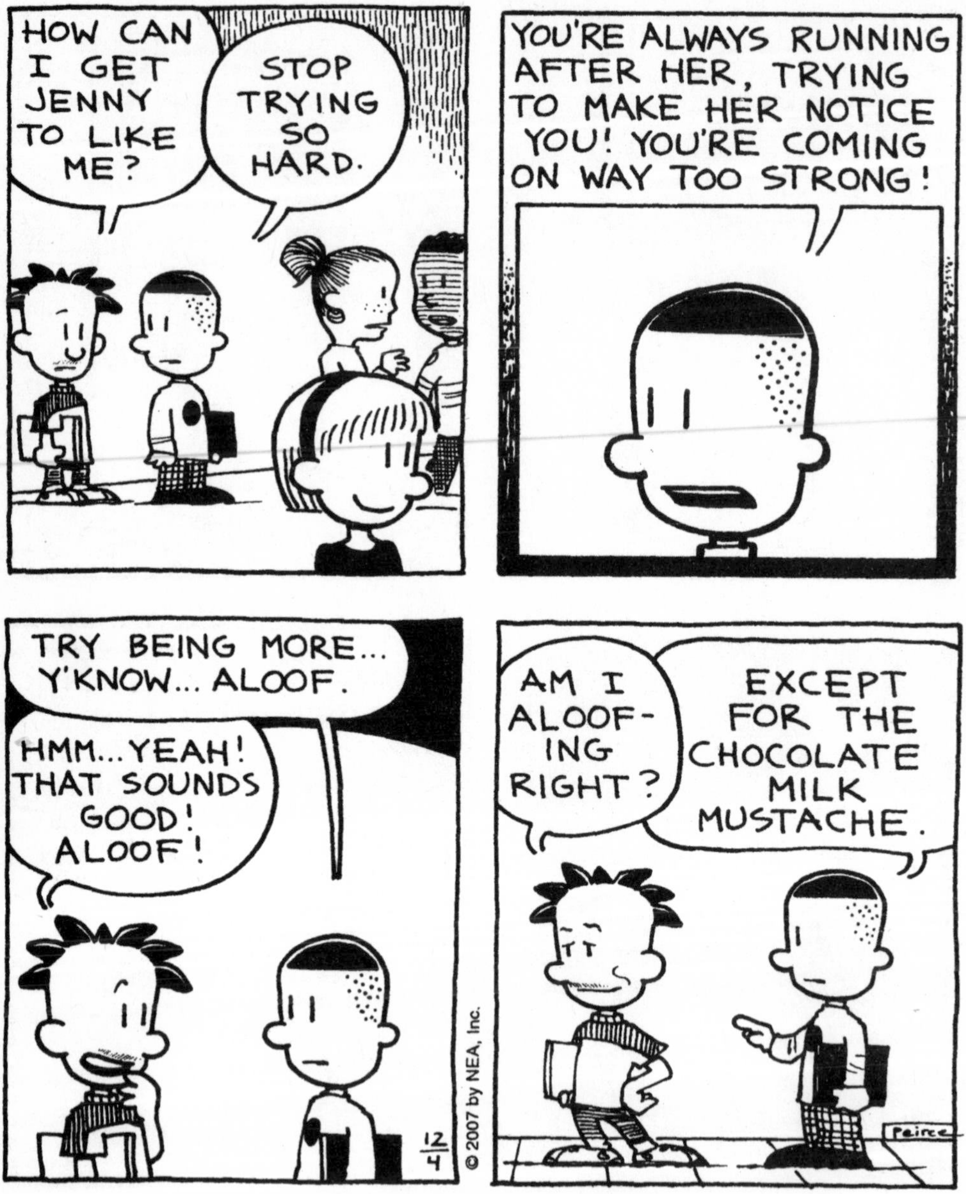
HOW CAN I GET JENNY TO LIKE ME?
STOP TRYING SO HARD.
YOU'RE ALWAYS RUNNING AFTER HER, TRYING TO MAKE HER NOTICE YOU! YOU'RE COMING ON WAY TOO STRONG!
TRY BEING MORE... Y'KNOW... ALOOF.
HMM... YEAH! THAT SOUNDS GOOD! ALOOF!
12/4
© 2007 by NEA, Inc.
AM I ALOOF-ING RIGHT?
EXCEPT FOR THE CHOCOLATE MILK MUSTACHE.
Peirce

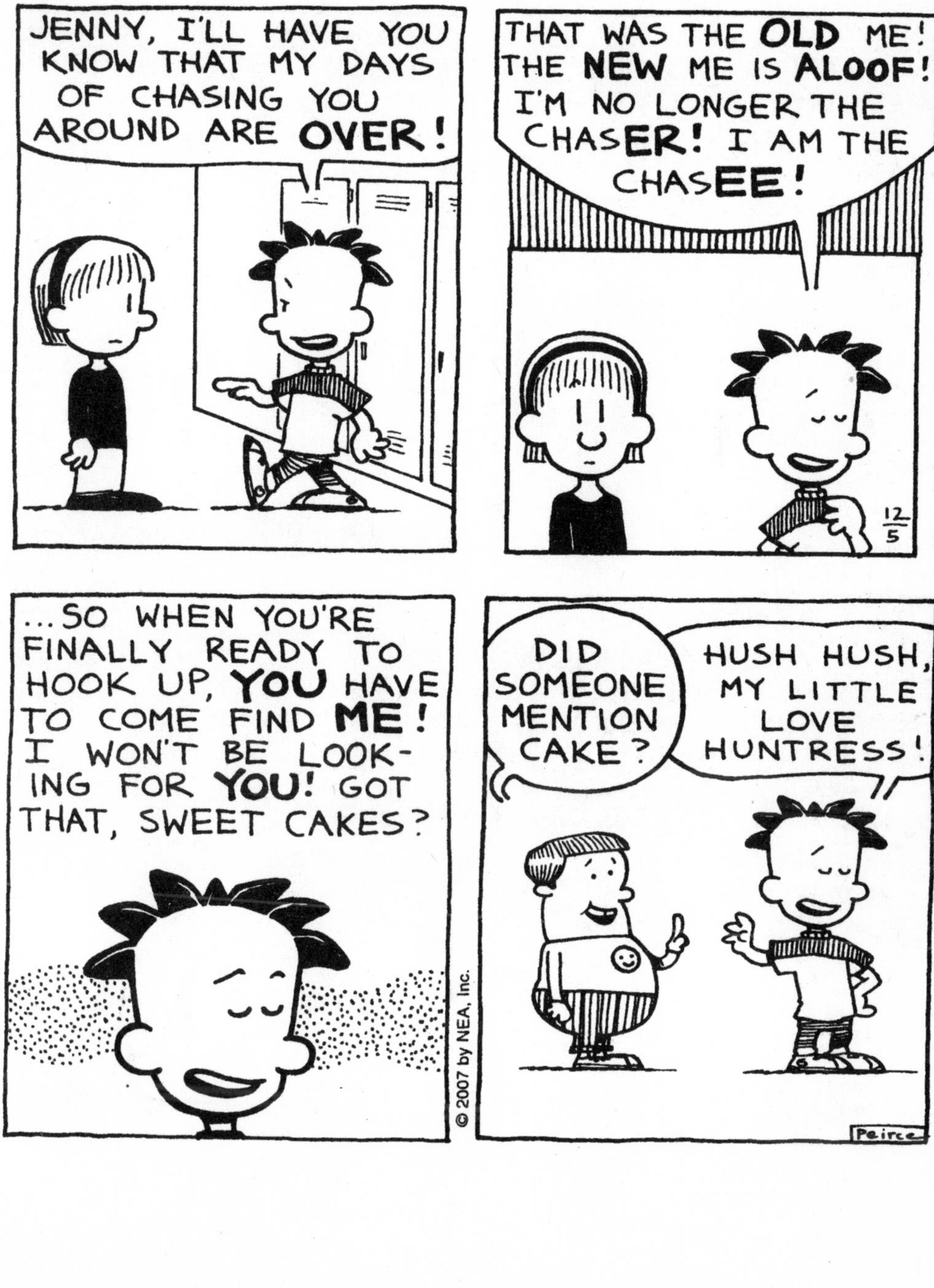
JENNY, I'LL HAVE YOU KNOW THAT MY DAYS OF CHASING YOU AROUND ARE **OVER**!
THAT WAS THE **OLD** ME! THE **NEW** ME IS **ALOOF**! I'M NO LONGER THE CHAS**ER**! I AM THE CHAS**EE**!
12/5
...SO WHEN YOU'RE FINALLY READY TO HOOK UP, **YOU** HAVE TO COME FIND **ME**! I WON'T BE LOOKING FOR **YOU**! GOT THAT, SWEET CAKES?
DID SOMEONE MENTION CAKE?
HUSH HUSH, MY LITTLE LOVE HUNTRESS!
Peirce

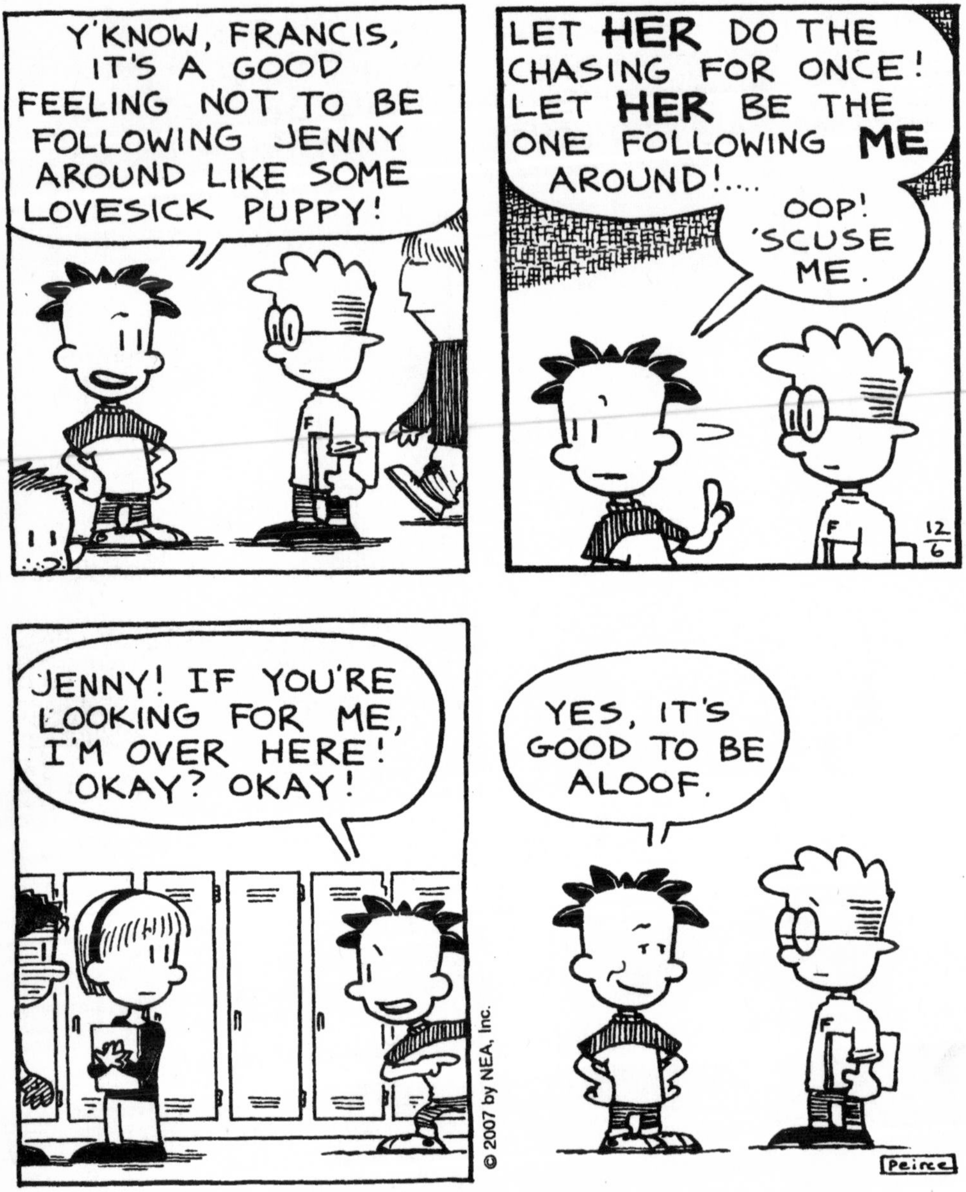
Y'KNOW, FRANCIS, IT'S A GOOD FEELING NOT TO BE FOLLOWING JENNY AROUND LIKE SOME LOVESICK PUPPY!
LET **HER** DO THE CHASING FOR ONCE! LET **HER** BE THE ONE FOLLOWING **ME** AROUND!....
OOP! 'SCUSE ME.
12/6
JENNY! IF YOU'RE LOOKING FOR ME, I'M OVER HERE! OKAY? OKAY!
YES, IT'S GOOD TO BE ALOOF.
PEIRCE

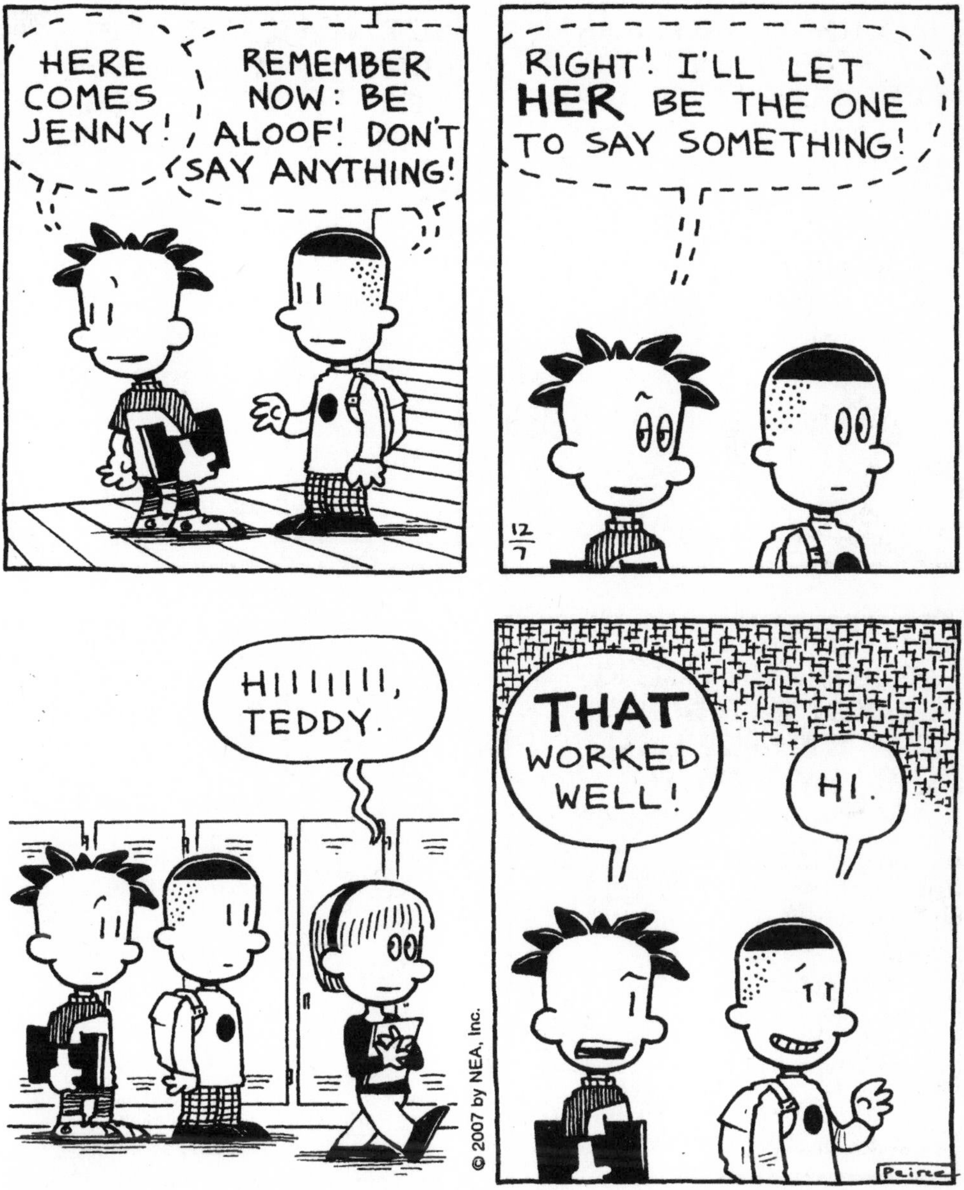
HERE COMES JENNY!
REMEMBER NOW: BE ALOOF! DON'T SAY ANYTHING!
RIGHT! I'LL LET **HER** BE THE ONE TO SAY SOMETHING!
12/7
HIIIIIII, TEDDY.
© 2007 by NEA, Inc.
THAT WORKED WELL!
HI.
PEIRCE

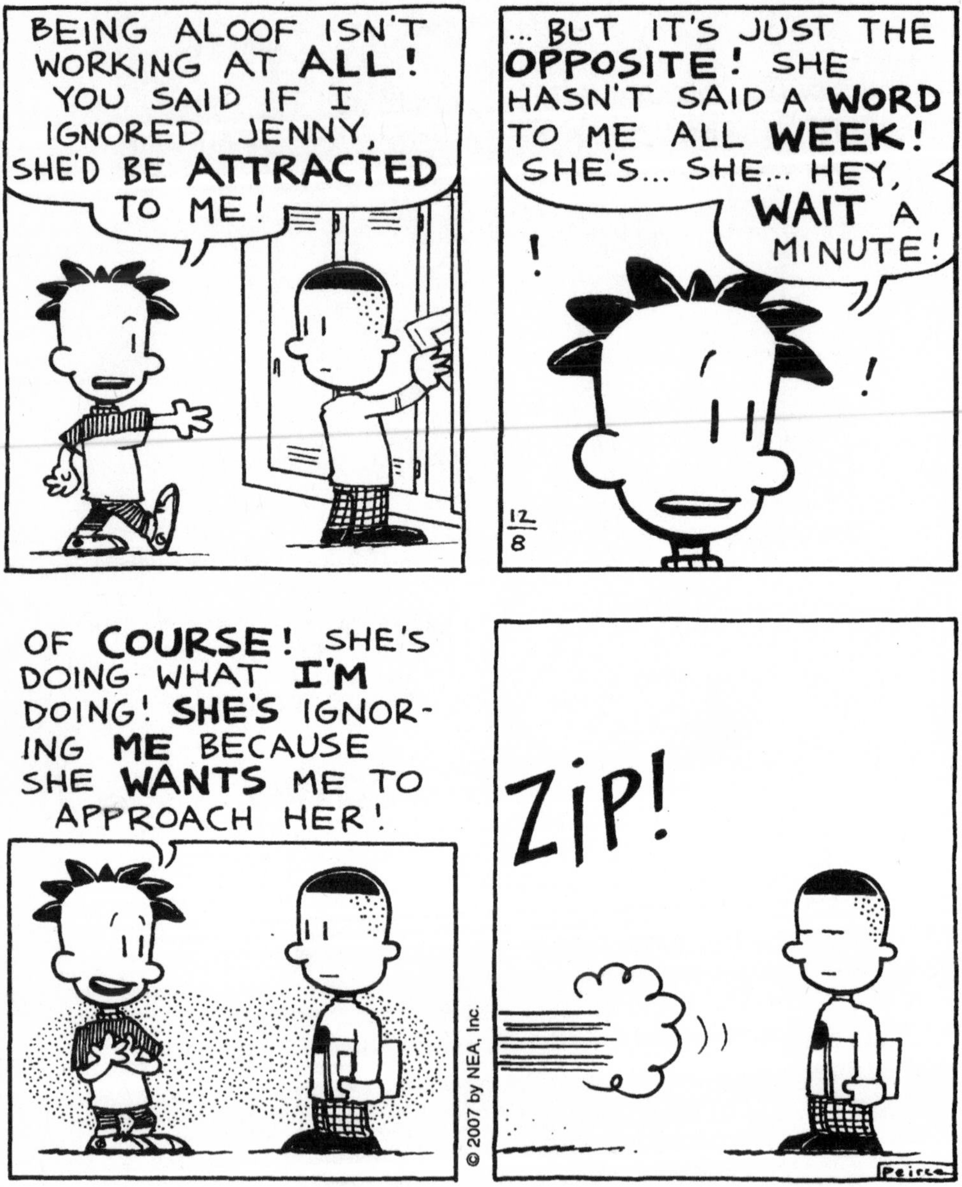
BEING ALOOF ISN'T WORKING AT ALL! YOU SAID IF I IGNORED JENNY, SHE'D BE ATTRACTED TO ME!
... BUT IT'S JUST THE OPPOSITE! SHE HASN'T SAID A WORD TO ME ALL WEEK! SHE'S... SHE... HEY, WAIT A MINUTE!
!
!
12
8
OF COURSE! SHE'S DOING WHAT I'M DOING! SHE'S IGNORING ME BECAUSE SHE WANTS ME TO APPROACH HER!
© 2007 by NEA, Inc.
ZIP!
Peirce

HEY, CHECK OUT TODAY'S SPORTS SECTION! "MIDDLE SCHOOL HOOPS PREVIEW" BY GARY GREEN!
OOH! ARE WE IN THERE?
YUP, THERE'S A WHOLE PARAGRAPH ON US!
"THE BOBCATS OF PUBLIC SCHOOL 38 WILL LOOK TO REBOUND FROM LAST SEASON'S 3-12 RECORD."
12/9
"A KEY PLAYER WILL BE CENTER CHESTER BUDRICK, WHOSE SIZE AND STRENGTH MAKE HIM A FORCE IN THE PIVOT."
THAT'S CHESTER, ALL RIGHT!
"OTHER BRIGHT SPOTS ARE LIKELY TO INCLUDE SMALL FORWARD FRANCIS POPE AND SHOOTING GUARD TEDDY ORTIZ."
DUDE!
WAIT A MINUTE! WHERE'S MY NAME? AREN'T I A BRIGHT SPOT?
I'M DEFINITELY A BRIGHT SPOT! WHY DIDN'T HE CALL ME A BRIGHT SPOT?
BECAUSE YOU'RE NOT VERY BRIGHT?
BUT WE KNEW THAT ALREADY!
PAT PAT
I'VE BEEN LIBELED.
Peirce

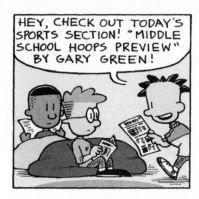

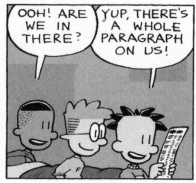

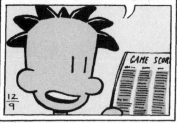

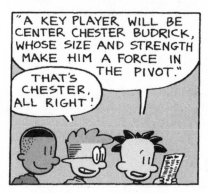

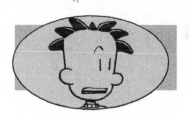

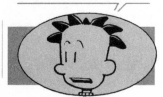

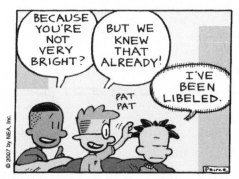

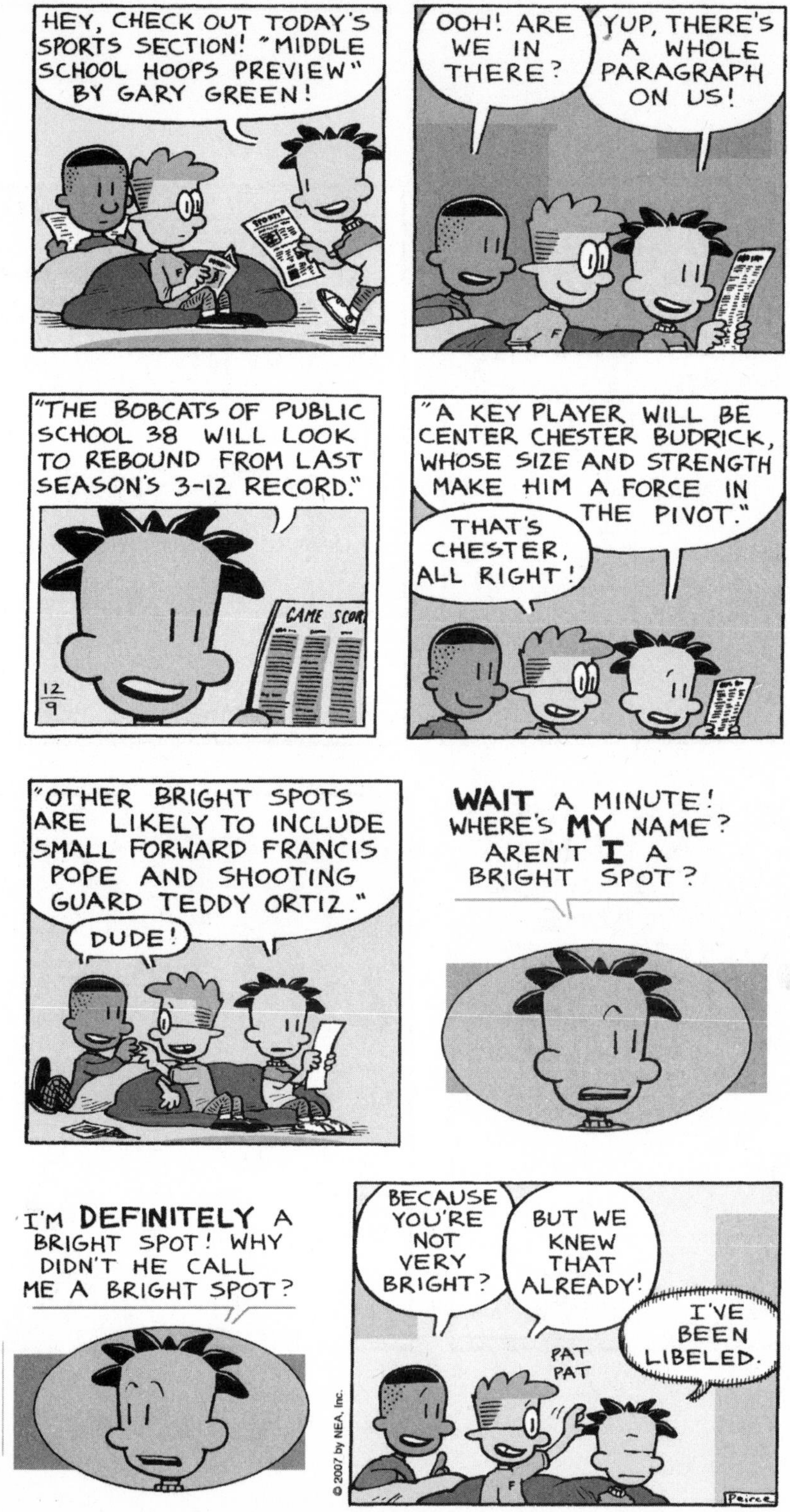

CHAMPS, OR NOT?

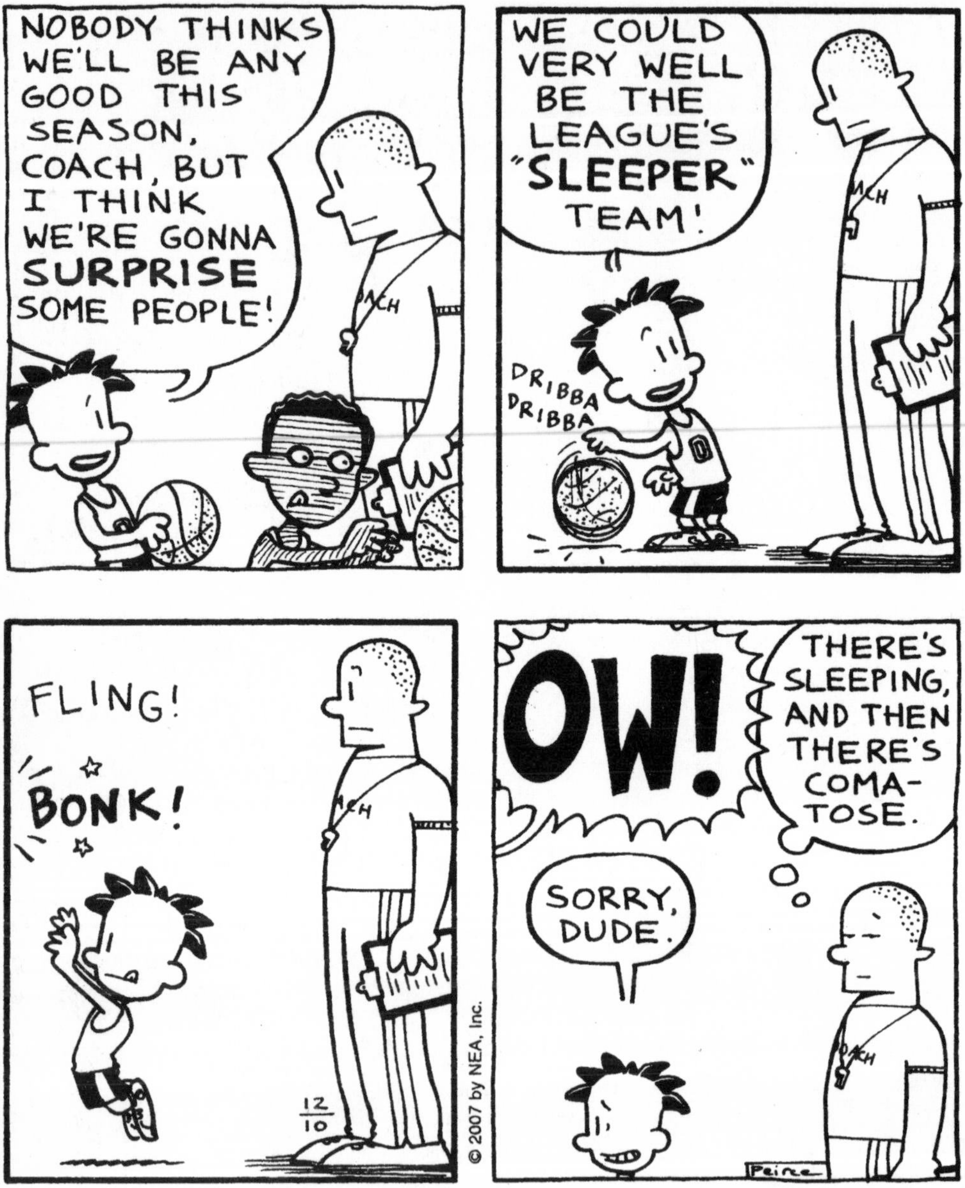
NOBODY THINKS WE'LL BE ANY GOOD THIS SEASON, COACH, BUT I THINK WE'RE GONNA SURPRISE SOME PEOPLE!
WE COULD VERY WELL BE THE LEAGUE'S "SLEEPER" TEAM!
DRIBBA DRIBBA
FLING!
BONK!
12/10
© 2007 by NEA, Inc.
OW!
THERE'S SLEEPING, AND THEN THERE'S COMA-TOSE.
SORRY, DUDE.
Peirce

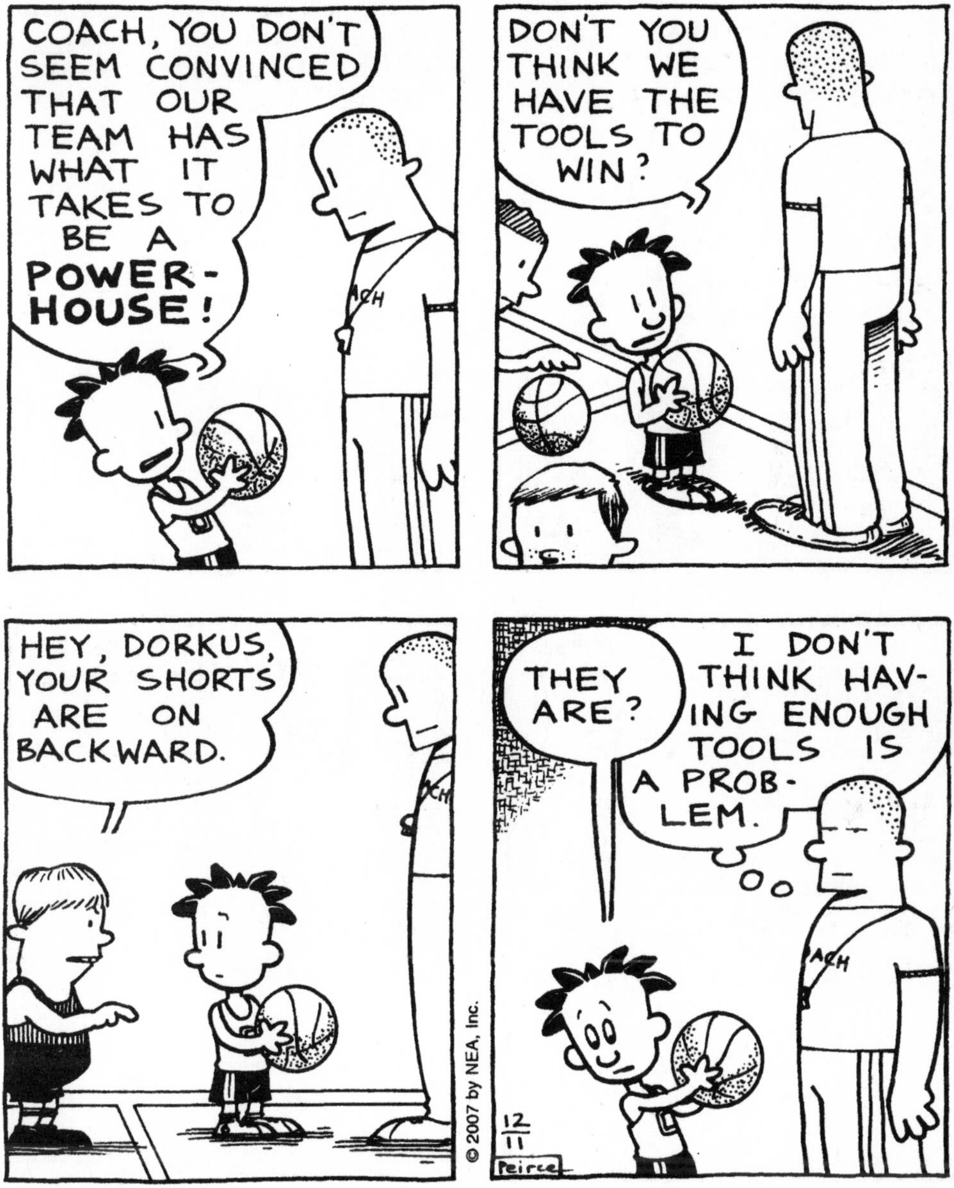
COACH, YOU DON'T SEEM CONVINCED THAT OUR TEAM HAS WHAT IT TAKES TO BE A **POWER-HOUSE!**
DON'T YOU THINK WE HAVE THE TOOLS TO WIN?
HEY, DORKUS, YOUR SHORTS ARE ON BACKWARD.
THEY ARE?
I DON'T THINK HAVING ENOUGH TOOLS IS A PROBLEM.
© 2007 by NEA, Inc.
12/11
Peirce

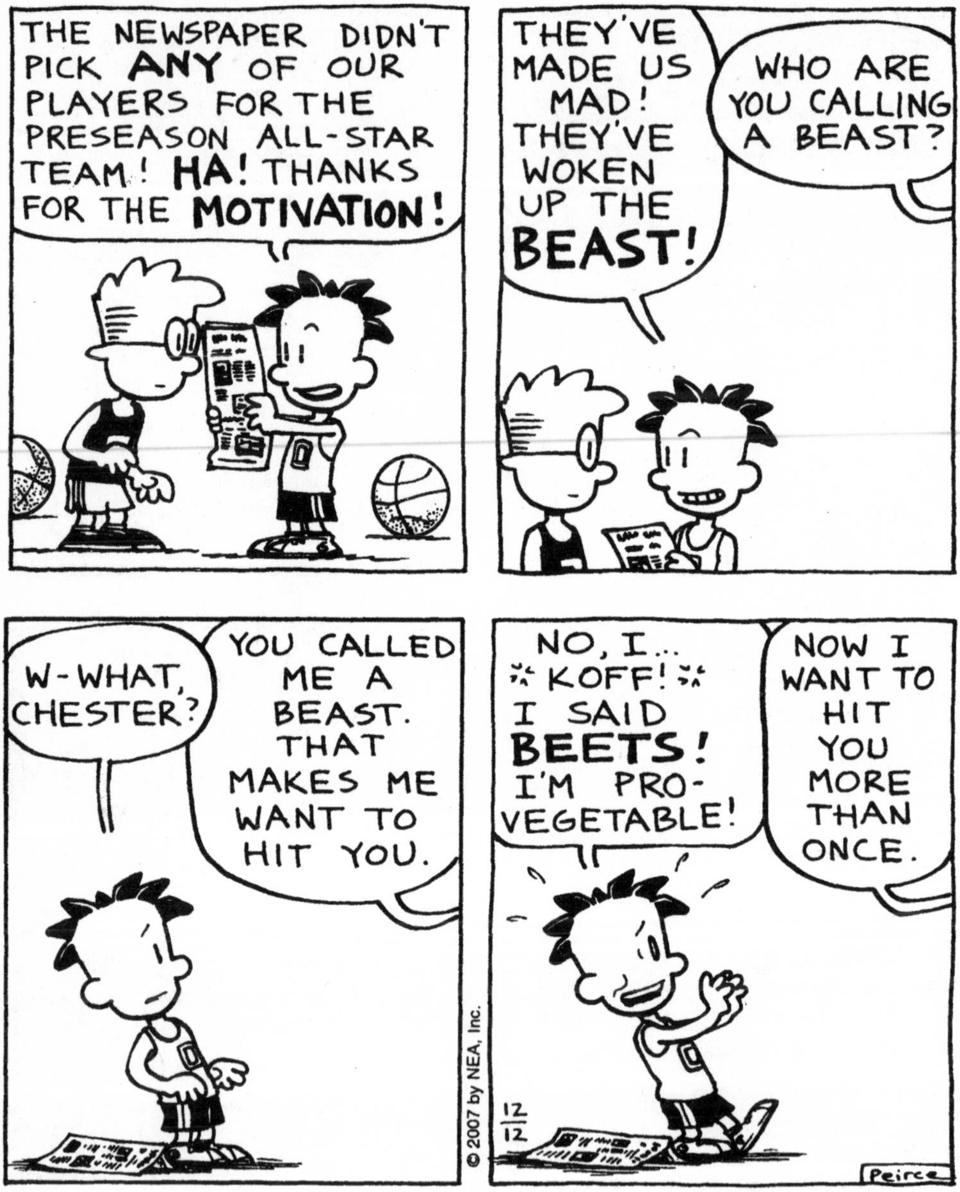
THE NEWSPAPER DIDN'T PICK **ANY** OF OUR PLAYERS FOR THE PRESEASON ALL-STAR TEAM! **HA!** THANKS FOR THE **MOTIVATION!**
THEY'VE MADE US MAD! THEY'VE WOKEN UP THE **BEAST!**
WHO ARE YOU CALLING A BEAST?
W-WHAT, CHESTER?
YOU CALLED ME A BEAST. THAT MAKES ME WANT TO HIT YOU.
NO, I... KOFF! I SAID **BEETS!** I'M PRO-VEGETABLE!
NOW I WANT TO HIT YOU MORE THAN ONCE.
© 2007 by NEA, Inc.
12/12
Peirce

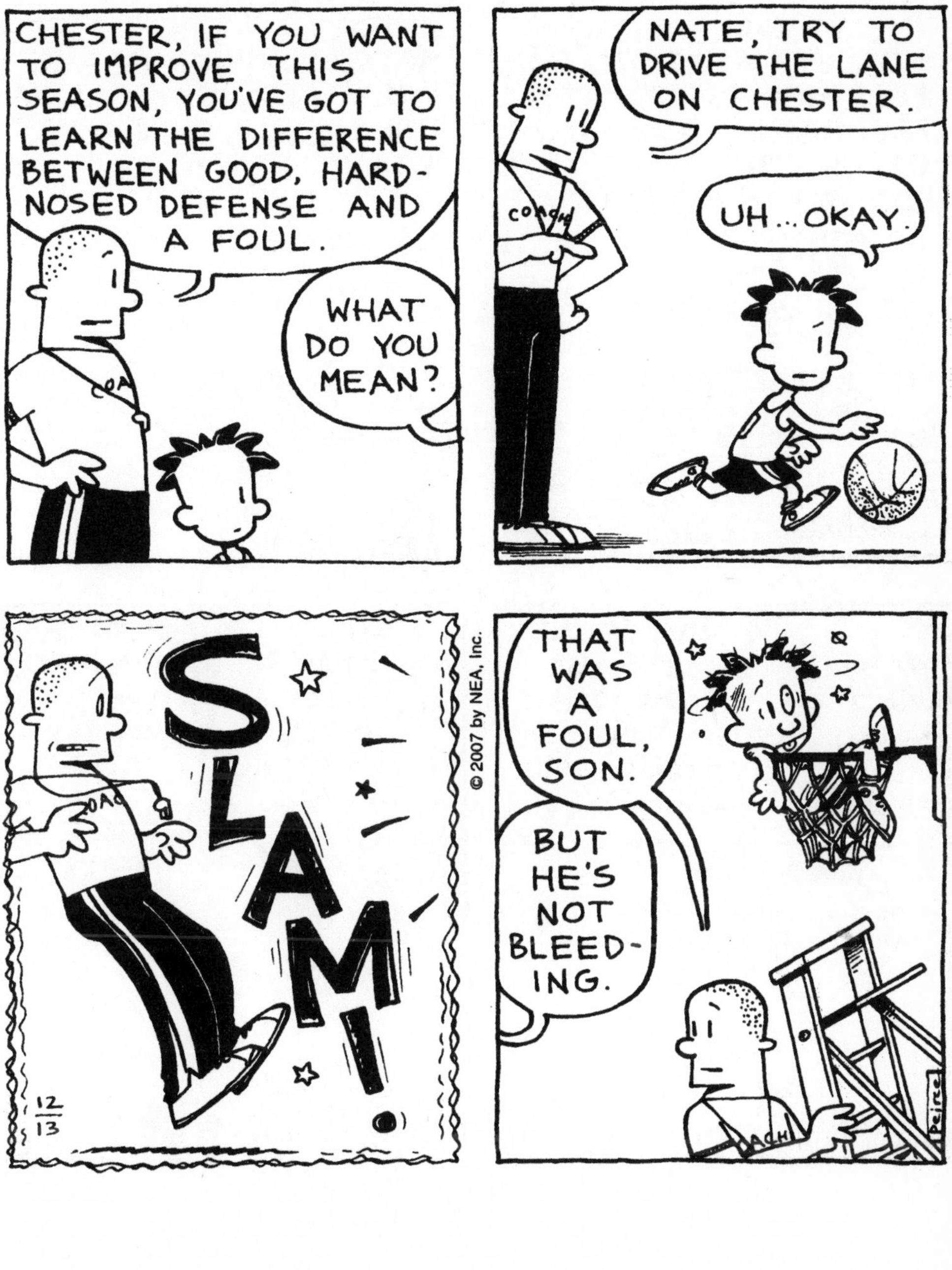
CHESTER, IF YOU WANT TO IMPROVE THIS SEASON, YOU'VE GOT TO LEARN THE DIFFERENCE BETWEEN GOOD, HARD-NOSED DEFENSE AND A FOUL.
WHAT DO YOU MEAN?
NATE, TRY TO DRIVE THE LANE ON CHESTER.
UH...OKAY.
SLAM!
THAT WAS A FOUL, SON.
BUT HE'S NOT BLEEDING.
12/13
Peirce
© 2007 by NEA, Inc.

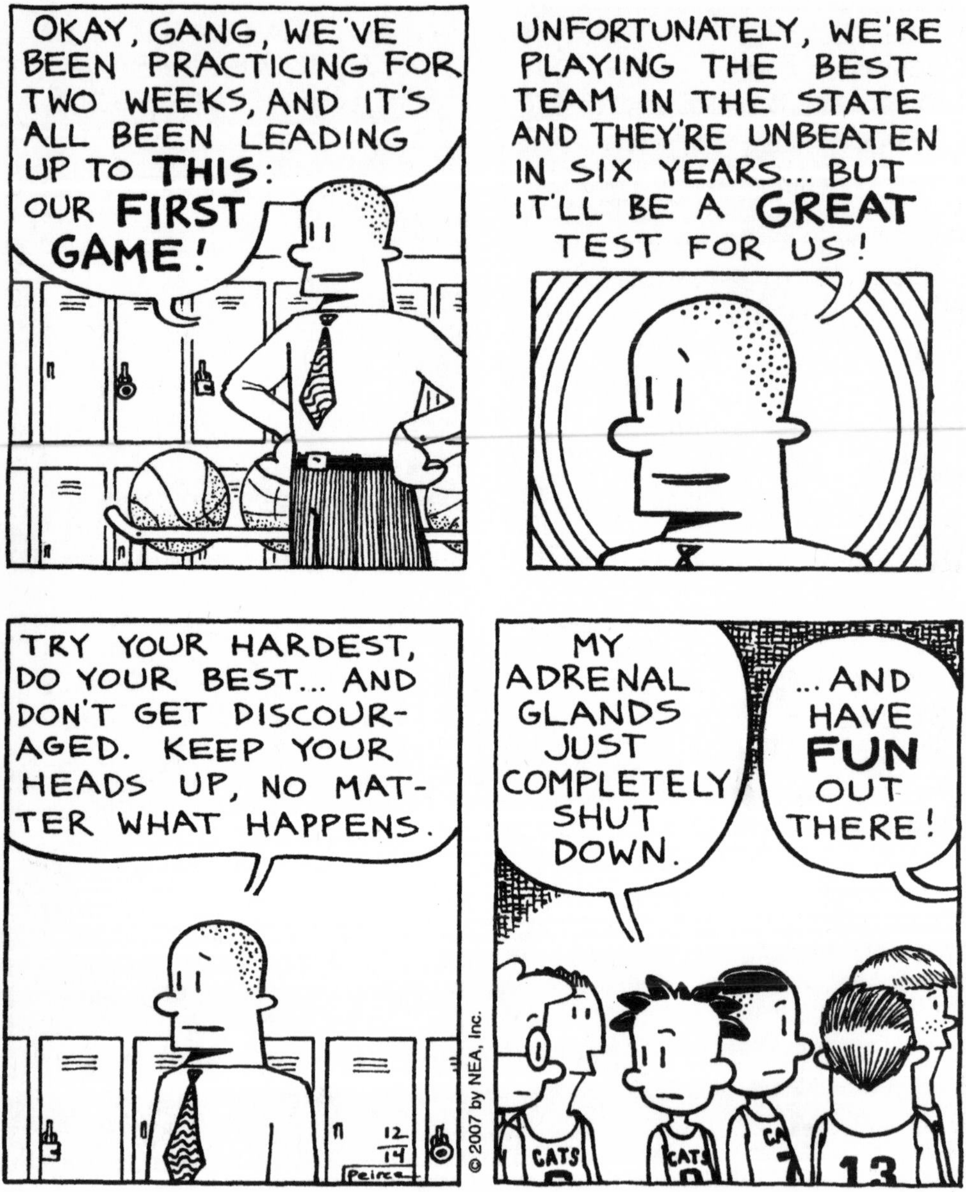
OKAY, GANG, WE'VE BEEN PRACTICING FOR TWO WEEKS, AND IT'S ALL BEEN LEADING UP TO THIS: OUR FIRST GAME!
UNFORTUNATELY, WE'RE PLAYING THE BEST TEAM IN THE STATE AND THEY'RE UNBEATEN IN SIX YEARS... BUT IT'LL BE A GREAT TEST FOR US!
TRY YOUR HARDEST, DO YOUR BEST... AND DON'T GET DISCOURAGED. KEEP YOUR HEADS UP, NO MATTER WHAT HAPPENS.
...AND HAVE FUN OUT THERE!
MY ADRENAL GLANDS JUST COMPLETELY SHUT DOWN.
12/14
Peirce
CATS
CATS
13

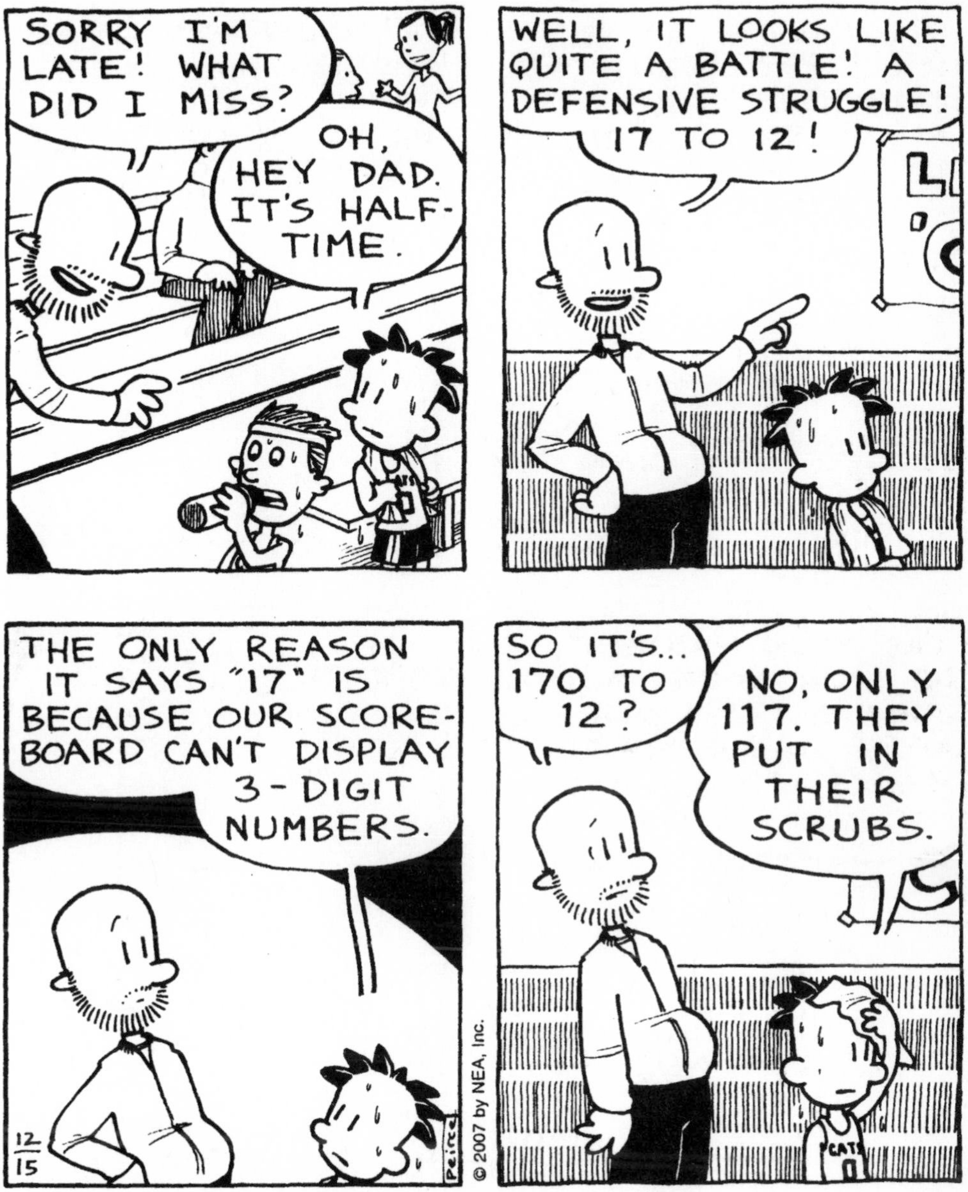
SORRY I'M LATE! WHAT DID I MISS?
OH, HEY DAD. IT'S HALF-TIME.
WELL, IT LOOKS LIKE QUITE A BATTLE! A DEFENSIVE STRUGGLE! 17 TO 12!
THE ONLY REASON IT SAYS "17" IS BECAUSE OUR SCORE-BOARD CAN'T DISPLAY 3-DIGIT NUMBERS.
12/15
Peirce
SO IT'S... 170 TO 12?
NO, ONLY 117. THEY PUT IN THEIR SCRUBS.

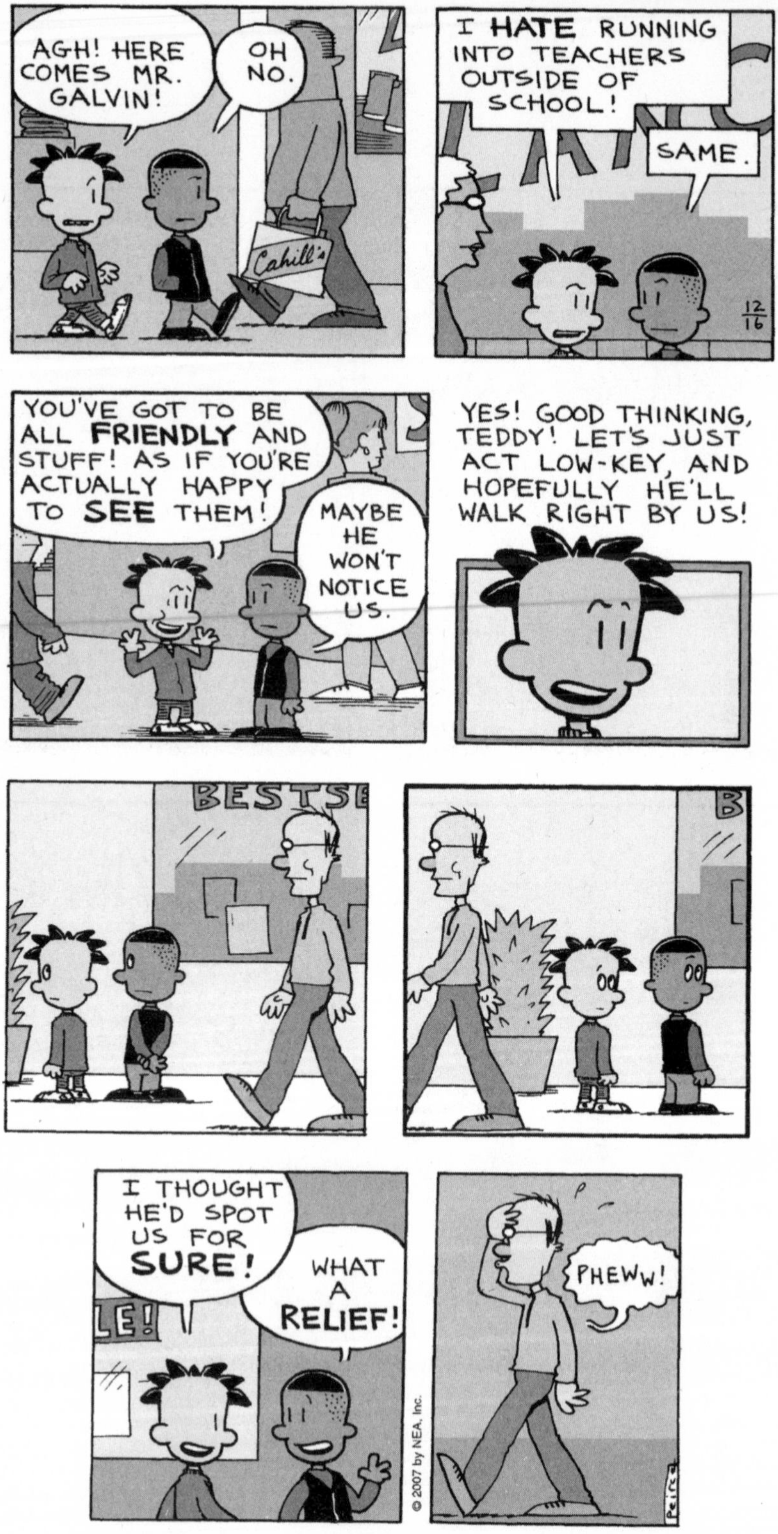
AGH! HERE COMES MR. GALVIN!
OH NO.
Cahill's
I **HATE** RUNNING INTO TEACHERS OUTSIDE OF SCHOOL!
SAME.
12/16
YOU'VE GOT TO BE ALL **FRIENDLY** AND STUFF! AS IF YOU'RE ACTUALLY HAPPY TO **SEE** THEM!
MAYBE HE WON'T NOTICE US.
YES! GOOD THINKING, TEDDY! LET'S JUST ACT LOW-KEY, AND HOPEFULLY HE'LL WALK RIGHT BY US!
BESTSE
I THOUGHT HE'D SPOT US FOR **SURE**!
WHAT A **RELIEF**!
LE!
© 2007 by NEA, Inc.
PHEWW!
Peirce

DOGS VS. CATS

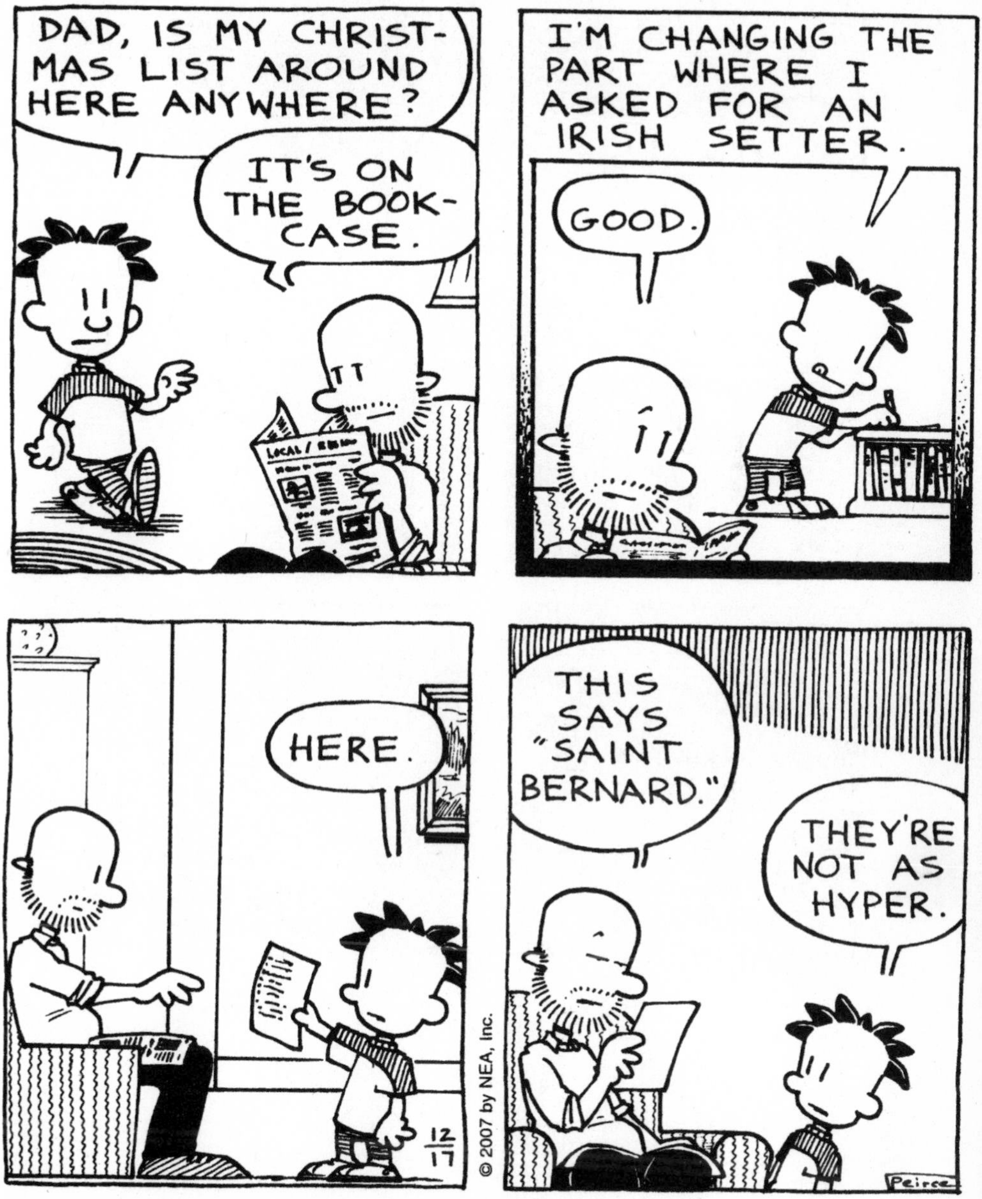
DAD, IS MY CHRISTMAS LIST AROUND HERE ANYWHERE?
IT'S ON THE BOOKCASE.
I'M CHANGING THE PART WHERE I ASKED FOR AN IRISH SETTER.
GOOD.
HERE.
12/17
THIS SAYS "SAINT BERNARD."
THEY'RE NOT AS HYPER.
Peirce

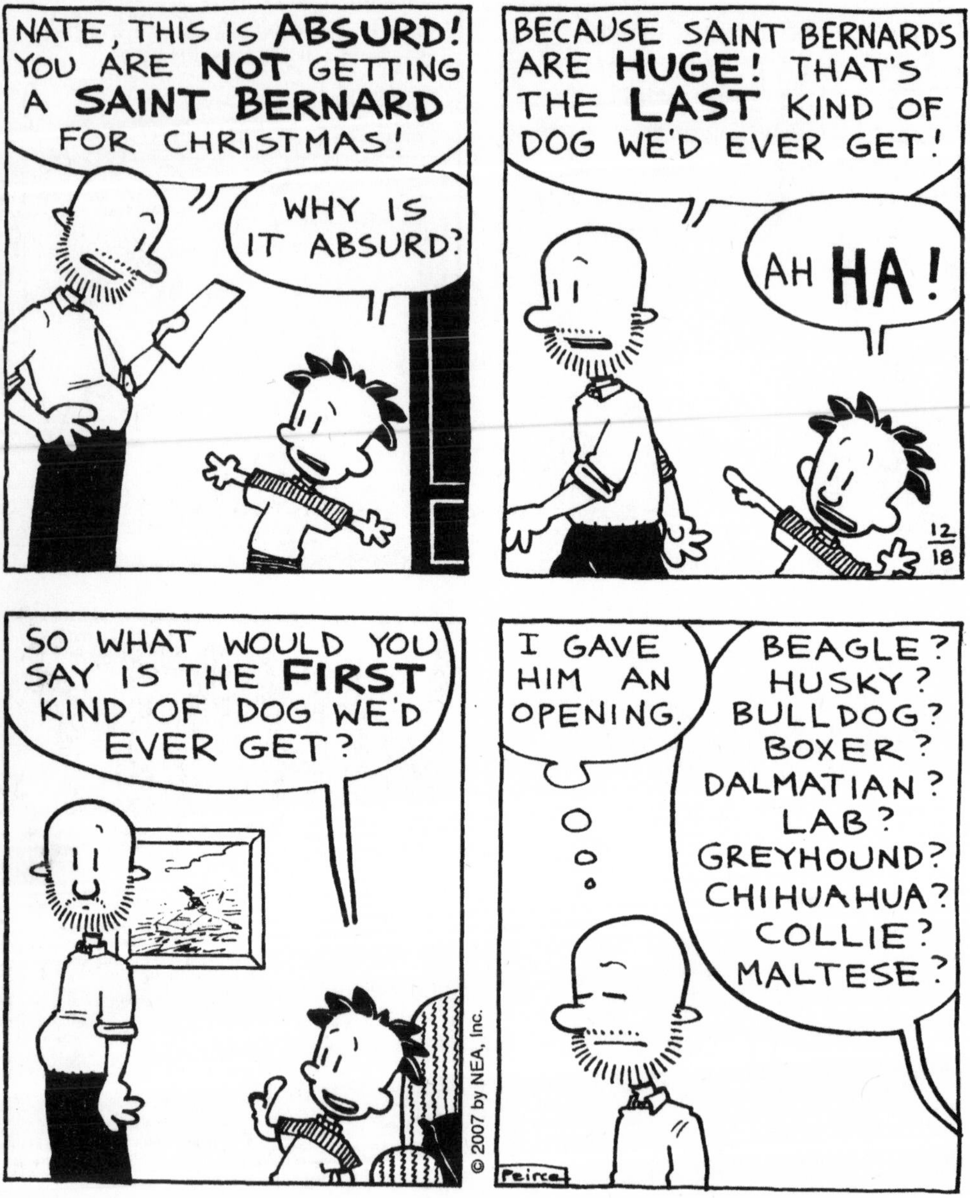
NATE, THIS IS ABSURD! YOU ARE NOT GETTING A SAINT BERNARD FOR CHRISTMAS!
WHY IS IT ABSURD?
BECAUSE SAINT BERNARDS ARE HUGE! THAT'S THE LAST KIND OF DOG WE'D EVER GET!
AH HA!
12/18
SO WHAT WOULD YOU SAY IS THE FIRST KIND OF DOG WE'D EVER GET?
© 2007 by NEA, Inc.
I GAVE HIM AN OPENING.
BEAGLE? HUSKY? BULLDOG? BOXER? DALMATIAN? LAB? GREYHOUND? CHIHUAHUA? COLLIE? MALTESE?
Peirce

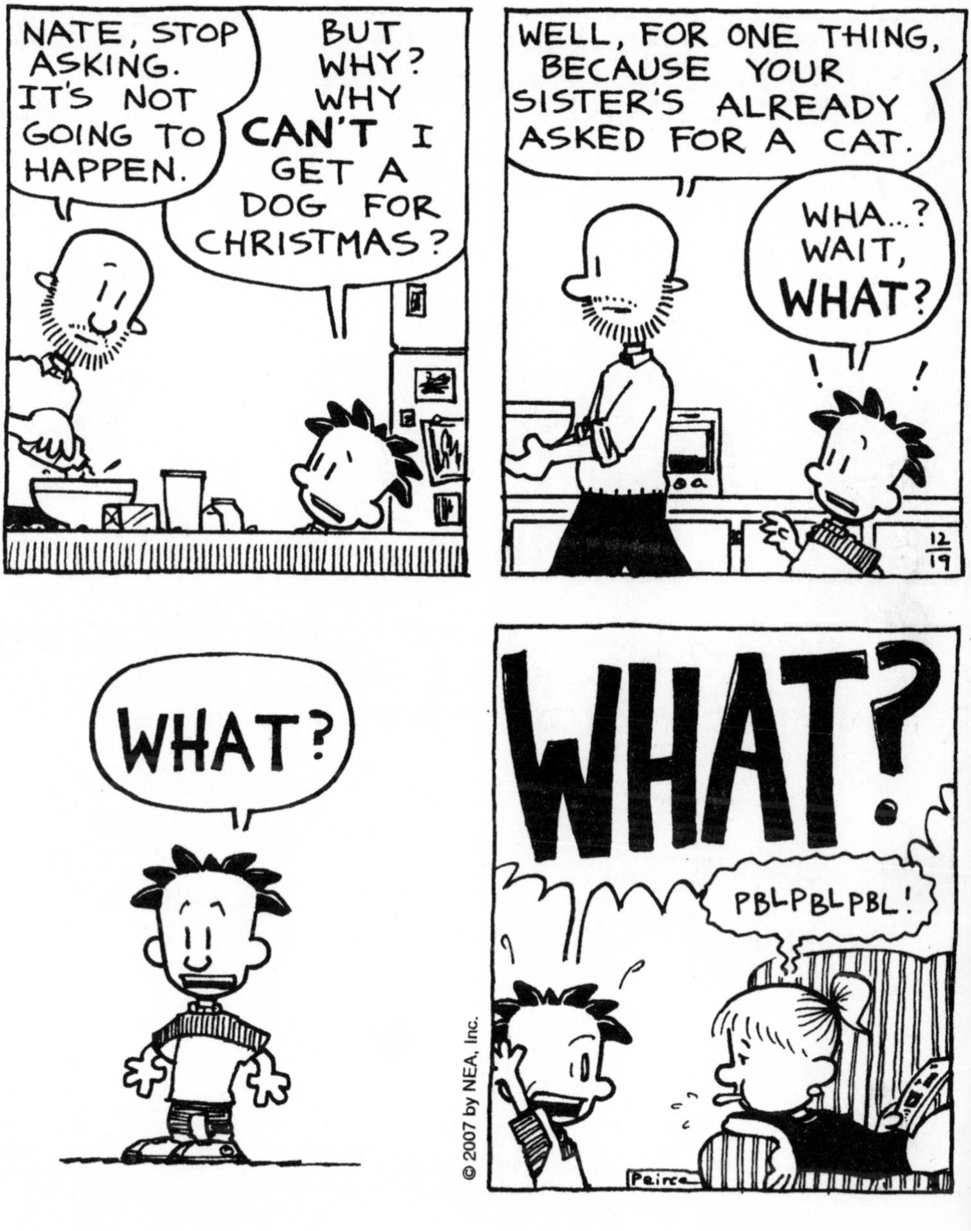
NATE, STOP ASKING. IT'S NOT GOING TO HAPPEN.
BUT WHY? WHY **CAN'T** I GET A DOG FOR CHRISTMAS?
WELL, FOR ONE THING, BECAUSE YOUR SISTER'S ALREADY ASKED FOR A CAT.
WHA...? WAIT, **WHAT?**
! !
12/19
WHAT?
WHAT?
PBLPBLPBL!
Peirce

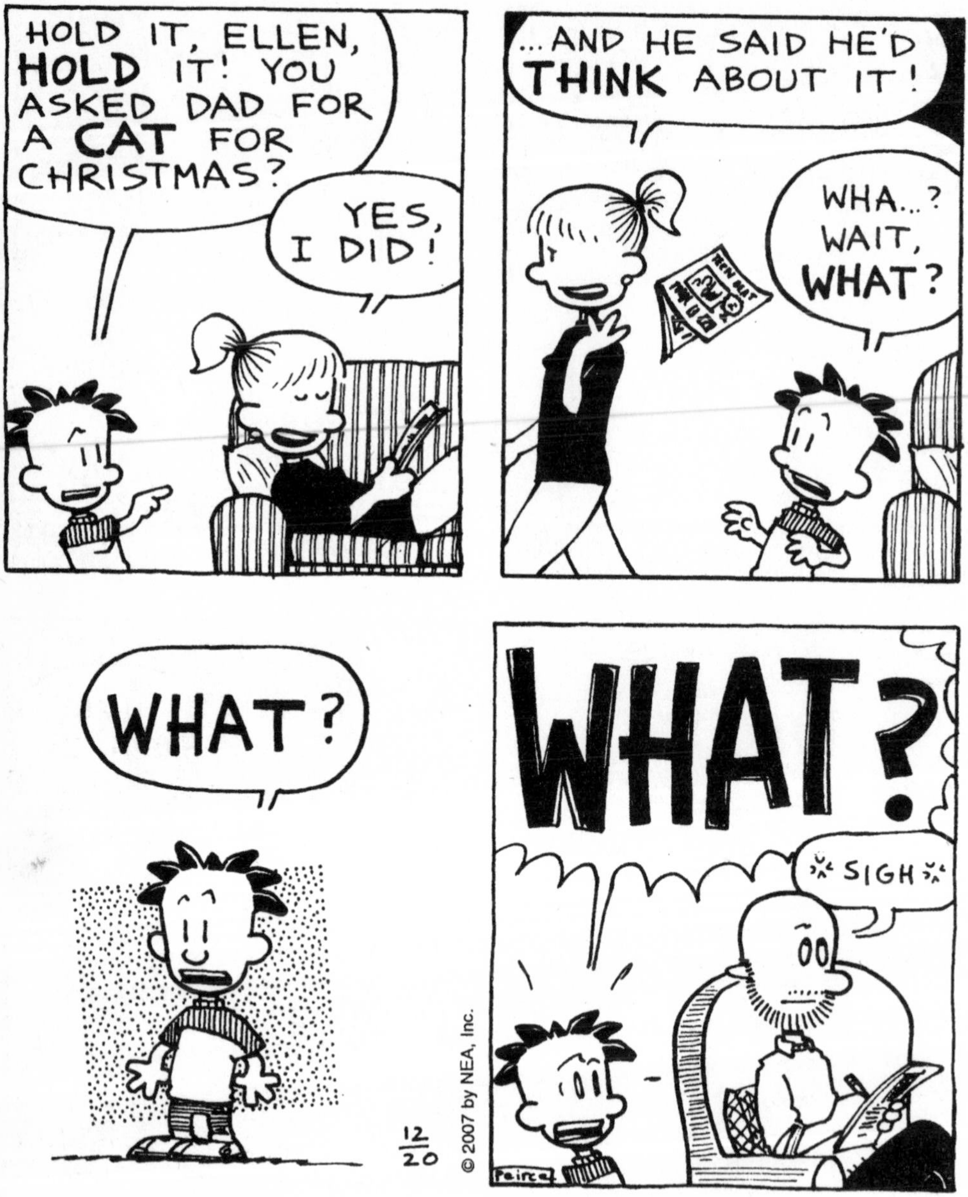
HOLD IT, ELLEN, HOLD IT! YOU ASKED DAD FOR A CAT FOR CHRISTMAS?
YES, I DID!
...AND HE SAID HE'D THINK ABOUT IT!
WHA...? WAIT, WHAT?
WHAT?
12/20
WHAT?
SIGH

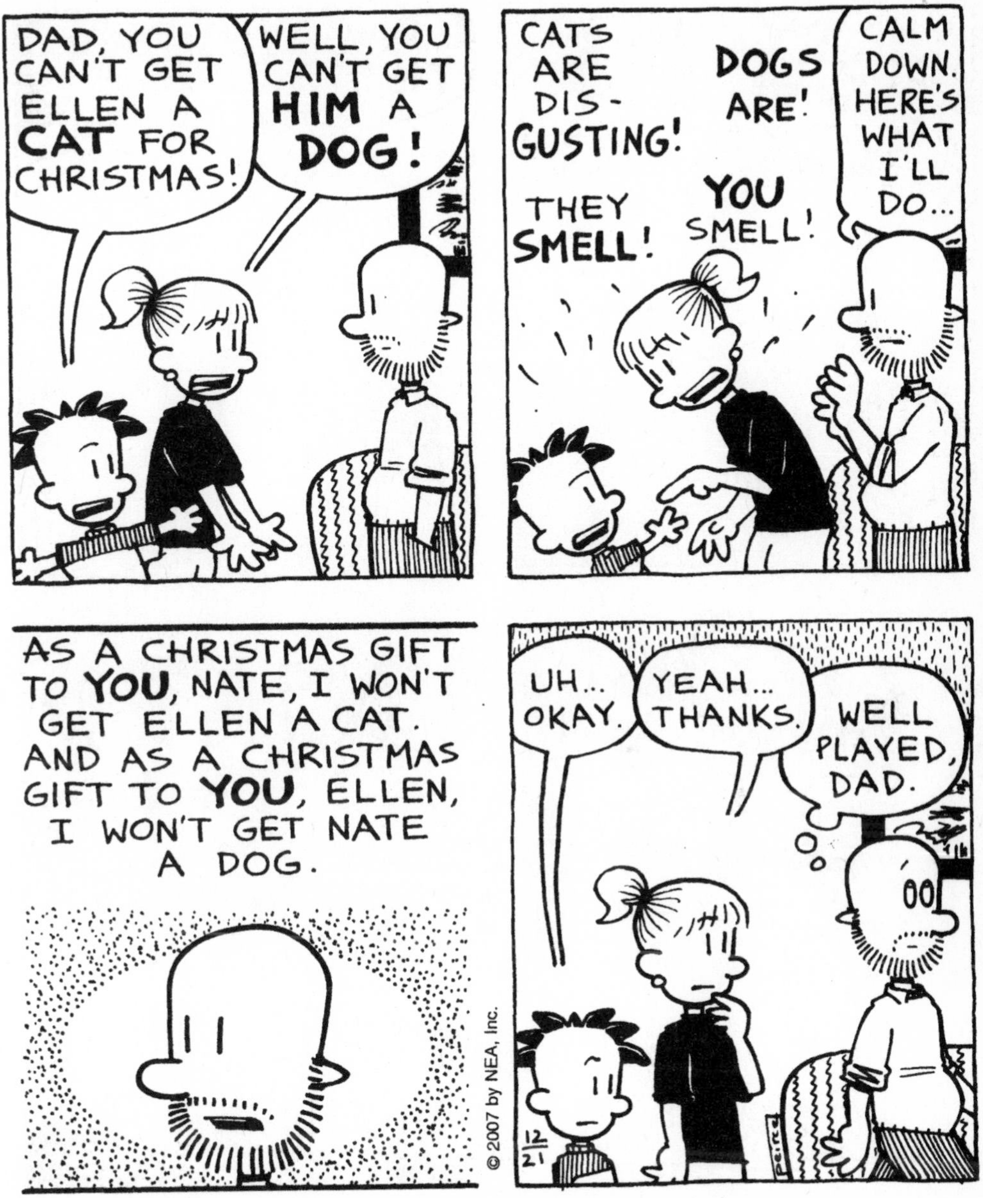
DAD, YOU CAN'T GET ELLEN A **CAT** FOR CHRISTMAS!
WELL, YOU CAN'T GET **HIM** A **DOG**!
CATS ARE DIS-GUSTING!
DOGS ARE!
THEY **SMELL**!
YOU SMELL!
CALM DOWN. HERE'S WHAT I'LL DO...
AS A CHRISTMAS GIFT TO **YOU**, NATE, I WON'T GET ELLEN A CAT. AND AS A CHRISTMAS GIFT TO **YOU**, ELLEN, I WON'T GET NATE A DOG.
UH... OKAY.
YEAH... THANKS.
WELL PLAYED, DAD.
© 2007 by NEA, Inc.
12/21

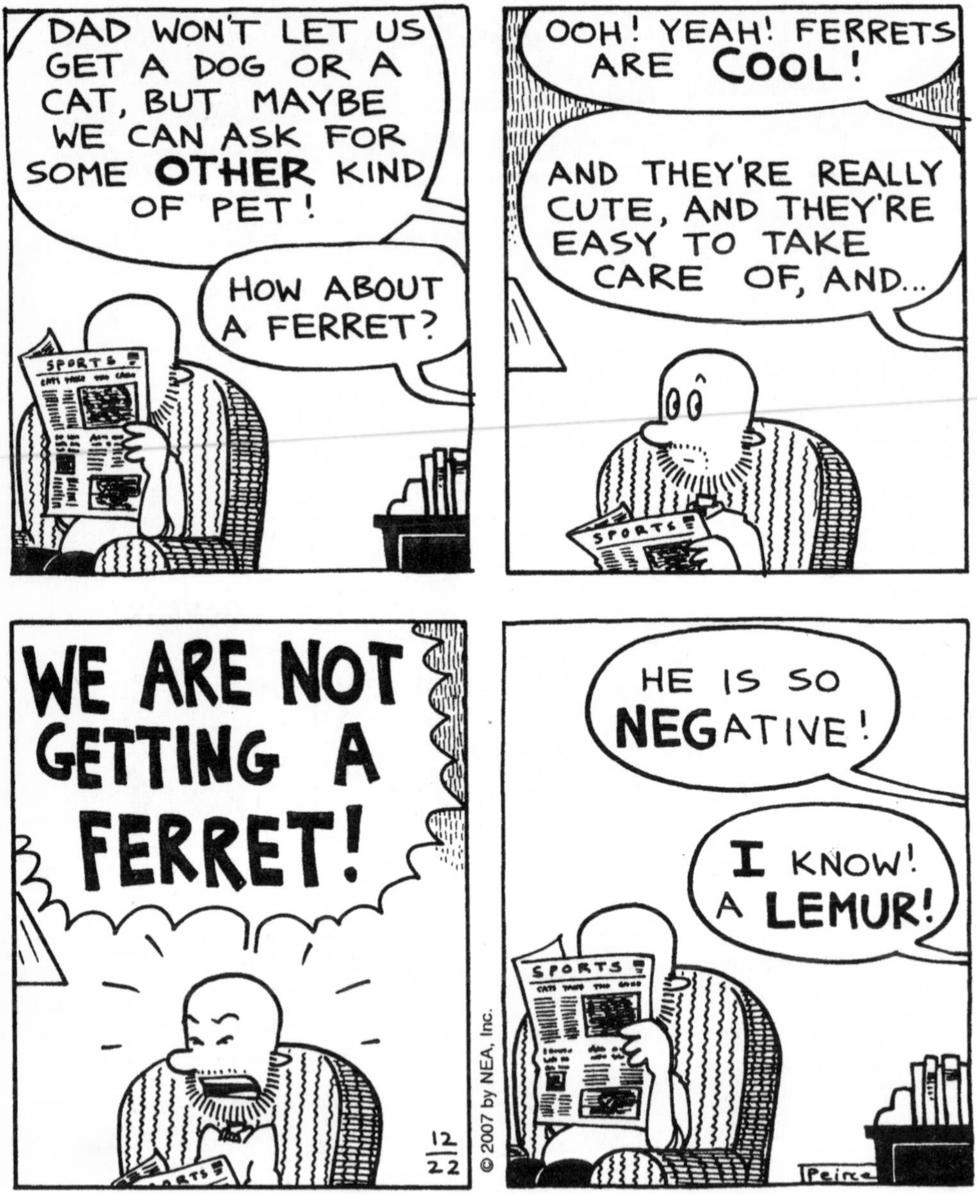
DAD WON'T LET US GET A DOG OR A CAT, BUT MAYBE WE CAN ASK FOR SOME OTHER KIND OF PET!
HOW ABOUT A FERRET?
SPORTS
OOH! YEAH! FERRETS ARE COOL!
AND THEY'RE REALLY CUTE, AND THEY'RE EASY TO TAKE CARE OF, AND...
SPORTS
WE ARE NOT GETTING A FERRET!
12/22
HE IS SO NEGATIVE!
I KNOW! A LEMUR!
SPORTS
Peirce

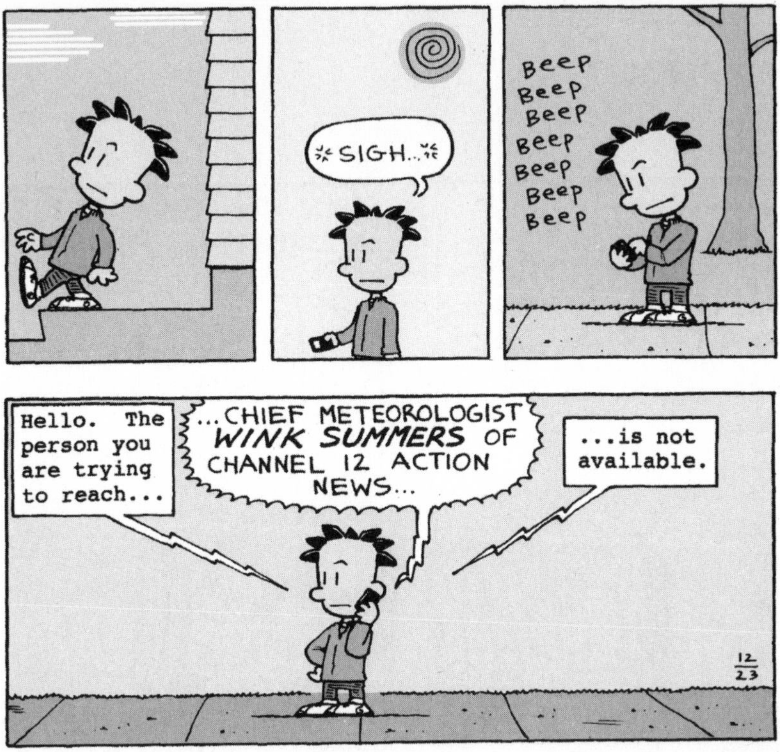
SIGH...
Beep Beep Beep Beep Beep Beep Beep
Hello. The person you are trying to reach...
...CHIEF METEOROLOGIST WINK SUMMERS OF CHANNEL 12 ACTION NEWS...
...is not available.
12
23

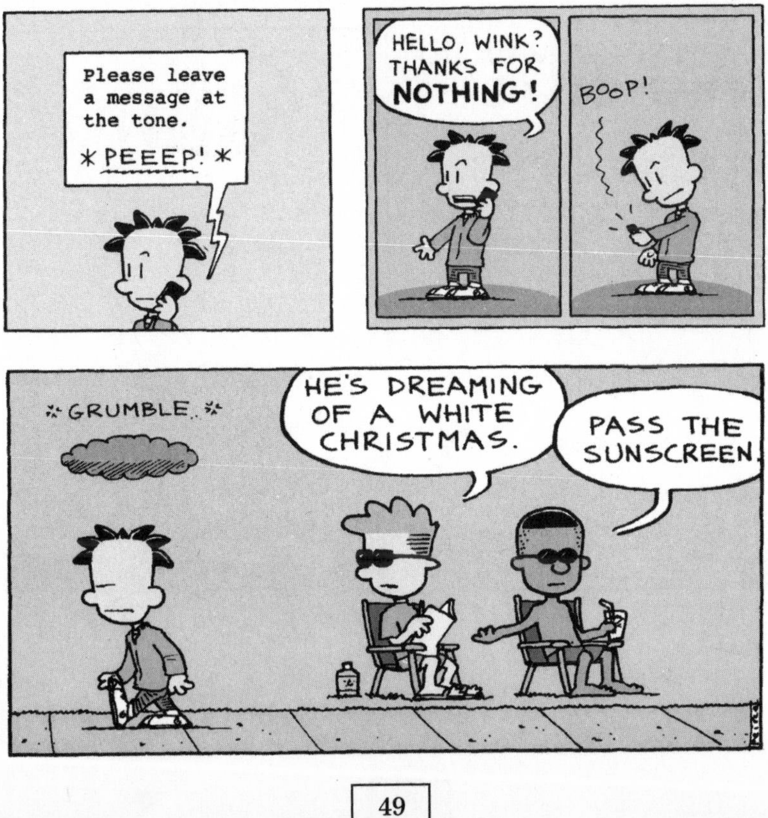
Please leave a message at the tone.
PEEEP!
HELLO, WINK? THANKS FOR NOTHING!
BOOP!
GRUMBLE..
HE'S DREAMING OF A WHITE CHRISTMAS.
PASS THE SUNSCREEN.

'TIS THE SEASON

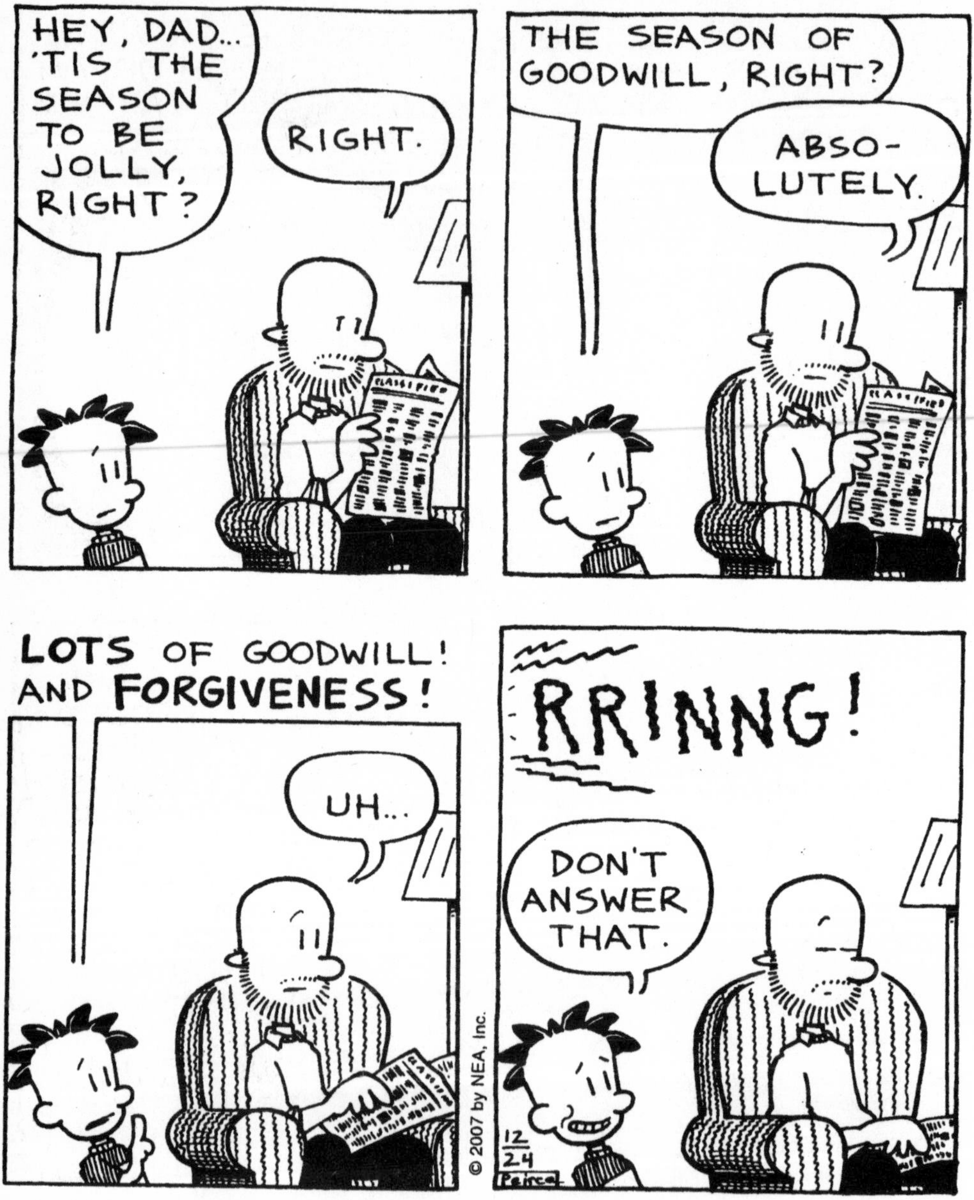
HEY, DAD... 'TIS THE SEASON TO BE JOLLY, RIGHT?
RIGHT.
THE SEASON OF GOODWILL, RIGHT?
ABSO-LUTELY.
LOTS OF GOODWILL! AND FORGIVENESS!
UH...
RRINNG!
DON'T ANSWER THAT.
© 2007 by NEA, Inc.
12 24
Peirce

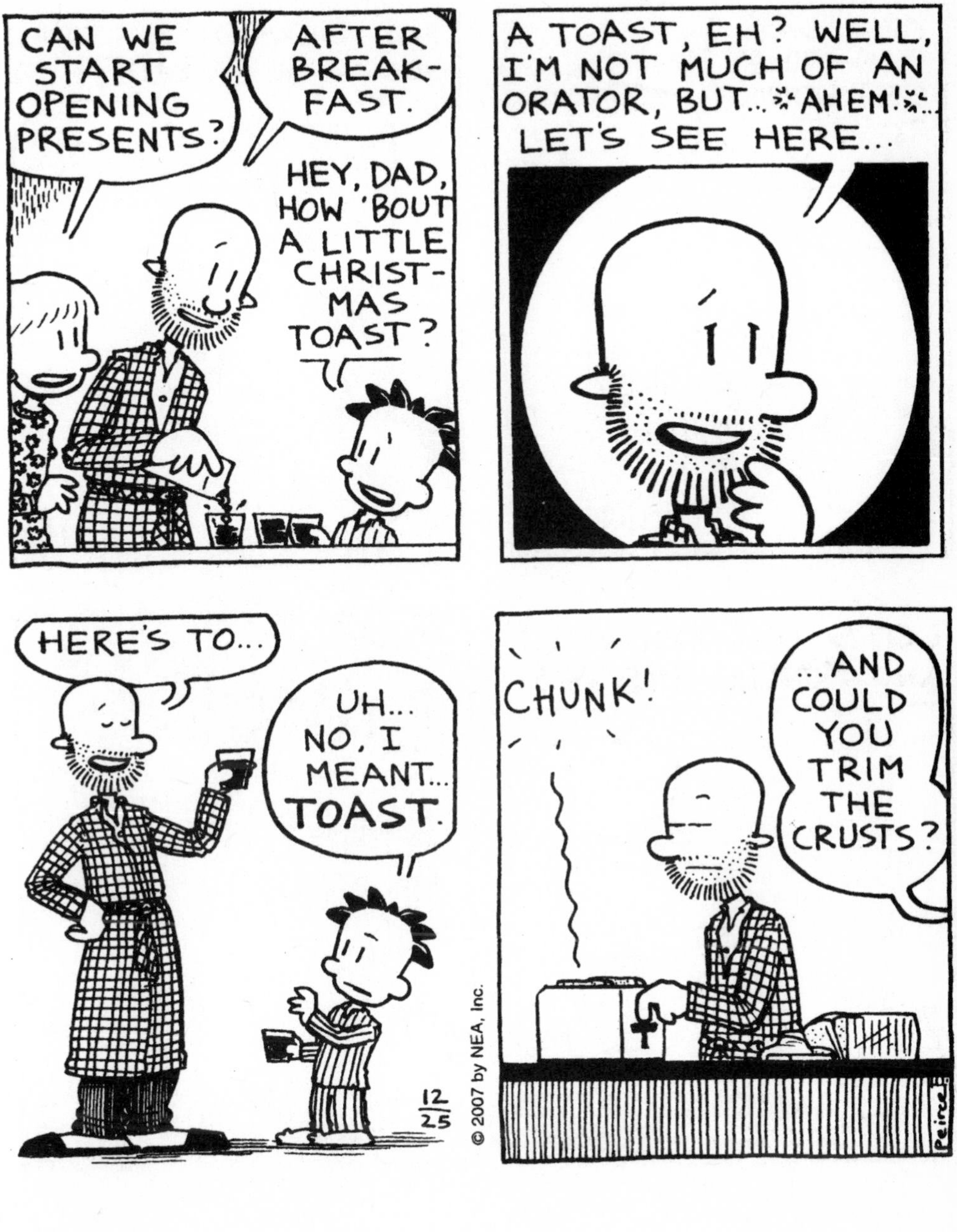
CAN WE START OPENING PRESENTS?
AFTER BREAK-FAST.
HEY, DAD, HOW 'BOUT A LITTLE CHRIST-MAS TOAST?
A TOAST, EH? WELL, I'M NOT MUCH OF AN ORATOR, BUT... *AHEM!*... LET'S SEE HERE...
HERE'S TO...
UH... NO, I MEANT... TOAST.
12/25
CHUNK!
...AND COULD YOU TRIM THE CRUSTS?
Peirce

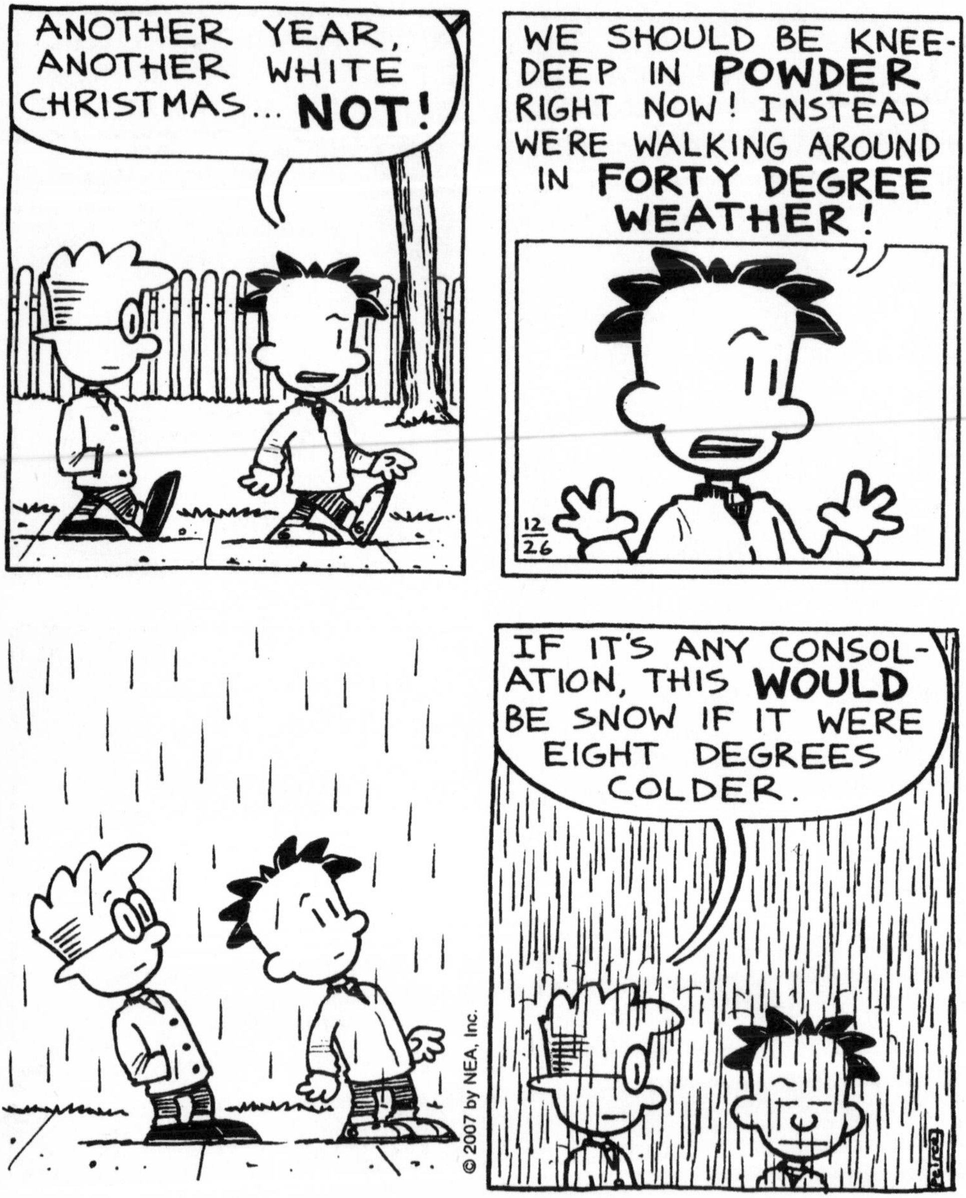
ANOTHER YEAR, ANOTHER WHITE CHRISTMAS... NOT!
WE SHOULD BE KNEE-DEEP IN POWDER RIGHT NOW! INSTEAD WE'RE WALKING AROUND IN FORTY DEGREE WEATHER!
12/26
© 2007 by NEA, Inc.
IF IT'S ANY CONSOLATION, THIS WOULD BE SNOW IF IT WERE EIGHT DEGREES COLDER.

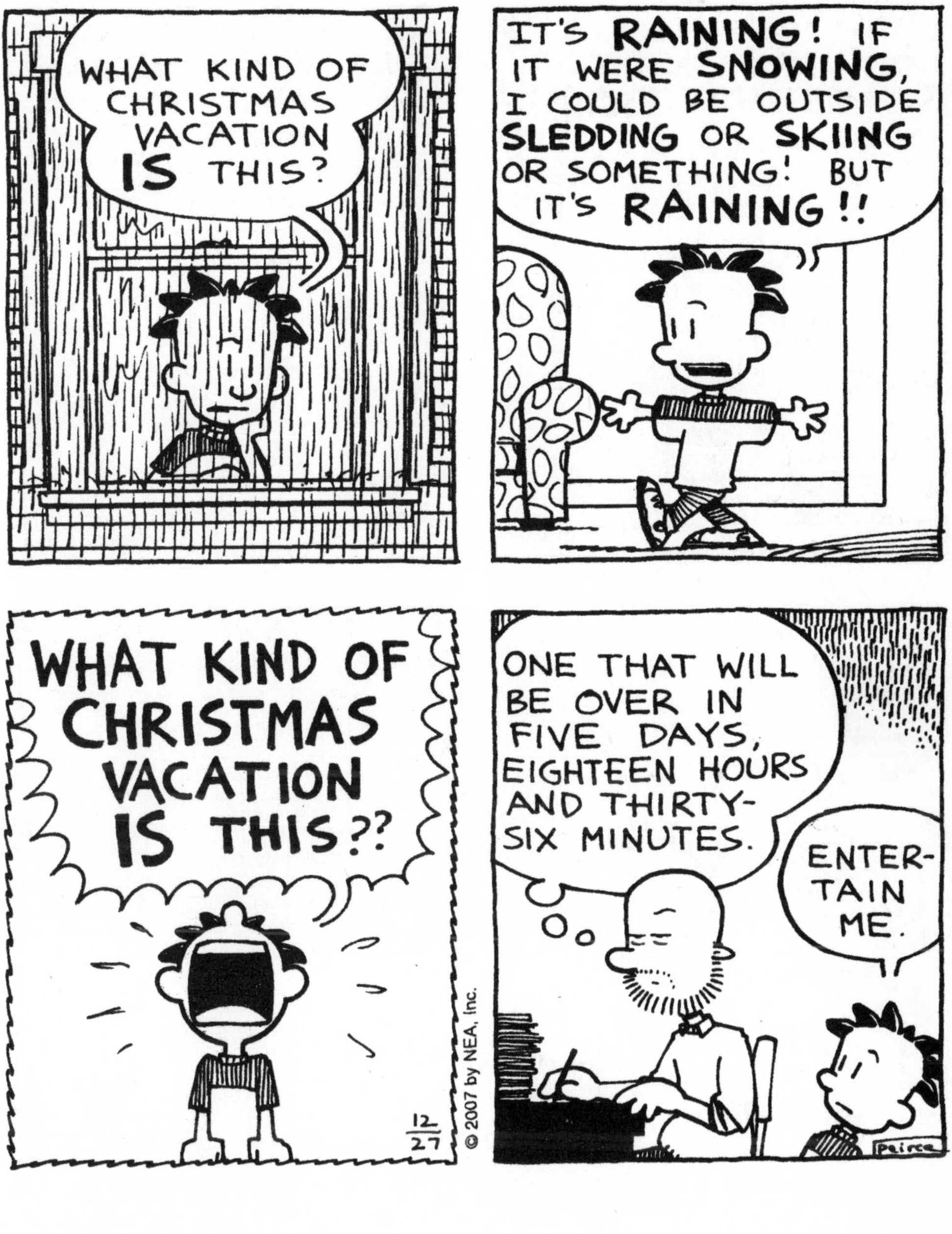
WHAT KIND OF CHRISTMAS VACATION IS THIS?
IT'S RAINING! IF IT WERE SNOWING, I COULD BE OUTSIDE SLEDDING OR SKIING OR SOMETHING! BUT IT'S RAINING!!
WHAT KIND OF CHRISTMAS VACATION IS THIS??
12/27
© 2007 by NEA, Inc.
ONE THAT WILL BE OVER IN FIVE DAYS, EIGHTEEN HOURS AND THIRTY-SIX MINUTES.
ENTERTAIN ME.
Peirce

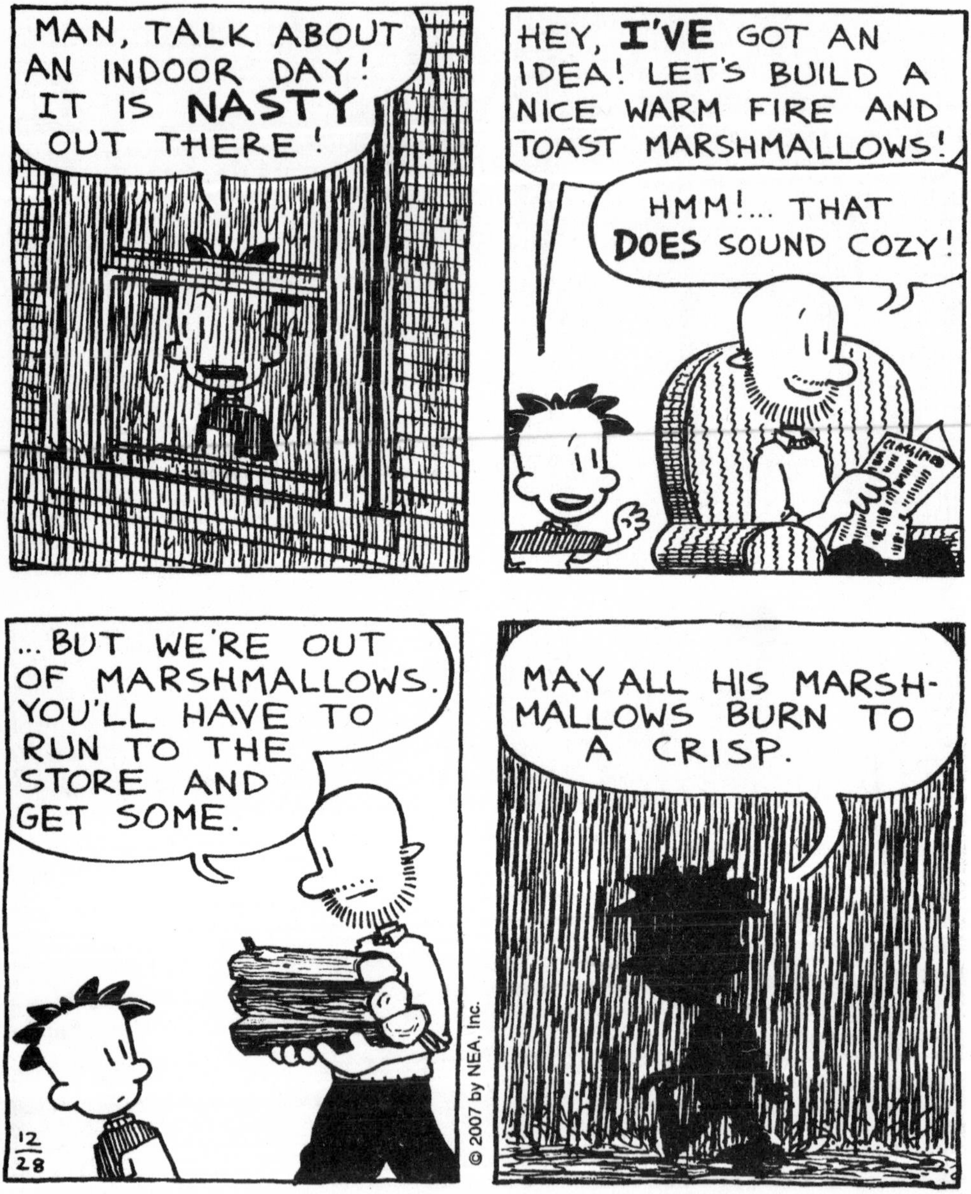
MAN, TALK ABOUT AN INDOOR DAY! IT IS NASTY OUT THERE!
HEY, I'VE GOT AN IDEA! LET'S BUILD A NICE WARM FIRE AND TOAST MARSHMALLOWS!
HMM!... THAT DOES SOUND COZY!
CLASSIFIED
...BUT WE'RE OUT OF MARSHMALLOWS. YOU'LL HAVE TO RUN TO THE STORE AND GET SOME.
12/28
© 2007 by NEA, Inc.
MAY ALL HIS MARSH-MALLOWS BURN TO A CRISP.

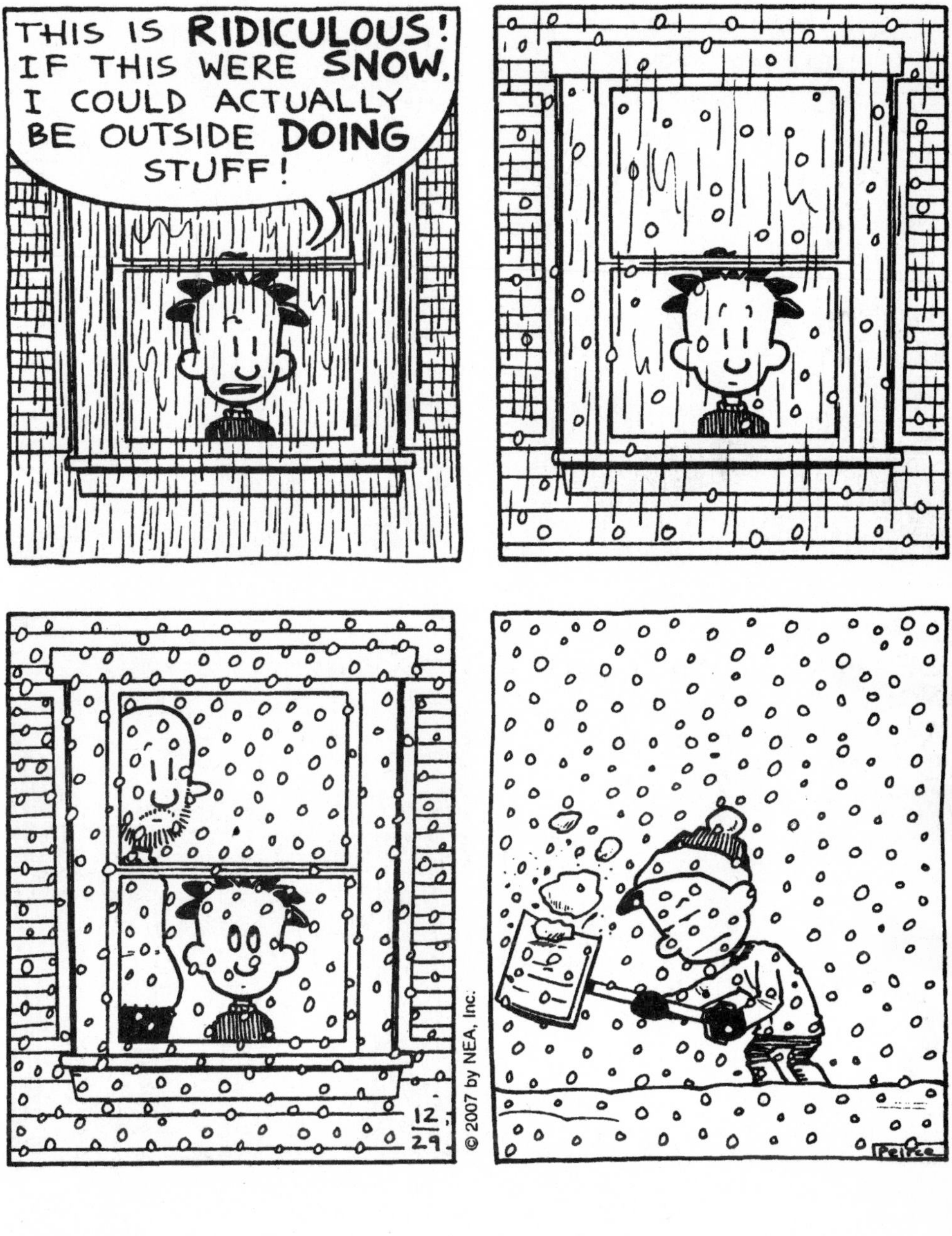
THIS IS RIDICULOUS! IF THIS WERE SNOW, I COULD ACTUALLY BE OUTSIDE DOING STUFF!
12/29
© 2007 by NEA, Inc.
Peirce

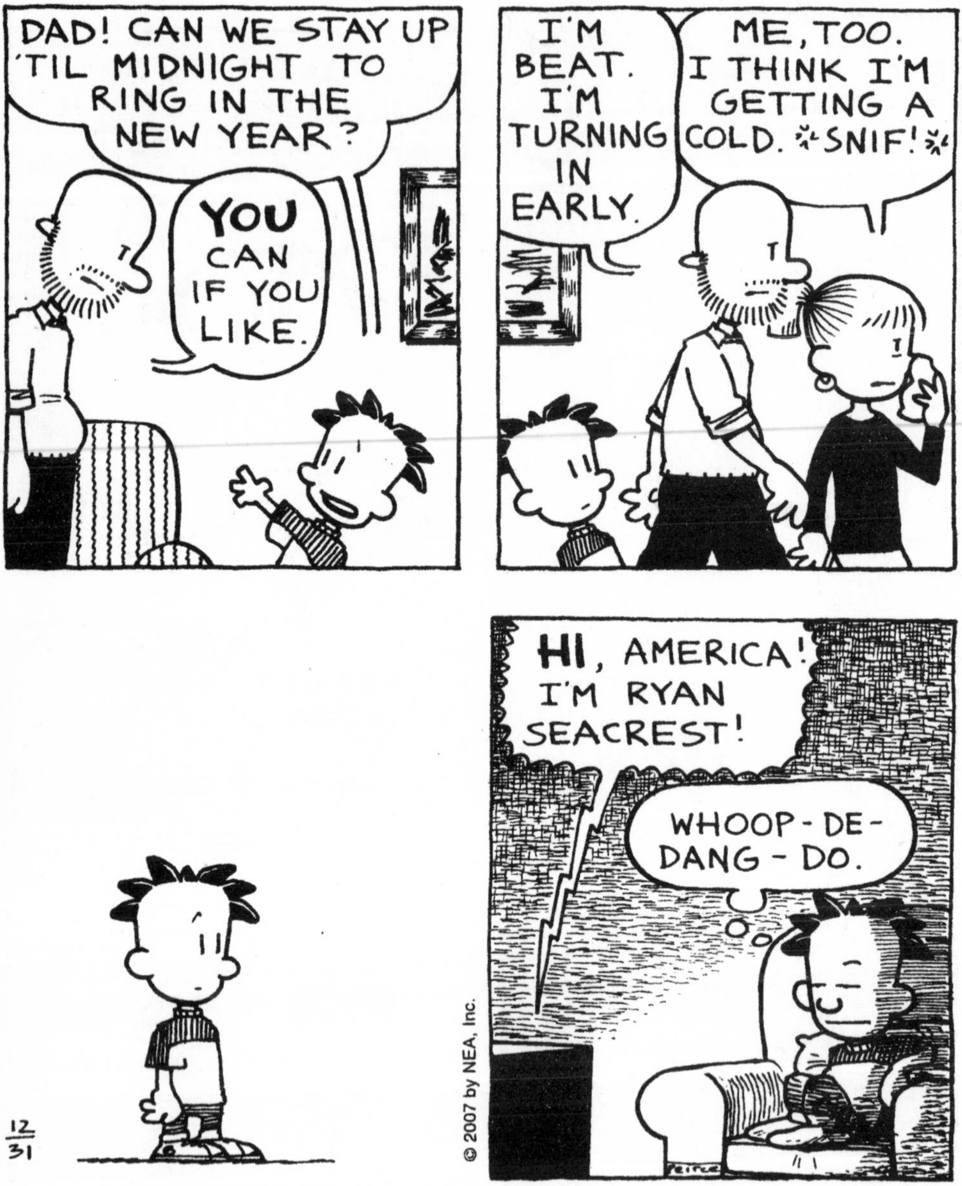
DAD! CAN WE STAY UP 'TIL MIDNIGHT TO RING IN THE NEW YEAR?
YOU CAN IF YOU LIKE.
I'M BEAT. I'M TURNING IN EARLY.
ME, TOO. I THINK I'M GETTING A COLD. *SNIF!*
HI, AMERICA! I'M RYAN SEACREST!
WHOOP-DE-DANG-DO.
12/31
© 2007 by NEA, Inc.

WELL? DID YOU GET A DOG FOR CHRIST-MAS?
HA! OF COURSE NOT!
...ALTHOUGH MY DAD CLAIMS HE GOT ME THE "NEXT BEST THING"!
1/1/08
WHAT'S THE NEXT BEST THING?
A UCONN HUSKIES T-SHIRT AND A COPY OF "OLD YELLER".
PARENTS ARE SO LAME.
I'LL BE RE-GIFTING.
Peirce
© 2008 by NEA, Inc.

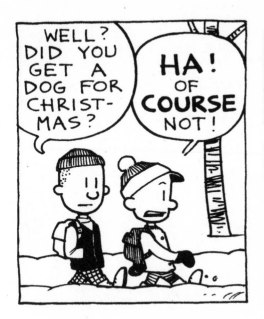

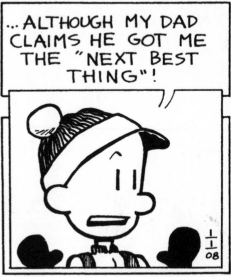

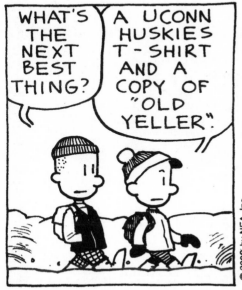

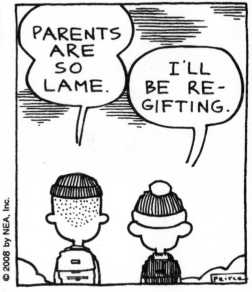

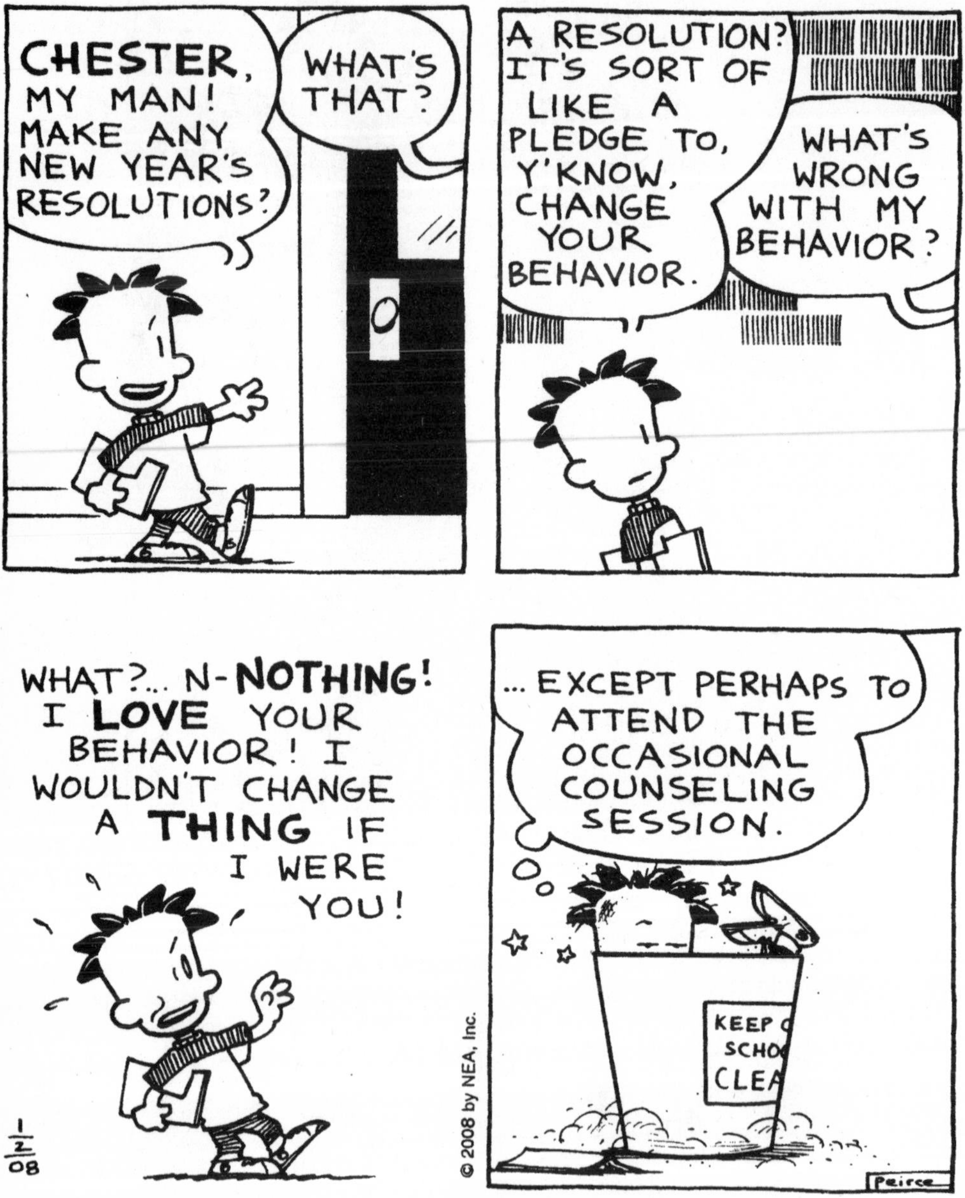
CHESTER, MY MAN! MAKE ANY NEW YEAR'S RESOLUTIONS?
WHAT'S THAT?
A RESOLUTION? IT'S SORT OF LIKE A PLEDGE TO, Y'KNOW, CHANGE YOUR BEHAVIOR.
WHAT'S WRONG WITH MY BEHAVIOR?
WHAT?... N-NOTHING! I LOVE YOUR BEHAVIOR! I WOULDN'T CHANGE A THING IF I WERE YOU!
...EXCEPT PERHAPS TO ATTEND THE OCCASIONAL COUNSELING SESSION.
KEEP O
SCHO
CLEA
1/2/08
© 2008 by NEA, Inc.
Peirce

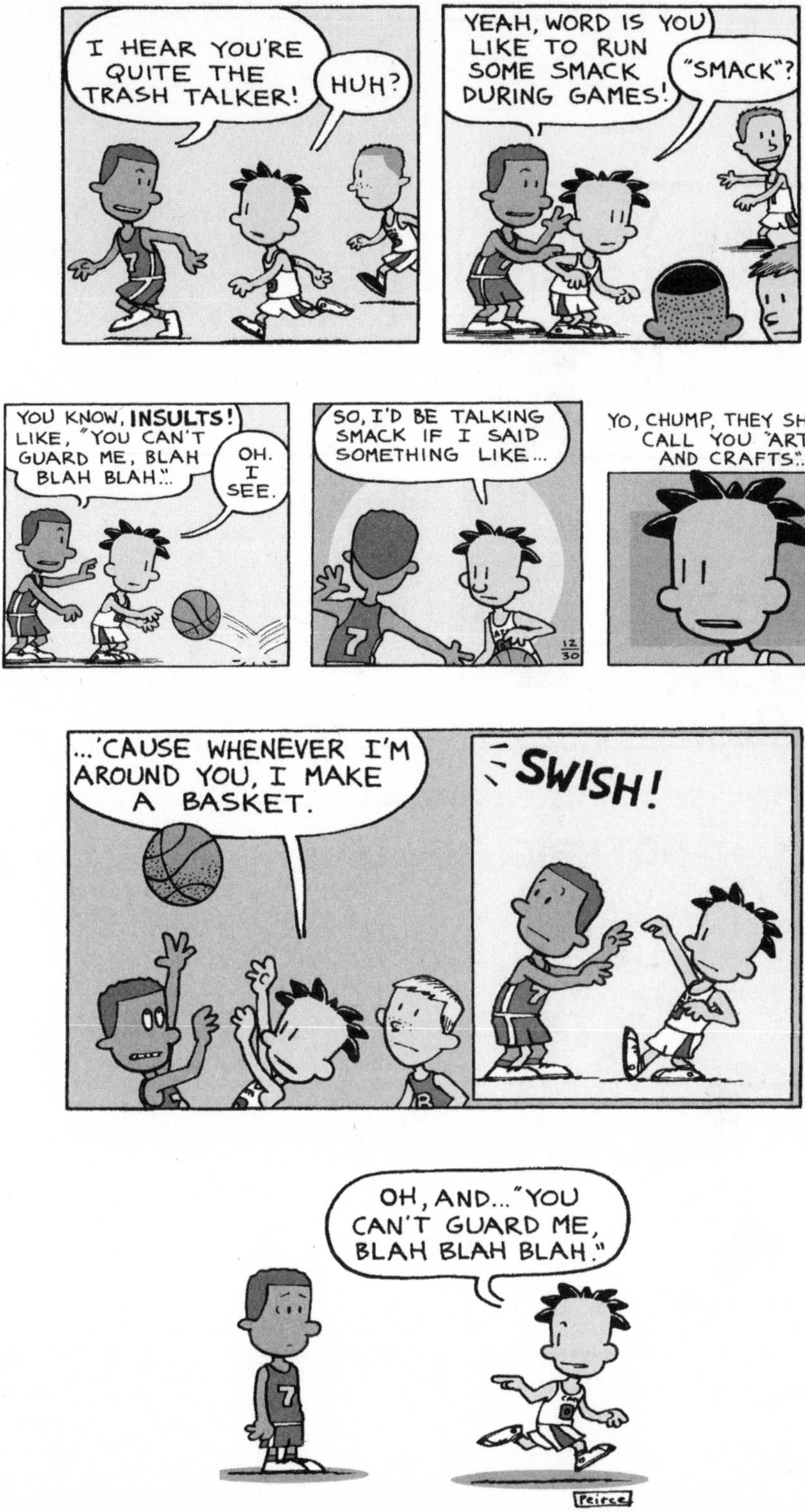
I HEAR YOU'RE QUITE THE TRASH TALKER!
HUH?
YEAH, WORD IS YOU LIKE TO RUN SOME SMACK DURING GAMES!
"SMACK"?
YOU KNOW, **INSULTS!** LIKE, "YOU CAN'T GUARD ME, BLAH BLAH BLAH."...
OH. I SEE.
SO, I'D BE TALKING SMACK IF I SAID SOMETHING LIKE...
12 30
YO, CHUMP, THEY SHOULD CALL YOU "ARTS AND CRAFTS"...
...'CAUSE WHENEVER I'M AROUND YOU, I MAKE A BASKET.
SWISH!
OH, AND... "YOU CAN'T GUARD ME, BLAH BLAH BLAH."
Peirce

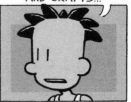

THE BOOK OF FACTS = BOR-ING!

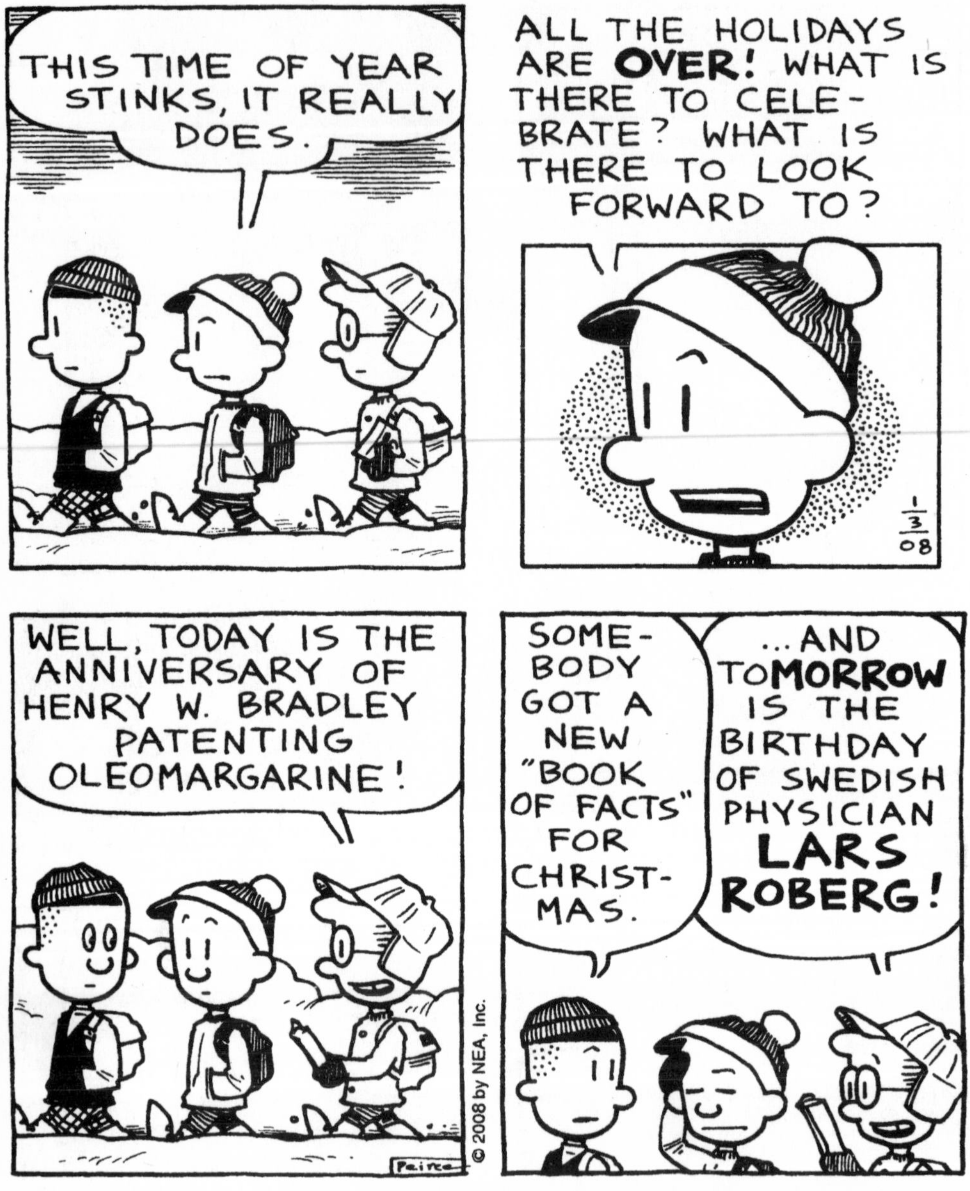
THIS TIME OF YEAR STINKS, IT REALLY DOES.
ALL THE HOLIDAYS ARE **OVER!** WHAT IS THERE TO CELE-BRATE? WHAT IS THERE TO LOOK FORWARD TO?
1/3/08
WELL, TODAY IS THE ANNIVERSARY OF HENRY W. BRADLEY PATENTING OLEOMARGARINE!
Peirce
© 2008 by NEA, Inc.
SOME-BODY GOT A NEW "BOOK OF FACTS" FOR CHRIST-MAS.
...AND TO**MORROW** IS THE BIRTHDAY OF SWEDISH PHYSICIAN **LARS ROBERG!**

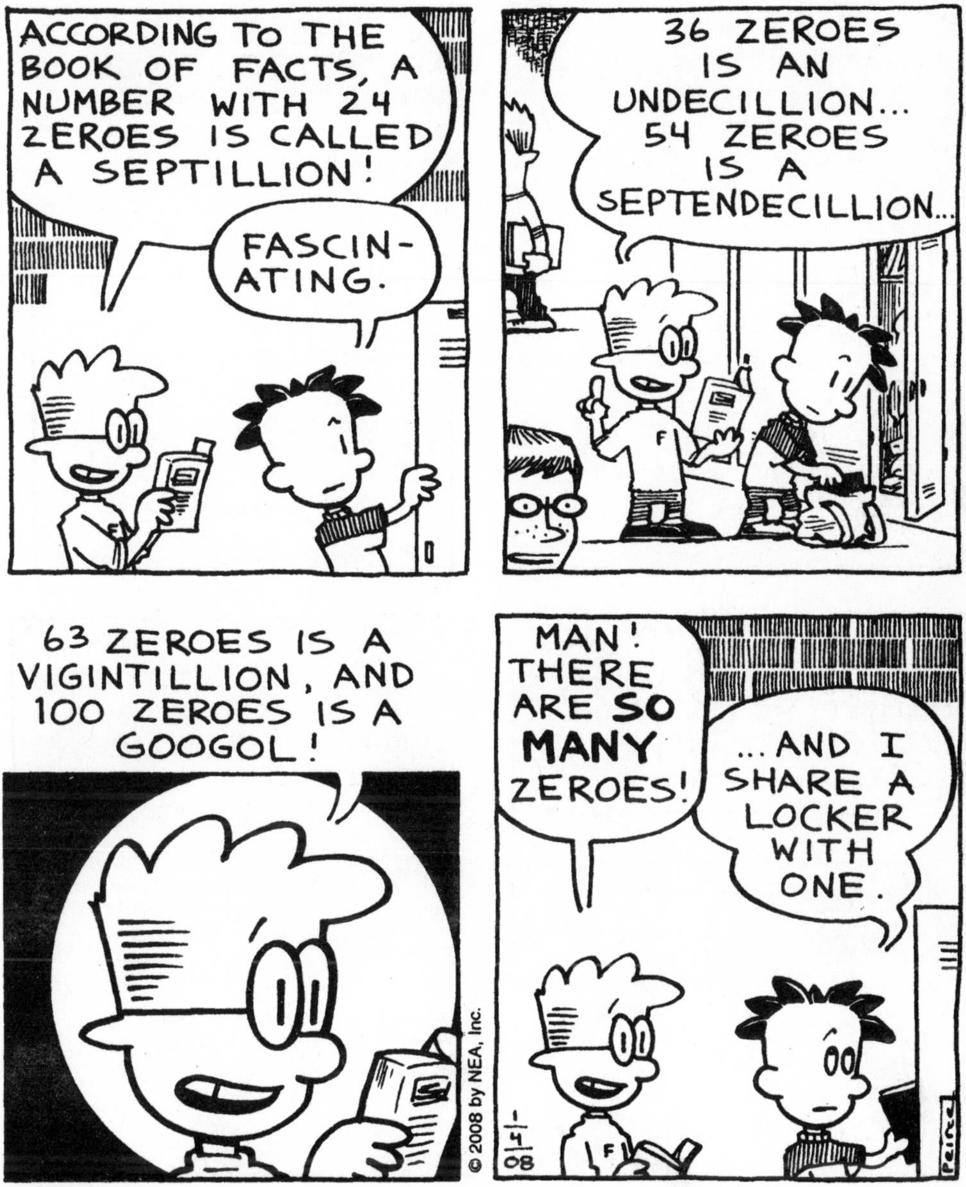
ACCORDING TO THE BOOK OF FACTS, A NUMBER WITH 24 ZEROES IS CALLED A SEPTILLION!
FASCIN-ATING.
36 ZEROES IS AN UNDECILLION... 54 ZEROES IS A SEPTENDECILLION...
63 ZEROES IS A VIGINTILLION, AND 100 ZEROES IS A GOOGOL!
MAN! THERE ARE **SO MANY** ZEROES!
...AND I SHARE A LOCKER WITH ONE.
© 2008 by NEA, Inc.
1-4-08
PEIRCE

NOW **HERE'S** AN INTERESTING FACT! DID YOU KNOW THAT THE AM... ...F MONEY IN CIR... ...HAS RISEN... ...DURIN... ...TWO DE...

THIS IS AWFUL.

I AGREE.

AND THAT'S NOT ALL! WHEN... ...MINT STA... ...NG MO... TH... ...EENTH... NT... ...IT B... AFT... ...WASN'T EVE... AND...

I DON'T KNOW HOW MUCH MORE OF THIS I CAN TAKE.

SAME.

AND LISTEN TO **THIS**: SINCE 1969, THE LARG... NOMINATION OF U.S. CU... RENCY THAT HAS BEEN... SSUED IS THE $100 BI... ...LARGER DENOMINATIO... ...LLS REACH THE FEDER... ...ERVE BANK, THEY'RE RE...

1/5/08

...OVE... ...CIRCULATI...

I COULD FIGHT BACK WITH SOME "STAR TREK: THE NEXT GENERATION" TRIVIA.

WHY NOT JUST STICK FORKS IN MY EYES?

© 2008 by NEA, Inc.

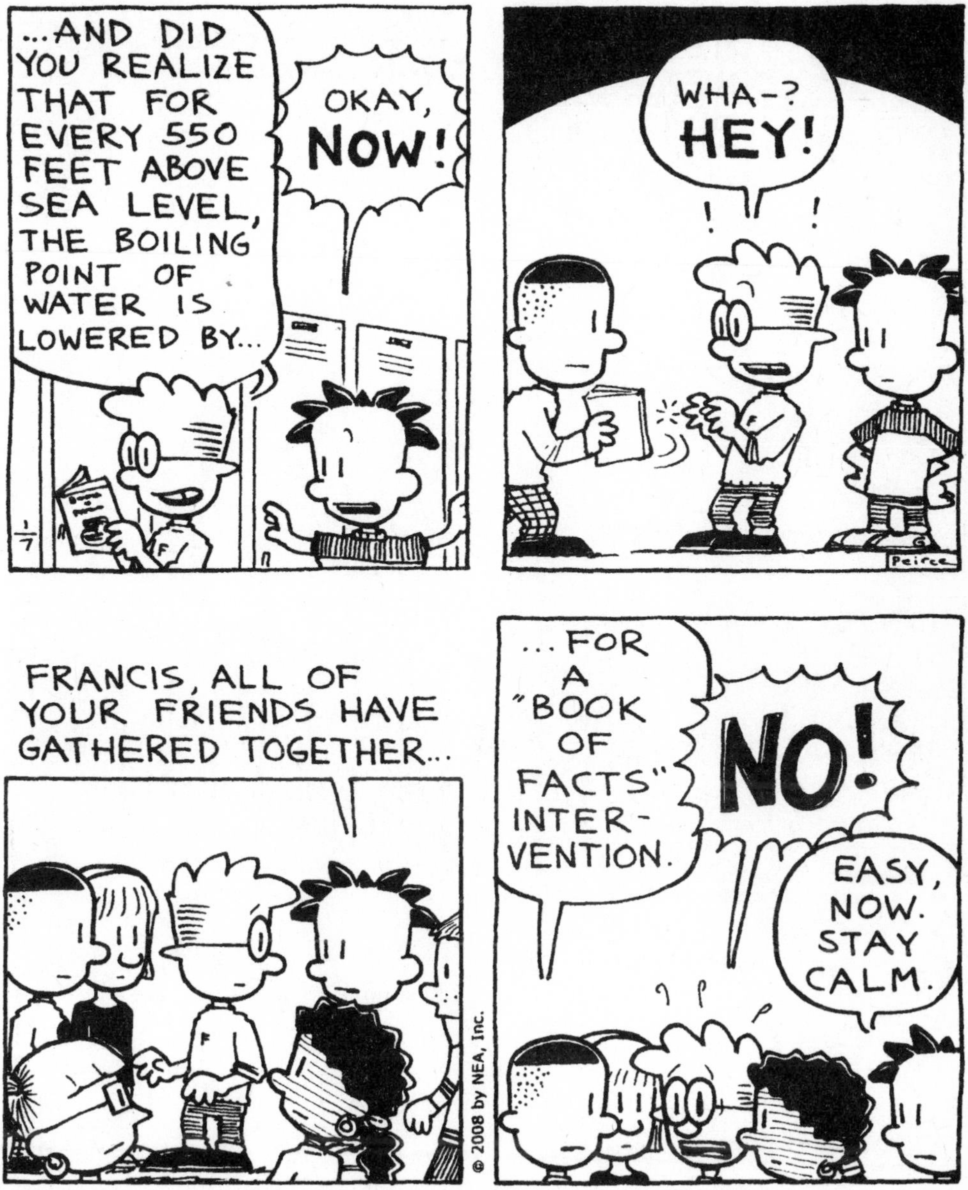
...AND DID YOU REALIZE THAT FOR EVERY 550 FEET ABOVE SEA LEVEL, THE BOILING POINT OF WATER IS LOWERED BY...
OKAY, NOW!
WHA-? HEY!
! !
FRANCIS, ALL OF YOUR FRIENDS HAVE GATHERED TOGETHER...
...FOR A "BOOK OF FACTS" INTER-VENTION.
NO!
EASY, NOW. STAY CALM.
Peirce
© 2008 by NEA, Inc.

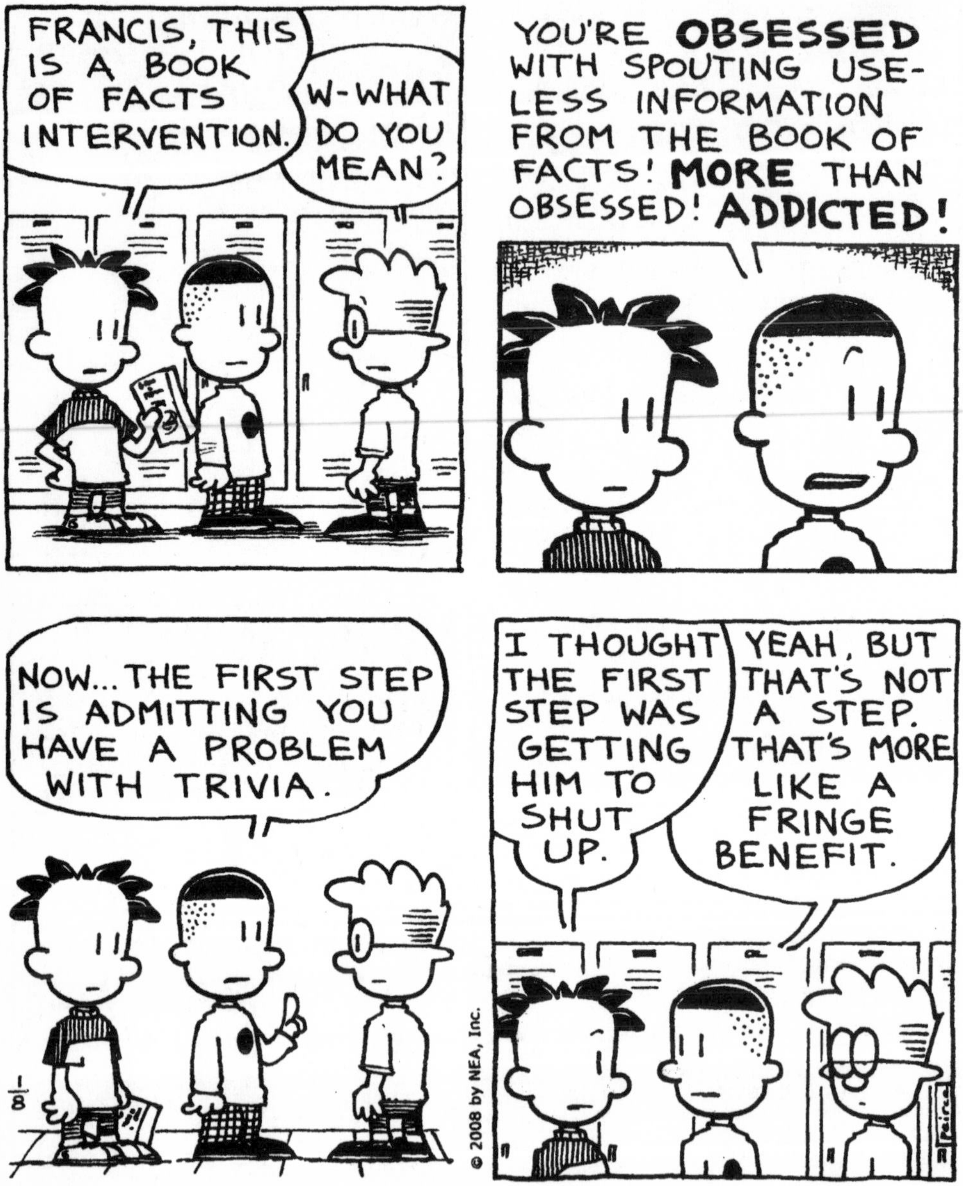
FRANCIS, THIS IS A BOOK OF FACTS INTERVENTION.
W-WHAT DO YOU MEAN?
YOU'RE **OBSESSED** WITH SPOUTING USELESS INFORMATION FROM THE BOOK OF FACTS! **MORE** THAN OBSESSED! **ADDICTED!**
NOW... THE FIRST STEP IS ADMITTING YOU HAVE A PROBLEM WITH TRIVIA.
1/8
© 2008 by NEA, Inc.
I THOUGHT THE FIRST STEP WAS GETTING HIM TO SHUT UP.
YEAH, BUT THAT'S NOT A STEP. THAT'S MORE LIKE A FRINGE BENEFIT.
Peirce

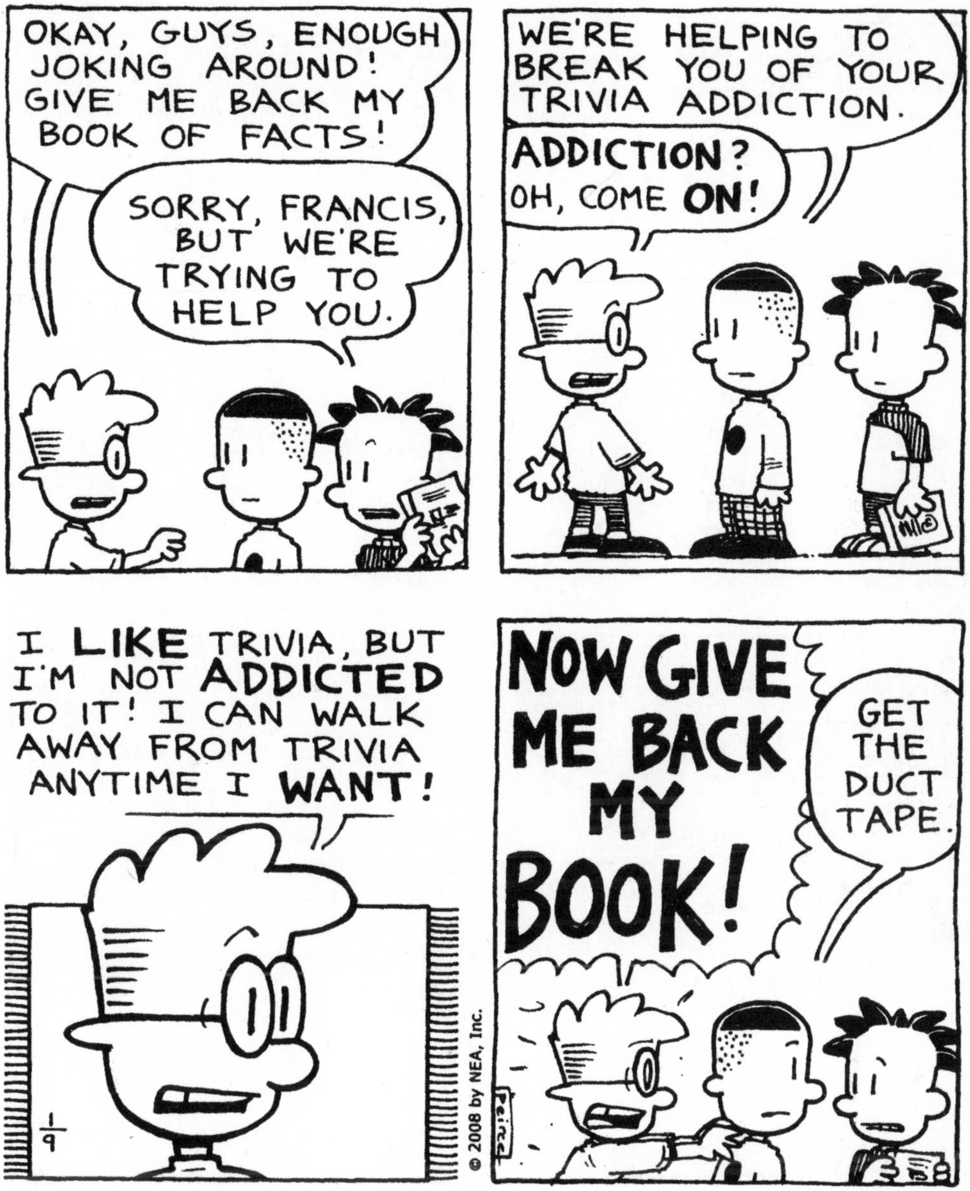
OKAY, GUYS, ENOUGH JOKING AROUND! GIVE ME BACK MY BOOK OF FACTS!
SORRY, FRANCIS, BUT WE'RE TRYING TO HELP YOU.
WE'RE HELPING TO BREAK YOU OF YOUR TRIVIA ADDICTION.
ADDICTION? OH, COME ON!
I LIKE TRIVIA, BUT I'M NOT ADDICTED TO IT! I CAN WALK AWAY FROM TRIVIA ANYTIME I WANT!
1/9
© 2008 by NEA, Inc.
NOW GIVE ME BACK MY BOOK!
GET THE DUCT TAPE.

HOW'S FRANCIS DOING WITHOUT HIS BOOK OF FACTS?

NOT GOOD.

DID YOU KNOW THAT THE CAPITAL OF DJIBOUTI IS ROSEAU? WAIT!... NO, THAT CAN'T BE RIGHT... UH... THE CAPITAL OF ROSEAU IS...

UH... HOLD IT, LET ME START OVER!... DID YOU KNOW THAT THE COMPOSER ARTURO "HOT LIPS" O'FARRILL WAS... UM... NO, WAIT, HIS NICKNAME WASN'T "HOT LIPS", IT WAS... DANG, WHAT **WAS** IT?...

1/10

OKAY, LET'S TALK ABOU AILROADS! THE NUMBER F T S OF TRACK IN 30 WAS OV A BRITNEY S W H A L B IN NO, DOES SENSE! 'LL HAVE G

HE'S TRYING TO FREE-STYLE.

THIS IS UGLY.

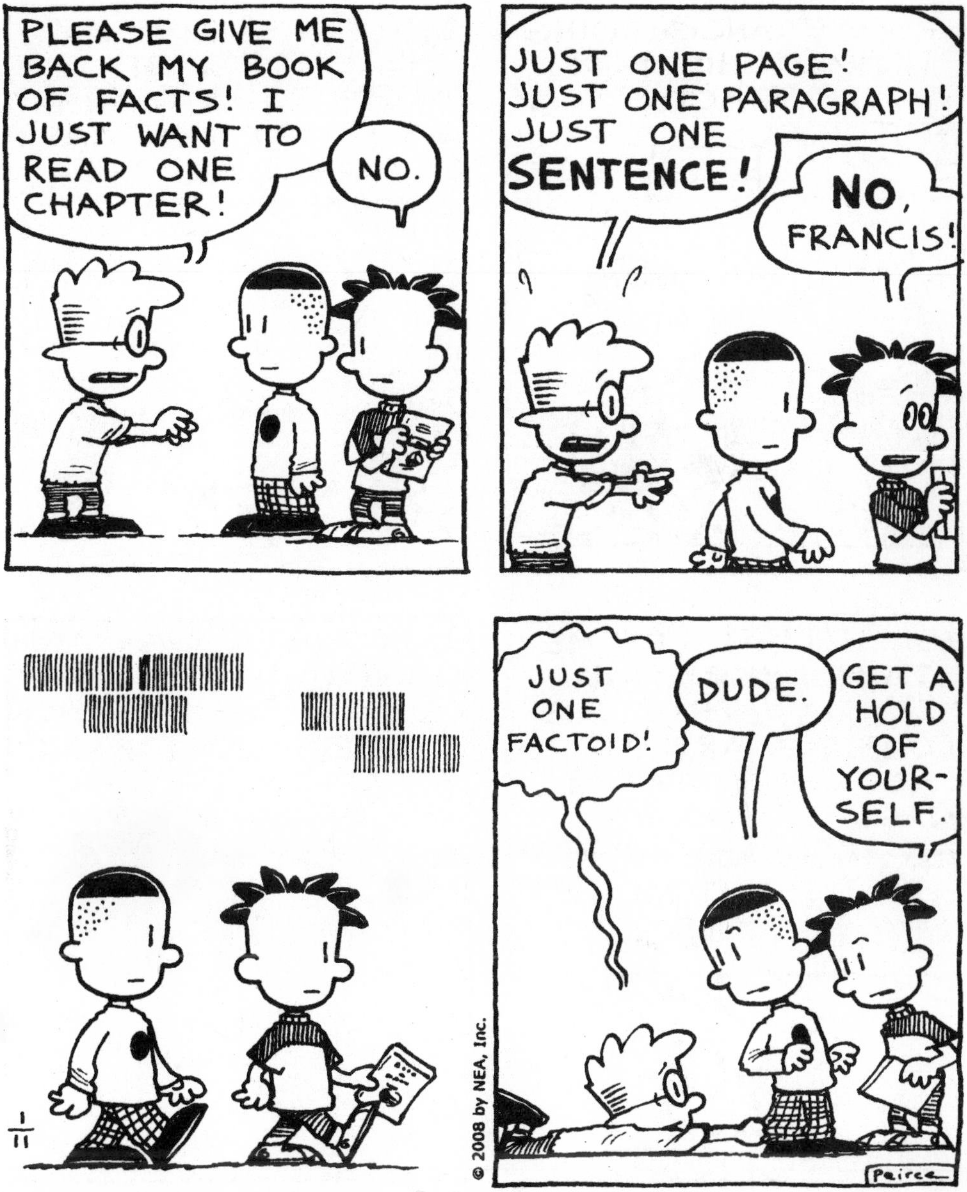
PLEASE GIVE ME BACK MY BOOK OF FACTS! I JUST WANT TO READ ONE CHAPTER!
NO.
JUST ONE PAGE! JUST ONE PARAGRAPH! JUST ONE SENTENCE!
NO, FRANCIS!
JUST ONE FACTOID!
DUDE.
GET A HOLD OF YOUR-SELF.
Peirce

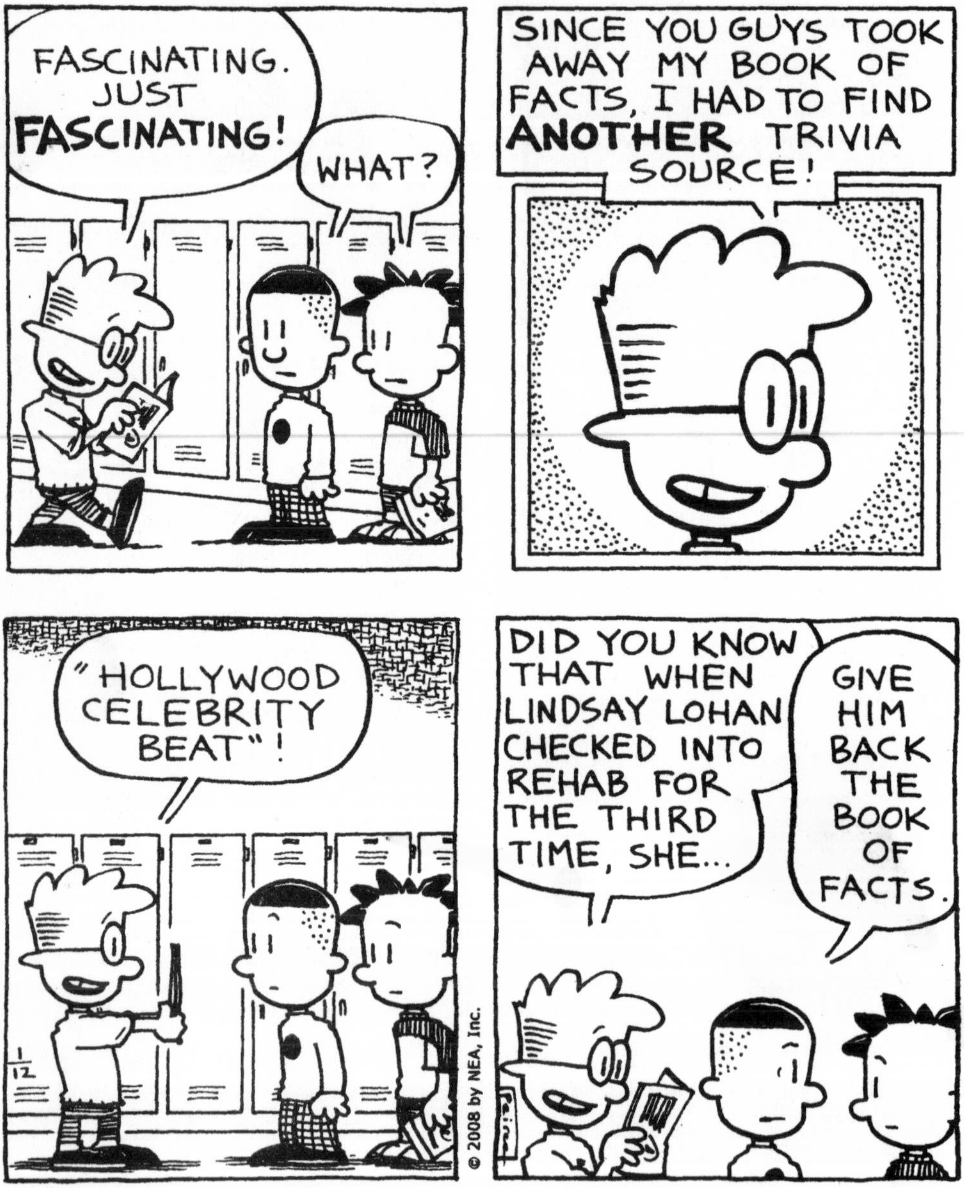
FASCINATING. JUST FASCINATING!
WHAT?
SINCE YOU GUYS TOOK AWAY MY BOOK OF FACTS, I HAD TO FIND ANOTHER TRIVIA SOURCE!
"HOLLYWOOD CELEBRITY BEAT"!
DID YOU KNOW THAT WHEN LINDSAY LOHAN CHECKED INTO REHAB FOR THE THIRD TIME, SHE...
GIVE HIM BACK THE BOOK OF FACTS.
© 2008 by NEA, Inc.

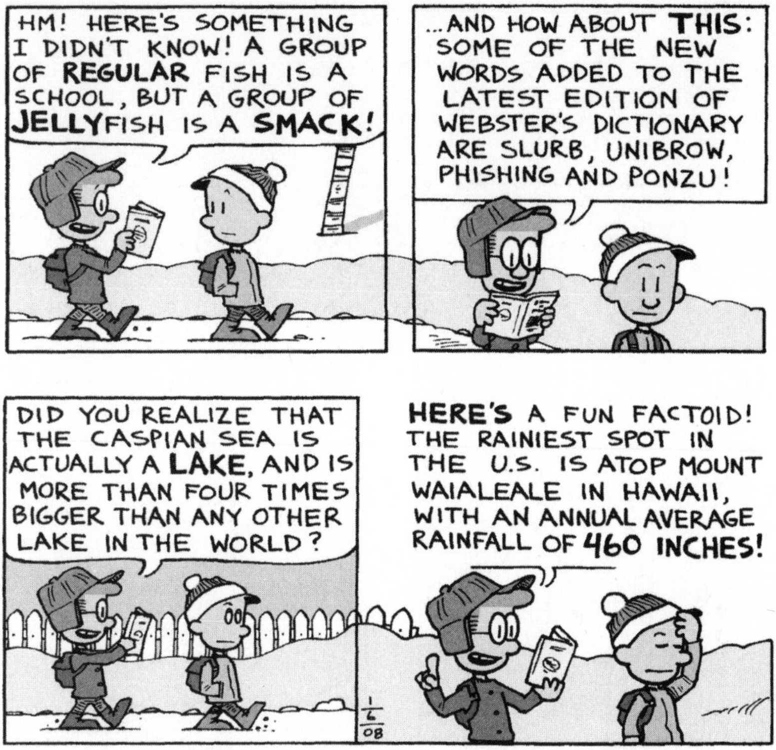
HM! HERE'S SOMETHING I DIDN'T KNOW! A GROUP OF REGULAR FISH IS A SCHOOL, BUT A GROUP OF JELLYFISH IS A SMACK!
...AND HOW ABOUT THIS: SOME OF THE NEW WORDS ADDED TO THE LATEST EDITION OF WEBSTER'S DICTIONARY ARE SLURB, UNIBROW, PHISHING AND PONZU!
DID YOU REALIZE THAT THE CASPIAN SEA IS ACTUALLY A LAKE, AND IS MORE THAN FOUR TIMES BIGGER THAN ANY OTHER LAKE IN THE WORLD?
1/6/08
HERE'S A FUN FACTOID! THE RAINIEST SPOT IN THE U.S. IS ATOP MOUNT WAIALEALE IN HAWAII, WITH AN ANNUAL AVERAGE RAINFALL OF 460 INCHES!

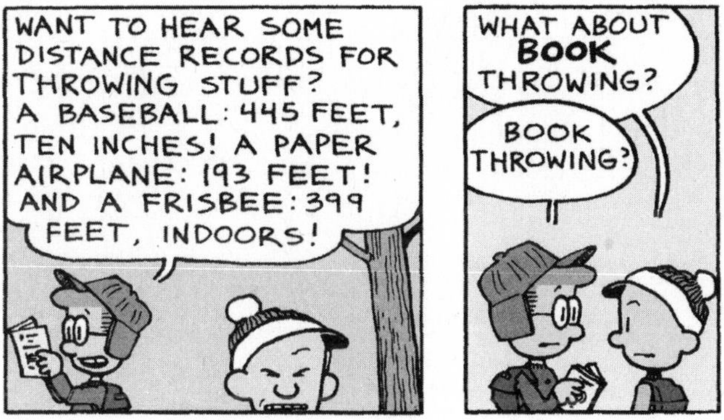
WANT TO HEAR SOME DISTANCE RECORDS FOR THROWING STUFF? A BASEBALL: 445 FEET, TEN INCHES! A PAPER AIRPLANE: 193 FEET! AND A FRISBEE: 399 FEET, INDOORS!
WHAT ABOUT BOOK THROWING?
BOOK THROWING?

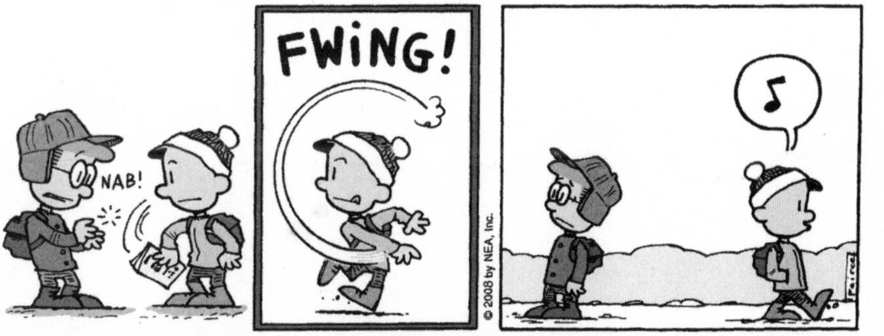
NAB!
FWING!
♪
© 2008 by NEA, Inc.

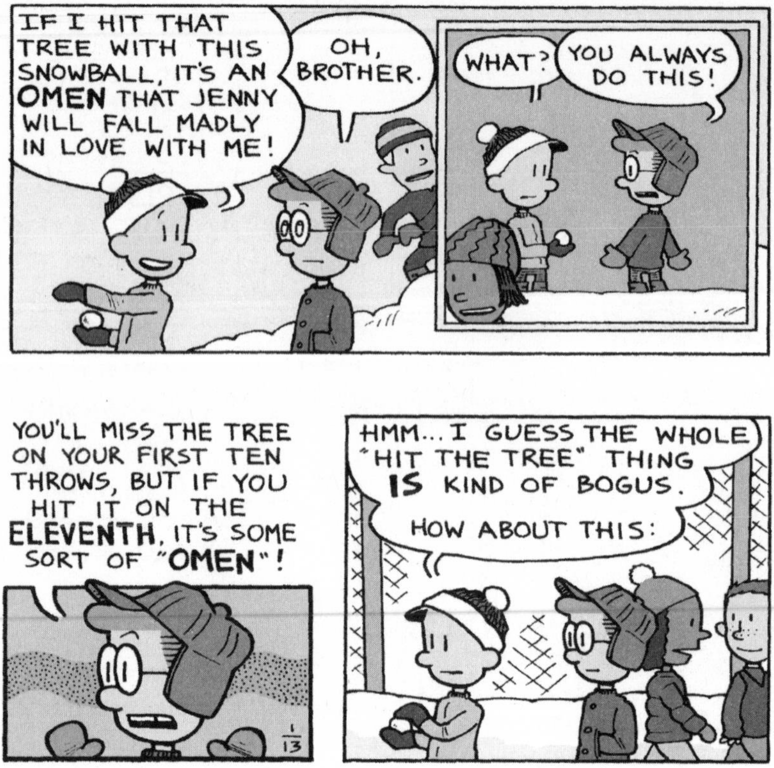
IF I HIT THAT TREE WITH THIS SNOWBALL, IT'S AN OMEN THAT JENNY WILL FALL MADLY IN LOVE WITH ME!
OH, BROTHER.
WHAT?
YOU ALWAYS DO THIS!
YOU'LL MISS THE TREE ON YOUR FIRST TEN THROWS, BUT IF YOU HIT IT ON THE ELEVENTH, IT'S SOME SORT OF "OMEN"!
1/13
HMM... I GUESS THE WHOLE "HIT THE TREE" THING IS KIND OF BOGUS.
HOW ABOUT THIS:

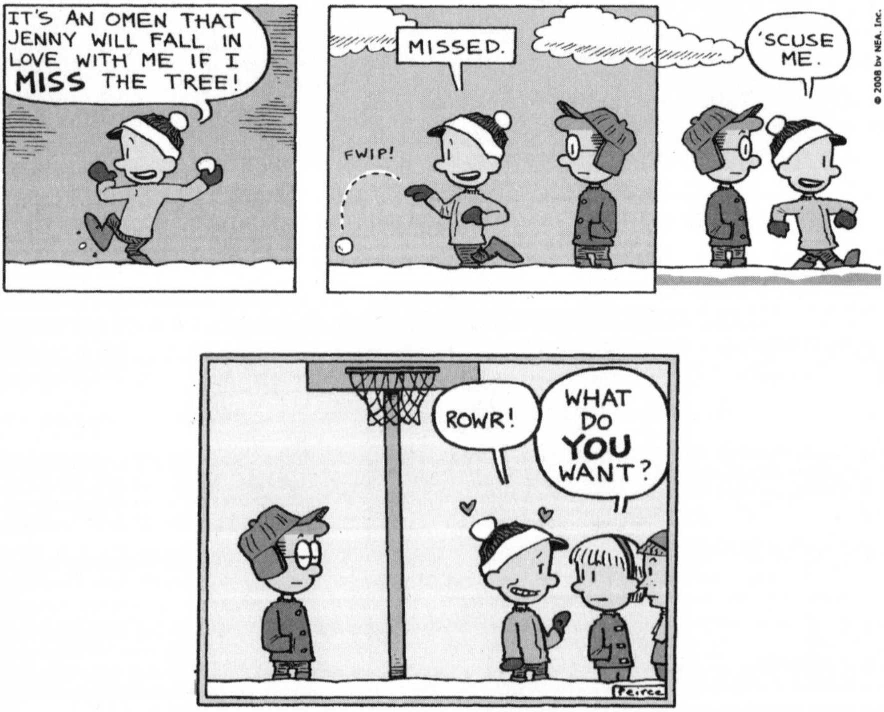
IT'S AN OMEN THAT JENNY WILL FALL IN LOVE WITH ME IF I MISS THE TREE!
FWIP!
MISSED.
'SCUSE ME.
© 2008 by NEA, Inc.
ROWR!
WHAT DO YOU WANT?
Peirce

RELAX...OR ELSE!

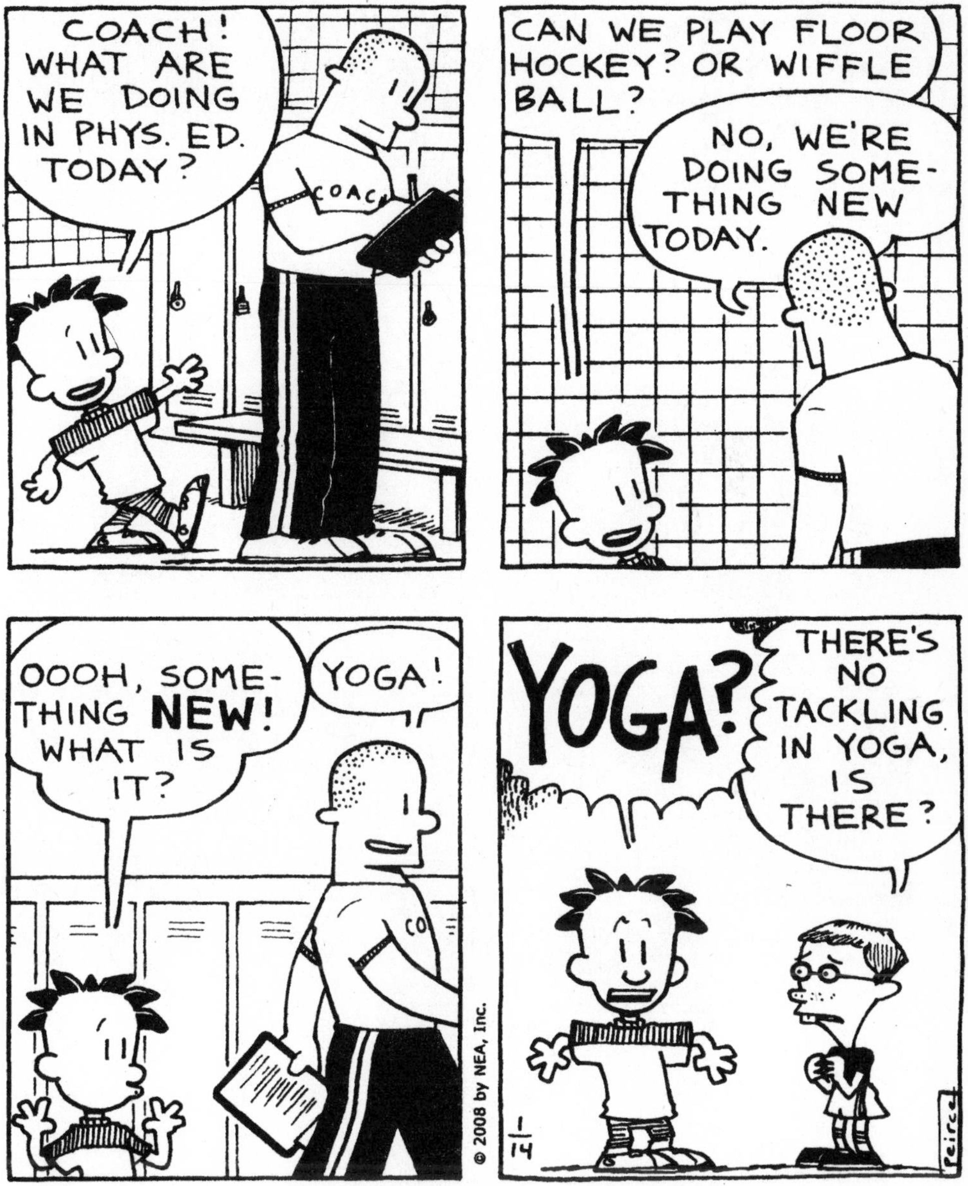
COACH! WHAT ARE WE DOING IN PHYS. ED. TODAY?
COACH
CAN WE PLAY FLOOR HOCKEY? OR WIFFLE BALL?
NO, WE'RE DOING SOMETHING NEW TODAY.
OOOH, SOMETHING **NEW**! WHAT IS IT?
YOGA!
CO
YOGA?
THERE'S NO TACKLING IN YOGA, IS THERE?
© 2008 by NEA, Inc.
1/14
Peirce

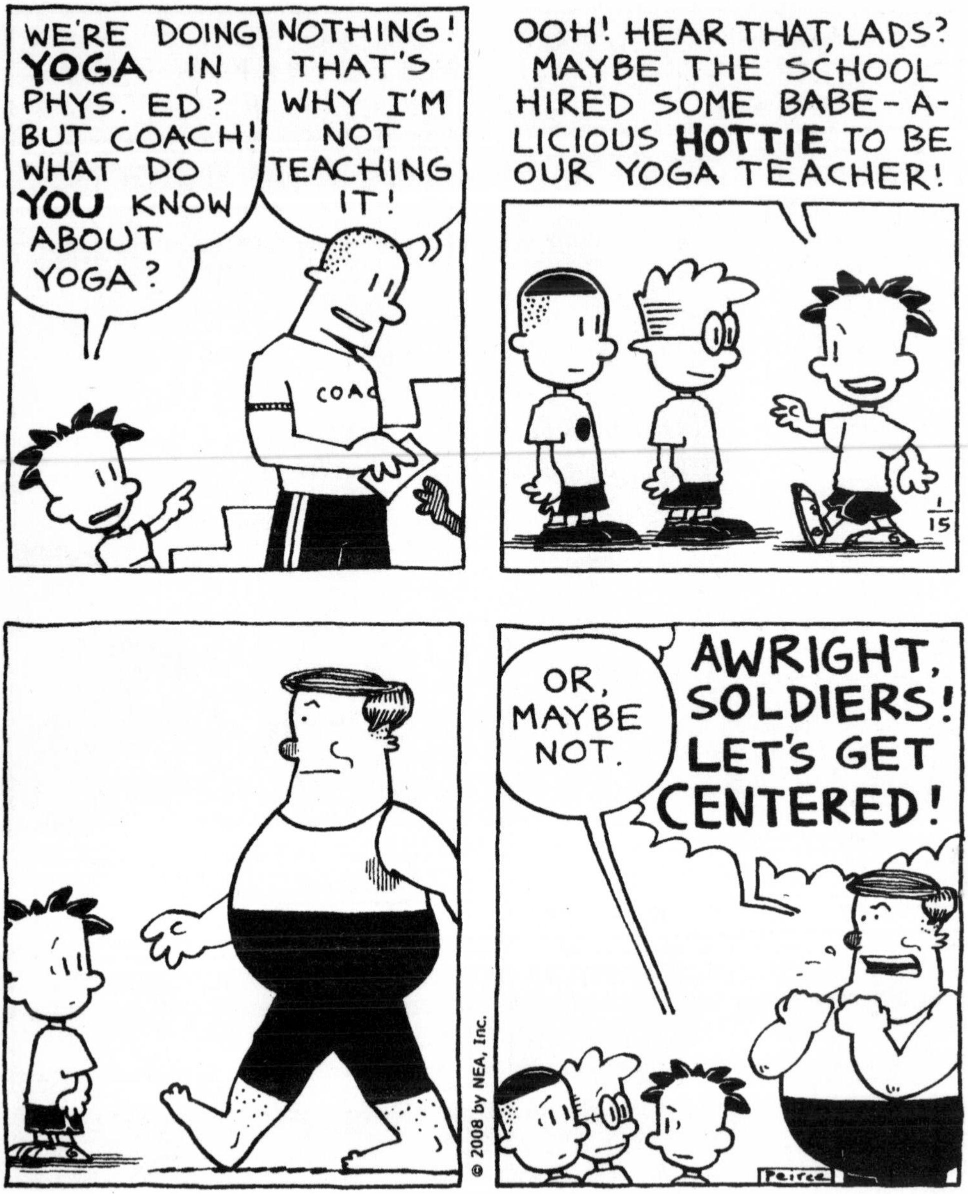

WE'RE DOING **YOGA** IN PHYS. ED? BUT COACH! WHAT DO **YOU** KNOW ABOUT YOGA?
NOTHING! THAT'S WHY I'M NOT TEACHING IT!
COAC
OOH! HEAR THAT, LADS? MAYBE THE SCHOOL HIRED SOME BABE-A-LICIOUS **HOTTIE** TO BE OUR YOGA TEACHER!
1 15
© 2008 by NEA, Inc.
AWRIGHT, SOLDIERS! LET'S GET CENTERED!
OR, MAYBE NOT.
Peirce

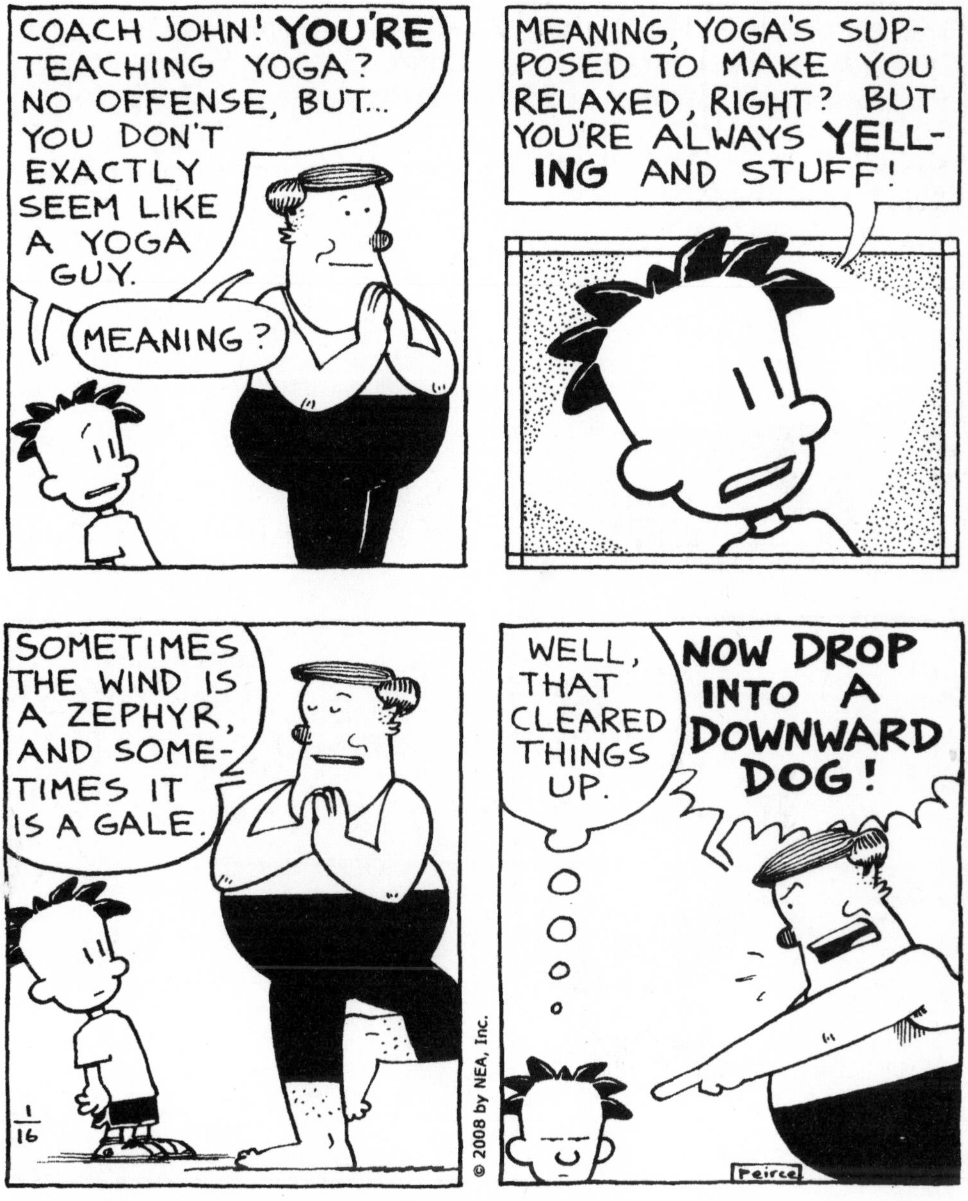
COACH JOHN! YOU'RE TEACHING YOGA? NO OFFENSE, BUT... YOU DON'T EXACTLY SEEM LIKE A YOGA GUY.
MEANING?
MEANING, YOGA'S SUPPOSED TO MAKE YOU RELAXED, RIGHT? BUT YOU'RE ALWAYS YELLING AND STUFF!
SOMETIMES THE WIND IS A ZEPHYR, AND SOMETIMES IT IS A GALE.
1/16
© 2008 by NEA, Inc.
WELL, THAT CLEARED THINGS UP.
NOW DROP INTO A DOWNWARD DOG!
Peirce

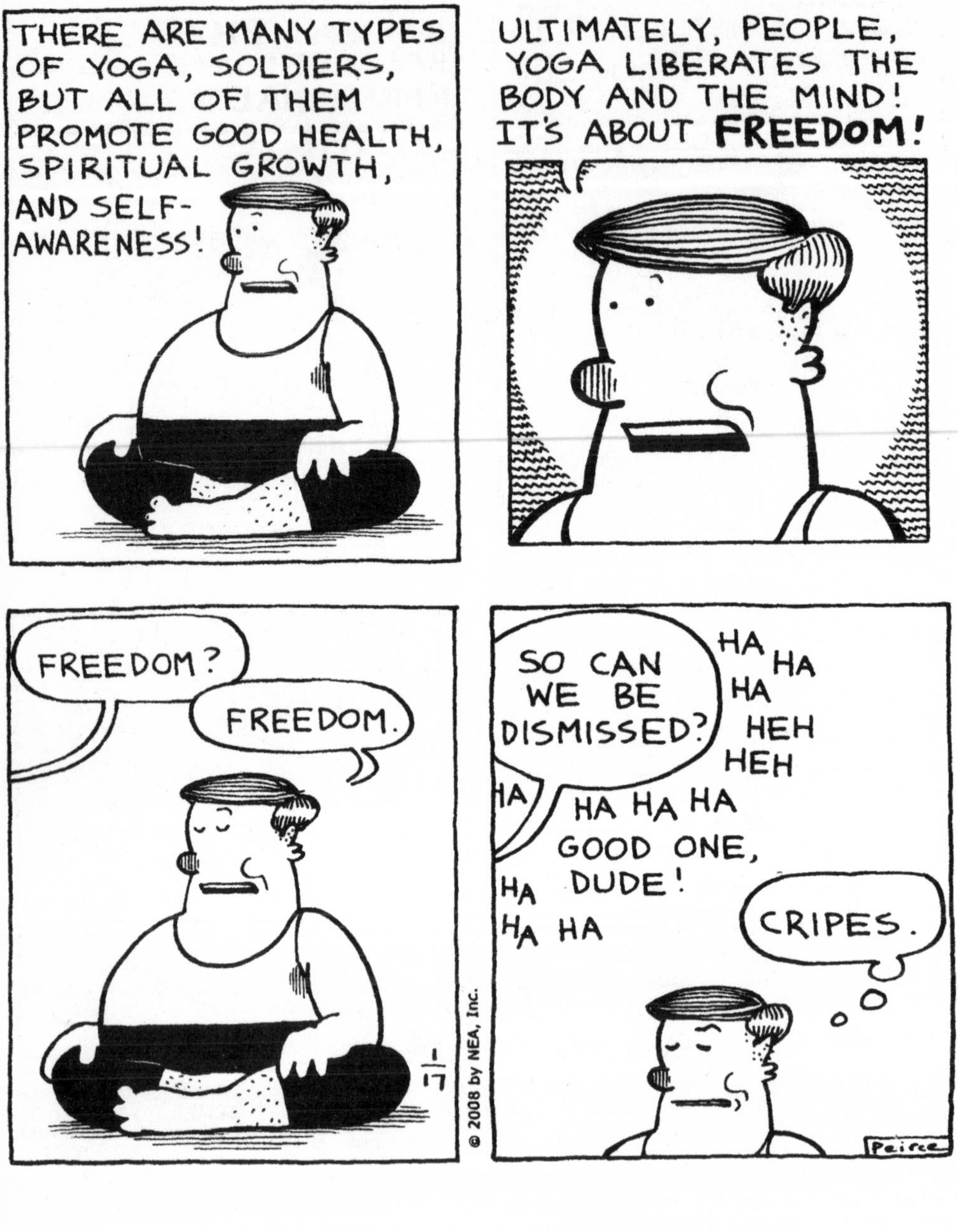
THERE ARE MANY TYPES OF YOGA, SOLDIERS, BUT ALL OF THEM PROMOTE GOOD HEALTH, SPIRITUAL GROWTH,
AND SELF-AWARENESS!
ULTIMATELY, PEOPLE, YOGA LIBERATES THE BODY AND THE MIND! IT'S ABOUT FREEDOM!
FREEDOM?
FREEDOM.
SO CAN WE BE DISMISSED?
HA HA HA HEH HEH
HA
HA HA HA GOOD ONE, DUDE!
HA HA HA
CRIPES.
1/17
© 2008 by NEA, Inc.
Peirce

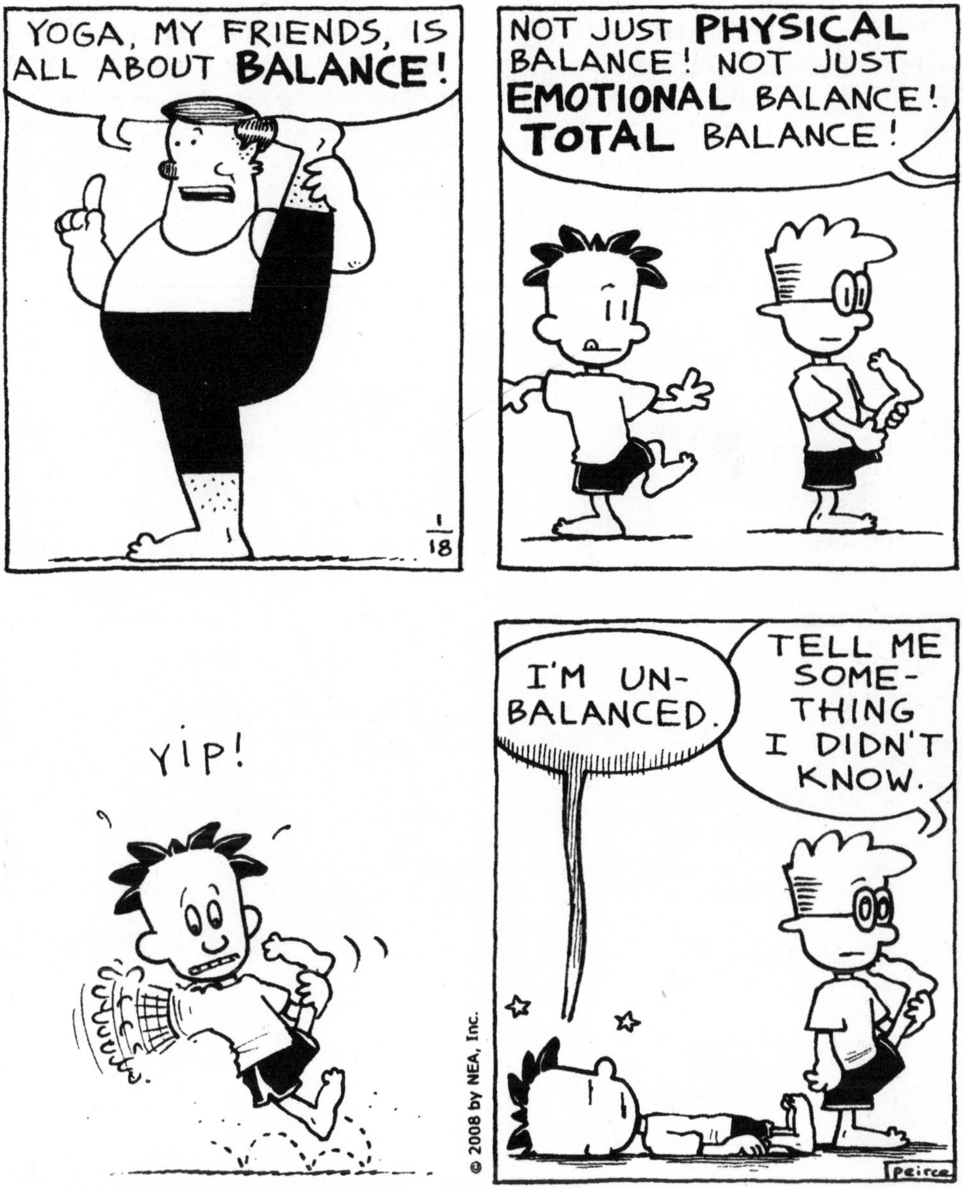
YOGA, MY FRIENDS, IS ALL ABOUT BALANCE!
1/18
NOT JUST PHYSICAL BALANCE! NOT JUST EMOTIONAL BALANCE! TOTAL BALANCE!
YIP!
I'M UN-BALANCED.
TELL ME SOME-THING I DIDN'T KNOW.
© 2008 by NEA, Inc.
Peirce

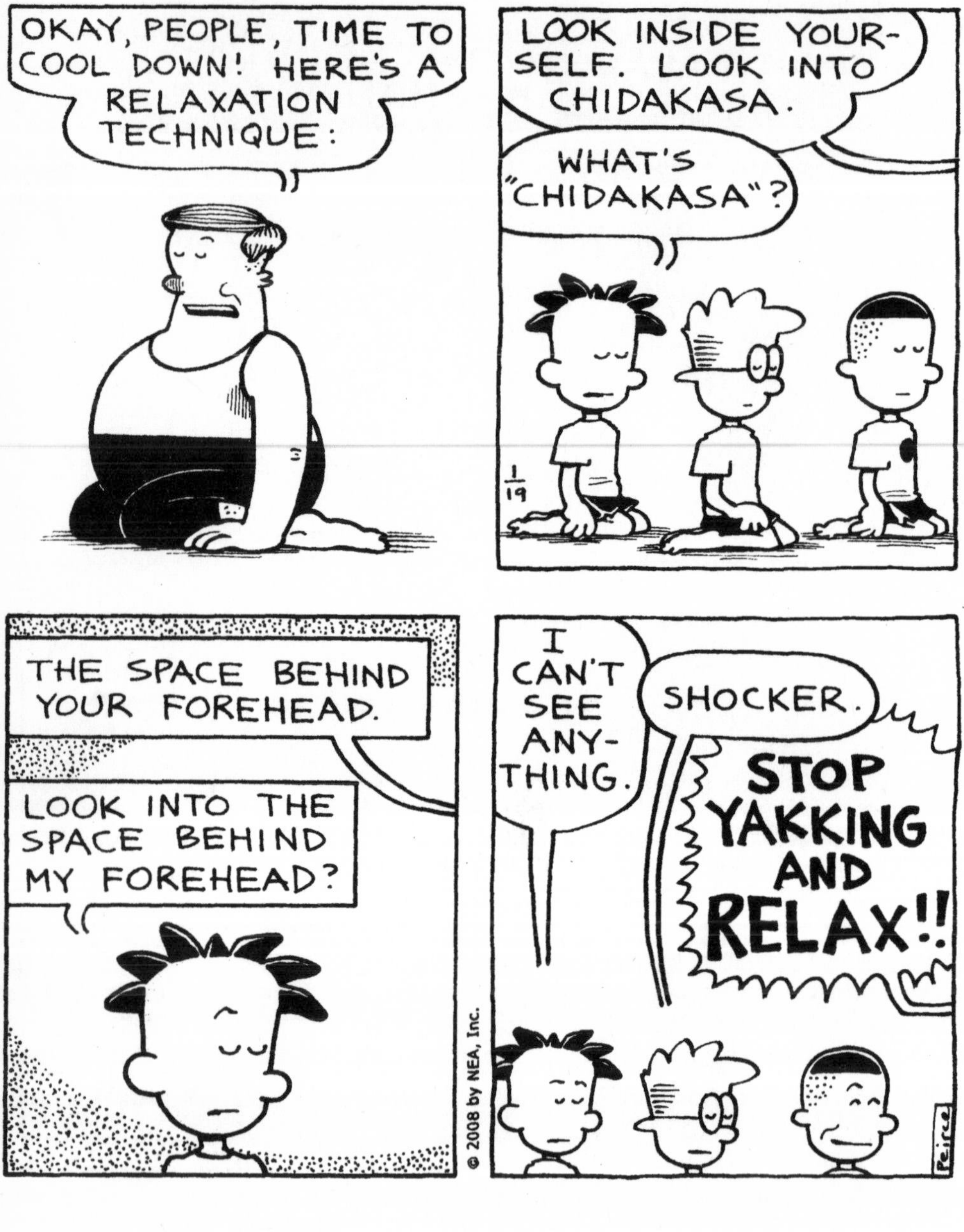
OKAY, PEOPLE, TIME TO COOL DOWN! HERE'S A RELAXATION TECHNIQUE:
LOOK INSIDE YOURSELF. LOOK INTO CHIDAKASA.
WHAT'S "CHIDAKASA"?
1/19
THE SPACE BEHIND YOUR FOREHEAD.
LOOK INTO THE SPACE BEHIND MY FOREHEAD?
I CAN'T SEE ANYTHING.
SHOCKER.
STOP YAKKING AND RELAX!!
Peirce

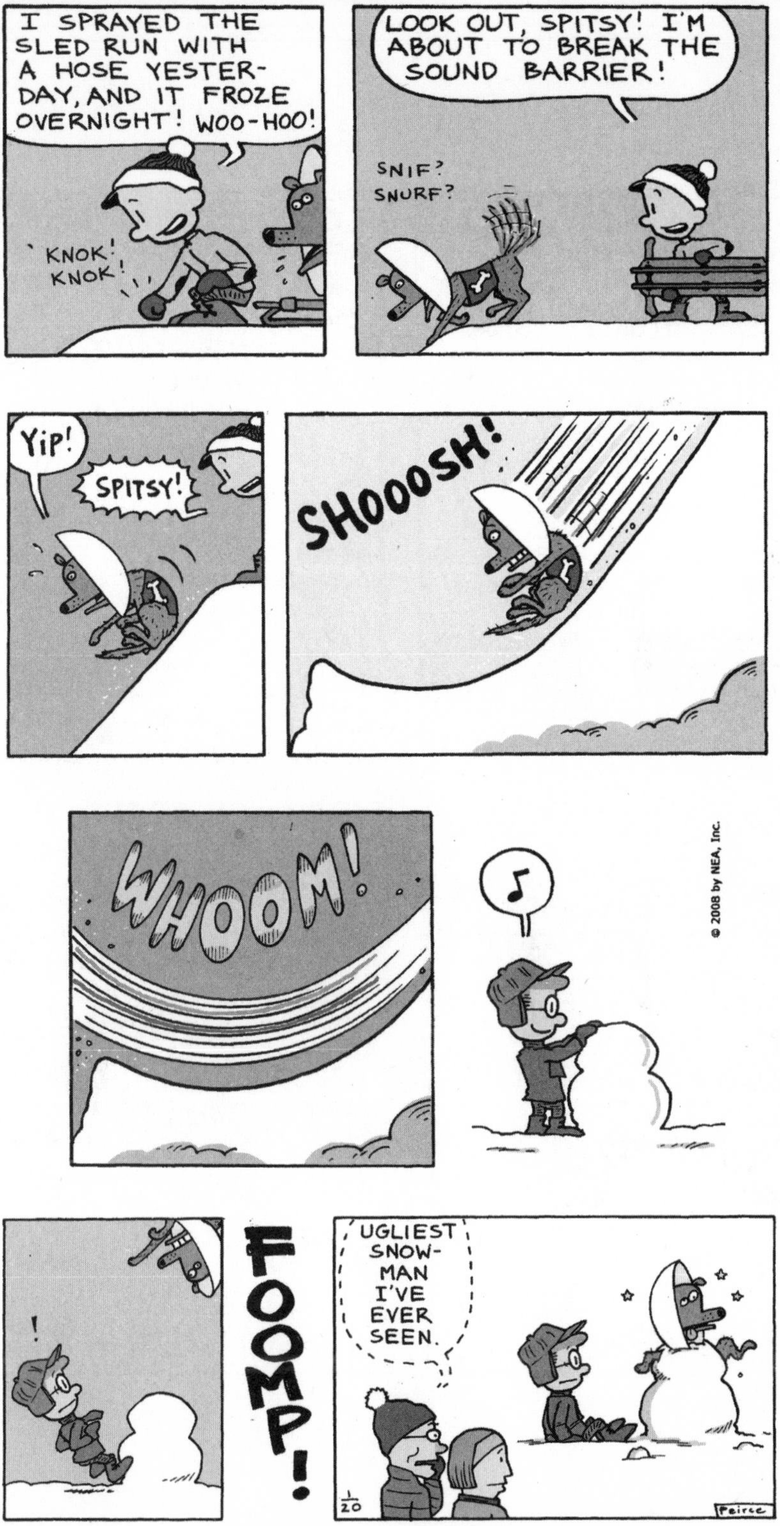
I SPRAYED THE SLED RUN WITH A HOSE YESTERDAY, AND IT FROZE OVERNIGHT! WOO-HOO!
KNOK! KNOK!
LOOK OUT, SPITSY! I'M ABOUT TO BREAK THE SOUND BARRIER!
SNIF? SNURF?
YIP!
SPITSY!
SHOOOSH!
WHOOM!
© 2008 by NEA, Inc.
!
FOOMP!
UGLIEST SNOW-MAN I'VE EVER SEEN.
1/20
Peirce

ART À LA NATE

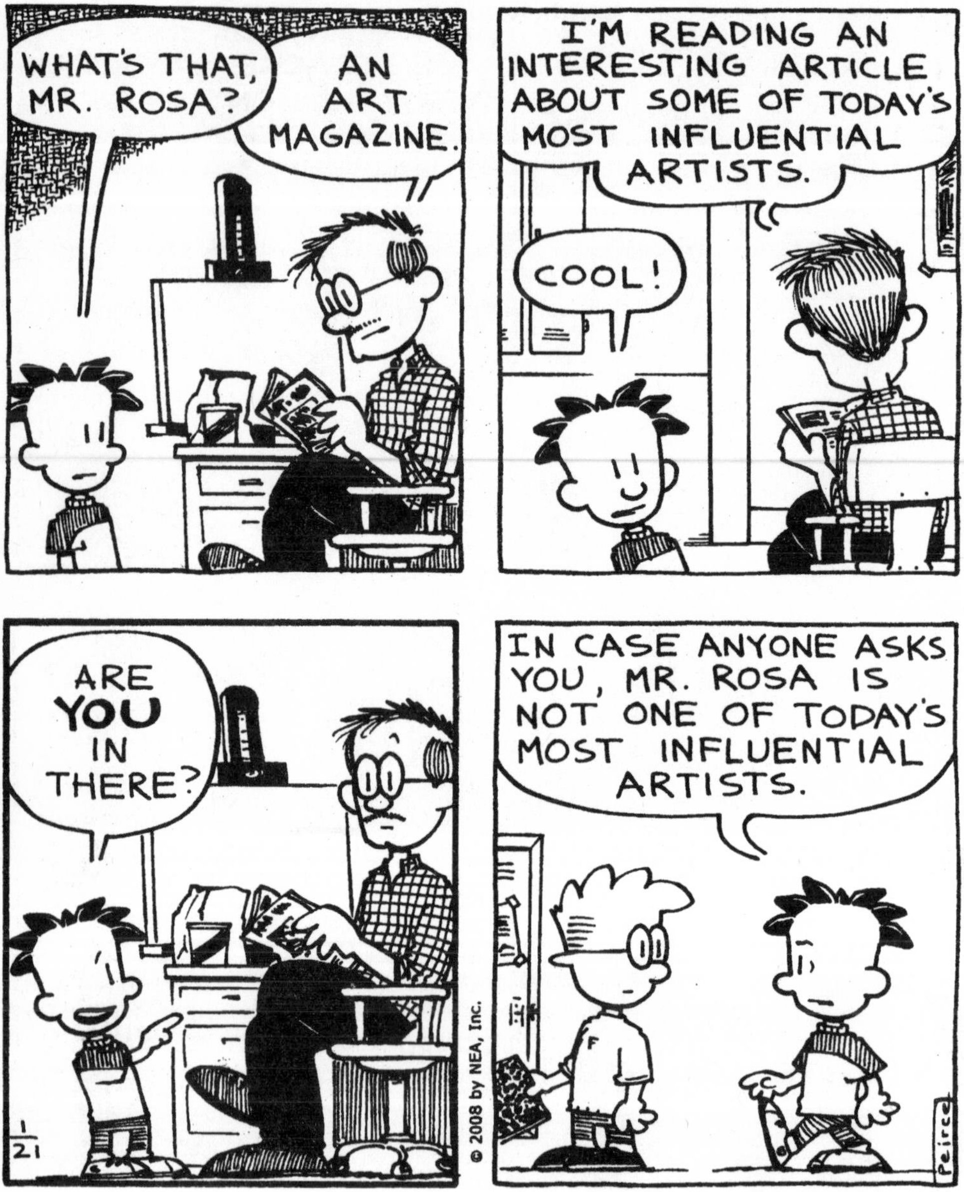

WHAT'S THAT, MR. ROSA?
AN ART MAGAZINE.
I'M READING AN INTERESTING ARTICLE ABOUT SOME OF TODAY'S MOST INFLUENTIAL ARTISTS.
COOL!
ARE **YOU** IN THERE?
IN CASE ANYONE ASKS YOU, MR. ROSA IS NOT ONE OF TODAY'S MOST INFLUENTIAL ARTISTS.
1/21
© 2008 by NEA, Inc.
Peirce

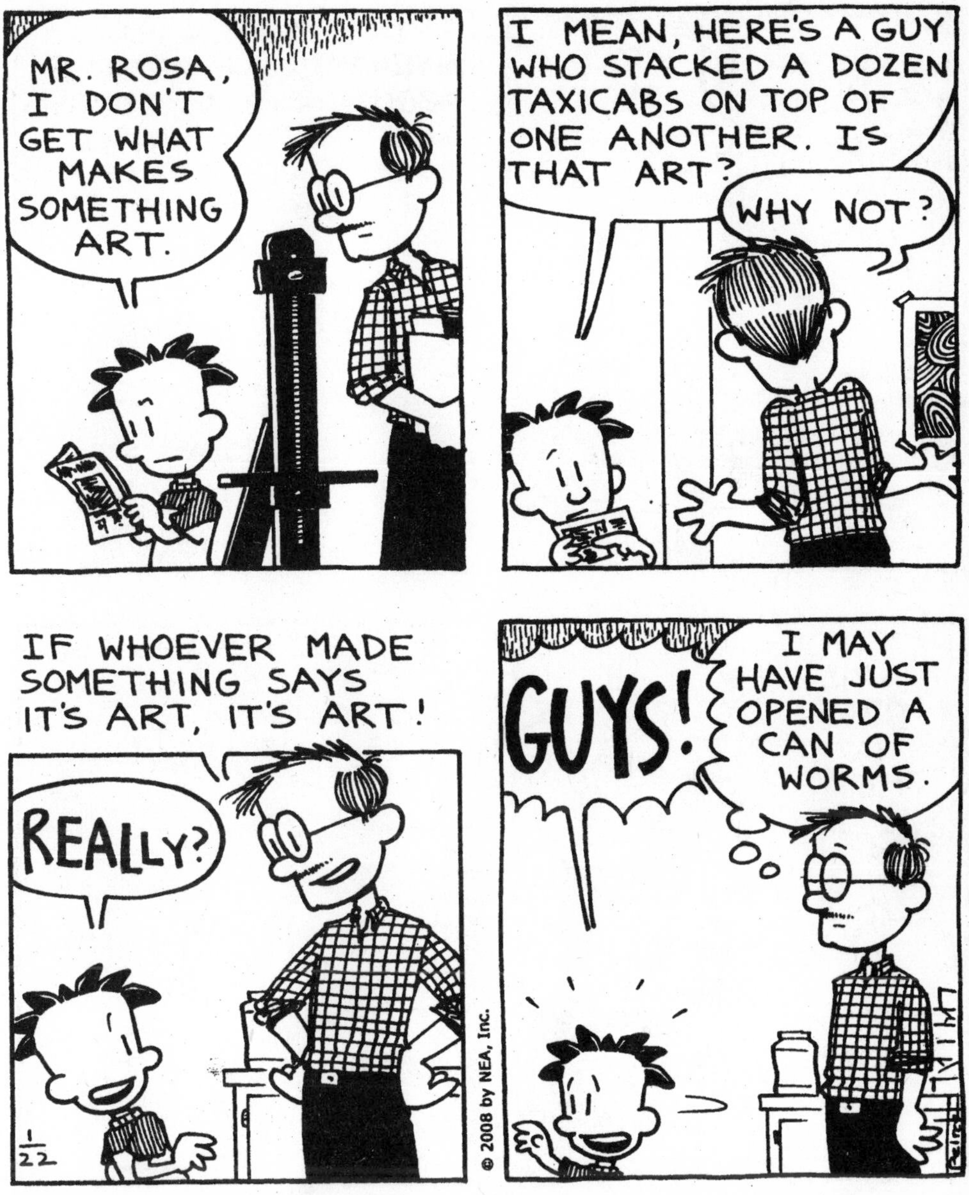
MR. ROSA, I DON'T GET WHAT MAKES SOMETHING ART.
I MEAN, HERE'S A GUY WHO STACKED A DOZEN TAXICABS ON TOP OF ONE ANOTHER. IS THAT ART?
WHY NOT?
IF WHOEVER MADE SOMETHING SAYS IT'S ART, IT'S ART!
REALLY?
GUYS!
I MAY HAVE JUST OPENED A CAN OF WORMS.
1/22
© 2008 by NEA, Inc.

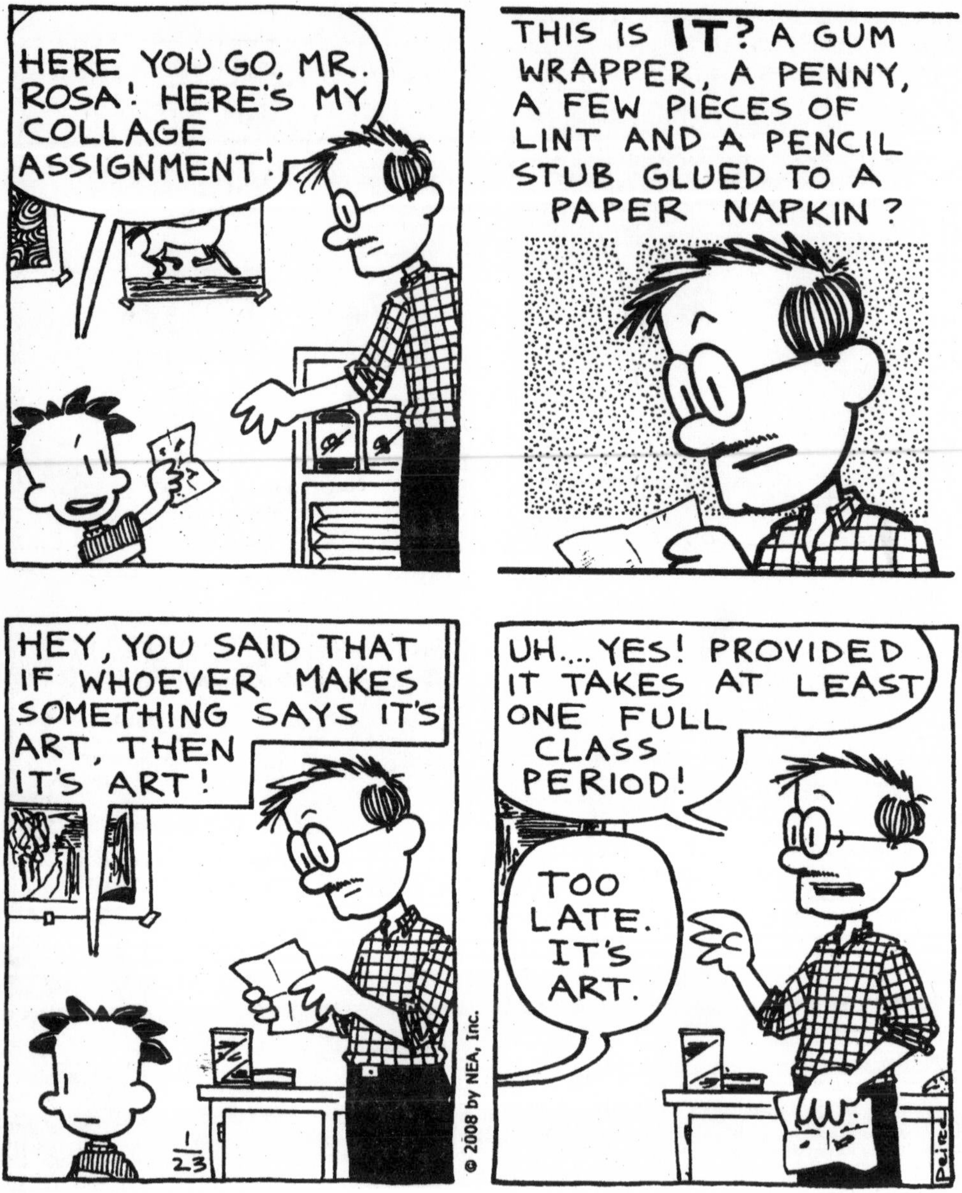
HERE YOU GO, MR. ROSA! HERE'S MY COLLAGE ASSIGNMENT!
THIS IS IT? A GUM WRAPPER, A PENNY, A FEW PIECES OF LINT AND A PENCIL STUB GLUED TO A PAPER NAPKIN?
HEY, YOU SAID THAT IF WHOEVER MAKES SOMETHING SAYS IT'S ART, THEN IT'S ART!
UH.... YES! PROVIDED IT TAKES AT LEAST ONE FULL CLASS PERIOD!
TOO LATE. IT'S ART.
1/23
© 2008 by NEA, Inc.
Peirce

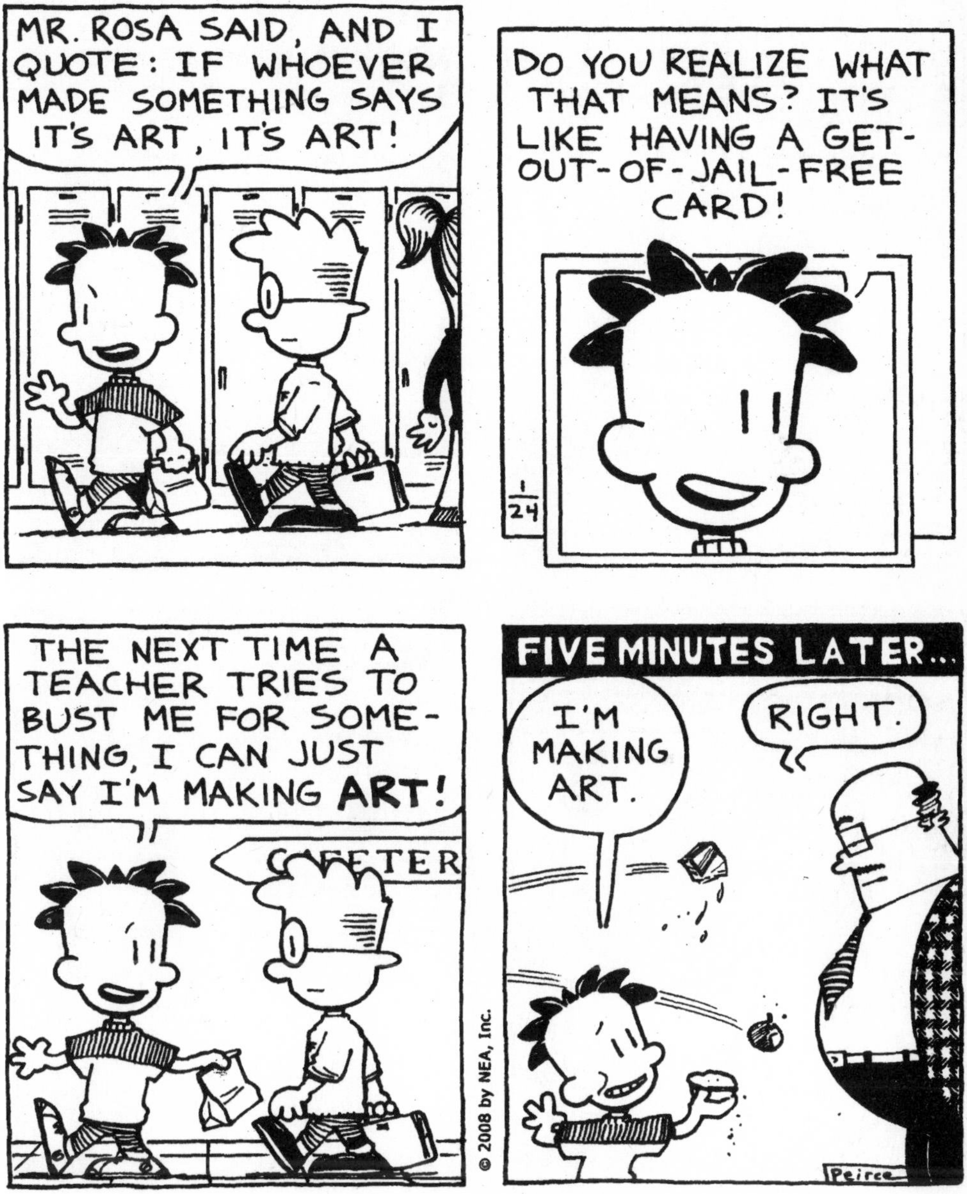
MR. ROSA SAID, AND I QUOTE: IF WHOEVER MADE SOMETHING SAYS IT'S ART, IT'S ART!
DO YOU REALIZE WHAT THAT MEANS? IT'S LIKE HAVING A GET-OUT-OF-JAIL-FREE CARD!
1/24
THE NEXT TIME A TEACHER TRIES TO BUST ME FOR SOME-THING, I CAN JUST SAY I'M MAKING **ART**!
© 2008 by NEA, Inc.
FIVE MINUTES LATER...
I'M MAKING ART.
RIGHT.
Peirce

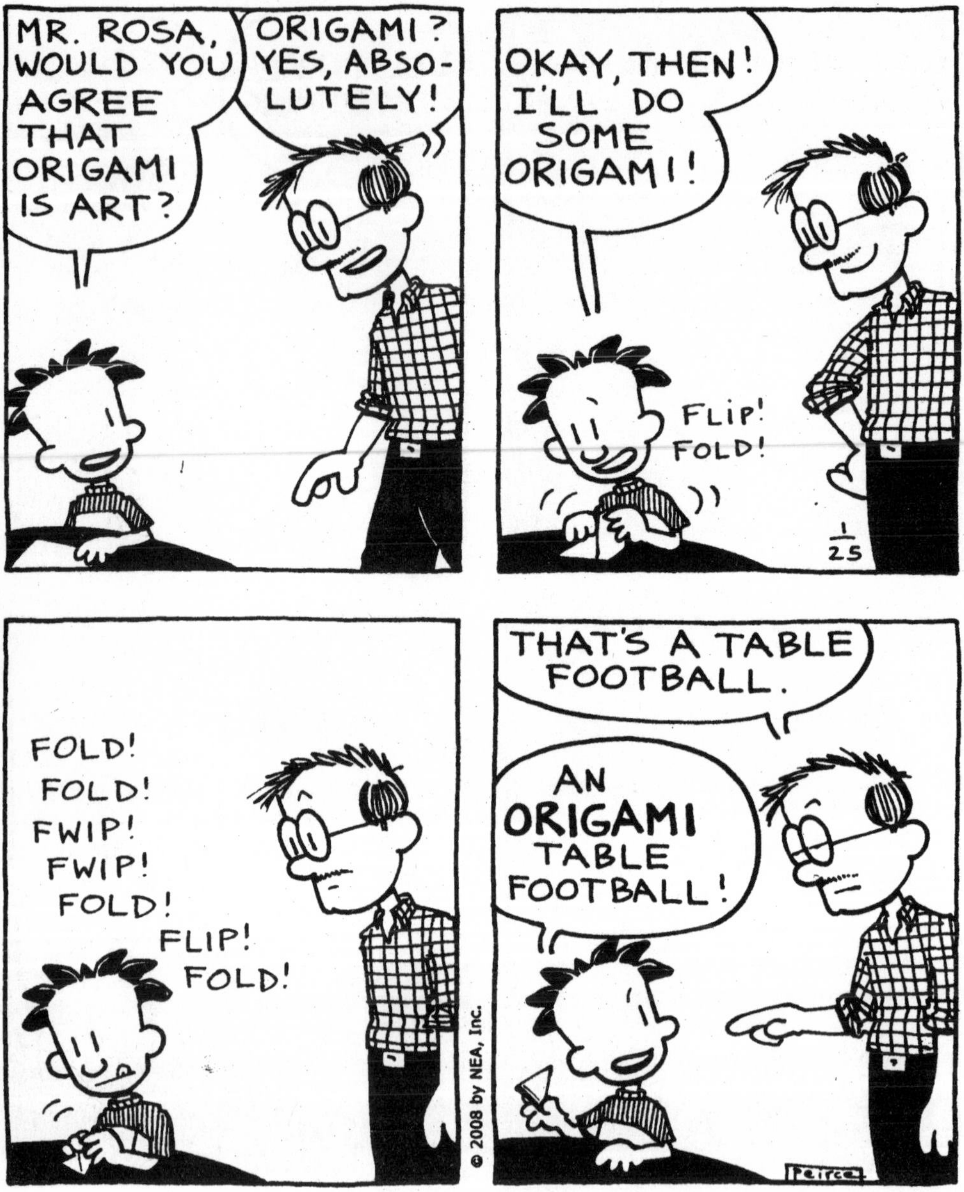
MR. ROSA, WOULD YOU AGREE THAT ORIGAMI IS ART?
ORIGAMI? YES, ABSOLUTELY!
OKAY, THEN! I'LL DO SOME ORIGAMI!
FLIP! FOLD!
1/25
FOLD! FOLD! FWIP! FWIP! FOLD! FLIP! FOLD!
© 2008 by NEA, Inc.
THAT'S A TABLE FOOTBALL.
AN ORIGAMI TABLE FOOTBALL!
Peirce

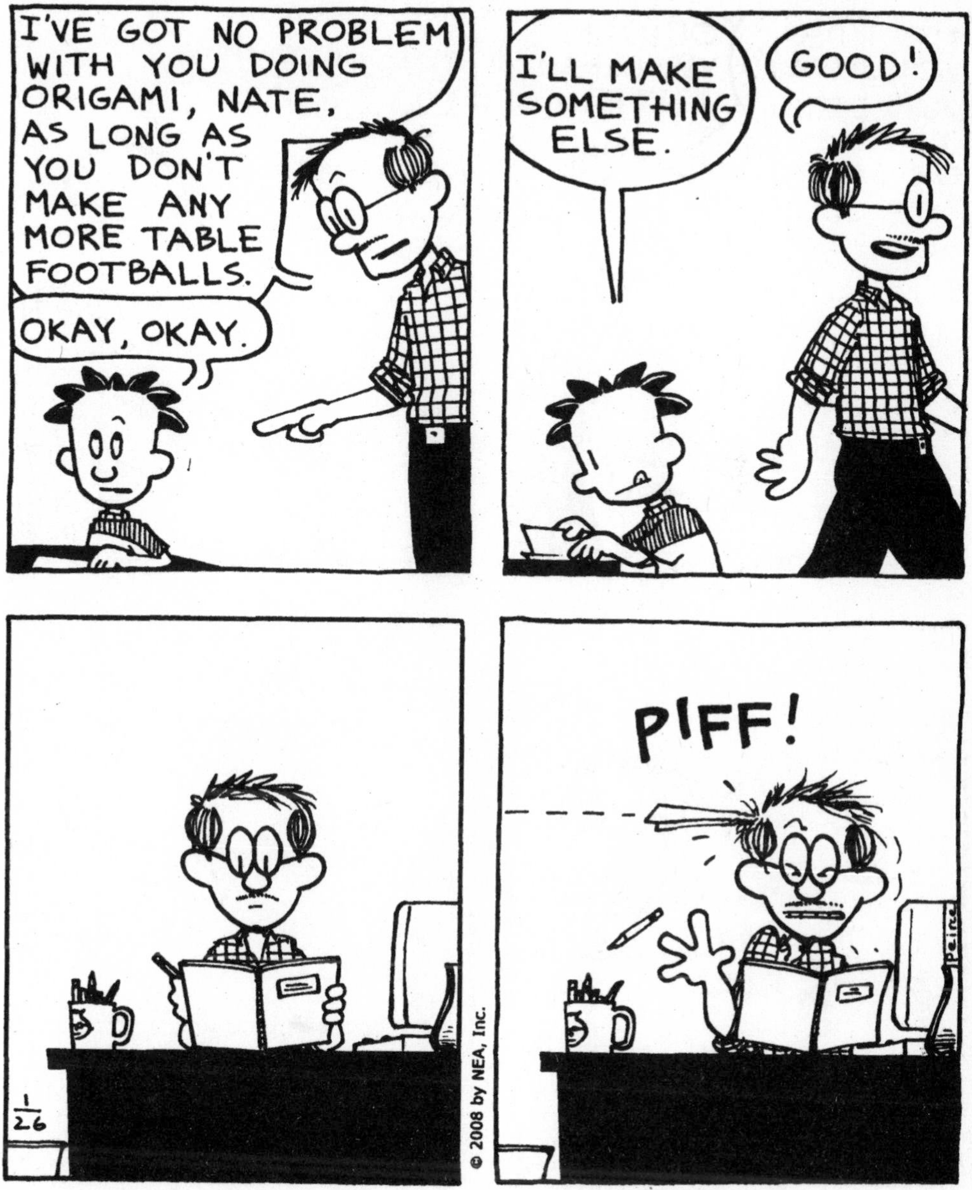
I'VE GOT NO PROBLEM WITH YOU DOING ORIGAMI, NATE, AS LONG AS YOU DON'T MAKE ANY MORE TABLE FOOTBALLS.
OKAY, OKAY.
I'LL MAKE SOMETHING ELSE.
GOOD!
PIFF!
1/26
© 2008 by NEA, Inc.
Peirce

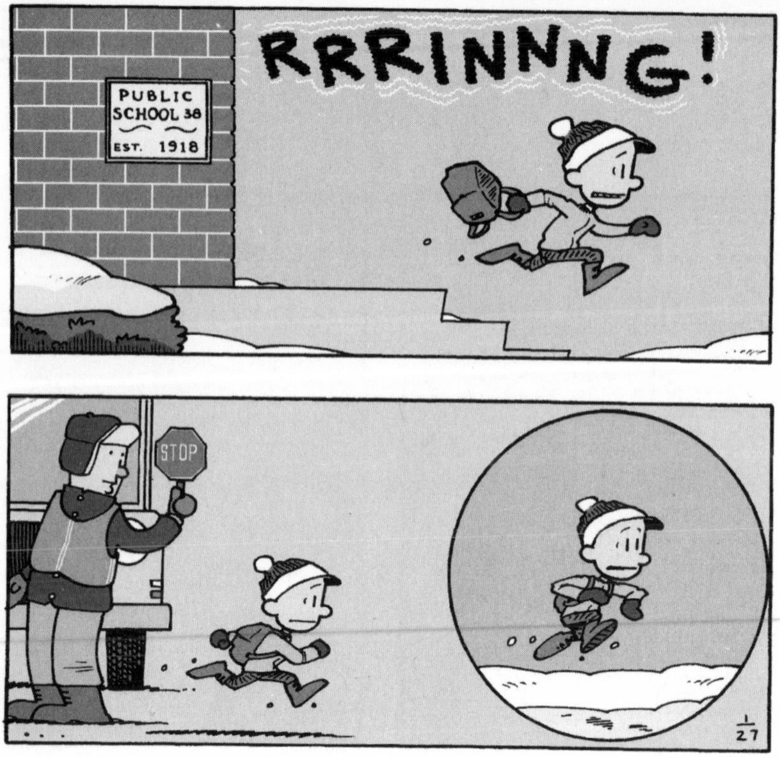
PUBLIC
SCHOOL 38
EST. 1918
RRRINNNG!
STOP
1/27

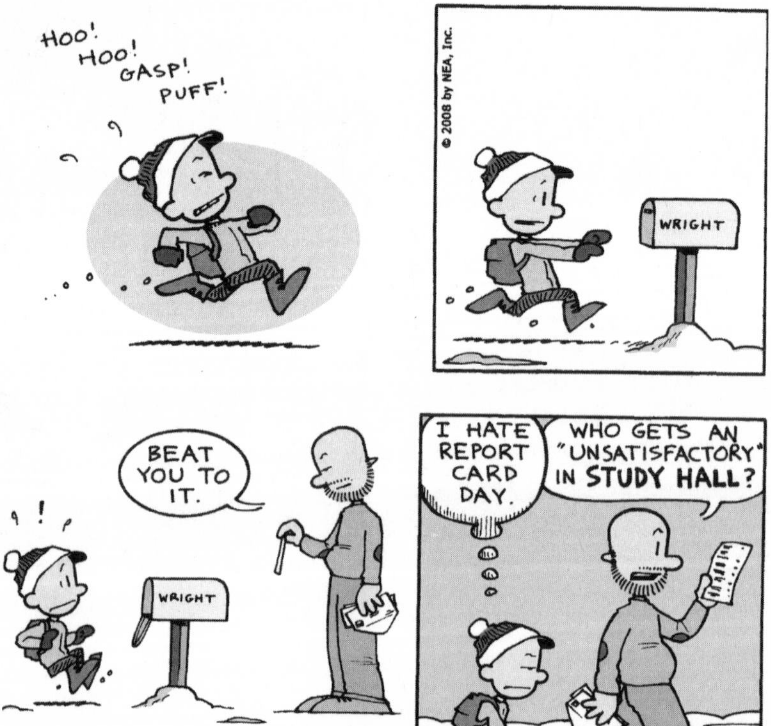
HOO! HOO! GASP! PUFF!
© 2008 by NEA, Inc.
WRIGHT
BEAT YOU TO IT.
WRIGHT
I HATE REPORT CARD DAY.
WHO GETS AN "UNSATISFACTORY" IN STUDY HALL?
Peirce

WHO'S THE PERFECT COUPLE?

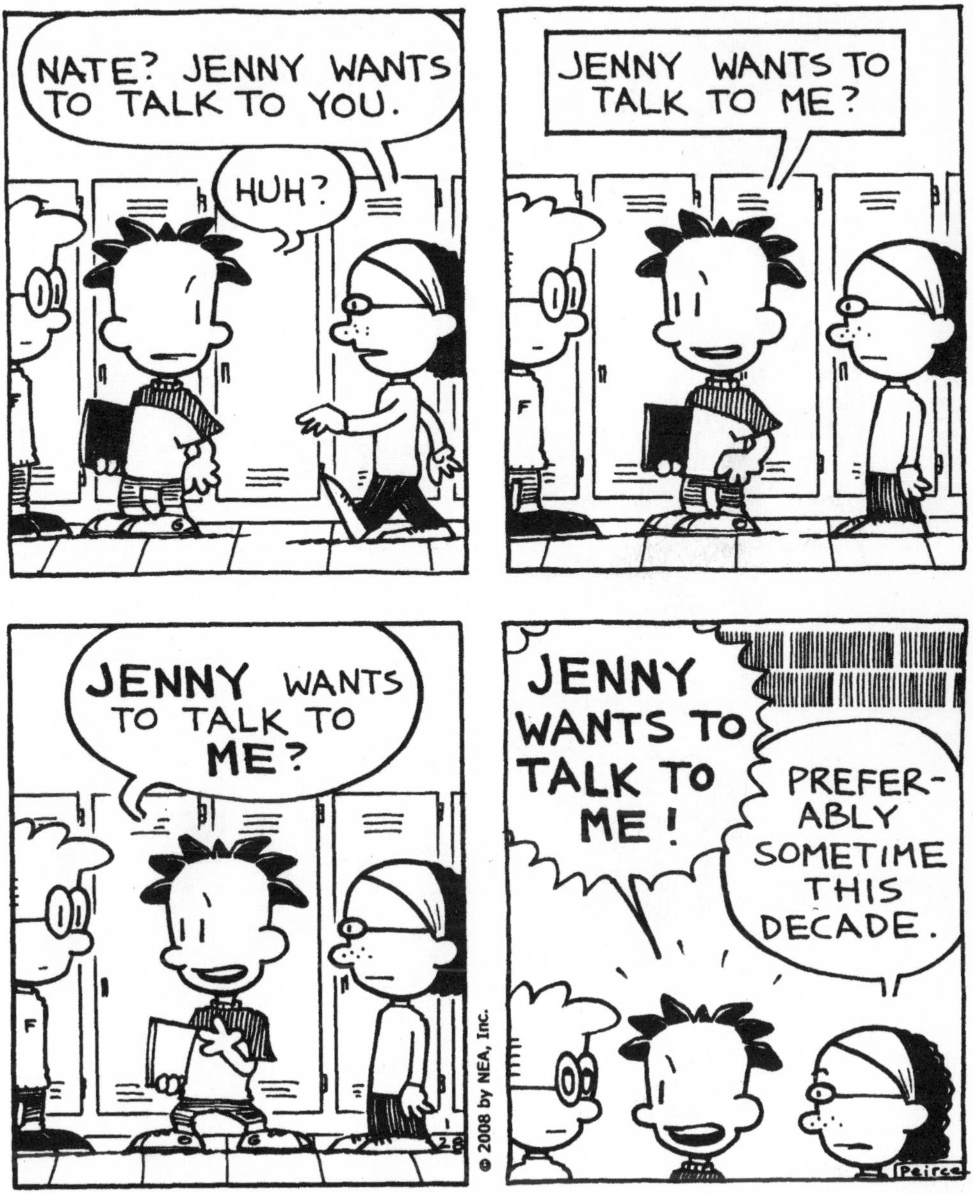
NATE? JENNY WANTS TO TALK TO YOU.
HUH?
JENNY WANTS TO TALK TO ME?
JENNY WANTS TO TALK TO ME?
JENNY WANTS TO TALK TO ME!
PREFER-ABLY SOMETIME THIS DECADE.
© 2008 by NEA, Inc.
Peirce

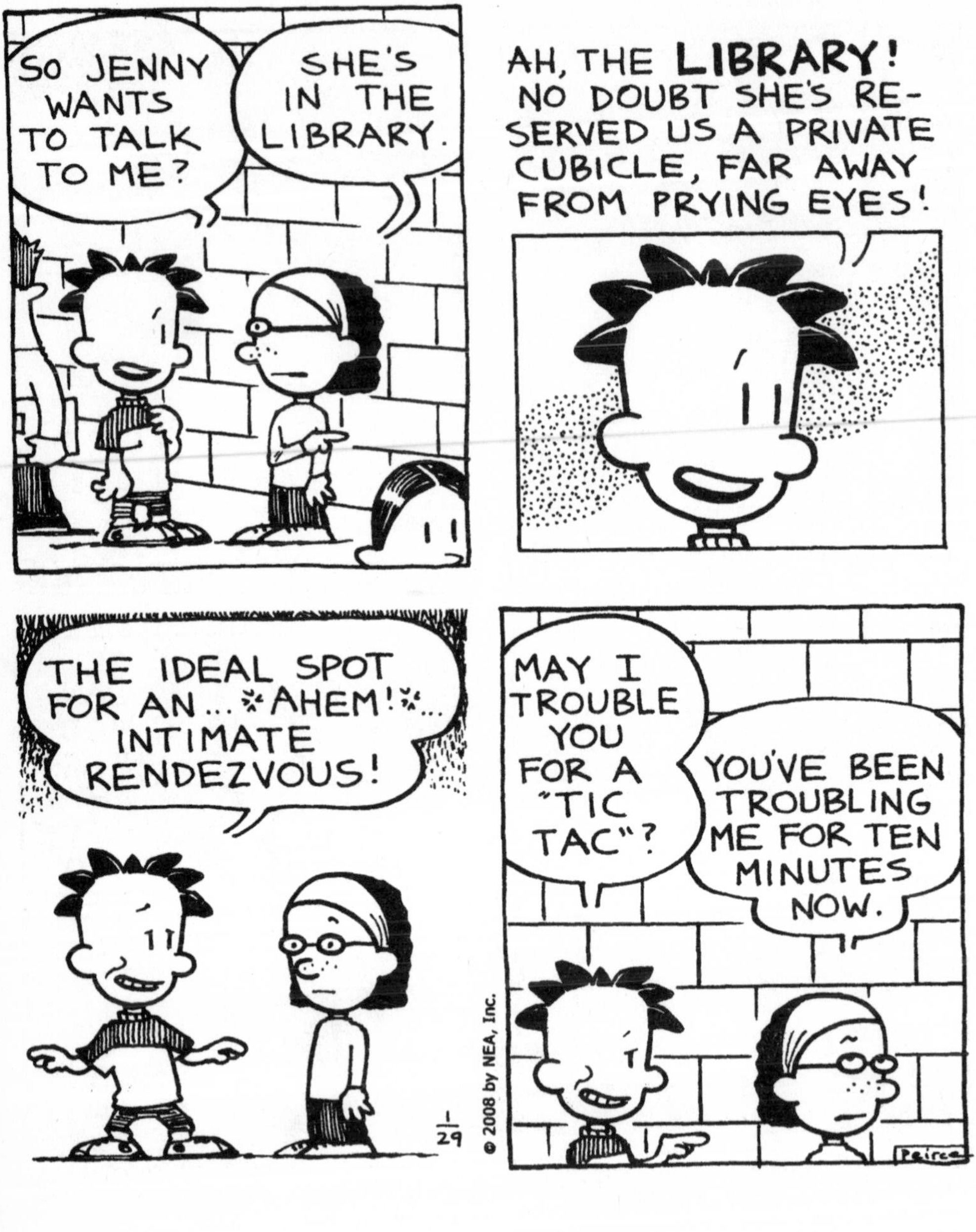
SO JENNY WANTS TO TALK TO ME?
SHE'S IN THE LIBRARY.
AH, THE LIBRARY! NO DOUBT SHE'S RESERVED US A PRIVATE CUBICLE, FAR AWAY FROM PRYING EYES!
THE IDEAL SPOT FOR AN... *AHEM!*... INTIMATE RENDEZVOUS!
MAY I TROUBLE YOU FOR A "TIC TAC"?
YOU'VE BEEN TROUBLING ME FOR TEN MINUTES NOW.
1/29
© 2008 by NEA, Inc.
Peirce

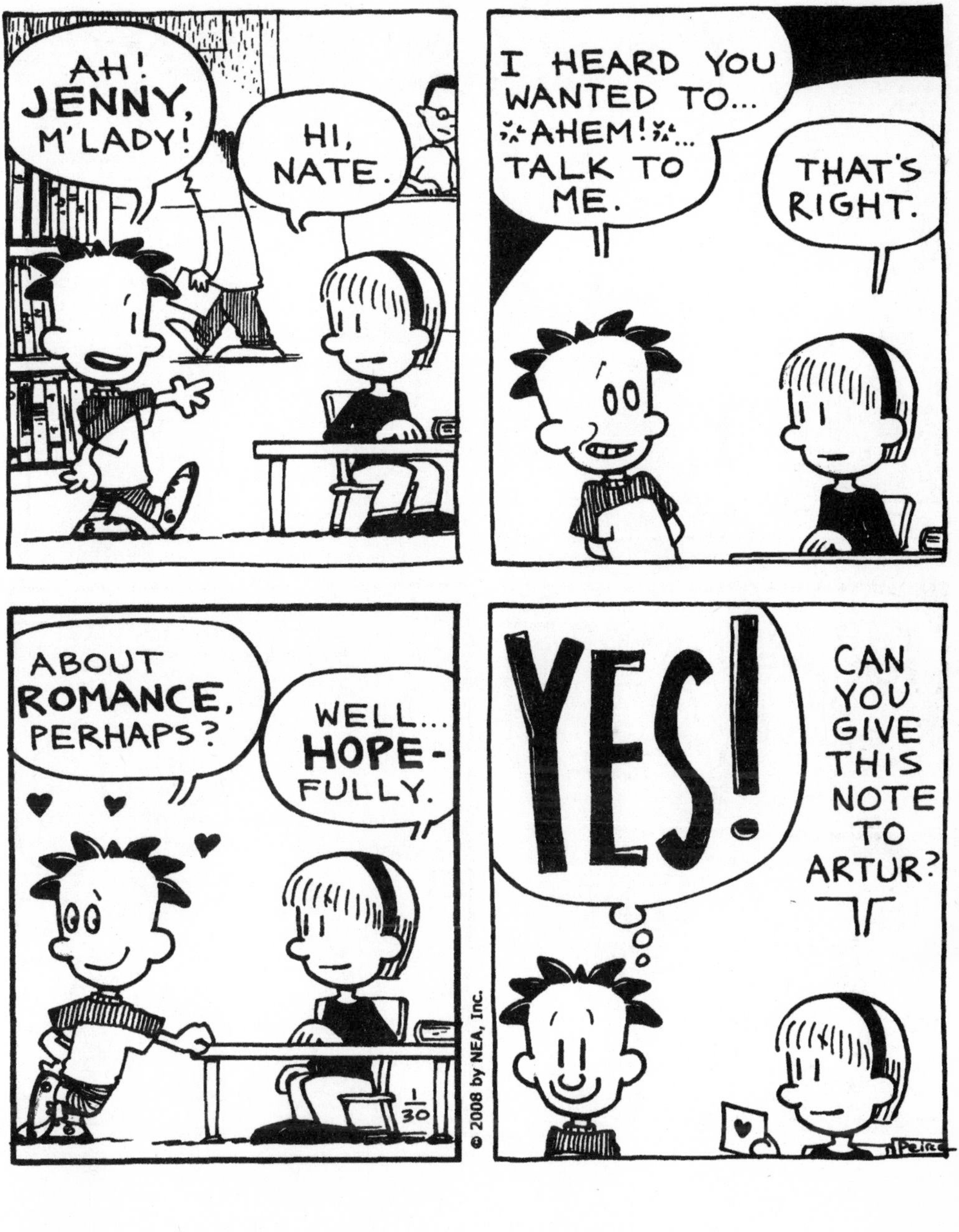
AH! JENNY, M'LADY!
HI, NATE.
I HEARD YOU WANTED TO... AHEM!... TALK TO ME.
THAT'S RIGHT.
ABOUT ROMANCE, PERHAPS?
WELL... HOPE-FULLY.
1/30
© 2008 by NEA, Inc.
YES!
CAN YOU GIVE THIS NOTE TO ARTUR?
Peirce

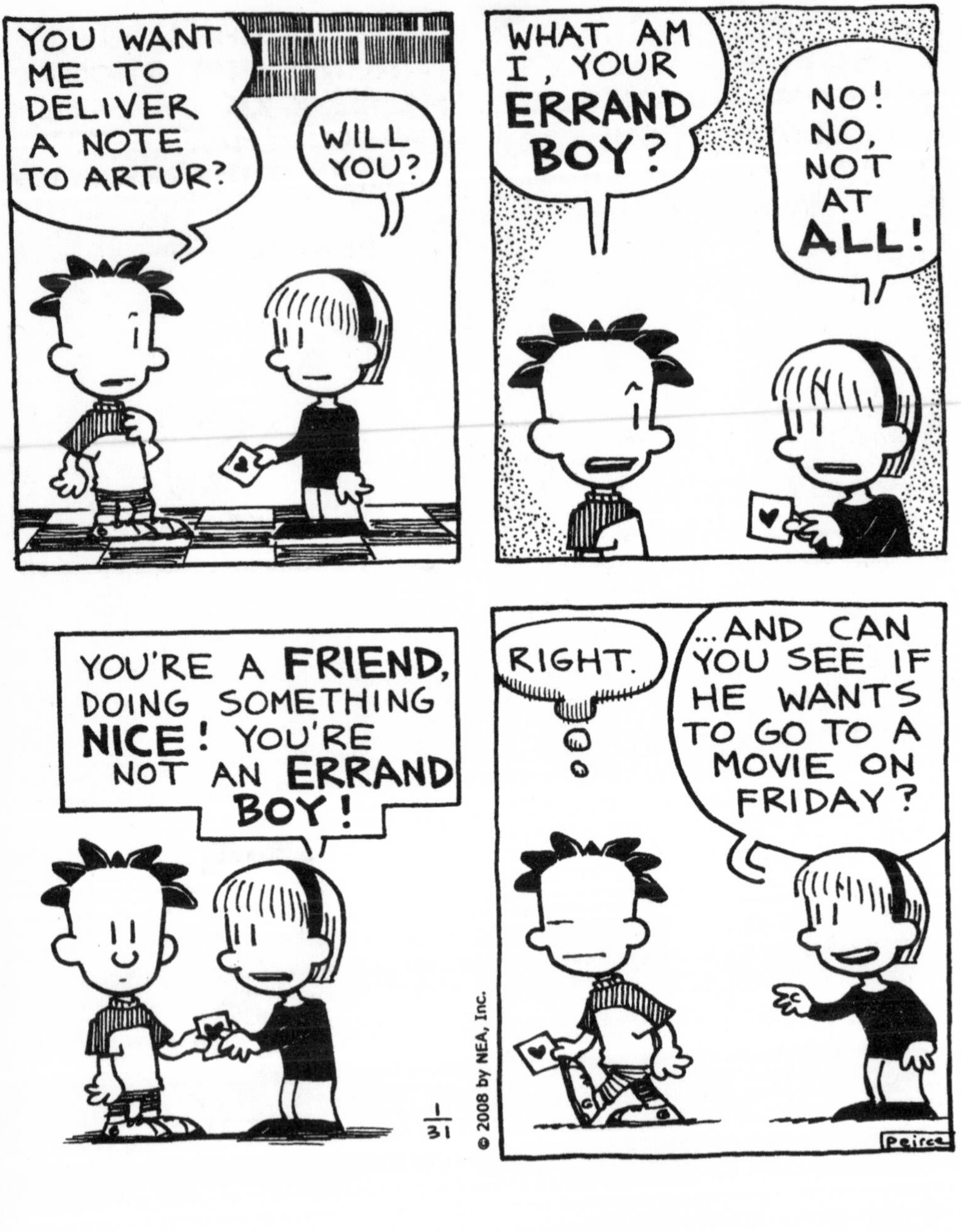
YOU WANT ME TO DELIVER A NOTE TO ARTUR?
WILL YOU?
WHAT AM I, YOUR ERRAND BOY?
NO! NO, NOT AT ALL!
YOU'RE A FRIEND, DOING SOMETHING NICE! YOU'RE NOT AN ERRAND BOY!
1/31
© 2008 by NEA, Inc.
RIGHT.
...AND CAN YOU SEE IF HE WANTS TO GO TO A MOVIE ON FRIDAY?
Peirce

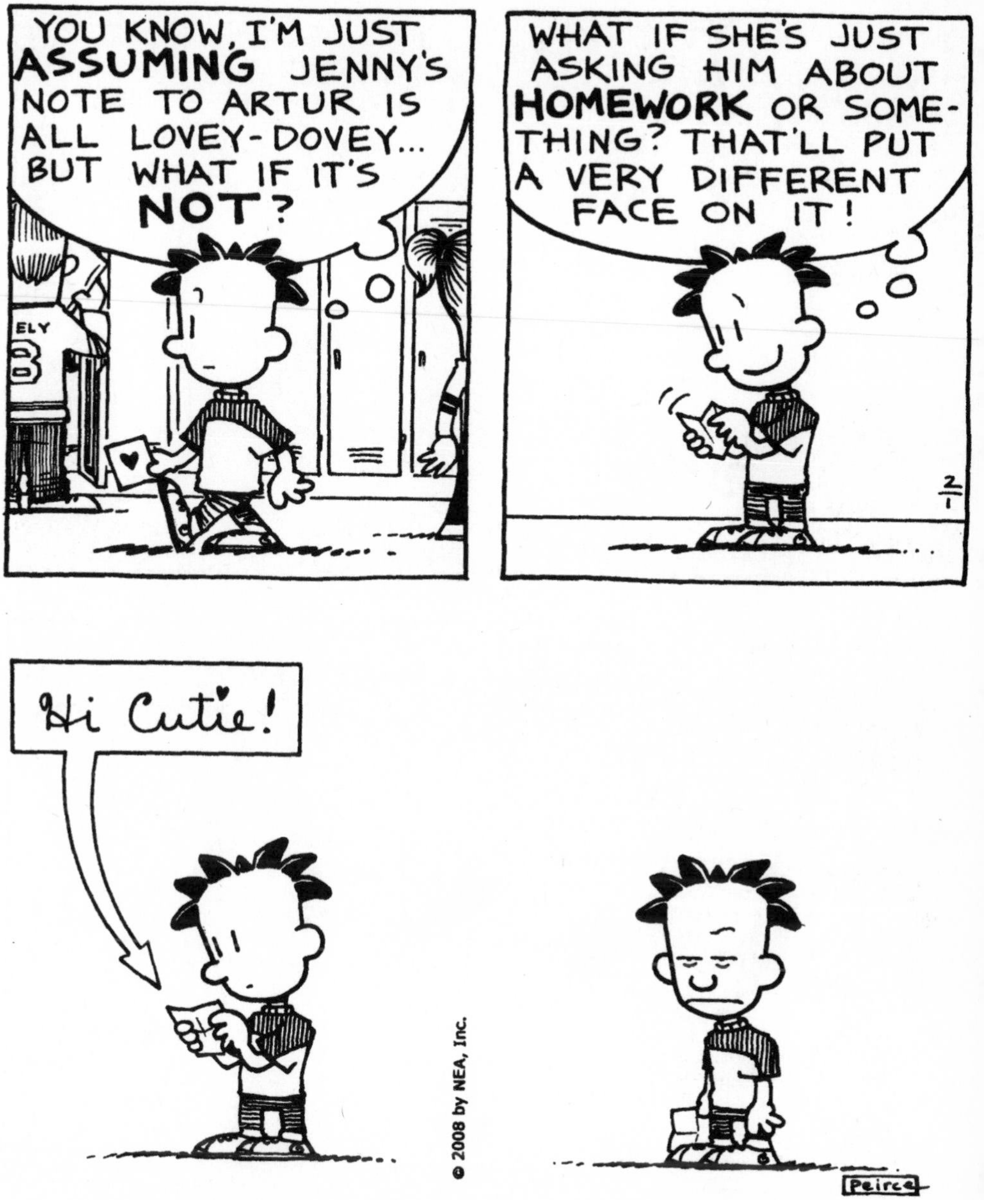
YOU KNOW, I'M JUST **ASSUMING** JENNY'S NOTE TO ARTUR IS ALL LOVEY-DOVEY... BUT WHAT IF IT'S **NOT**?
WHAT IF SHE'S JUST ASKING HIM ABOUT **HOMEWORK** OR SOME-THING? THAT'LL PUT A VERY DIFFERENT FACE ON IT!
Hi Cutie!
© 2008 by NEA, Inc.
Peirce

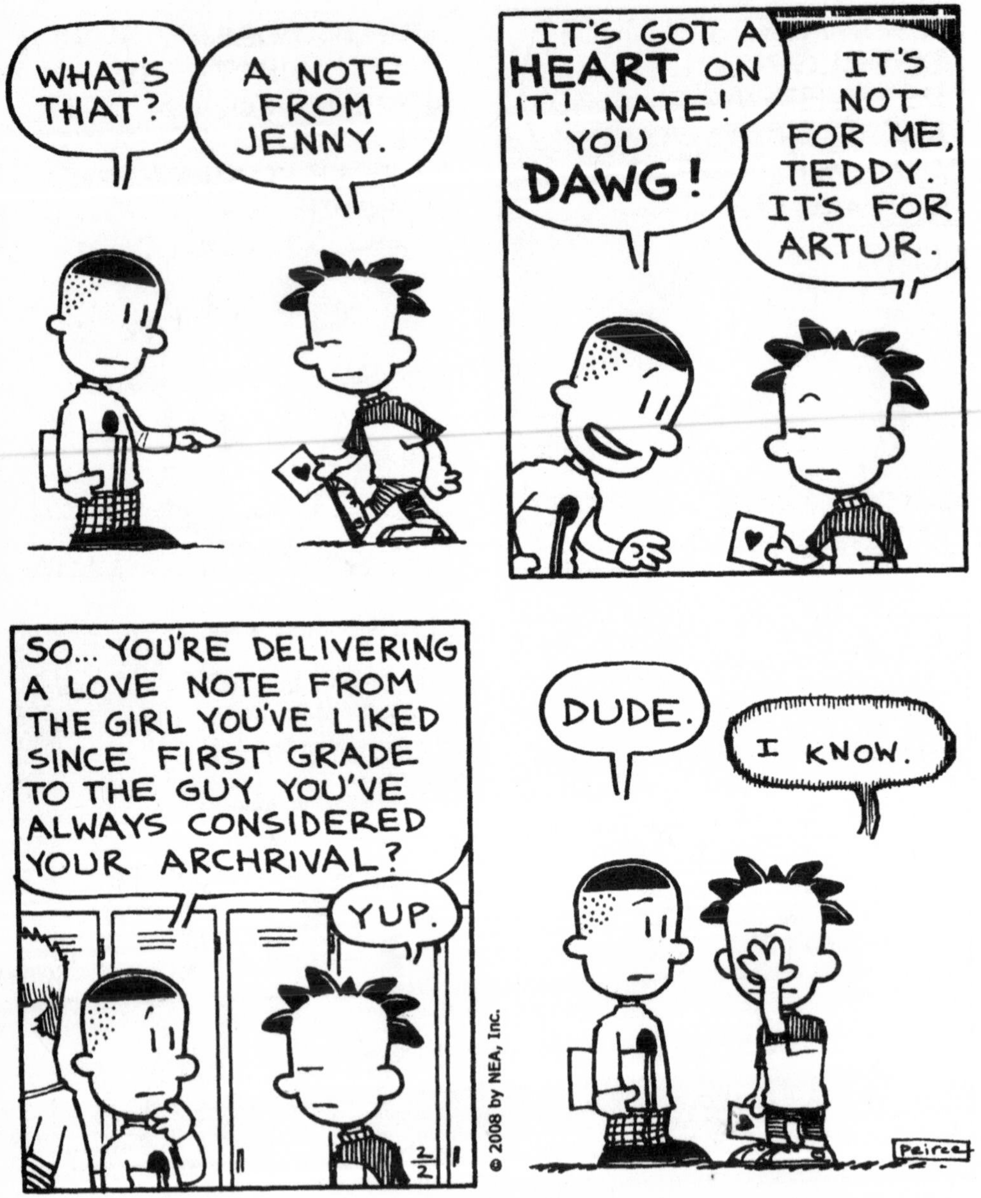
WHAT'S THAT?
A NOTE FROM JENNY.
IT'S GOT A HEART ON IT! NATE! YOU DAWG!
IT'S NOT FOR ME, TEDDY. IT'S FOR ARTUR.
SO... YOU'RE DELIVERING A LOVE NOTE FROM THE GIRL YOU'VE LIKED SINCE FIRST GRADE TO THE GUY YOU'VE ALWAYS CONSIDERED YOUR ARCHRIVAL?
YUP.
2/2
© 2008 by NEA, Inc.
DUDE.
I KNOW.
Peirce

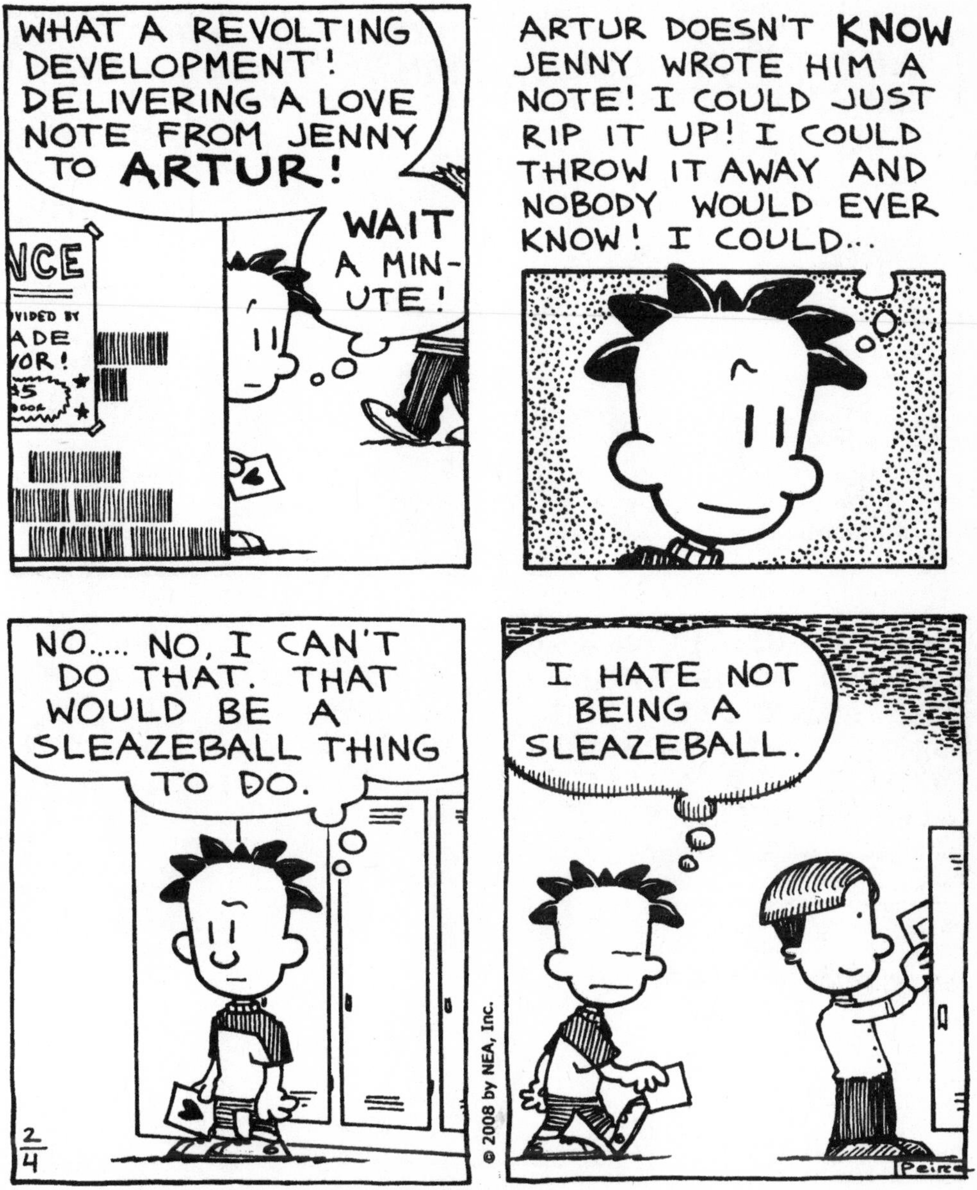
WHAT A REVOLTING DEVELOPMENT! DELIVERING A LOVE NOTE FROM JENNY TO ARTUR!
WAIT A MINUTE!
ARTUR DOESN'T KNOW JENNY WROTE HIM A NOTE! I COULD JUST RIP IT UP! I COULD THROW IT AWAY AND NOBODY WOULD EVER KNOW! I COULD...
NO..... NO, I CAN'T DO THAT. THAT WOULD BE A SLEAZEBALL THING TO DO.
I HATE NOT BEING A SLEAZEBALL.
2/4
© 2008 by NEA, Inc.
PEIRCE

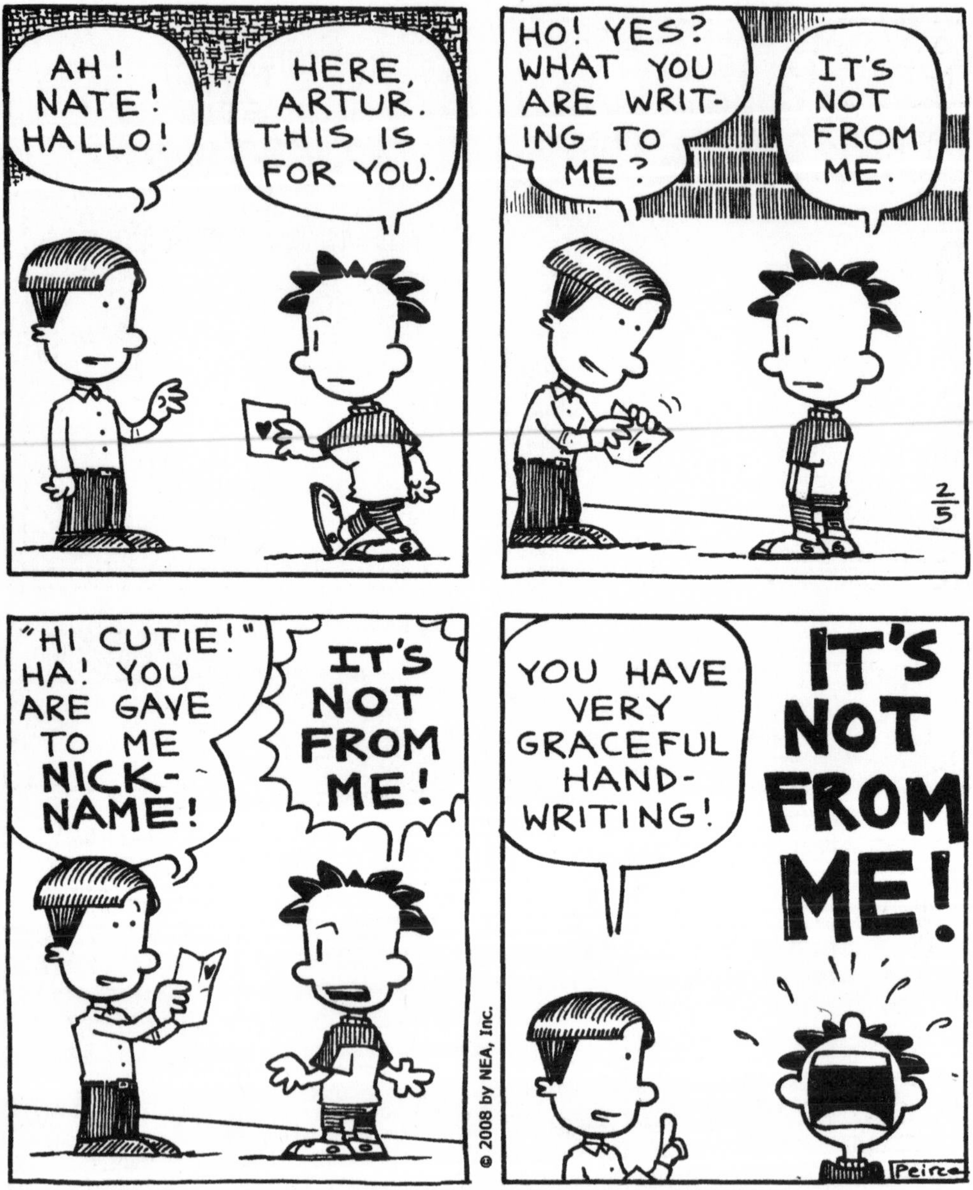
AH! NATE! HALLO!
HERE, ARTUR. THIS IS FOR YOU.
HO! YES? WHAT YOU ARE WRITING TO ME?
IT'S NOT FROM ME.
2/5
"HI CUTIE!" HA! YOU ARE GAVE TO ME NICKNAME!
IT'S NOT FROM ME!
© 2008 by NEA, Inc.
YOU HAVE VERY GRACEFUL HANDWRITING!
IT'S NOT FROM ME!
Peirce

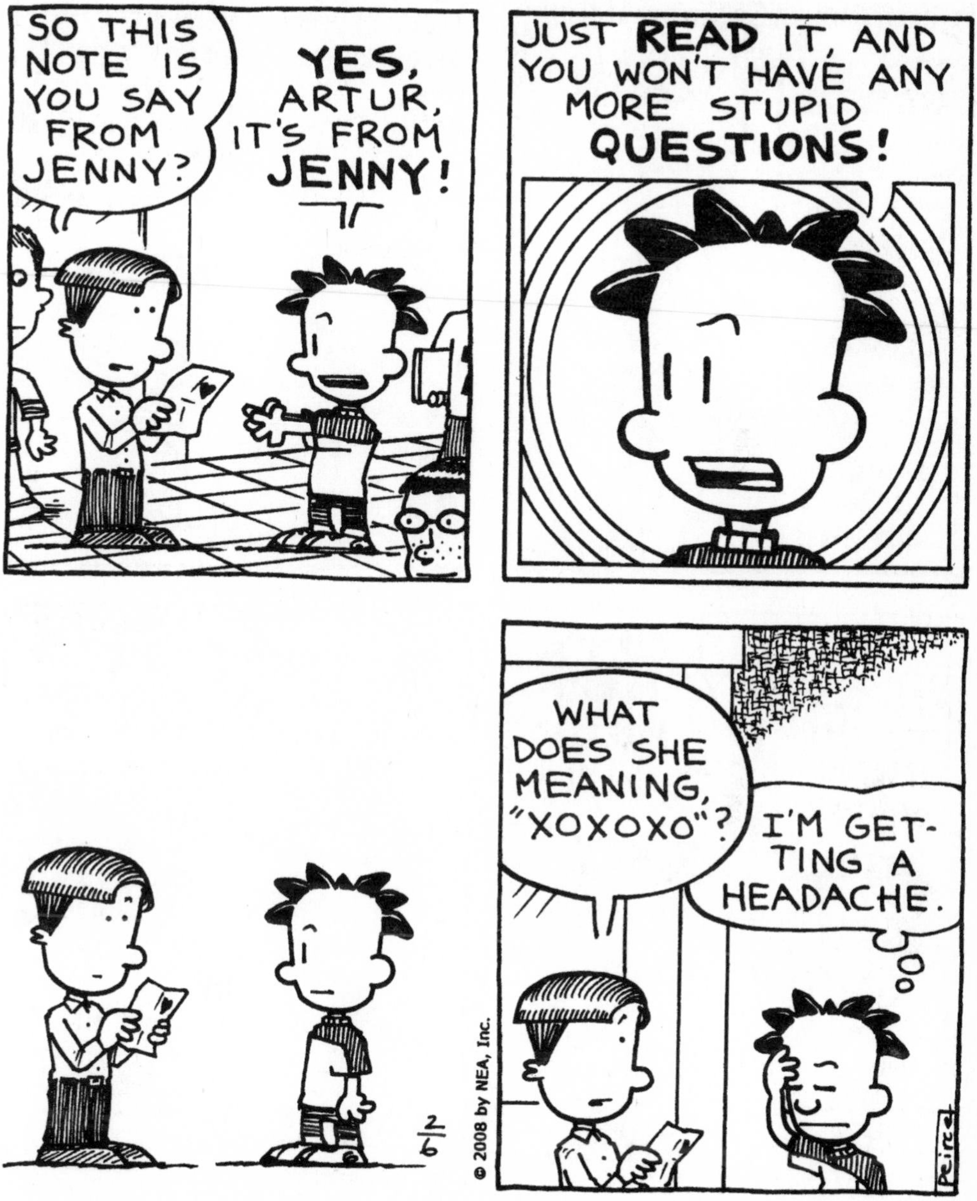
SO THIS NOTE IS YOU SAY FROM JENNY?
YES, ARTUR, IT'S FROM JENNY!
JUST READ IT, AND YOU WON'T HAVE ANY MORE STUPID QUESTIONS!
WHAT DOES SHE MEANING, "XOXOXO"?
I'M GETTING A HEADACHE.
2/6
© 2008 by NEA, Inc.
Peirce

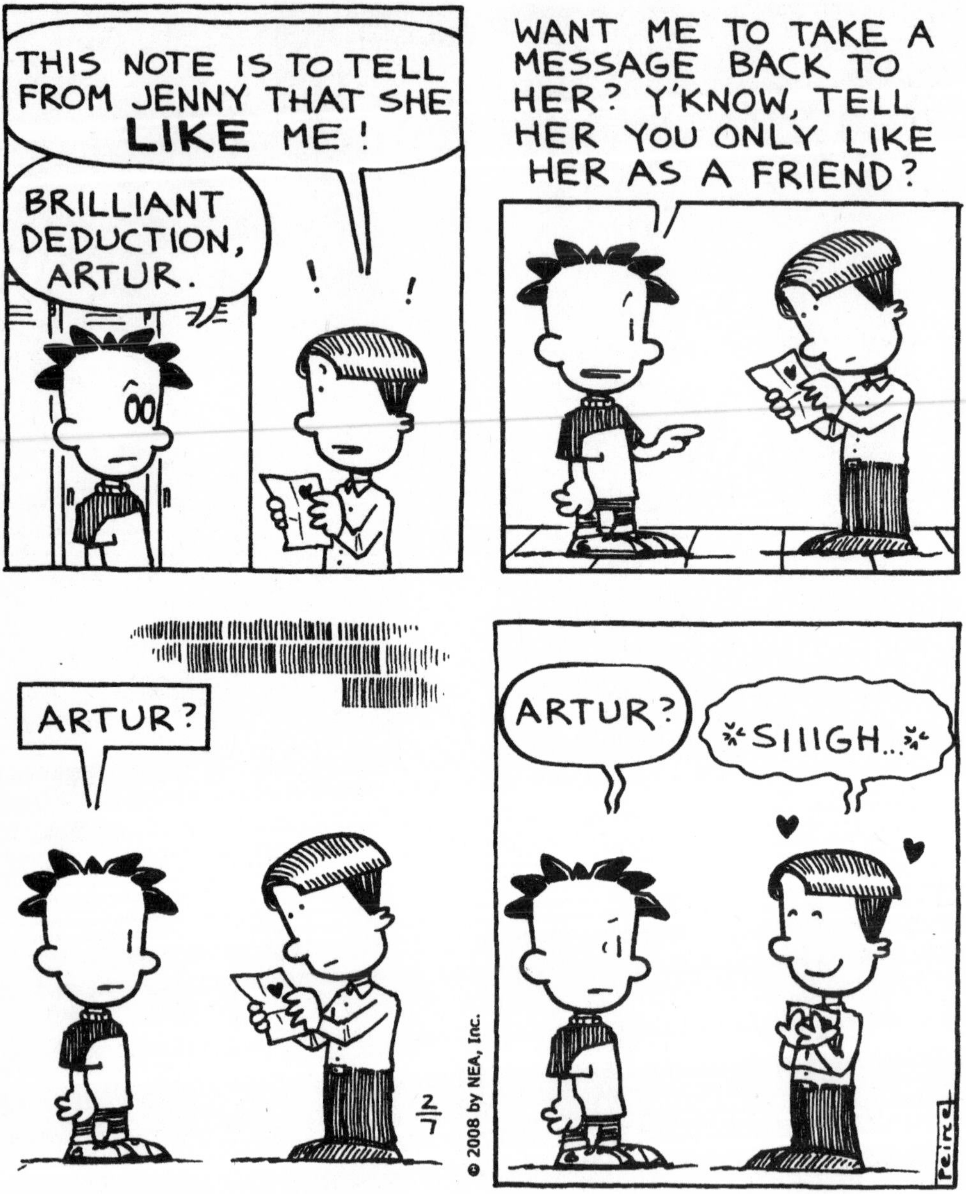
THIS NOTE IS TO TELL FROM JENNY THAT SHE LIKE ME!
BRILLIANT DEDUCTION, ARTUR.
!
!
WANT ME TO TAKE A MESSAGE BACK TO HER? Y'KNOW, TELL HER YOU ONLY LIKE HER AS A FRIEND?
ARTUR?
ARTUR?
SIIIGH...
2/7
© 2008 by NEA, Inc.
Peirce

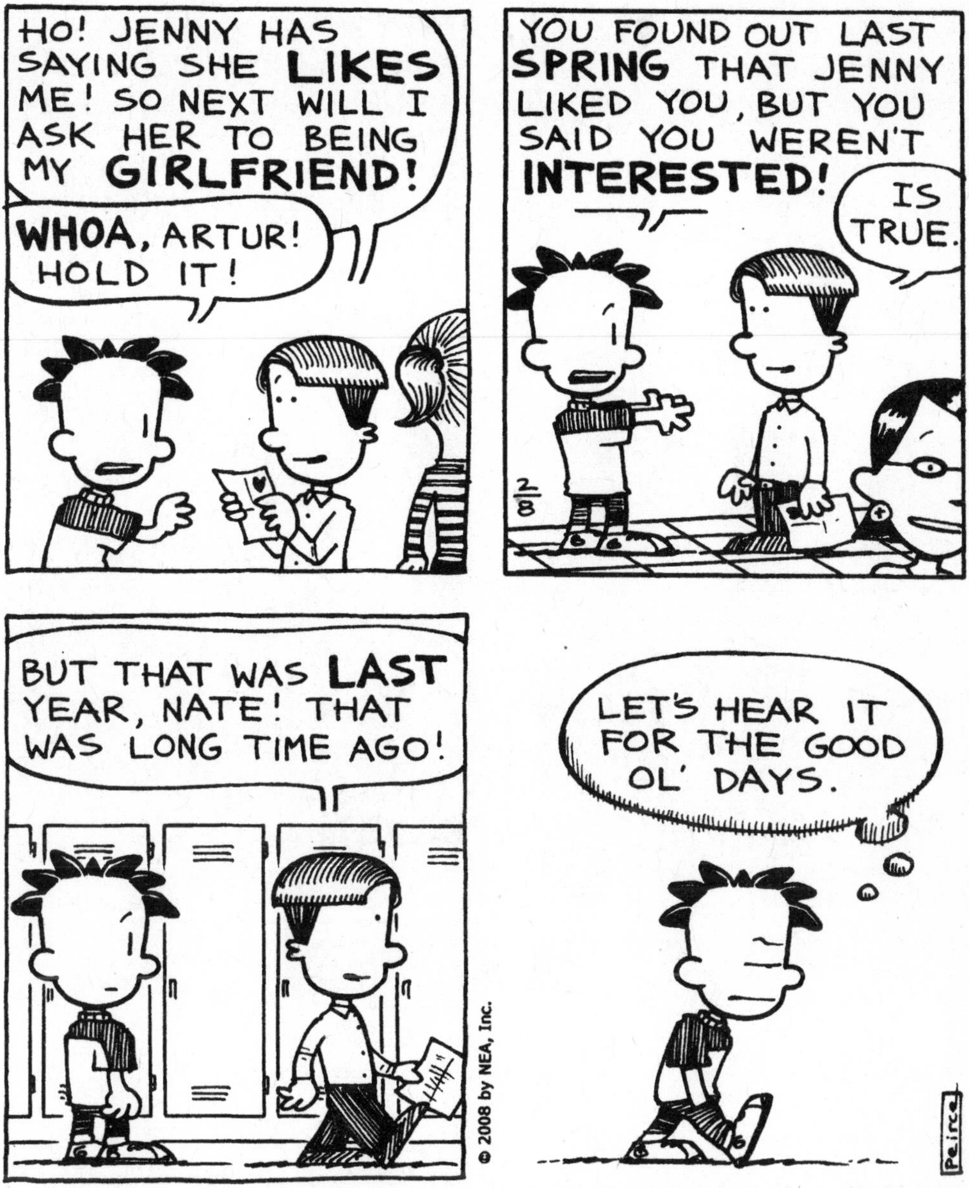
HO! JENNY HAS SAYING SHE LIKES ME! SO NEXT WILL I ASK HER TO BEING MY GIRLFRIEND!
WHOA, ARTUR! HOLD IT!
YOU FOUND OUT LAST SPRING THAT JENNY LIKED YOU, BUT YOU SAID YOU WEREN'T INTERESTED!
IS TRUE.
2/8
BUT THAT WAS LAST YEAR, NATE! THAT WAS LONG TIME AGO!
LET'S HEAR IT FOR THE GOOD OL' DAYS.
Peirce

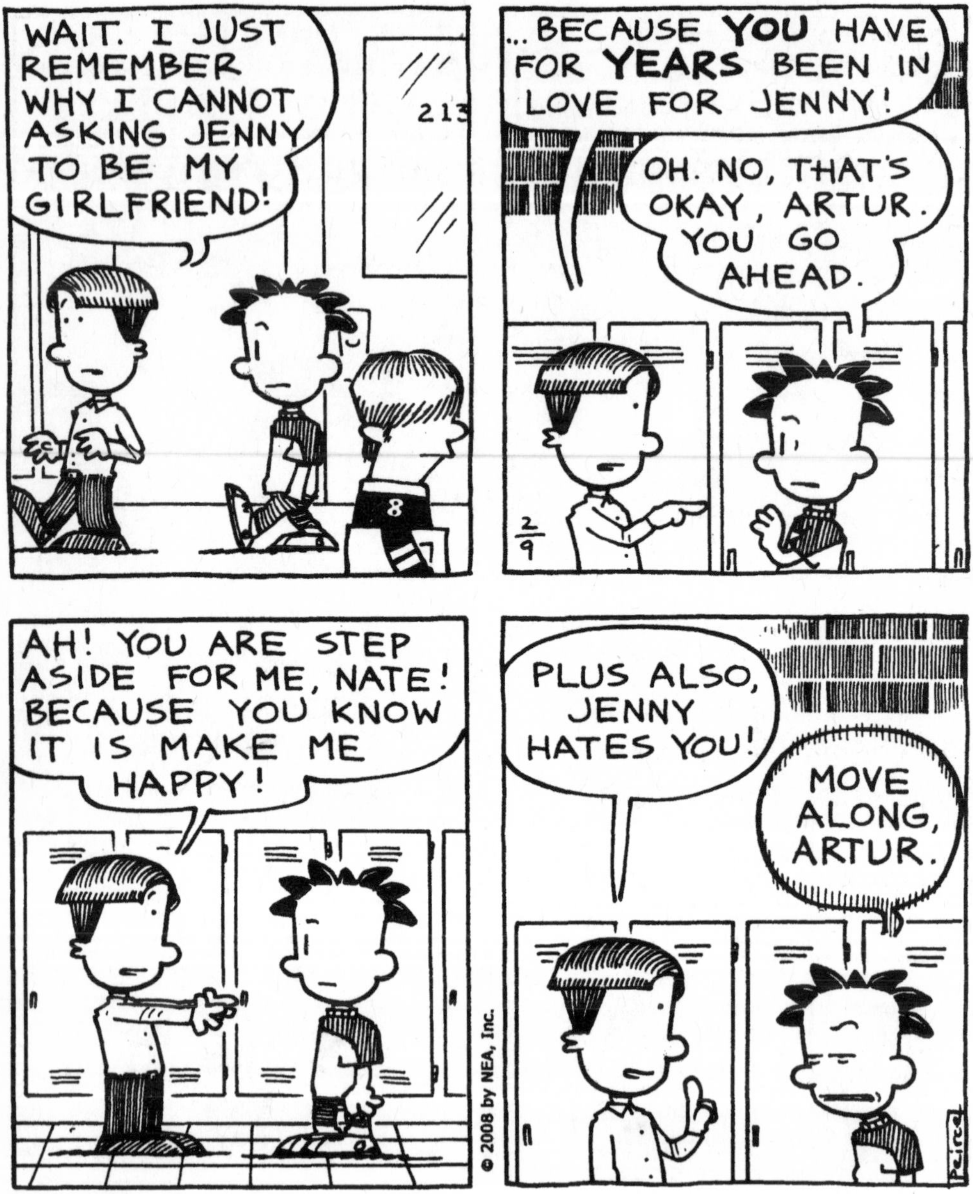
WAIT. I JUST REMEMBER WHY I CANNOT ASKING JENNY TO BE MY GIRLFRIEND!
213
...BECAUSE YOU HAVE FOR YEARS BEEN IN LOVE FOR JENNY!
OH. NO, THAT'S OKAY, ARTUR. YOU GO AHEAD.
2/9
AH! YOU ARE STEP ASIDE FOR ME, NATE! BECAUSE YOU KNOW IT IS MAKE ME HAPPY!
PLUS ALSO, JENNY HATES YOU!
MOVE ALONG, ARTUR.
Peirce

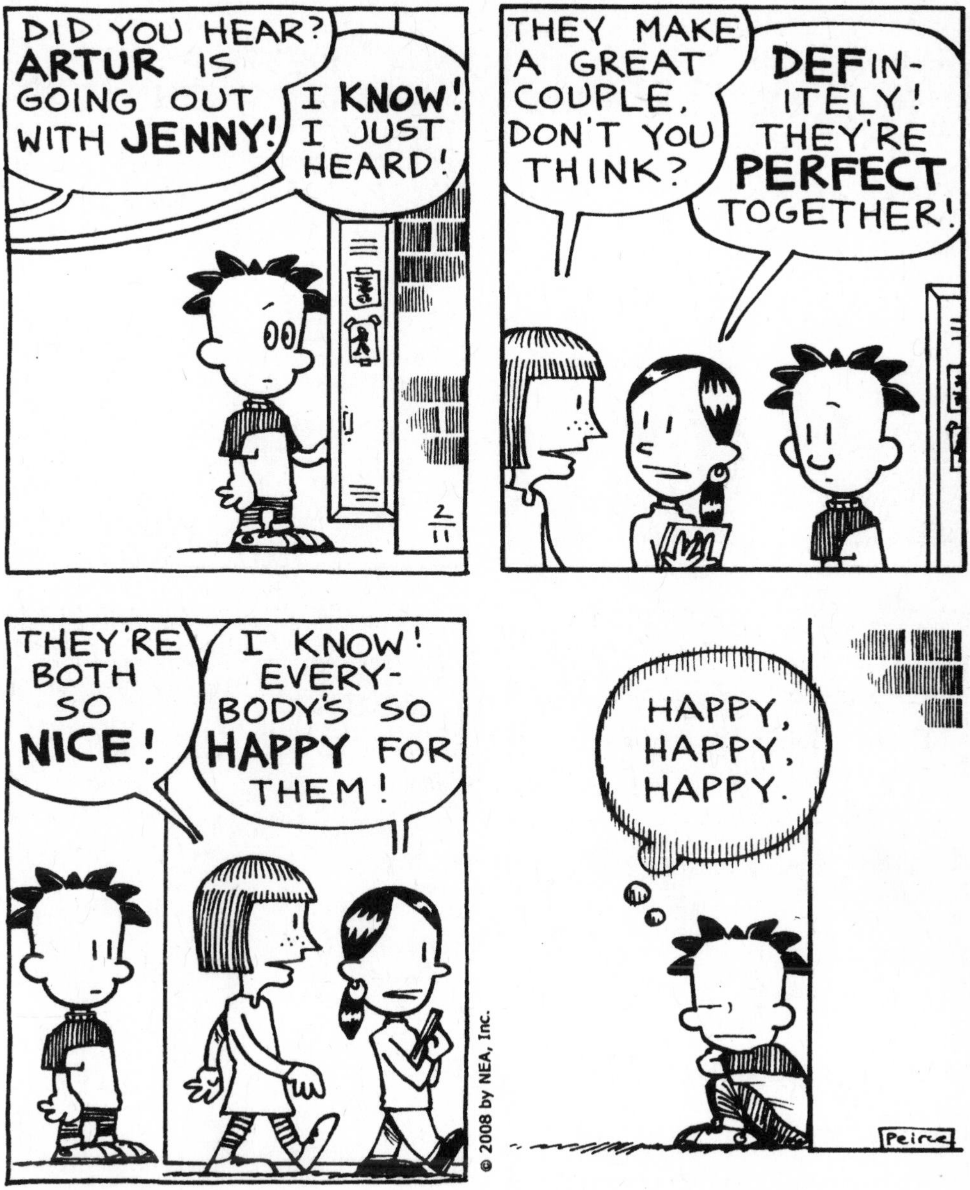
DID YOU HEAR? ARTUR IS GOING OUT WITH JENNY!
I KNOW! I JUST HEARD!
2/11
THEY MAKE A GREAT COUPLE, DON'T YOU THINK?
DEFIN-ITELY! THEY'RE PERFECT TOGETHER!
THEY'RE BOTH SO NICE!
I KNOW! EVERY-BODY'S SO HAPPY FOR THEM!
HAPPY, HAPPY, HAPPY.
Peirce

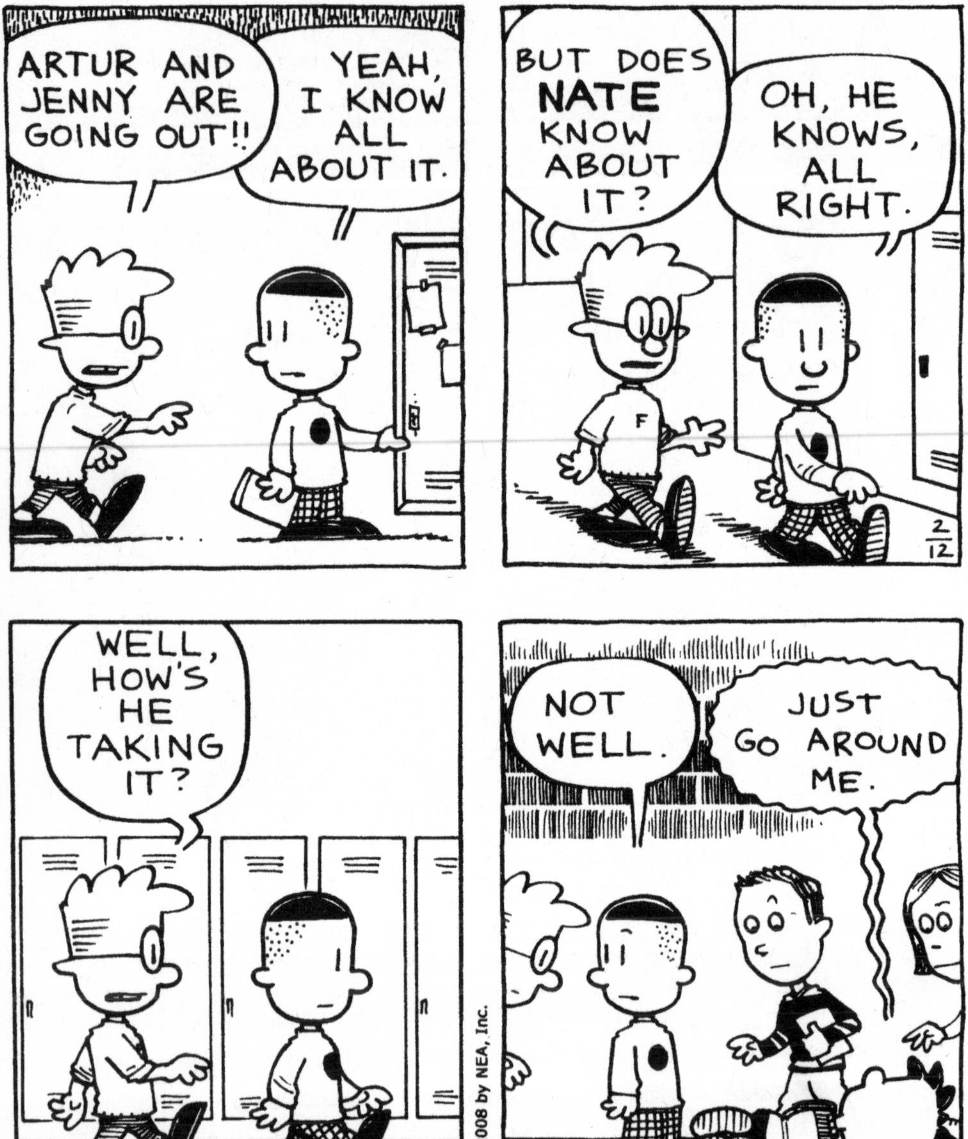
ARTUR AND JENNY ARE GOING OUT!!
YEAH, I KNOW ALL ABOUT IT.
BUT DOES NATE KNOW ABOUT IT?
OH, HE KNOWS, ALL RIGHT.
2/12
WELL, HOW'S HE TAKING IT?
© 2008 by NEA, Inc.
NOT WELL.
JUST GO AROUND ME.
Peirce

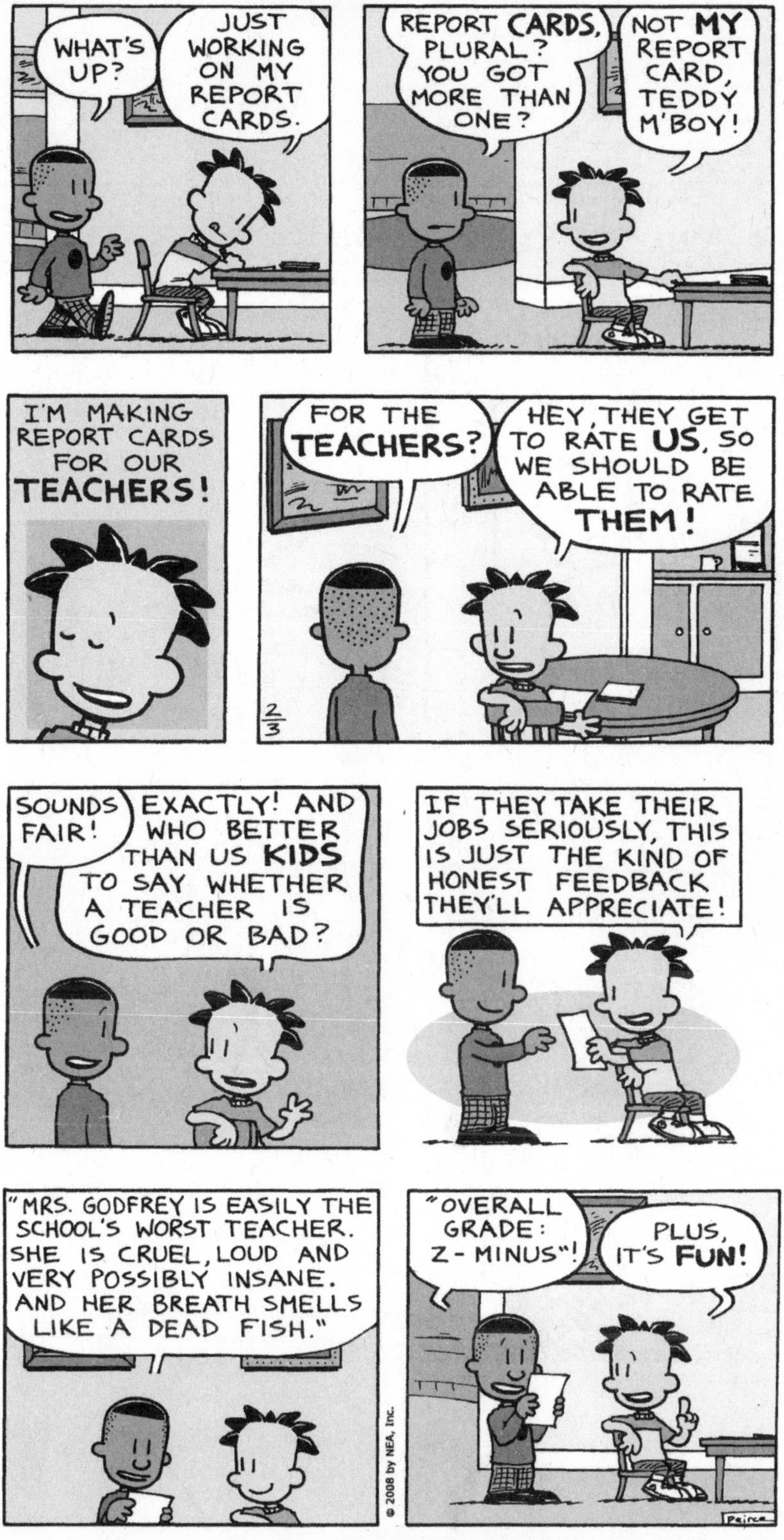
WHAT'S UP?
JUST WORKING ON MY REPORT CARDS.
REPORT CARDS, PLURAL? YOU GOT MORE THAN ONE?
NOT MY REPORT CARD, TEDDY M'BOY!
I'M MAKING REPORT CARDS FOR OUR TEACHERS!
FOR THE TEACHERS?
HEY, THEY GET TO RATE US, SO WE SHOULD BE ABLE TO RATE THEM!
SOUNDS FAIR!
EXACTLY! AND WHO BETTER THAN US KIDS TO SAY WHETHER A TEACHER IS GOOD OR BAD?
IF THEY TAKE THEIR JOBS SERIOUSLY, THIS IS JUST THE KIND OF HONEST FEEDBACK THEY'LL APPRECIATE!
"MRS. GODFREY IS EASILY THE SCHOOL'S WORST TEACHER. SHE IS CRUEL, LOUD AND VERY POSSIBLY INSANE. AND HER BREATH SMELLS LIKE A DEAD FISH."
"OVERALL GRADE: Z-MINUS"!
PLUS, IT'S FUN!
© 2008 by NEA, Inc.
Peirce

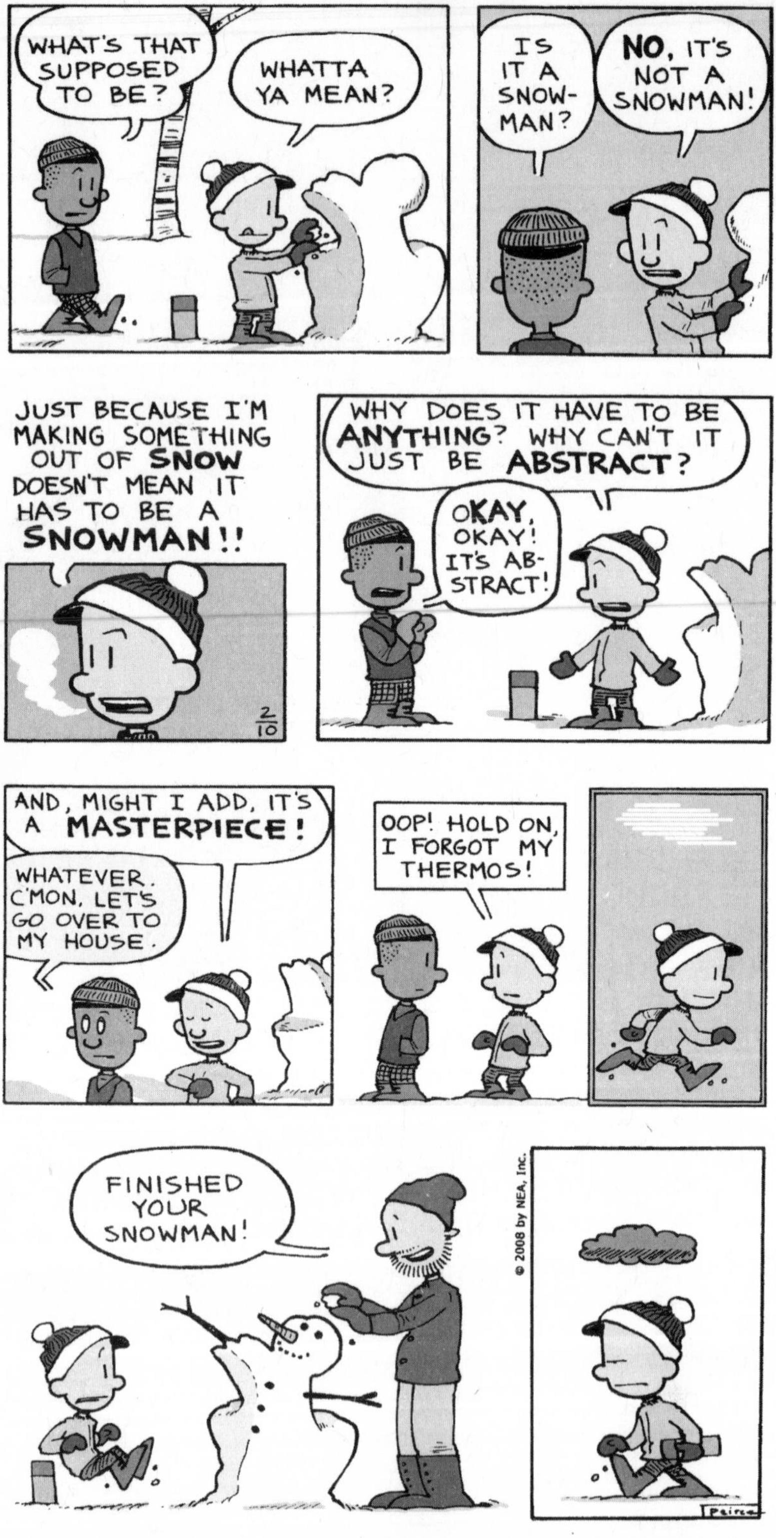
WHAT'S THAT SUPPOSED TO BE?
WHATTA YA MEAN?
IS IT A SNOW-MAN?
NO, IT'S NOT A SNOWMAN!
JUST BECAUSE I'M MAKING SOMETHING OUT OF SNOW DOESN'T MEAN IT HAS TO BE A SNOWMAN!!
2/10
WHY DOES IT HAVE TO BE ANYTHING? WHY CAN'T IT JUST BE ABSTRACT?
OKAY, OKAY! IT'S AB-STRACT!
AND, MIGHT I ADD, IT'S A MASTERPIECE!
WHATEVER. C'MON, LET'S GO OVER TO MY HOUSE.
OOP! HOLD ON, I FORGOT MY THERMOS!
FINISHED YOUR SNOWMAN!
Peirce

LUNCH BLUES

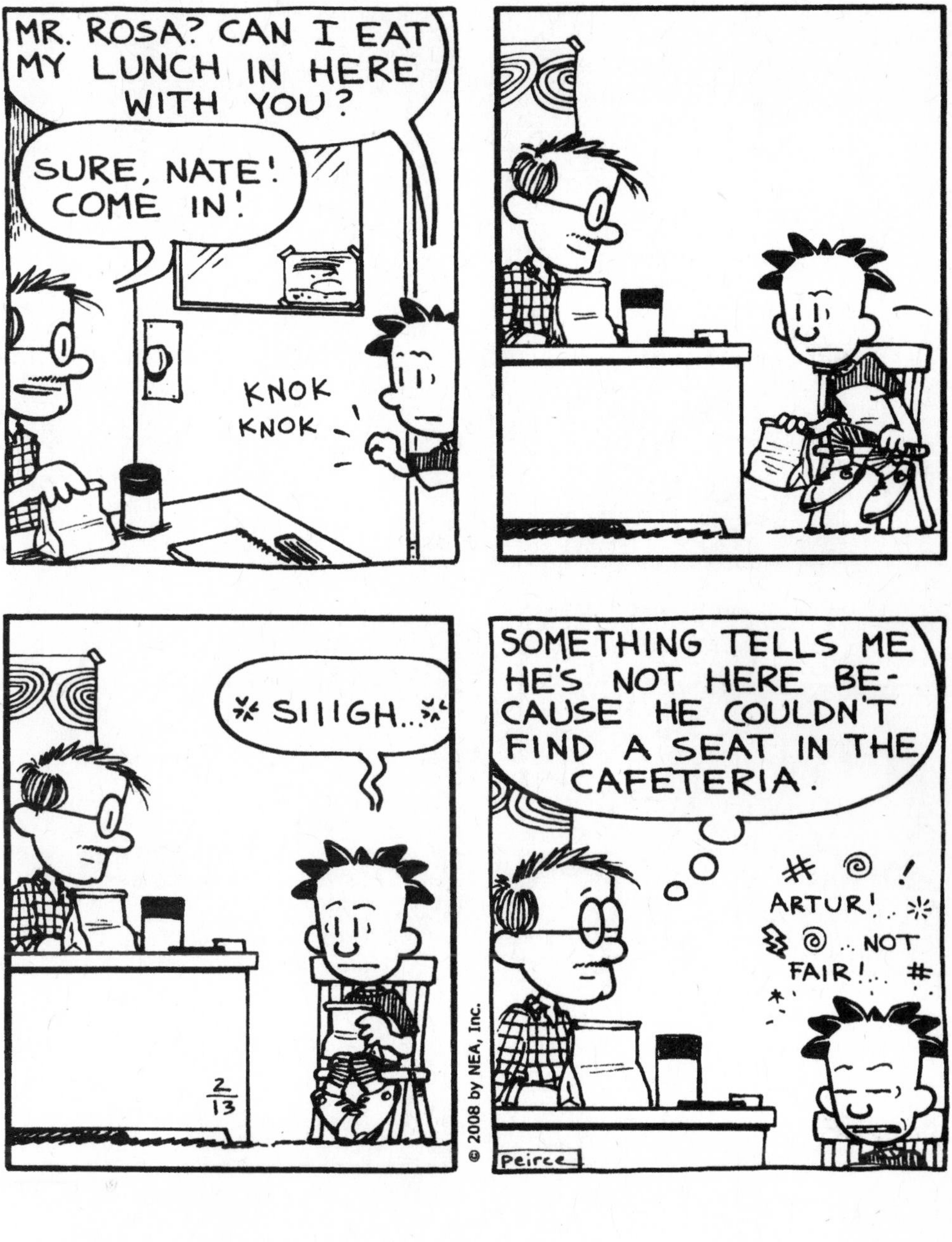
MR. ROSA? CAN I EAT MY LUNCH IN HERE WITH YOU?
SURE, NATE! COME IN!
KNOK KNOK
SIIIGH...
2/13
© 2008 by NEA, Inc.
SOMETHING TELLS ME HE'S NOT HERE BE-CAUSE HE COULDN'T FIND A SEAT IN THE CAFETERIA.
@ ! ARTUR! .. @ .. NOT FAIR!..
Peirce

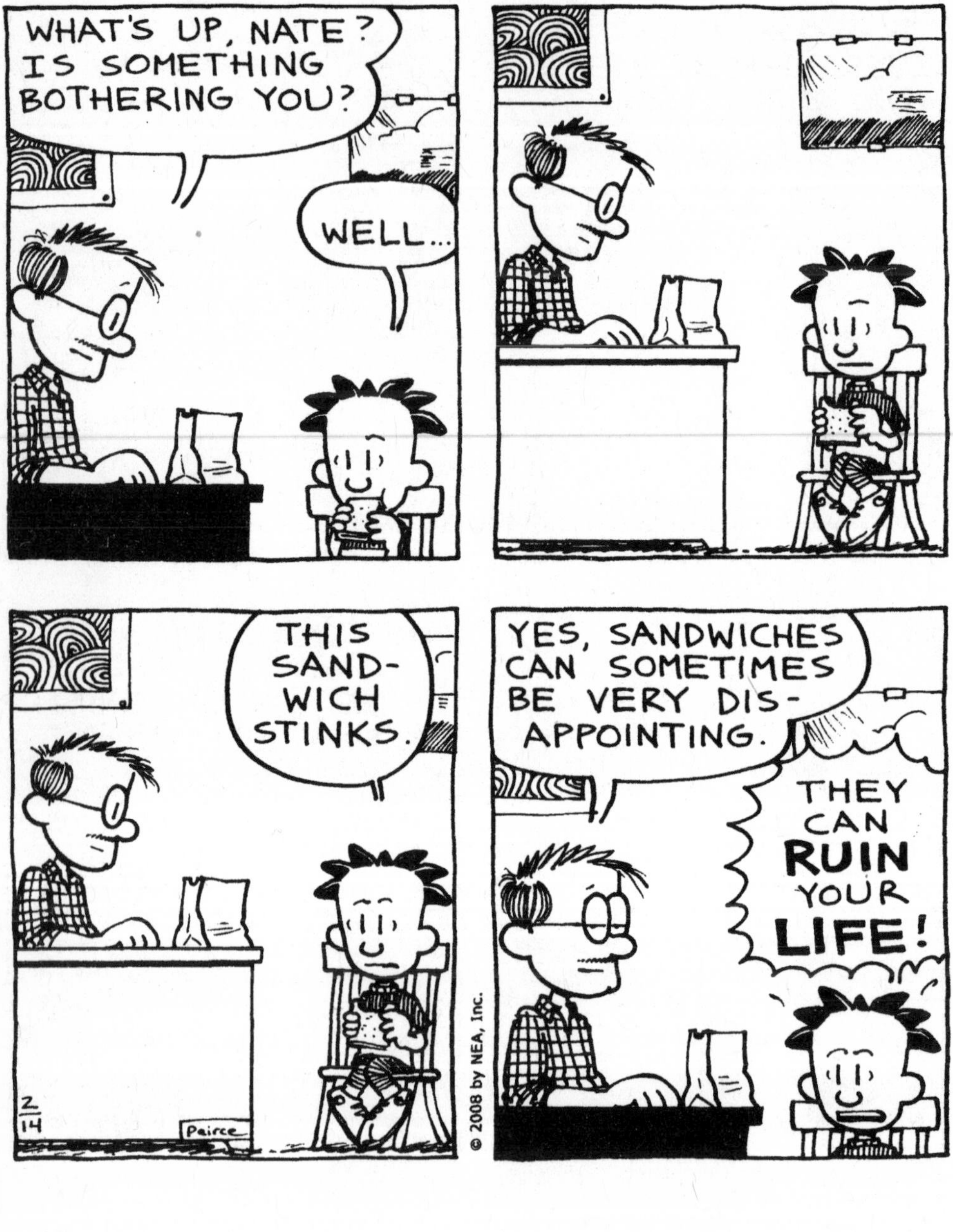
WHAT'S UP, NATE? IS SOMETHING BOTHERING YOU?
WELL...
THIS SAND-WICH STINKS.
YES, SANDWICHES CAN SOMETIMES BE VERY DIS-APPOINTING.
THEY CAN RUIN YOUR LIFE!
2/14
Peirce
© 2008 by NEA, Inc.

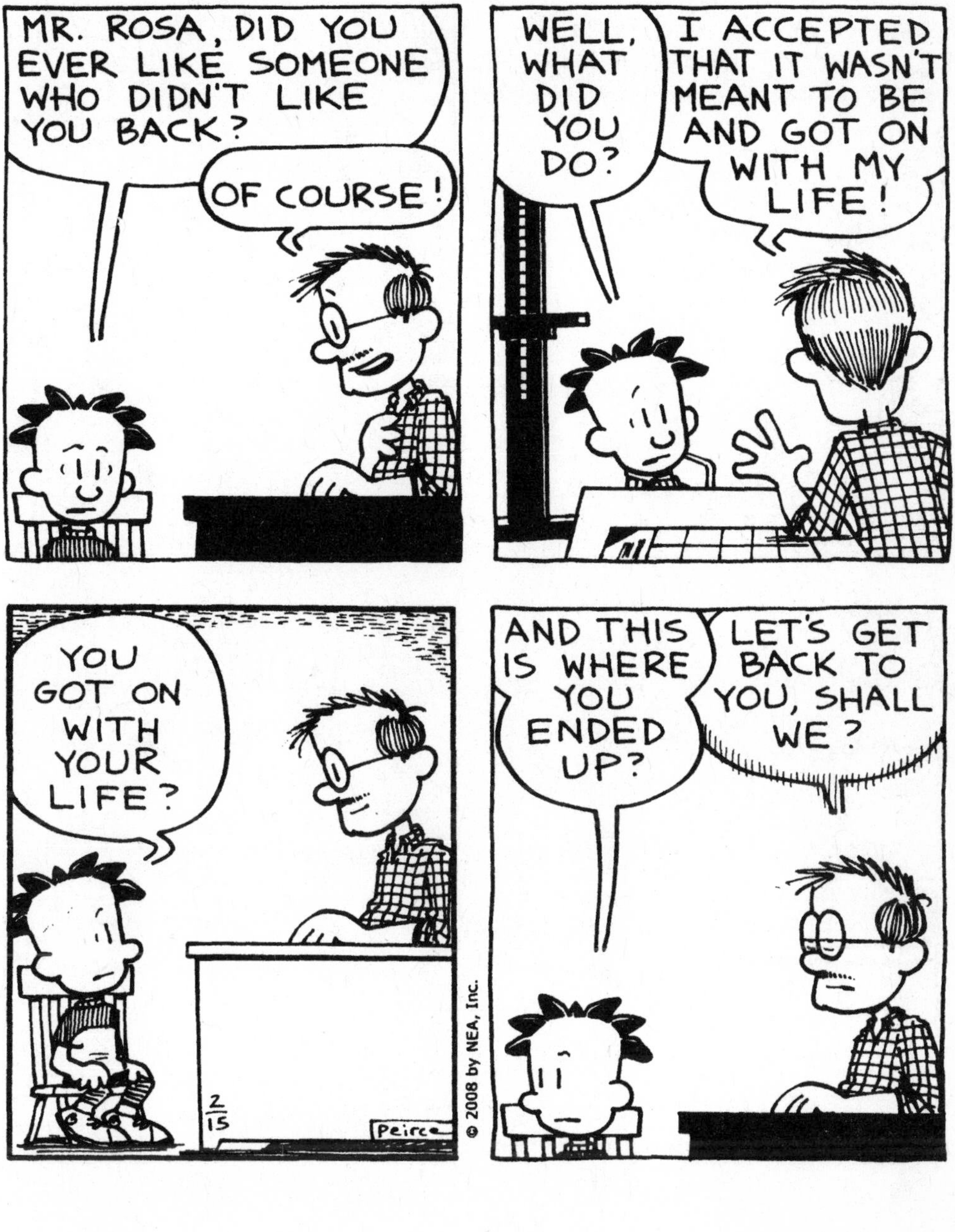
MR. ROSA, DID YOU EVER LIKE SOMEONE WHO DIDN'T LIKE YOU BACK?
OF COURSE!
WELL, WHAT DID YOU DO?
I ACCEPTED THAT IT WASN'T MEANT TO BE AND GOT ON WITH MY LIFE!
YOU GOT ON WITH YOUR LIFE?
2/15
Peirce
© 2008 by NEA, Inc.
AND THIS IS WHERE YOU ENDED UP?
LET'S GET BACK TO YOU, SHALL WE?

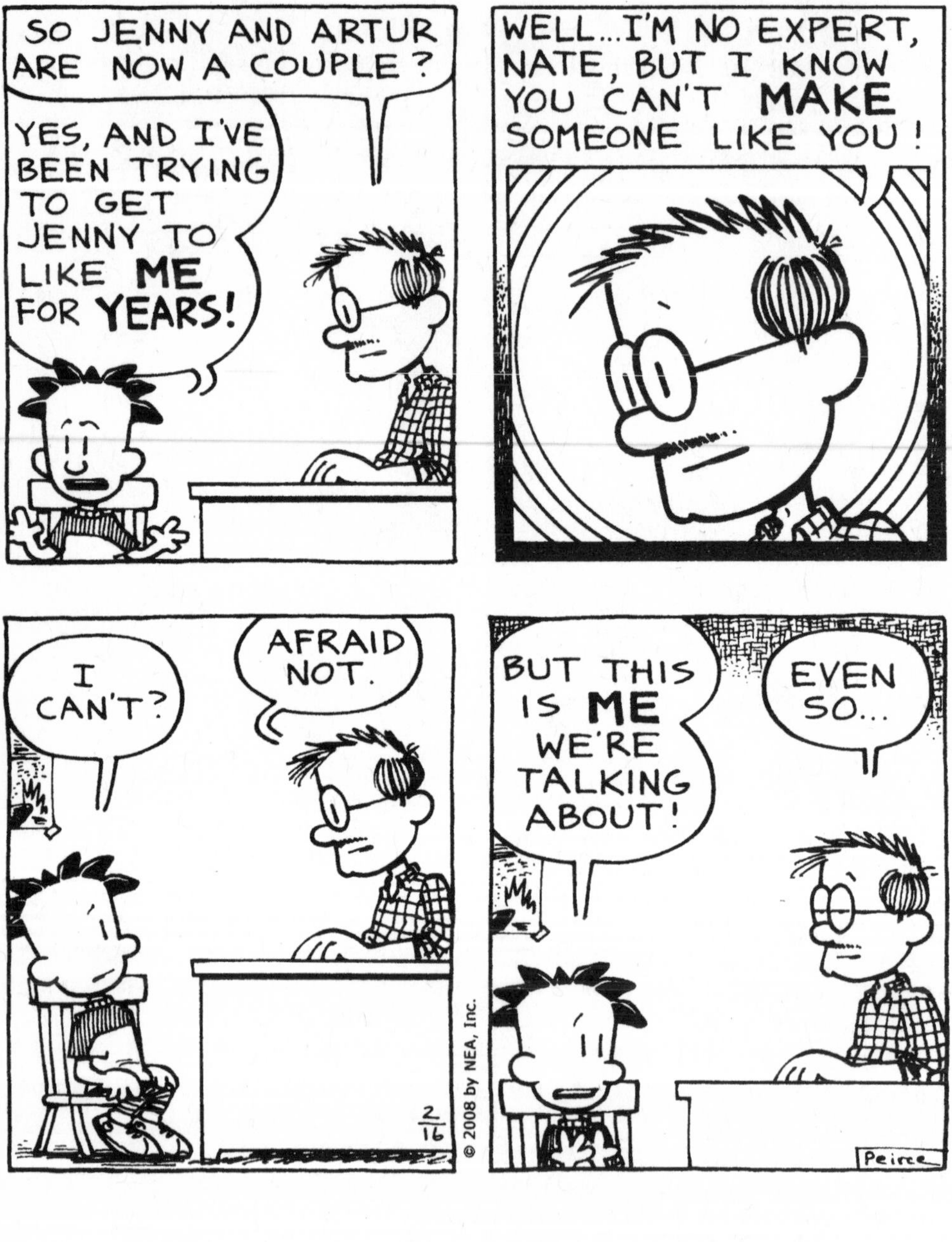
SO JENNY AND ARTUR ARE NOW A COUPLE?
YES, AND I'VE BEEN TRYING TO GET JENNY TO LIKE ME FOR YEARS!
WELL...I'M NO EXPERT, NATE, BUT I KNOW YOU CAN'T MAKE SOMEONE LIKE YOU!
I CAN'T?
AFRAID NOT.
BUT THIS IS ME WE'RE TALKING ABOUT!
EVEN SO...
2/16
© 2008 by NEA, Inc.
Peirce

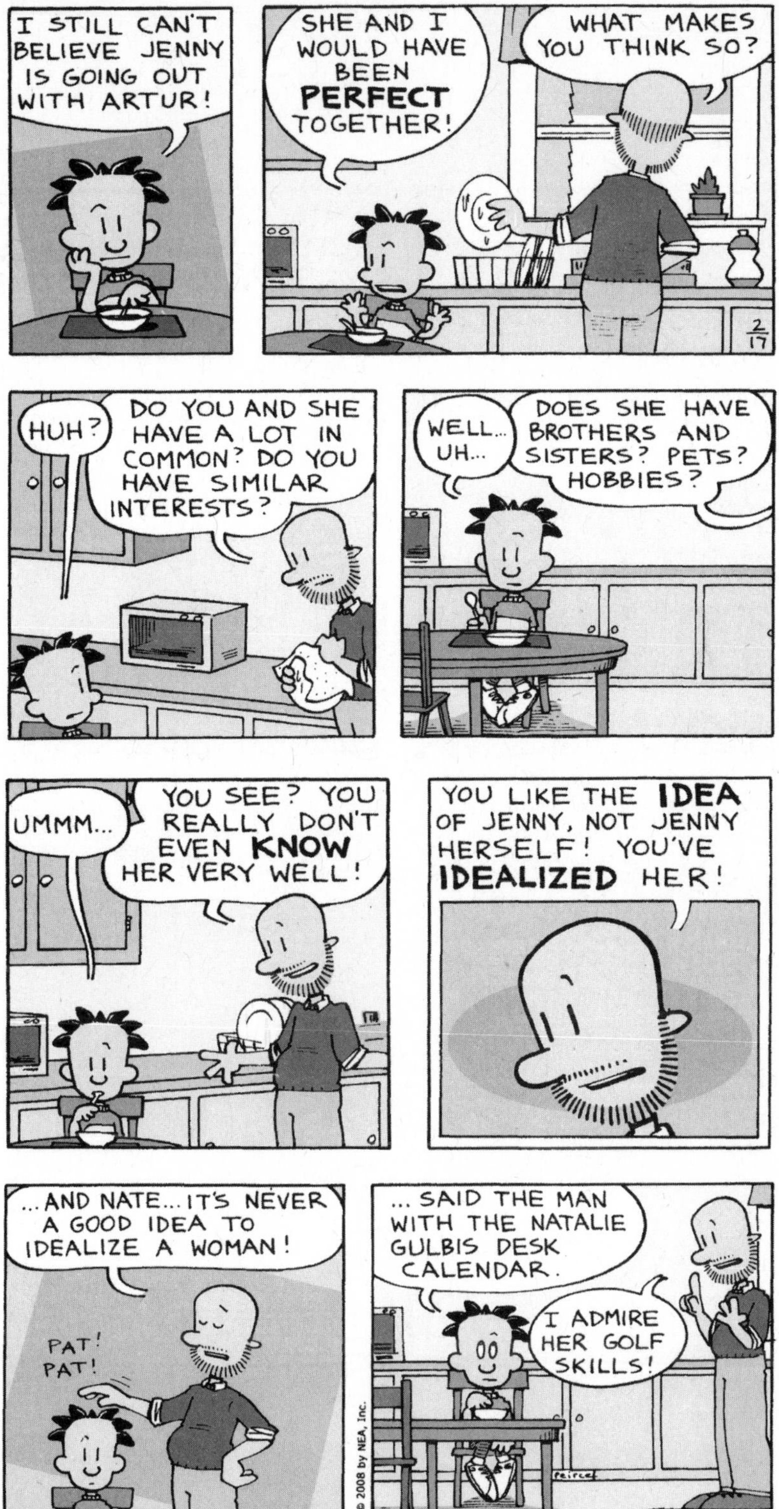
I STILL CAN'T BELIEVE JENNY IS GOING OUT WITH ARTUR!
SHE AND I WOULD HAVE BEEN **PERFECT** TOGETHER!
WHAT MAKES YOU THINK SO?
2/17
HUH?
DO YOU AND SHE HAVE A LOT IN COMMON? DO YOU HAVE SIMILAR INTERESTS?
WELL... UH...
DOES SHE HAVE BROTHERS AND SISTERS? PETS? HOBBIES?
UMMM...
YOU SEE? YOU REALLY DON'T EVEN **KNOW** HER VERY WELL!
YOU LIKE THE **IDEA** OF JENNY, NOT JENNY HERSELF! YOU'VE **IDEALIZED** HER!
...AND NATE... IT'S NEVER A GOOD IDEA TO IDEALIZE A WOMAN!
PAT! PAT!
... SAID THE MAN WITH THE NATALIE GULBIS DESK CALENDAR.
I ADMIRE HER GOLF SKILLS!

NATE WRIGHT, FOOD CRITIC

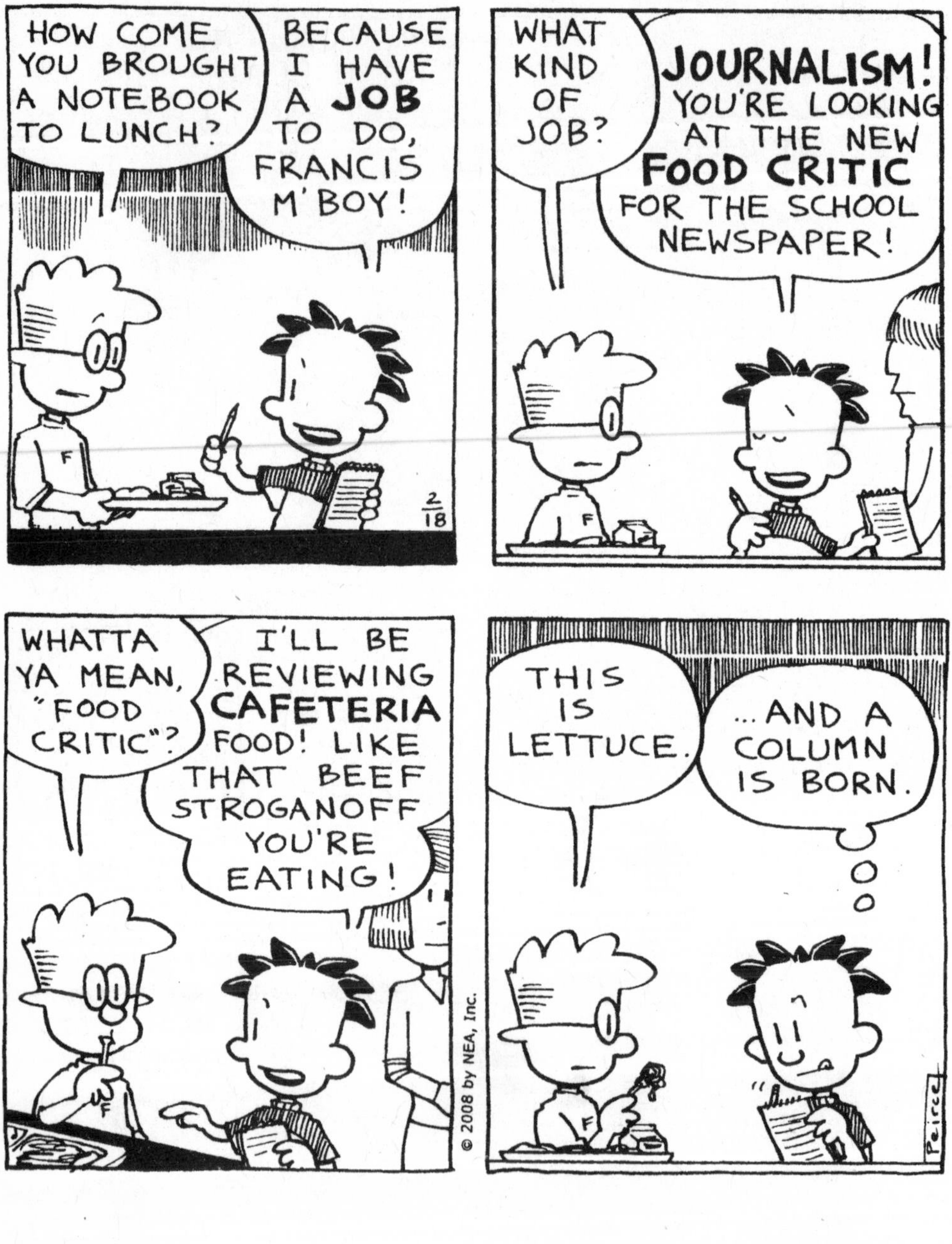

HOW COME YOU BROUGHT A NOTEBOOK TO LUNCH?
BECAUSE I HAVE A **JOB** TO DO, FRANCIS M'BOY!
2/18
WHAT KIND OF JOB?
JOURNALISM! YOU'RE LOOKING AT THE NEW **FOOD CRITIC** FOR THE SCHOOL NEWSPAPER!
WHATTA YA MEAN, "FOOD CRITIC"?
I'LL BE REVIEWING **CAFETERIA** FOOD! LIKE THAT BEEF STROGANOFF YOU'RE EATING!
© 2008 by NEA, Inc.
THIS IS LETTUCE.
...AND A COLUMN IS BORN.
Peirce

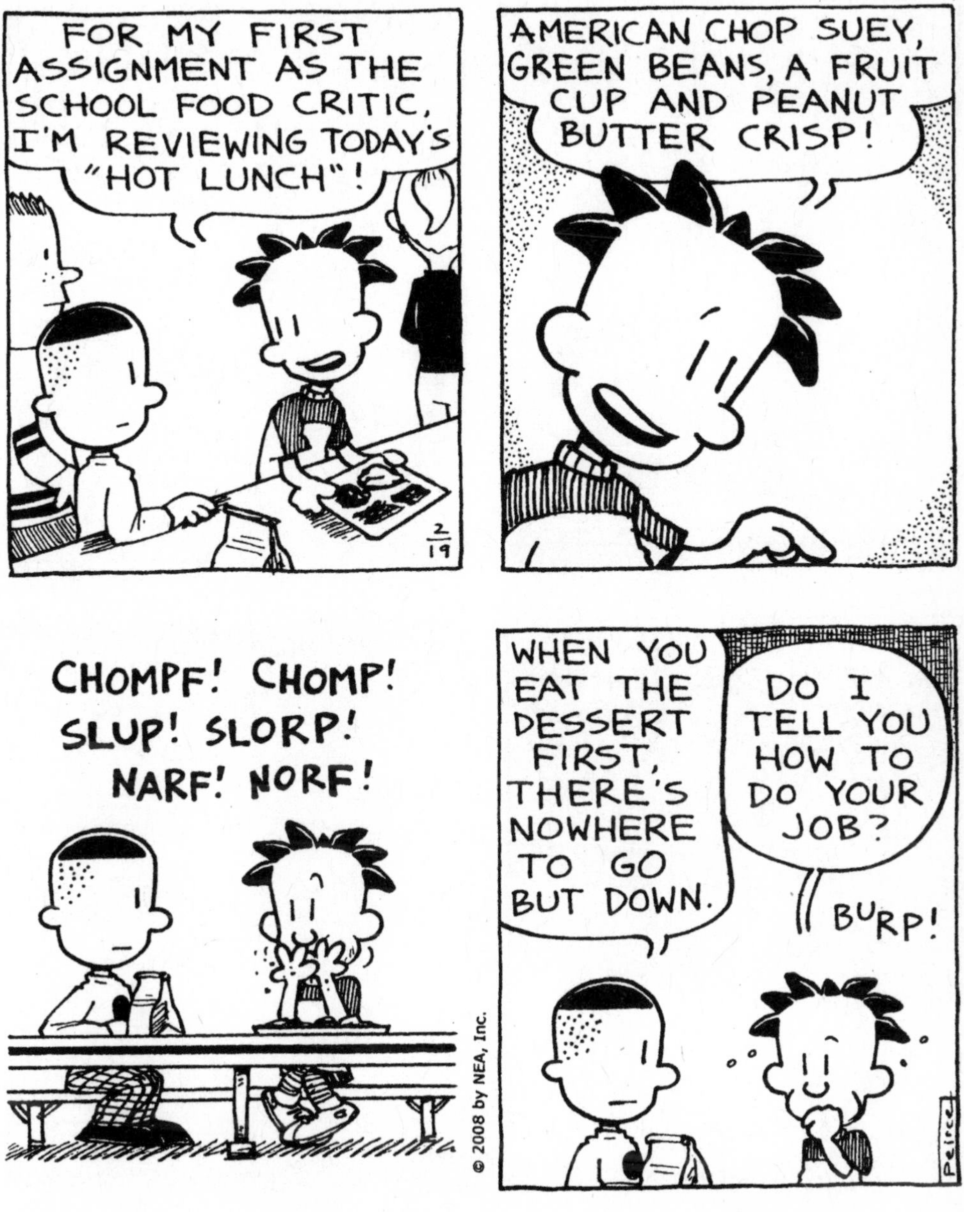
FOR MY FIRST ASSIGNMENT AS THE SCHOOL FOOD CRITIC, I'M REVIEWING TODAY'S "HOT LUNCH"!
2/19
AMERICAN CHOP SUEY, GREEN BEANS, A FRUIT CUP AND PEANUT BUTTER CRISP!
CHOMPF! CHOMP! SLUP! SLORP! NARF! NORF!
© 2008 by NEA, Inc.
WHEN YOU EAT THE DESSERT FIRST, THERE'S NOWHERE TO GO BUT DOWN.
DO I TELL YOU HOW TO DO YOUR JOB?
BURP!
Peirce

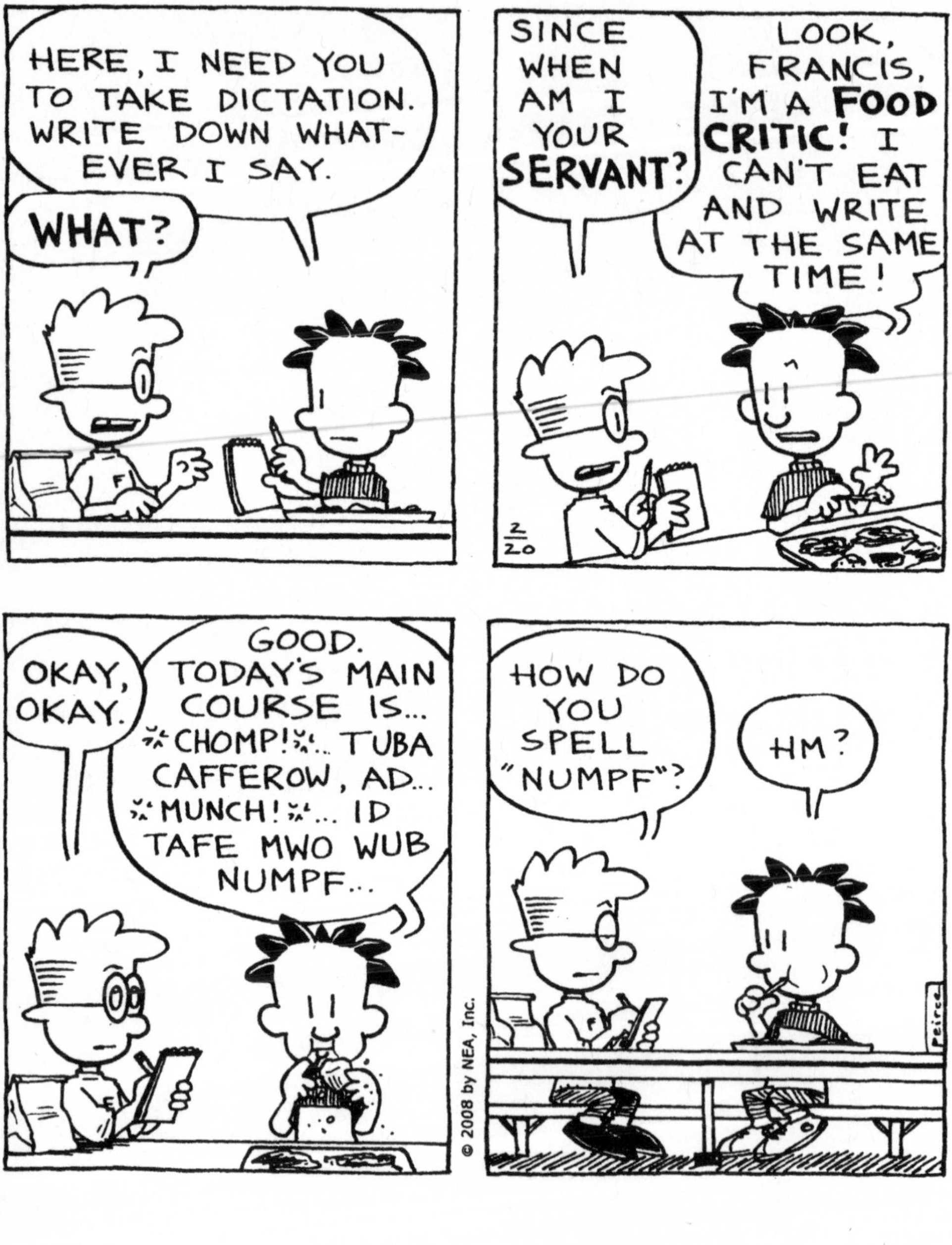
HERE, I NEED YOU TO TAKE DICTATION. WRITE DOWN WHATEVER I SAY.
WHAT?
SINCE WHEN AM I YOUR SERVANT?
LOOK, FRANCIS, I'M A FOOD CRITIC! I CAN'T EAT AND WRITE AT THE SAME TIME!
2/20
OKAY, OKAY.
GOOD. TODAY'S MAIN COURSE IS... CHOMP!... TUBA CAFFEROW, AD... MUNCH!... ID TAFE MWO WUB NUMPF...
© 2008 by NEA, Inc.
HOW DO YOU SPELL "NUMPF"?
HM?
Peirce

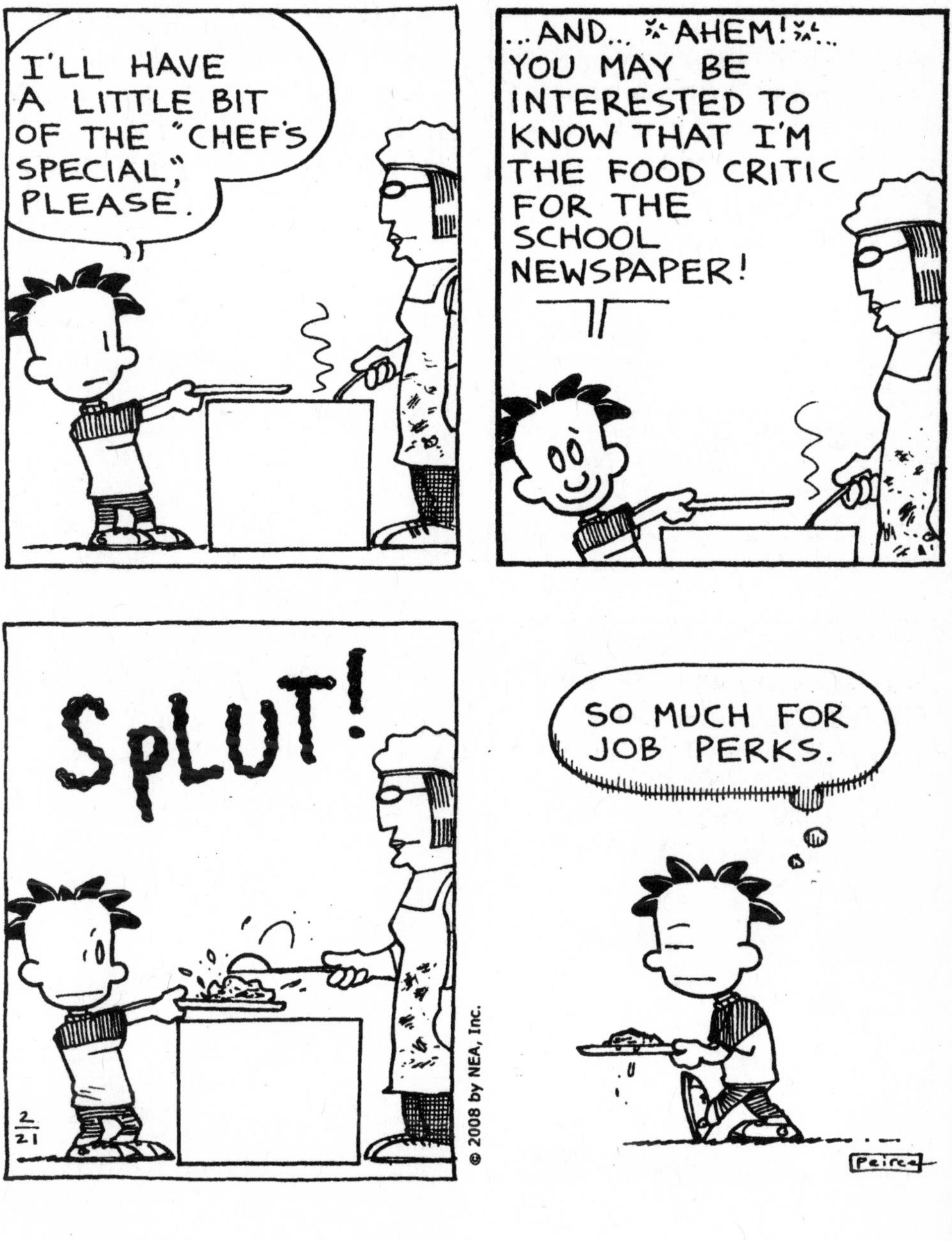
I'LL HAVE A LITTLE BIT OF THE "CHEF'S SPECIAL," PLEASE.
...AND... *AHEM!*... YOU MAY BE INTERESTED TO KNOW THAT I'M THE FOOD CRITIC FOR THE SCHOOL NEWSPAPER!
SPLUT!
2/21
© 2008 by NEA, Inc.
SO MUCH FOR JOB PERKS.
Peirce

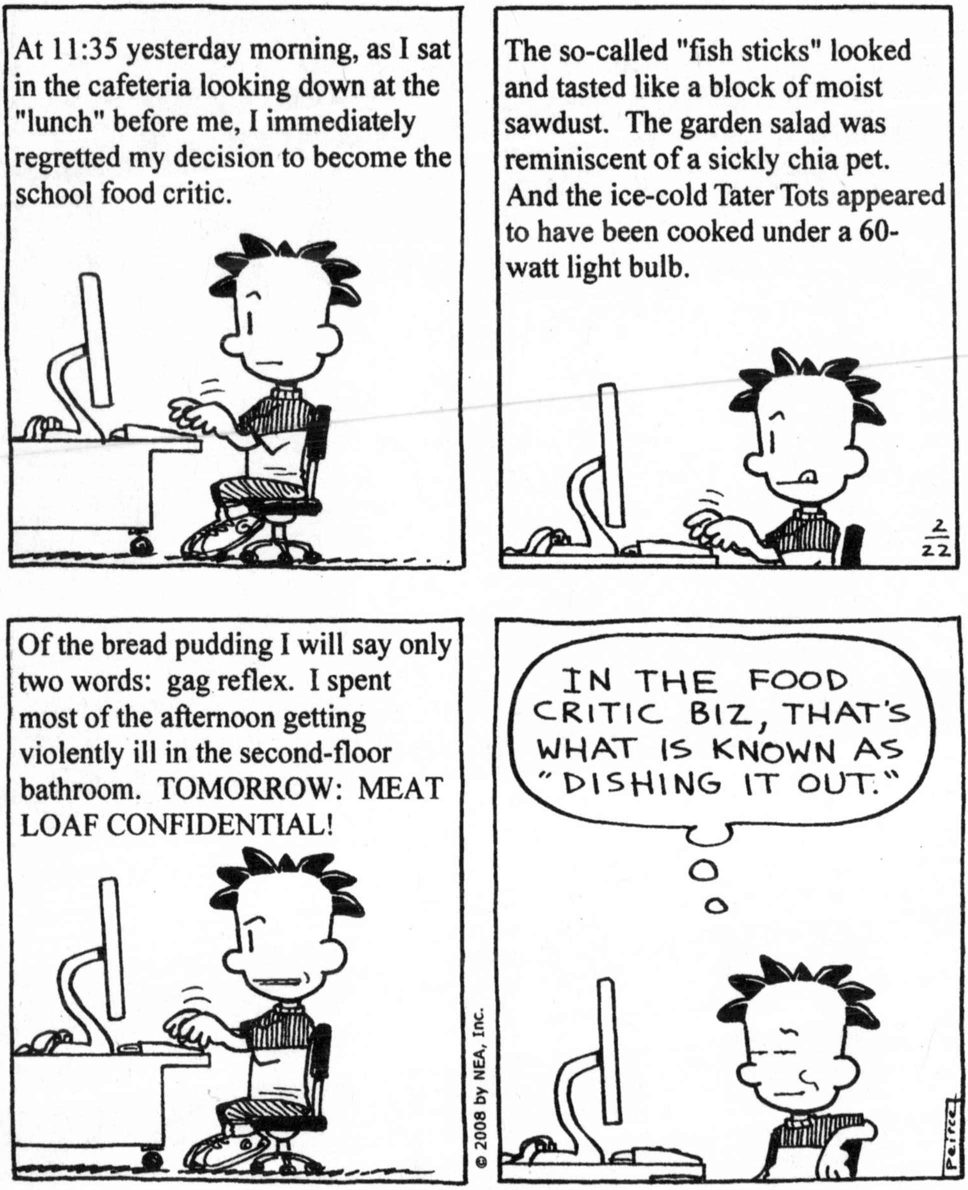
At 11:35 yesterday morning, as I sat in the cafeteria looking down at the "lunch" before me, I immediately regretted my decision to become the school food critic.
The so-called "fish sticks" looked and tasted like a block of moist sawdust. The garden salad was reminiscent of a sickly chia pet. And the ice-cold Tater Tots appeared to have been cooked under a 60-watt light bulb.
2/22
Of the bread pudding I will say only two words: gag reflex. I spent most of the afternoon getting violently ill in the second-floor bathroom. TOMORROW: MEAT LOAF CONFIDENTIAL!
IN THE FOOD CRITIC BIZ, THAT'S WHAT IS KNOWN AS "DISHING IT OUT."
Peirce

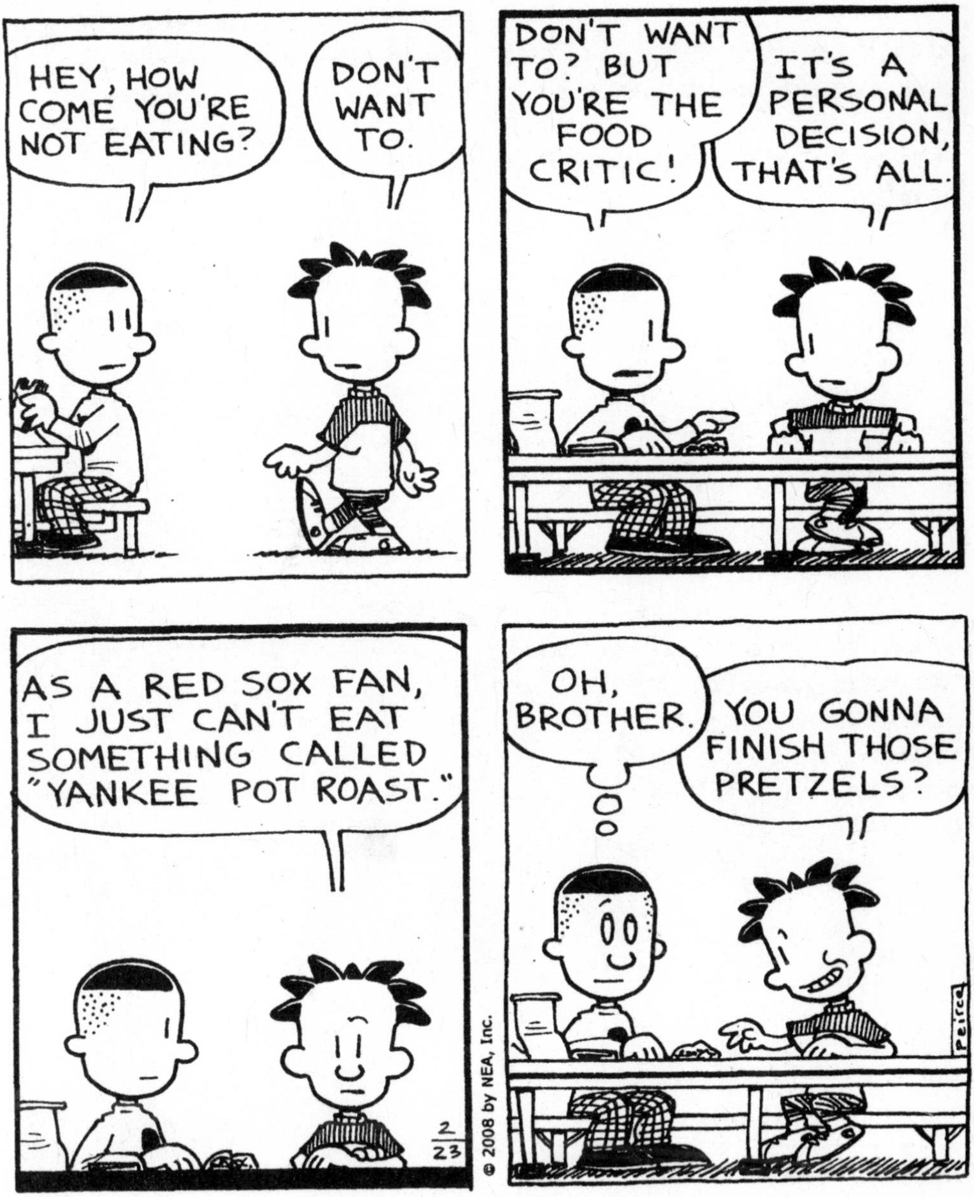
HEY, HOW COME YOU'RE NOT EATING?
DON'T WANT TO.
DON'T WANT TO? BUT YOU'RE THE FOOD CRITIC!
IT'S A PERSONAL DECISION, THAT'S ALL.
AS A RED SOX FAN, I JUST CAN'T EAT SOMETHING CALLED "YANKEE POT ROAST."
2/23
© 2008 by NEA, Inc.
OH, BROTHER.
YOU GONNA FINISH THOSE PRETZELS?
Peirce

PRINCIPAL NICHOLS?

YES! WHAT CAN I DO FOR YOU, NATE?

I WAS WONDERING IF I COULD EAT LUNCH IN YOUR OFFICE.

YOU'RE PRETTY MUCH MY LAST HOPE.

GOODNESS! WELL, I'M GLAD YOU CAME TO ME, SON.

REMEMBER, THE LAST THREE LETTERS OF "PRINCIPAL" ARE P-A-L!

I'M A **FRIEND** THAT STUDENTS CAN **TRUST** AND **CONFIDE** IN! THAT'S WHY I'M **HERE**!

NOW... WHAT SEEMS TO BE THE PROBLEM?

I COULDN'T FIND ANYONE TO TRADE LUNCHES WITH.

WHAT'LL YOU GIVE ME FOR A CHICKEN SALAD PITA?

CRIPES.

WHAT'S WITH BODY LANGUAGE?

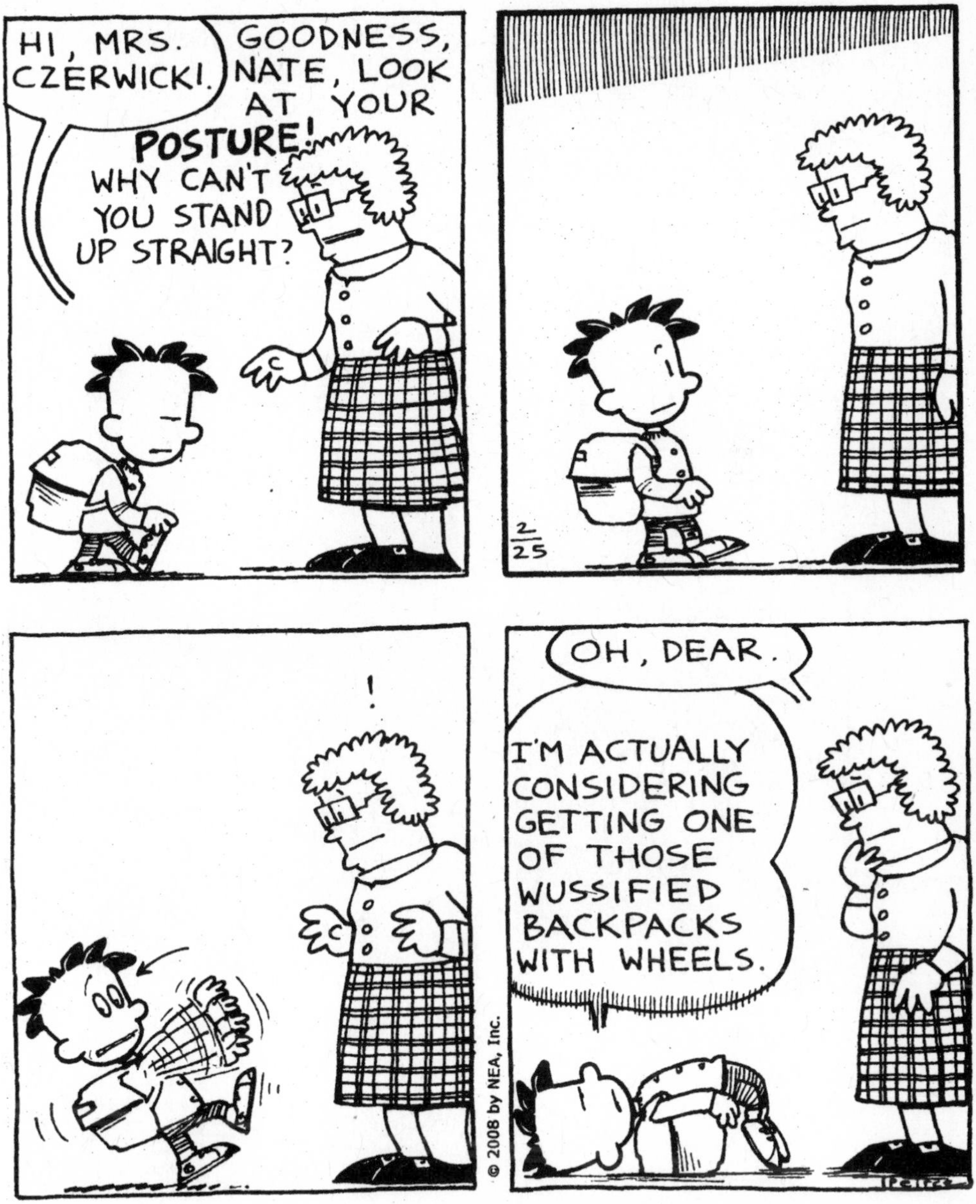
HI, MRS. CZERWICKI.
GOODNESS, NATE, LOOK AT YOUR **POSTURE**! WHY CAN'T YOU STAND UP STRAIGHT?
2/25
!
© 2008 by NEA, Inc.
OH, DEAR.
I'M ACTUALLY CONSIDERING GETTING ONE OF THOSE WUSSIFIED BACKPACKS WITH WHEELS.

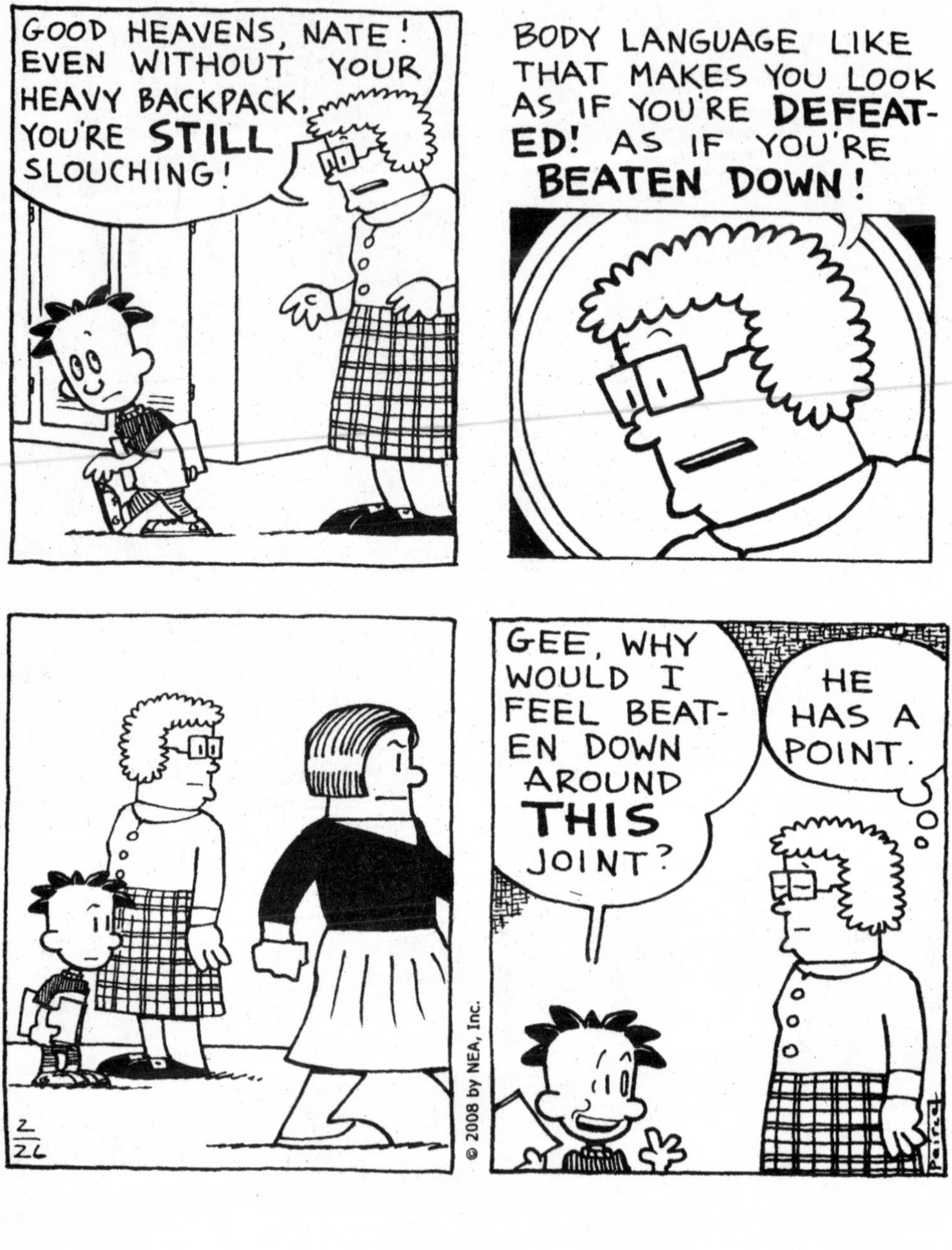
GOOD HEAVENS, NATE! EVEN WITHOUT YOUR HEAVY BACKPACK, YOU'RE **STILL** SLOUCHING!
BODY LANGUAGE LIKE THAT MAKES YOU LOOK AS IF YOU'RE **DEFEATED!** AS IF YOU'RE **BEATEN DOWN!**
GEE, WHY WOULD I FEEL BEATEN DOWN AROUND **THIS** JOINT?
HE HAS A POINT.
2/26
Peirce

© 2008 by NEA, Inc.

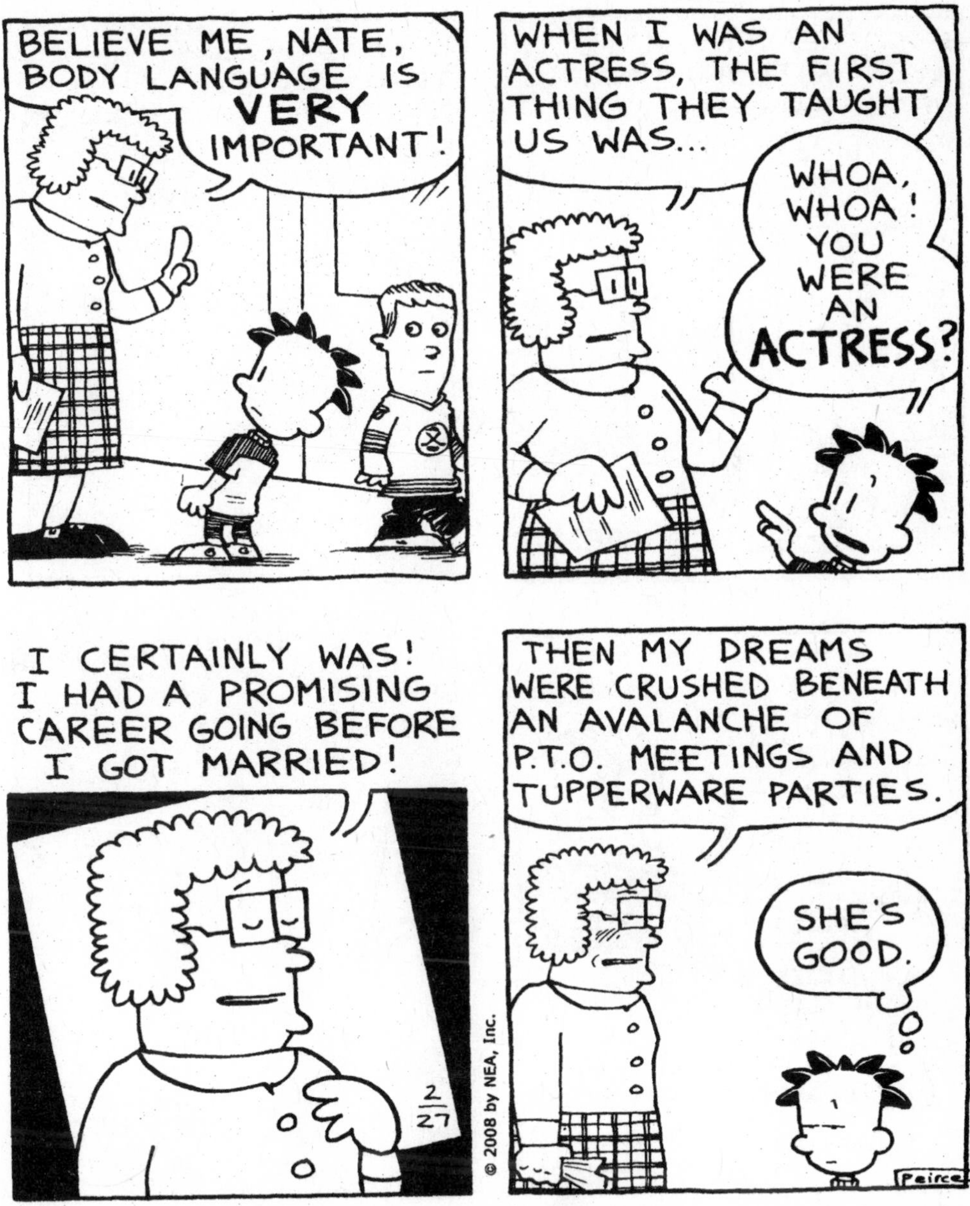
BELIEVE ME, NATE, BODY LANGUAGE IS VERY IMPORTANT!
WHEN I WAS AN ACTRESS, THE FIRST THING THEY TAUGHT US WAS...
WHOA, WHOA! YOU WERE AN ACTRESS?
I CERTAINLY WAS! I HAD A PROMISING CAREER GOING BEFORE I GOT MARRIED!
2/27
© 2008 by NEA, Inc.
THEN MY DREAMS WERE CRUSHED BENEATH AN AVALANCHE OF P.T.O. MEETINGS AND TUPPERWARE PARTIES.
SHE'S GOOD.
Peirce

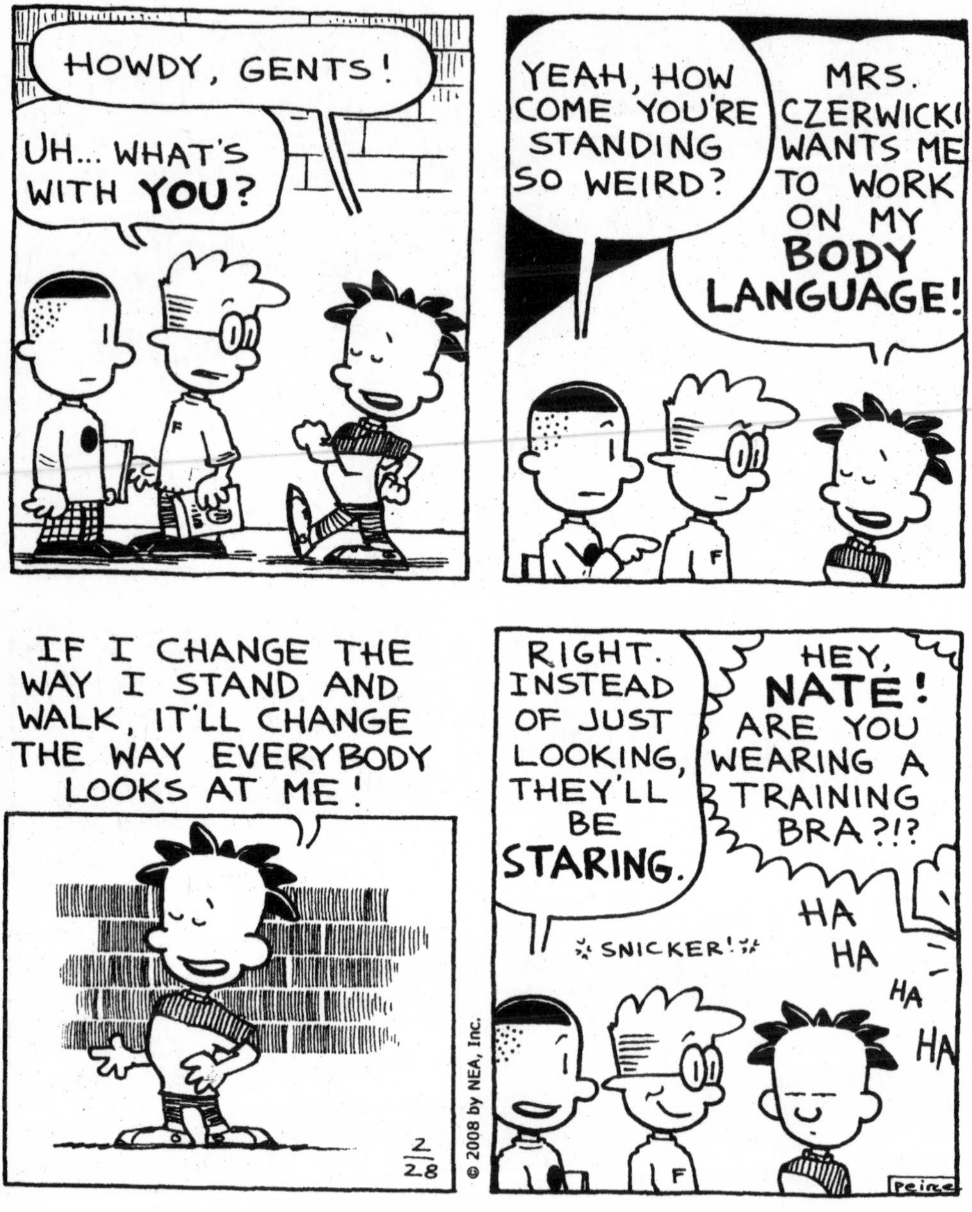
HOWDY, GENTS!
UH... WHAT'S WITH **YOU**?
YEAH, HOW COME YOU'RE STANDING SO WEIRD?
MRS. CZERWICKI WANTS ME TO WORK ON MY **BODY LANGUAGE**!
IF I CHANGE THE WAY I STAND AND WALK, IT'LL CHANGE THE WAY EVERYBODY LOOKS AT ME!
2 28
RIGHT. INSTEAD OF JUST LOOKING, THEY'LL BE **STARING**.
HEY, **NATE**! ARE YOU WEARING A TRAINING BRA?!?
SNICKER!
HA HA HA HA
PEIRCE

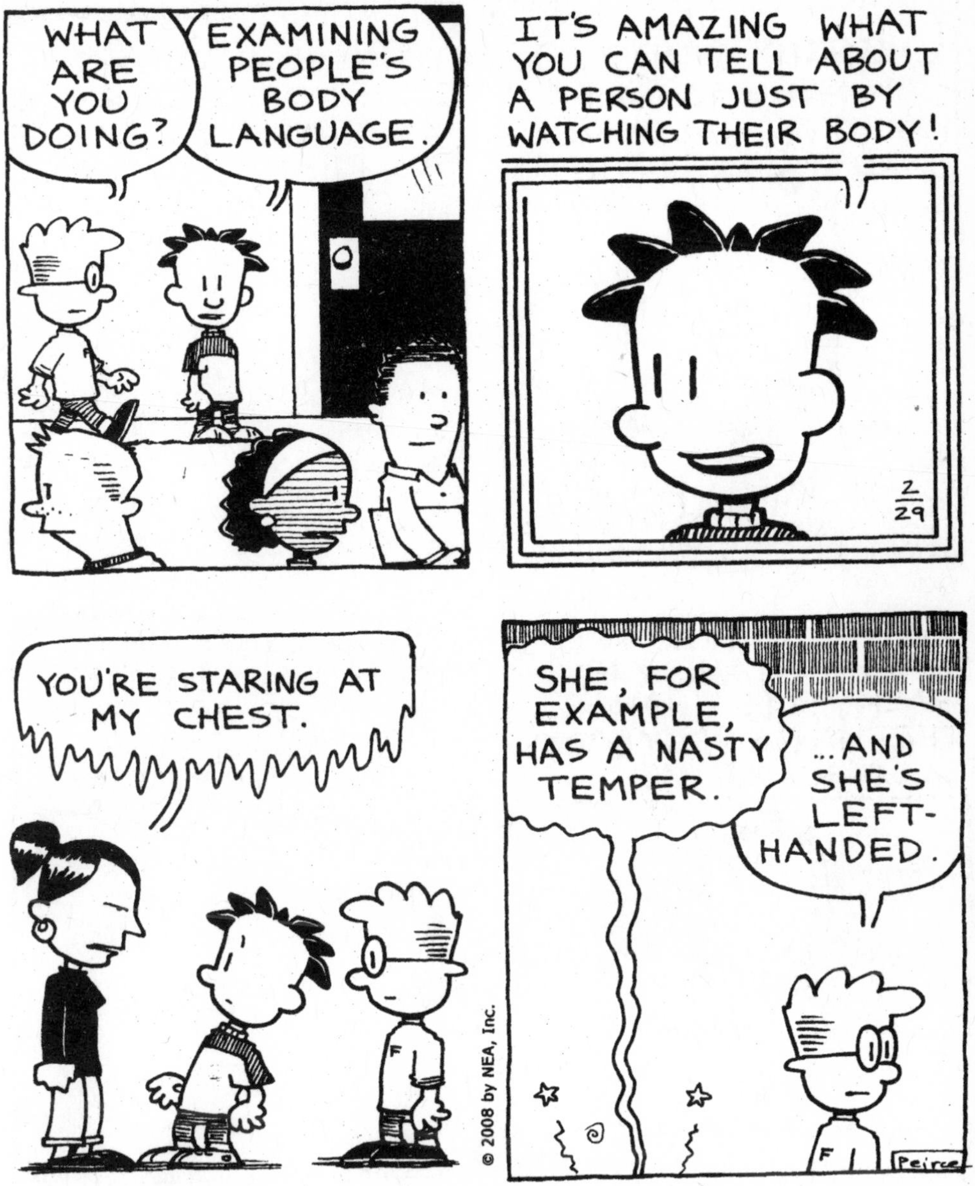
WHAT ARE YOU DOING?
EXAMINING PEOPLE'S BODY LANGUAGE.
IT'S AMAZING WHAT YOU CAN TELL ABOUT A PERSON JUST BY WATCHING THEIR BODY!
2/29
YOU'RE STARING AT MY CHEST.
© 2008 by NEA, Inc.
SHE, FOR EXAMPLE, HAS A NASTY TEMPER.
...AND SHE'S LEFT-HANDED.
Peirce

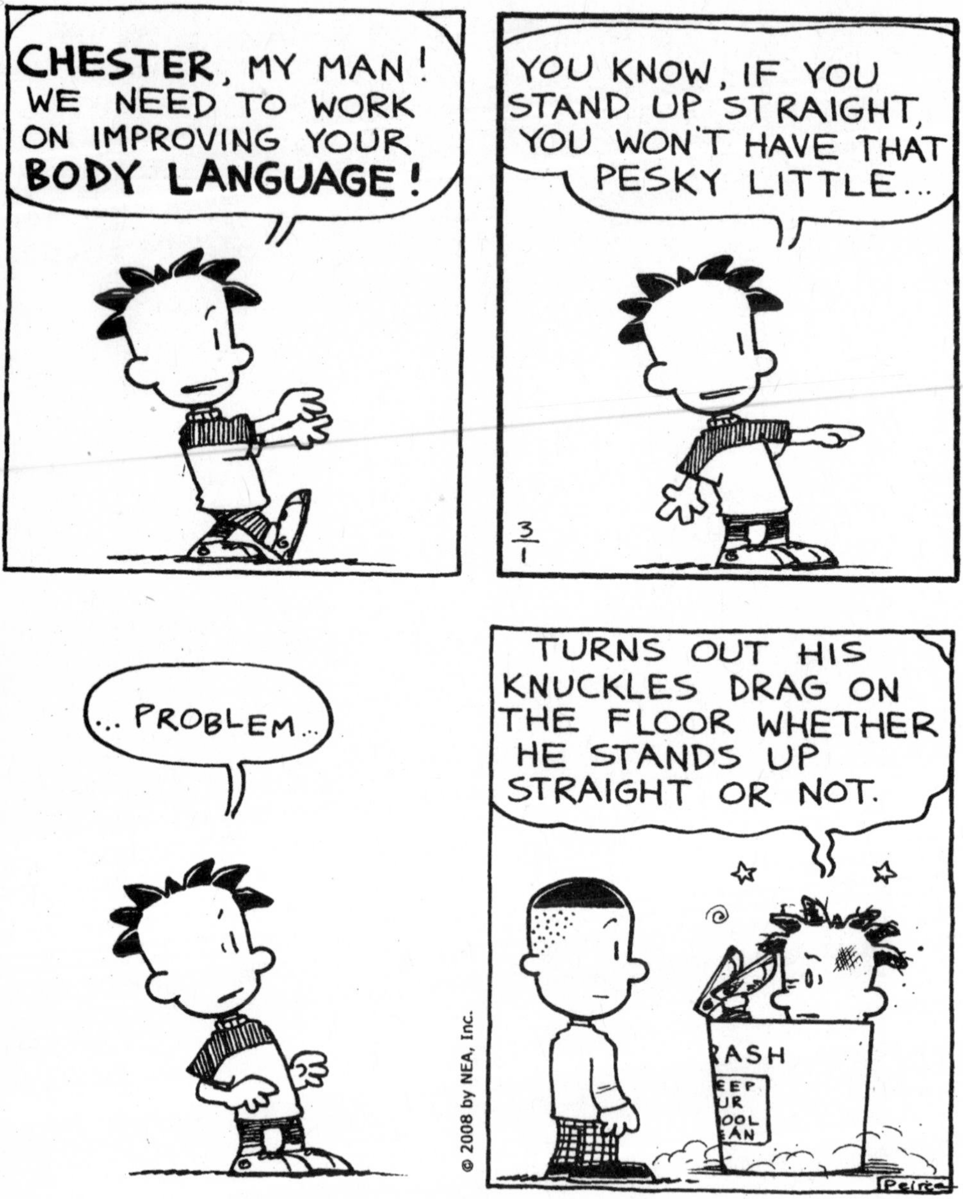
CHESTER, MY MAN! WE NEED TO WORK ON IMPROVING YOUR BODY LANGUAGE!
YOU KNOW, IF YOU STAND UP STRAIGHT, YOU WON'T HAVE THAT PESKY LITTLE...
... PROBLEM...
TURNS OUT HIS KNUCKLES DRAG ON THE FLOOR WHETHER HE STANDS UP STRAIGHT OR NOT.

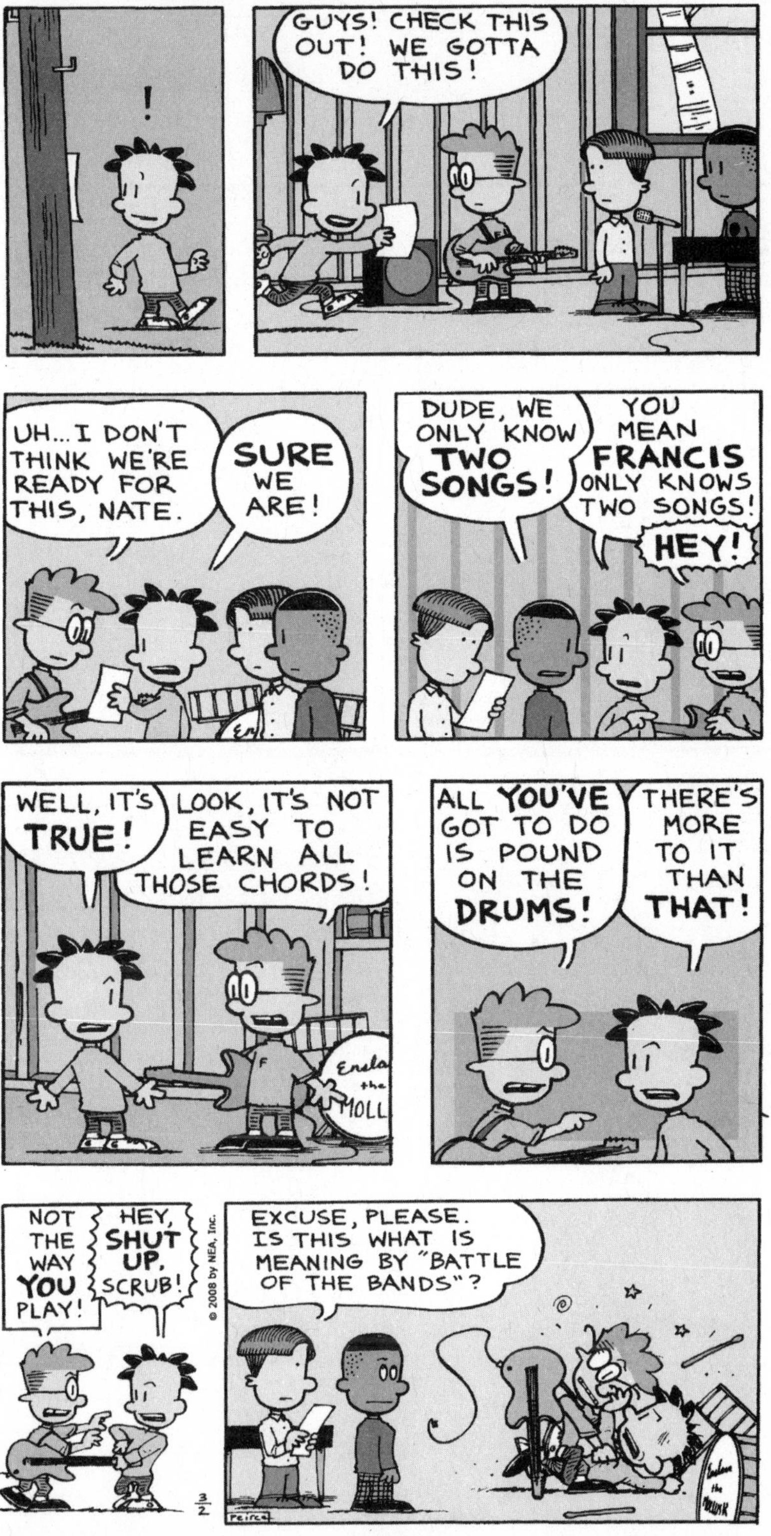
!
GUYS! CHECK THIS OUT! WE GOTTA DO THIS!
UH... I DON'T THINK WE'RE READY FOR THIS, NATE.
SURE WE ARE!
DUDE, WE ONLY KNOW TWO SONGS!
YOU MEAN FRANCIS ONLY KNOWS TWO SONGS!
HEY!
WELL, IT'S TRUE!
LOOK, IT'S NOT EASY TO LEARN ALL THOSE CHORDS!
ALL YOU'VE GOT TO DO IS POUND ON THE DRUMS!
THERE'S MORE TO IT THAN THAT!
NOT THE WAY YOU PLAY!
HEY, SHUT UP, SCRUB!
© 2008 by NEA, Inc.
EXCUSE, PLEASE. IS THIS WHAT IS MEANING BY "BATTLE OF THE BANDS"?
3/2
Peirce

RUBBER BANDS RULE!

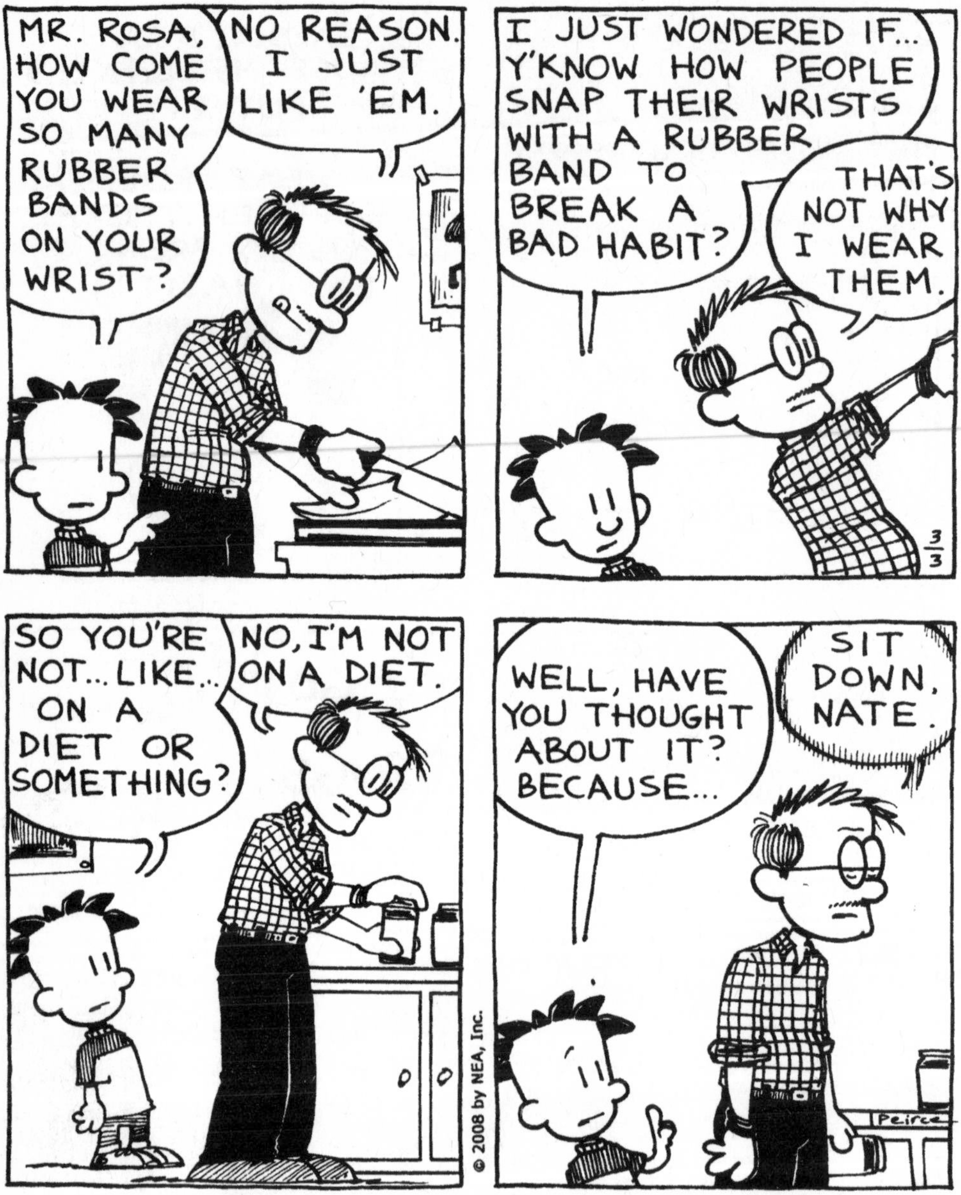
MR. ROSA, HOW COME YOU WEAR SO MANY RUBBER BANDS ON YOUR WRIST?
NO REASON. I JUST LIKE 'EM.
I JUST WONDERED IF... Y'KNOW HOW PEOPLE SNAP THEIR WRISTS WITH A RUBBER BAND TO BREAK A BAD HABIT?
THAT'S NOT WHY I WEAR THEM.
3/3
SO YOU'RE NOT... LIKE... ON A DIET OR SOMETHING?
NO, I'M NOT ON A DIET.
© 2008 by NEA, Inc.
WELL, HAVE YOU THOUGHT ABOUT IT? BECAUSE...
SIT DOWN, NATE.
Peirce

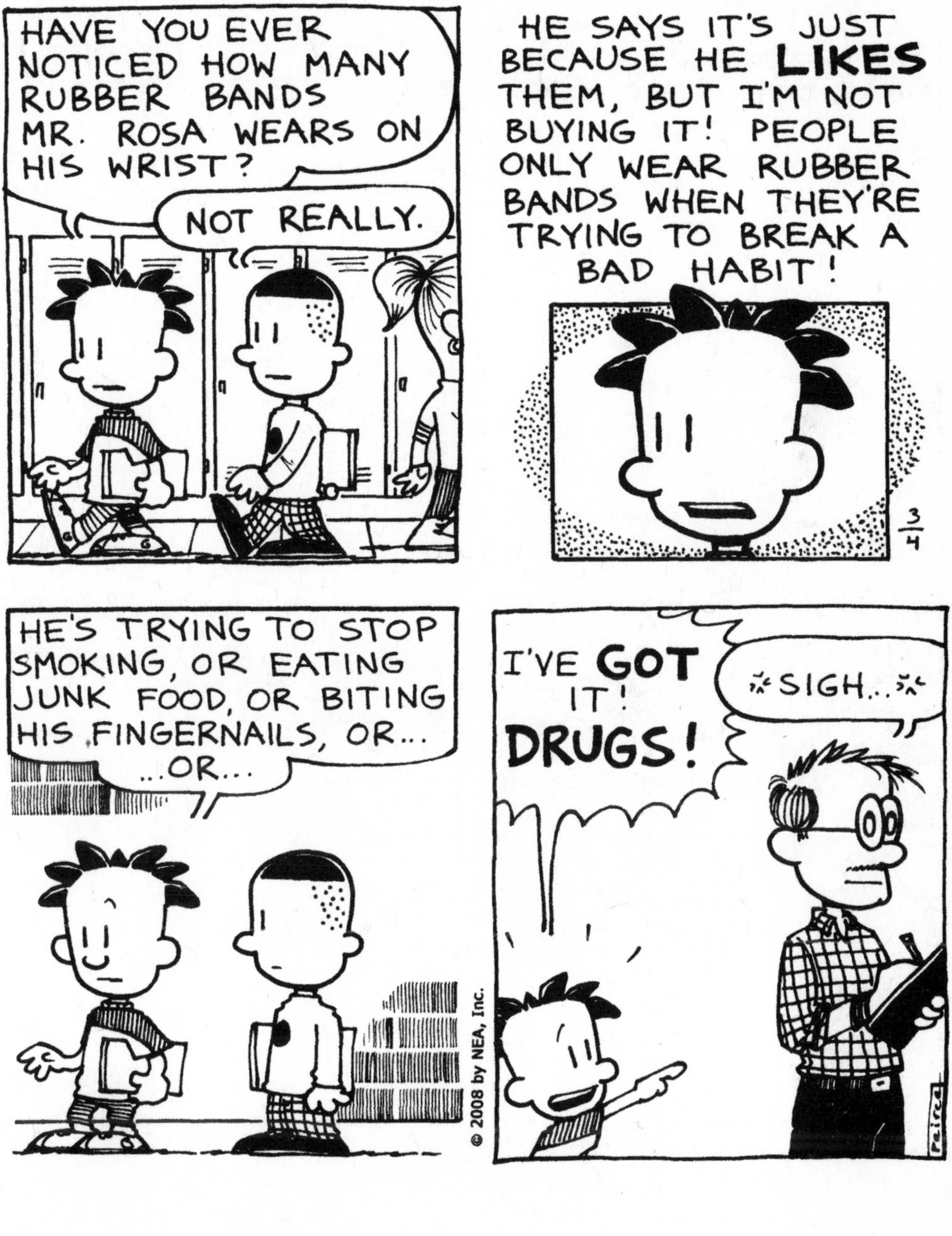
HAVE YOU EVER NOTICED HOW MANY RUBBER BANDS MR. ROSA WEARS ON HIS WRIST?
NOT REALLY.
HE SAYS IT'S JUST BECAUSE HE **LIKES** THEM, BUT I'M NOT BUYING IT! PEOPLE ONLY WEAR RUBBER BANDS WHEN THEY'RE TRYING TO BREAK A BAD HABIT!
3/4
HE'S TRYING TO STOP SMOKING, OR EATING JUNK FOOD, OR BITING HIS FINGERNAILS, OR... ...OR...
© 2008 by NEA, Inc.
I'VE **GOT** IT! **DRUGS!**
SIGH...
Peirce

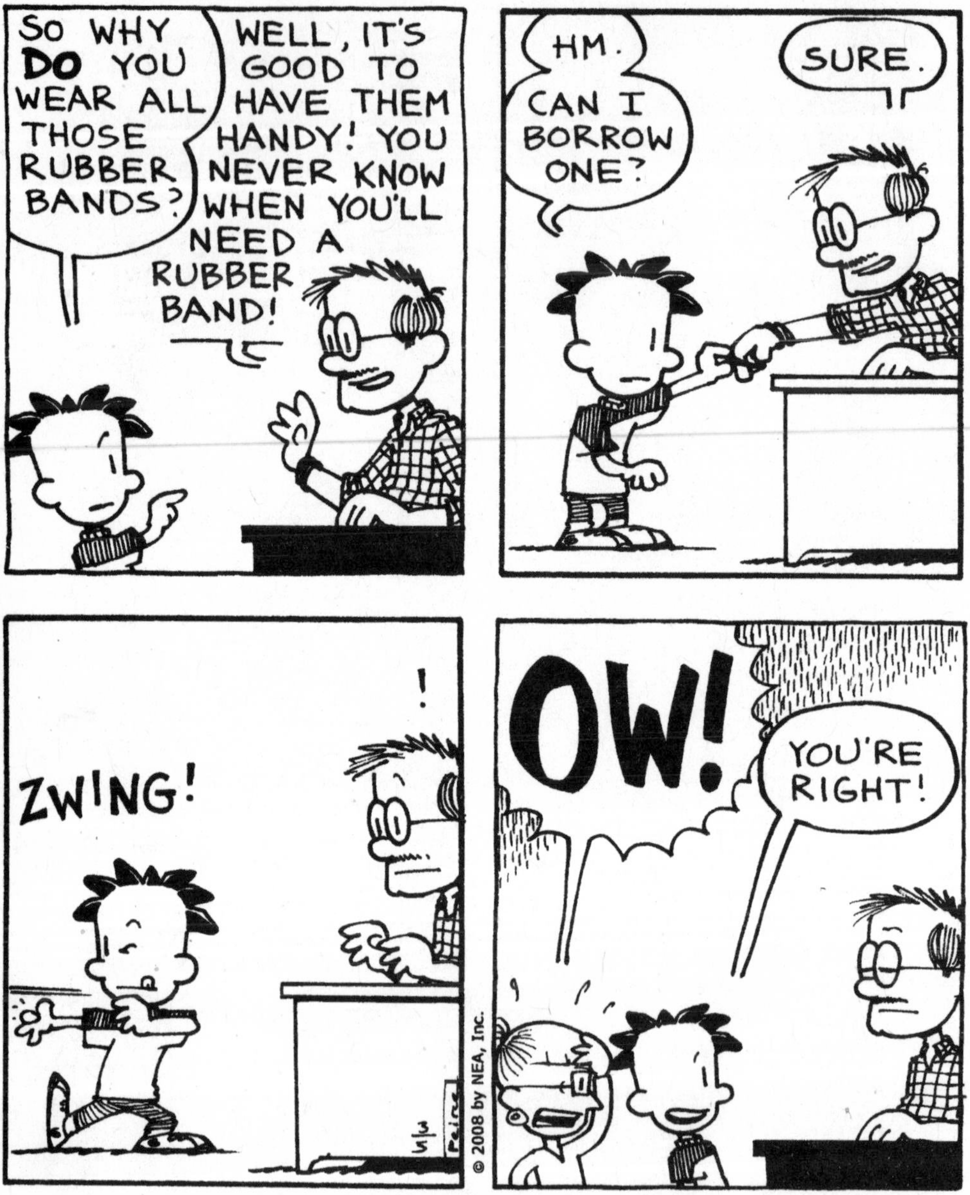
SO WHY DO YOU WEAR ALL THOSE RUBBER BANDS?
WELL, IT'S GOOD TO HAVE THEM HANDY! YOU NEVER KNOW WHEN YOU'LL NEED A RUBBER BAND!
HM.
CAN I BORROW ONE?
SURE.
!
ZWING!
© 2008 by NEA, Inc.
OW!
YOU'RE RIGHT!

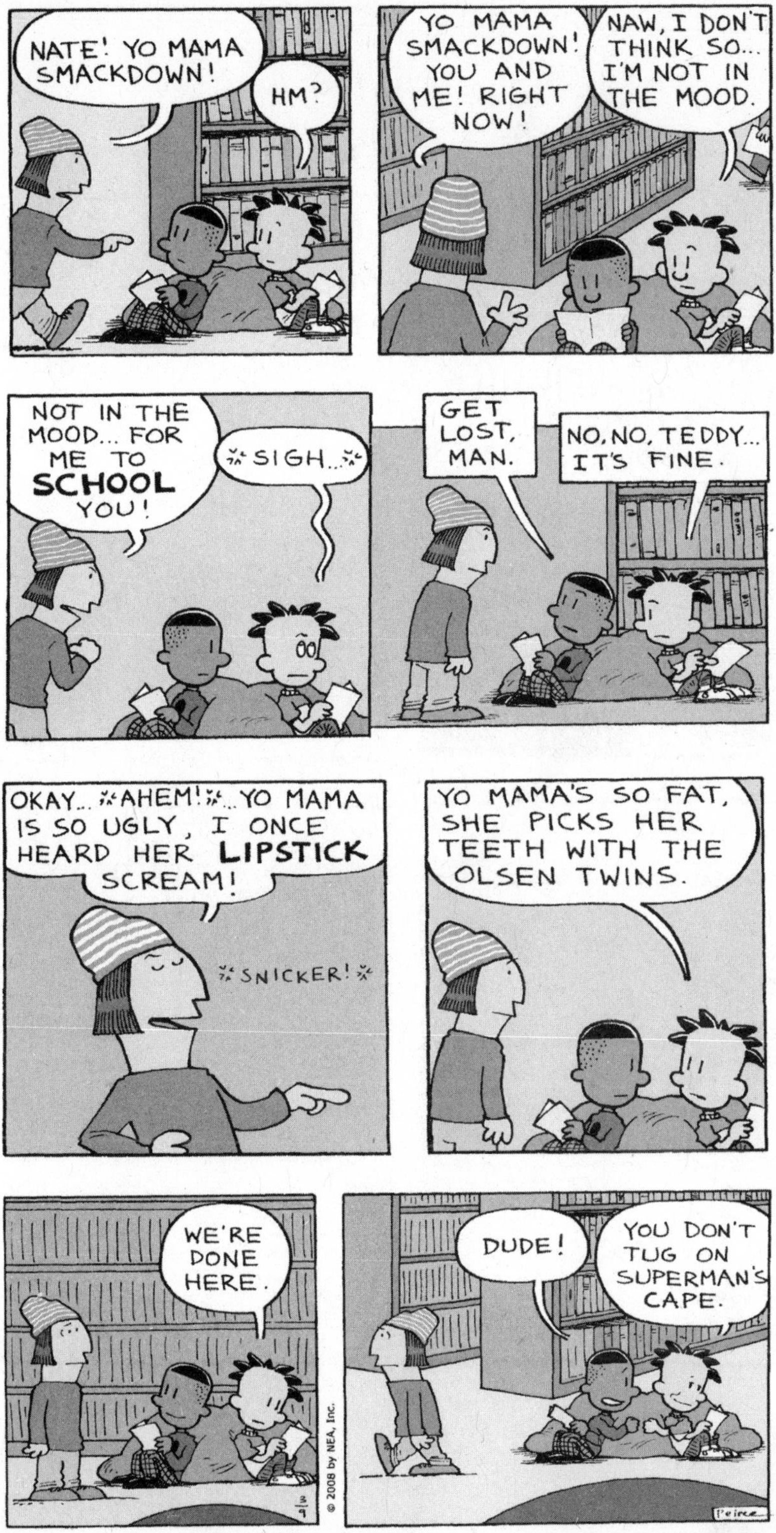
NATE! YO MAMA SMACKDOWN!
HM?
YO MAMA SMACKDOWN! YOU AND ME! RIGHT NOW!
NAW, I DON'T THINK SO... I'M NOT IN THE MOOD.
NOT IN THE MOOD... FOR ME TO **SCHOOL** YOU!
SIGH...
GET LOST, MAN.
NO, NO, TEDDY... IT'S FINE.
OKAY... *AHEM!*... YO MAMA IS SO UGLY, I ONCE HEARD HER **LIPSTICK** SCREAM!
SNICKER!
YO MAMA'S SO FAT, SHE PICKS HER TEETH WITH THE OLSEN TWINS.
WE'RE DONE HERE.
DUDE!
YOU DON'T TUG ON SUPERMAN'S CAPE.
© 2008 by NEA, Inc.
Peirce

ARE YOU COOL ENOUGH?

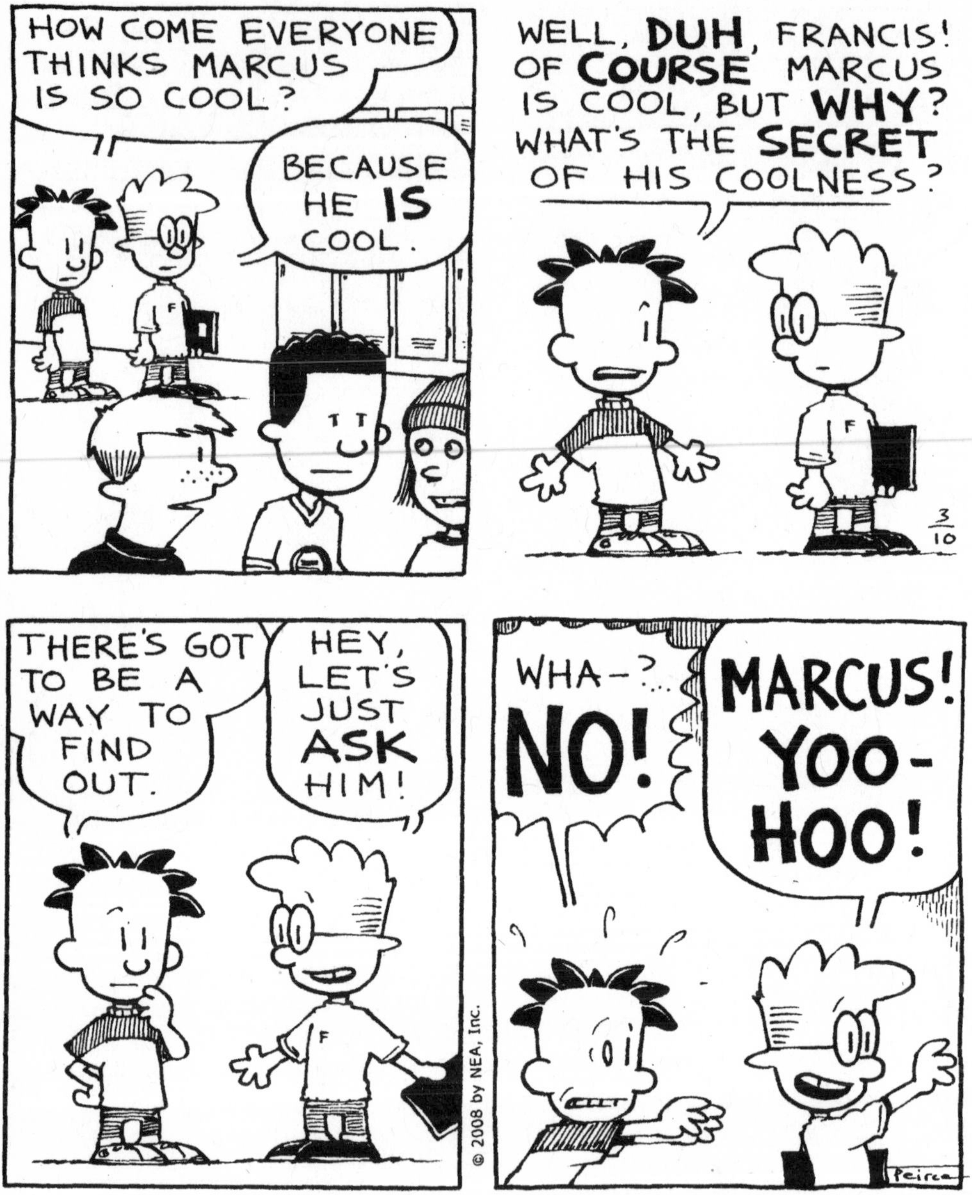
HOW COME EVERYONE THINKS MARCUS IS SO COOL?
BECAUSE HE **IS** COOL.
WELL, **DUH**, FRANCIS! OF **COURSE** MARCUS IS COOL, BUT **WHY**? WHAT'S THE **SECRET** OF HIS COOLNESS?
3/10
THERE'S GOT TO BE A WAY TO FIND OUT.
HEY, LET'S JUST **ASK** HIM!
© 2008 by NEA, Inc.
WHA-?... **NO!**
MARCUS! YOO-HOO!
Peirce

FRANCIS, **NO!** WE CAN'T JUST WALK UP TO MARCUS AND ASK HIM WHY HE'S **COOL!**

WHY NOT?

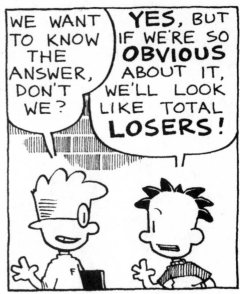

WE WANT TO KNOW THE ANSWER, DON'T WE?

YES, BUT IF WE'RE SO **OBVIOUS** ABOUT IT, WE'LL LOOK LIKE TOTAL **LOSERS!**

IF WE WANT TO FIND OUT MARCUS' SECRET OF COOLNESS, WE'VE GOT TO BE... TO BE...

...COOL ABOUT IT?

IT'S SO STINKIN' IRONIC.

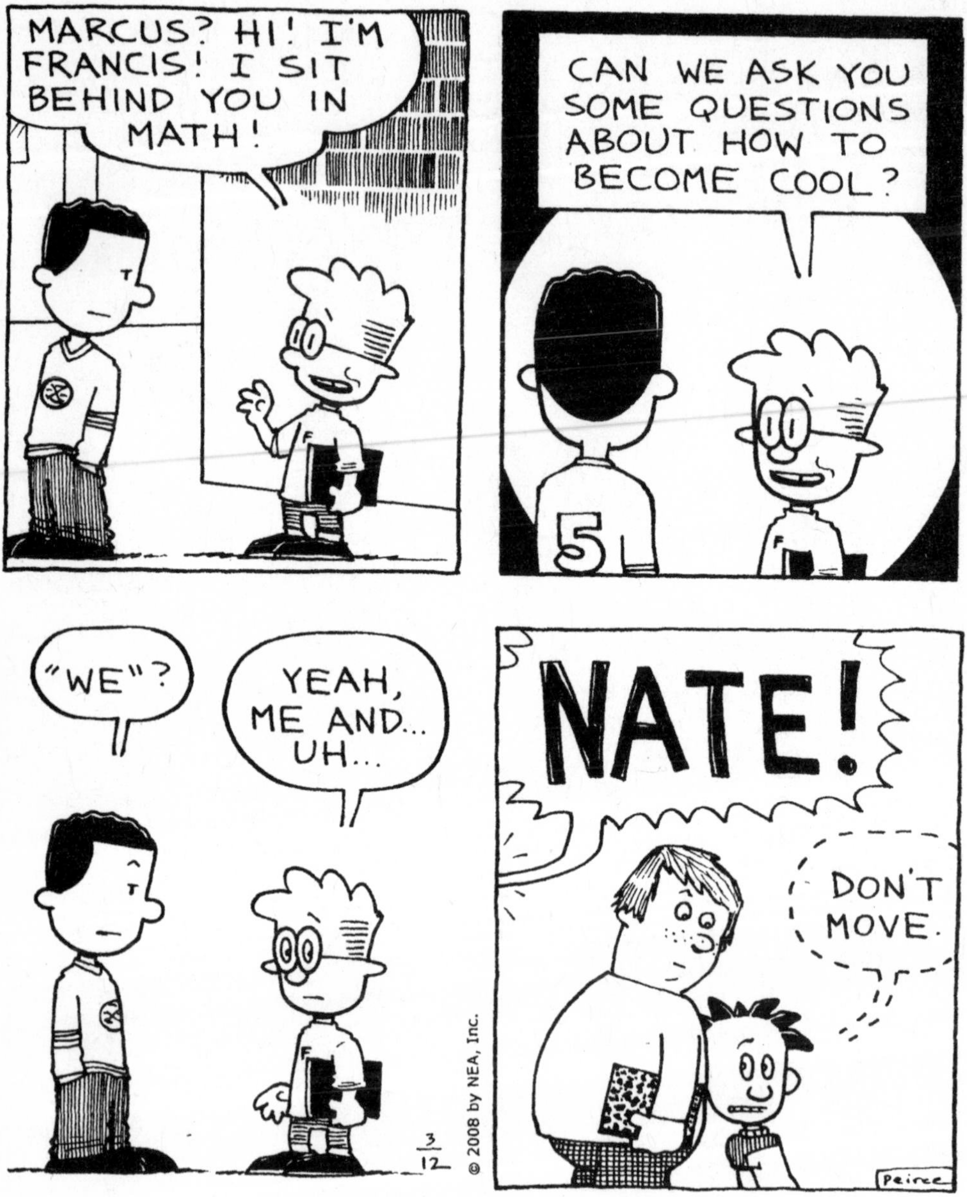
MARCUS? HI! I'M FRANCIS! I SIT BEHIND YOU IN MATH!
CAN WE ASK YOU SOME QUESTIONS ABOUT HOW TO BECOME COOL?
5
"WE"?
YEAH, ME AND... UH...
3/12
© 2008 by NEA, Inc.
NATE!
DON'T MOVE.
Peirce

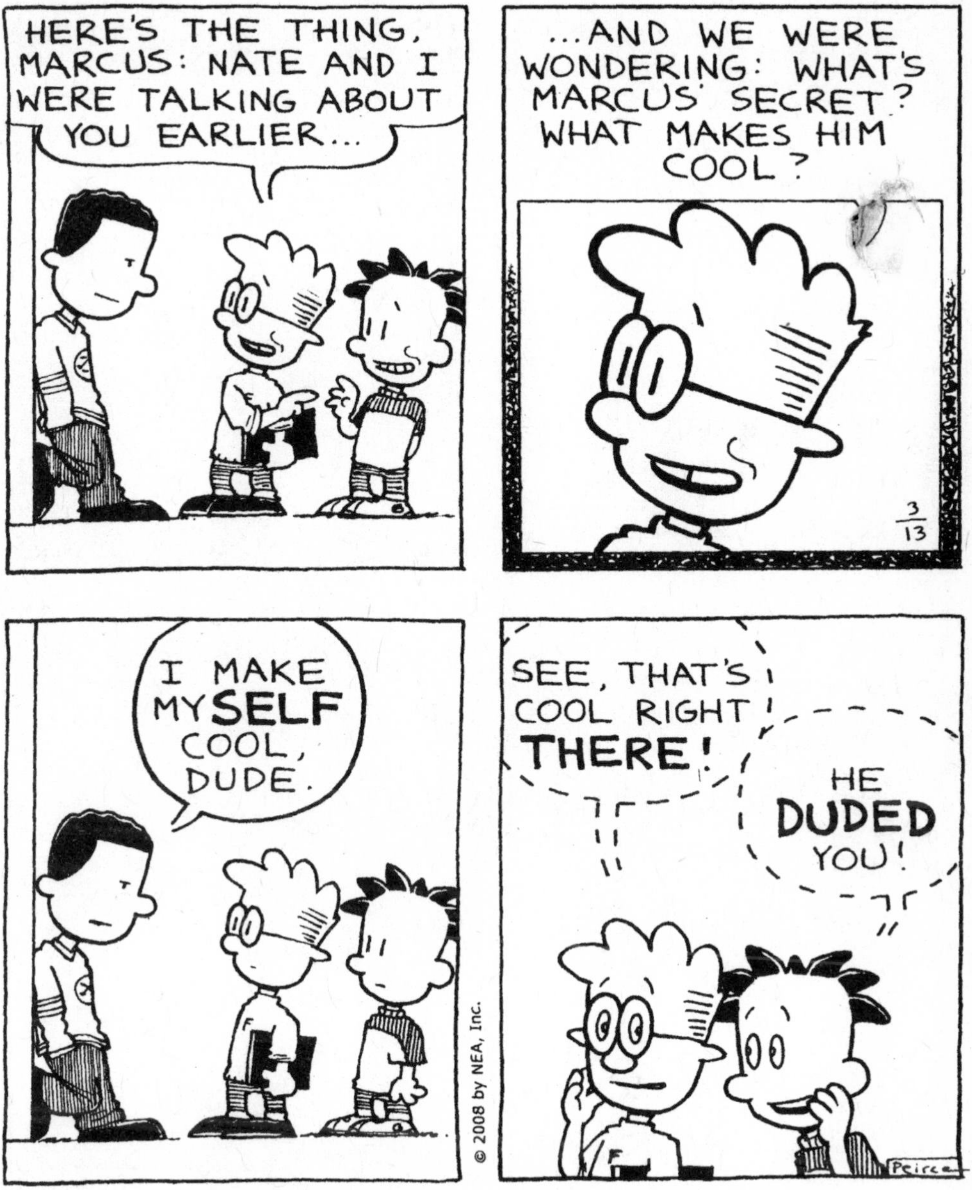
HERE'S THE THING, MARCUS: NATE AND I WERE TALKING ABOUT YOU EARLIER...
...AND WE WERE WONDERING: WHAT'S MARCUS' SECRET? WHAT MAKES HIM COOL?
I MAKE MY**SELF** COOL, DUDE.
SEE, THAT'S COOL RIGHT **THERE**!
HE **DUDED** YOU!

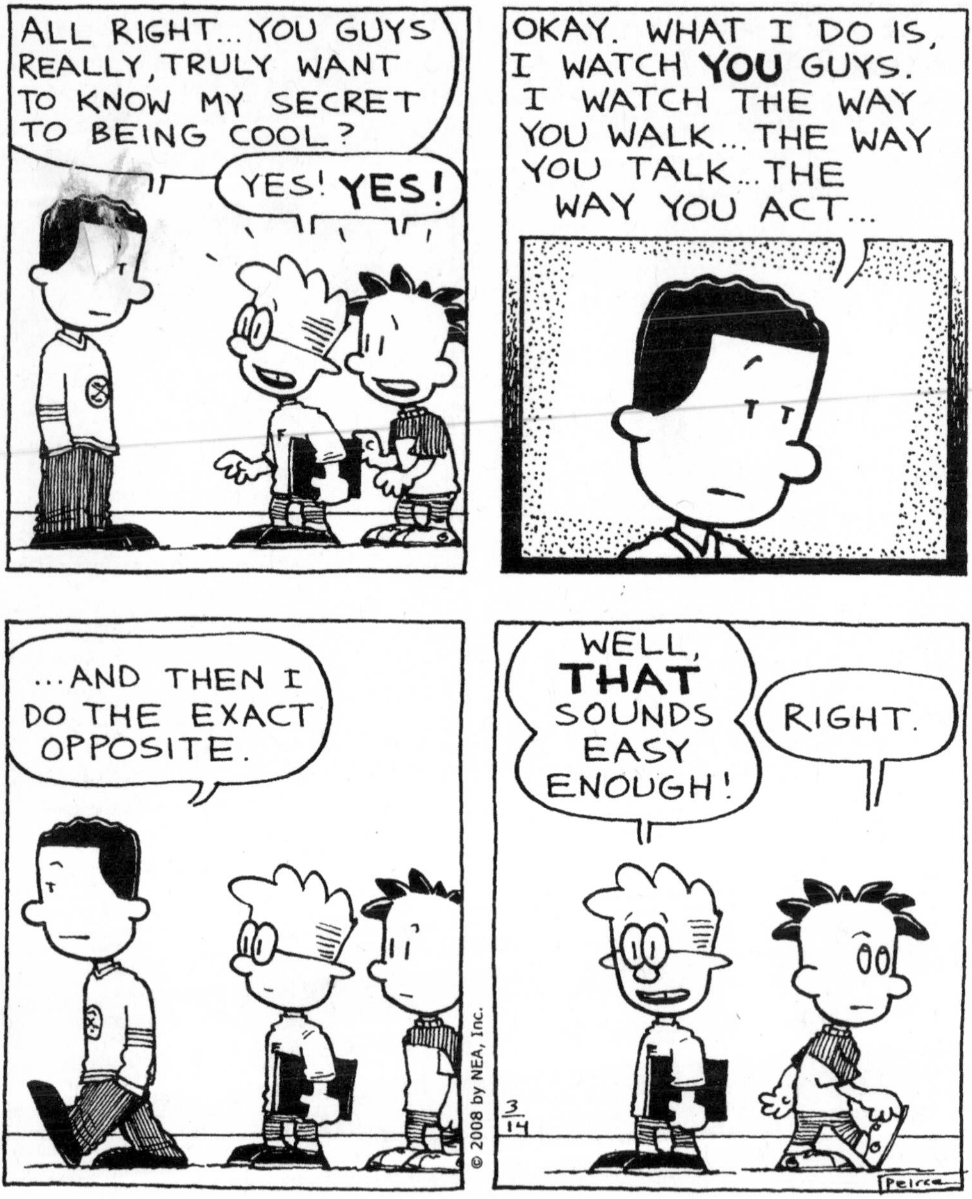
ALL RIGHT... YOU GUYS REALLY, TRULY WANT TO KNOW MY SECRET TO BEING COOL?
YES! **YES!**
OKAY. WHAT I DO IS, I WATCH **YOU** GUYS. I WATCH THE WAY YOU WALK... THE WAY YOU TALK... THE WAY YOU ACT...
...AND THEN I DO THE EXACT OPPOSITE.
WELL, **THAT** SOUNDS EASY ENOUGH!
RIGHT.
© 2008 by NEA, Inc.
3/14
Peirce

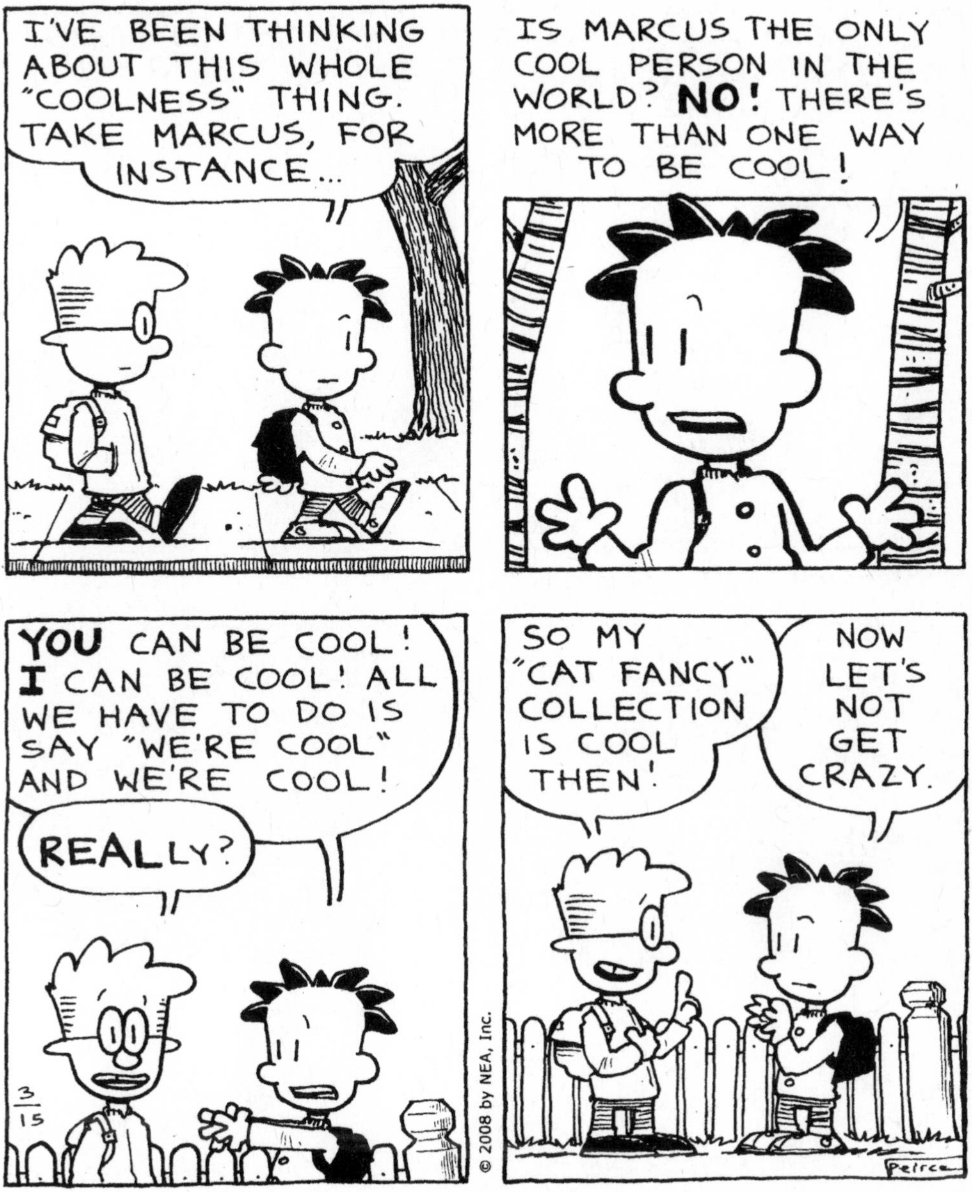

I'VE BEEN THINKING ABOUT THIS WHOLE "COOLNESS" THING. TAKE MARCUS, FOR INSTANCE...
IS MARCUS THE ONLY COOL PERSON IN THE WORLD? NO! THERE'S MORE THAN ONE WAY TO BE COOL!
YOU CAN BE COOL! I CAN BE COOL! ALL WE HAVE TO DO IS SAY "WE'RE COOL" AND WE'RE COOL!
REALLY?
3/15
© 2008 by NEA, Inc.
SO MY "CAT FANCY" COLLECTION IS COOL THEN!
NOW LET'S NOT GET CRAZY.
Peirce

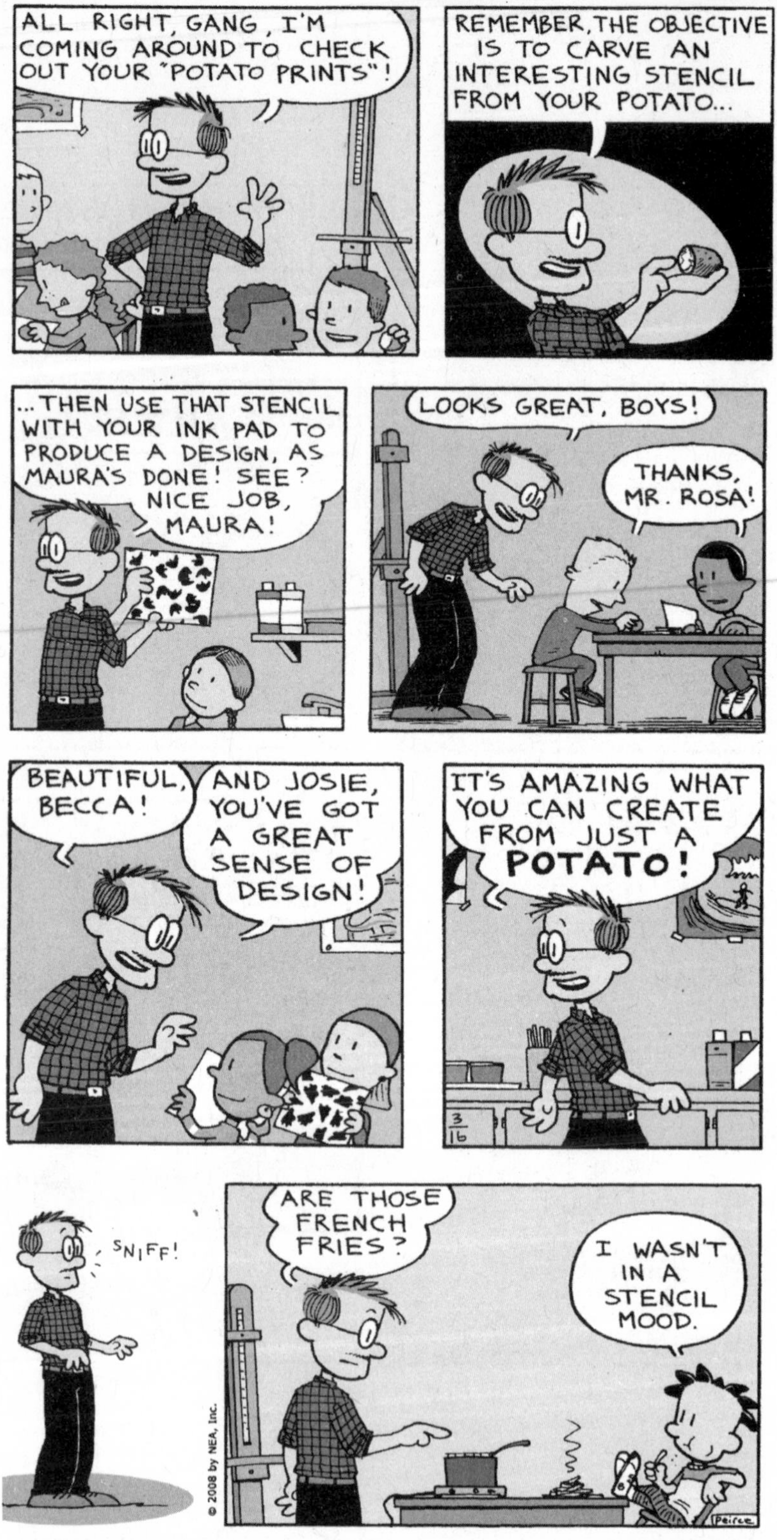
ALL RIGHT, GANG, I'M COMING AROUND TO CHECK OUT YOUR "POTATO PRINTS"!
REMEMBER, THE OBJECTIVE IS TO CARVE AN INTERESTING STENCIL FROM YOUR POTATO...
...THEN USE THAT STENCIL WITH YOUR INK PAD TO PRODUCE A DESIGN, AS MAURA'S DONE! SEE?
NICE JOB, MAURA!
LOOKS GREAT, BOYS!
THANKS, MR. ROSA!
BEAUTIFUL, BECCA!
AND JOSIE, YOU'VE GOT A GREAT SENSE OF DESIGN!
IT'S AMAZING WHAT YOU CAN CREATE FROM JUST A POTATO!
3/16
SNIFF!
ARE THOSE FRENCH FRIES?
I WASN'T IN A STENCIL MOOD.
© 2008 by NEA, Inc.
Peirce

THE PERFECT DATE

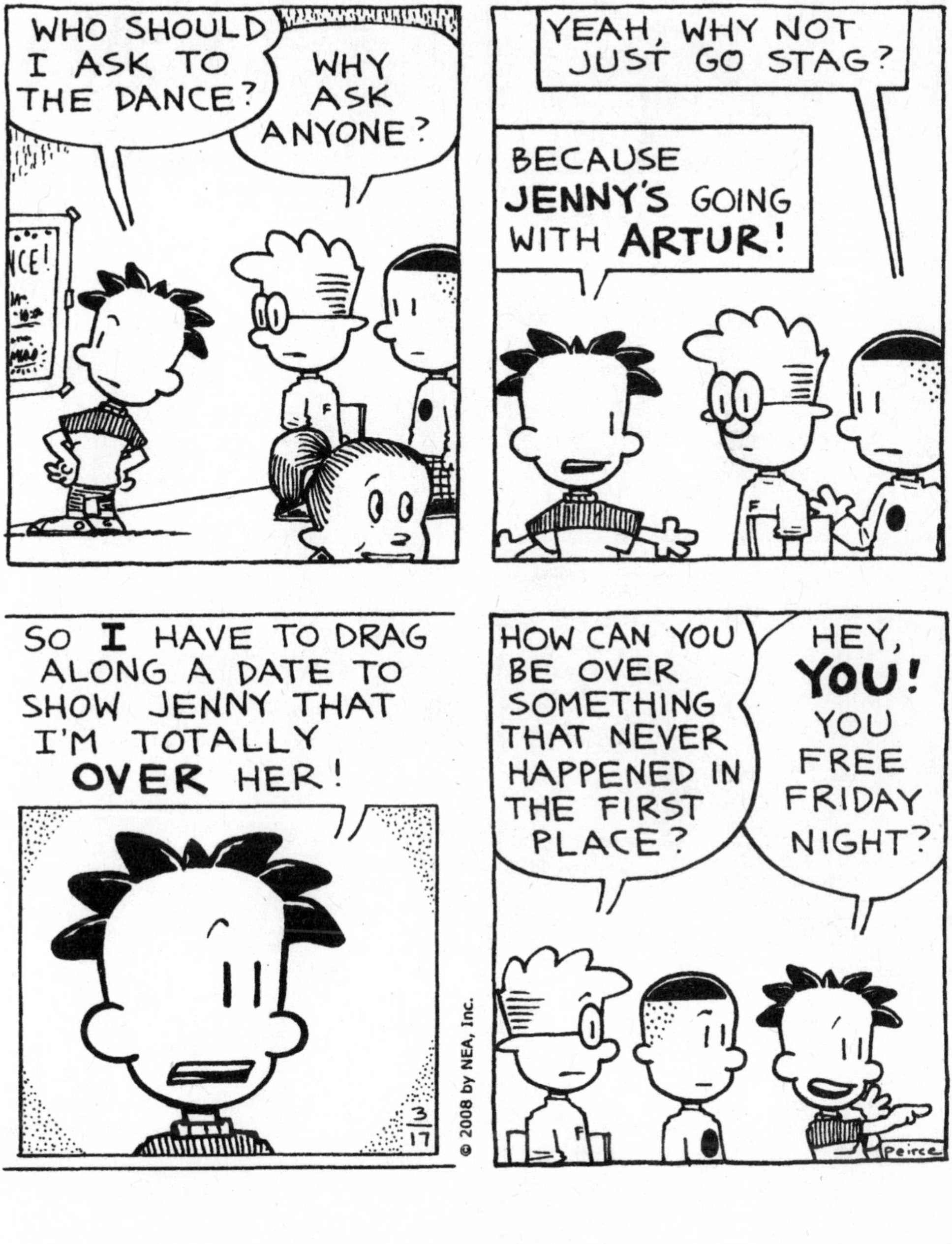
WHO SHOULD I ASK TO THE DANCE?
WHY ASK ANYONE?
YEAH, WHY NOT JUST GO STAG?
BECAUSE JENNY'S GOING WITH ARTUR!
SO I HAVE TO DRAG ALONG A DATE TO SHOW JENNY THAT I'M TOTALLY OVER HER!
3/17
HOW CAN YOU BE OVER SOMETHING THAT NEVER HAPPENED IN THE FIRST PLACE?
HEY, YOU! YOU FREE FRIDAY NIGHT?
PEIRCE

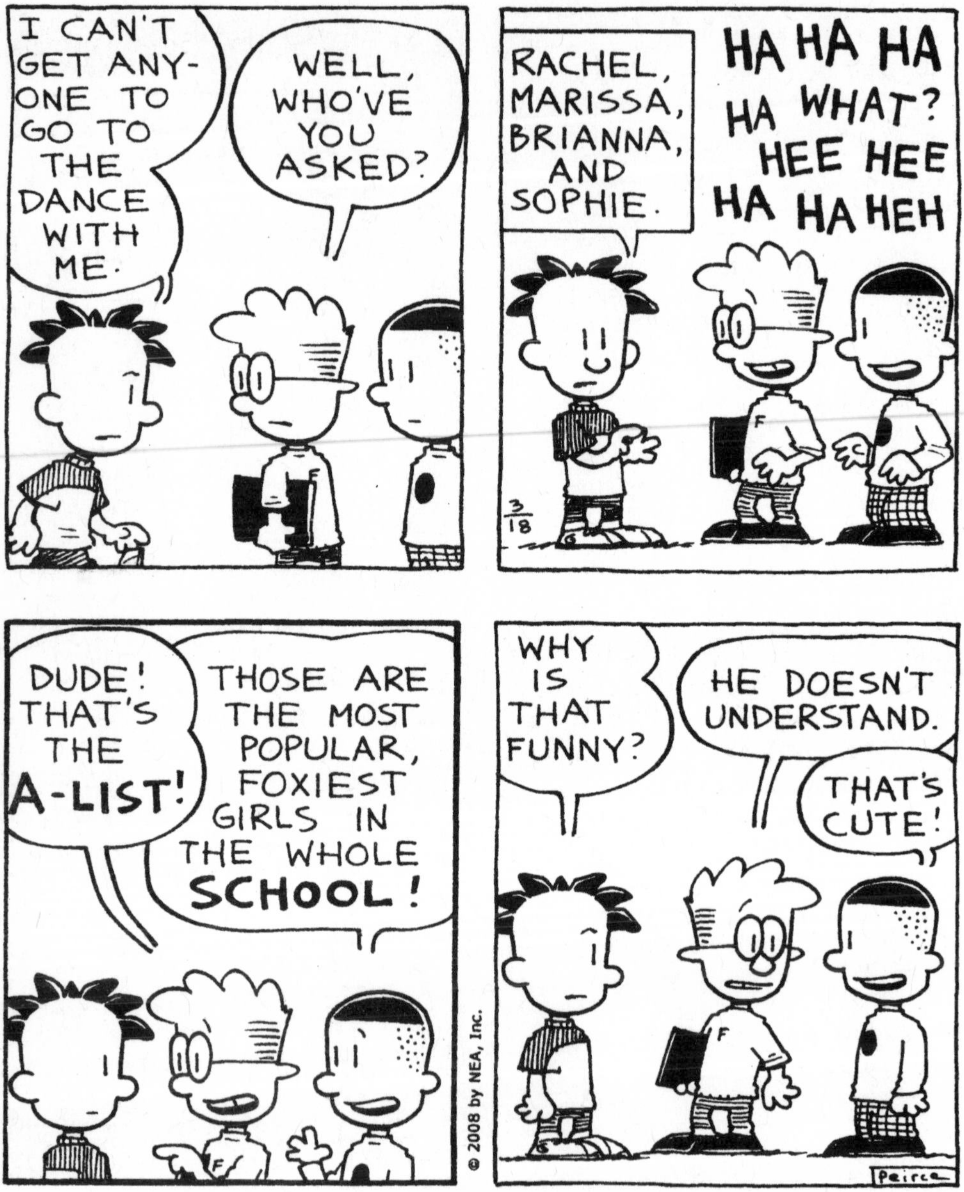
I CAN'T GET ANYONE TO GO TO THE DANCE WITH ME.
WELL, WHO'VE YOU ASKED?
RACHEL, MARISSA, BRIANNA, AND SOPHIE.
HA HA HA HA WHAT? HEE HEE HA HA HEH
3/18
DUDE! THAT'S THE A-LIST!
THOSE ARE THE MOST POPULAR, FOXIEST GIRLS IN THE WHOLE SCHOOL!
© 2008 by NEA, Inc.
WHY IS THAT FUNNY?
HE DOESN'T UNDERSTAND.
THAT'S CUTE!
Peirce

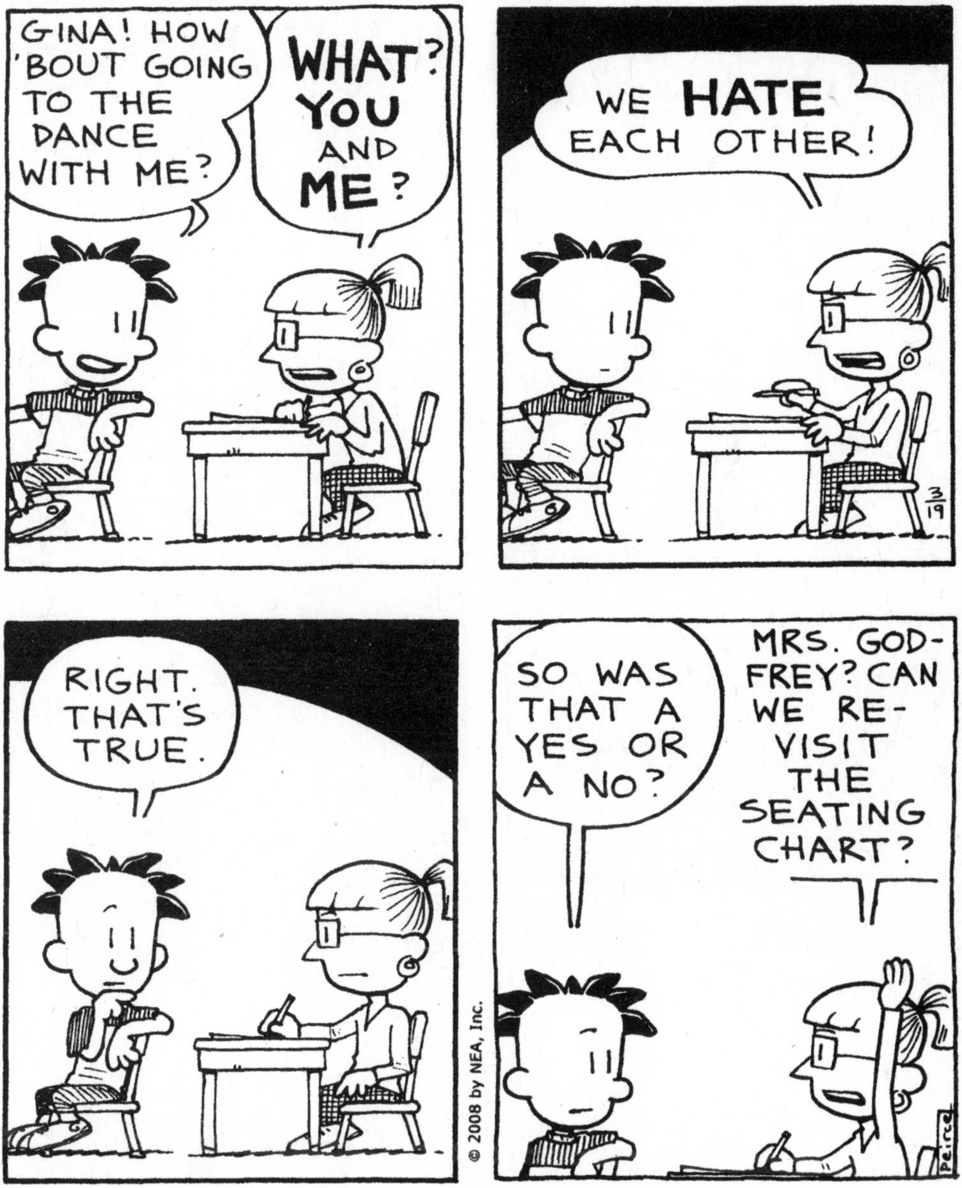
GINA! HOW 'BOUT GOING TO THE DANCE WITH ME?
WHAT? YOU AND ME?
WE HATE EACH OTHER!
3/19
RIGHT. THAT'S TRUE.
© 2008 by NEA, Inc.
SO WAS THAT A YES OR A NO?
MRS. GODFREY? CAN WE REVISIT THE SEATING CHART?
Peirce

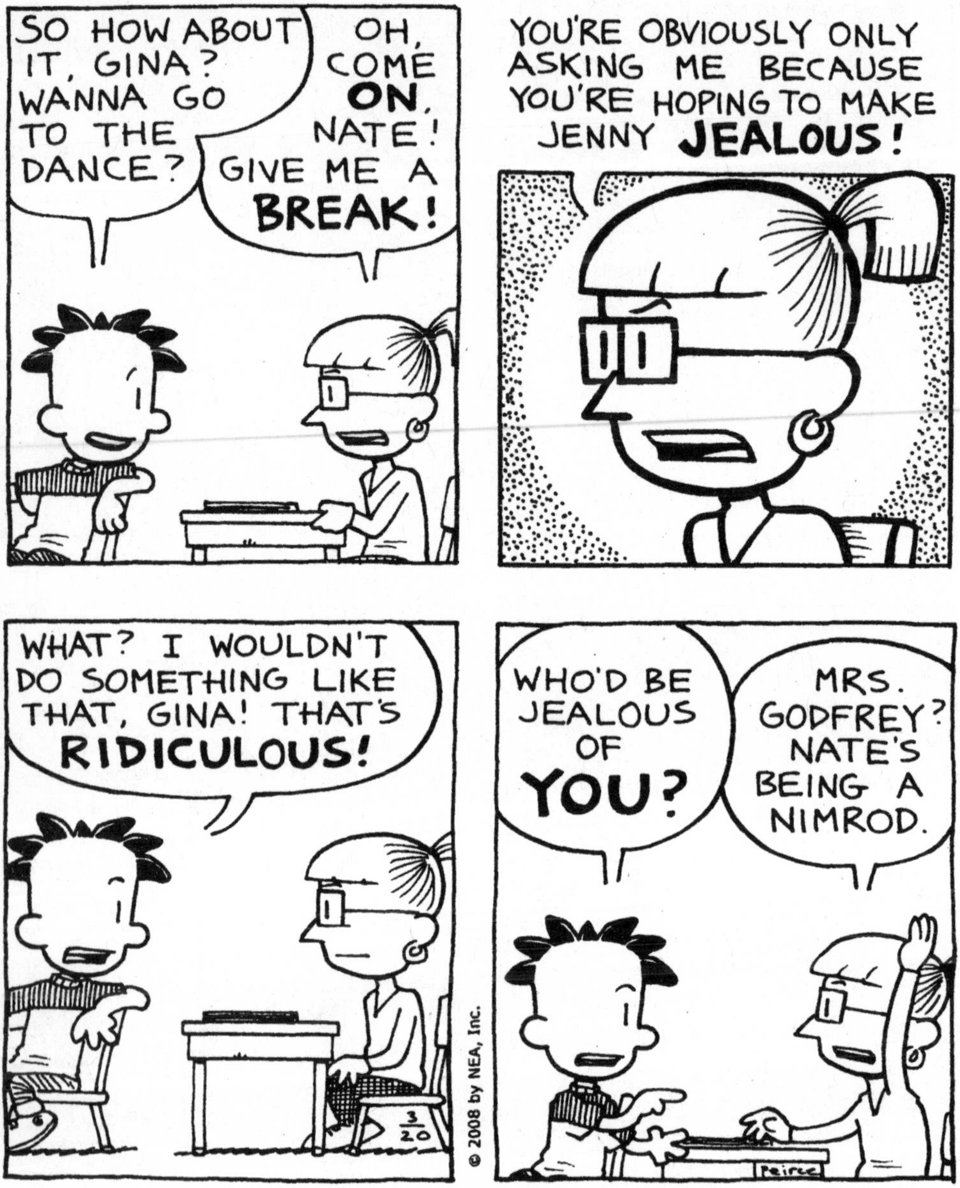
SO HOW ABOUT IT, GINA? WANNA GO TO THE DANCE?
OH, COME **ON**, NATE! GIVE ME A **BREAK!**
YOU'RE OBVIOUSLY ONLY ASKING ME BECAUSE YOU'RE HOPING TO MAKE JENNY **JEALOUS!**
WHAT? I WOULDN'T DO SOMETHING LIKE THAT, GINA! THAT'S **RIDICULOUS!**
3/20
© 2008 by NEA, Inc.
WHO'D BE JEALOUS OF **YOU?**
MRS. GODFREY? NATE'S BEING A NIMROD.
Peirce

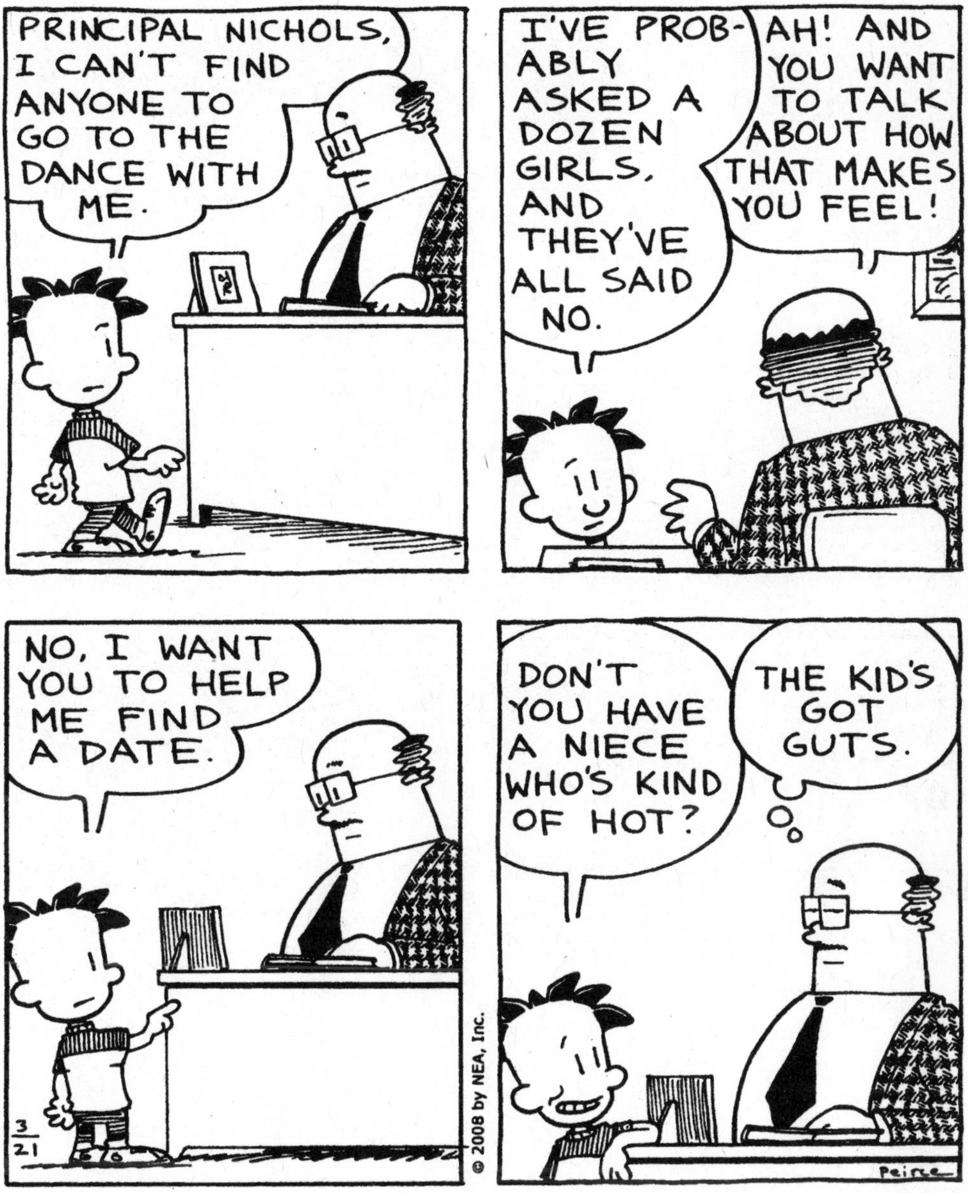
PRINCIPAL NICHOLS, I CAN'T FIND ANYONE TO GO TO THE DANCE WITH ME.
I'VE PROBABLY ASKED A DOZEN GIRLS, AND THEY'VE ALL SAID NO.
AH! AND YOU WANT TO TALK ABOUT HOW THAT MAKES YOU FEEL!
NO, I WANT YOU TO HELP ME FIND A DATE.
3/21
© 2008 by NEA, Inc.
DON'T YOU HAVE A NIECE WHO'S KIND OF HOT?
THE KID'S GOT GUTS.
Peirce

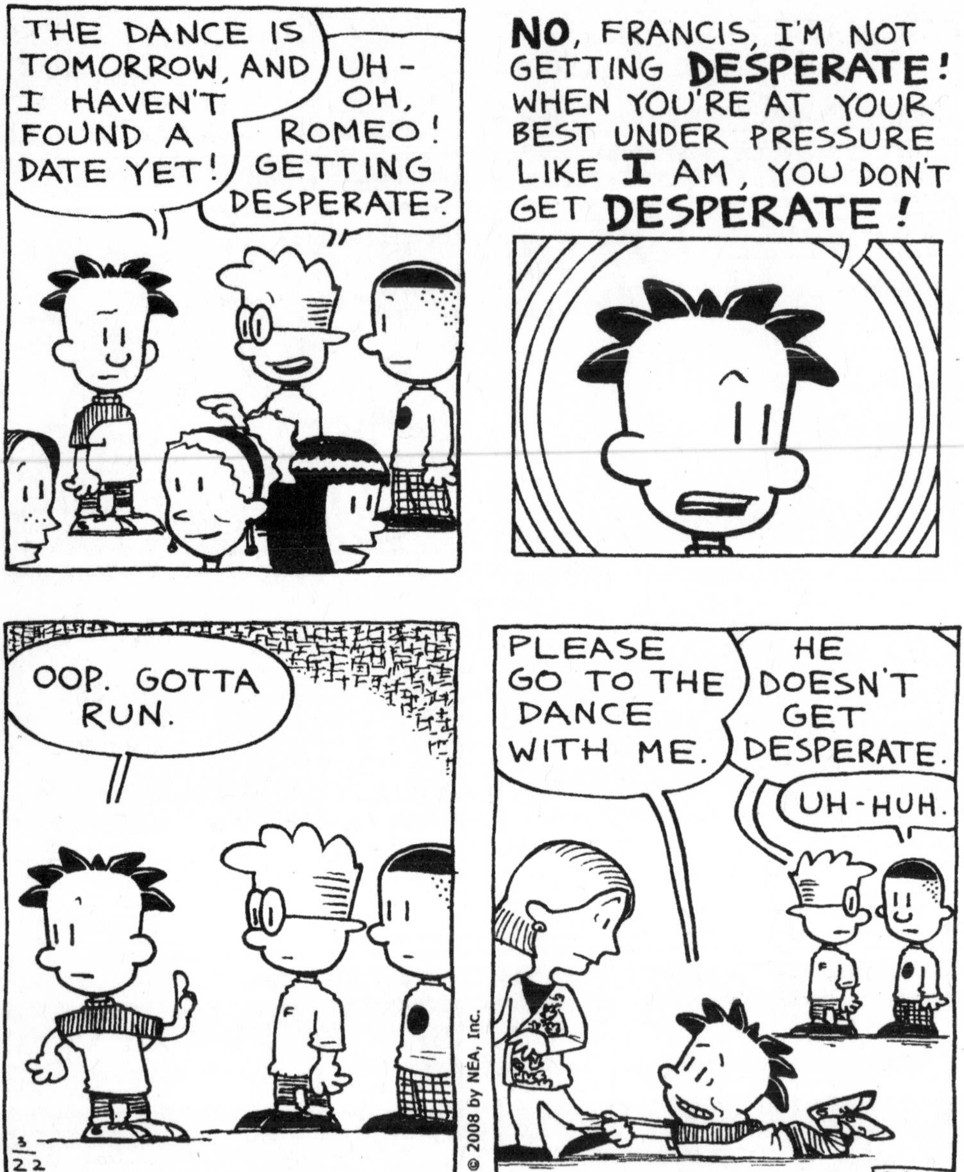
THE DANCE IS TOMORROW, AND I HAVEN'T FOUND A DATE YET!
UH-OH, ROMEO! GETTING DESPERATE?
NO, FRANCIS, I'M NOT GETTING DESPERATE! WHEN YOU'RE AT YOUR BEST UNDER PRESSURE LIKE I AM, YOU DON'T GET DESPERATE!
OOP. GOTTA RUN.
3/22
© 2008 by NEA, Inc.
PLEASE GO TO THE DANCE WITH ME.
HE DOESN'T GET DESPERATE.
UH-HUH.
Peirce

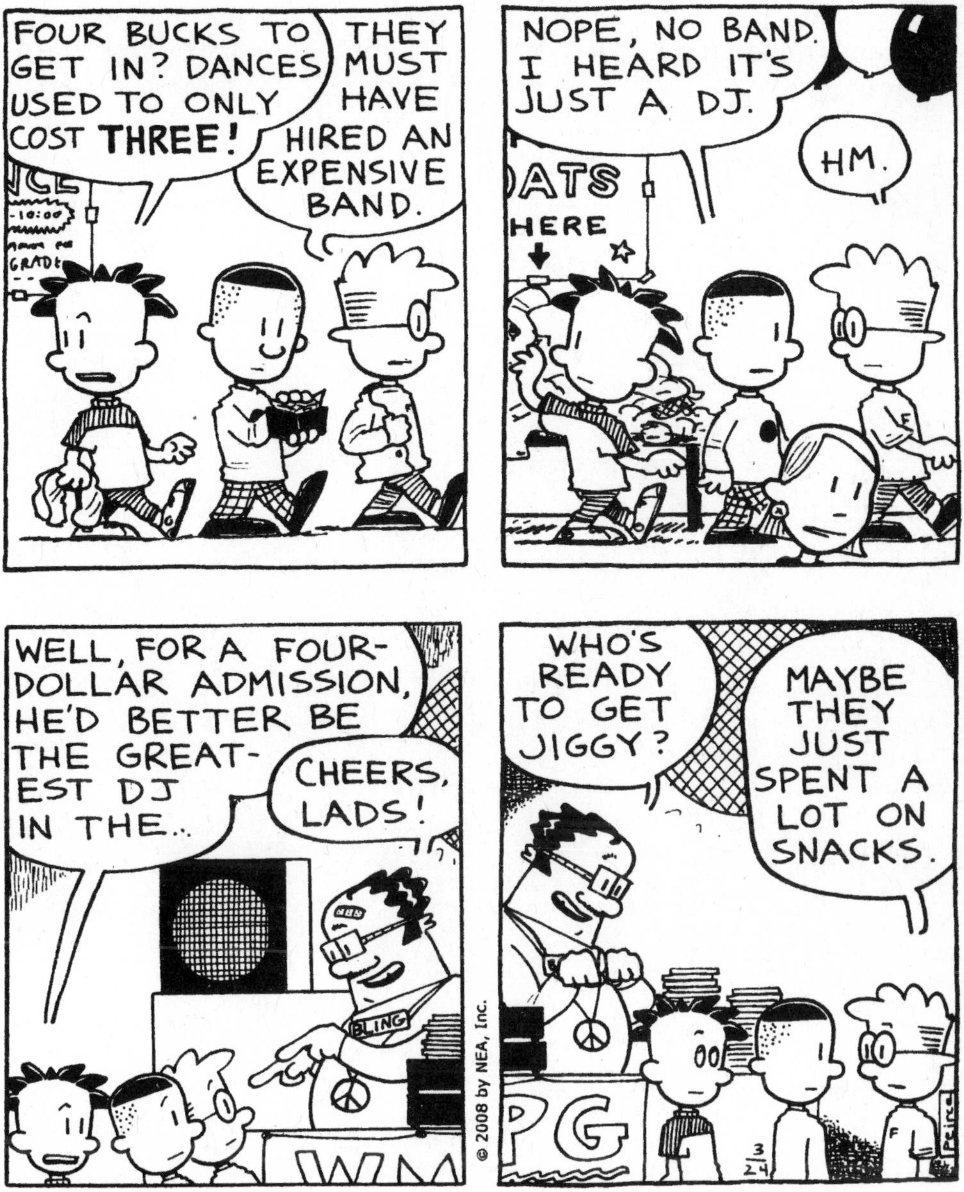
FOUR BUCKS TO GET IN? DANCES USED TO ONLY COST THREE!
THEY MUST HAVE HIRED AN EXPENSIVE BAND.
NOPE, NO BAND. I HEARD IT'S JUST A DJ.
HM.
WELL, FOR A FOUR-DOLLAR ADMISSION, HE'D BETTER BE THE GREATEST DJ IN THE...
CHEERS, LADS!
BLING
WHO'S READY TO GET JIGGY?
MAYBE THEY JUST SPENT A LOT ON SNACKS.
3/24
Peirce

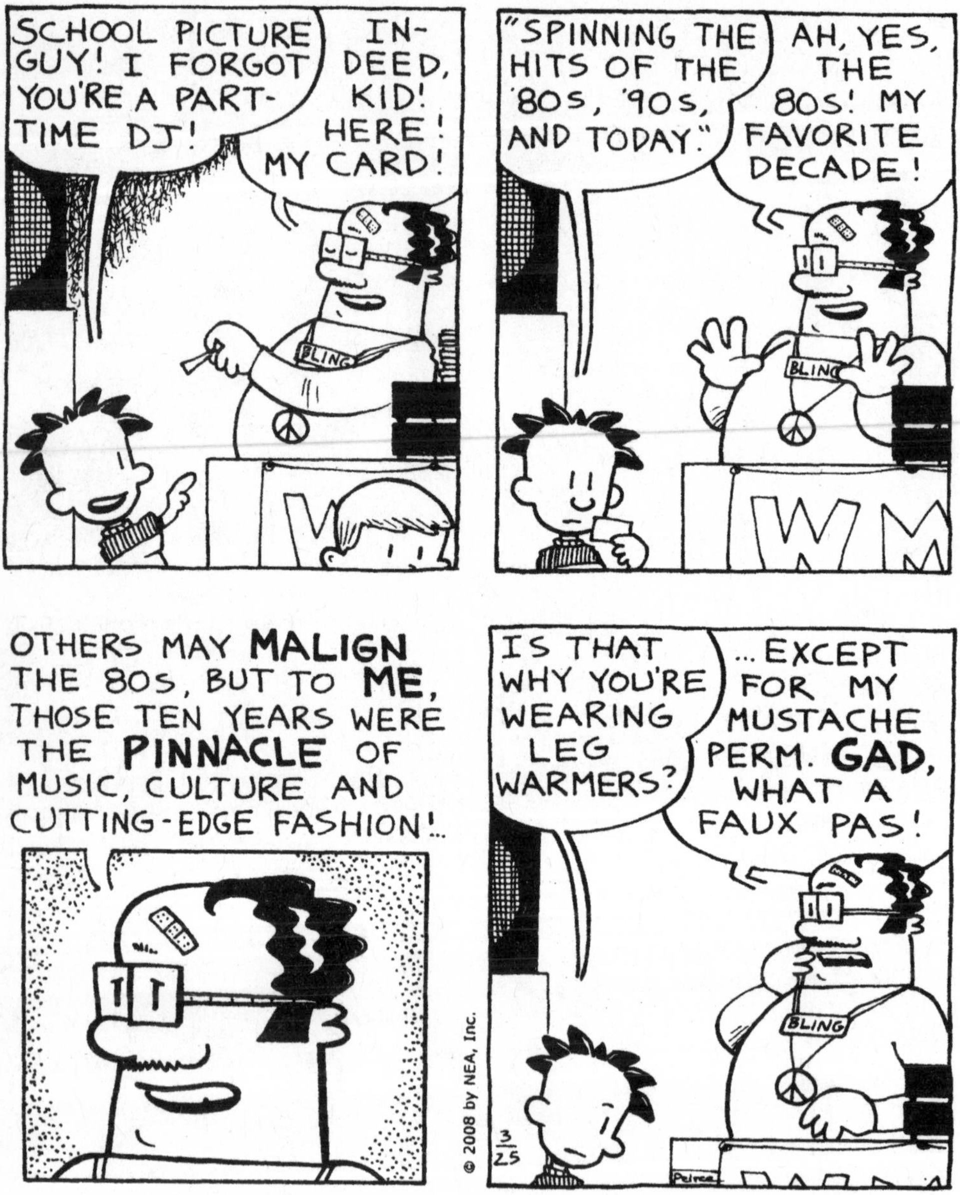
SCHOOL PICTURE GUY! I FORGOT YOU'RE A PART-TIME DJ!
INDEED, KID! HERE! MY CARD!
BLING
"SPINNING THE HITS OF THE '80s, '90s, AND TODAY."
AH, YES, THE 80s! MY FAVORITE DECADE!
BLING
OTHERS MAY **MALIGN** THE 80s, BUT TO **ME**, THOSE TEN YEARS WERE THE **PINNACLE** OF MUSIC, CULTURE AND CUTTING-EDGE FASHION!..
IS THAT WHY YOU'RE WEARING LEG WARMERS?
...EXCEPT FOR MY MUSTACHE PERM. **GAD**, WHAT A FAUX PAS!
BLING
© 2008 by NEA, Inc.
3 25

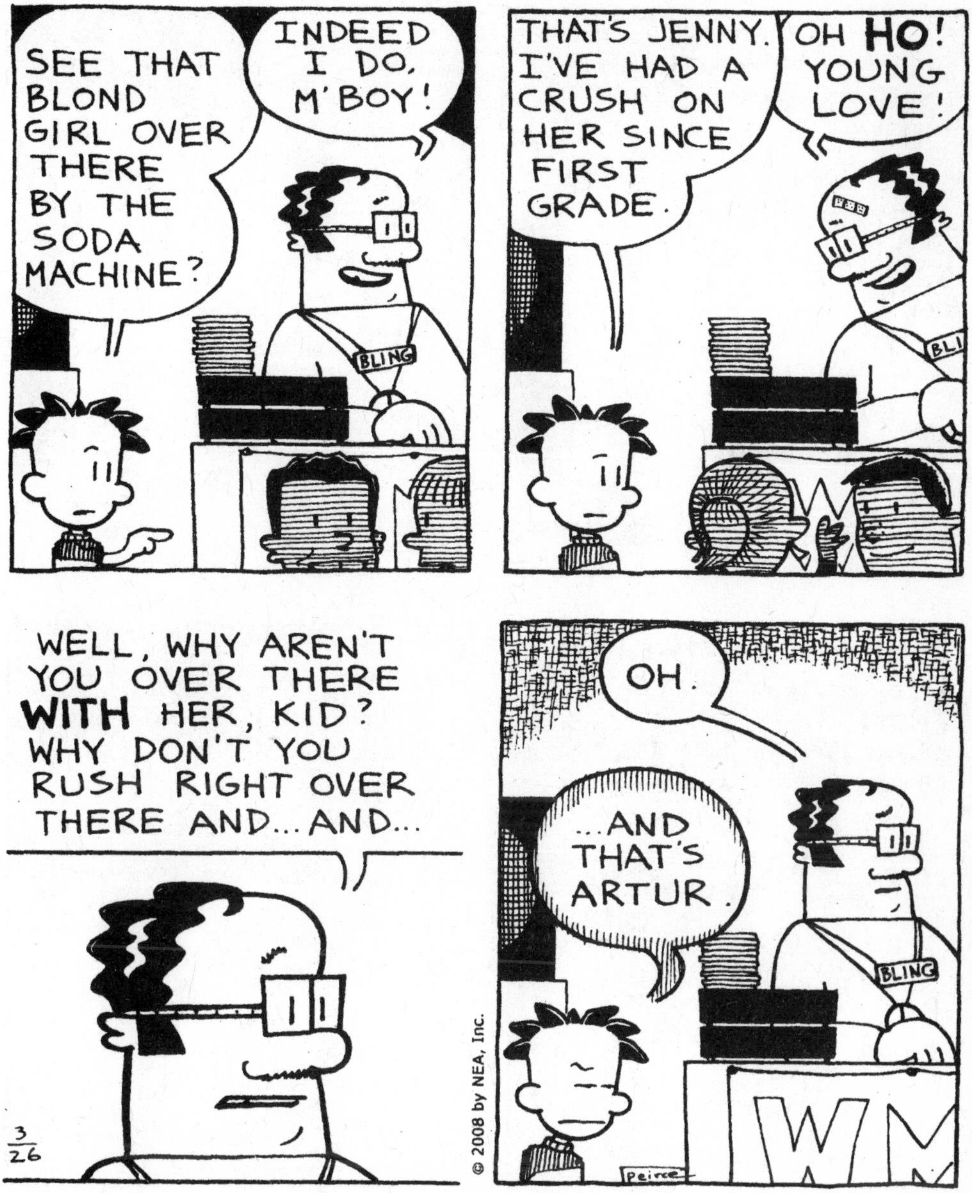
SEE THAT BLOND GIRL OVER THERE BY THE SODA MACHINE?
INDEED I DO, M'BOY!
BLING
THAT'S JENNY. I'VE HAD A CRUSH ON HER SINCE FIRST GRADE.
OH **HO**! YOUNG LOVE!
WELL, WHY AREN'T YOU OVER THERE **WITH** HER, KID? WHY DON'T YOU RUSH RIGHT OVER THERE AND... AND...
3/26
OH.
...AND THAT'S ARTUR.
BLING
Peirce

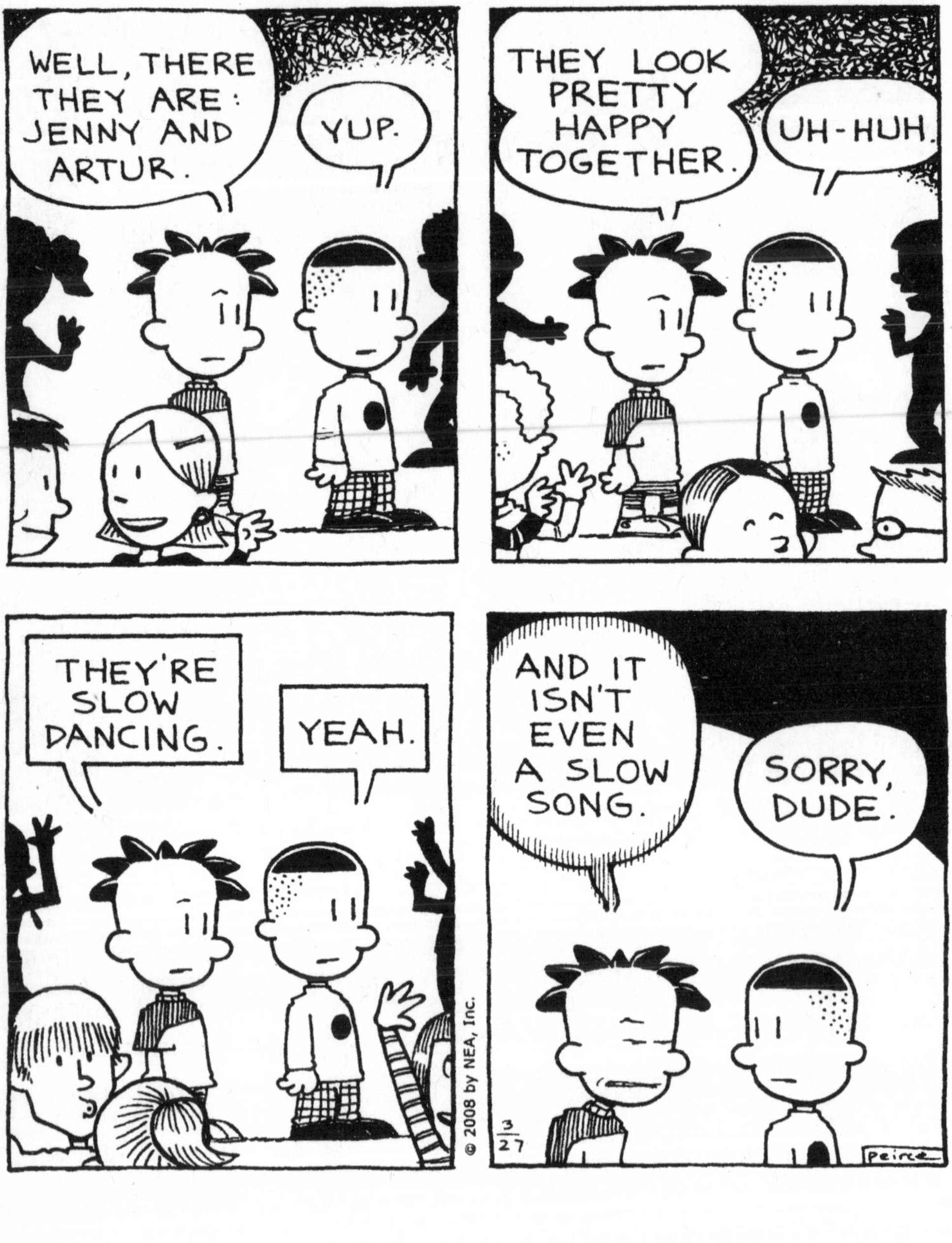
WELL, THERE THEY ARE: JENNY AND ARTUR.
YUP.
THEY LOOK PRETTY HAPPY TOGETHER.
UH-HUH.
THEY'RE SLOW DANCING.
YEAH.
AND IT ISN'T EVEN A SLOW SONG.
SORRY, DUDE.
© 2008 by NEA, Inc.
3/27
peirce

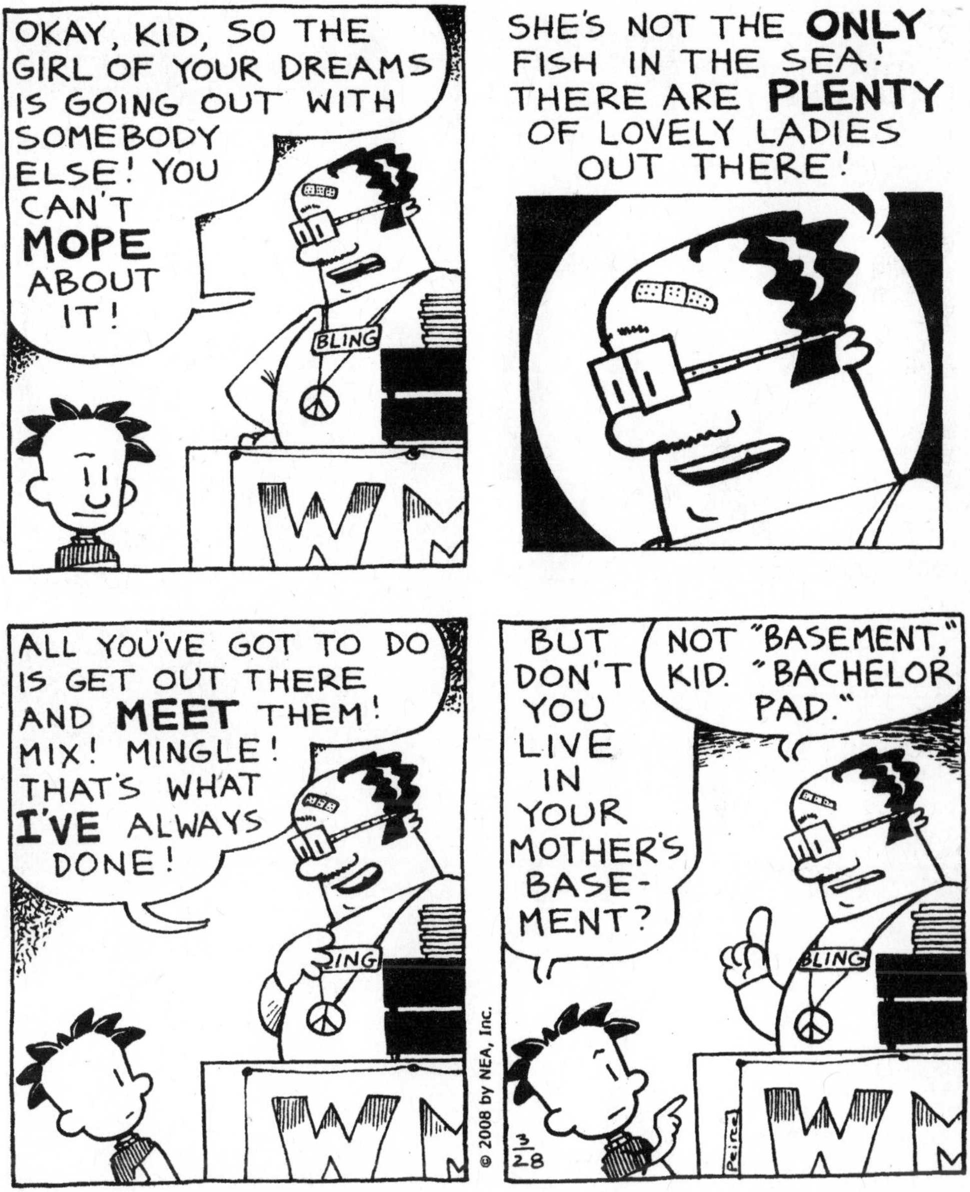
OKAY, KID, SO THE GIRL OF YOUR DREAMS IS GOING OUT WITH SOMEBODY ELSE! YOU CAN'T **MOPE** ABOUT IT!
BLING
SHE'S NOT THE **ONLY** FISH IN THE SEA! THERE ARE **PLENTY** OF LOVELY LADIES OUT THERE!
ALL YOU'VE GOT TO DO IS GET OUT THERE AND **MEET** THEM! MIX! MINGLE! THAT'S WHAT **I'VE** ALWAYS DONE!
BUT DON'T YOU LIVE IN YOUR MOTHER'S BASEMENT?
NOT "BASEMENT," KID. "BACHELOR PAD."
BLING
© 2008 by NEA, Inc.
3/28
Peirce

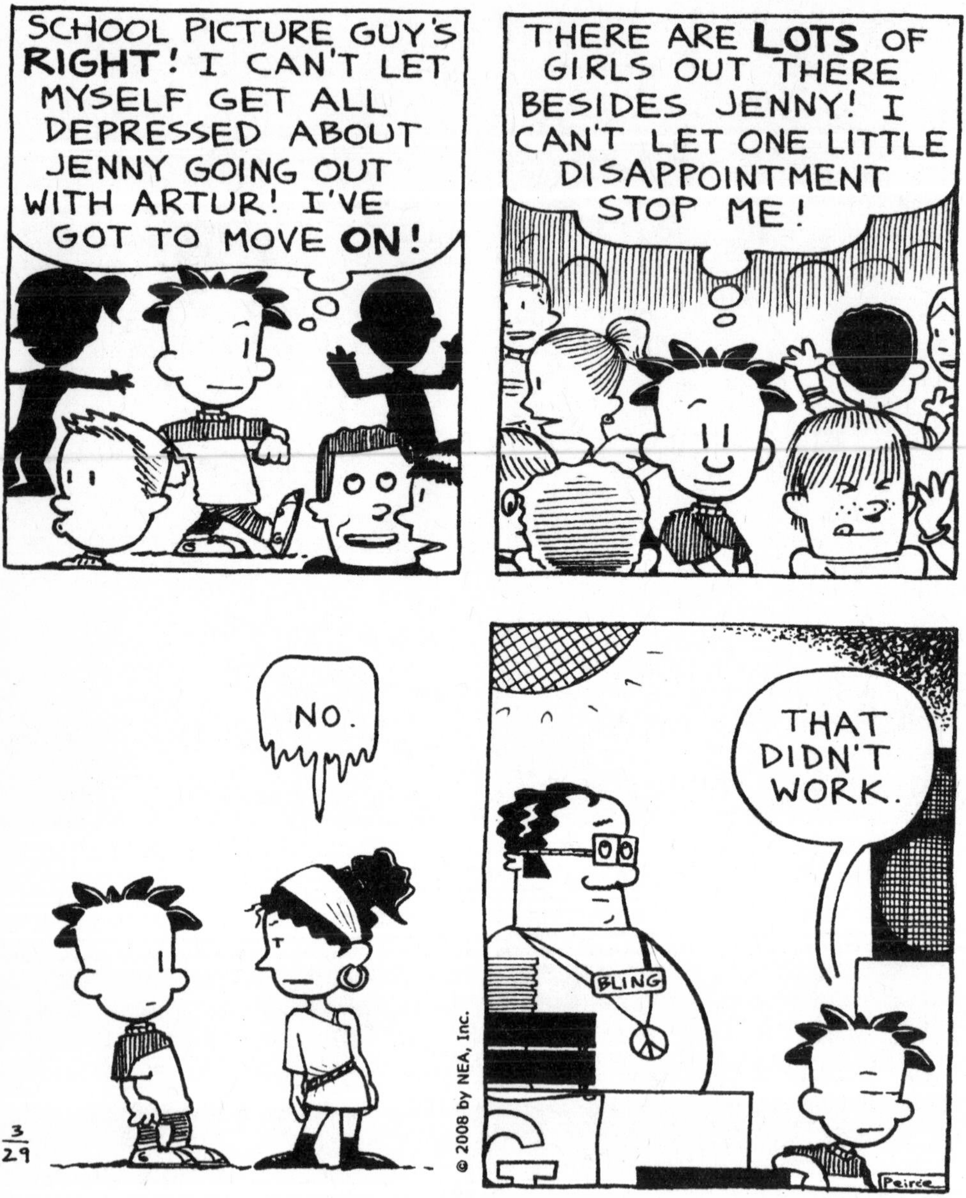
SCHOOL PICTURE GUY'S RIGHT! I CAN'T LET MYSELF GET ALL DEPRESSED ABOUT JENNY GOING OUT WITH ARTUR! I'VE GOT TO MOVE ON!
THERE ARE LOTS OF GIRLS OUT THERE BESIDES JENNY! I CAN'T LET ONE LITTLE DISAPPOINTMENT STOP ME!
NO.
3/29
© 2008 by NEA, Inc.
THAT DIDN'T WORK.
BLING
Peirce

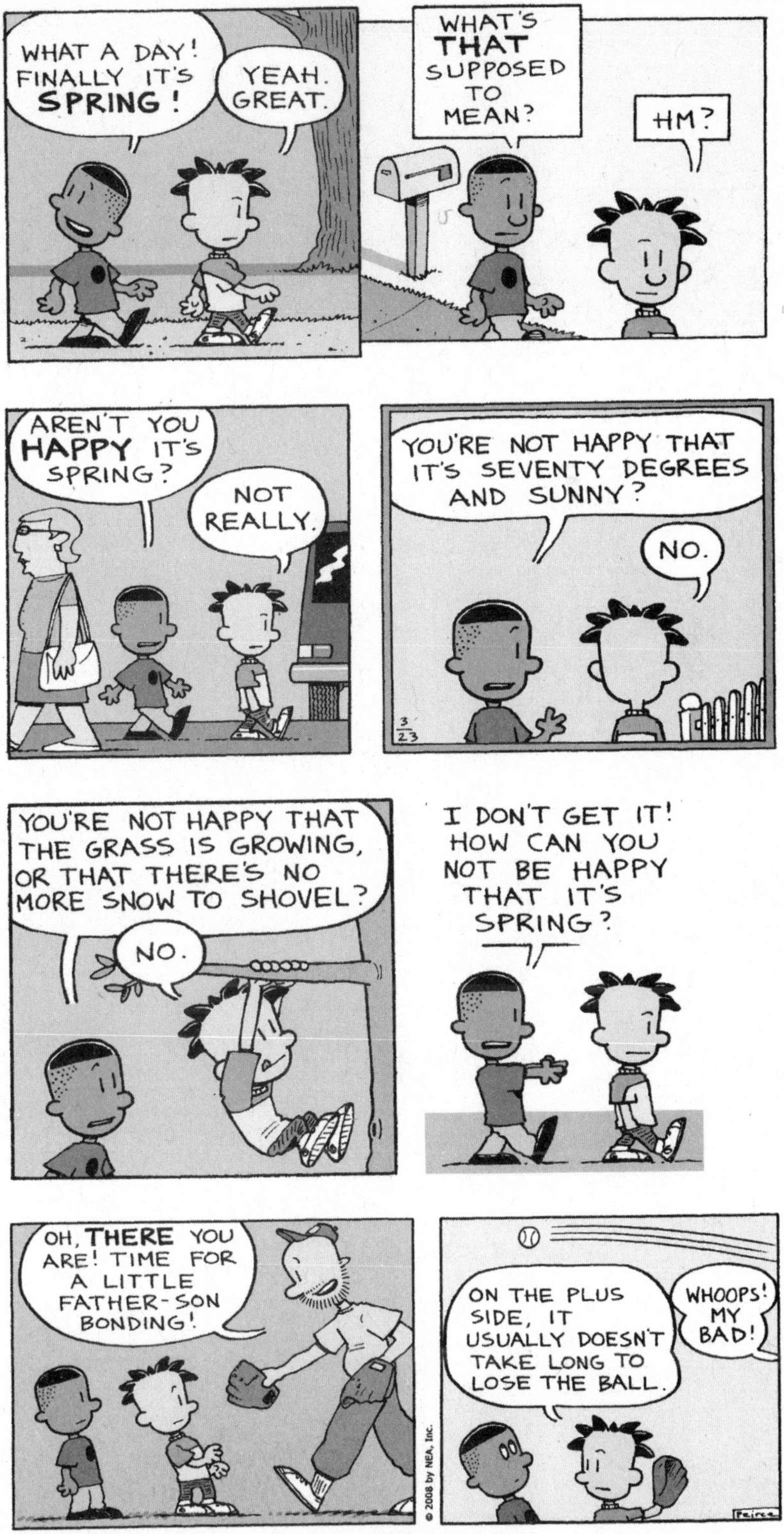
WHAT A DAY! FINALLY IT'S SPRING!
YEAH. GREAT.
WHAT'S THAT SUPPOSED TO MEAN?
HM?
AREN'T YOU HAPPY IT'S SPRING?
NOT REALLY.
YOU'RE NOT HAPPY THAT IT'S SEVENTY DEGREES AND SUNNY?
NO.
3/23
YOU'RE NOT HAPPY THAT THE GRASS IS GROWING, OR THAT THERE'S NO MORE SNOW TO SHOVEL?
NO.
I DON'T GET IT! HOW CAN YOU NOT BE HAPPY THAT IT'S SPRING?
OH, THERE YOU ARE! TIME FOR A LITTLE FATHER-SON BONDING!
© 2008 by NEA, Inc.
ON THE PLUS SIDE, IT USUALLY DOESN'T TAKE LONG TO LOSE THE BALL.
WHOOPS! MY BAD!
Peirce

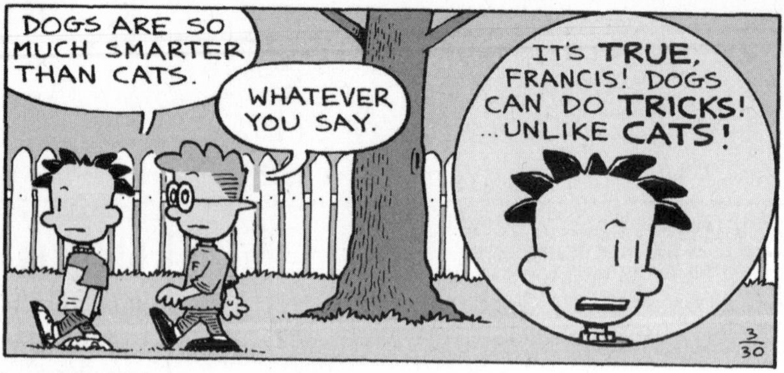
DOGS ARE SO MUCH SMARTER THAN CATS.
WHATEVER YOU SAY.
IT'S TRUE, FRANCIS! DOGS CAN DO TRICKS! ...UNLIKE CATS!
3/30

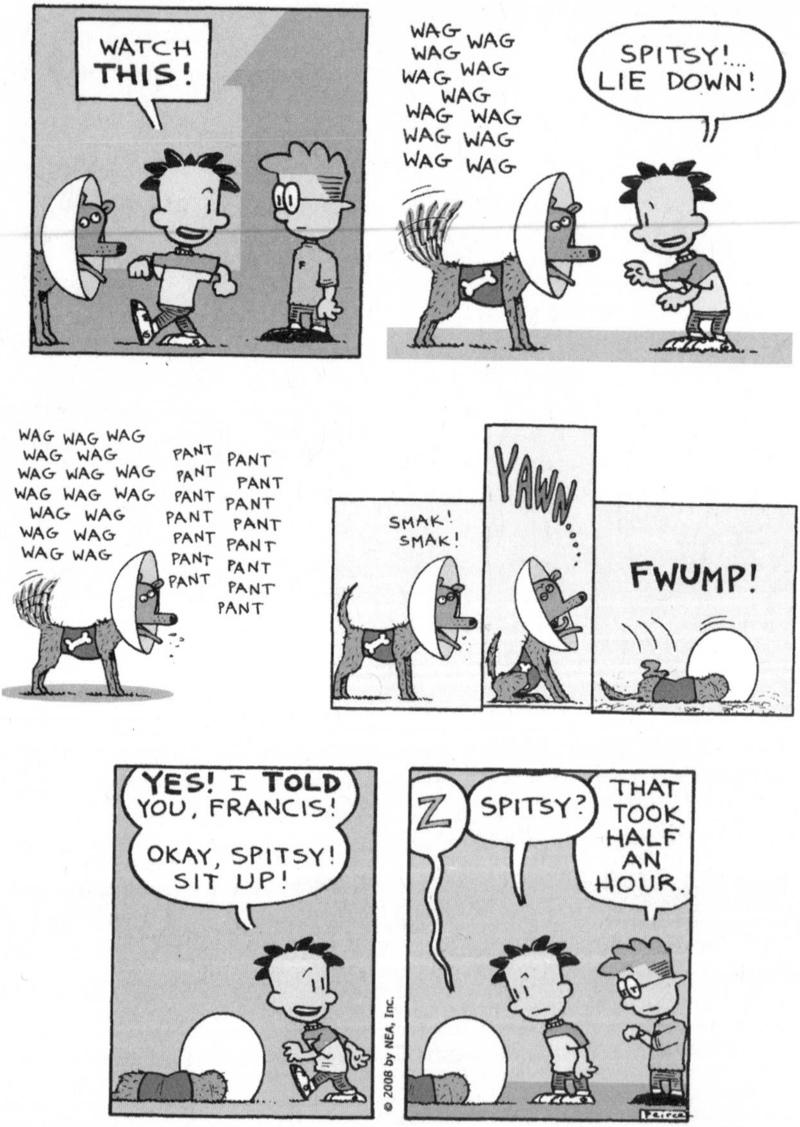
WATCH THIS!
WAG WAG WAG WAG WAG WAG WAG WAG WAG WAG WAG WAG WAG
SPITSY!... LIE DOWN!
WAG WAG WAG WAG WAG WAG WAG WAG WAG WAG WAG WAG WAG WAG WAG WAG WAG
PANT PANT PANT PANT PANT PANT PANT PANT PANT PANT PANT PANT PANT PANT PANT
SMAK! SMAK!
YAWN
FWUMP!
YES! I TOLD YOU, FRANCIS!
OKAY, SPITSY! SIT UP!
© 2008 by NEA, Inc.
Z
SPITSY?
THAT TOOK HALF AN HOUR.

DETENTION, AGAIN

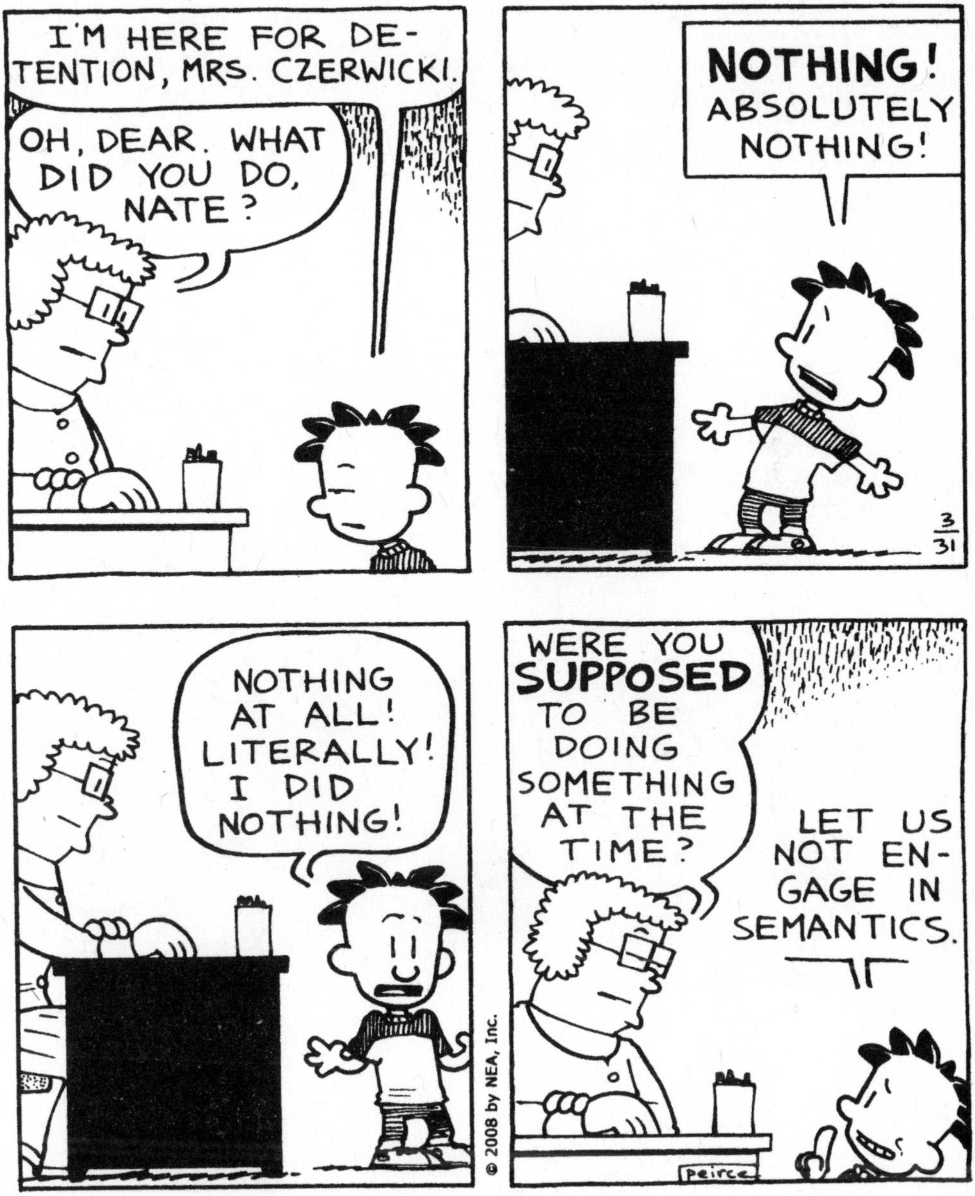
I'M HERE FOR DETENTION, MRS. CZERWICKI.
OH, DEAR. WHAT DID YOU DO, NATE?
NOTHING! ABSOLUTELY NOTHING!
3/31
NOTHING AT ALL! LITERALLY! I DID NOTHING!
© 2008 by NEA, Inc.
WERE YOU SUPPOSED TO BE DOING SOMETHING AT THE TIME?
LET US NOT ENGAGE IN SEMANTICS.
peirce

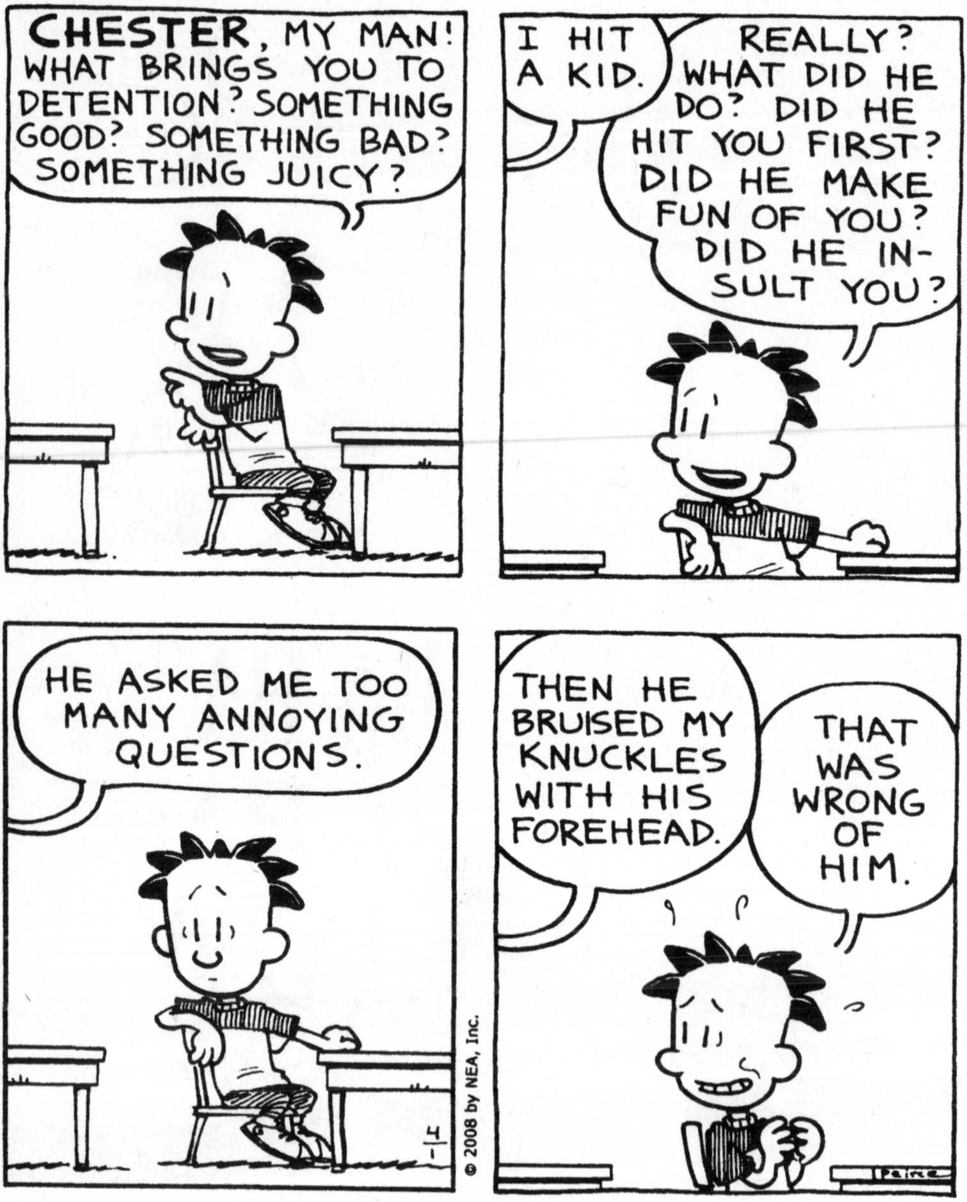
CHESTER, MY MAN! WHAT BRINGS YOU TO DETENTION? SOMETHING GOOD? SOMETHING BAD? SOMETHING JUICY?
I HIT A KID.
REALLY? WHAT DID HE DO? DID HE HIT YOU FIRST? DID HE MAKE FUN OF YOU? DID HE IN-SULT YOU?
HE ASKED ME TOO MANY ANNOYING QUESTIONS.
THEN HE BRUISED MY KNUCKLES WITH HIS FOREHEAD.
THAT WAS WRONG OF HIM.
1-4
© 2008 by NEA, Inc.
PEIRCE

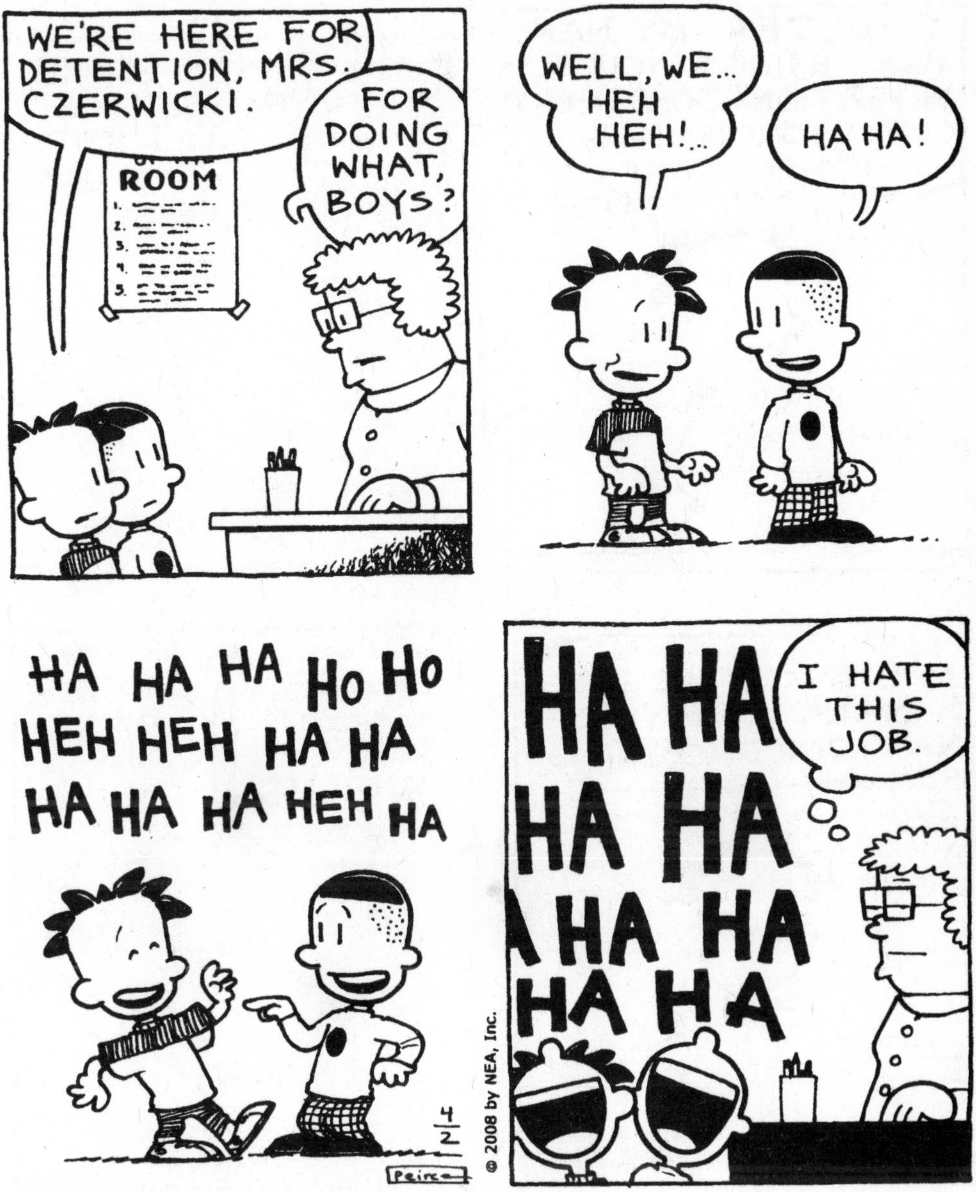
WE'RE HERE FOR DETENTION, MRS. CZERWICKI.
FOR DOING WHAT, BOYS?
ROOM
WELL, WE... HEH HEH!...
HA HA!
HA HA HA HO HO HEH HEH HA HA HA HA HA HEH HA
4/2
Peirce
© 2008 by NEA, Inc.
HA HA HA HA HA HA HA HA HA
I HATE THIS JOB.

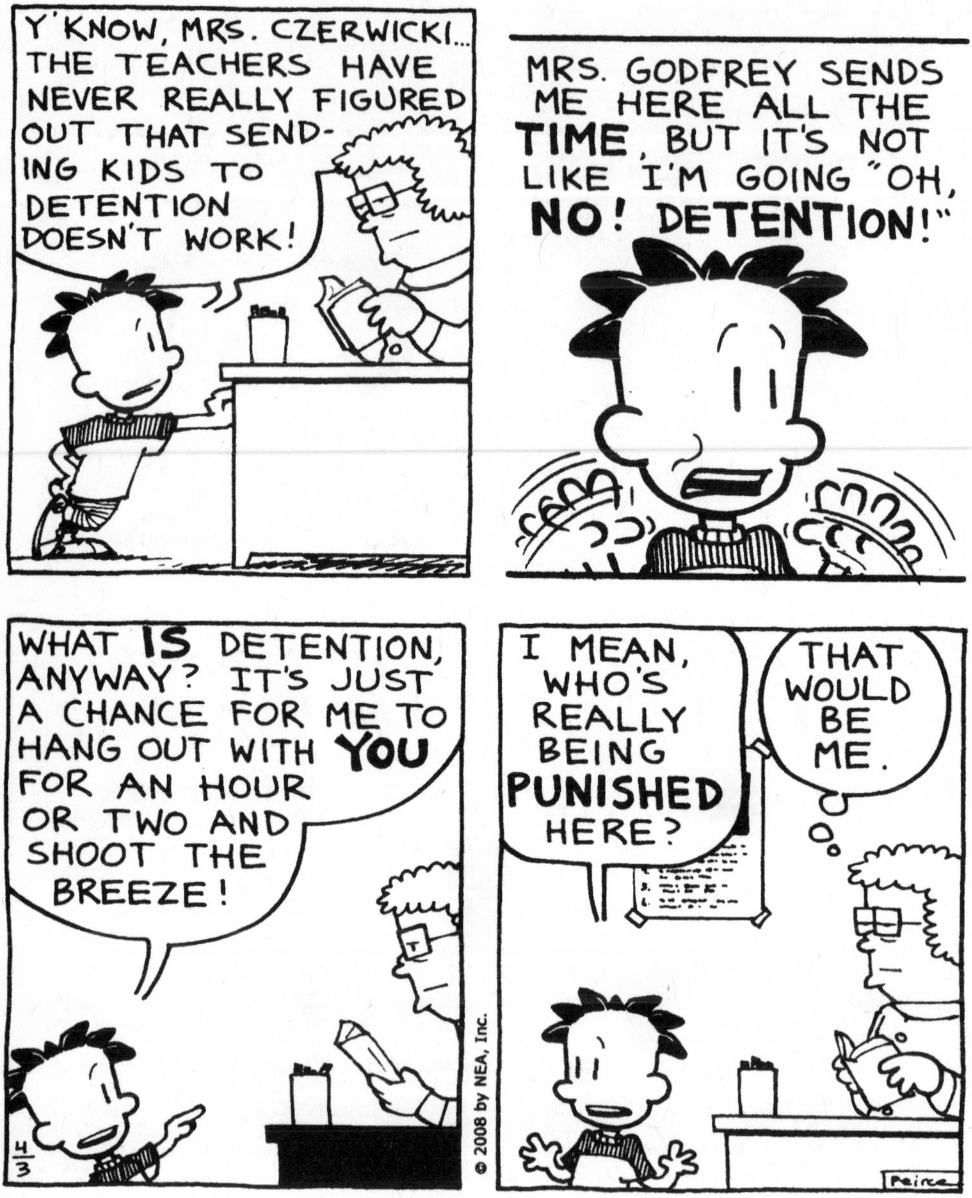
Y'KNOW, MRS. CZERWICKI... THE TEACHERS HAVE NEVER REALLY FIGURED OUT THAT SENDING KIDS TO DETENTION DOESN'T WORK!
MRS. GODFREY SENDS ME HERE ALL THE TIME, BUT IT'S NOT LIKE I'M GOING "OH, NO! DETENTION!"
WHAT IS DETENTION, ANYWAY? IT'S JUST A CHANCE FOR ME TO HANG OUT WITH YOU FOR AN HOUR OR TWO AND SHOOT THE BREEZE!
4/3
© 2008 by NEA, Inc.
I MEAN, WHO'S REALLY BEING PUNISHED HERE?
THAT WOULD BE ME.
Peirce

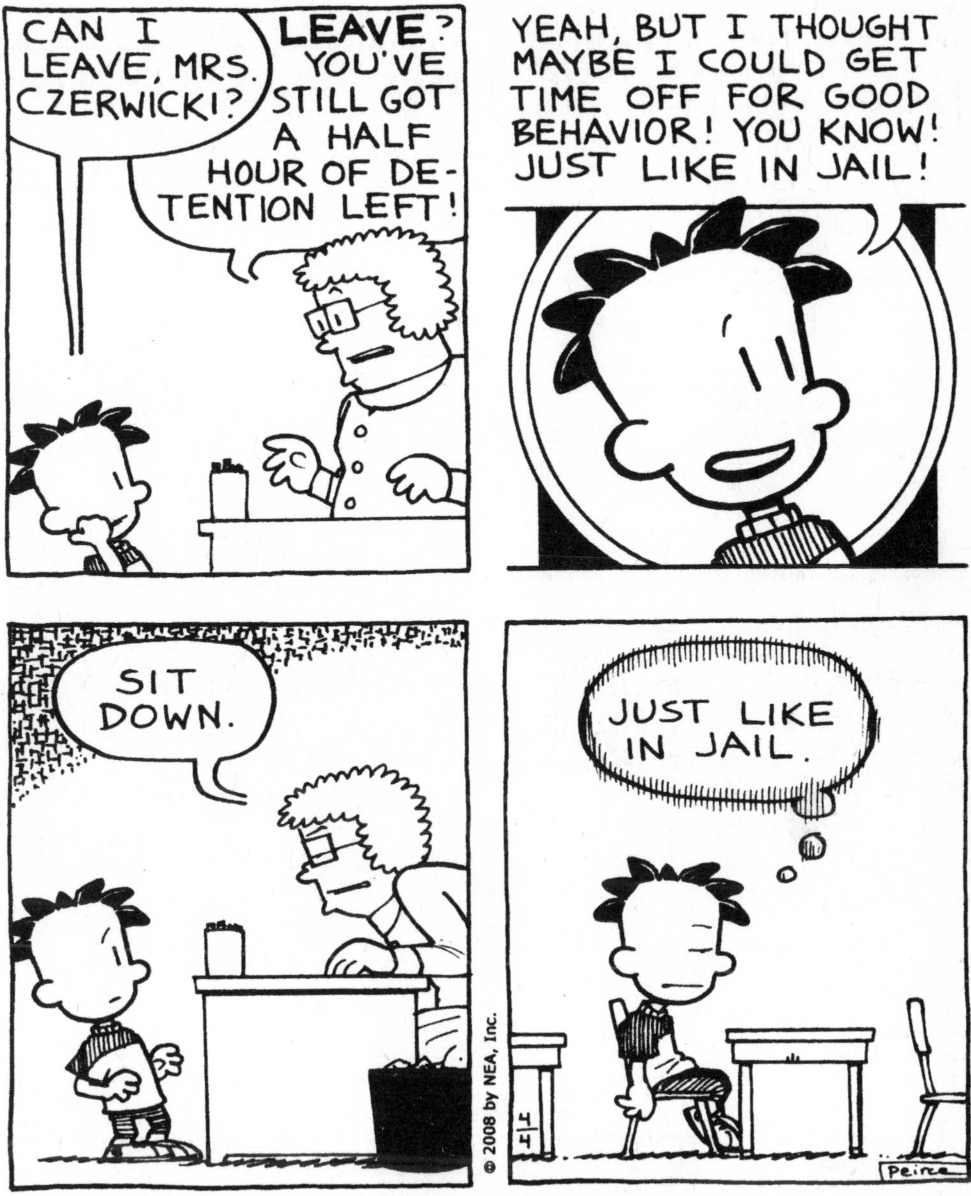
CAN I LEAVE, MRS. CZERWICKI?
LEAVE? YOU'VE STILL GOT A HALF HOUR OF DETENTION LEFT!
YEAH, BUT I THOUGHT MAYBE I COULD GET TIME OFF FOR GOOD BEHAVIOR! YOU KNOW! JUST LIKE IN JAIL!
SIT DOWN.
JUST LIKE IN JAIL.
© 2008 by NEA, Inc.
4/4
Peirce

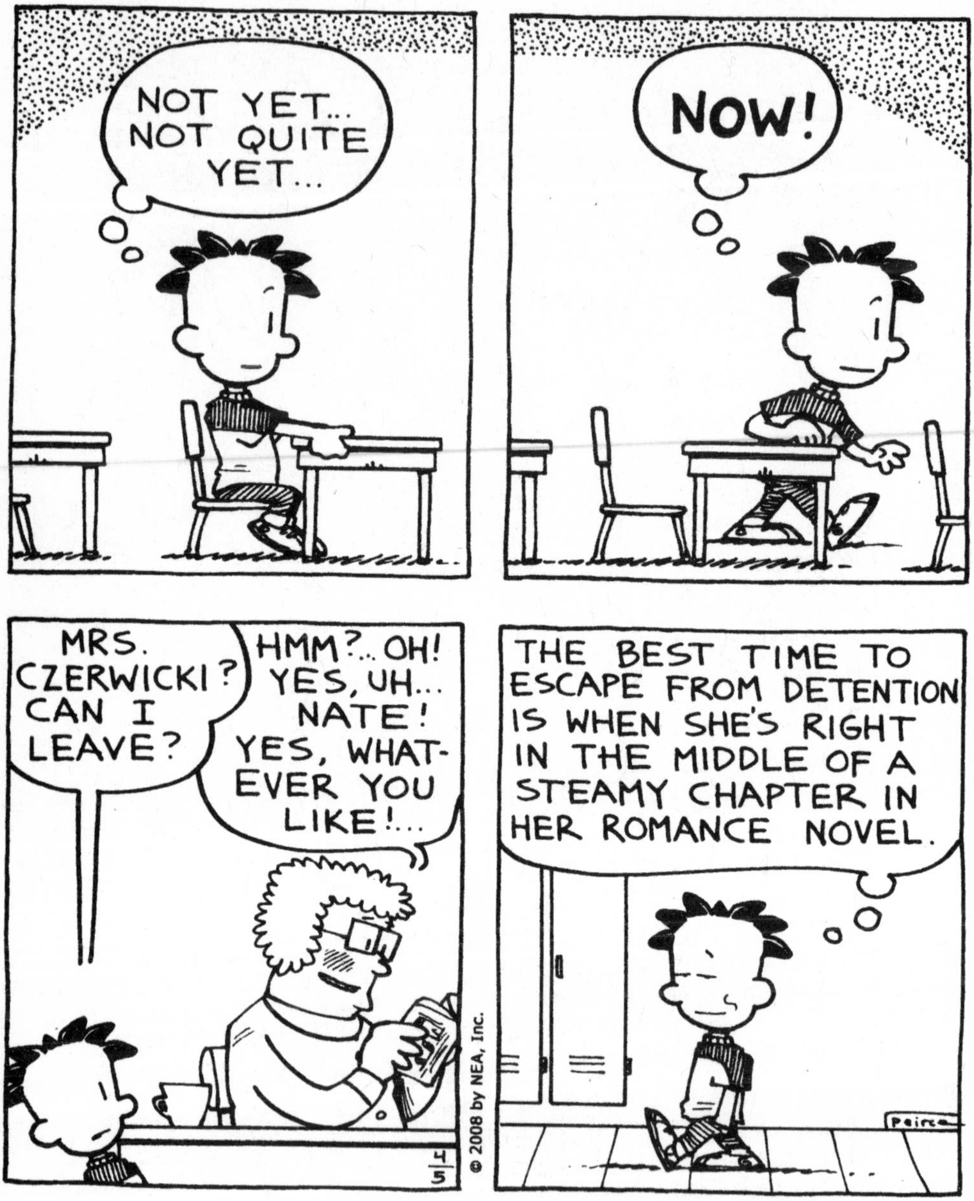
NOT YET... NOT QUITE YET...
NOW!
MRS. CZERWICKI? CAN I LEAVE?
HMM?... OH! YES, UH... NATE! YES, WHATEVER YOU LIKE!...
THE BEST TIME TO ESCAPE FROM DETENTION IS WHEN SHE'S RIGHT IN THE MIDDLE OF A STEAMY CHAPTER IN HER ROMANCE NOVEL.
4/5
Peirce

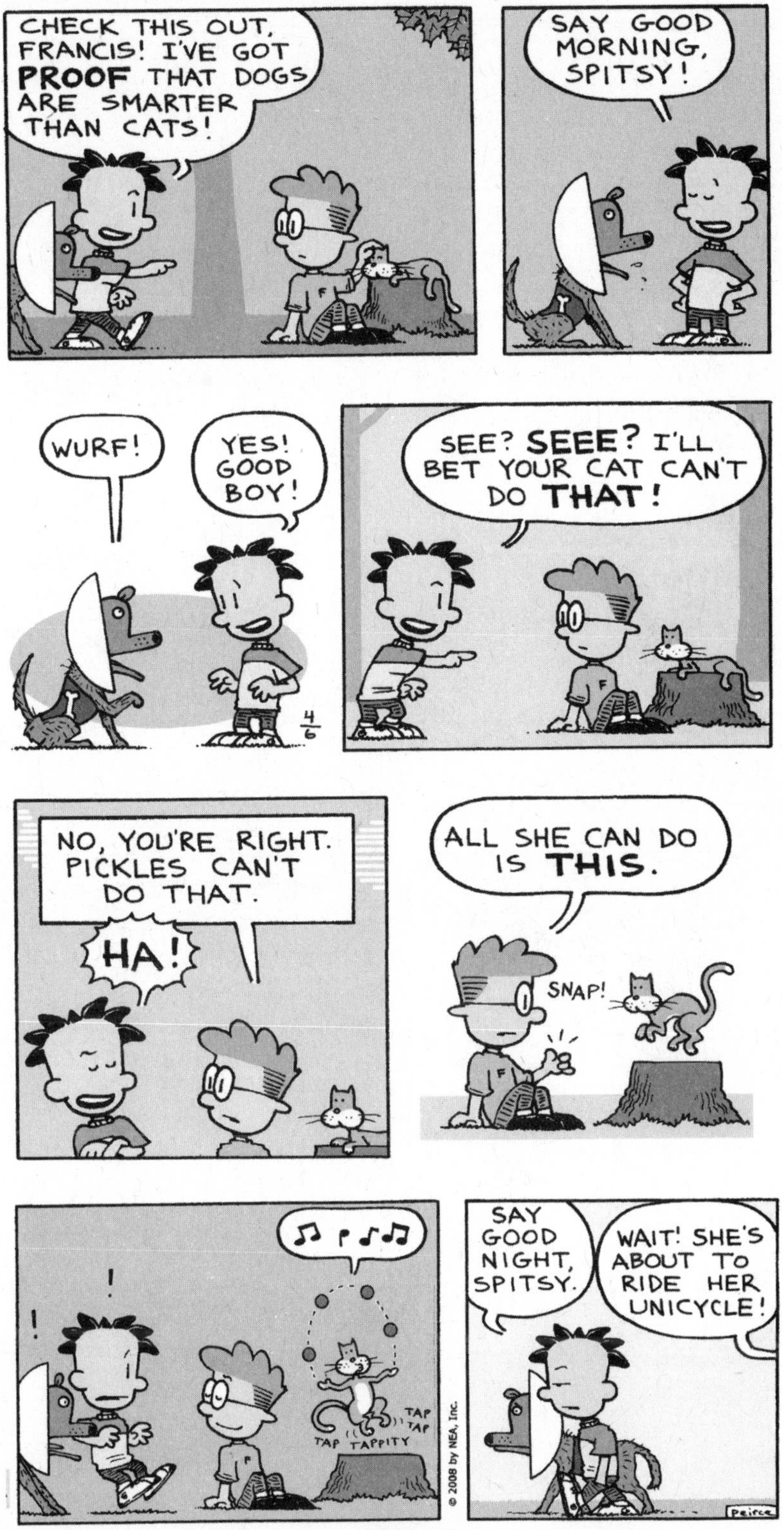
CHECK THIS OUT, FRANCIS! I'VE GOT PROOF THAT DOGS ARE SMARTER THAN CATS!
SAY GOOD MORNING, SPITSY!
WURF!
YES! GOOD BOY!
4/6
SEE? SEEE? I'LL BET YOUR CAT CAN'T DO THAT!
NO, YOU'RE RIGHT. PICKLES CAN'T DO THAT.
HA!
ALL SHE CAN DO IS THIS.
SNAP!
!
!
TAP TAP
TAP TAPPITY
© 2008 by NEA, Inc.
SAY GOOD NIGHT, SPITSY.
WAIT! SHE'S ABOUT TO RIDE HER UNICYCLE!
Peirce

BOOK BUDDIES, NATE'S WAY

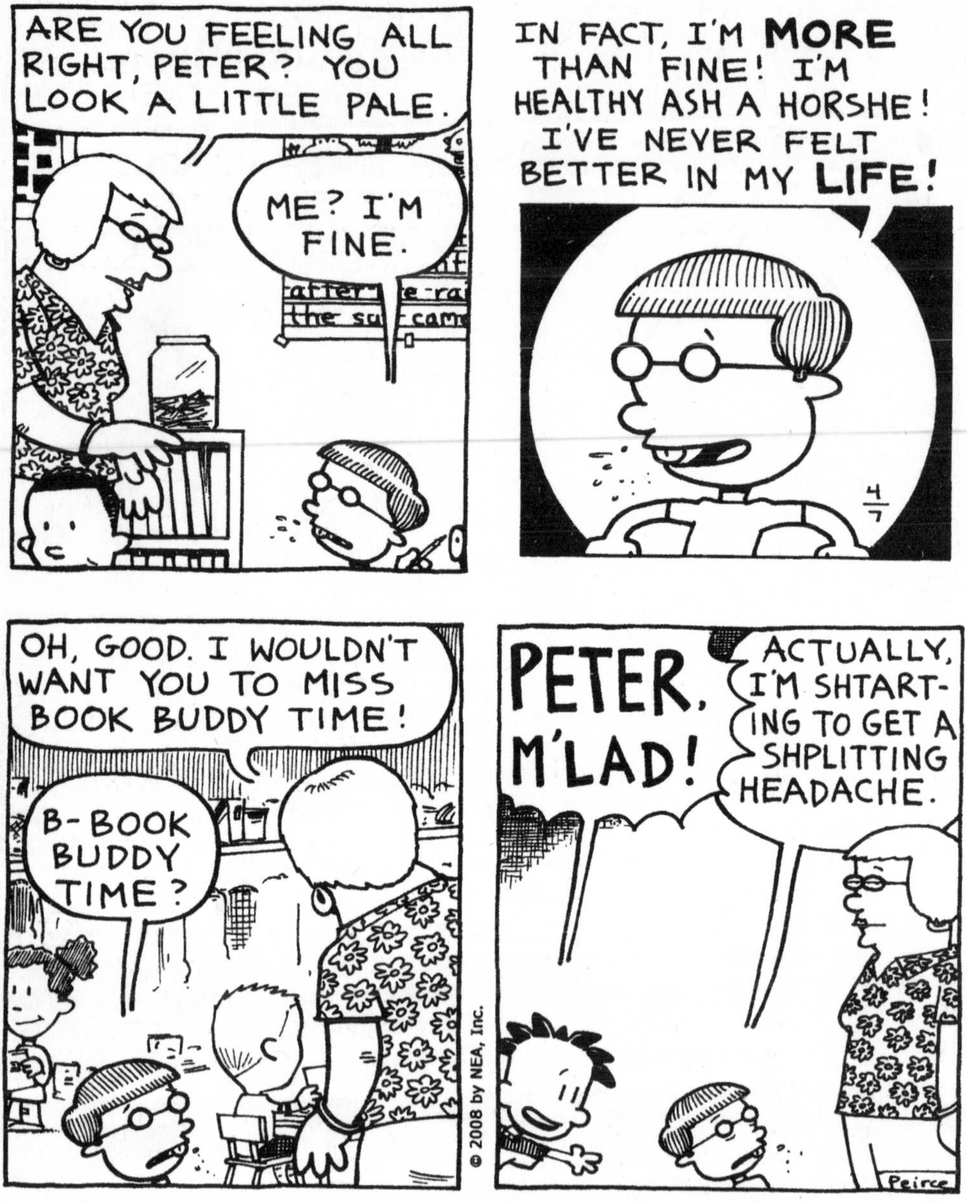
ARE YOU FEELING ALL RIGHT, PETER? YOU LOOK A LITTLE PALE.
ME? I'M FINE.
IN FACT, I'M **MORE** THAN FINE! I'M HEALTHY ASH A HORSHE! I'VE NEVER FELT BETTER IN MY **LIFE**!
4/7
OH, GOOD. I WOULDN'T WANT YOU TO MISS BOOK BUDDY TIME!
B-BOOK BUDDY TIME?
© 2008 by NEA, Inc.
PETER, M'LAD!
ACTUALLY, I'M SHTART-ING TO GET A SHPLITTING HEADACHE.
Peirce

LOOK... NO OFFENSHE, BUT YOU DON'T NEED TO BE HERE.

PETER, I'M SUP- POSED TO HELP YOU WITH YOUR READING!

I DON'T **NEED** HELP! JUSHT GO HANG OUT IN THE COMPUTER LAB OR SHOME- THING!

THAT WOULD BE NEGLECT- ING MY ROLE AS YOUR BOOK BUDDY!

SEE? "BOOK BUDDIES MENTOR AND ENCOUR- AGE FIRST-GRADERS IN THEIR READING, FOSTERING A LOVE OF BOOKS AND PROMOTING..."

BOOK BUDDIES

and Muff pond to-t even

4/8

© 2008 by NEA, Inc.

...WHAT'S THAT WORD?

"LITERACY."

BOOK BUDDIES

LEVEL I

LEVEL

Peirce

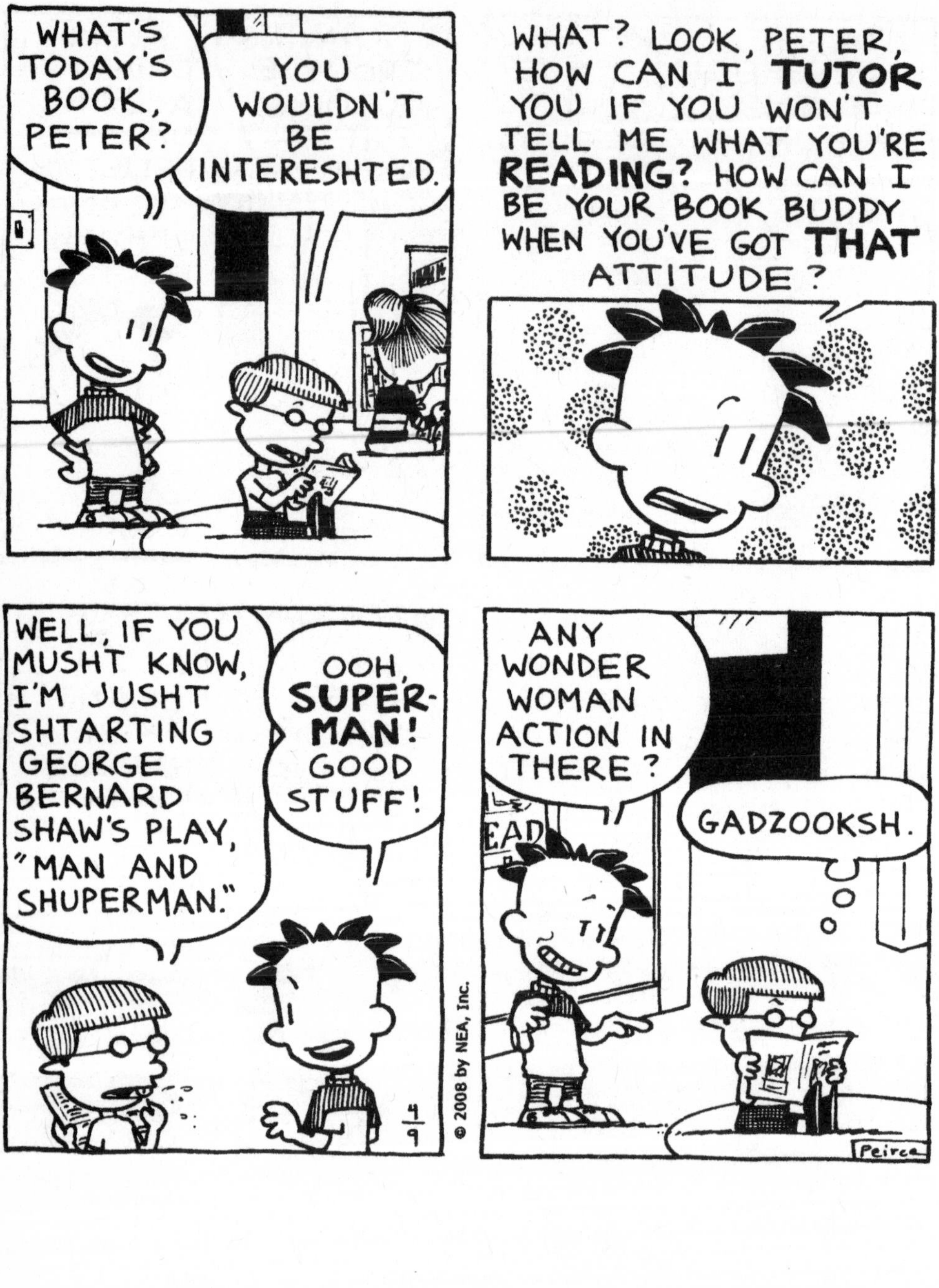
WHAT'S TODAY'S BOOK, PETER?
YOU WOULDN'T BE INTERESHTED.
WHAT? LOOK, PETER, HOW CAN I **TUTOR** YOU IF YOU WON'T TELL ME WHAT YOU'RE **READING**? HOW CAN I BE YOUR BOOK BUDDY WHEN YOU'VE GOT **THAT** ATTITUDE?
WELL, IF YOU MUSHT KNOW, I'M JUSHT SHTARTING GEORGE BERNARD SHAW'S PLAY, "MAN AND SHUPERMAN."
OOH, **SUPER-MAN**! GOOD STUFF!
4/9
© 2008 by NEA, Inc.
ANY WONDER WOMAN ACTION IN THERE?
GADZOOKSH.
Peirce

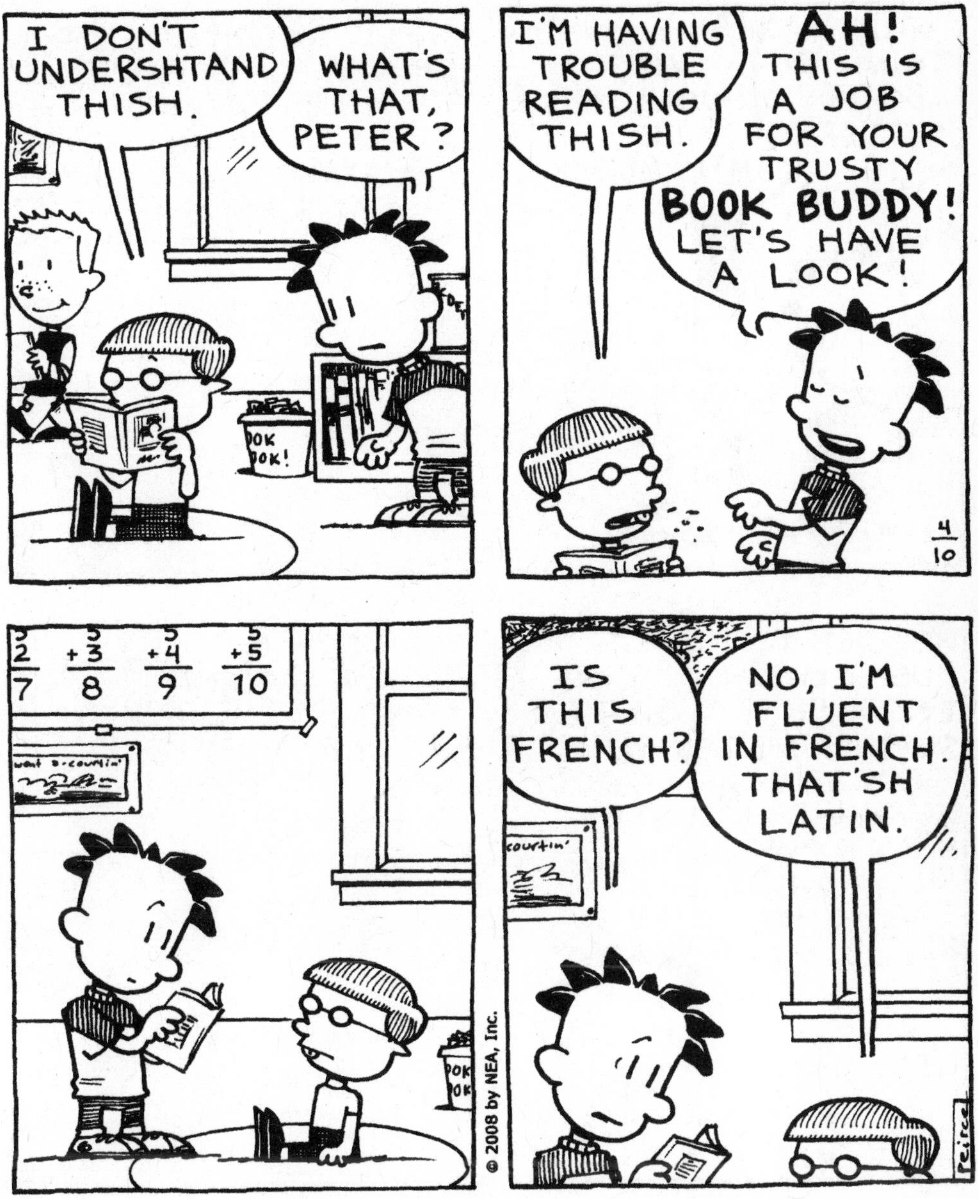
I DON'T UNDERSHTAND THISH.
WHAT'S THAT, PETER?
I'M HAVING TROUBLE READING THISH.
AH! THIS IS A JOB FOR YOUR TRUSTY BOOK BUDDY! LET'S HAVE A LOOK!
4/10
IS THIS FRENCH?
NO, I'M FLUENT IN FRENCH. THAT'SH LATIN.
© 2008 by NEA, Inc.
Peirce

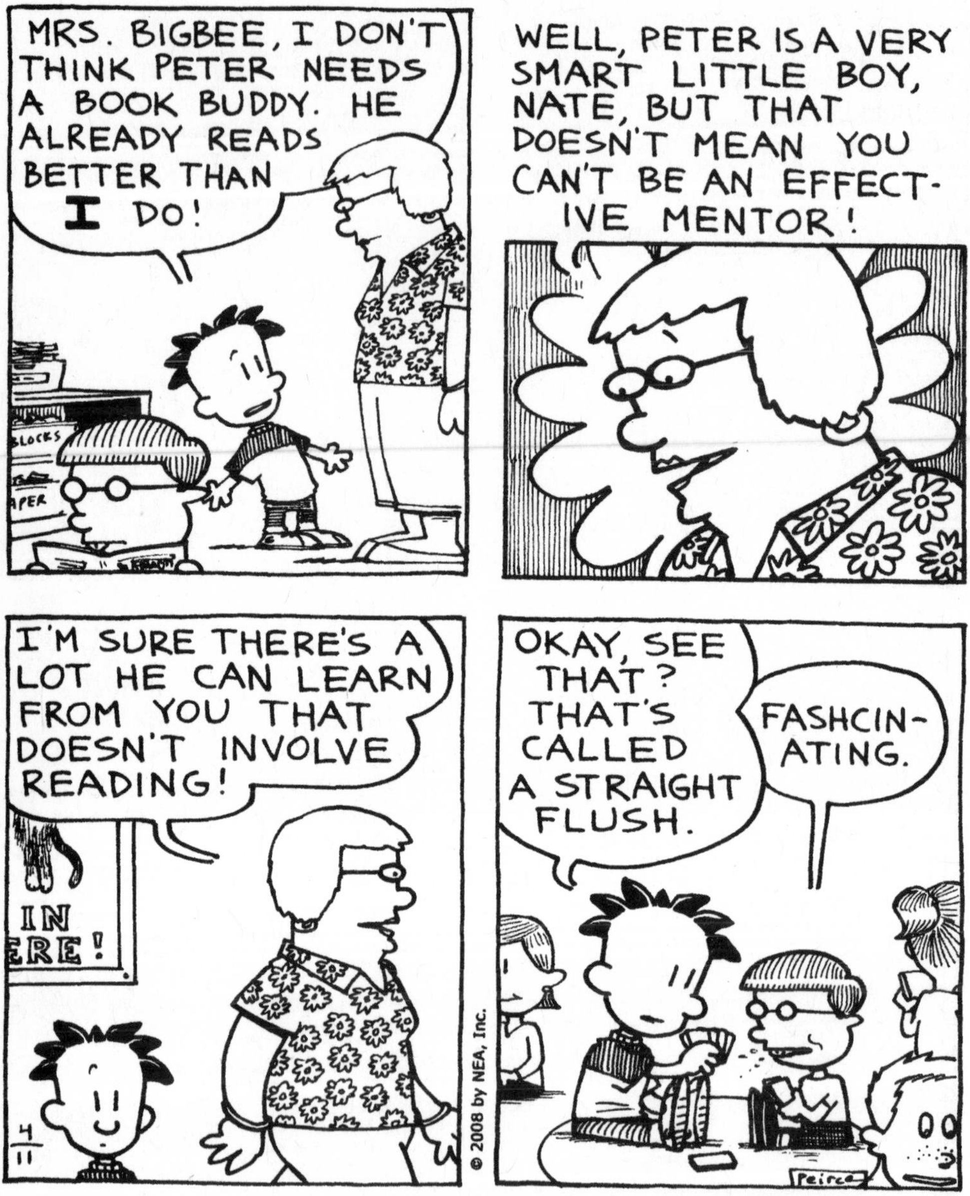
MRS. BIGBEE, I DON'T THINK PETER NEEDS A BOOK BUDDY. HE ALREADY READS BETTER THAN I DO!
BLOCKS
APER
WELL, PETER IS A VERY SMART LITTLE BOY, NATE, BUT THAT DOESN'T MEAN YOU CAN'T BE AN EFFECT-IVE MENTOR!
I'M SURE THERE'S A LOT HE CAN LEARN FROM YOU THAT DOESN'T INVOLVE READING!
IN
ERE!
4/11
© 2008 by NEA, Inc.
OKAY, SEE THAT? THAT'S CALLED A STRAIGHT FLUSH.
FASHCIN-ATING.
Peirce

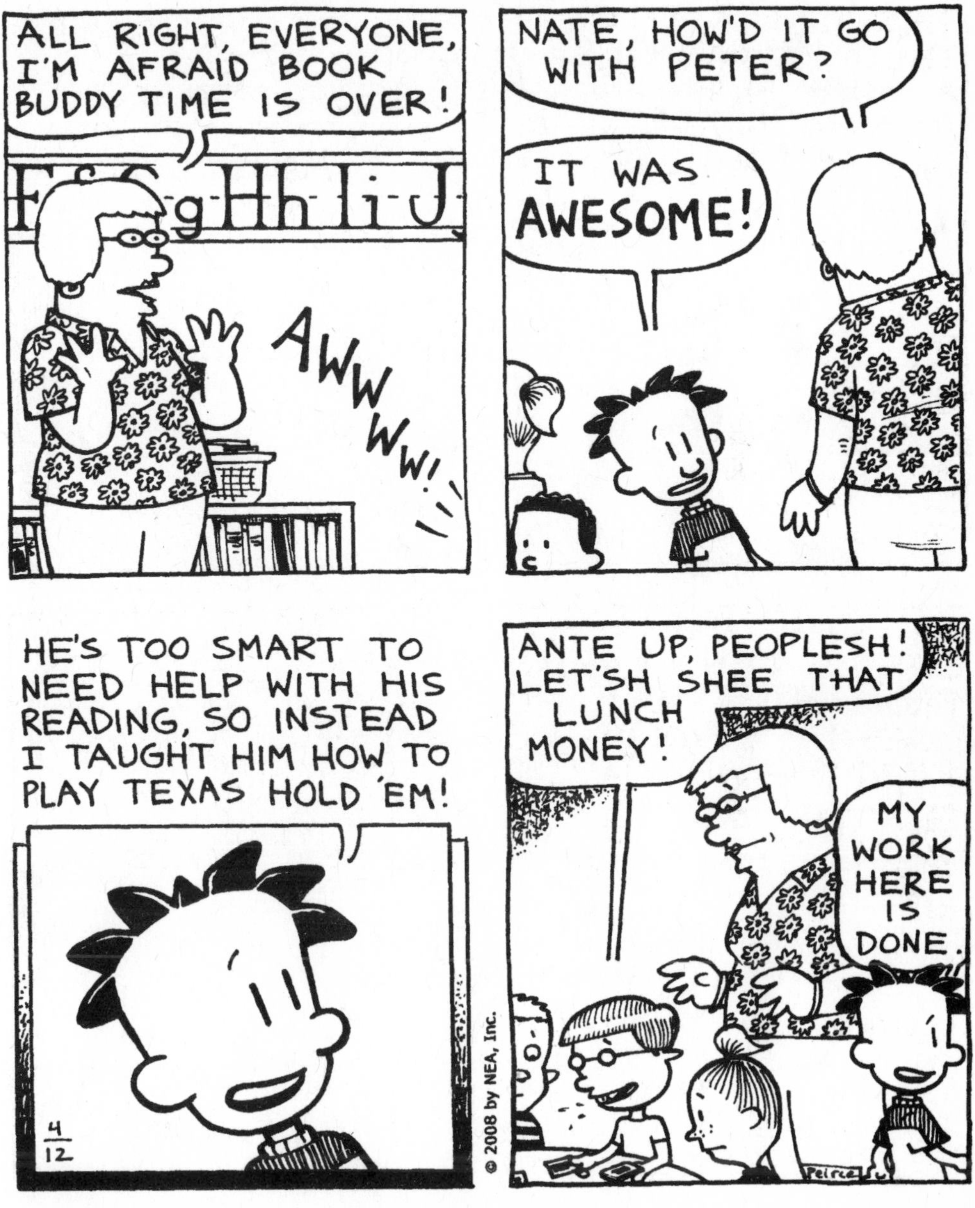
ALL RIGHT, EVERYONE, I'M AFRAID BOOK BUDDY TIME IS OVER!
AWWWWW!
NATE, HOW'D IT GO WITH PETER?
IT WAS **AWESOME!**
HE'S TOO SMART TO NEED HELP WITH HIS READING, SO INSTEAD I TAUGHT HIM HOW TO PLAY TEXAS HOLD 'EM!
4/12
© 2008 by NEA, Inc.
ANTE UP, PEOPLESH! LET'SH SHEE THAT LUNCH MONEY!
MY WORK HERE IS DONE.
Peirce

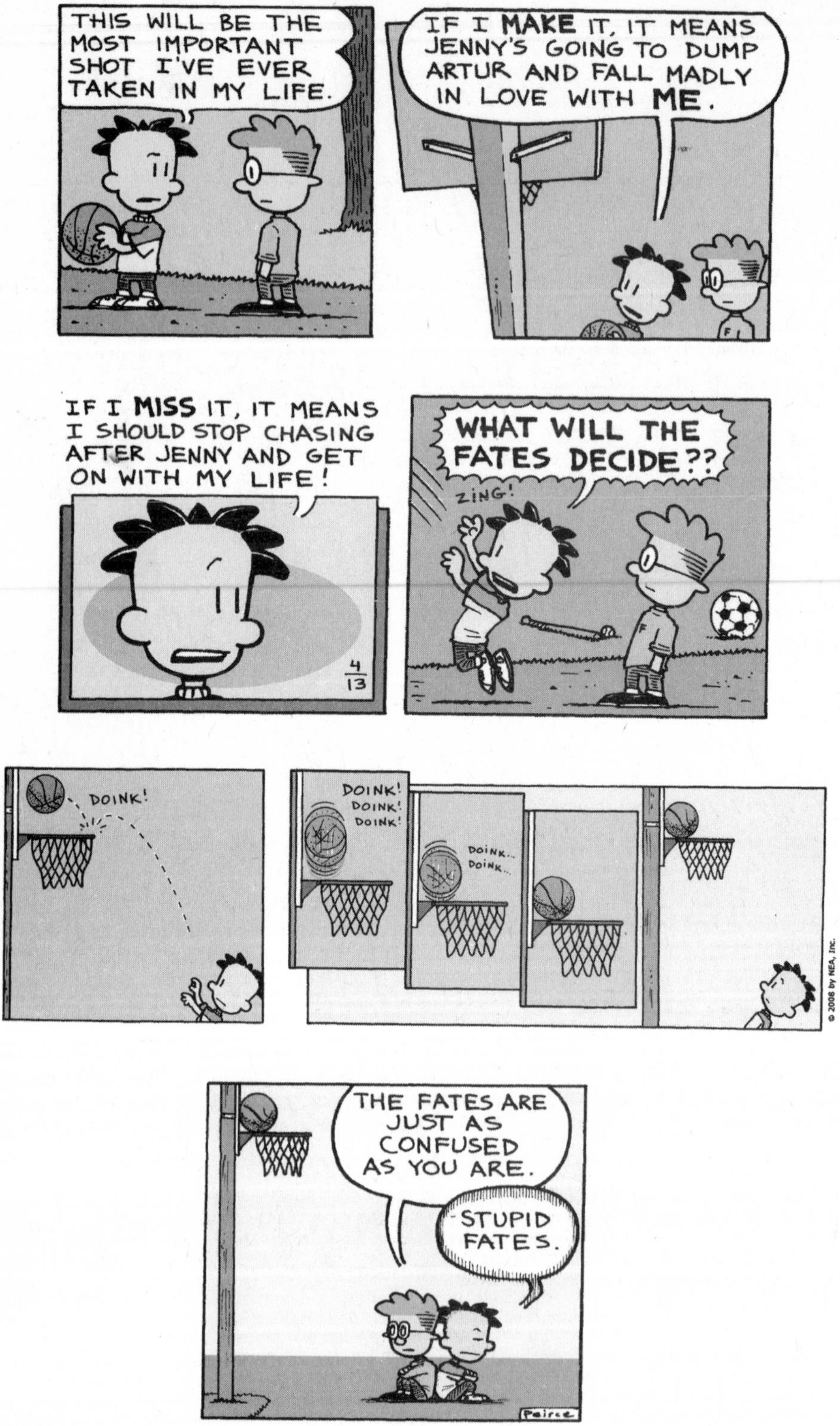
THIS WILL BE THE MOST IMPORTANT SHOT I'VE EVER TAKEN IN MY LIFE.
IF I MAKE IT, IT MEANS JENNY'S GOING TO DUMP ARTUR AND FALL MADLY IN LOVE WITH ME.
IF I MISS IT, IT MEANS I SHOULD STOP CHASING AFTER JENNY AND GET ON WITH MY LIFE!
4/13
WHAT WILL THE FATES DECIDE??
ZING!
DOINK!
DOINK! DOINK! DOINK!
DOINK... DOINK...
© 2008 by NEA, Inc.
THE FATES ARE JUST AS CONFUSED AS YOU ARE.
STUPID FATES.
Peirce

CRUSHED

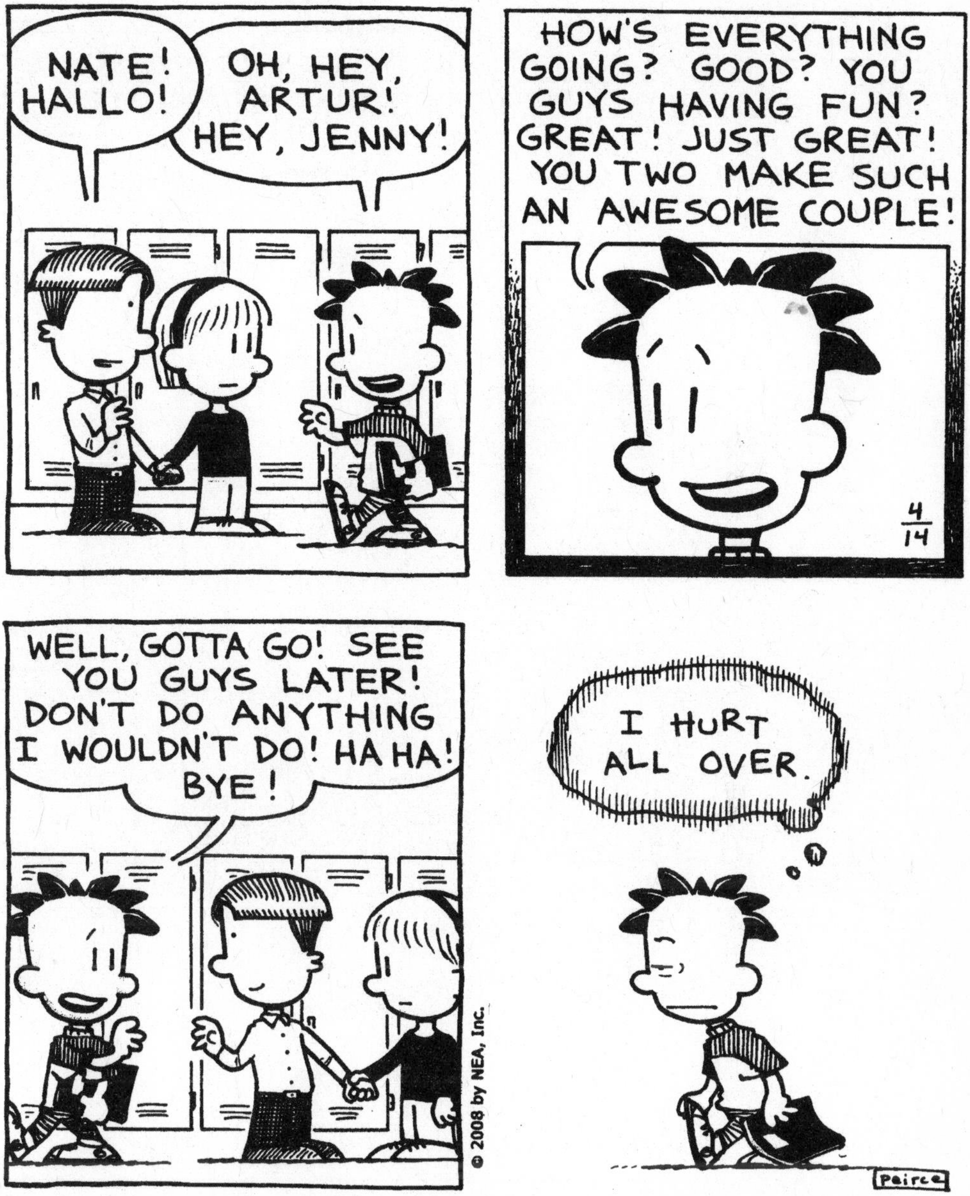
NATE! HALLO!
OH, HEY, ARTUR! HEY, JENNY!
HOW'S EVERYTHING GOING? GOOD? YOU GUYS HAVING FUN? GREAT! JUST GREAT! YOU TWO MAKE SUCH AN AWESOME COUPLE!
4/14
WELL, GOTTA GO! SEE YOU GUYS LATER! DON'T DO ANYTHING I WOULDN'T DO! HA HA! BYE!
© 2008 by NEA, Inc.
I HURT ALL OVER.
peirce

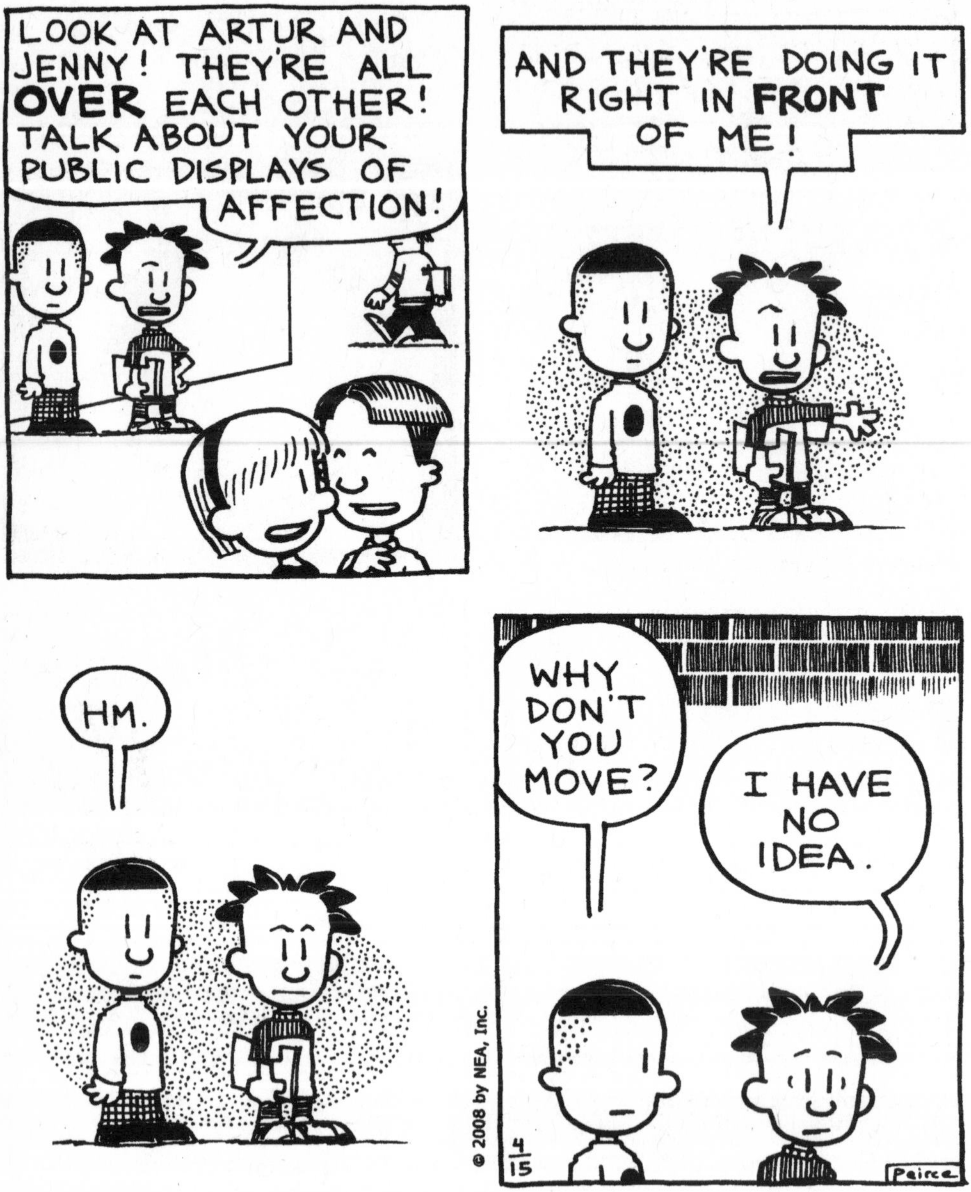
LOOK AT ARTUR AND JENNY! THEY'RE ALL **OVER** EACH OTHER! TALK ABOUT YOUR PUBLIC DISPLAYS OF AFFECTION!
AND THEY'RE DOING IT RIGHT IN **FRONT** OF ME!
HM.
WHY DON'T YOU MOVE?
I HAVE NO IDEA.
© 2008 by NEA, Inc.
4/15
Peirce

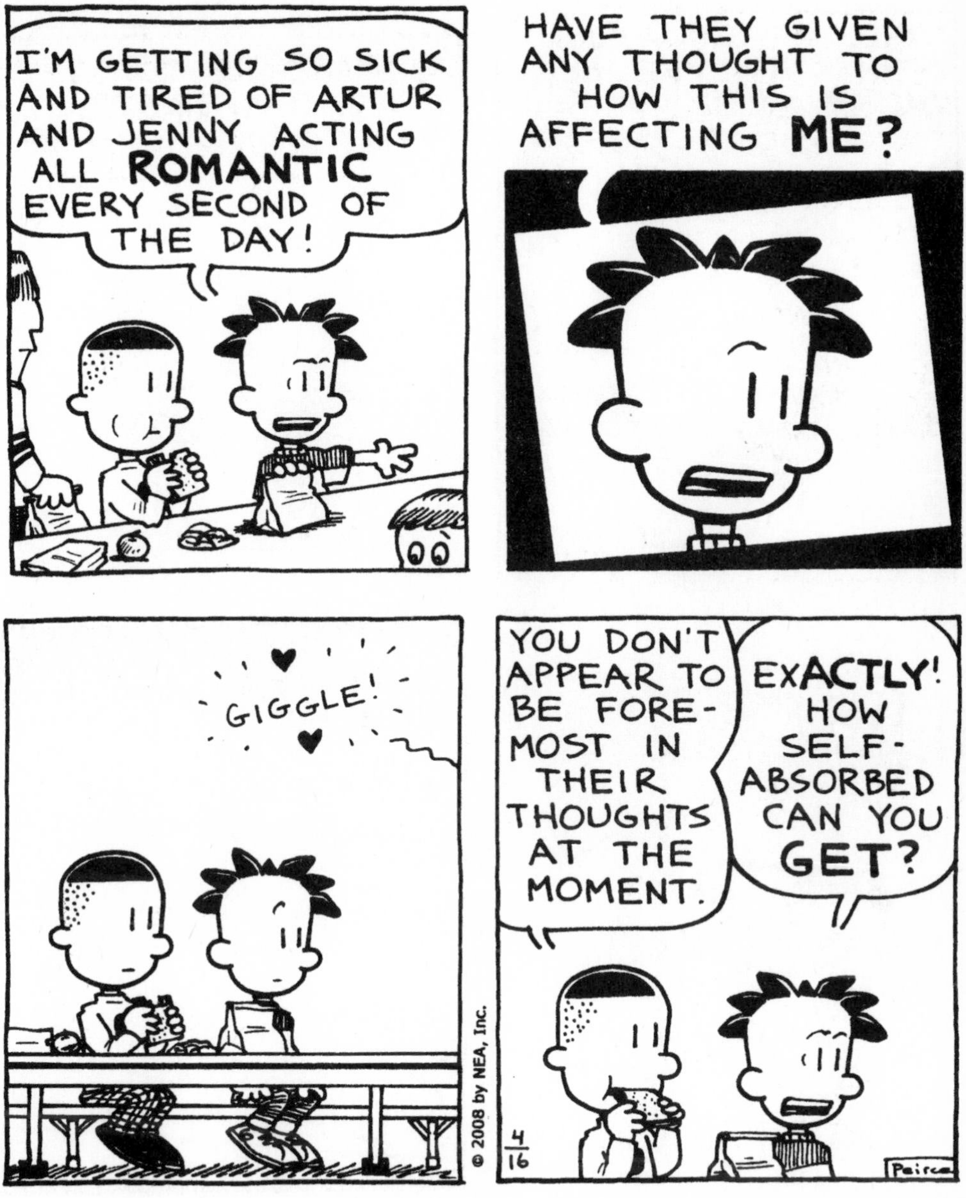
I'M GETTING SO SICK AND TIRED OF ARTUR AND JENNY ACTING ALL ROMANTIC EVERY SECOND OF THE DAY!
HAVE THEY GIVEN ANY THOUGHT TO HOW THIS IS AFFECTING ME?
GIGGLE!
© 2008 by NEA, Inc.
4/16
YOU DON'T APPEAR TO BE FORE-MOST IN THEIR THOUGHTS AT THE MOMENT.
EXACTLY! HOW SELF-ABSORBED CAN YOU GET?
Peirce

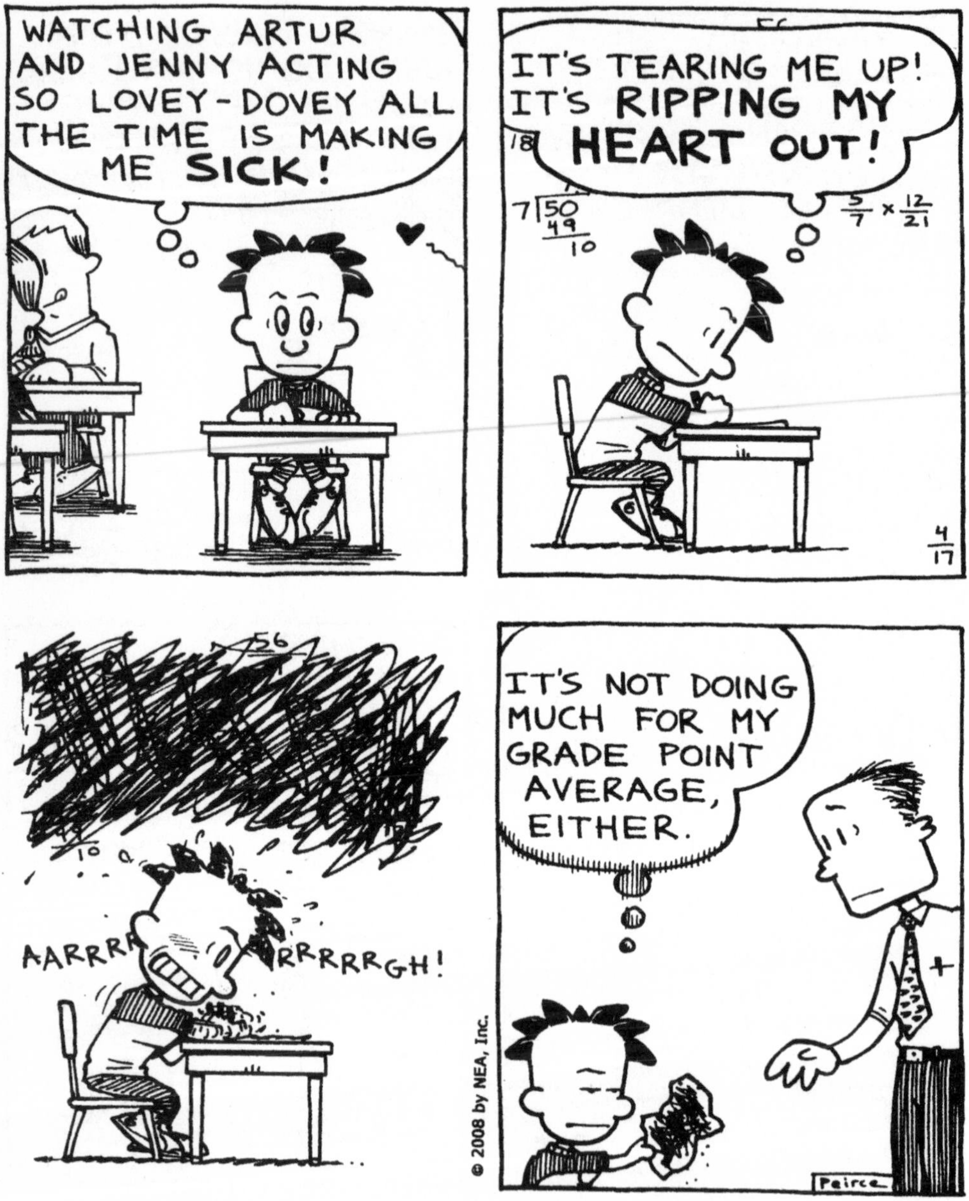
WATCHING ARTUR AND JENNY ACTING SO LOVEY-DOVEY ALL THE TIME IS MAKING ME SICK!
IT'S TEARING ME UP! IT'S RIPPING MY HEART OUT!
4/17
AARRRRRRRRRGH!
IT'S NOT DOING MUCH FOR MY GRADE POINT AVERAGE, EITHER.
Peirce

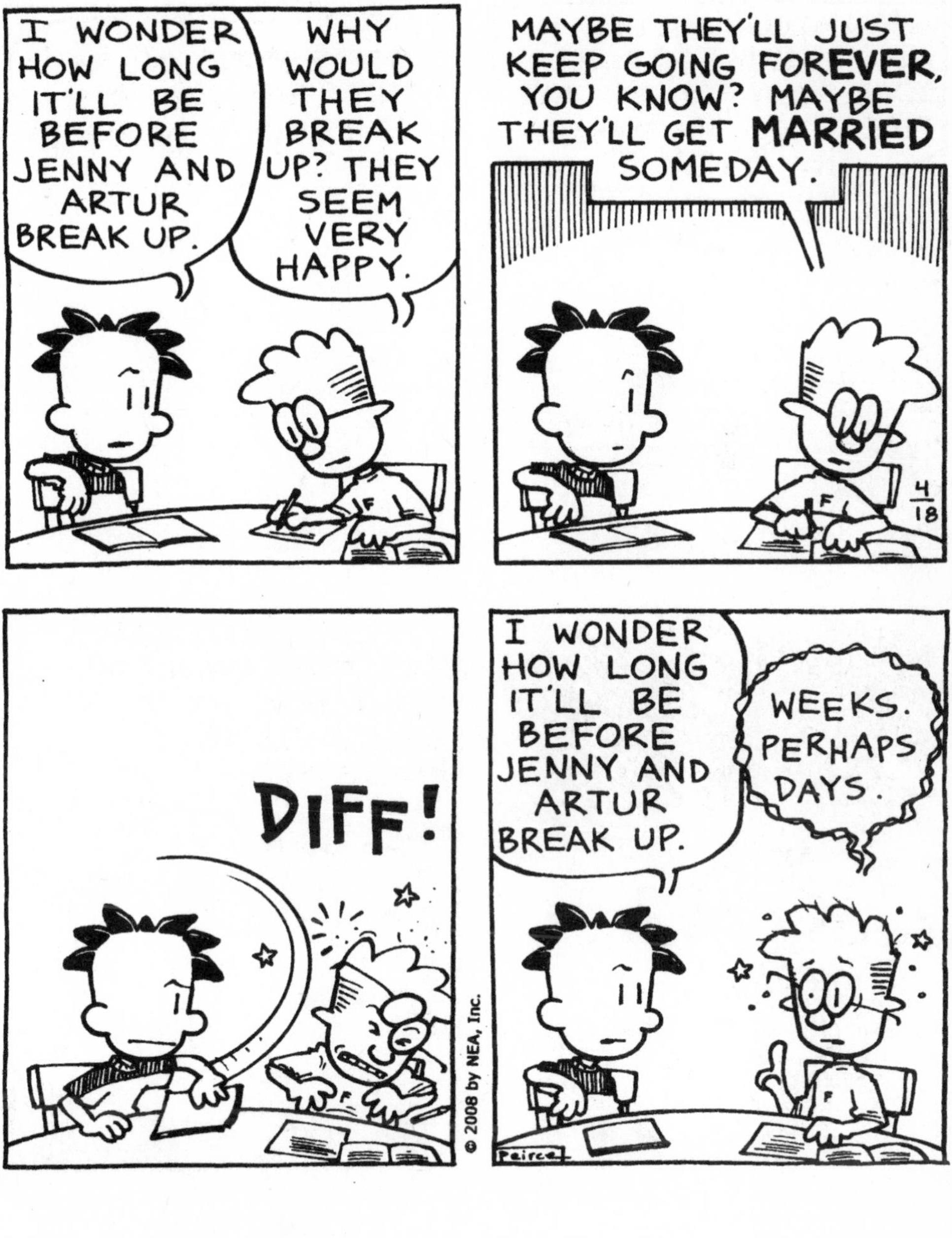
I WONDER HOW LONG IT'LL BE BEFORE JENNY AND ARTUR BREAK UP.
WHY WOULD THEY BREAK UP? THEY SEEM VERY HAPPY.
MAYBE THEY'LL JUST KEEP GOING FOREVER, YOU KNOW? MAYBE THEY'LL GET MARRIED SOMEDAY.
4/18
DIFF!
© 2008 by NEA, Inc.
I WONDER HOW LONG IT'LL BE BEFORE JENNY AND ARTUR BREAK UP.
WEEKS. PERHAPS DAYS.
Peirce

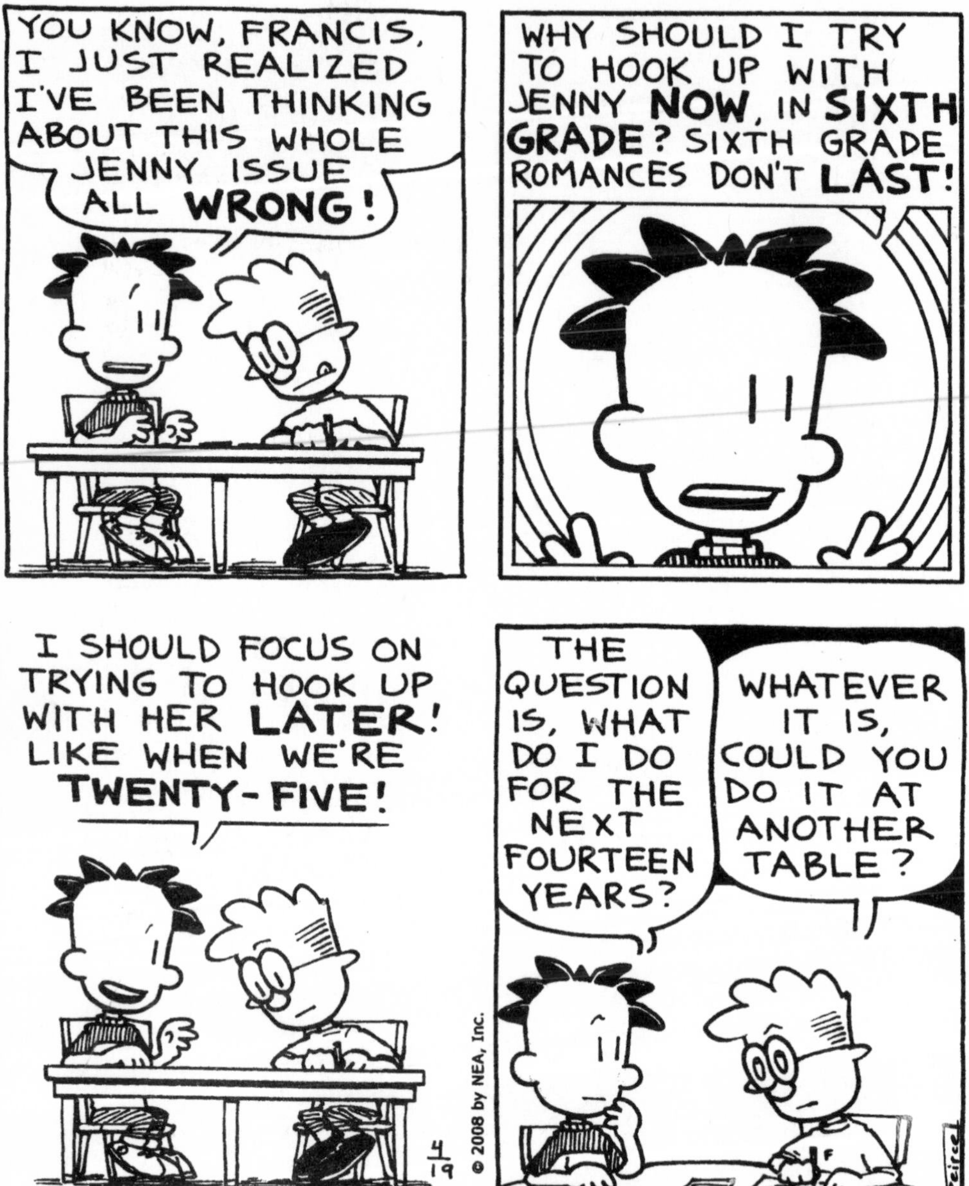
YOU KNOW, FRANCIS, I JUST REALIZED I'VE BEEN THINKING ABOUT THIS WHOLE JENNY ISSUE ALL WRONG!
WHY SHOULD I TRY TO HOOK UP WITH JENNY NOW, IN SIXTH GRADE? SIXTH GRADE ROMANCES DON'T LAST!
I SHOULD FOCUS ON TRYING TO HOOK UP WITH HER LATER! LIKE WHEN WE'RE TWENTY-FIVE!
THE QUESTION IS, WHAT DO I DO FOR THE NEXT FOURTEEN YEARS?
WHATEVER IT IS, COULD YOU DO IT AT ANOTHER TABLE?
4/19
Peirce

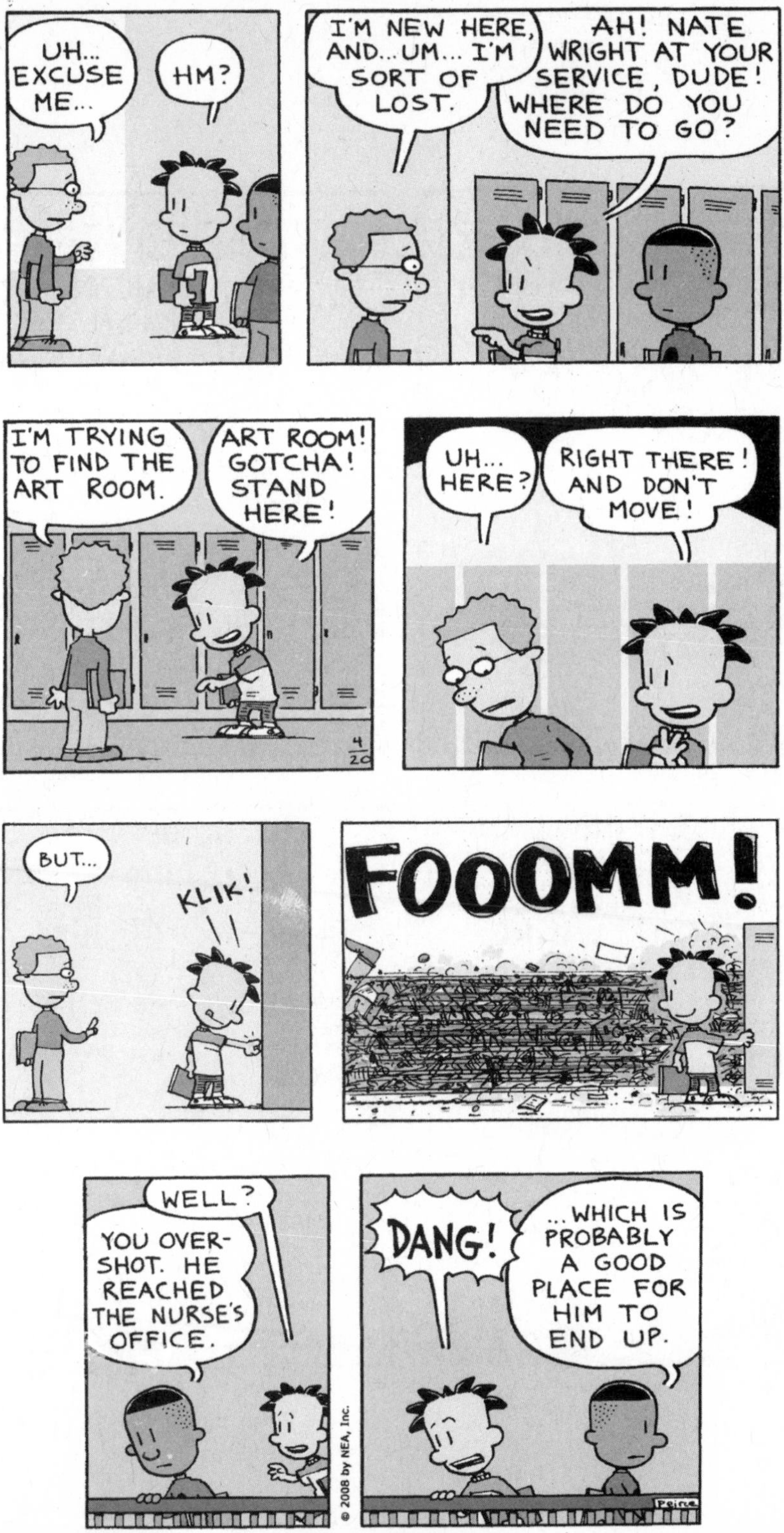
UH... EXCUSE ME...
HM?
I'M NEW HERE, AND... UM... I'M SORT OF LOST.
AH! NATE WRIGHT AT YOUR SERVICE, DUDE! WHERE DO YOU NEED TO GO?
I'M TRYING TO FIND THE ART ROOM.
ART ROOM! GOTCHA! STAND HERE!
4/20
UH... HERE?
RIGHT THERE! AND DON'T MOVE!
BUT...
KLIK!
FOOOMM!
WELL?
YOU OVER-SHOT. HE REACHED THE NURSE'S OFFICE.
DANG!
...WHICH IS PROBABLY A GOOD PLACE FOR HIM TO END UP.
© 2008 by NEA, Inc.
Peirce

SECRET FAN

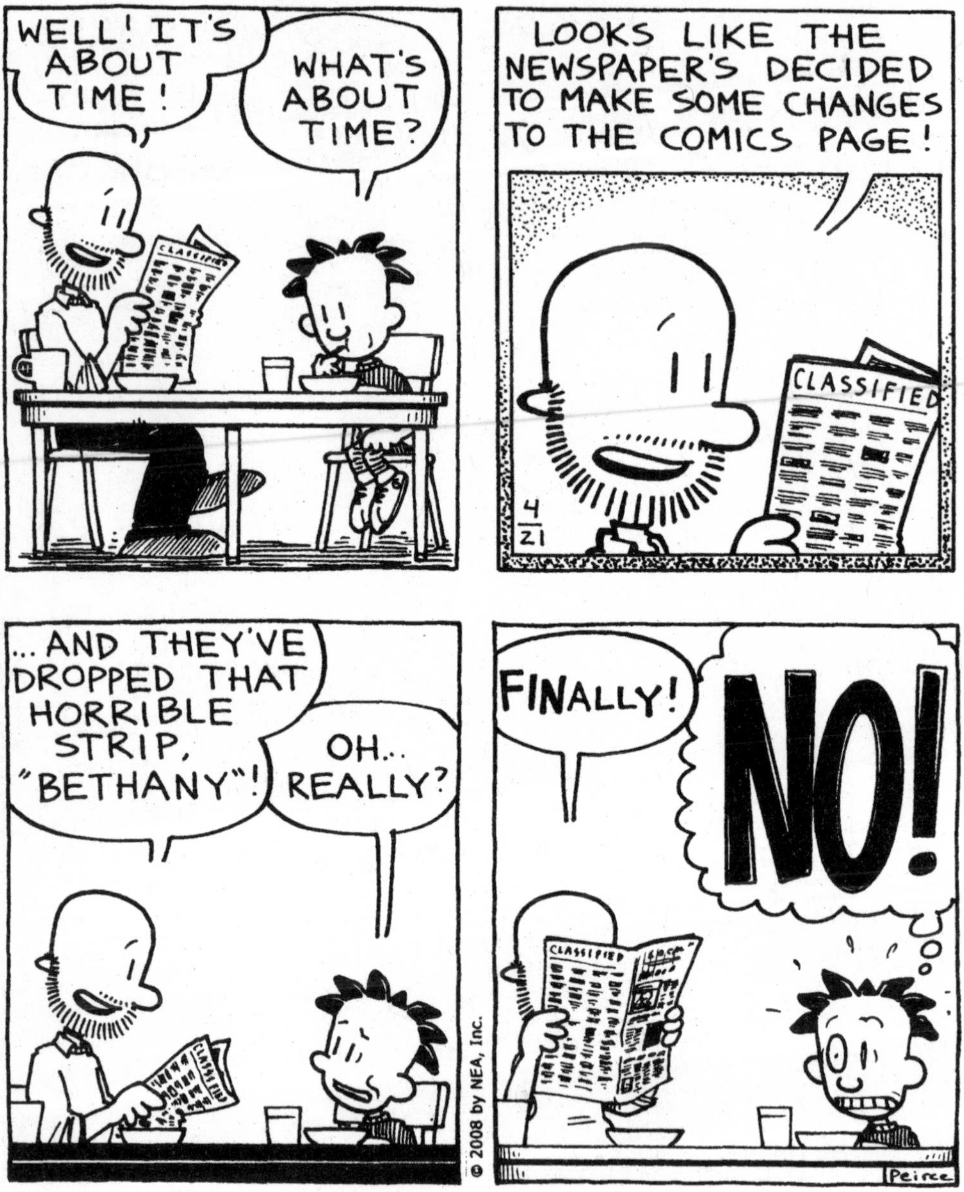
WELL! IT'S ABOUT TIME!
WHAT'S ABOUT TIME?
LOOKS LIKE THE NEWSPAPER'S DECIDED TO MAKE SOME CHANGES TO THE COMICS PAGE!
CLASSIFIED
4/21
... AND THEY'VE DROPPED THAT HORRIBLE STRIP, "BETHANY"!
OH... REALLY?
© 2008 by NEA, Inc.
FINALLY!
NO!
CLASSIFIED
Peirce

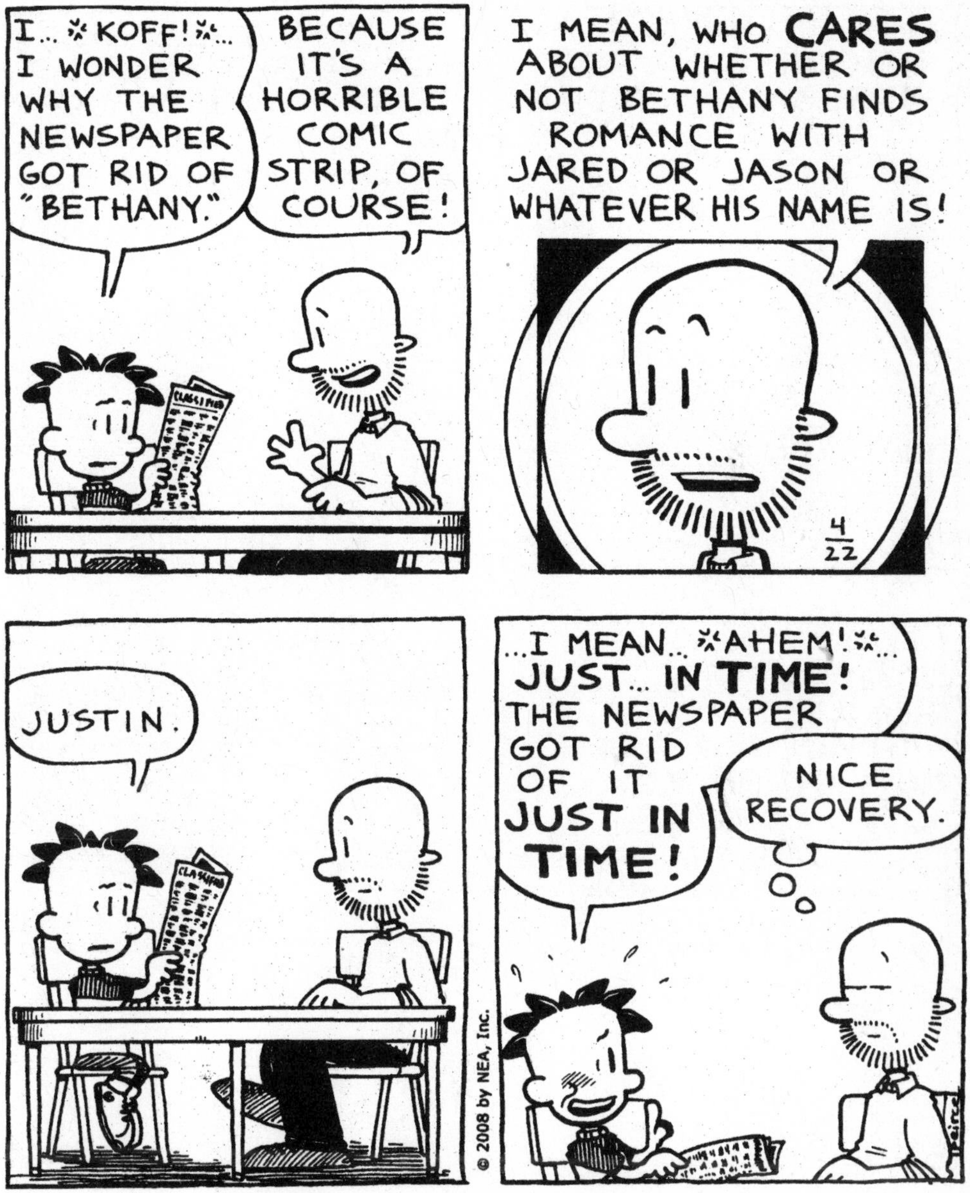
I... *KOFF!*... I WONDER WHY THE NEWSPAPER GOT RID OF "BETHANY."
BECAUSE IT'S A HORRIBLE COMIC STRIP, OF COURSE!
I MEAN, WHO CARES ABOUT WHETHER OR NOT BETHANY FINDS ROMANCE WITH JARED OR JASON OR WHATEVER HIS NAME IS!
4/22
JUSTIN.
...I MEAN... *AHEM!*... JUST... IN TIME! THE NEWSPAPER GOT RID OF IT JUST IN TIME!
NICE RECOVERY.
© 2008 by NEA, Inc.

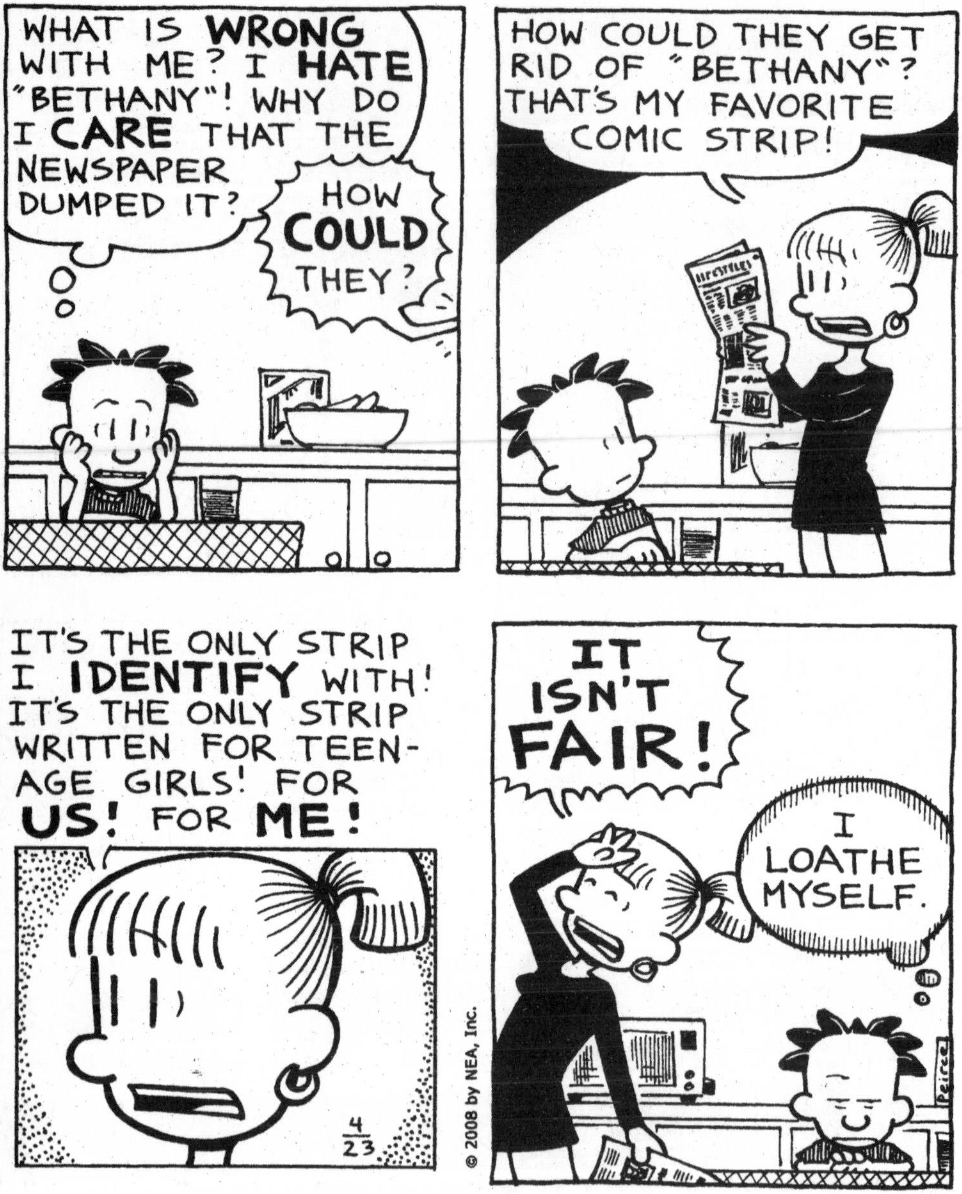
WHAT IS WRONG WITH ME? I HATE "BETHANY"! WHY DO I CARE THAT THE NEWSPAPER DUMPED IT?
HOW COULD THEY?
HOW COULD THEY GET RID OF "BETHANY"? THAT'S MY FAVORITE COMIC STRIP!
IT'S THE ONLY STRIP I IDENTIFY WITH! IT'S THE ONLY STRIP WRITTEN FOR TEEN-AGE GIRLS! FOR US! FOR ME!
4 23
© 2008 by NEA, Inc.
IT ISN'T FAIR!
I LOATHE MYSELF.
Peirce

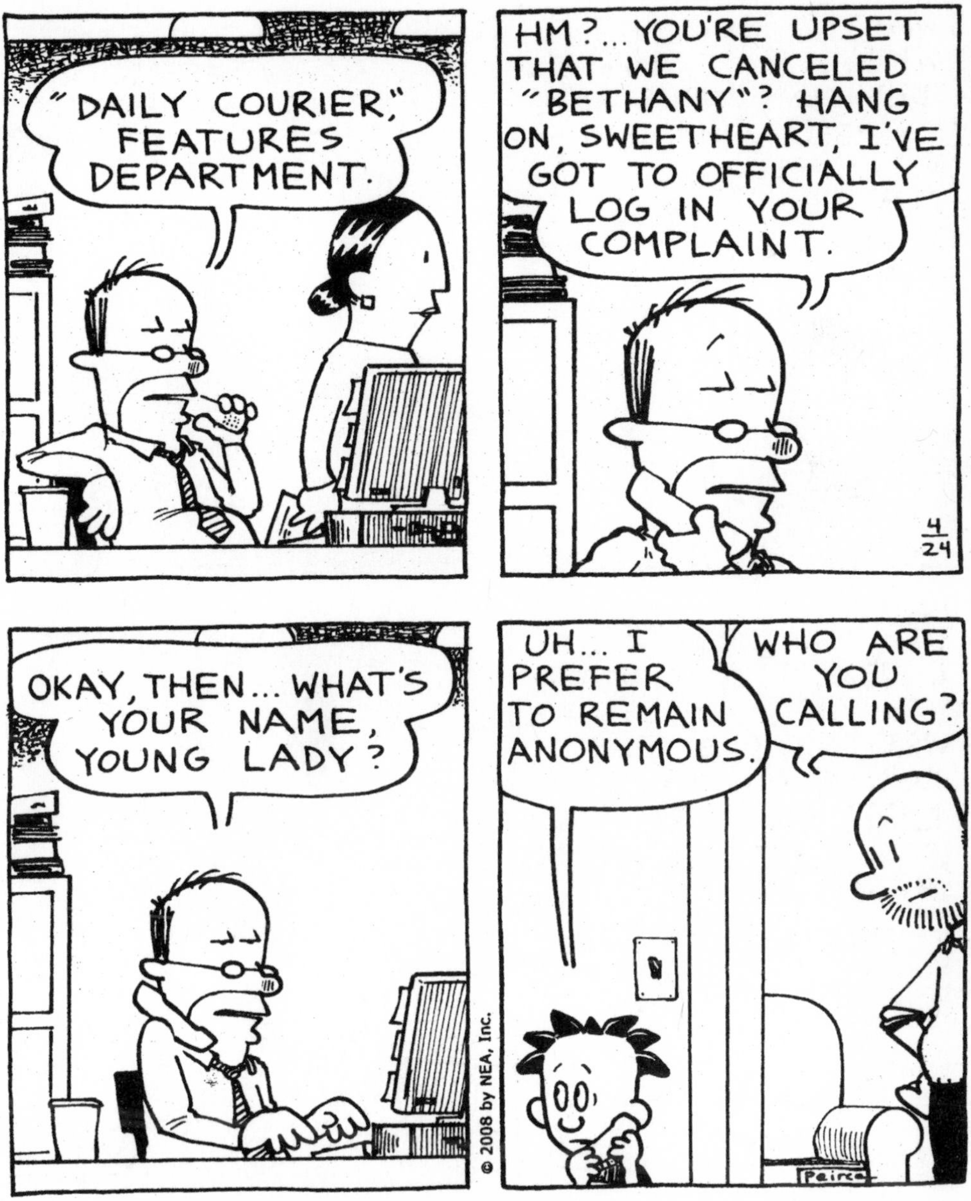

"DAILY COURIER," FEATURES DEPARTMENT.
HM?... YOU'RE UPSET THAT WE CANCELED "BETHANY"? HANG ON, SWEETHEART, I'VE GOT TO OFFICIALLY LOG IN YOUR COMPLAINT.
4/24
OKAY, THEN... WHAT'S YOUR NAME, YOUNG LADY?
UH... I PREFER TO REMAIN ANONYMOUS.
WHO ARE YOU CALLING?
Peirce

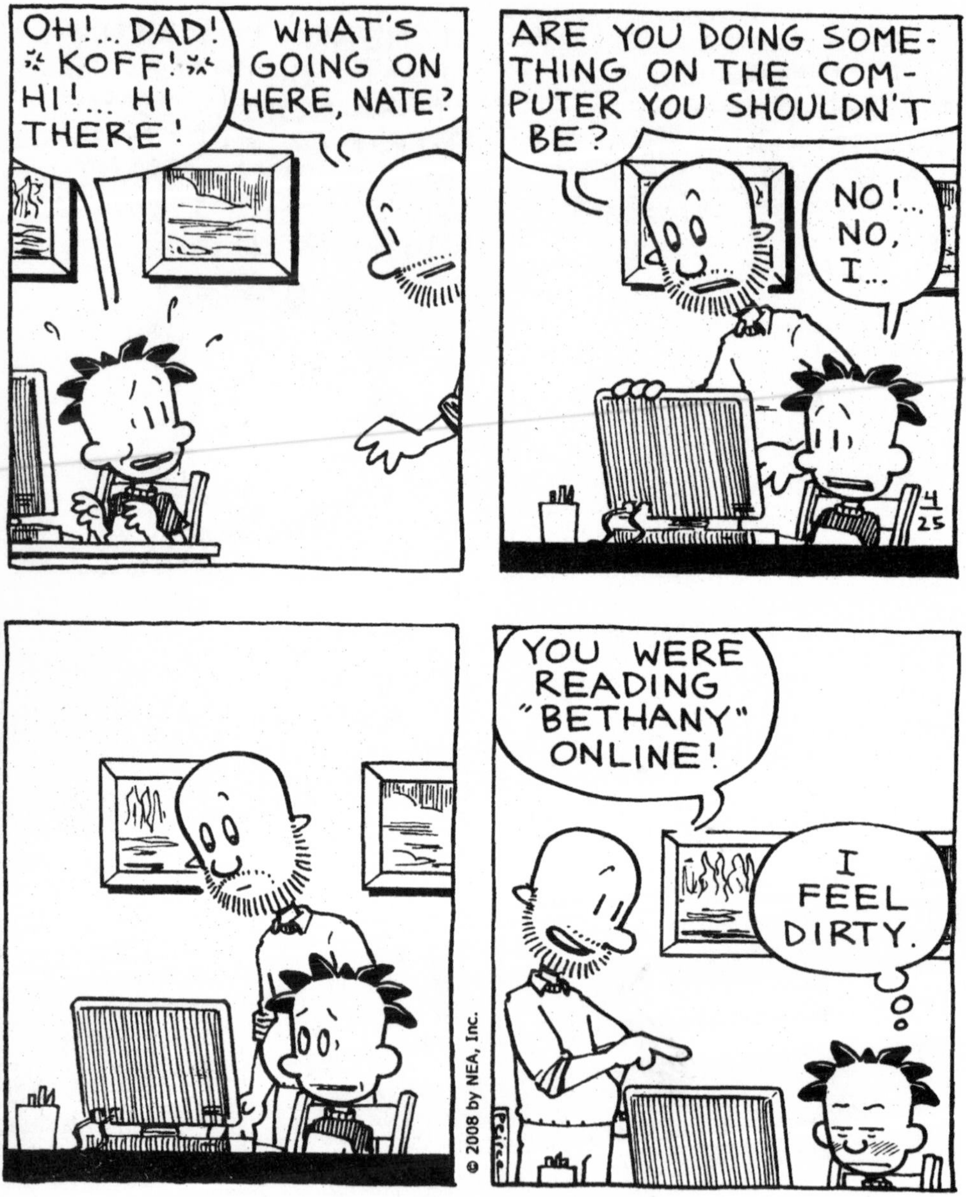
OH!... DAD! KOFF! HI!... HI THERE!
WHAT'S GOING ON HERE, NATE?
ARE YOU DOING SOMETHING ON THE COMPUTER YOU SHOULDN'T BE?
NO!... NO, I...
4/25
© 2008 by NEA, Inc.
YOU WERE READING "BETHANY" ONLINE!
I FEEL DIRTY.

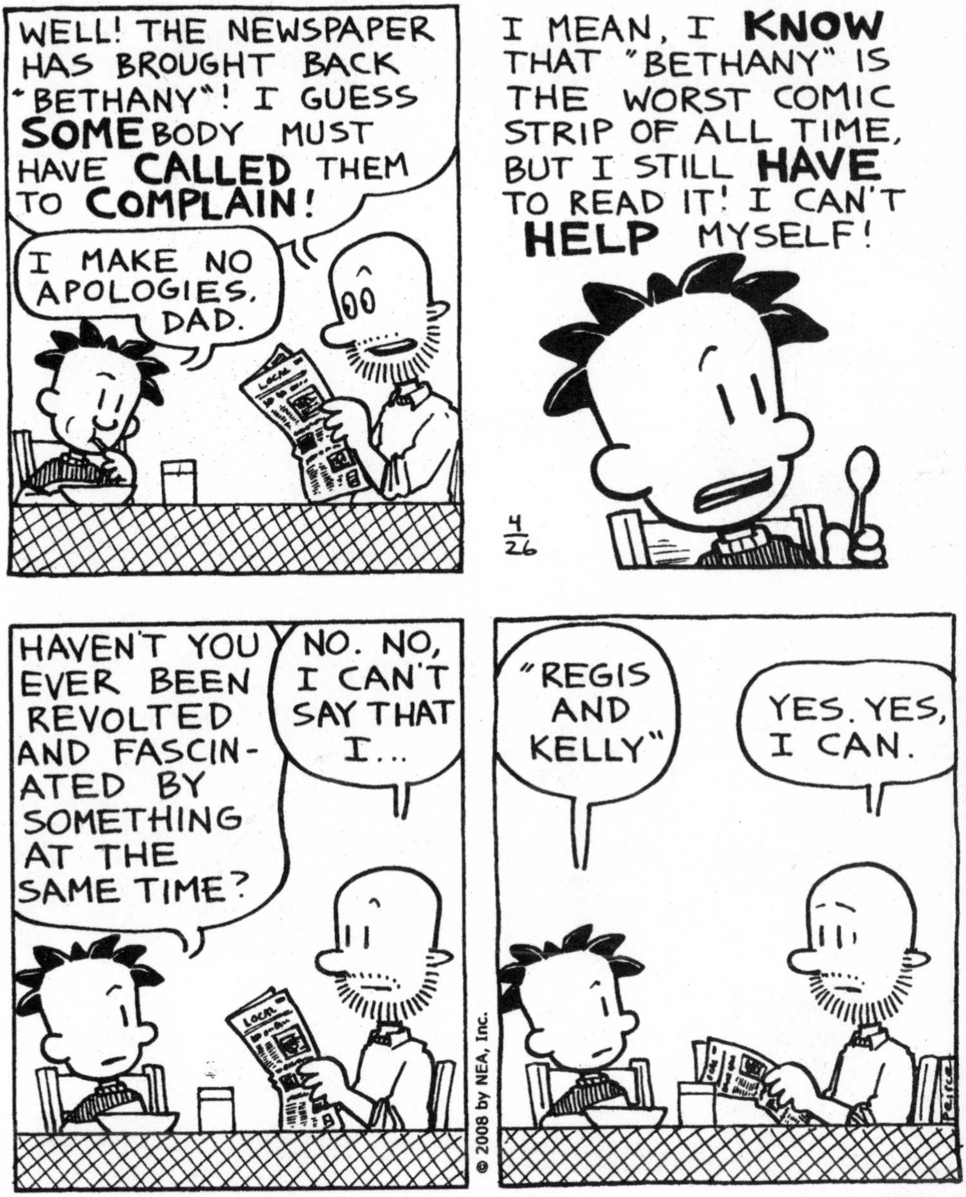
WELL! THE NEWSPAPER HAS BROUGHT BACK "BETHANY"! I GUESS **SOME**BODY MUST HAVE **CALLED** THEM TO **COMPLAIN**!
I MAKE NO APOLOGIES, DAD.
LOCAL
I MEAN, I **KNOW** THAT "BETHANY" IS THE WORST COMIC STRIP OF ALL TIME, BUT I STILL **HAVE** TO READ IT! I CAN'T **HELP** MYSELF!
4/26
HAVEN'T YOU EVER BEEN REVOLTED AND FASCINATED BY SOMETHING AT THE SAME TIME?
NO. NO, I CAN'T SAY THAT I...
LOCAL
"REGIS AND KELLY"
YES. YES, I CAN.
PEIRCE

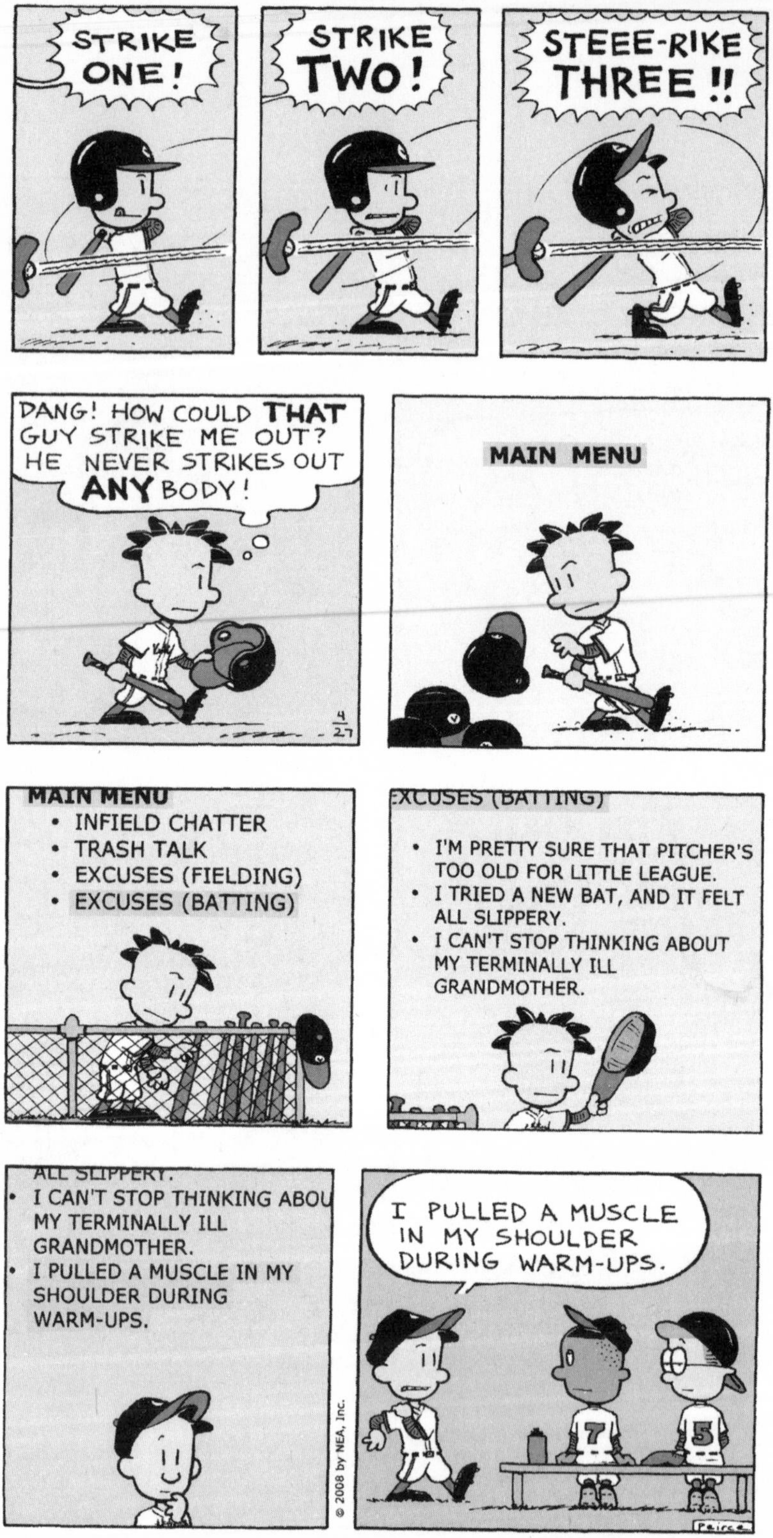
STRIKE ONE!
STRIKE TWO!
STEEE-RIKE THREE!!
DANG! HOW COULD THAT GUY STRIKE ME OUT? HE NEVER STRIKES OUT ANYBODY!
4
27
MAIN MENU
MAIN MENU
• INFIELD CHATTER
• TRASH TALK
• EXCUSES (FIELDING)
• EXCUSES (BATTING)
EXCUSES (BATTING)
• I'M PRETTY SURE THAT PITCHER'S TOO OLD FOR LITTLE LEAGUE.
• I TRIED A NEW BAT, AND IT FELT ALL SLIPPERY.
• I CAN'T STOP THINKING ABOUT MY TERMINALLY ILL GRANDMOTHER.
ALL SLIPPERY.
• I CAN'T STOP THINKING ABOU
MY TERMINALLY ILL GRANDMOTHER.
• I PULLED A MUSCLE IN MY SHOULDER DURING WARM-UPS.
© 2008 by NEA, Inc.
I PULLED A MUSCLE IN MY SHOULDER DURING WARM-UPS.
7
5
Peirce

BATTER UP!

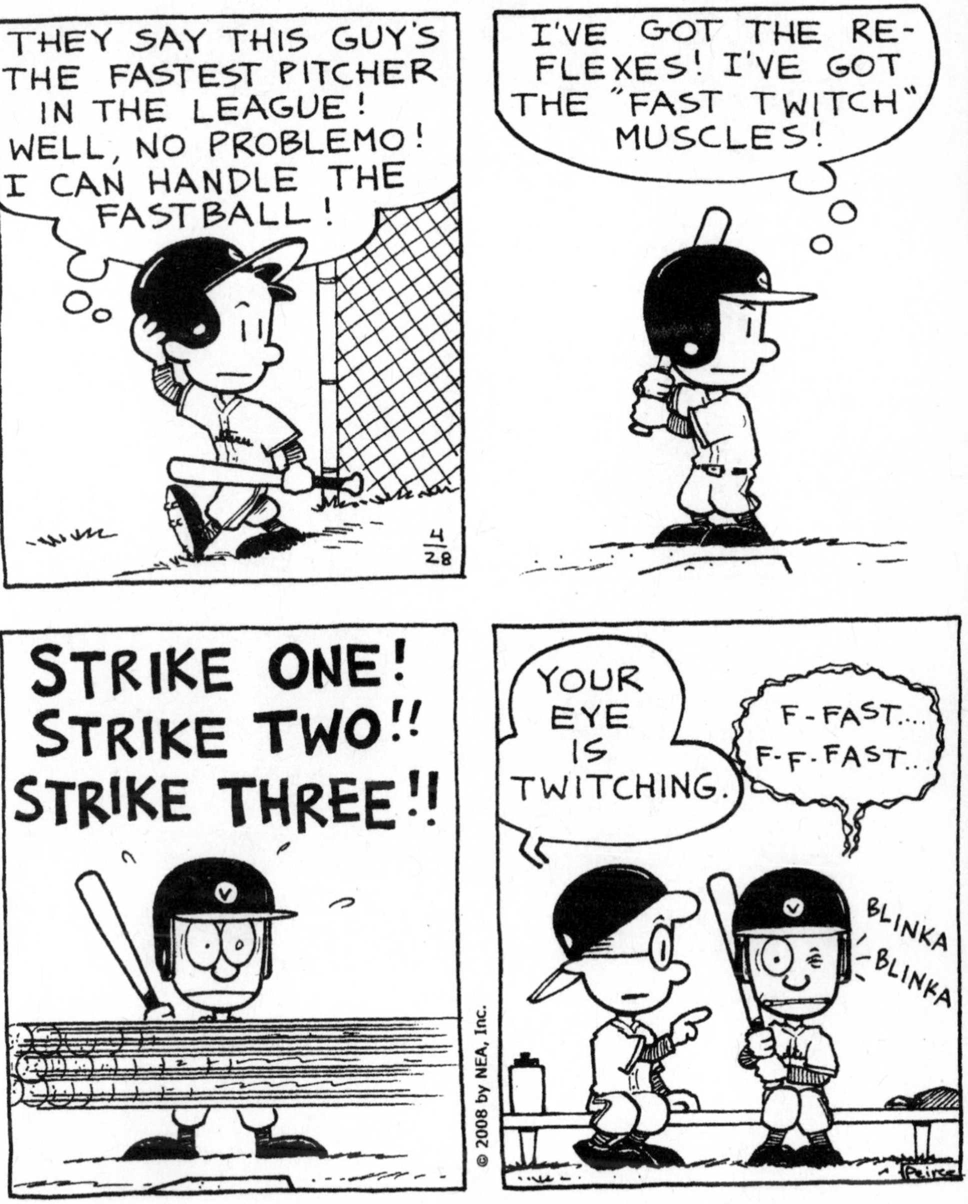
THEY SAY THIS GUY'S THE FASTEST PITCHER IN THE LEAGUE! WELL, NO PROBLEMO! I CAN HANDLE THE FASTBALL!
4/28
I'VE GOT THE RE-FLEXES! I'VE GOT THE "FAST TWITCH" MUSCLES!
STRIKE ONE!
STRIKE TWO!!
STRIKE THREE!!
YOUR EYE IS TWITCHING.
F-FAST... F-F-FAST...
BLINKA
BLINKA
Peirce

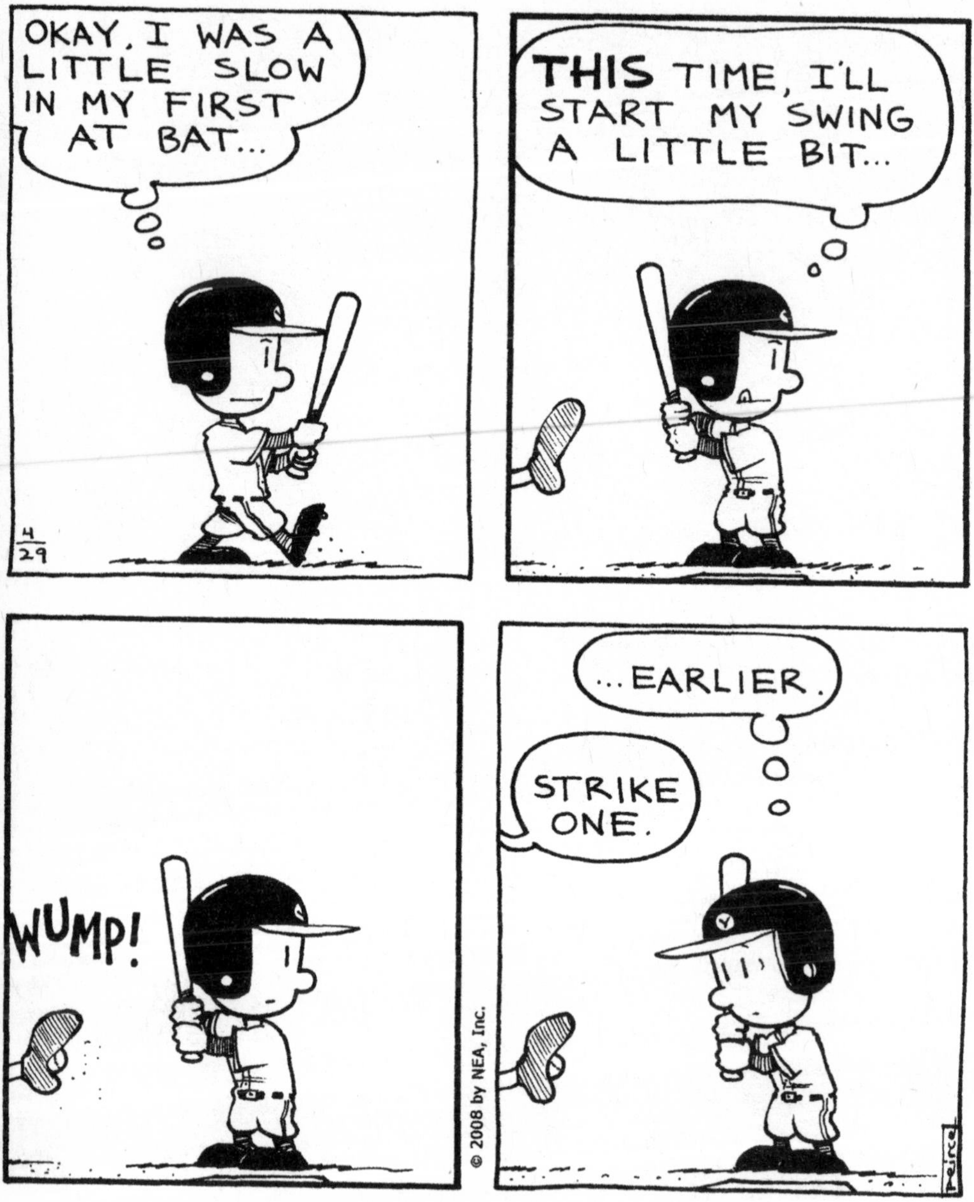
OKAY, I WAS A LITTLE SLOW IN MY FIRST AT BAT...
THIS TIME, I'LL START MY SWING A LITTLE BIT...
WUMP!
...EARLIER.
STRIKE ONE.
© 2008 by NEA, Inc.

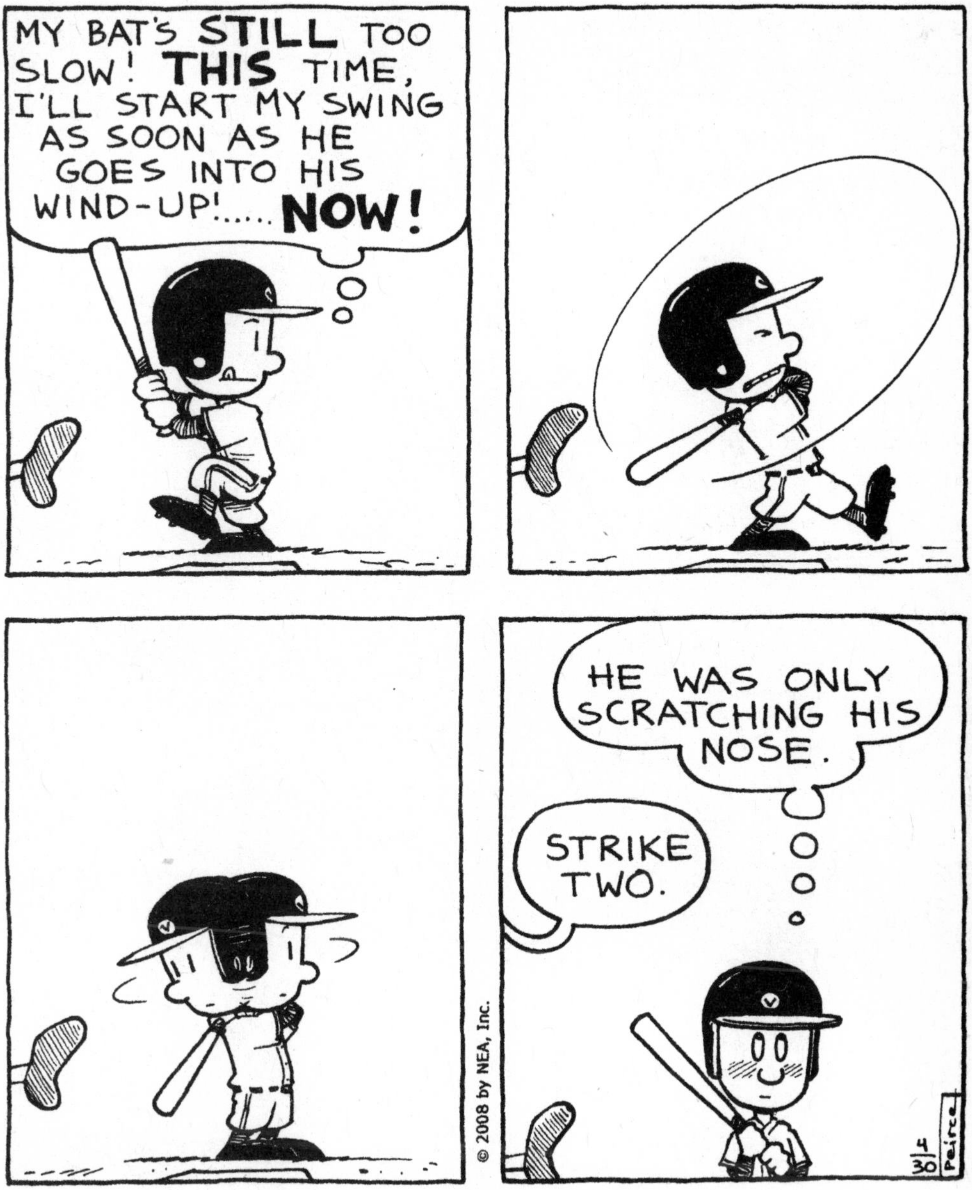
MY BAT'S STILL TOO SLOW! THIS TIME, I'LL START MY SWING AS SOON AS HE GOES INTO HIS WIND-UP!..... NOW!
STRIKE TWO.
HE WAS ONLY SCRATCHING HIS NOSE.
© 2008 by NEA, Inc.
4 30 Peirce

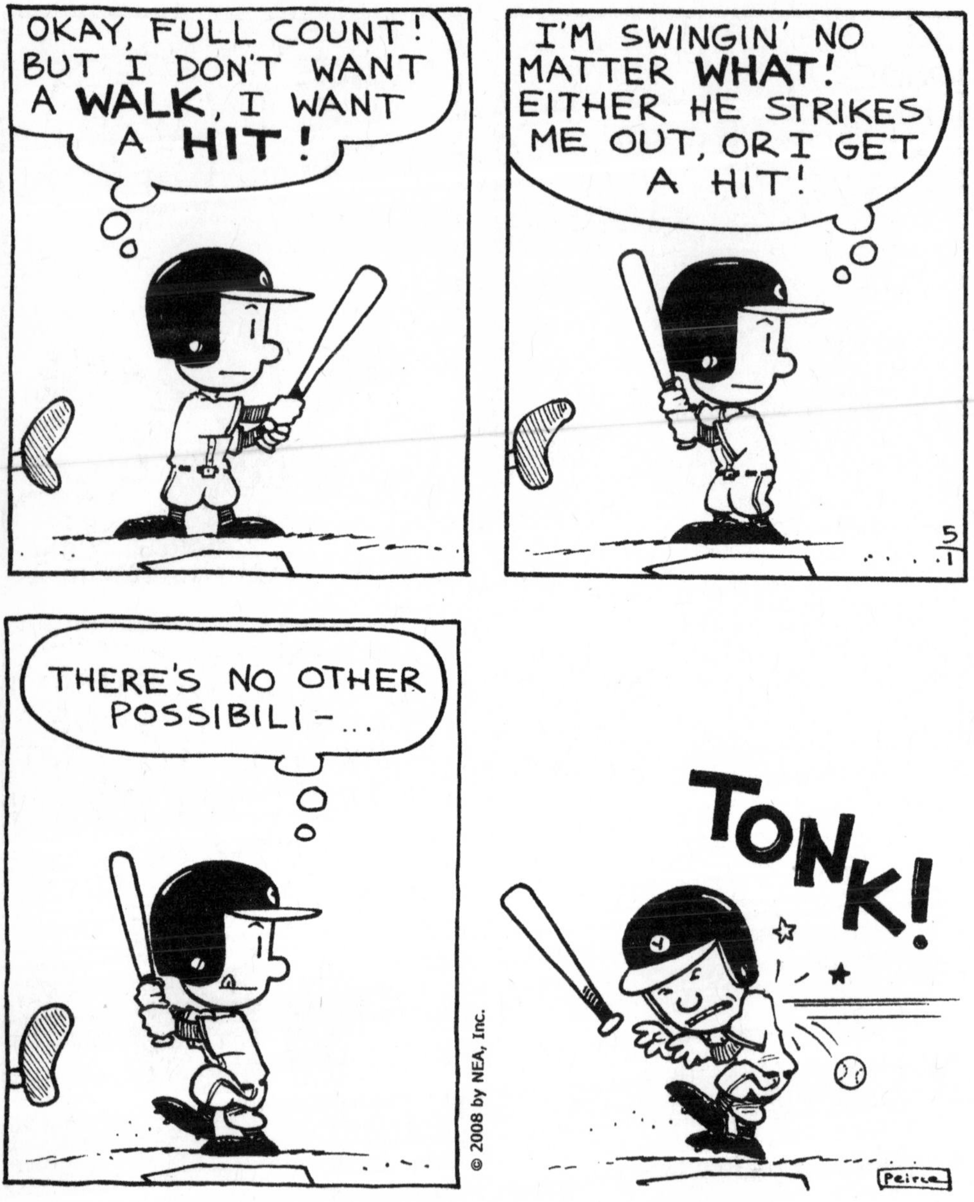
OKAY, FULL COUNT! BUT I DON'T WANT A **WALK**, I WANT A **HIT**!
I'M SWINGIN' NO MATTER **WHAT**! EITHER HE STRIKES ME OUT, OR I GET A HIT!
5/1
THERE'S NO OTHER POSSIBILI-...
TONK!
Peirce

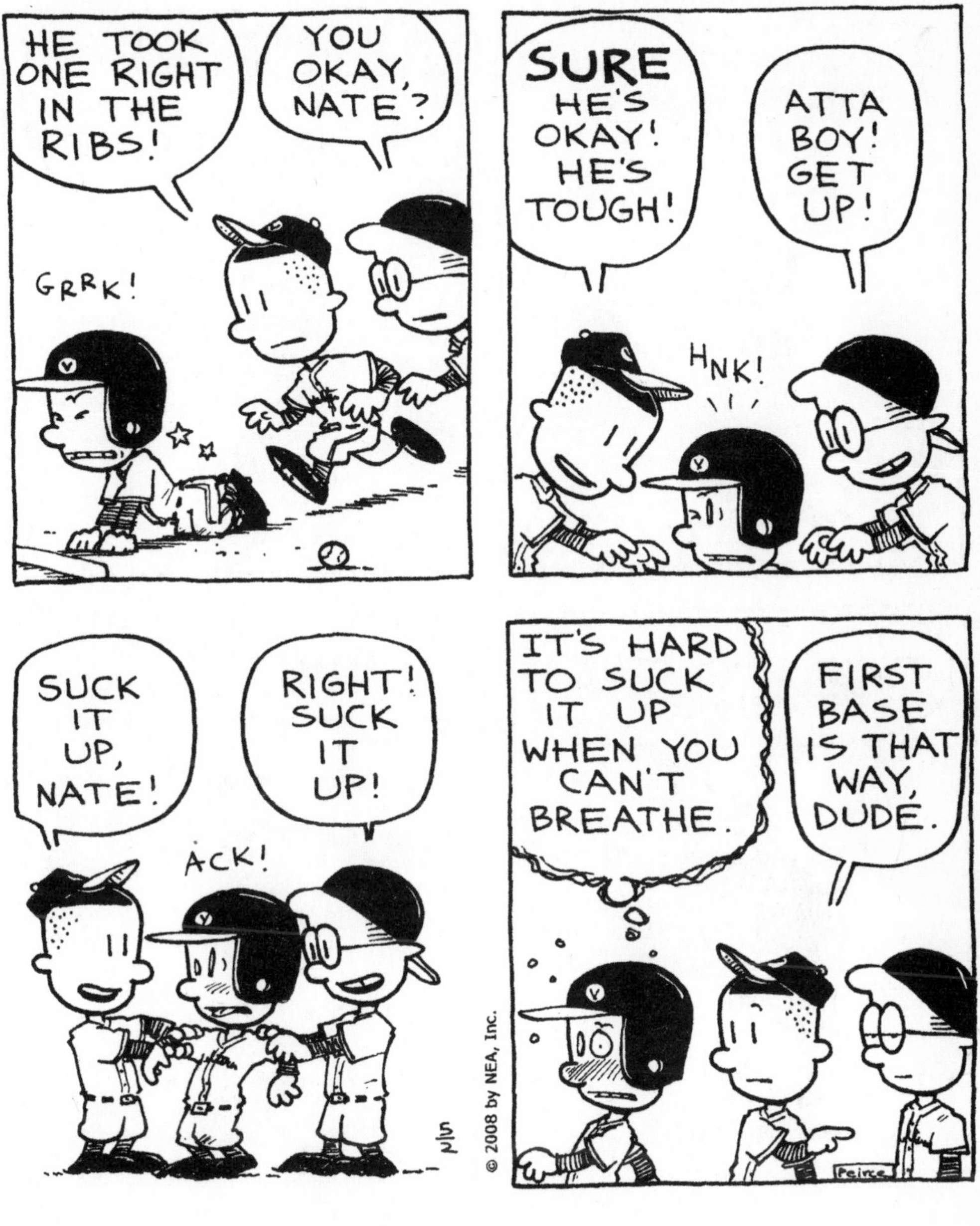
HE TOOK ONE RIGHT IN THE RIBS!
YOU OKAY, NATE?
GRRK!
SURE HE'S OKAY! HE'S TOUGH!
ATTA BOY! GET UP!
HNK!
SUCK IT UP, NATE!
RIGHT! SUCK IT UP!
ACK!
IT'S HARD TO SUCK IT UP WHEN YOU CAN'T BREATHE.
FIRST BASE IS THAT WAY, DUDE.
Peirce

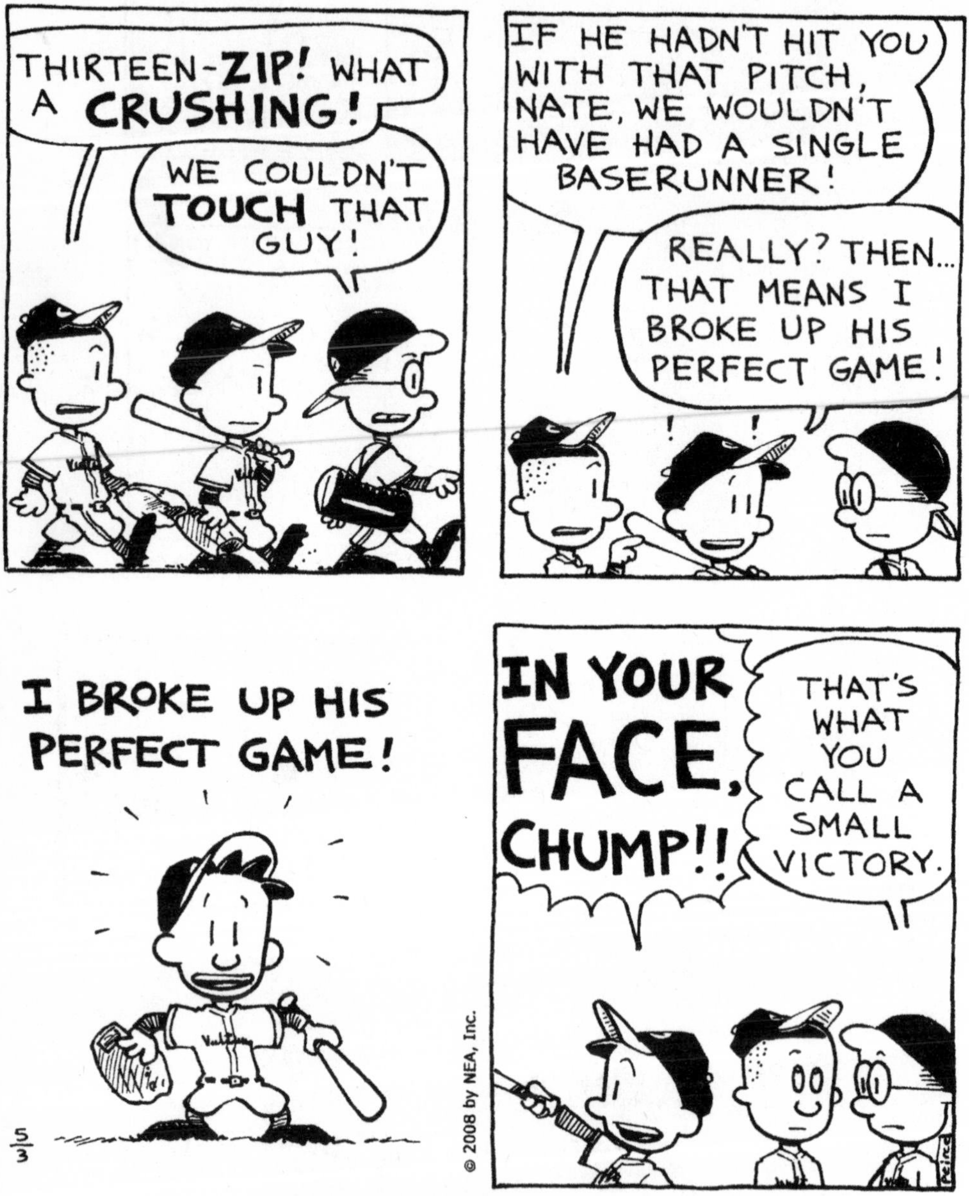

THIRTEEN-ZIP! WHAT A CRUSHING!
WE COULDN'T TOUCH THAT GUY!
IF HE HADN'T HIT YOU WITH THAT PITCH, NATE, WE WOULDN'T HAVE HAD A SINGLE BASERUNNER!
REALLY? THEN... THAT MEANS I BROKE UP HIS PERFECT GAME!
! !
I BROKE UP HIS PERFECT GAME!
5/3
© 2008 by NEA, Inc.
IN YOUR FACE, CHUMP!!
THAT'S WHAT YOU CALL A SMALL VICTORY.

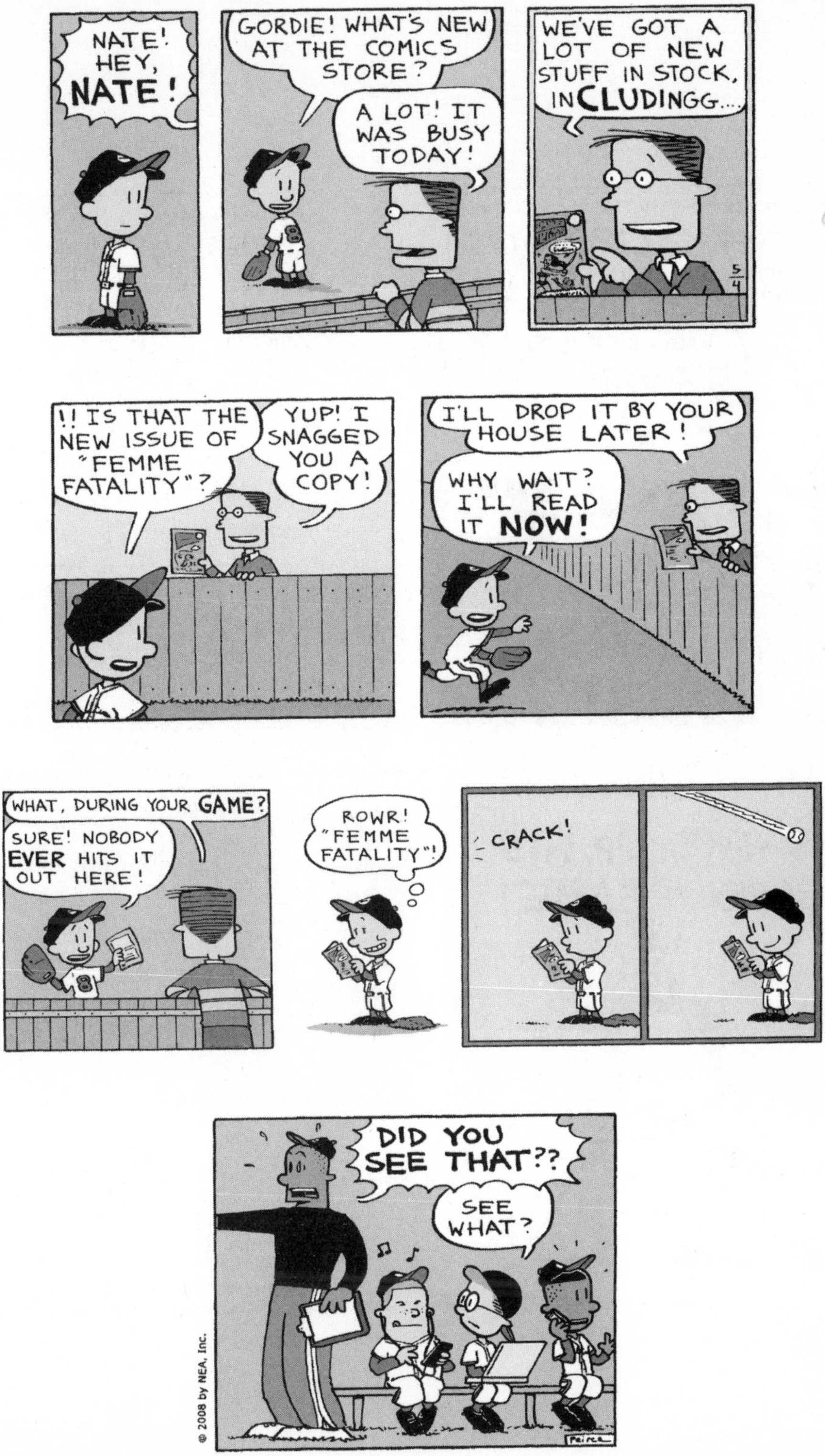

NATE! HEY, NATE!
GORDIE! WHAT'S NEW AT THE COMICS STORE?
A LOT! IT WAS BUSY TODAY!
WE'VE GOT A LOT OF NEW STUFF IN STOCK, INCLUDINGG...
5/4
!! IS THAT THE NEW ISSUE OF "FEMME FATALITY"?
YUP! I SNAGGED YOU A COPY!
I'LL DROP IT BY YOUR HOUSE LATER!
WHY WAIT? I'LL READ IT NOW!
WHAT, DURING YOUR GAME?
SURE! NOBODY EVER HITS IT OUT HERE!
ROWR! "FEMME FATALITY"!
CRACK!
DID YOU SEE THAT??
SEE WHAT?
© 2008 by NEA, Inc.
Peirce

WHAT COULD POSSIBLY GO WRONG?

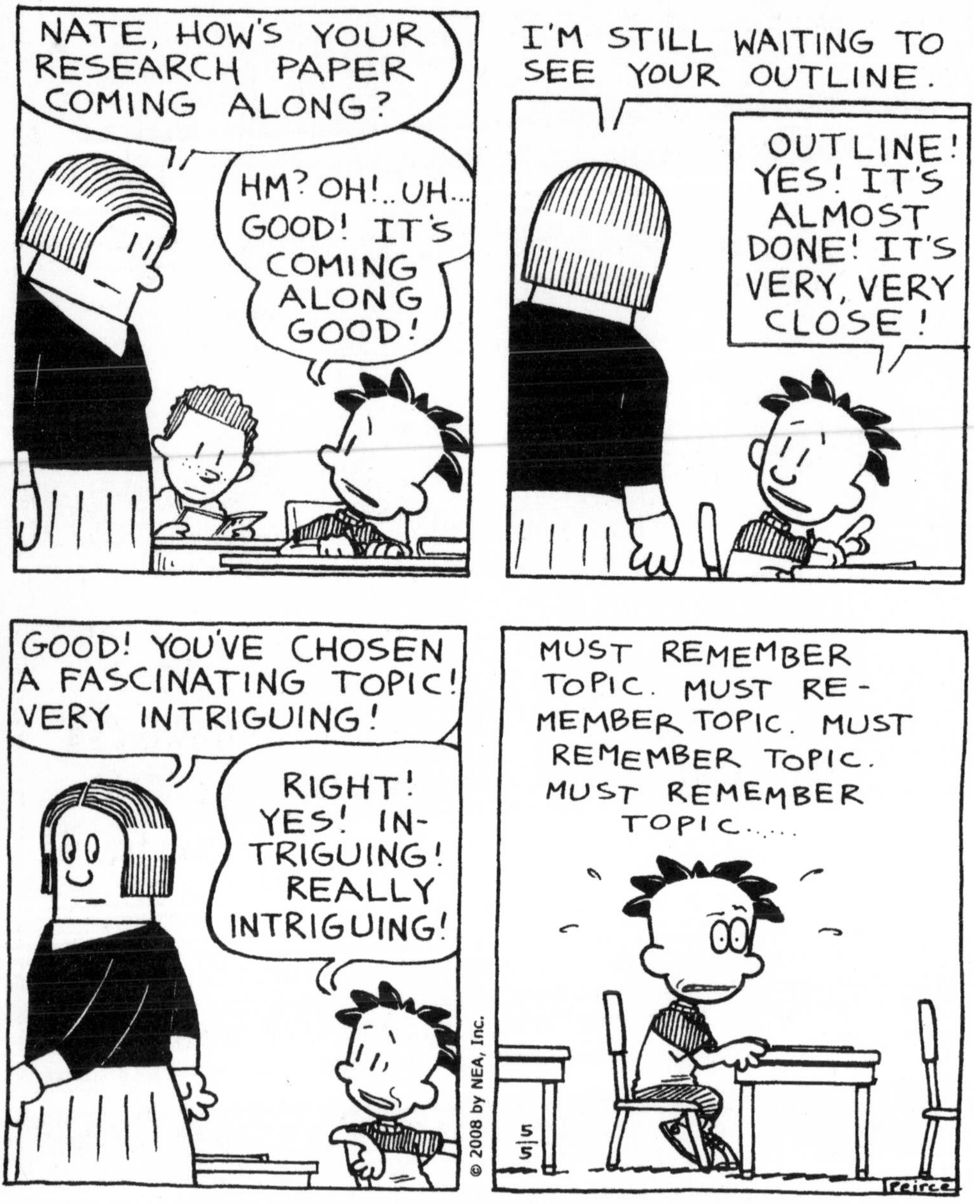
NATE, HOW'S YOUR RESEARCH PAPER COMING ALONG?
HM? OH!..UH... GOOD! IT'S COMING ALONG GOOD!
I'M STILL WAITING TO SEE YOUR OUTLINE.
OUTLINE! YES! IT'S ALMOST DONE! IT'S VERY, VERY CLOSE!
GOOD! YOU'VE CHOSEN A FASCINATING TOPIC! VERY INTRIGUING!
RIGHT! YES! INTRIGUING! REALLY INTRIGUING!
© 2008 by NEA, Inc.
MUST REMEMBER TOPIC. MUST REMEMBER TOPIC. MUST REMEMBER TOPIC. MUST REMEMBER TOPIC.....
Peirce

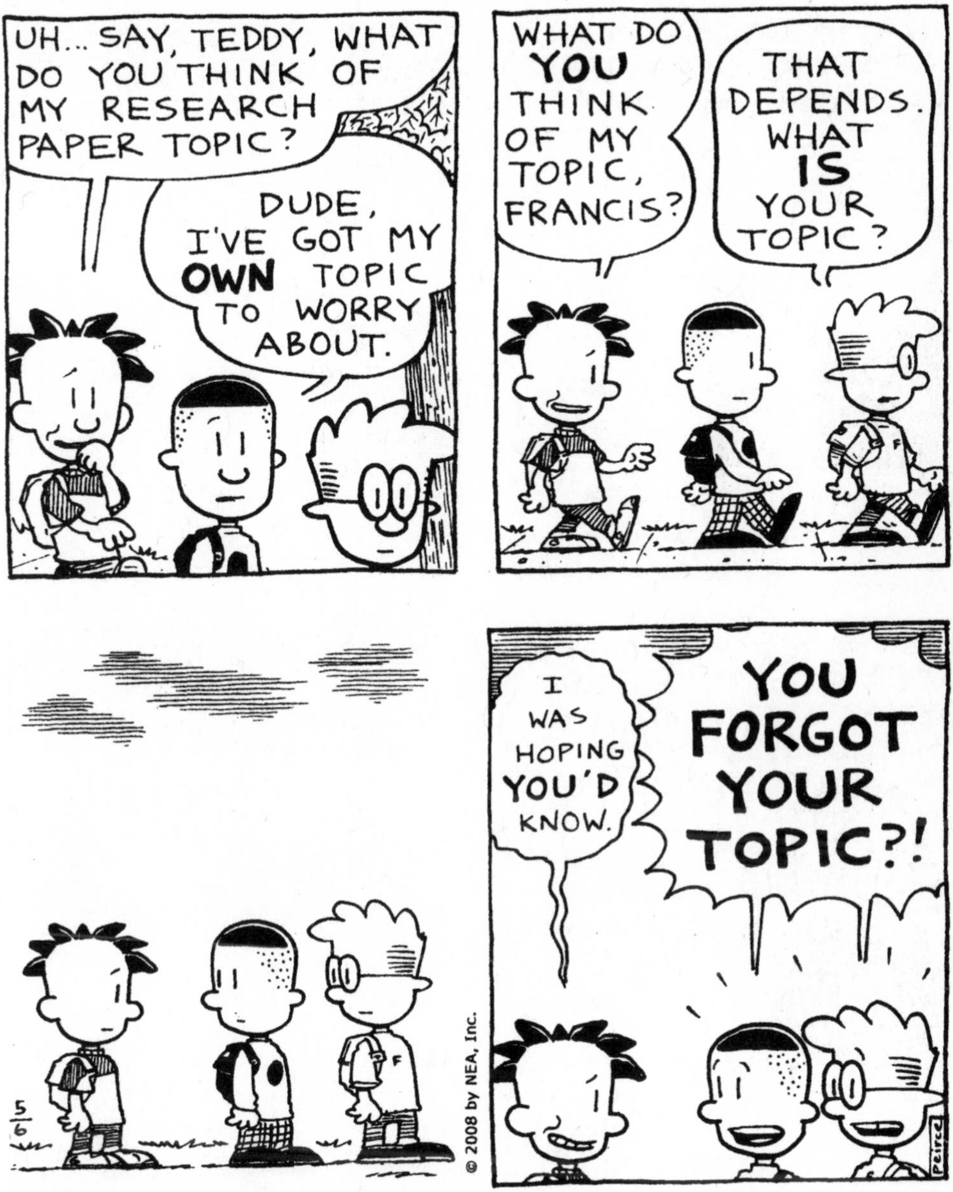
UH... SAY, TEDDY, WHAT DO YOU THINK OF MY RESEARCH PAPER TOPIC?
DUDE, I'VE GOT MY OWN TOPIC TO WORRY ABOUT.
WHAT DO YOU THINK OF MY TOPIC, FRANCIS?
THAT DEPENDS. WHAT IS YOUR TOPIC?
I WAS HOPING YOU'D KNOW.
YOU FORGOT YOUR TOPIC?!
5/6
Peirce

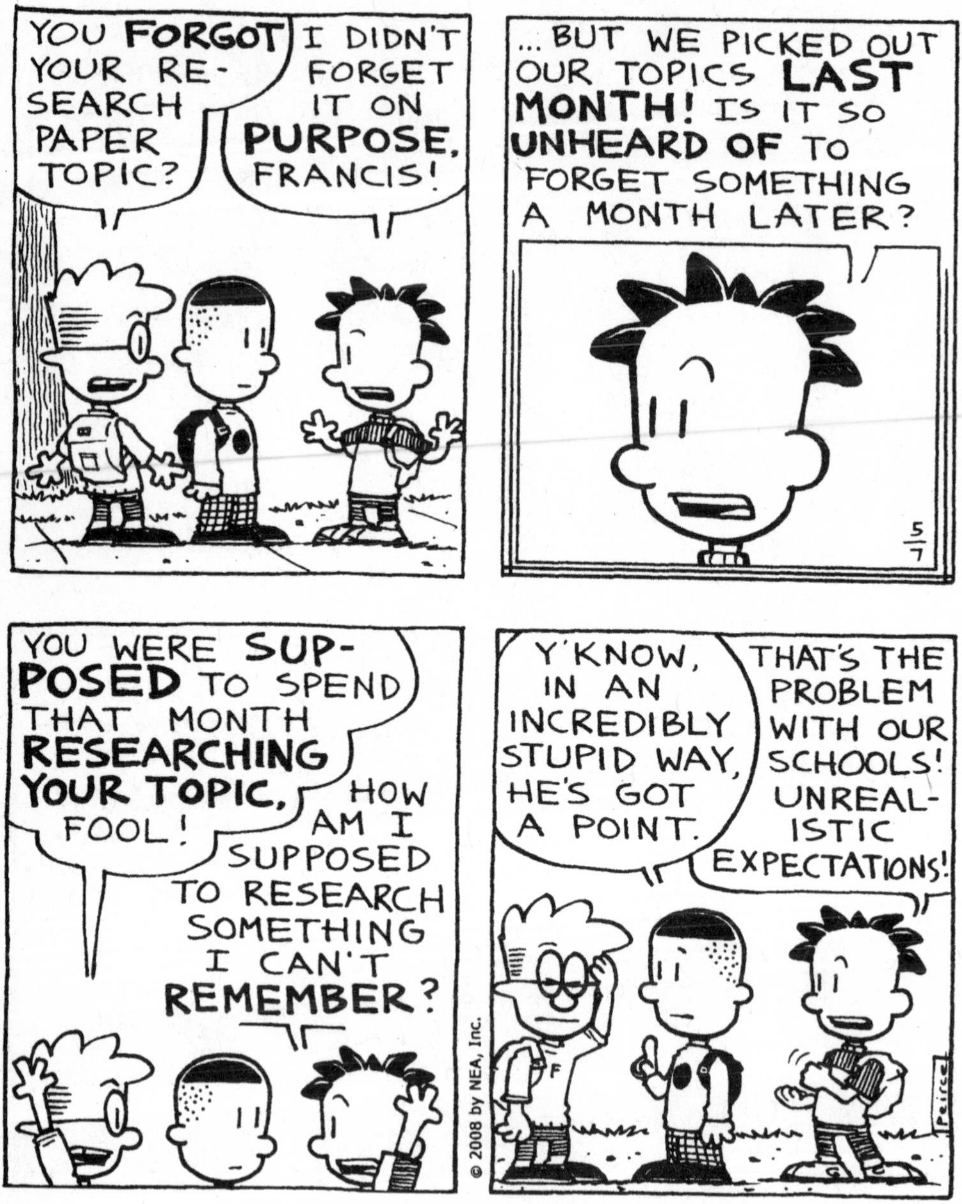
YOU FORGOT YOUR RE-SEARCH PAPER TOPIC?
I DIDN'T FORGET IT ON PURPOSE, FRANCIS!
... BUT WE PICKED OUT OUR TOPICS LAST MONTH! IS IT SO UNHEARD OF TO FORGET SOMETHING A MONTH LATER?
5/7
YOU WERE SUP-POSED TO SPEND THAT MONTH RESEARCHING YOUR TOPIC, FOOL!
HOW AM I SUPPOSED TO RESEARCH SOMETHING I CAN'T REMEMBER?
© 2008 by NEA, Inc.
Y'KNOW, IN AN INCREDIBLY STUPID WAY, HE'S GOT A POINT.
THAT'S THE PROBLEM WITH OUR SCHOOLS! UNREAL-ISTIC EXPECTATIONS!
Peirce

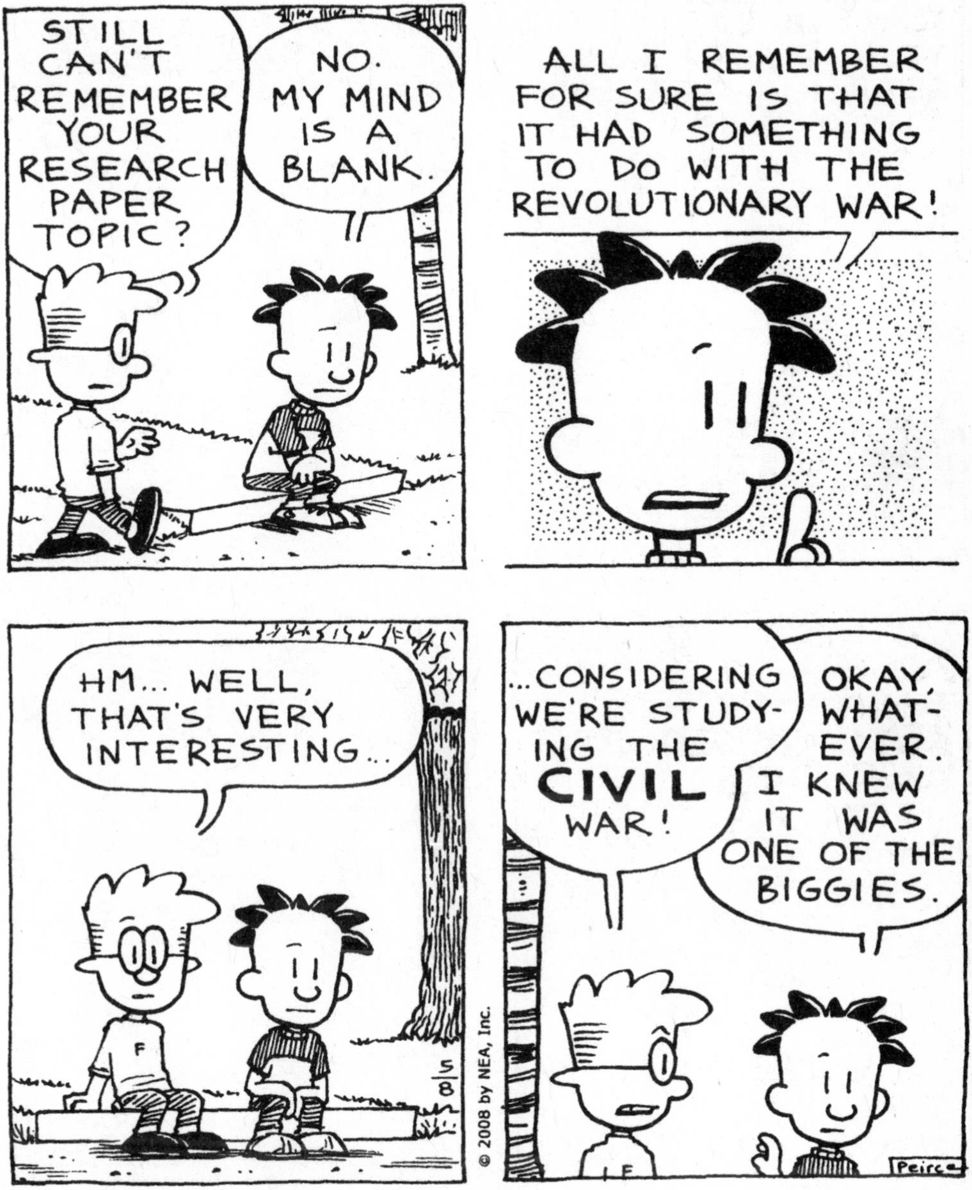
STILL CAN'T REMEMBER YOUR RESEARCH PAPER TOPIC?
NO. MY MIND IS A BLANK.
ALL I REMEMBER FOR SURE IS THAT IT HAD SOMETHING TO DO WITH THE REVOLUTIONARY WAR!
HM... WELL, THAT'S VERY INTERESTING...
...CONSIDERING WE'RE STUDYING THE CIVIL WAR!
OKAY, WHATEVER. I KNEW IT WAS ONE OF THE BIGGIES.
5/8
© 2008 by NEA, Inc.
Peirce

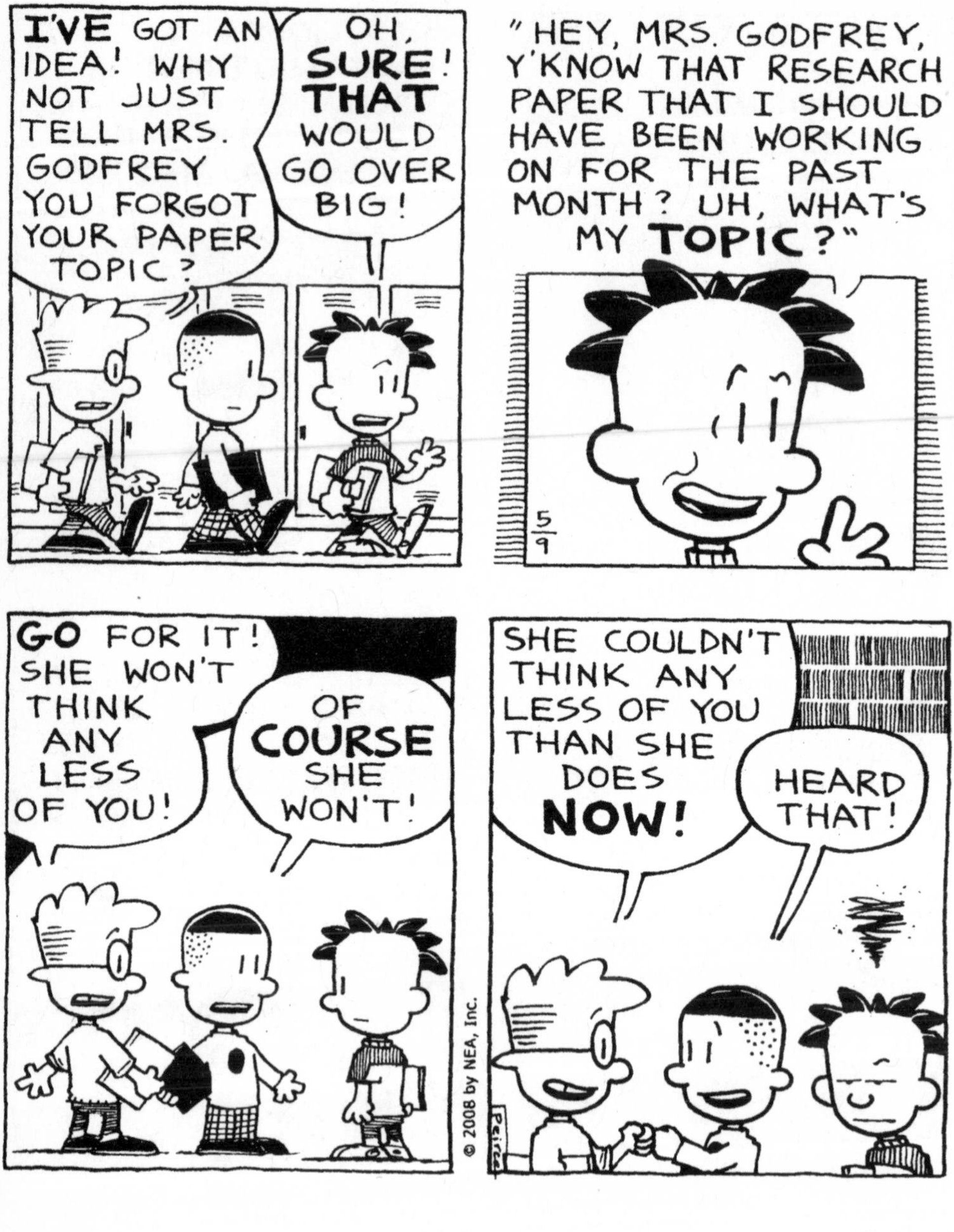
I'VE GOT AN IDEA! WHY NOT JUST TELL MRS. GODFREY YOU FORGOT YOUR PAPER TOPIC?
OH, SURE! THAT WOULD GO OVER BIG!
"HEY, MRS. GODFREY, Y'KNOW THAT RESEARCH PAPER THAT I SHOULD HAVE BEEN WORKING ON FOR THE PAST MONTH? UH, WHAT'S MY TOPIC?"
5/9
GO FOR IT! SHE WON'T THINK ANY LESS OF YOU!
OF COURSE SHE WON'T!
© 2008 by NEA, Inc.
SHE COULDN'T THINK ANY LESS OF YOU THAN SHE DOES NOW!
HEARD THAT!

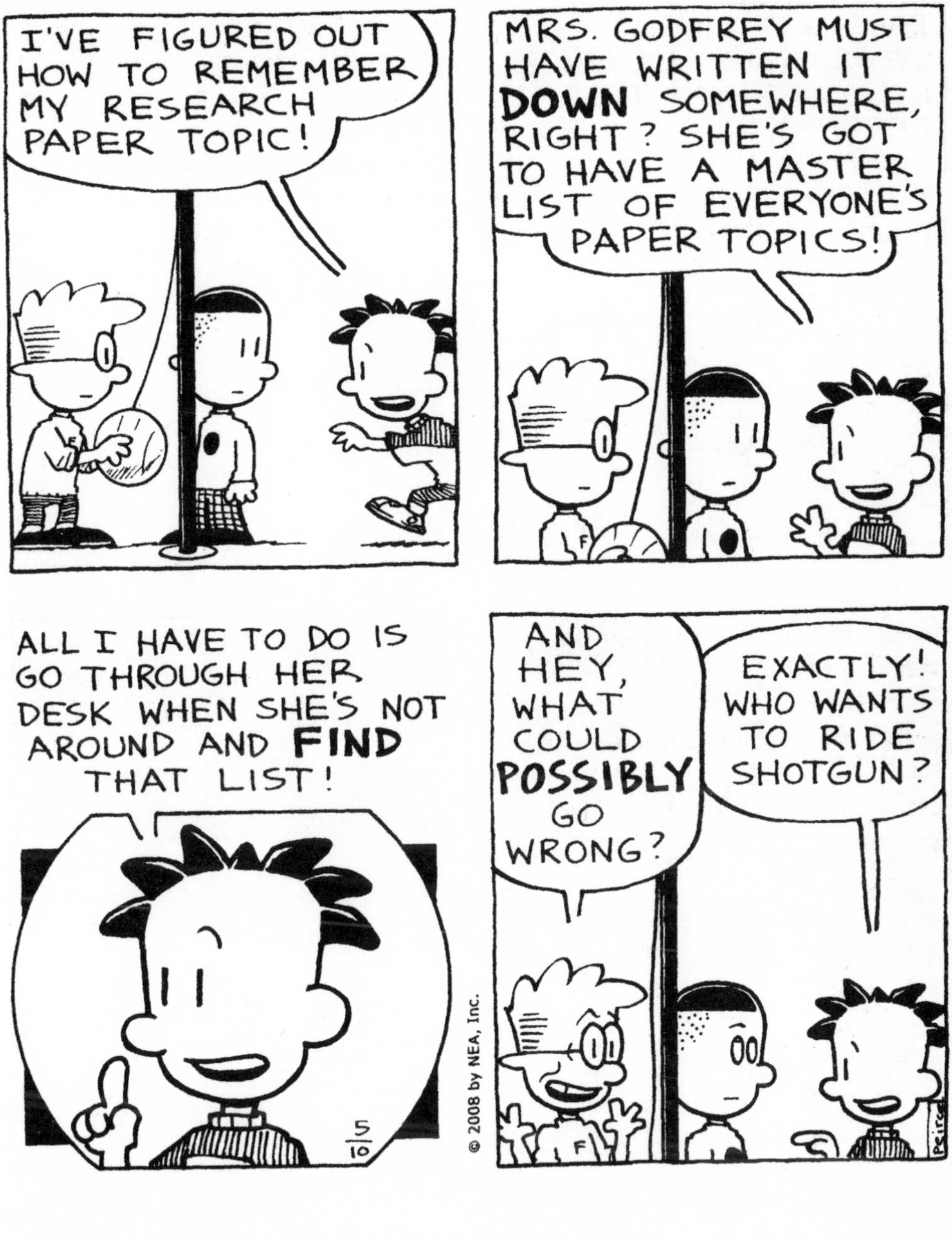
I'VE FIGURED OUT HOW TO REMEMBER MY RESEARCH PAPER TOPIC!
MRS. GODFREY MUST HAVE WRITTEN IT DOWN SOMEWHERE, RIGHT? SHE'S GOT TO HAVE A MASTER LIST OF EVERYONE'S PAPER TOPICS!
ALL I HAVE TO DO IS GO THROUGH HER DESK WHEN SHE'S NOT AROUND AND FIND THAT LIST!
AND HEY, WHAT COULD POSSIBLY GO WRONG?
EXACTLY! WHO WANTS TO RIDE SHOTGUN?
5/10
© 2008 by NEA, Inc.
PEIRCE

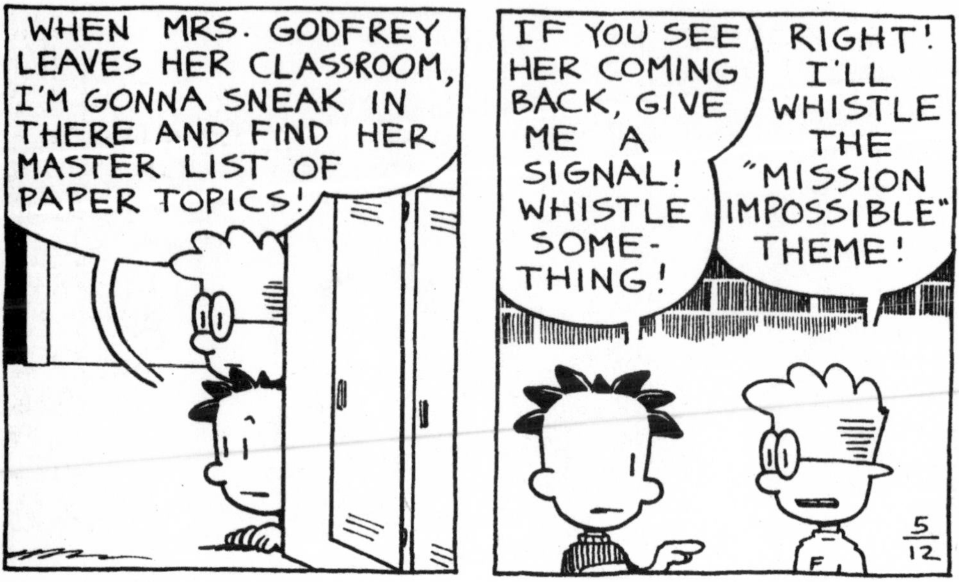
WHEN MRS. GODFREY LEAVES HER CLASSROOM, I'M GONNA SNEAK IN THERE AND FIND HER MASTER LIST OF PAPER TOPICS!
IF YOU SEE HER COMING BACK, GIVE ME A SIGNAL! WHISTLE SOMETHING!
RIGHT! I'LL WHISTLE THE "MISSION IMPOSSIBLE" THEME!
5/12

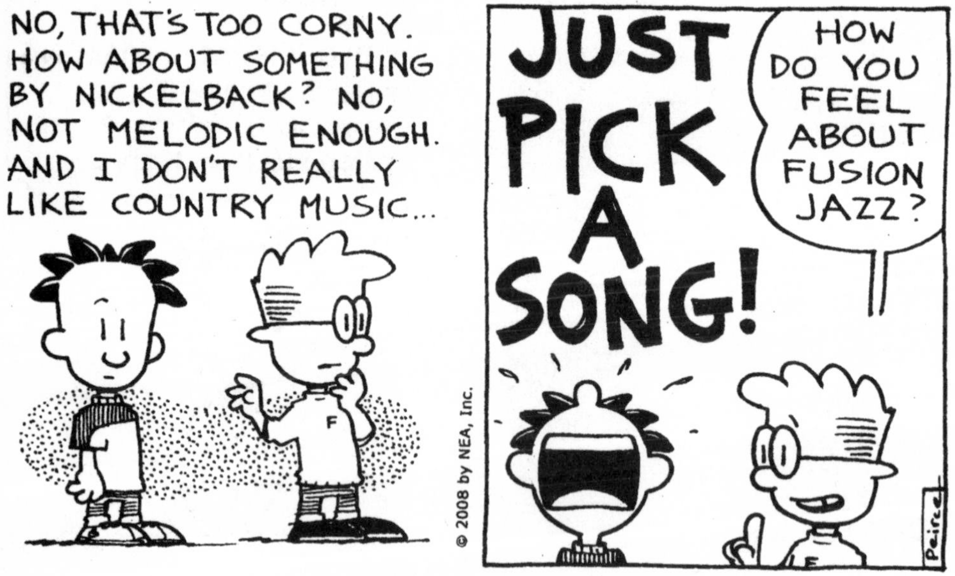
NO, THAT'S TOO CORNY. HOW ABOUT SOMETHING BY NICKELBACK? NO, NOT MELODIC ENOUGH. AND I DON'T REALLY LIKE COUNTRY MUSIC...
JUST PICK A SONG!
HOW DO YOU FEEL ABOUT FUSION JAZZ?
Peirce

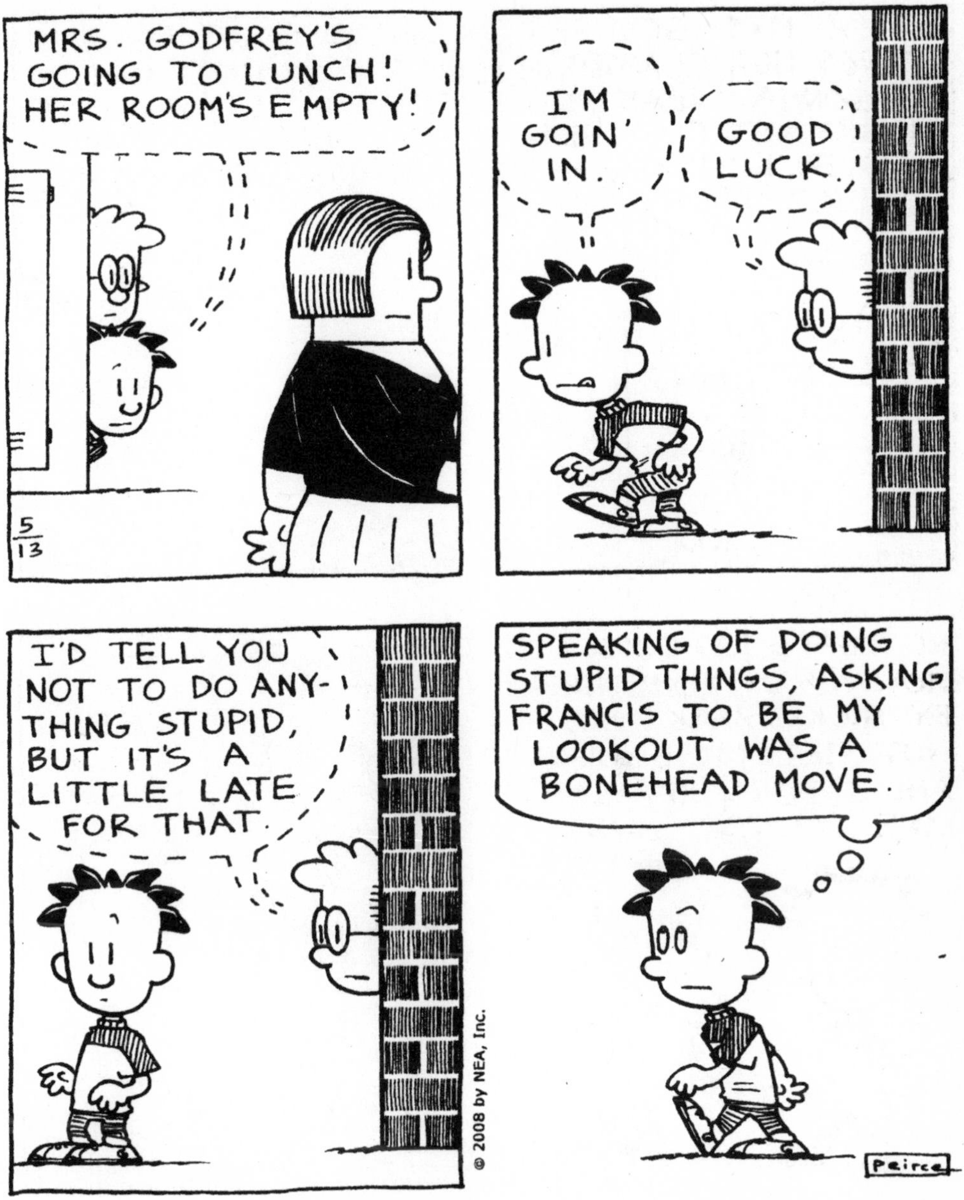

MRS. GODFREY'S GOING TO LUNCH! HER ROOM'S EMPTY!
5/13
I'M GOIN' IN.
GOOD LUCK.
I'D TELL YOU NOT TO DO ANY-THING STUPID, BUT IT'S A LITTLE LATE FOR THAT.
SPEAKING OF DOING STUPID THINGS, ASKING FRANCIS TO BE MY LOOKOUT WAS A BONEHEAD MOVE.
PEIRCE

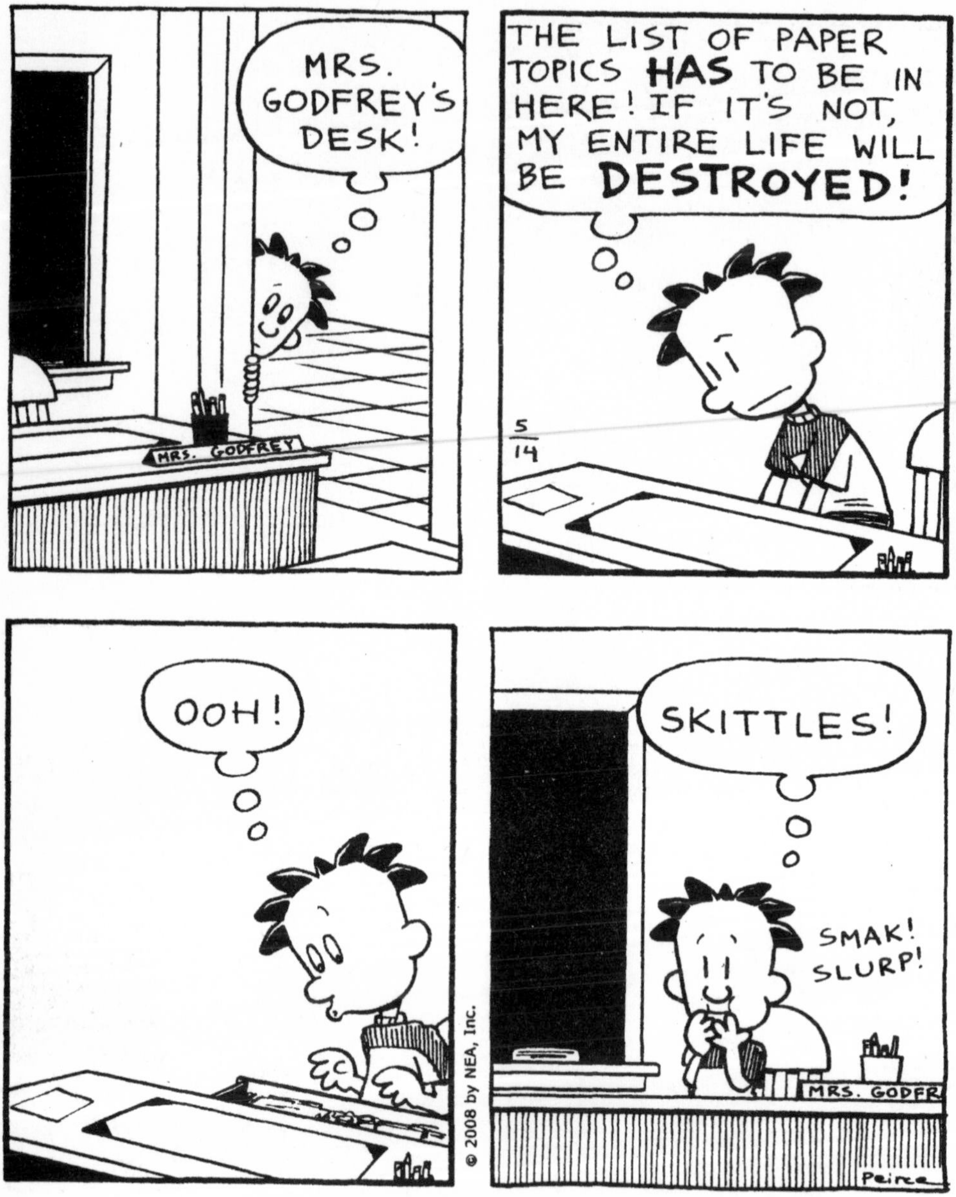
MRS. GODFREY'S DESK!
MRS. GODFREY
THE LIST OF PAPER TOPICS HAS TO BE IN HERE! IF IT'S NOT, MY ENTIRE LIFE WILL BE DESTROYED!
5/14
OOH!
© 2008 by NEA, Inc.
SKITTLES!
SMAK! SLURP!
MRS. GODFR
Peirce

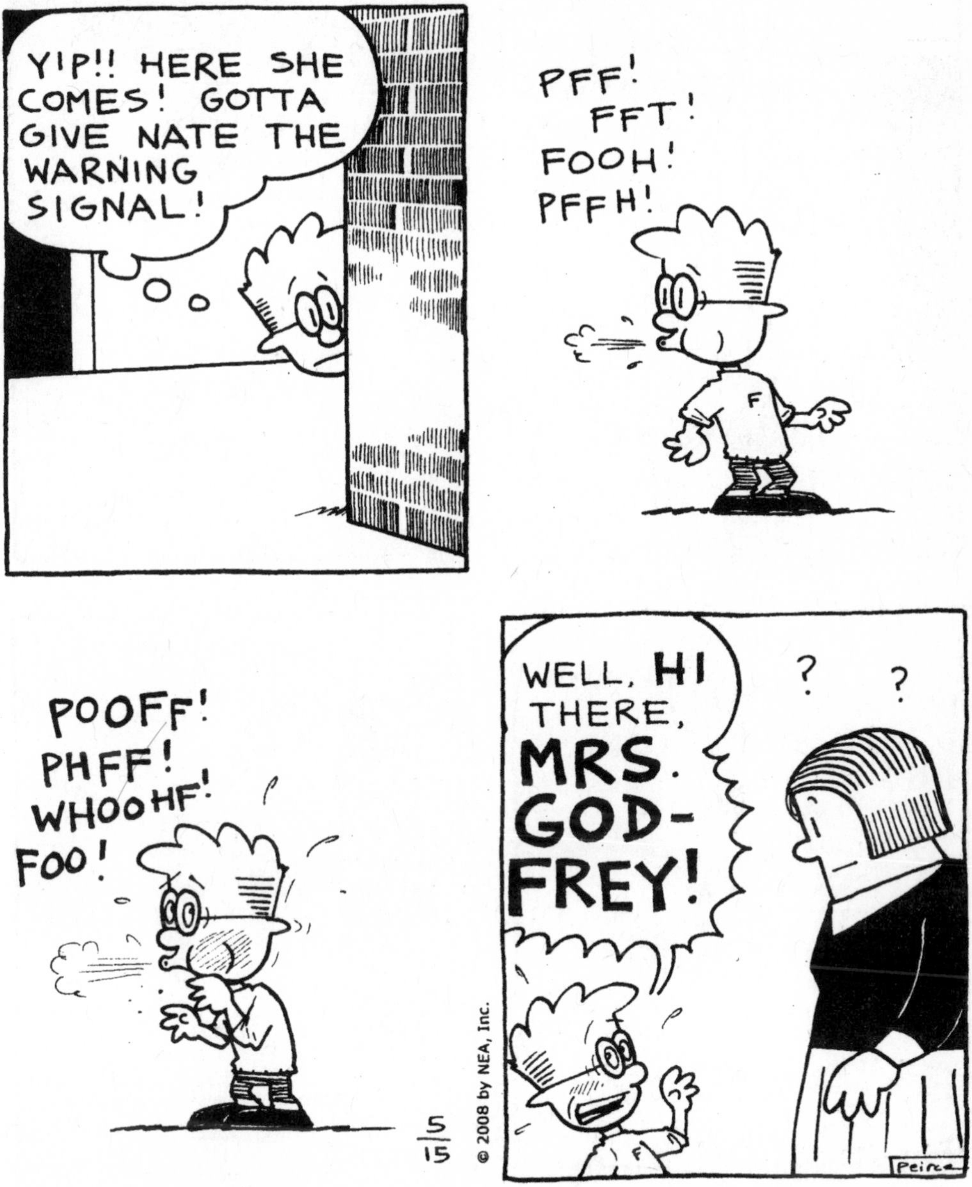
YIP!! HERE SHE COMES! GOTTA GIVE NATE THE WARNING SIGNAL!
PFF! FFT! FOOH! PFFH!
POOFF! PHFF! WHOOHF! FOO!
WELL, HI THERE, MRS. GOD-FREY!
? ?
5/15
© 2008 by NEA, Inc.
Peirce

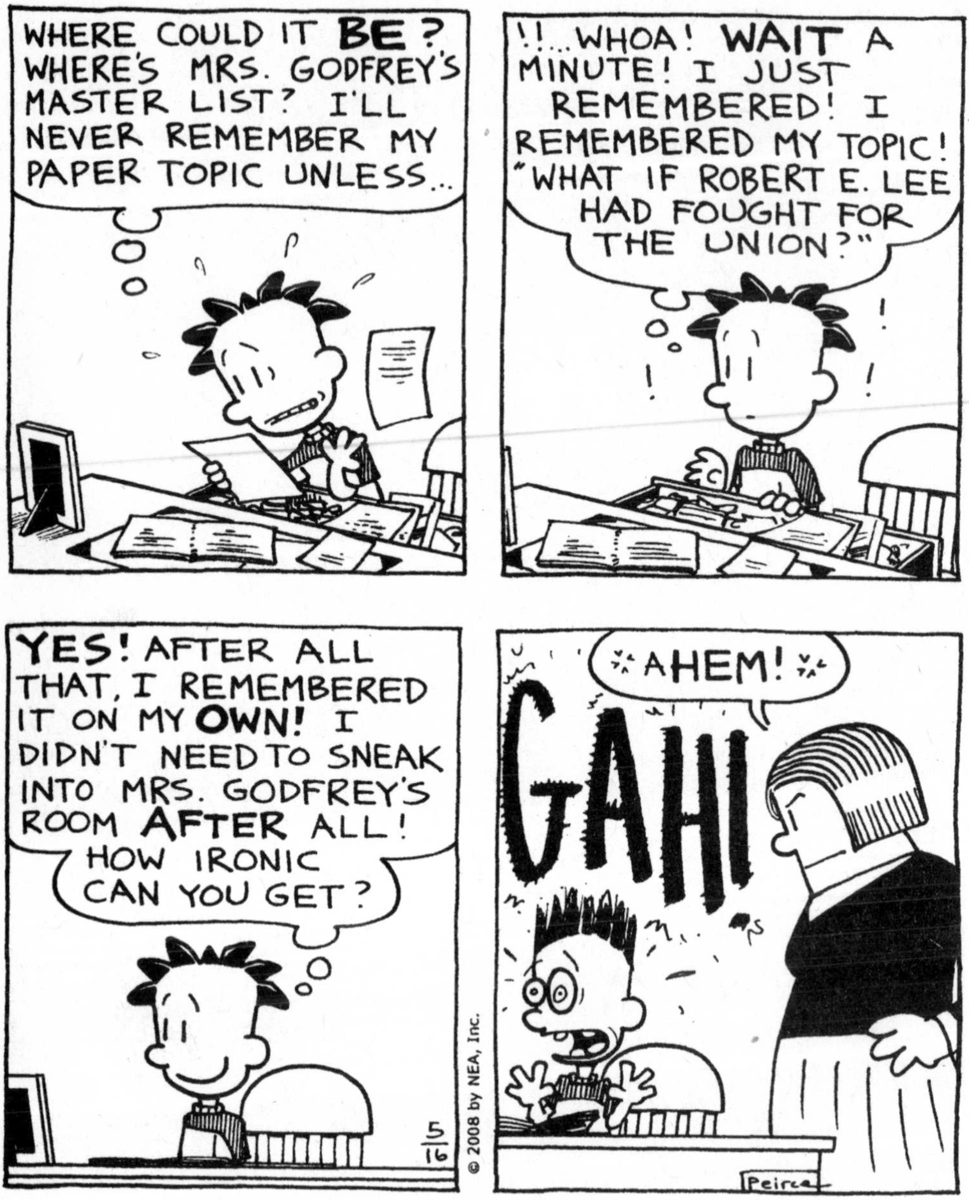
WHERE COULD IT BE? WHERE'S MRS. GODFREY'S MASTER LIST? I'LL NEVER REMEMBER MY PAPER TOPIC UNLESS...
!!...WHOA! WAIT A MINUTE! I JUST REMEMBERED! I REMEMBERED MY TOPIC! "WHAT IF ROBERT E. LEE HAD FOUGHT FOR THE UNION?"
YES! AFTER ALL THAT, I REMEMBERED IT ON MY OWN! I DIDN'T NEED TO SNEAK INTO MRS. GODFREY'S ROOM AFTER ALL! HOW IRONIC CAN YOU GET?
5/16
© 2008 by NEA, Inc.
AHEM!
GAH!
Peirce

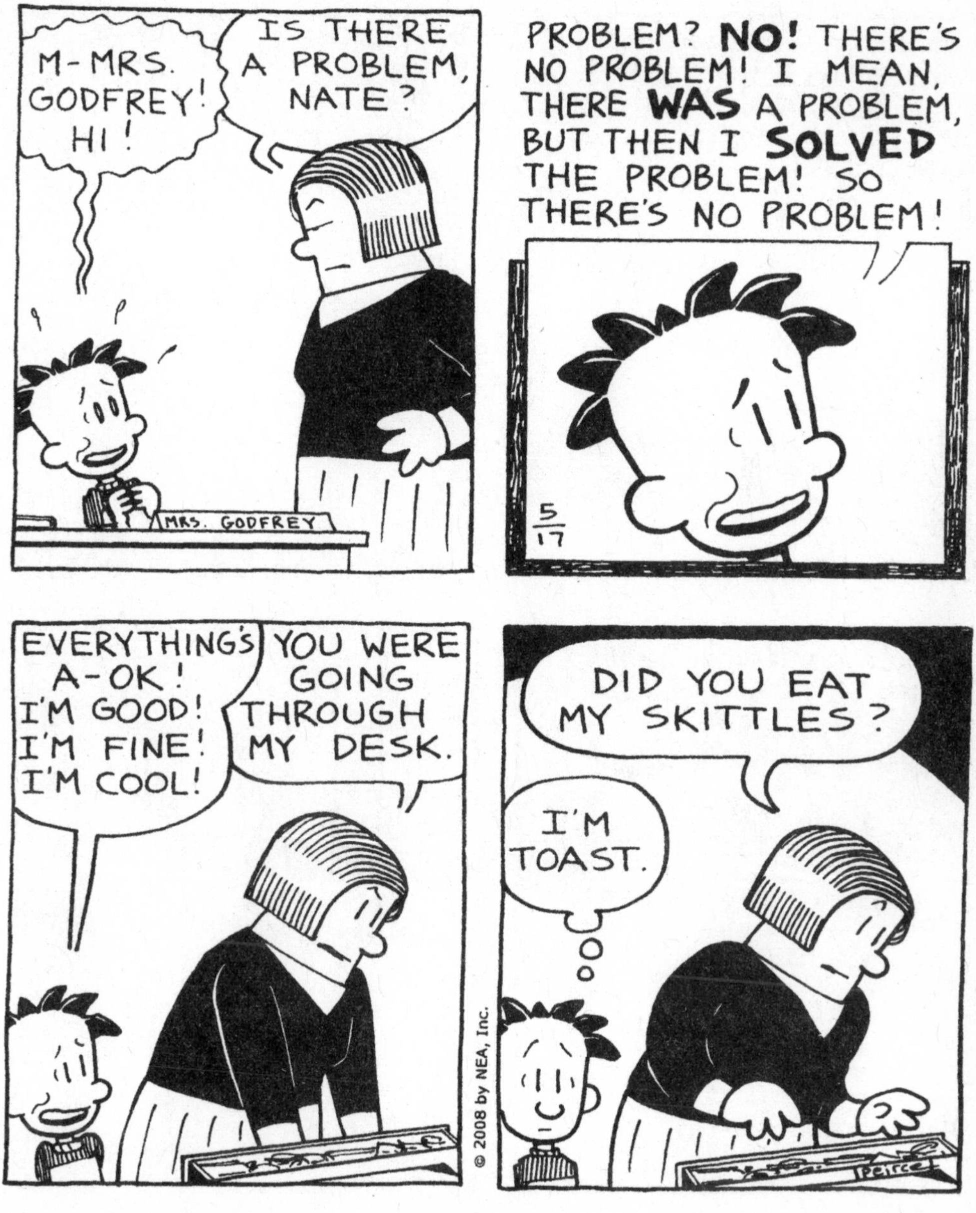
M-MRS. GODFREY! HI!
IS THERE A PROBLEM, NATE?
MRS. GODFREY
PROBLEM? **NO!** THERE'S NO PROBLEM! I MEAN, THERE **WAS** A PROBLEM, BUT THEN I **SOLVED** THE PROBLEM! SO THERE'S NO PROBLEM!
5/17
EVERYTHING'S A-OK! I'M GOOD! I'M FINE! I'M COOL!
YOU WERE GOING THROUGH MY DESK.
© 2008 by NEA, Inc.
DID YOU EAT MY SKITTLES?
I'M TOAST.
Peirce

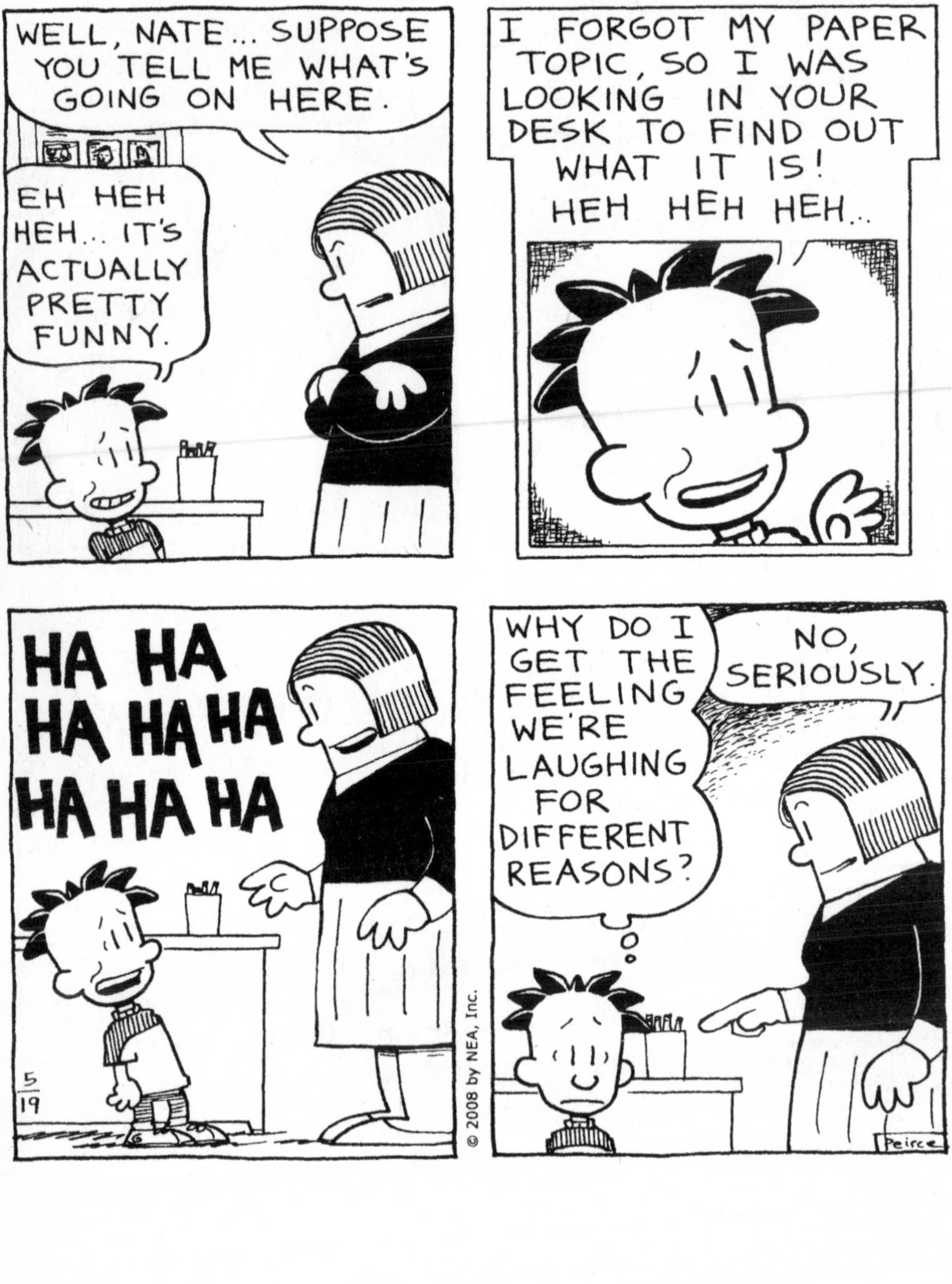
WELL, NATE... SUPPOSE YOU TELL ME WHAT'S GOING ON HERE.
EH HEH HEH... IT'S ACTUALLY PRETTY FUNNY.
I FORGOT MY PAPER TOPIC, SO I WAS LOOKING IN YOUR DESK TO FIND OUT WHAT IT IS! HEH HEH HEH..
HA HA HA HA HA HA HA HA
5/19
WHY DO I GET THE FEELING WE'RE LAUGHING FOR DIFFERENT REASONS?
NO, SERIOUSLY.
Peirce

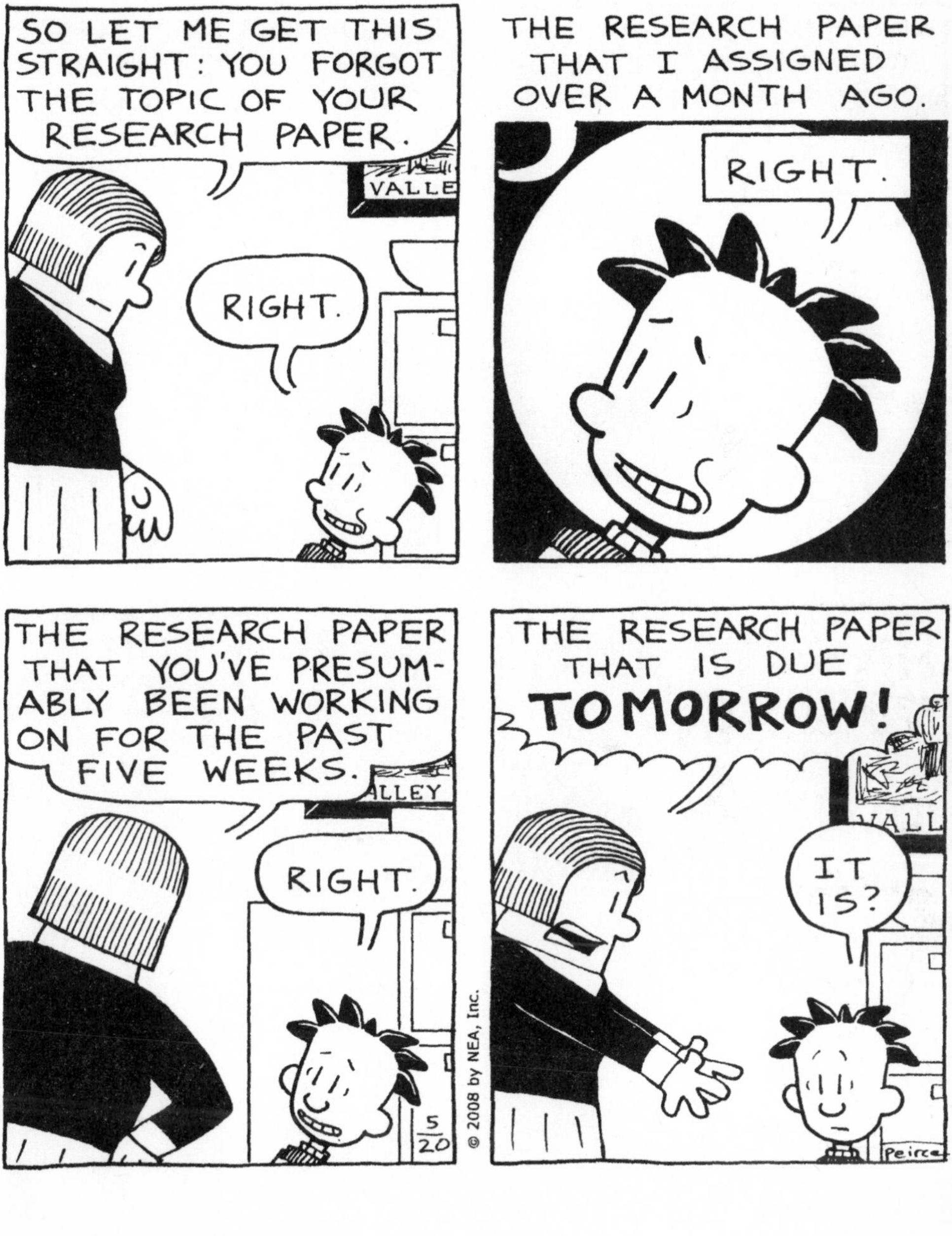
SO LET ME GET THIS STRAIGHT: YOU FORGOT THE TOPIC OF YOUR RESEARCH PAPER.
RIGHT.
THE RESEARCH PAPER THAT I ASSIGNED OVER A MONTH AGO.
RIGHT.
THE RESEARCH PAPER THAT YOU'VE PRESUMABLY BEEN WORKING ON FOR THE PAST FIVE WEEKS.
RIGHT.
5/20
© 2008 by NEA, Inc.
THE RESEARCH PAPER THAT IS DUE **TOMORROW!**
IT IS?
Peirce

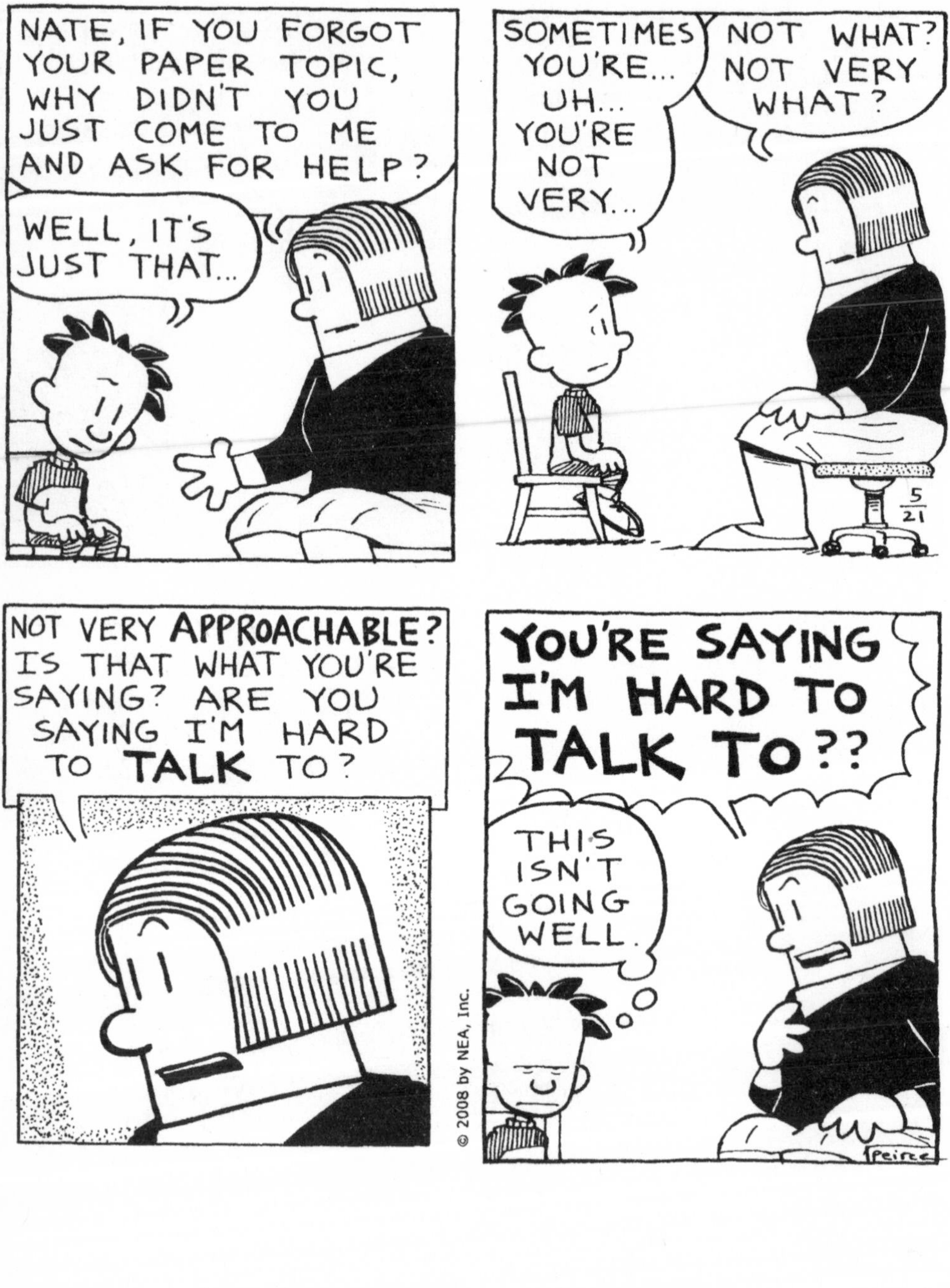
NATE, IF YOU FORGOT YOUR PAPER TOPIC, WHY DIDN'T YOU JUST COME TO ME AND ASK FOR HELP?
WELL, IT'S JUST THAT...
SOMETIMES YOU'RE... UH... YOU'RE NOT VERY...
NOT WHAT? NOT VERY WHAT?
5/21
NOT VERY APPROACHABLE? IS THAT WHAT YOU'RE SAYING? ARE YOU SAYING I'M HARD TO TALK TO?
YOU'RE SAYING I'M HARD TO TALK TO??
THIS ISN'T GOING WELL.
PEIRCE

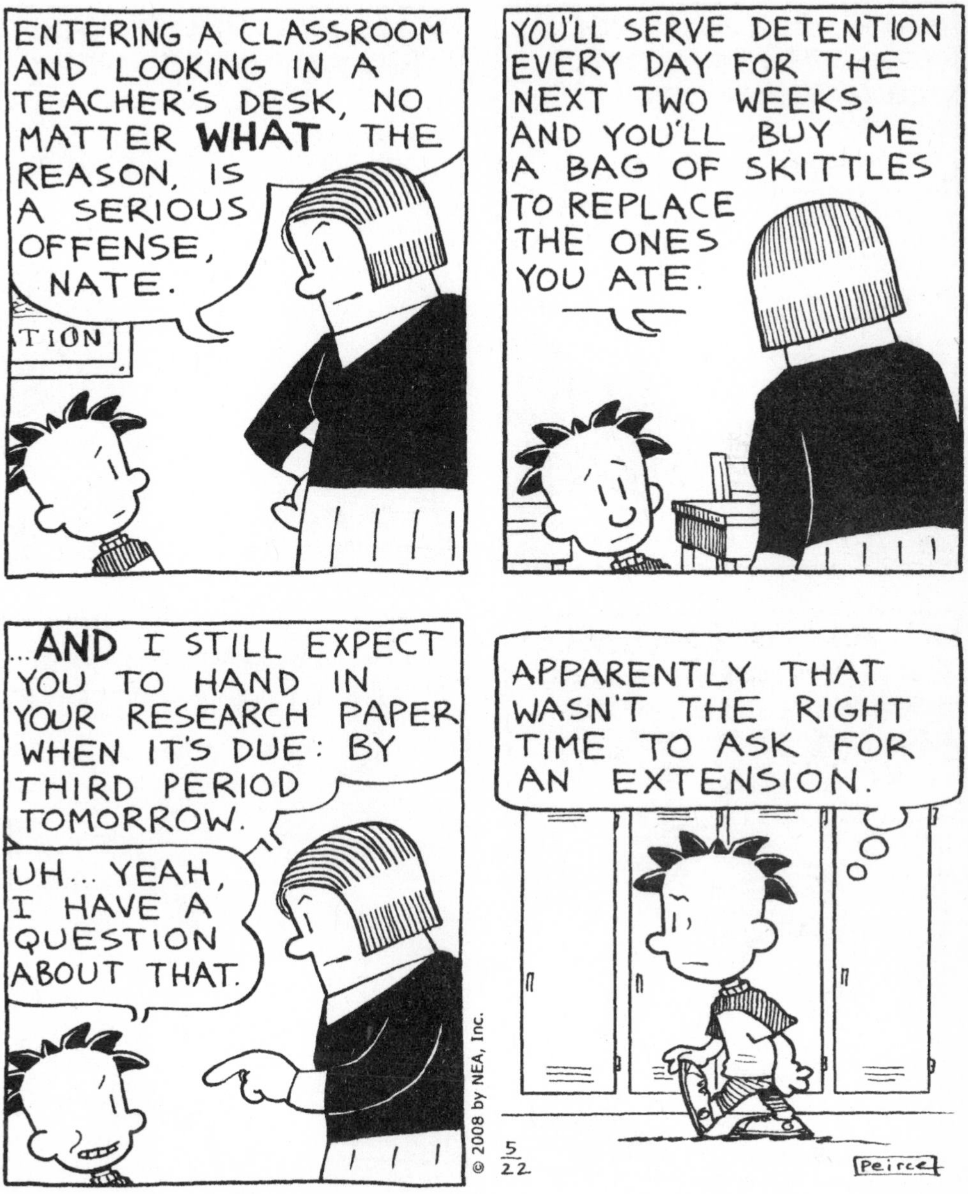
ENTERING A CLASSROOM AND LOOKING IN A TEACHER'S DESK, NO MATTER WHAT THE REASON, IS A SERIOUS OFFENSE, NATE.
TION
YOU'LL SERVE DETENTION EVERY DAY FOR THE NEXT TWO WEEKS, AND YOU'LL BUY ME A BAG OF SKITTLES TO REPLACE THE ONES YOU ATE.
...AND I STILL EXPECT YOU TO HAND IN YOUR RESEARCH PAPER WHEN IT'S DUE: BY THIRD PERIOD TOMORROW.
UH... YEAH, I HAVE A QUESTION ABOUT THAT.
© 2008 by NEA, Inc.
5/22
APPARENTLY THAT WASN'T THE RIGHT TIME TO ASK FOR AN EXTENSION.
Peirce

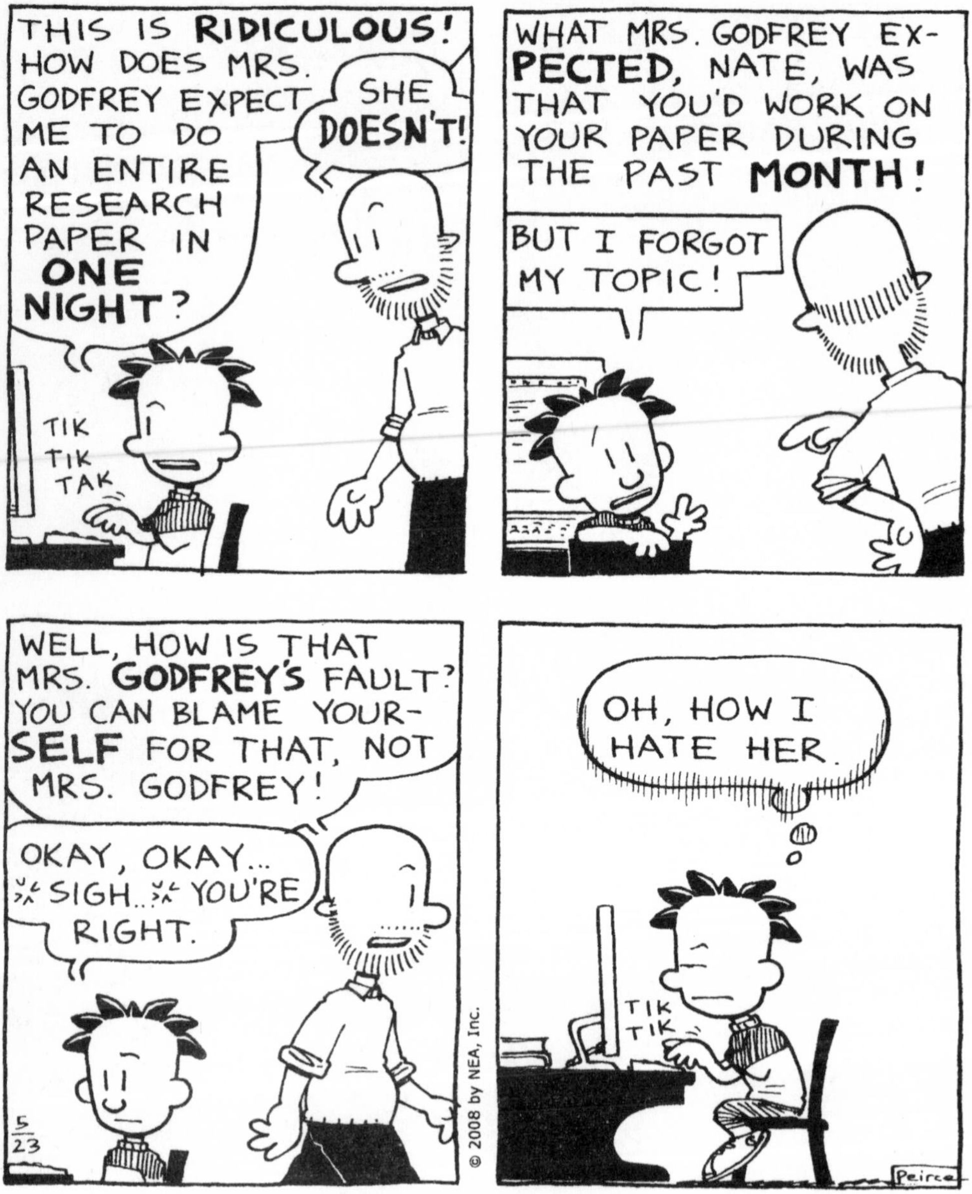
THIS IS RIDICULOUS! HOW DOES MRS. GODFREY EXPECT ME TO DO AN ENTIRE RESEARCH PAPER IN ONE NIGHT?
SHE DOESN'T!
TIK TIK TAK
WHAT MRS. GODFREY EXPECTED, NATE, WAS THAT YOU'D WORK ON YOUR PAPER DURING THE PAST MONTH!
BUT I FORGOT MY TOPIC!
WELL, HOW IS THAT MRS. GODFREY'S FAULT? YOU CAN BLAME YOURSELF FOR THAT, NOT MRS. GODFREY!
OKAY, OKAY... SIGH... YOU'RE RIGHT.
5/23
© 2008 by NEA, Inc.
OH, HOW I HATE HER.
TIK TIK
Peirce

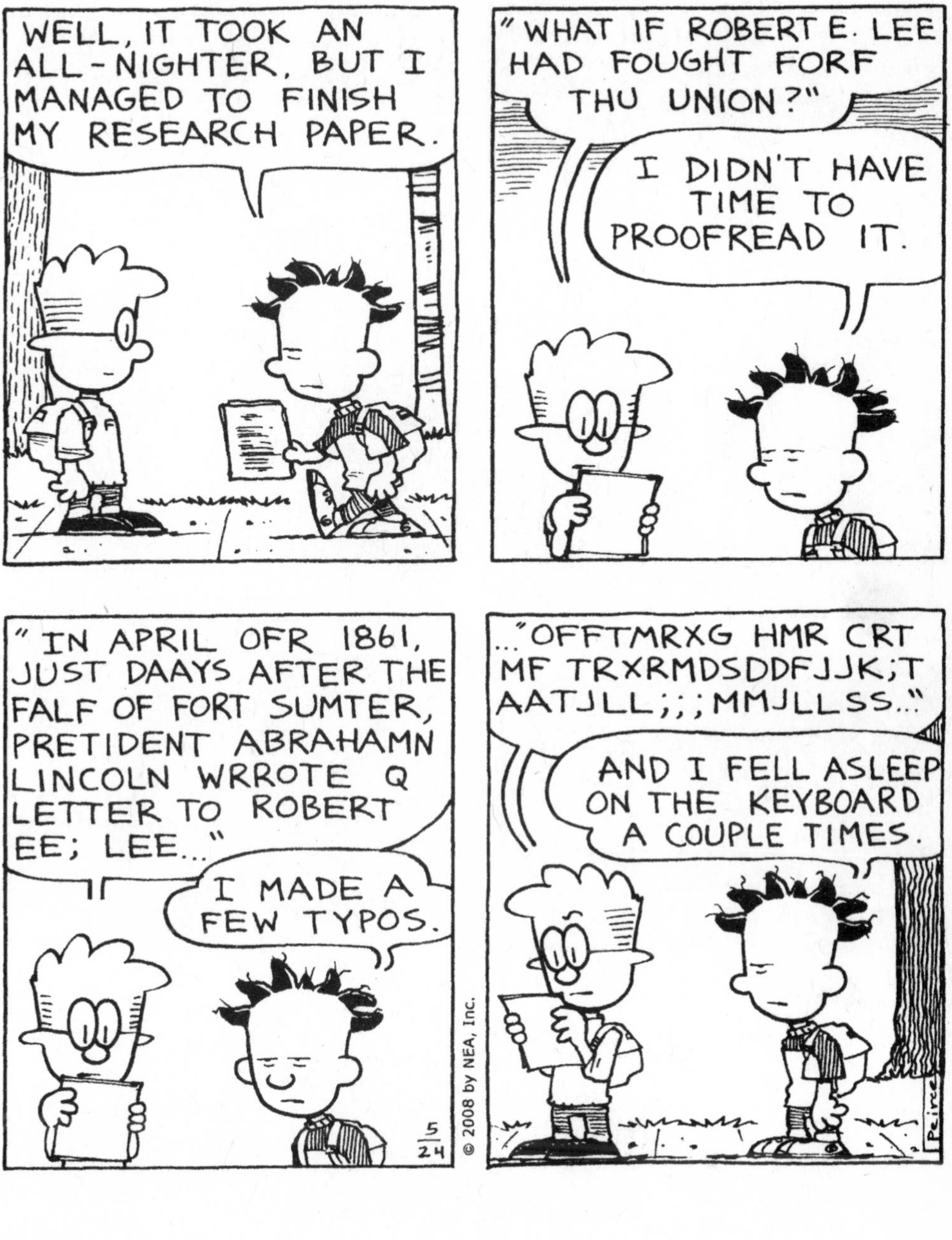
WELL, IT TOOK AN ALL-NIGHTER, BUT I MANAGED TO FINISH MY RESEARCH PAPER.
"WHAT IF ROBERT E. LEE HAD FOUGHT FORF THU UNION?"
I DIDN'T HAVE TIME TO PROOFREAD IT.
"IN APRIL OFR 1861, JUST DAAYS AFTER THE FALF OF FORT SUMTER, PRETIDENT ABRAHAMN LINCOLN WRROTE Q LETTER TO ROBERT EE; LEE..."
I MADE A FEW TYPOS.
..."OFFTMRXG HMR CRT MF TRXRMDSDDFJJK;T AATJLL;;;MMJLLSS..."
AND I FELL ASLEEP ON THE KEYBOARD A COUPLE TIMES.
5/24
© 2008 by NEA, Inc.
Peirce

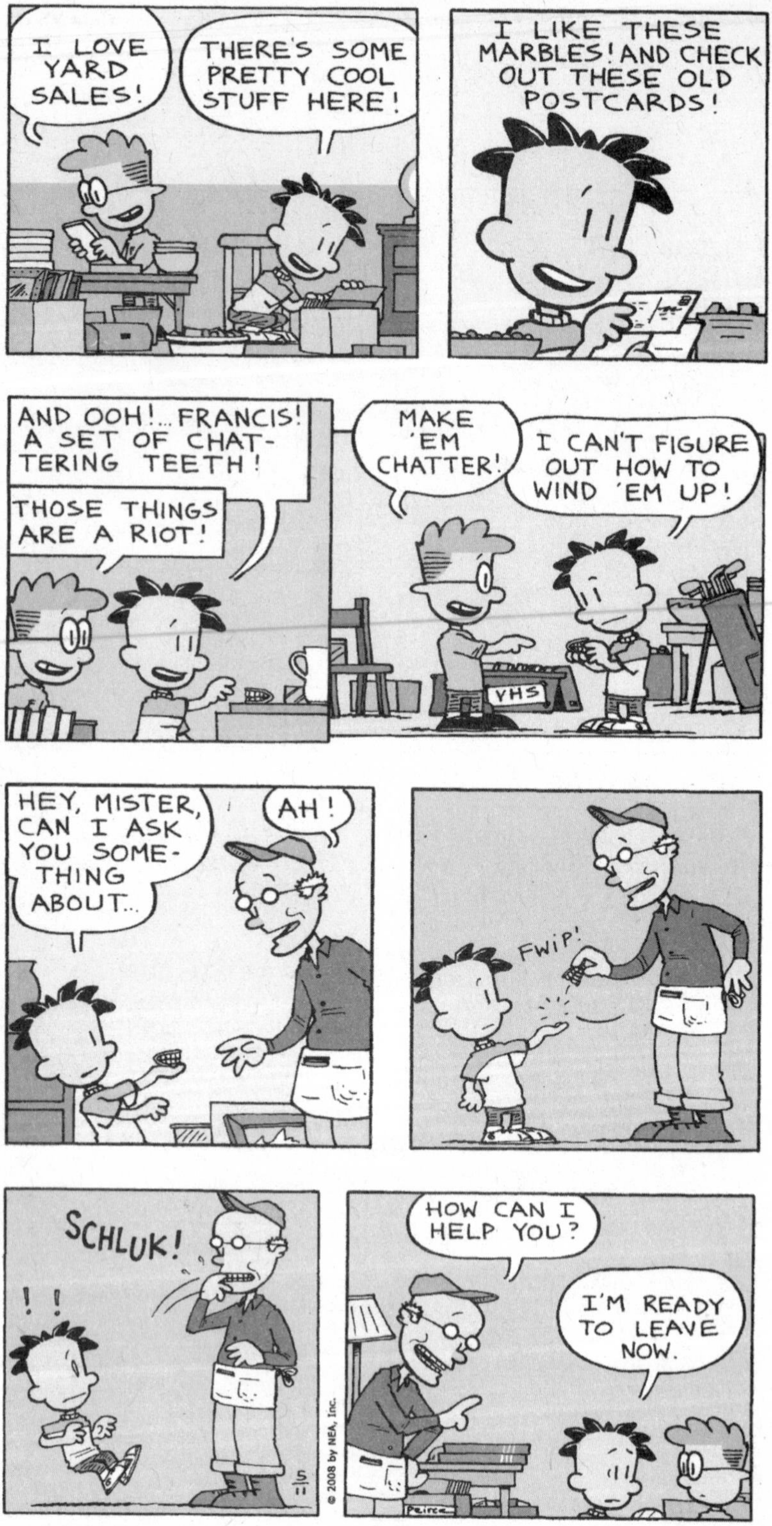
I LOVE YARD SALES!
THERE'S SOME PRETTY COOL STUFF HERE!
I LIKE THESE MARBLES! AND CHECK OUT THESE OLD POSTCARDS!
AND OOH!... FRANCIS! A SET OF CHATTERING TEETH!
THOSE THINGS ARE A RIOT!
MAKE 'EM CHATTER!
I CAN'T FIGURE OUT HOW TO WIND 'EM UP!
VHS
HEY, MISTER, CAN I ASK YOU SOMETHING ABOUT...
AH!
FWIP!
SCHLUK!
! !
© 2008 by NEA, Inc.
HOW CAN I HELP YOU?
I'M READY TO LEAVE NOW.

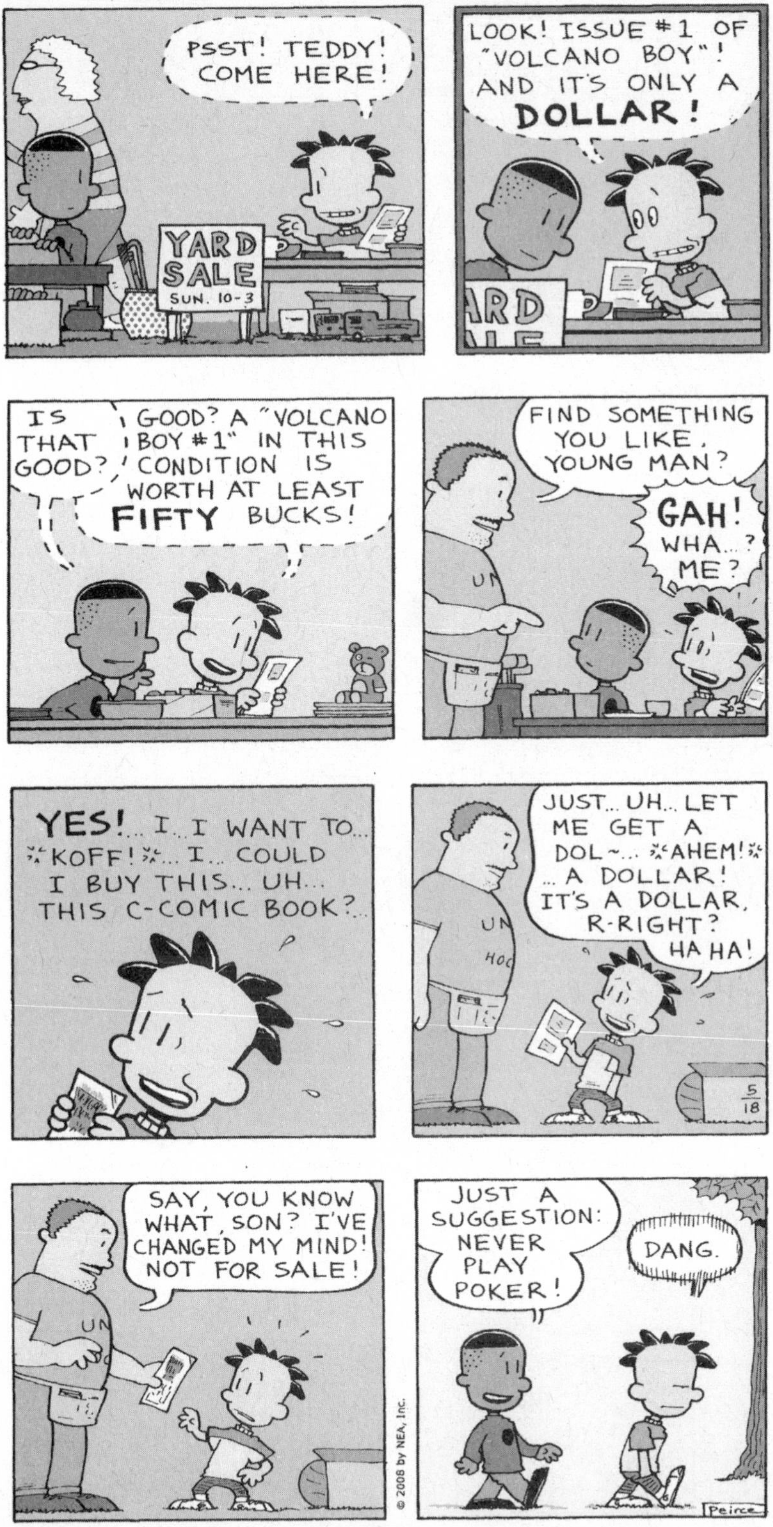
PSST! TEDDY! COME HERE!
YARD SALE SUN. 10-3
LOOK! ISSUE #1 OF "VOLCANO BOY"! AND IT'S ONLY A DOLLAR!
IS THAT GOOD?
GOOD? A "VOLCANO BOY #1" IN THIS CONDITION IS WORTH AT LEAST FIFTY BUCKS!
FIND SOMETHING YOU LIKE, YOUNG MAN?
GAH! WHA...? ME?
YES!... I... I WANT TO... *KOFF!*... I... COULD I BUY THIS... UH... THIS C-COMIC BOOK?...
JUST... UH... LET ME GET A DOL~... *AHEM!* ... A DOLLAR! IT'S A DOLLAR, R-RIGHT? HA HA!
SAY, YOU KNOW WHAT, SON? I'VE CHANGED MY MIND! NOT FOR SALE!
JUST A SUGGESTION: NEVER PLAY POKER!
DANG.
© 2008 by NEA, Inc.
Peirce

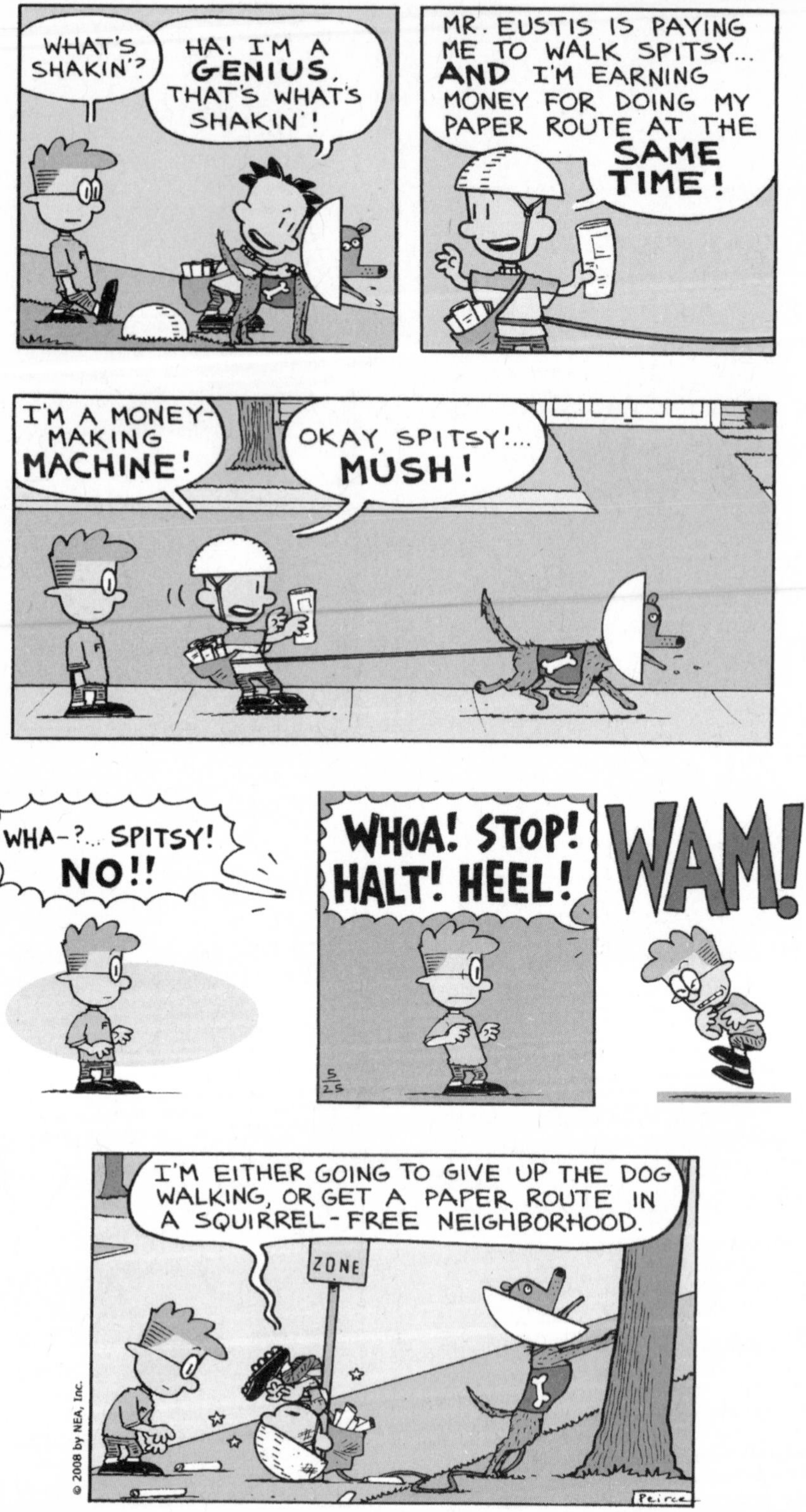
WHAT'S SHAKIN'?
HA! I'M A GENIUS, THAT'S WHAT'S SHAKIN'!
MR. EUSTIS IS PAYING ME TO WALK SPITSY... AND I'M EARNING MONEY FOR DOING MY PAPER ROUTE AT THE SAME TIME!
I'M A MONEY-MAKING MACHINE!
OKAY, SPITSY!... MUSH!
WHA-?... SPITSY! NO!!
WHOA! STOP! HALT! HEEL!
5/25
WAM!
I'M EITHER GOING TO GIVE UP THE DOG WALKING, OR GET A PAPER ROUTE IN A SQUIRREL-FREE NEIGHBORHOOD.
ZONE
© 2008 by NEA, Inc.
Peirce

THE LIST

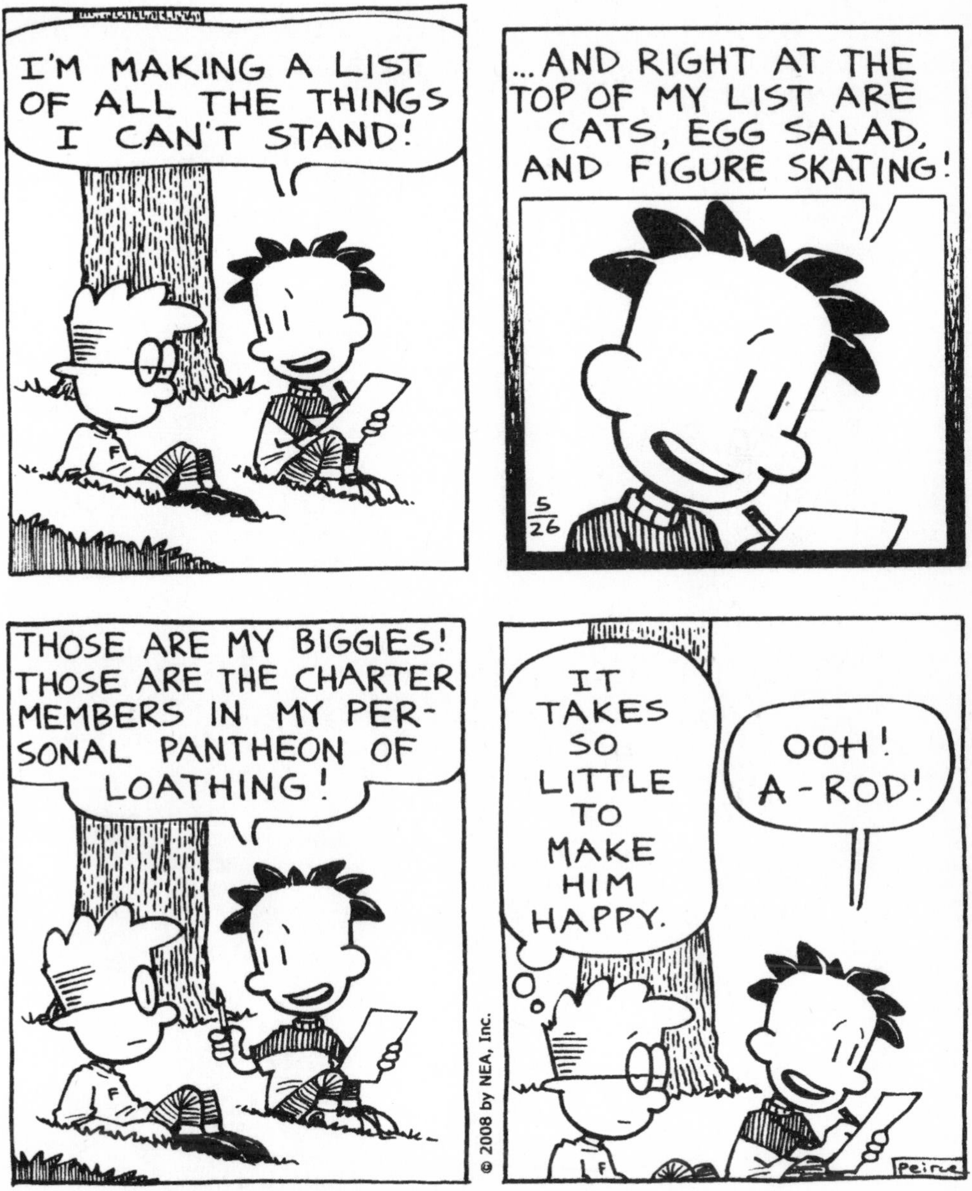
I'M MAKING A LIST OF ALL THE THINGS I CAN'T STAND!
...AND RIGHT AT THE TOP OF MY LIST ARE CATS, EGG SALAD, AND FIGURE SKATING!
5/26
THOSE ARE MY BIGGIES! THOSE ARE THE CHARTER MEMBERS IN MY PERSONAL PANTHEON OF LOATHING!
IT TAKES SO LITTLE TO MAKE HIM HAPPY.
OOH! A-ROD!
Peirce
© 2008 by NEA, Inc.

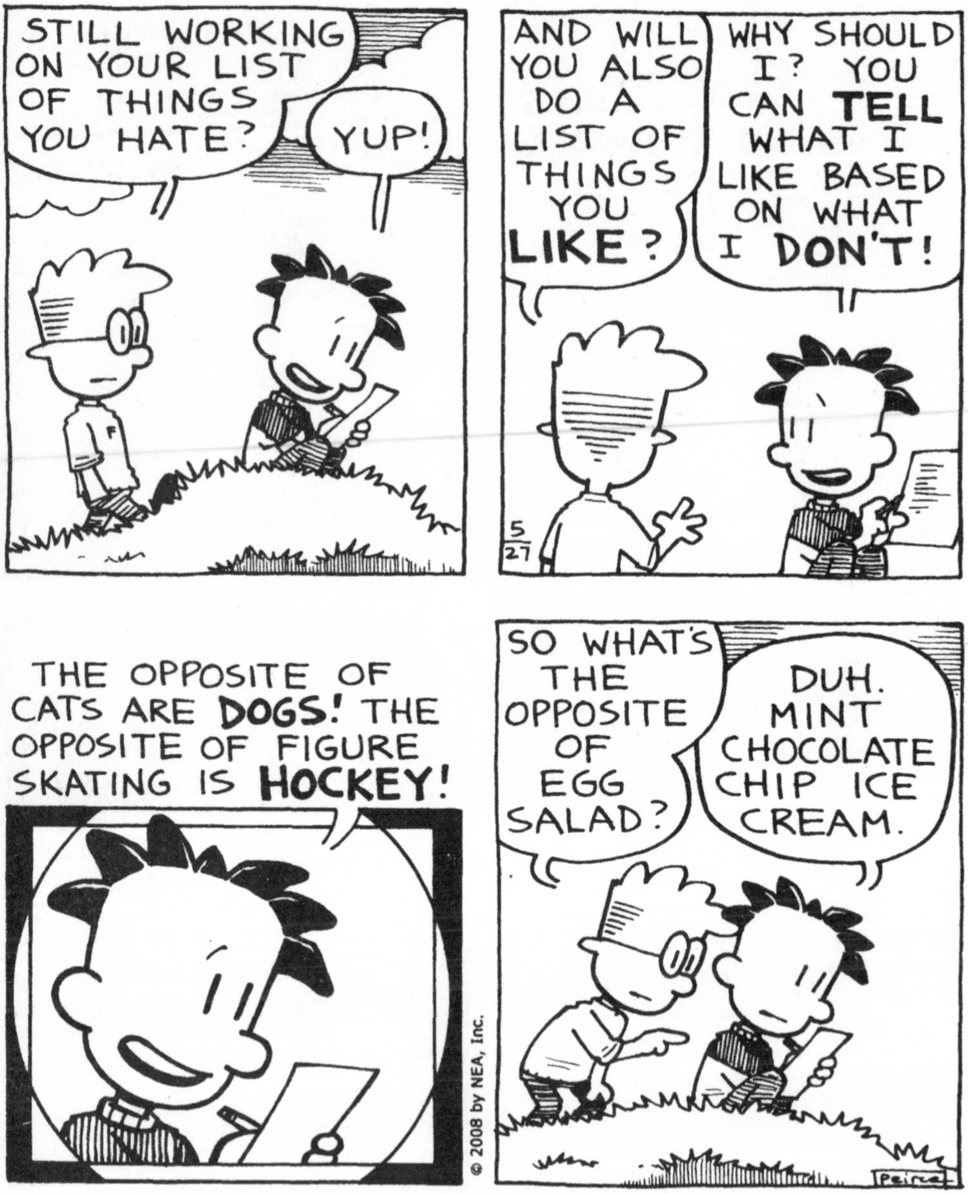
STILL WORKING ON YOUR LIST OF THINGS YOU HATE?
YUP!
AND WILL YOU ALSO DO A LIST OF THINGS YOU LIKE?
WHY SHOULD I? YOU CAN TELL WHAT I LIKE BASED ON WHAT I DON'T!
5
27
THE OPPOSITE OF CATS ARE DOGS! THE OPPOSITE OF FIGURE SKATING IS HOCKEY!
SO WHAT'S THE OPPOSITE OF EGG SALAD?
DUH. MINT CHOCOLATE CHIP ICE CREAM.
Peirce

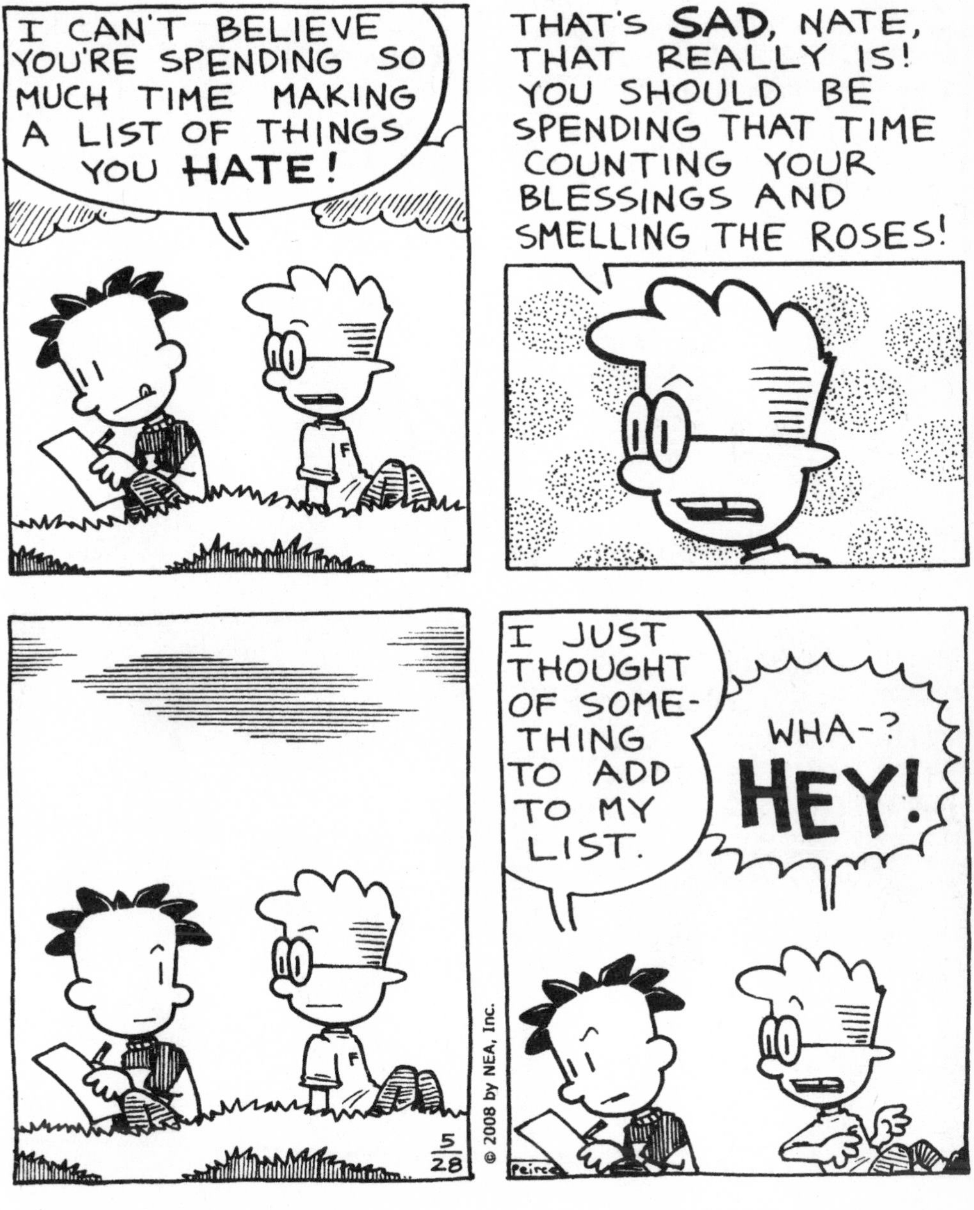
I CAN'T BELIEVE YOU'RE SPENDING SO MUCH TIME MAKING A LIST OF THINGS YOU HATE!
THAT'S SAD, NATE, THAT REALLY IS! YOU SHOULD BE SPENDING THAT TIME COUNTING YOUR BLESSINGS AND SMELLING THE ROSES!
5/28
© 2008 by NEA, Inc.
I JUST THOUGHT OF SOME-THING TO ADD TO MY LIST.
WHA-?
HEY!
Peirce

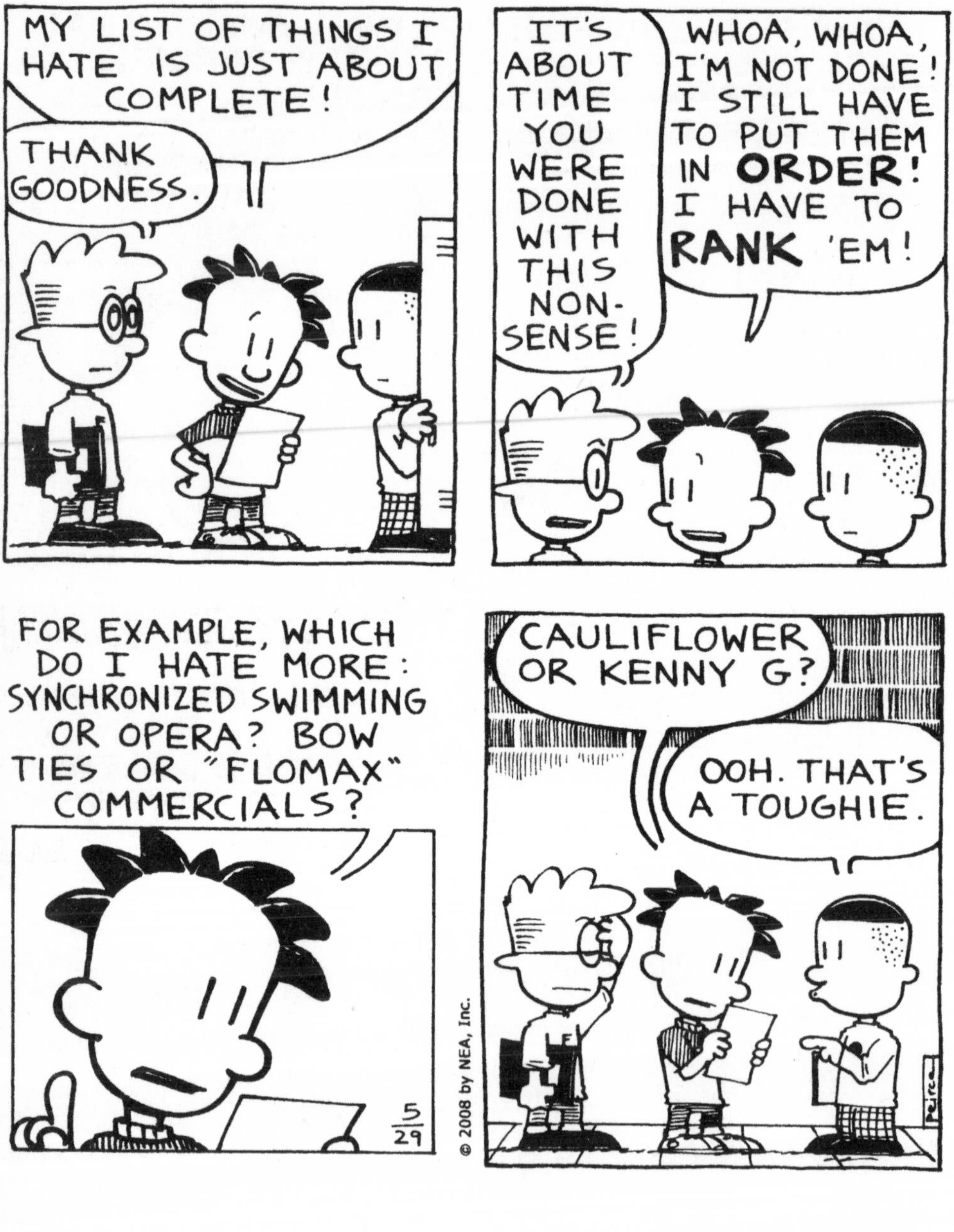
MY LIST OF THINGS I HATE IS JUST ABOUT COMPLETE!
THANK GOODNESS.
IT'S ABOUT TIME YOU WERE DONE WITH THIS NON-SENSE!
WHOA, WHOA, I'M NOT DONE! I STILL HAVE TO PUT THEM IN **ORDER**! I HAVE TO **RANK** 'EM!
FOR EXAMPLE, WHICH DO I HATE MORE: SYNCHRONIZED SWIMMING OR OPERA? BOW TIES OR "FLOMAX" COMMERCIALS?
5/29
CAULIFLOWER OR KENNY G?
OOH. THAT'S A TOUGHIE.
Peirce
© 2008 by NEA, Inc.

BRAINIAC

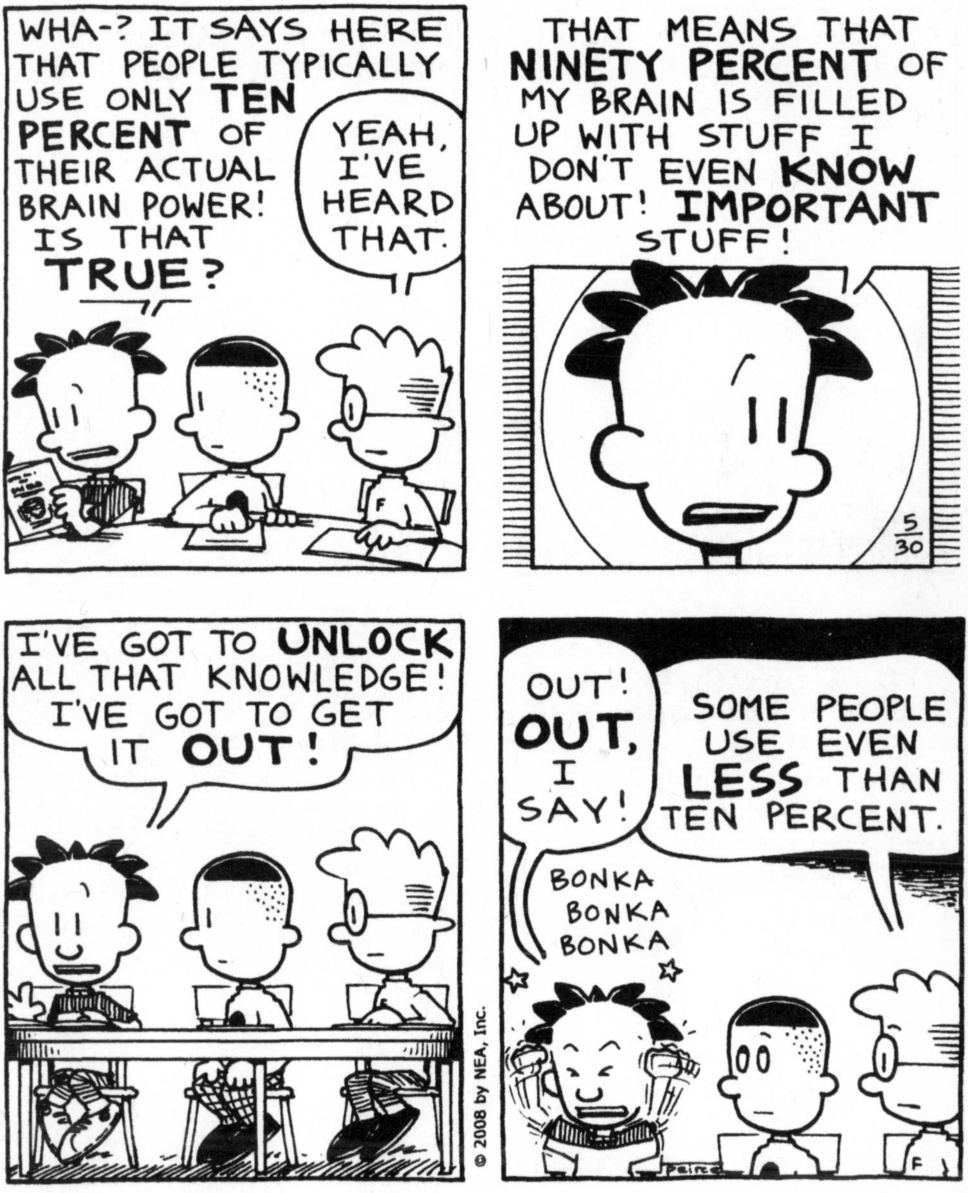
WHA-? IT SAYS HERE THAT PEOPLE TYPICALLY USE ONLY **TEN PERCENT** OF THEIR ACTUAL BRAIN POWER! IS THAT **TRUE**?
YEAH, I'VE HEARD THAT.
THAT MEANS THAT **NINETY PERCENT** OF MY BRAIN IS FILLED UP WITH STUFF I DON'T EVEN **KNOW** ABOUT! **IMPORTANT** STUFF!
5/30
I'VE GOT TO **UNLOCK** ALL THAT KNOWLEDGE! I'VE GOT TO GET IT **OUT**!
© 2008 by NEA, Inc.
OUT! **OUT**, I SAY!
SOME PEOPLE USE EVEN **LESS** THAN TEN PERCENT.
BONKA BONKA BONKA

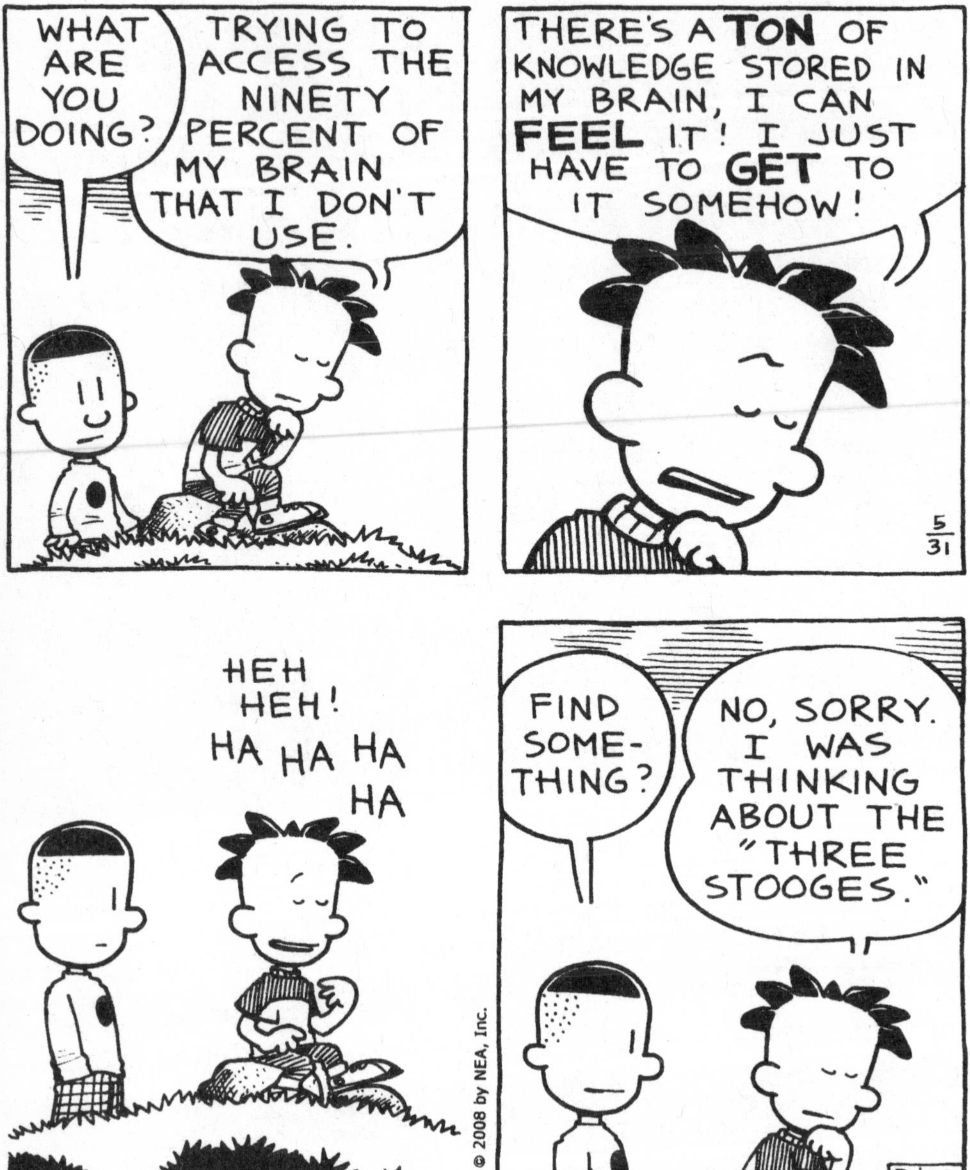
WHAT ARE YOU DOING?
TRYING TO ACCESS THE NINETY PERCENT OF MY BRAIN THAT I DON'T USE.
THERE'S A **TON** OF KNOWLEDGE STORED IN MY BRAIN, I CAN **FEEL** IT! I JUST HAVE TO **GET** TO IT SOMEHOW!
5/31
HEH HEH!
HA HA HA HA
FIND SOME-THING?
NO, SORRY. I WAS THINKING ABOUT THE "THREE STOOGES."
Peirce

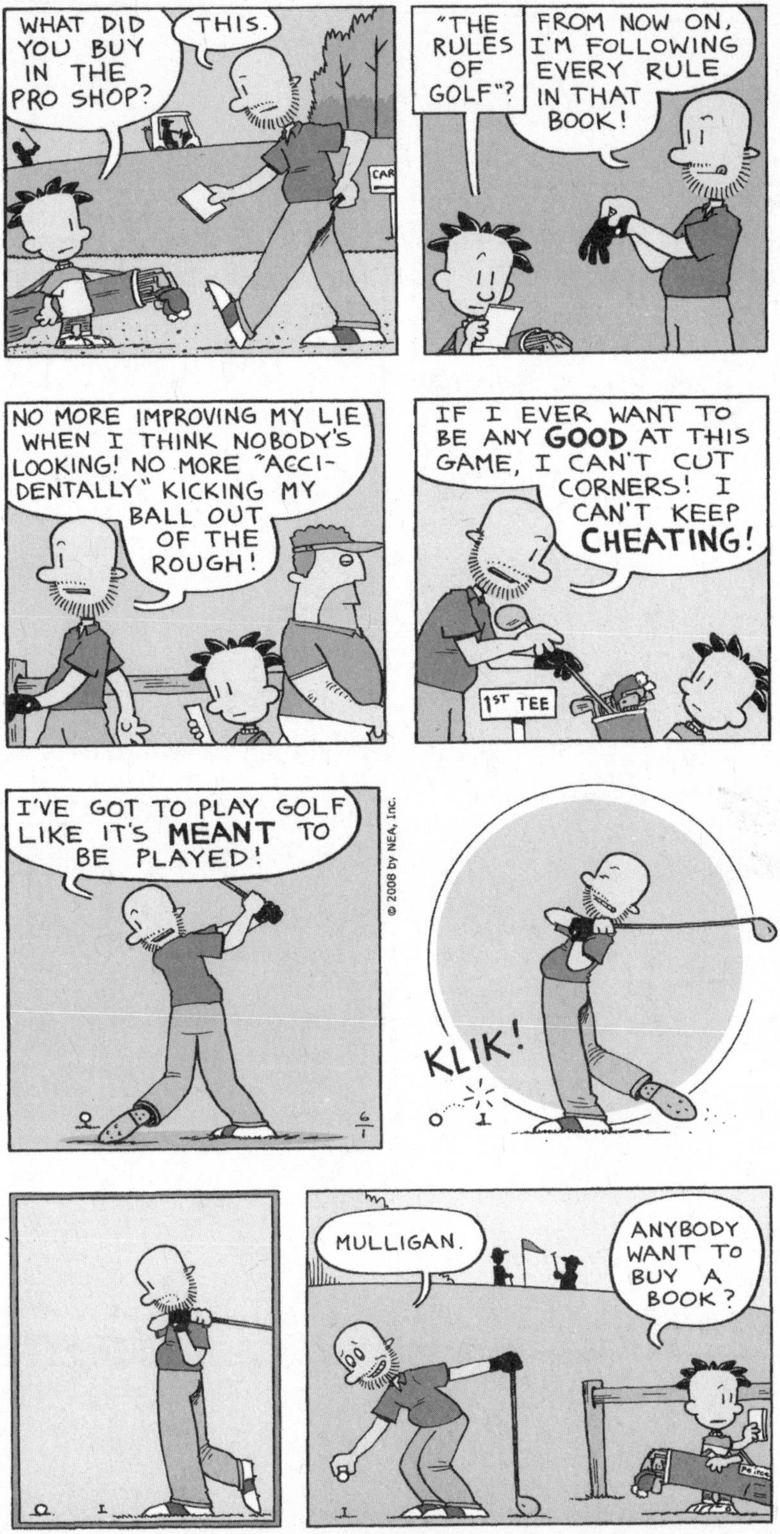
WHAT DID YOU BUY IN THE PRO SHOP?
THIS.
CAR
"THE RULES OF GOLF"?
FROM NOW ON, I'M FOLLOWING EVERY RULE IN THAT BOOK!
NO MORE IMPROVING MY LIE WHEN I THINK NOBODY'S LOOKING! NO MORE "ACCIDENTALLY" KICKING MY BALL OUT OF THE ROUGH!
IF I EVER WANT TO BE ANY **GOOD** AT THIS GAME, I CAN'T CUT CORNERS! I CAN'T KEEP **CHEATING**!
1ST TEE
I'VE GOT TO PLAY GOLF LIKE IT'S **MEANT** TO BE PLAYED!
© 2008 by NEA, Inc.
6/1
KLIK!
MULLIGAN.
ANYBODY WANT TO BUY A BOOK?

ROCKIN' OUT

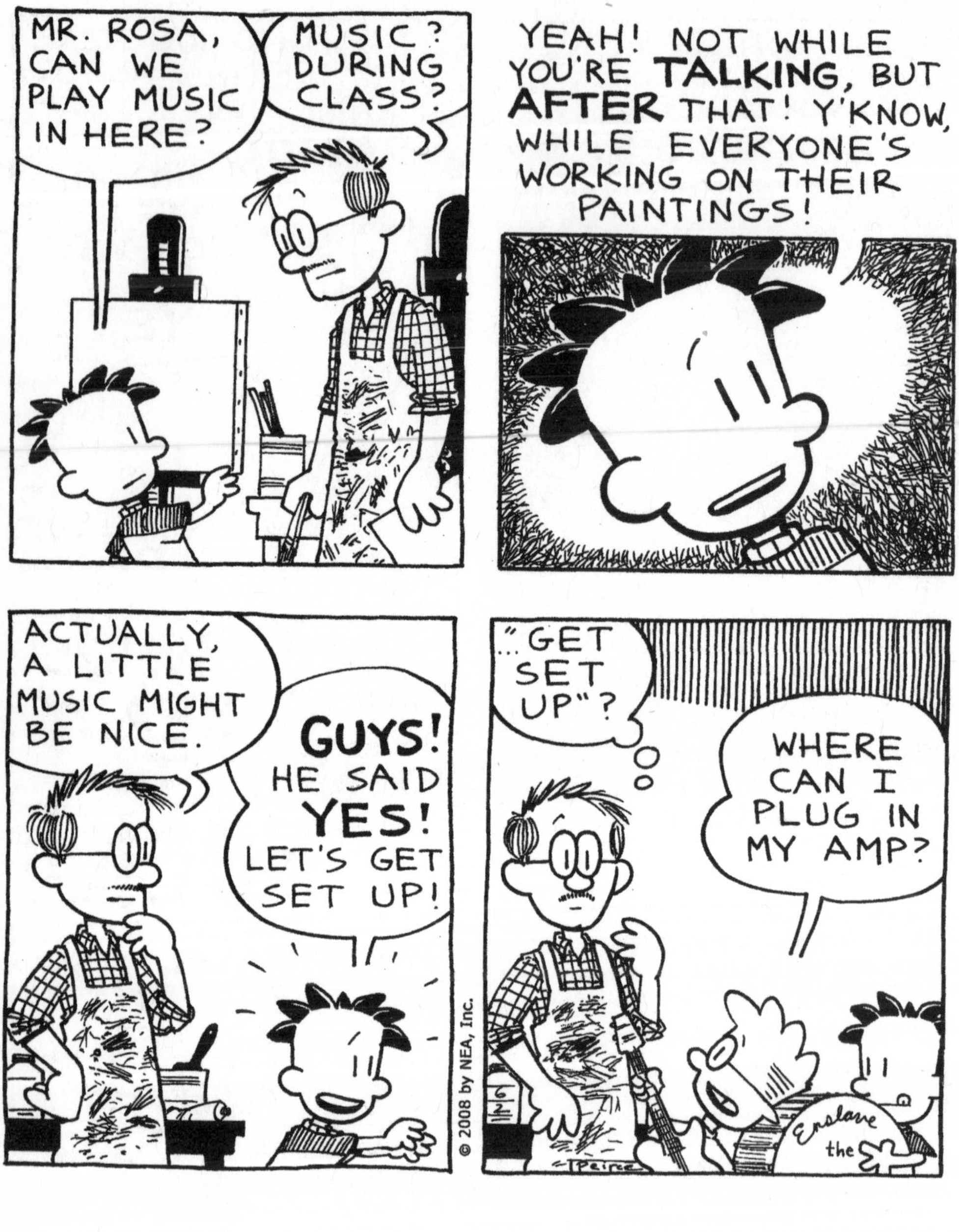
MR. ROSA, CAN WE PLAY MUSIC IN HERE?
MUSIC? DURING CLASS?
YEAH! NOT WHILE YOU'RE **TALKING**, BUT **AFTER** THAT! Y'KNOW, WHILE EVERYONE'S WORKING ON THEIR PAINTINGS!
ACTUALLY, A LITTLE MUSIC MIGHT BE NICE.
GUYS! HE SAID **YES!** LET'S GET SET UP!
..."GET SET UP"?
WHERE CAN I PLUG IN MY AMP?
Enslave the
© 2008 by NEA, Inc.

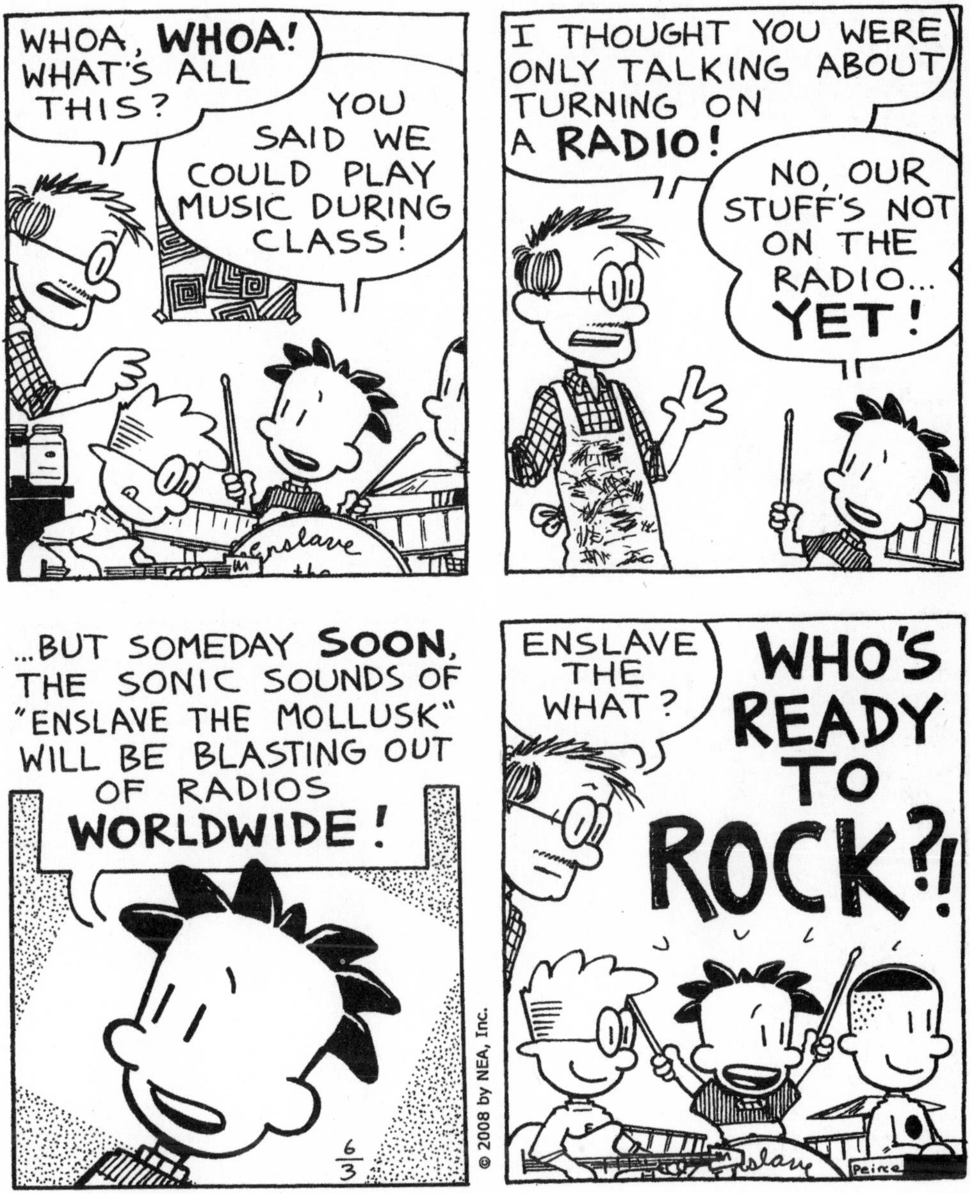
WHOA, WHOA! WHAT'S ALL THIS?
YOU SAID WE COULD PLAY MUSIC DURING CLASS!
I THOUGHT YOU WERE ONLY TALKING ABOUT TURNING ON A RADIO!
NO, OUR STUFF'S NOT ON THE RADIO... YET!
...BUT SOMEDAY SOON, THE SONIC SOUNDS OF "ENSLAVE THE MOLLUSK" WILL BE BLASTING OUT OF RADIOS WORLDWIDE!
6/3
ENSLAVE THE WHAT?
WHO'S READY TO ROCK?!
Peirce
© 2008 by NEA, Inc.

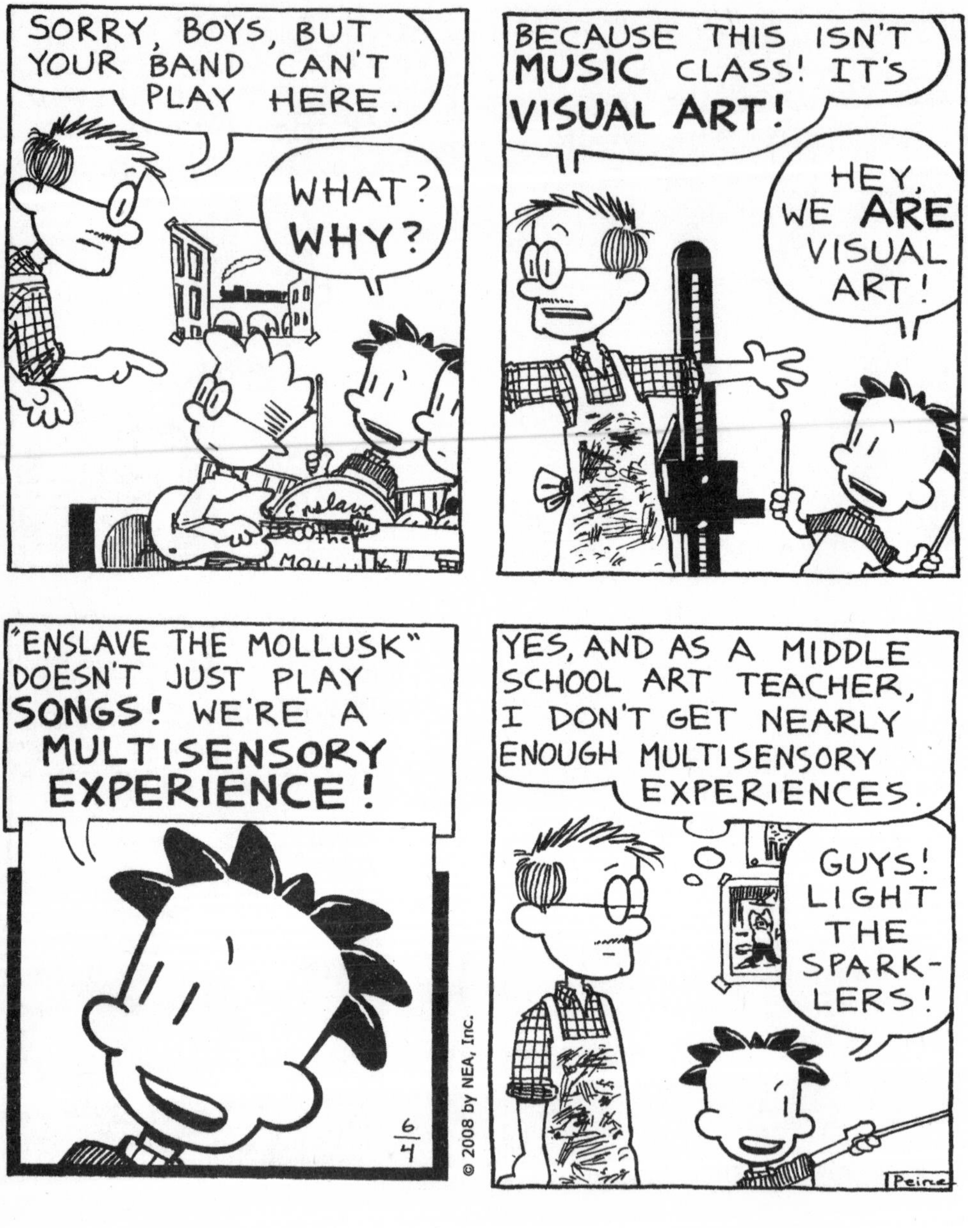
SORRY, BOYS, BUT YOUR BAND CAN'T PLAY HERE.
WHAT? WHY?
BECAUSE THIS ISN'T MUSIC CLASS! IT'S VISUAL ART!
HEY, WE ARE VISUAL ART!
"ENSLAVE THE MOLLUSK" DOESN'T JUST PLAY SONGS! WE'RE A MULTISENSORY EXPERIENCE!
6/4
YES, AND AS A MIDDLE SCHOOL ART TEACHER, I DON'T GET NEARLY ENOUGH MULTISENSORY EXPERIENCES.
GUYS! LIGHT THE SPARK-LERS!
Peirce

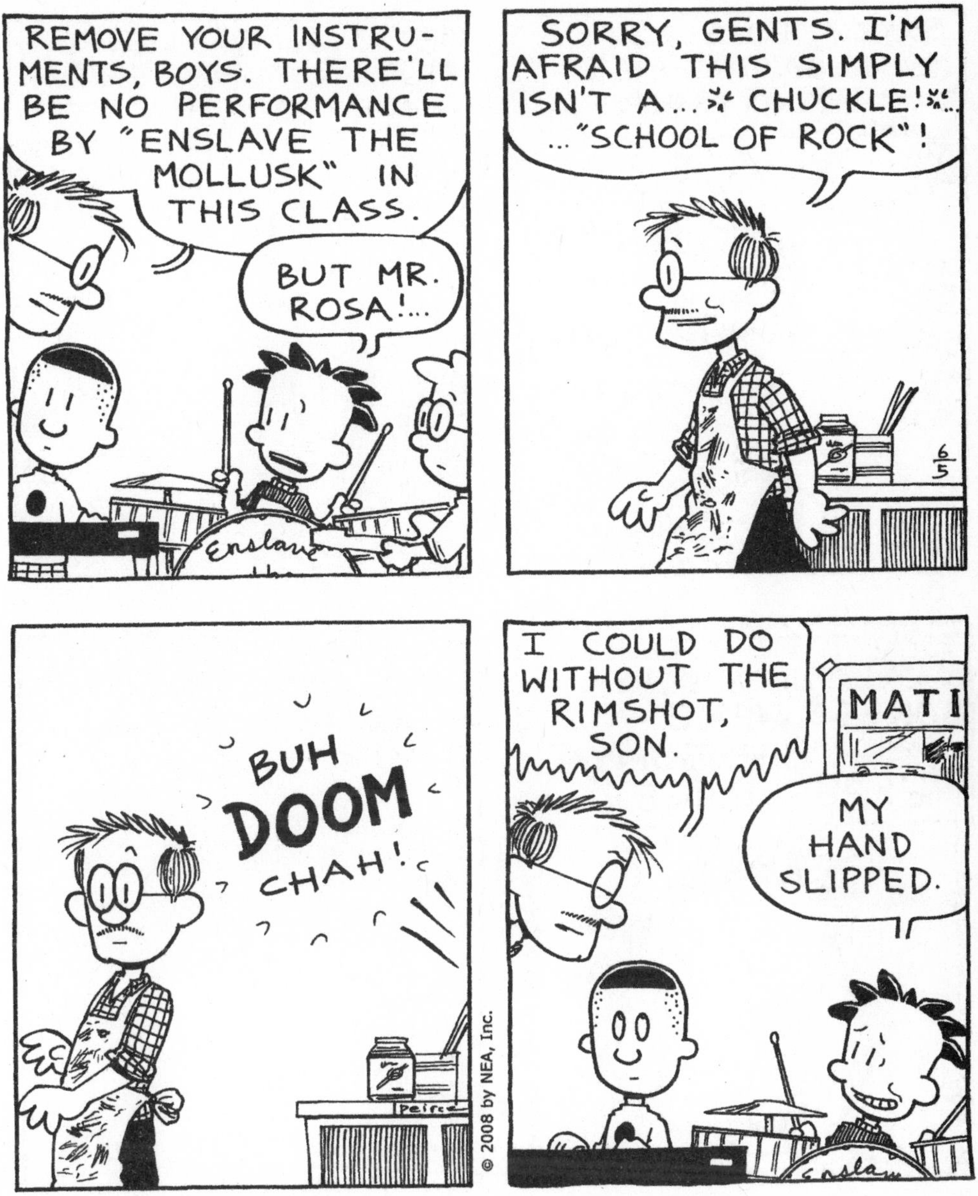
REMOVE YOUR INSTRUMENTS, BOYS. THERE'LL BE NO PERFORMANCE BY "ENSLAVE THE MOLLUSK" IN THIS CLASS.
BUT MR. ROSA!...
Enslave
SORRY, GENTS. I'M AFRAID THIS SIMPLY ISN'T A... CHUCKLE!... ..."SCHOOL OF ROCK"!
6/5
BUH DOOM CHAH!
Peirce
© 2008 by NEA, Inc.
I COULD DO WITHOUT THE RIMSHOT, SON.
MATI
MY HAND SLIPPED.

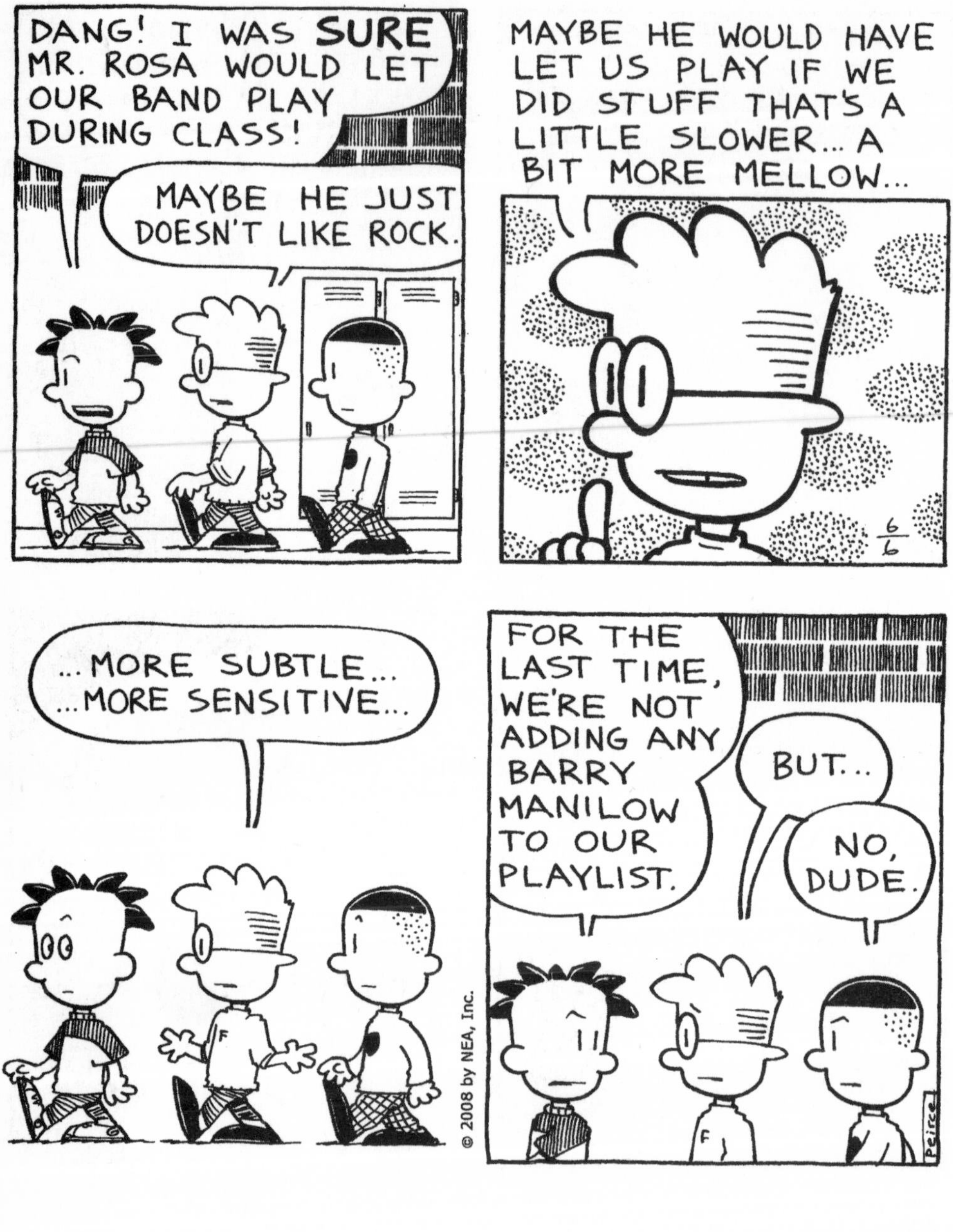
DANG! I WAS SURE MR. ROSA WOULD LET OUR BAND PLAY DURING CLASS!
MAYBE HE JUST DOESN'T LIKE ROCK.
MAYBE HE WOULD HAVE LET US PLAY IF WE DID STUFF THAT'S A LITTLE SLOWER... A BIT MORE MELLOW...
...MORE SUBTLE... ...MORE SENSITIVE...
FOR THE LAST TIME, WE'RE NOT ADDING ANY BARRY MANILOW TO OUR PLAYLIST.
BUT...
NO, DUDE.
Peirce

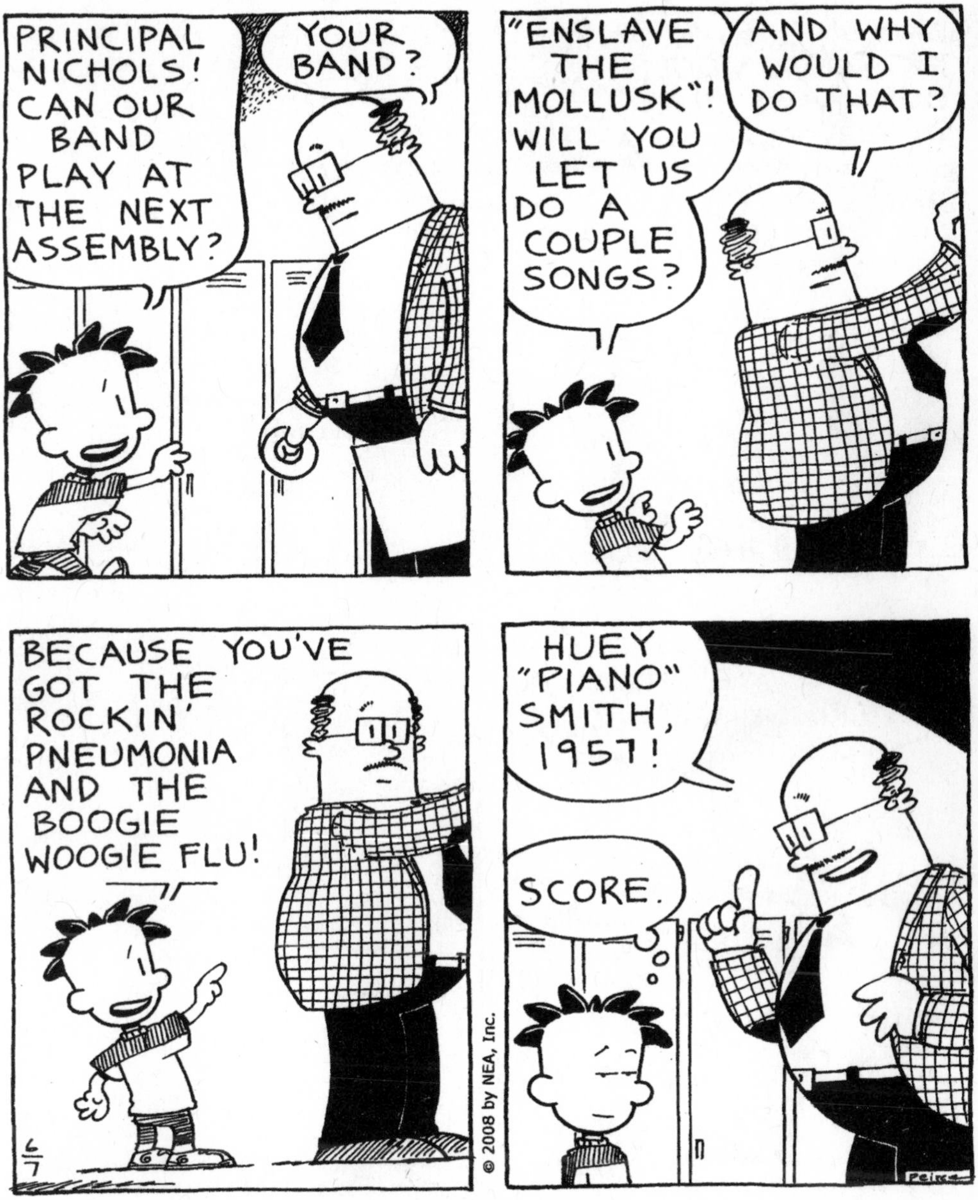
PRINCIPAL NICHOLS! CAN OUR BAND PLAY AT THE NEXT ASSEMBLY?
YOUR BAND?
"ENSLAVE THE MOLLUSK"! WILL YOU LET US DO A COUPLE SONGS?
AND WHY WOULD I DO THAT?
BECAUSE YOU'VE GOT THE ROCKIN' PNEUMONIA AND THE BOOGIE WOOGIE FLU!
HUEY "PIANO" SMITH, 1957!
SCORE.
6/7
© 2008 by NEA, Inc.

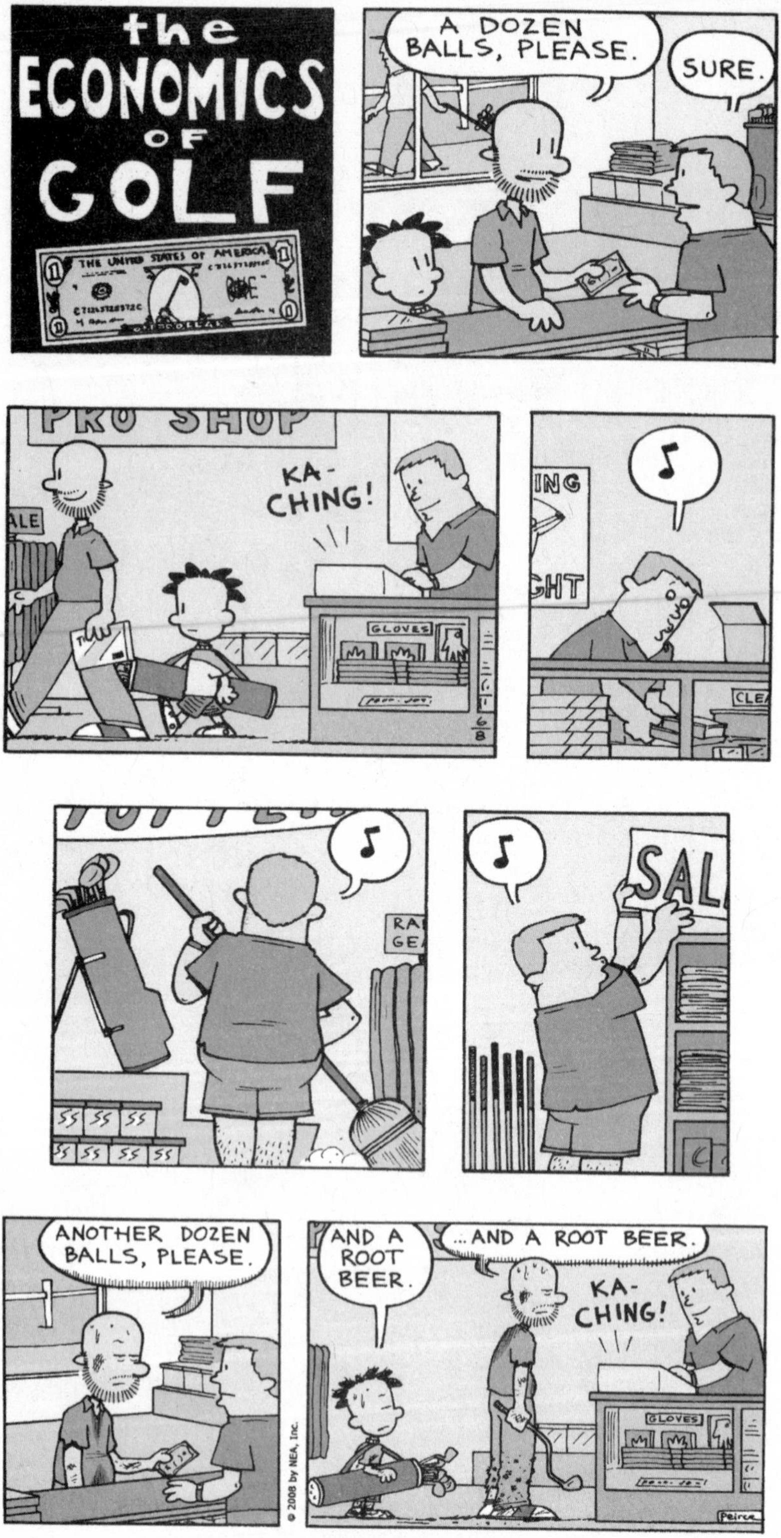
the ECONOMICS OF GOLF
THE UNITED STATES OF AMERICA
A DOZEN BALLS, PLEASE.
SURE.
PRO SHOP
KA-CHING!
GLOVES
♪
♪
♪
SAL
ANOTHER DOZEN BALLS, PLEASE.
AND A ROOT BEER.
...AND A ROOT BEER.
KA-CHING!
GLOVES
© 2008 by NEA, Inc.
Peirce

STUCK ON NATE

BONUS ACTIVITIES TO CRACK YOU UP!

ALL MIXED UP

Can you match each of Nate's sketches to the correct strip?

1

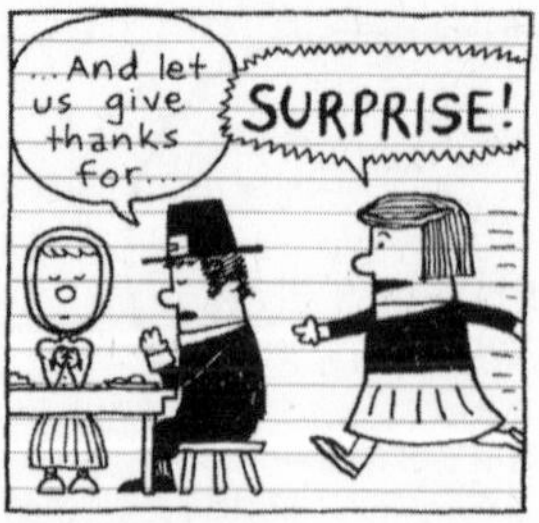
...And let us give thanks for...
SURPRISE!

2

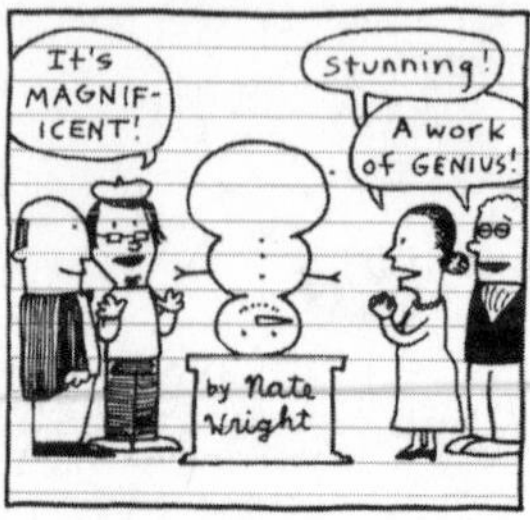
It's MAGNIF-ICENT!
Stunning!
A work of GENIUS!
by Nate Wright

3

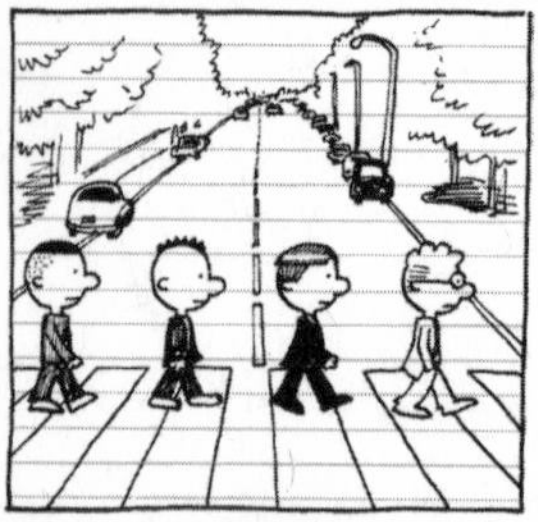

4

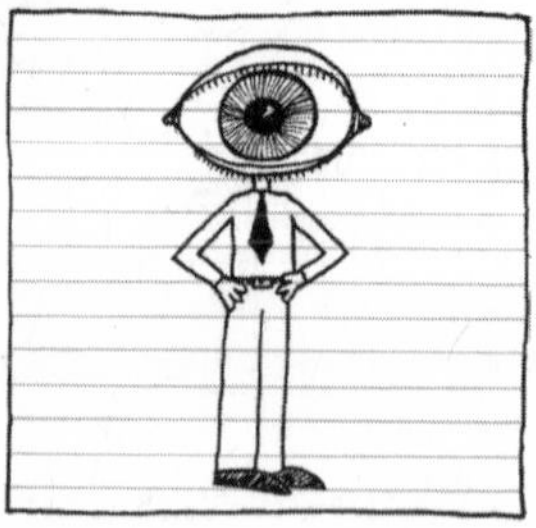

5

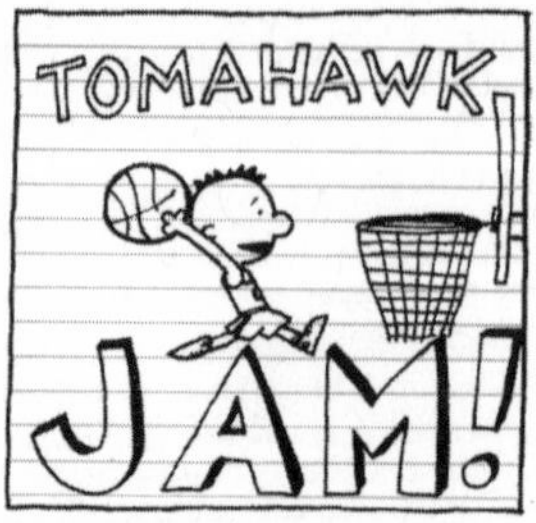
TOMAHAWK
JAM!

A

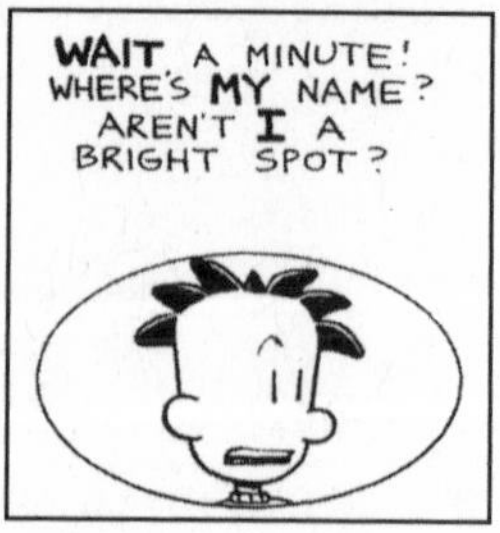
WAIT A MINUTE! WHERE'S MY NAME? AREN'T I A BRIGHT SPOT?

B

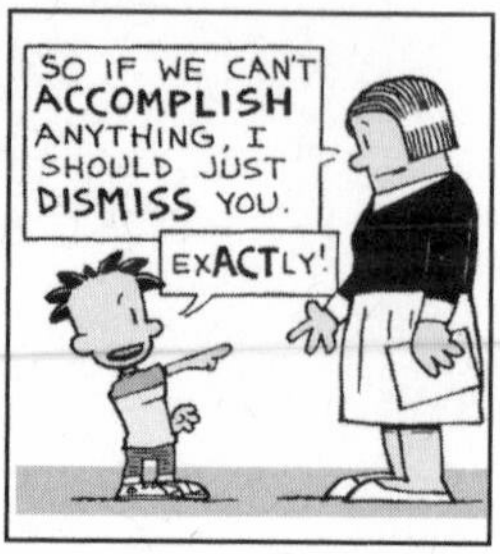
SO IF WE CAN'T ACCOMPLISH ANYTHING, I SHOULD JUST DISMISS YOU.
EXACTLY!

C

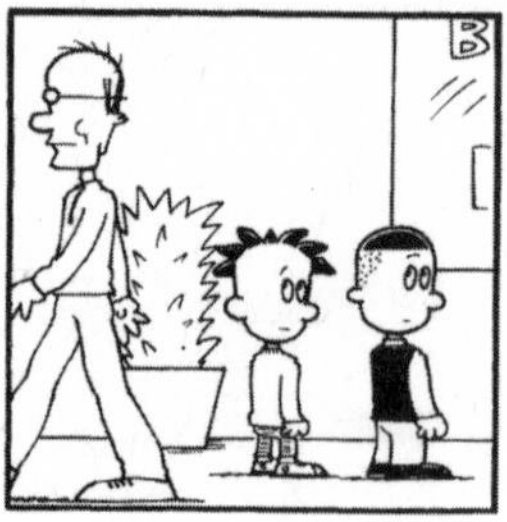

D

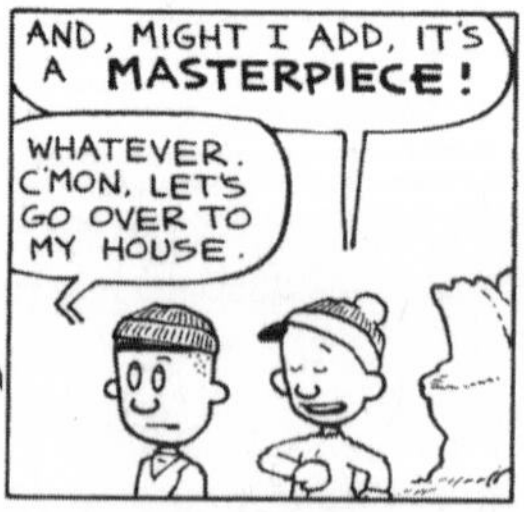
AND, MIGHT I ADD, IT'S A MASTERPIECE!
WHATEVER. C'MON, LET'S GO OVER TO MY HOUSE.

E

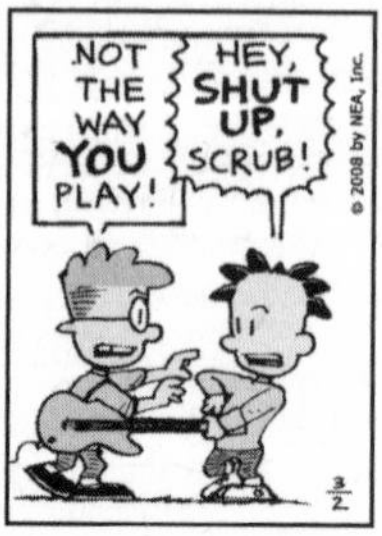
NOT THE WAY YOU PLAY!
HEY, SHUT UP, SCRUB!
© 2008 by NEA, Inc.

Answers: 1B, 2D, 3E, 4C, 5A

SUPERCOOL CAPTIONS

Can you come up with captions for Nate's sketches?

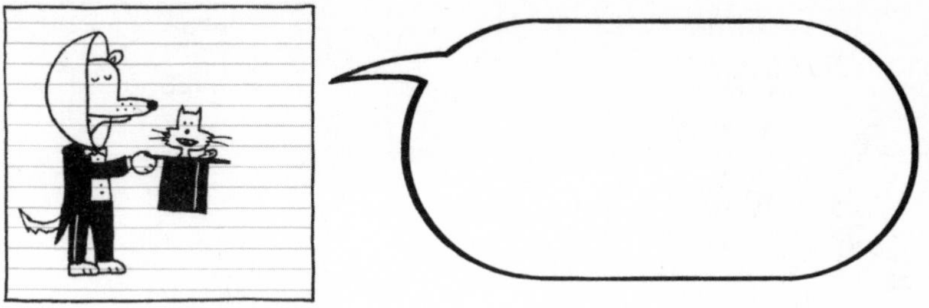

A

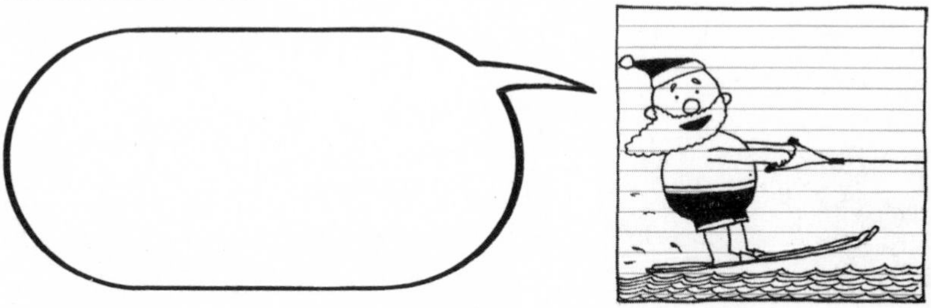

B

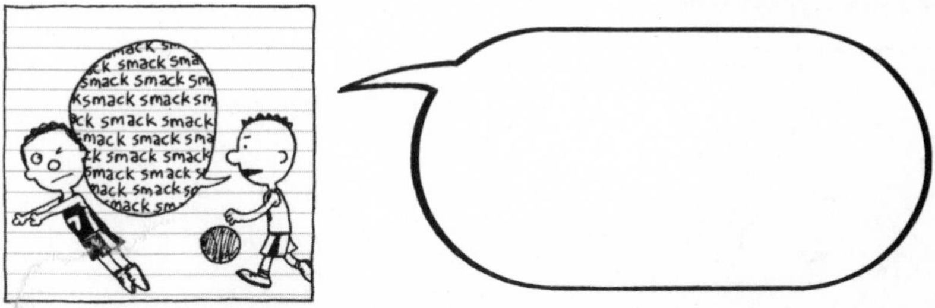

C

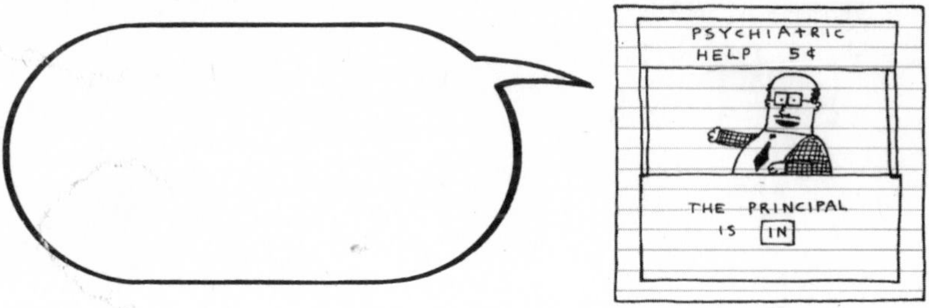
PSYCHIATRIC HELP 5¢
THE PRINCIPAL IS IN

D

SUPER CHALLENGE: Guess which sketch goes with the Sunday comic strips on pages 49, 59, 112, 151:

Comic A goes on page ____________.

Comic B goes on page ____________.

Comic C goes on page ____________.

Comic D goes on page ____________.

Answers: A: 151; B: 49; C: 59; D: 112

NATE ≠ NEAT

Have you ever scrambled the letters in your name to see if they spell anything else? Well, **I** have. And guess what: **MY** letters spell **N·E·A·T!**

KSSSCH!

Pretty ironic, right? Hey, I realize I'm not exactly Joe Tidy. **EVERYBODY** knows it. But that doesn't stop Francis, who color-codes his underwear, from pointing it out about a jillion times a day.

Your desk is **DISGUSTING**. You have paint on your shirt. Oh, and you have Cheez Doodle stains all over your face. What a SLOB you are!

Francis has been telling me to clean up my act since I poured applesauce down his pants back in kindergarten. Of course, I've always ignored him. But then last week my sloppiness got Francis in trouble... and he **NEVER** gets in trouble!

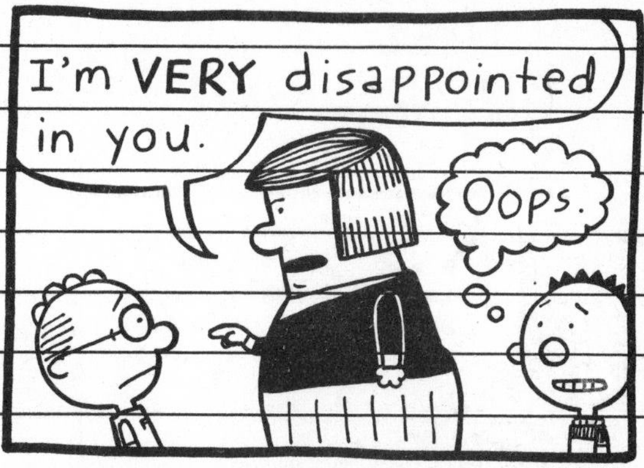
I'm VERY disappointed in you.
Oops.

I felt so bad about it, I decided to actually try to get neater. And thanks to Teddy and his uncle Pedro, the hypnotist, it's working... **TOO** well. All of the sudden, I'm starting to act **JUST LIKE FRANCIS!** Frankly, I think I'm losing my mind.

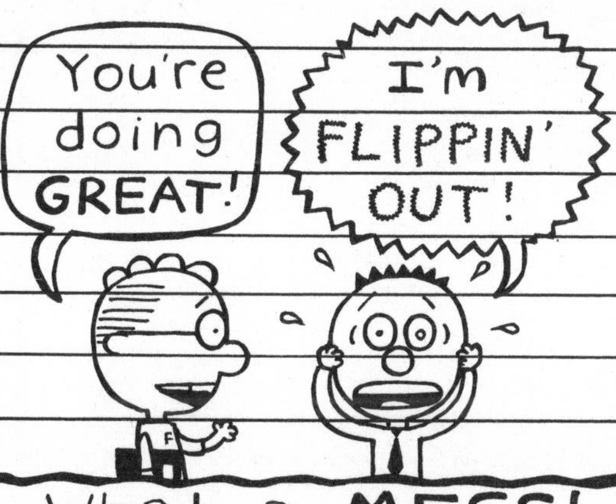
You're doing GREAT!
I'm FLIPPIN' OUT!

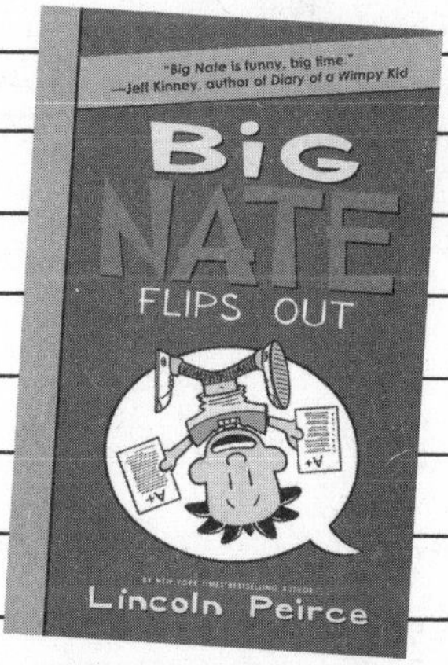
"Big Nate is funny, big time."
—Jeff Kinney, author of Diary of a Wimpy Kid
BIG NATE
FLIPS OUT
Lincoln Peirce

What a **MESS!**

Read all about it in

BIG NATE FLIPS OUT!!

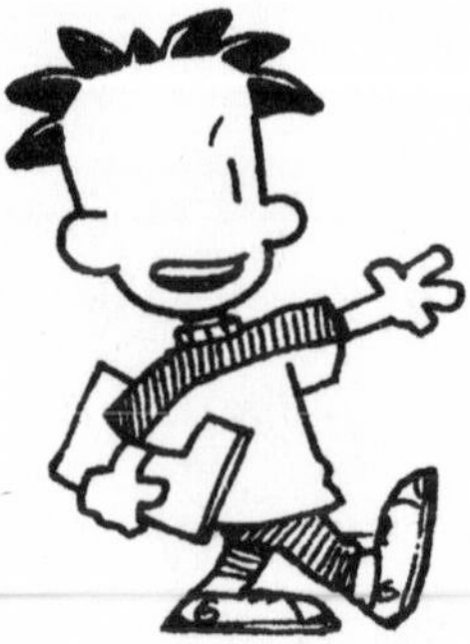

These comic strips first appeared in newspapers
from November 5, 2007, through June 8, 2008.

www.harpercollinschildrens.com
www.bignatebooks.com

Go to www.bignate.com to read the *Big Nate* comic strip.

Library of Congress catalog card number: 2011930716
ISBN 978-0-06-208694-5 (pbk.)

Typography by Andrea Vandergrift
18 19 CG/LSCH 13
❖
First Edition

Lincoln Peirce

(pronounced "purse") is a cartoonist/writer and *New York Times* bestselling author of the hilarious Big Nate book series (www.bignatebooks.com), now published in twenty-two countries worldwide. He is also the creator of the comic strip *Big Nate*, which appears in over two hundred and fifty U.S. newspapers and online daily at www.bignate.com. Lincoln's boyhood idol was Charles Schulz of *Peanuts* fame, but his main inspiration for Big Nate has always been his own experience as a sixth grader. Just like Nate, Lincoln loves comics, ice hockey, and Cheez Doodles (and dislikes cats, figure skating, and egg salad). His Big Nate books have been featured on *Good Morning America* and in *USA Today*, the *Washington Post*, and the *Boston Globe*. He has also written for Cartoon Network and Nickelodeon. Lincoln lives with his wife and two children in Portland, Maine.

NATE RATES ALL THE BIG NATE BOOKS!

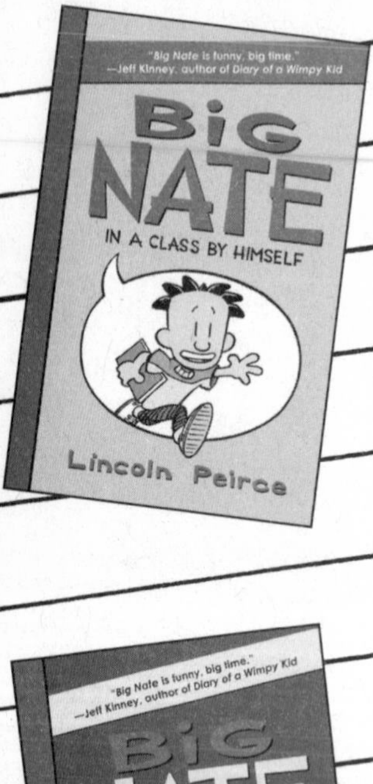
"Big Nate is funny, big time."
—Jeff Kinney, author of Diary of a Wimpy Kid
BIG NATE
IN A CLASS BY HIMSELF
Lincoln Peirce

Grade: A+

Comments: I surpass all others! How could you improve on that?

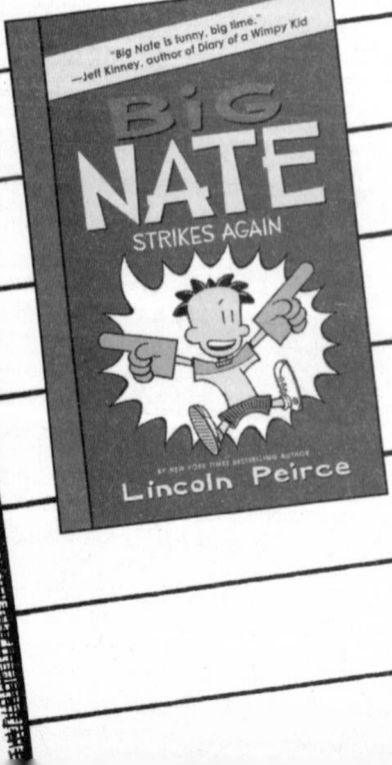
"Big Nate is funny, big time."
—Jeff Kinney, author of Diary of a Wimpy Kid
BIG NATE
STRIKES AGAIN
Lincoln Peirce

Grade: A+

Comments: Guess who wins the face-off with Gina, my all-time enemy?